WALLID

Third Novel in the Series
The Siddhi Wars

By

CURTIS MITCHELL

Please direct all correspondence
and book orders to:
Flying Key Ventures
PO Box 505
Hampstead MD 21074

flyingkey@earthlink.net

Library of Congress Control Number 2022908416

ISBN 978-0-9907067-4-8
eISBN 978-0-9907067-5-5

Printed in the United States of America

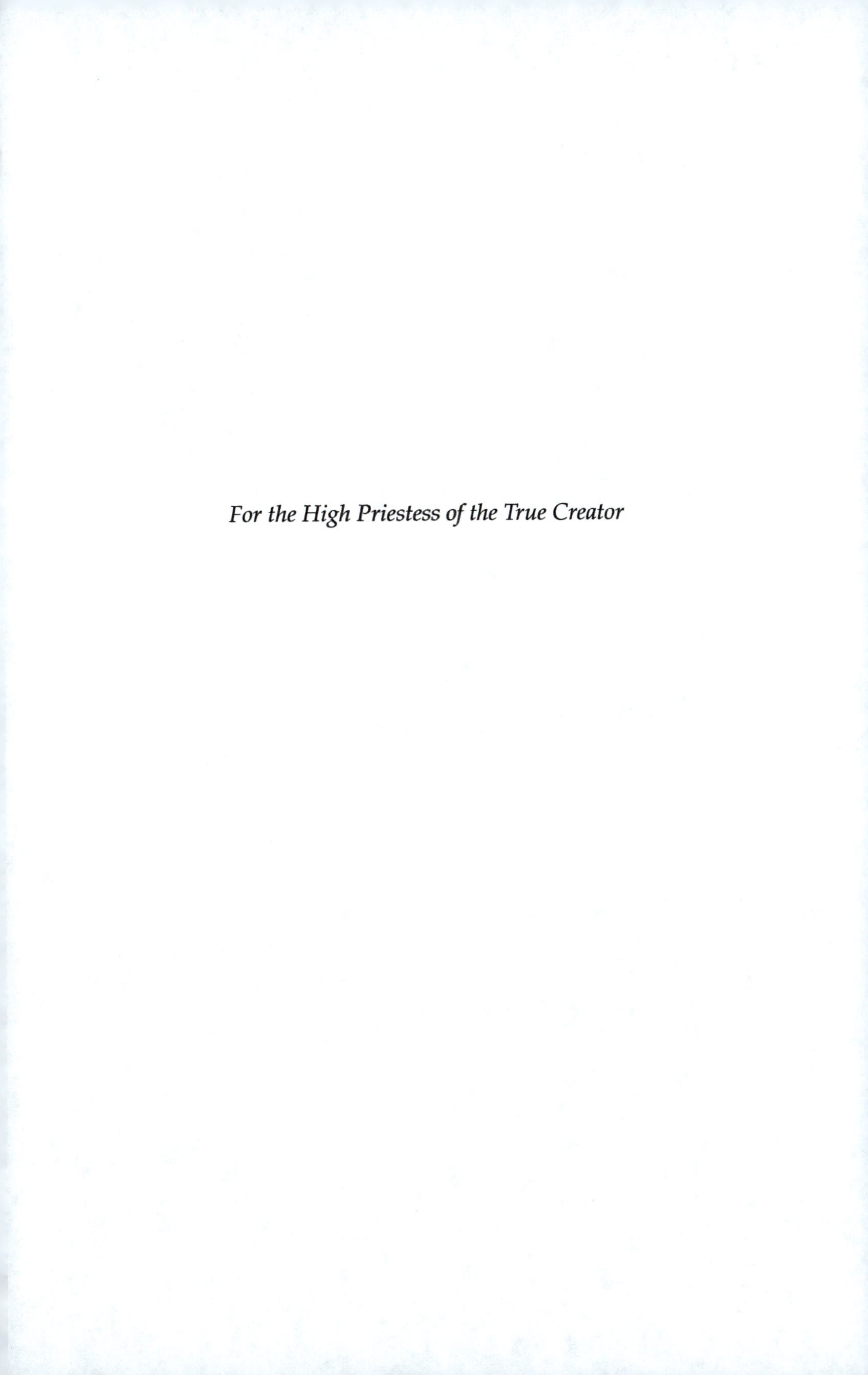

For the High Priestess of the True Creator

"Ecstasy is your birthright."

Table of Contents

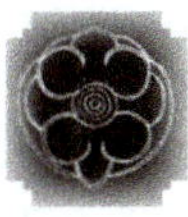

1

THE WATERFALLS OF JASMINE EVERYWHERE

Jasmine loved the heat. She'd learned just which clothes to wear and just which way to wear her hair, fine tuning her presence for equanimity. And when she was in the mood for extremes she'd lay out naked in the yard next to the small salt water pool ever-splashing over the edges until she was in a full sweat and then plunge into the cool water, rolling out onto the deck again into a sweat, darkening her skin. With her long dark hair she could walk down the streets now and shop. With her knowledge of the local languages, both the legal and the local banned language, the shopkeepers she was closest to could almost forget she was an American. And when she went into a new shop, the keepers would speculate about where she was from, arguing for the fun of it that, no, she couldn't be.

She'd taken work in the international yoga school, run via shell corporations by the Order. She was paid enough to cover her groceries, and she would purchase something fresh almost every day, which established a predictable order in her life that put everyone who would see her come and go at ease. Soon she became almost invisible to everyone in that section of town. This gave her the opportunity to study the statuary and the stonework, and feel into it, discerning its innate capacities.

For there was incredible stonework everywhere. Most people lived in extended families, several generations living together inside walled compounds. Even most of the single family houses were in walled compounds. The older, more traditional compounds had stone guardians, fearsome warriors, on either side of the gate. The gate itself was carved to resemble the outline of the sacred volcano on one end of the island, which rose directly out of the sea, bulging its massive shoulders up over ten thousand feet. The legend was that these gates represented a split in the mountain—a split where the spirits of the ancestors could come through and abide with their descendants. In every courtyard there were low towers with small houses at the top occupied by the ashes of the ancestors. The legend also told that in the event of a grave threat the gates would slide together and the split would close, making the way impassable for all, spirit or soma-bound.

In every courtyard there were also altars, some to nature spirits, some small thrones also on towers for the deities or the syncreatic god, the titular chief deity, depicted as a being suspended in the air with flames coming from all its joints, and a halo of flames; the one god that kept the Meemons of the Invader's faithful accepting that the islanders' pantheon was, in essence, monotheistic. Every morning small offerings would be set out on woven grass trays made the day before, offerings of food and water, flowers and incense, such that by noon the smell of the incense would rise above and mask the fecund and rotting smells of the jungle, and cover the city smells of sewage and cooking oil. The breeze smelled sweet all afternoon, until the night flowering plants would take over.

There was art—painting and statuary—everywhere. Stones carved with faces, masks from characters in the local heroic tales, and monumental carvings from the legends of the old religion and the old practices of Winduism. Temples to the old deities were everywhere, some set for tourists, others set for the practice of the old ways, of course now all watched over by the flaming god at the top.

Wade couldn't stand the city with its narrow streets and scowling shopkeepers. He would never fit in there. He decided to take a vacation house in the country where he could at least get out and walk the terraced rice fields. The farmers in the village grew used to him quickly and would share lunch with him when he would pass them in their thatched huts on raised platforms. When he understood the value, he even began to leave small flower offerings to their garden deities in their tiny beribboned temples raised above the waving grain.

The Priests of the village approved, but among themselves he was always regarded with skepticism. It wasn't clear, exactly, why the big American was there. He was an unlikely type to stay for weeks, reading, sunning himself, and often going into town. He had rented a scooter to take him into town to be with Jasmine when his duties as a Consort called him in. But the Priests didn't care enough to have him followed to see where he went every day. They assumed he was simply touring the island and taking in the sights.

Jasmine, for her part, was engaged in the accumulation of power using archaic alchemical and tantric practices. She had a vague idea of what she was accumulating power for, and what her role would be. The Divine Feminine, in one face or another, would visit her every day during her devotions and either show her, or tell her, what she was to do that particular day, or for several days in a row, instructing her in the work of the internal movement and manipulation of energies, giving her exercises in how to manipulate and direct energies, working on her control of inanimate objects, or her ability to separate her psychic and spiritual bodies from her soma. Her focus at the moment was small stones, several of which, carved and painted, she had set up in salient locations around her house.

Another focus was on the selection of young men from whom she could feed, deriving the energy she needed from the energy they were only too willing to expend. She employed a modified version of a ritual pattern established by the Order of the Red Phoenix in Waitan.

Young men, referred to as Little Phoenixes, were invited to participate in some form of physical interaction with the Priestess that released energy, sexual energy, that they held in excess of their needs. In exchange they received only the minimal energetic feedback—being bathed in the fields of the Priestess, which enhanced their pleasure and ensured their silence and loyalty.

The men chosen for this role were not on the path of the Consort, and, indeed, had no interest in what they did not know. Jasmine trolled the men from the yoga classes she would teach. She had no qualms about this, because most of the men she accumulated were simply in class to troll the wen students in the first place.

It was dangerous work, this gathering of substances. The men could always become aggressive and demand more than was being offered. Because of this possibility, a Priestess's Consort was always required to be nearby, able to perceive what was happening with the Priestess and her Little Phoenii. If a direct visual perspective on what was happening couldn't be manufactured then direct audio was required. Shouting distance was too far away.

Wade was finding himself less and less interested in performing his duties to Jasmine in this regard.

Jasmine's house had been occupied for a long time. It was on a lot on the old road that ran along the crest of the Crack the Rock gorge. The gorge was narrow—Jasmine could shoot an arrow across it. The walls of the gorge went almost straight down, and were covered in impenetrable jungle except in places where the bare rock showed through. The river was more than two hundred feet down, and fast, crashing between rocks with such speed it raised little clouds of mist, which on cool mornings would rise to the level of her house and wrap it in light fog. Forms would appear in it while she was sitting, observing the rising sun. Sometimes she felt she was engaging directly with the Spirits of the Land, and these forms would interact with her in ways she could only describe as sentient, although in their manifestation they were always quite temporary.

The oldest part of the house, closest to the street, was two rooms made with block and cement plaster and painted off-white. These were now used as the kitchen and a pantry. There were raised thresholds between the rooms.

Closer to the gorge was a long, sunken living room with windows along the north side with a second story that included a large master bedroom with its own bath and two smaller bedrooms, which used the bath at the back of the living room below under the staircase. On the west end of the house were sliding glass doors that led from the staircase landing to a deck. In the middle of the deck was the raised pool surrounded with foliage. The deck extended beyond the pool and hung over the gorge on cantilevered wooden beams. A railing kept one from falling. Beyond, the far wall of the gorge rose steeply, covered in vines and trees. Too steep for any dwelling, the mists that rose from the river below snaked among the trunks and flowers.

There were two gates on the street side; one for pedestrian traffic and the second, with two doors, that would open to a parking pad for scooters or a small car. A wooden privacy fence, almost ten feet tall, ran along the north boundary of the lot and met the deck at the west end. There was room for flowers, and a small tropical garden along this side of the lot. Jasmine flowers hung like waterfalls along the fence.

She loved it here. She loved the town and the tropics. The humidity made her dark hair thick and wavy. She loved being able to dress in tropical clothes and the freedom to swim and sunbathe nude.

Every morning on her way to the yoga studio she would walk past a family compound that drew her attention. The gate would be open and she could look in through the heavily carved mountain shoulders, or through the wider auto gate, and either walk by slowly or stand in the shadows on the street and observe. What drew her attention was two old wen screaming at each other, often with a young wen caught in the middle space between them, sometimes pulling on her by the arm or by her clothes or hair one way or the other.

Jasmine came to understand, through her knowledge of Windonesian, and the local banned language Nahasi, that the old wen were the young wen's grandmothers, and they were competing in their commands over what their granddaughter should do and say and what roles she should play in the family. One grandmother would demand that she be served first after the family meal, at which neither was welcome. The other grandmother would demand that the young wen be allowed to eat with the family and help her mother clean up first, before the grandmothers would be fed. The one grandmother demanded that the young wen clean up her shelter, the other insisted, with much name calling, that the lazy old wen should clean up after herself.

Jasmine knew that Moon Halter would be arriving on the island soon to explain it all to her, even though she had known that it was the custom here to treat the old wen badly once their husbands had died, allowing them only cast-off clothes, making them sleep not in the family house but on low platforms under lean-to structures attached to the compound walls with only ragged mat curtains to block the wind and rain, open to the mosquitoes. And old wen were not allowed to sit with the family for meals, except on certain holy days.

It was as if the old wen had no worth without their husbands, and this was something Jasmine simply could not understand. Jasmine came to think of them as Good Grandmother and Bad Grandmother. Usually, every day that she went to work she would hear the loud screechings of Bad Grandmother at the young wen demanding something, some service or another, and the defensive screeching of Good Grandmother to leave her alone, that she was a good girl. In this way she learned the girl's name was Napat.

Jasmine couldn't be sure about how old she was. From watching her Jasmine guessed she might be fourteen or fifteen. Sometimes Jasmine would arrange to be on Napat's street when she left her compound for school. Jasmine would practice her urban escape and evasion skills following Napat. Education on the island required uniforms and Jasmine had learned that the Good Grandmother had been washing rags in the poor people's laundry pool downstream from the bathing pool in Crack the Rock gorge. There was a long and winding set of steps from the street level down to the pools. Grandmother had been washing rags to help Napat pay for school uniforms and supplies. Napat was her parent's seventh child, and the family's resources were already strained.

Jasmine had gone down to the pool one day, following Grandmother. A short falls fed the bathing pool. The water of the bathing section spread out into a shallow flat before gathering itself into a short falls again. There were pounding stones for the laundry, worn in by countless hands of wen over generations. Most houses in town now had running water or laundry services. Now only the poor came down to what was once a pristine river filled with clear water.

Jasmine was surprised to find a shrine at the bottom alongside the pools. From the platform where the steps down ended, another short flight of steps ran back up along the face of a huge rock. There was another smaller platform with a fine chair and a ceremonial umbrella for the deity to sit during an invocation. A spring emerged from the top of the rock and the water sheeted thinly down over its entire surface. A small plant with little round leaves covered the surface, anchored in the rock, and the sheeting water would drip from the ends of the leaves, each drop golden in the light of the sun. The drops would fall from the leaves in a golden curtain into the pool below.

The grandmother had hitched up her sarong to mid-thigh, tucking it into her waistline, and crossed the laundry pool to the other side and carefully removed her shirt and hung it on a branch. Jasmine had seen the old wen arguing over the girl through the open gate, each having a hold on one of Napat's arms, pulling her one way then the other. They'd both been topless then, in the old way, Jasmine knew. Wen had only been required to wear shirts or tops covering their breasts when the law had been changed when Windonesia became a nation. The vast majority practiced the Wuzlim religion, more or less strictly. The Grandmother squatted down and pulled the dirty squares of the cloth from the sling basket she'd carried. She wet all the rags at once, and then, using a bar of soap, rubbing it into the rags, she got to work, scrubbing the cloth into the pounding stone, rinsing each rag and holding it up to the light for inspection. Sometimes she'd see a spot and rub the soap in again, then bundle it up, rubbing the cloth with a hand stone into the pounding stone.

As she worked the old wen glanced sideways at Jasmine repeatedly. Jasmine, studying the shrine, was aware of the gaze. Jasmine noticed a depression in the rock on the far side of the altar platform that could not be seen from where she stood. She took off her sandals, tucked up her sarong as she had seen the old wen do, and waded into the pool. When she got around the platform she discovered a small cave, the floor just above the waterline. At the mouth of the cave was a pipe driven into a crack in the rock, a valved spigot at the end. Below that was a rock carving sitting in the back of the shallow hollow.

The stone was a little more than a foot tall, flat on its base, and cylindrical. About two thirds of the way up a line like a collar had been carved into it, and above that it came to a rounded, almost hemispherical head. As Jasmine reached out a hand to touch the stone, the old wen spoke to her in Nahasi, "Queen Old Woman."

Jasmine gasped and withdrew her hand quickly. She'd read about the Queen Old Woman stones in her studies. They were supposedly hidden, or at least out of common sight, at the old temples and shrines all through the island, usually near the bottom, and along the many streams and rivers. She was the representation of the Goddess Salakta, mother of the ruling Trimerid, the True Creator. And sometimes their lover, as the Goddess of Tantra. In some places there were still the old Skreeva standing stones, and often near them would be found a Salakta stone. And now here she was, closer to the ancient representation of the old Goddess in situ, than she had imagined . She turned to the old wen and asked in Nahasi, "May I touch it?"

The old wen barked with laughter at the language, and said, "Yes, daughter, you may. The priests come here to get holy water from the pipe and take it to use in their ceremonies, but they never touch the stone. And they never call Her to the throne any more, only their new god. But sometimes I do, and She sits there, and we talk. She told me a young woman would come. Maybe you."

Jasmine removed her sarong, placing it on the platform. She squatted down all the way, her butt immersed in the cool water, and then kneeling, leaned forward and touched it with both hands. A shiver of energy poured through her, a small quick orgasm.

The old wen could see her backside quiver and laughed out loud. "You see? Much power there," she said. "The priests are afraid to touch Her. But they know She protects the spring, and keeps it clean from all the filth above."

Jasmine returned the laughter and, taking her sarong, crossed the river and, wrapping her sarong around her waist she removed her shirt and sat on a stone next to the old grandmother. They exchanged names—the old wen was named Red Flowers. She translated Jasmine's name into Nahasi, and approved of the choice. After a moment Jasmine reached over to the pile of dirty rags and began helping with the laundry. She got the whole family story.

The grandmother talked some about the old days, and how only the ruling class practiced the Windu traditions of casting off the old wen upon the death of the husband. In many cases the wen had been expected to throw themselves on the cremation fire. But it had never been that way for the everyday people, the common people. Grandmothers used to be respected but now the people adopted more and more ways of the ruling caste. It was illegal now for widows to be burned with their husbands, but to be spurned and ignored was close enough to death. Her daughter would make sure she had enough to eat when her husband wasn't looking, but the Bad Grandmother's daughter did little for her, and she would steal from Good Grandmother when she could. Good Grandmother would often hide small amounts of food, and sometimes money, where she knew the Bad Grandmother would find them and take them, hoping that it might make her more calm, if not more generous. It had not worked so far, and the Bad Grandmother took out her anger and hatred at the way her life had turned out on Napat because she had a future. The Good Grandmother tried to intervene, but she had been knocked down more than once and was afraid of falling.

Jasmine carried the damp rags up the three hundred steps and pushed some paper money into the old woman's hand at the top. Jasmine promised to come visit her at the pools again. In this way she learned about the old ways. Before the Windu invaders had come a thousand years earlier there was a path to the spirits of the land. They worked with the people, and with the elements, and life was abundant and good. There were healers and miracle workers. Both men and wen could pursue knowledge in this way.

Now, the everyday people worked for the ruling caste and their priests. The priests had even suspended the activities of the temple to the Goddess Wahsastami, a Goddess of Healing and Knowledge from their own pantheon, except for certain high holy days. New priestesses were only rarely allowed to learn the ways of the Order, and she was afraid that these ways would die out. But the people still kept the old ways alive, quiet and in the background. The old wen even told Jasmine some of the ceremonies, and where she could find the plants and the little black mushroom that gave visions of the spirits.

Then one day the old wen didn't come. Jasmine walked by the family compound and a black flag was tied to a bar in the gate. Good Grandmother was dead.

On subsequent mornings on her walk to work Jasmine could hear the Bad Grandmother screeching at the girl Napat. Once she heard Napat weeping and screaming back to her grandmother to let go of her hair. Jasmine followed Napat when she could, tracking the girl's grief in her slumped posture, her sunken eyes, the way she would stop on the street and sigh. Even the girl's hair had lost its luster. Once Jasmine found her sitting on the steps of a neighboring compound, weeping, great sobs wracking her body, hands over her mouth to keep the neighbors from hearing her wail. Napat's misery was palpable, even at a distance. Jasmine could only imagine how the old wen tortured her.

A month after Good Grandmother's death she heard something remarkable. She heard Good Grandmother's voice, shouting over Bad Grandmother's hoarse screams of terror. "You will let her go!" the voice of Good Grandmother shouted. Jasmine was so surprised that she ran up the steps, pushed open the gate and looked in. She saw Napat had a grip on the old woman's forearm and had forced her to her knees. Napat looked fierce and the old woman terrified. Jasmine called out, "Napat!"

Napat looked at her, but it was not Napat's face she saw. It was the face of the Good Grandmother, shimmering over Napat's. Bad Grandmother started crying out, "The ghost! The ghost!"

"Let her go," Jasmine ordered. Napat did, staring at Jasmine.

"I know you," the ghost face said.

"Yes Grandmother, you do," Jasmine replied humbly.

"You take her," Good Grandmother said. "She is not safe here."

"Yes, Grandmother." Jasmine held out her hand and Napat let the Bad Grandmother's arm go, sleep walked to the gate and took Jasmine's hand. They walked to the yoga studio, Napat holding Jasmine's hand, Jasmine talking to her, and sometimes to the Grandmother's ghost, the whole way. She posted a hastily written note on a nail in the door saying classes were cancelled for today and would resume the next day as usual. They walked back to Jasmine's house that overlooked Crack the Rock gorge.

Jasmine sat Napat down on the deck besides the small pool. She brought her a glass of water from the bottle in the kitchen and sat down next to her, talking in quiet words. She looked intently at the downturned face; looking to see if it was Napat's face, or Grandmother's face she was dealing with.

Napat started to weep.

Jasmine saw the Grandmother's face shimmer briefly over Napat's, then flit away. It was just Napat present. She hid her face in her hand and Jasmine let her. She wept the long weeping—the weeping when you become afraid that the tears will never stop. Weeping not just for the loss of someone—for the sake of the one lost—but then for oneself, and for the life that one has to live with a hole in it, a hole that may never fill in.

Jasmine called upon She Who Comes to be near her, and guide her, should Napat's grief become so great that she would break—that her mind would break, or her capacity for feelings. The young wen had to be psychically fragile from the possession by her Grandmother.

Jasmine stilled herself and opened her feelings. She felt into Napat, feeling what Napat felt. Napat wept until Jasmine feared that she was nearing the edge of the Great Weeping, and the connection with the Sea of Grief, the Grief of all the Unshed Unwept Tears, waiting just a few meters above her head, waiting to pour through any susceptible soul. It would be too much for Napat's mind.

Jasmine called upon the Goddess. She could feel the coalescence behind her, then a touch of golden warmth on her shoulders. Her mind filled with the image of what she was to do. She touched Napat on her shoulders, and transmitted through the energy, the light, the vibration. She laid Napat over on her side on the deck. She took a pillow from a deck chair and placed it under her head. She kneeled down on the cushion at Napat's head and laid it in her lap, stroking the long damp hair away from her cheek.

Jasmine turned Napat's head until she was looking up. She leaned forward, shrouding the young wen with her hair and placed her fingers lightly on the girl's temples. She vibrated the Resonance until she found the frequency that soothed the sobbing and stilled the wails. With a hiccup and a shiver Napat fell asleep.

Jasmine arose and retrieved two shawls from her living room and returned and covered the girl. She dropped her shirt on the deck, then her sarong, and slipped naked into the pool, reveling in the closeness of the Divine.

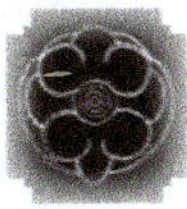

2

DROPPING INTO SHADOW

Napat woke up when the deck dropped into shadow from the setting sun. Jasmine had been sunning herself dry and was walking past Napat when she sat up. Jasmine, still naked, walked toward her, smiling and nodding. Napat saw her as outlined in golden light. She saw the shadow at the top of Jasmine's thighs illuminated as though from within. She stared at it and felt a thrill of longing pierce her between her own thighs. When Jasmine passed Napat she touched her shoulder and said, "Welcome, little friend," in Nahasi. Jasmine scooped up the sarongs and flung them over her shoulder, looked back and said, "Come in."

Napat, still dazed from the possession by her Grandmother, was seeing everything in a glow, but the one around Jasmine was particularly bright, and wide. She squinted at the gorgeous wen as she walked away. Napat felt overcome, overpowered by the beauty that just passed her by. She fell deeply in love, no, deeper than that. She fell immediately into devotion. Her memory of what she'd been through earlier that day, and what Jasmine had done to save her, came flooding back, threatening to re-evoke those emotions, but she inhaled instead. She inhaled the scent of the High Priestess. Some particular shade of light from Jasmine entered into the cloud of her essence, a mixture of sweat and sex that equated with power. The power sank down in Napat and buzzed behind her clitoris, making her inhale sharply again. The emotions subsided completely.

She was still staring at Jasmine when Jasmine stuck her head back through the kitchen door, her hair swinging forward when she stopped. Jasmine said "Come in," again, beckoning. Then she smiled at Napat and Napat felt a melting sensation in her heart.

Jasmine had been feeling all this, knowing that Napat was at risk of imprinting on Jasmine, and losing her will in the process, Napat instead subsuming herself into Jasmine's will. It was something Jasmine wouldn't allow. Jasmine's role, as it was with all Priestesses in the Order, was to empower wen and help them to individuate themselves in the higher and more ecstatic levels of experience.

Napat's devotion would be damaging to her nascent soul, and a binding on Jasmine, and thus an impediment to Jasmine's spirit.

When Napat stepped into the kitchen Jasmine was leaving it, and told her, again over her shoulder, to make tea.

Napat filled the teapot from the bottled water on a stand and put it on the large burner of the small four-burner stove. She sat down on one of the three chairs at the small table.

Jasmine returned wearing western style clothes, a skirt and a button-down shirt, both in tropical weight cotton. The shirt was open four buttons, the lines of her breasts visible in the shadows. She sat down on the other side of the table from Napat. Napat watched her, eyes glittering like a hawk's. Jasmine sighed, smiled at her, and then stood up, getting a jar of tea from a cabinet behind her. The tea was a special black tea, with additional stimulants added to promote alertness and attentiveness.

Pointing to a cabinet on the left of the sink she said to Napat, "Get the honey from that cabinet, would you? And the tea balls hanging from the hook, and a spoon from the drawer below them?"

Jasmine watched as Napat struggled to turn her head away to and search out the items. She had a sudden image of Napat on her knees and Jasmine standing over her, holding Napat's hair balled in her fist. She couldn't be sure what kind of image it was, and it gave her a small thrill she didn't understand. Then she knew—it was a small taste of the power of being worshipped. It made her smile, but instead of identifying with it, she used it to reinforce the principles of her training.

Jasmine brought cups from the cabinet and they both returned to their seats. Jasmine filled the tea balls and laid them in the cups. She sat with her hands folded on the table waiting for the water to boil. Napat sat at right angles to her, leaning forward, her elbows on her knees.

When the kettle whistled, she got up, turned the burner off, and poured the water into a ceramic teapot on the counter. Bringing it to the table she poured water in both cups, set the pot down and waited a moment before she started swirling the ball around the cup by the chain. Napat, watching sideways, sat up and did the same. It seemed much prettier to do it that way, rather than bouncing the ball up and down in the water, or simply putting them in the pot.

Removing the ball and pouring in some honey, stirring it with her spoon, ever so swirly. Napat did the same, mirroring Jasmine. With Napat's attention drawn into the swirls, at the edge of hypnosis, ("Hyp-gnosis," she thought, smiling), she said, "Do you know who I am? Did your Grandmother tell you about me?"

Suddenly realizing it, Napat said, "You are the foreigner who came to visit her, and help, when she went to the pool to wash rags."

Jasmine answered, "Yes. I am she."

Napat lowered her head. "How can I thank you?"

Jasmine said, "Drink your tea. I will escort you home, it is already late. We will say I walked past you on the sidewalk, you were crying for your Grandmother, and I stopped to help. Beyond that, we shall see."

As she drank the tea, its enhancements began to work on her immediately. The more present Napat became, the more distant from the fog of the possession she became, farther by the minute from the stepping into the downspout from the Sea of Grief.

When Jasmine had first stepped into that space, into the downspout from the Sea of Grief, she had wept for a day, and then off and on for days. This Sea, composed of unwept tears, tears that should have been wept by the living but were left behind energetically in the atmosphere, was the most easily accessible transpersonal liminal region in the planet's magnetosphere. The energy, emotional energy stored like rain in a cloud, was just over the heads of the people, not very far, and it took only that someone be in a grieving state of consciousness, and then to think beyond themselves, think to the suffering of others, and the tears of the Sea of Grief would press upon someone, weighing on them until the grief burst through. It could pour through someone in a torrent, scouring them out like a flash flood in a stream bed. Or it could press steadily through, like a downpour, or slow to a trickle. The stones of one's ego would be washed away, pushed out or ground down, eventually exposing the core, the cylinder of the True Self, to be intuited. And from that intuition the Higher Heart could manifest. It could manifest through Love for others, knowing that their suffering was so much greater than one's own.

They rose from the table, retrieved Napat's backpack of books from the deck, and went down the streets to her home, rehearsing details of the story that they would tell her parents. Pushing open the gate, Napat looked over her shoulder at Jasmine. Jasmine nodded and followed her through the gate. Jasmine saw the figure of the surviving Grandmother move further into the shadows behind the screen of her shelter.

After introductions were made, and the story told, leaving out the part about the ghost of Good Grandmother, Jasmine was invited to eat, which she accepted. The family had just been finishing. Napat's older brothers and sisters vanished into the house while Napat's mother and father stayed on the dining platform, sitting cross legged at the low table, regarding Jasmine while she ate.

"Tell me again what happened today," Napat's father said. So they did. In Nahasi. This included Jasmine telling about where she was from and why she was here, exoterically speaking. She talked about walking past their gate every day, and about how she had befriended the deceased matriarch at the laundry pool, and how she had found Napat weeping and befriended her. She was here to teach yoga at the studio, and to live in their beautiful city. Jasmine did not intend to stay long, and when she finished, she stepped off the platform and stood up. Then she said something surprising. "I have been impressed by your daughter today. I am impressed by her intelligence and her learning. I am in need of a personal assistant. I would like to hire her to work for me in the afternoons, after school."

The impact of what Jasmine said was visible. Her father looked down contemplatively. Her mother's eyes lit up, as did Napat's, although she suppressed her smile. Her parents came down from the platform with her to see Jasmine to the gate.

As Jasmine shook the father's hand she pressed a substantial amount of folded cash into it, which he immediately, unseen by either his wife or his daughter, slipped into the waist line of his sarong. "Please, consider my request. I will pay her well. I will stop by tomorrow for your decision." She nodded at everyone, and thanked them, bowing, then went home herself.

The decision, of course, was affirmative. The next afternoon Jasmine knocked at the gate. It was answered by the mother and Jasmine stepped in. Napat appeared from the house, dressed traditionally, rather than in her school uniform. The mother said, "My husband says yes, Napat may work for you. But you are to pay him, once a week, for the privilege."

Jasmine said, "Yes, of course." She gestured to Napat, who could no longer suppress her smile. Her mother smiled also. "She will be home before dark. I have some correspondence I need her to translate for me. I will also help her learn to read and write English."

As they walked to Jasmine's house, Napat turned her head to Jasmine and asked, "Why are you doing this?"

"Your Grandmother would have wanted me to. She had big ideas for you. That is why she prevailed upon your father to keep you in school. She convinced him that his best hope for you was that you be educated well, and able to move to the capital and find a good job, and send money home. We have simply started early."

After walking a little in silence, Napat digesting what Jasmine had just said, Jasmine continued. "I was your Grandmother's friend, and she was mine. I cannot help but to continue to help her dream for you to manifest. Tomorrow when you come, bring clothes to leave at my house. That way you can come there straight from school, and not soil your uniforms. I will give you money to give to your father every week."

After a pause, Jasmine said, "You must understand. It will be your job to help me. You will do as I ask. There will be not only correspondence, or running errands for me, but other tasks, like cleaning the house and doing the dishes. Some cooking, as well. I need someone to make my life easier, and you are that someone. And I will also give you some money to keep for yourself."

Napat smiled, looking down. She thought, "Anything. Anything. I will do anything." Which, of course, Jasmine could hear with the Higher Hearing, but she chose to say nothing. Nothing yet, anyway. Jasmine had been trained to be aware of the seductiveness of power, and to use it, rather than surrender to its seduction in herself to use it over others—unless that was a path that served her Mission and She Who Comes.

At Jasmine's place she opened the gate with a key. They walked past the pool to the entrance to the house, entering with another key. "Do you know where to get copies of these keys made?"

"Yes," Napat replied.

"Are they still open? And are they far?"

"Probably, and not too far."

"I want you to get a set made for yourself. You will need them, so that you can come and go while I am not here."

Napat marveled at the trust Jasmine was showing her so quickly.

Jasmine took down an embroidered cloth shoulder bag and put

the keys in it and passed it to Napat. She handed Napat some cash and said, "Put it in the bag. It should be enough. Keep the change, only give me the receipt. There will be other purchases."

Napat stood glued to the spot. "Go, now," Jasmine said smiling. She put her hand on Napat's shoulder and a spark entered Napat from the hand. "Come back, and we will make supper together."

Jasmine turned away, unbuttoning her shirt and dropping it from her shoulders. "Jasmine? If they are closed, is there anything else?"

Jasmine turned back, her breasts swaying with the turn. Napat felt her breath catch. "Not tonight. Just come back so we can eat."

Napat and Jasmine turned away from each other at the same moment, both biting their lower lips. Napat was filled with longings she didn't understand.

Jasmine untied the string from her pants and let them drop away also, heading for the stairs. She heard Napat lock the gate behind her. Before she had even fallen to her bed she began to masturbate furiously, the activation from the tensions of the power had left her hot, and wet, soaking into her hand almost immediately.

She worked the little man so hard her hand became a blur that could only be intuited rather than discerned. Her mind was filled with visions of dominion. She rolled out of the bed and stood up, legs spread. She came, hard, in three sustained squirts. Her legs began shaking as she came and she settled slowly on her knees, coming once more, and then resting, her head and one arm on the edge of the bed, her hair spread out, covering her face.

She opened her lips and blew out once, moving some hair across her face. She settled down on her heels, and shook her head, saying "Whew. That was a fast one." Then she laughed out loud, and, standing up, went to the bathroom for a towel to dry the floor.

As she soaked up the rain she remembered the visions she'd had. She didn't remember seeing Wade in them. He wasn't there. She "hmm'd" when each vision ended with a still life. She studied these, analyzing the power content—the way each one showed her in a position of power and dominion. She looked, tracking the flow of energy within her. Settling on her heels again, holding the wet towel in her lap, she prayed.

"Great One, True Creator, spare me the excess of ego, and foster in me instead the power of Service to you."

The image of She Who Comes appeared in her fore-mind, smiling, and Jasmine smiled back. She gasped as She Who Comes initiated a stream of images in her mind about the near future, and how Jasmine was to mentor Napat.

When Napat returned Jasmine joined her in the kitchen dressed in a sarong and shawl. She asked Napat to cook—rice and vegetables— so Jasmine could watch how she handled herself in the kitchen. This also gave Jasmine the chance to invite Napat to talk more about her life, her dreams and ambitions, and to observe Napat's reactions when the subject veered towards Grandmother.

Napat seemed steady enough, and there were no intrusions upon her psyche. Grandmother was quiescent. Jasmine's role was to promote stability for now. And when sufficient stability was achieved they would begin the work of training Napat to use the ghost of Grandmother as a psychic source of information, and eventually introduce Napat to She Who Comes Herself.

3

SULKING

When they'd first arrived on Wallid, Wade had delusions that he would be spending more time with Jasmine, as if they were a couple on vacation, or even newlyweds. He was considerate and helpful and supportive. The first week—a week of rest—went just about as he'd planned. They spent a lot of time in bed together, sleeping, having sex, going out to eat.

The Order leased several properties on the island, and the small house in town with the pool was just right for two, although it had been built for someone smaller than Wade. He would occasionally bump his head on the wall coming down the staircase from the bedroom, or trip over the high threshold between the kitchen and the living room.

At the end of the week they met with the couple, the Priestess and her Consort, from whom they would be taking over management of the yoga studio. They worked to bring Jasmine and Wade up to speed on the management of the Studio, the class schedules, and the relations with the local contractors that kept the studio clean and supplied with water and refreshments.

In addition to their own place in town, the couple, Belinda and Mark, had a small place in the country, perched on the side of a gorge, isolated by the jungle from the view and hearing of others. It was to there they retreated, beyond the nosiness of neighbors, to practice their ritual engagements, the tantras of transition and the high tantra of Divine Union.

As the Hostess, Belinda was honored first with being bathed, her hair washed and combed, shaved and scented. The men paid more honor to her by following her directions as to where to place their hands, their lips, and their phalli. In the bed, a grand four poster draped in fine netting that still let air from the ceiling fan above, and light from the low bedside tables, and from a recess over the headboard. Jasmine sat up against this, leaning back on large pillows, Belinda reclining on her. Jasmine would whisper in her ear, or direct her hands, so Belinda learned from Jasmine—the Priestess from the High Priestess.

When the first ritual was done they ate lightly and conversed, retiring together in the huge bed. In the morning they rose, had tea, swam in the cantilevered salt water infinity pool, bathed, and then repeated the ritual of the night before, this time with Jasmine as the focus of attention.

The touch turned worshipful.

In response the High Priestess summoned the Resonance of the Higher Heart and blessed each one's face and lips, their fingertips and their sex, with the vibration and transferred Love along each path. This in turn led to the advent of the Presence of the Divine, Her image settling slowly over and into Jasmine. Worship was engaged in anew. This led to a fresh transfer of energy, enlivening all until their entire bodies resonated with the pulse.

Wade mounted, Mark coupled at Her head, Belinda reclined against Jasmine, drinking it in, her hand between her legs, and Jasmine's hand over her's, guiding it, feeling with it and through it, pounding with energy though it scarcely moved. Minds immersed in the golden light of bliss, all of them, Consorts and Priestess, High Priestess and the Divine Feminine, feeding each other, feeding the High Priestess, and feeding the Goddess, they exploded in orgiastic orgasm, spines arching, shouts and cries echoing into the canyon, startling the birds from the canopy.

Over a light brunch of dragon fruit and sparkling water Jasmine informed Mark and Belinda that they had been assigned to stay on the Island working down in the capital on the coast in an art gallery owned by the Order. If they wished, Jasmine would work with them every weekend if they were willing to make the trip up to the interior highlands city where they now were. They both agreed readily. Then Jasmine asked them to consider staying employed at the Yoga School. There was too much for her to do, and she told them she'd appreciate it if they would still stay on as managers, and instructors. They were delighted, and happy to know that they'd not be reassigned somewhere else.

Wade was mildly taken aback when the offer was made. She'd

not consulted with him first—as was her prerogative—but it made him, and what he might want to do, feel overlooked. Jasmine glanced quickly at him, noting his reaction.

On the way home, following Jasmine on their scooters, Wade felt something dissatisfied in his belly. He felt the difference between his status as a Consort and Jasmine's status as someone who had been through the High Initiation. He felt keenly that he was at the same status, the same level, as Mark, and it didn't seem fair to him, although he knew that he was, after all, Jasmine's Consort. At least that was something. But he didn't like it.

4

WORK

The Yoga Studio was a small two-story former warehouse with a girder extending out from the second story wall over a sliding door with a pulley for raising pallets. The entrance to the compound had both a rolling gate and a walk-through gate. There were offices along one side on the ground floor, which had a raised wooden floor for classes. Upstairs was mostly used for storage, but had a nice floor that could be used for additional classes. Up against the back wall of the compound there was a small cabin with a kitchenette, a bathroom, and divan that could be converted to a bed. It had a loft with a railing used for storage.

It was this cabin that Jasmine used for her other work: that of accumulating power for her impending role in the Liberation, as she thought of it. Her Consort, whose principal job was to provide security during her trysts, could hide in the loft. She thought of him as her "Big Phoenix", ready to swoop down and rescue her from the ashes of the energetic fires she might ignite in any of her "little phoenixes". Or in her own self—the alchemy generated a lot of heat, a lot of chi, or life-force energy, as she would complete the processes within her. In her mind she'd wondered what to call them when she thought of them: the plural of phoenix was what? Phoenii? When she realized she could use the aspirated 'h' rather than the 'f' sound she practiced saying it, "my little P'heenii" until she'd giggled.

Jasmine recruited her p'heenii only from among the expatriates, focusing on yoga students whom she knew would not be staying long on the island. This gave them a limited time to fall in love with her, and made their obedience to her conditions more likely. Local men were mostly locked into the patriarchal patterns of the Skreevic cult on the island, and would cause nothing but trouble if they suspected her of exercising any control, not to mention problems it would cause her Consort in dealing with them. This way the p'heenii could take home a lovely memory and there would be no attachment troubles for either them or herself.

Her schedule, worked out with the guidance of Madeleine, was to see her p'heenii only two days a week, with two sessions scheduled in the morning on those days. This would leave her time to teach an early class and one in the afternoon if there was demand. Otherwise Belinda would handle the overflow. There was always a breeze through the studio, and she was always amazed at how many people loved practicing during the heat of the day. She currently had three men she was seeing, and wouldn't give a second session in the week to any of them, preferring to wait for a fourth to appear and then she would add his mix to the recipe. Today, however, she had something planned for the next day, and would do three sessions back-to-back, in addition to the attention she would pay to her Consort. He could always serve as the fourth.

She had told her first p'heeni to come at 9:00 on this morning, another at 11:00. This would give the earlier one time to clear out and give her at least a half hour to meditate into the alchemy between each one, and then time to make it to her afternoon class.

The Consort's routine was to arrive by 7:30 on those days and make himself comfortable in the loft, out of sight. He could open the shutters if it wasn't raining, and ceiling fans would provide some measure of coolness.

She prepared herself with the lightest of paint and scent, putting her hair up with and old-style barrette that had dangling beadwork from the pin, or in a coil held in place with a pin the length of a chopstick. She would wear different outfits—a just above the knee length belted silk top made from an old kimono, or a white linen collared button front shirt that fell to mid-thigh. She had an ankle length loose slip made of transparent fabric with thin straps over the shoulders and a tuck under her breasts. And she had her old standby priestess outfits—tropical beach sarongs tied at the waist with a light weight shawl that would hang over her shoulders and down her front but leave her arms and breasts free; it was something she could shed in moment, or let fall artfully to the side.

She would arrange herself on the divan, covered with a tasseled cloth and overfilled with pillows. When she sat she would be framed with slender panels of painted flowers on the wall behind her. Off to her right but just within reach was a small table holding a tea service and another small table holding a bowl of fruit on the left.

Wade arrived an hour and half early, as scheduled. She washed him, fed him, and dressed him in a white tropical weight long-tailed shirt that came to his mid-thigh. They sat together in the traditional way, knees touching. She extended her ghost-chi body toward him, touching her little rod to him and holding it there while he shivered into an erection. She brought her ghost-chi body back, and extended her ghost-chi hands to envelope him, stroking him like a velvet glove. His erection poked through the folds of his shirt, then she leaned her ghost-chi body forward and sucked him with her mouth until she felt him swell even larger between her ghost-chi lips. When he gasped, and started to practice the fast breath, she stopped and opened her eyes, and smiled at him, holding the smile until he opened his eyes as well.

She laughed then, and leaned forward and breathed on him, and he twitched. She extended just the tip of her tongue to remove the drop of wetness there. 'It is time" she said. She sat back and bid him rise. He sighed and smiled, then stood and bowed, stepping back. "I will see the first one down here," she said. He said, "I am not sure any of them are ready for upstairs yet. Even for the taste."

She said, "I agree, and you know we will consult before I do." He nodded and stepped back again and turned toward the closet under the steps to the loft, sitting on the cushions and began to meditate, leaving the door open until the last minute.

He said, "I feel the need to remain close today."

She went to him and kissed him, murmured her love and gratitude for him in his ear and sent him on to the loft to serve as her hidden guardian.

The first little phoenix arrived while she was still sitting on the cushions finishing a cup of tea. She set the cup down and leaned back on her left arm, and dropped her right foot to the floor. She closed her eyes as if she was in meditation. She knew what she looked like. She looked like a Goddess, and she knew which one. She bid him enter, and then bar the door behind him.

He knew the drill. This was his eighth time. He knew the routine, it excited him every time. Jasmine had spotted him in class his first week there, and invited him over for tea the next day, and persuaded him to her service that first morning. He was only too happy to do it. She was strange, this teacher, and he had told no one, fearing she would know. He was humble about it, and grateful, which is what she had told him to practice feeling, and what he would actually feel, bringing those feelings back to her. And she frightened him a little. He had some ambivalence about going back to Germany in two weeks, but knew that, ultimately, he would feel relieved.

The first time she had sat him down and talked to him about her situation, claiming a congenital condition that made sex extremely painful but she still needed sex, and was able to get her pleasure from pleasing men orally. He had agreed to help her in this way (only too quickly) then she had taken him into the bathroom, disrobed him, and washed him, thoroughly inspecting him. And she had gone down on him right there, with his ass backed up against the sink stand. He had lasted only a few minutes, and she was pleased, and had actually come.

They had progressed. She would occasionally let him touch her hair and lightly hold the sides of her head. She never touched herself, but she always came. Sometimes she would even squirt a little, but she never exposed herself to him, nor touched herself, instead orgasming in the way she had been trained. And she would visit the Palace when she knew she could allow herself.

He came into the room and dropped his clothes on the floor. He waited there, watching her, his erection growing without even being touched. She sensed this and smiled in her meditation, opened her eyes and beamed a larger smile at him, and beckoned to him. He came to edge of the couch, and she leaned forward and put both her feet on the floor. She reached for him with one hand, turning his cock one way, then the other, examining him, then leaning forward, smelling him deeply, smelling the cleanliness of him. She let down her hair. She brought her other hand toward him, and slowly, softly, touching him, stroking him up and down with her fingertips, she grasped him, and sat forward, parting her lips, and enveloped him.

He was completely erect when she took him in. She knew his rhythms by now, and she took care to prolong his erection, and help him prolong it. She gripped him tightly at the base with one hand, and slowly stroked the shaft with the other. She kept her mouth still on the head, and made slow sucking motions with her mouth. The reduced motion and friction gave him time to become relaxed with what was happening and not let his excitement get the better of him. Jasmine had come to like him a little, and wanted to give him a relationship to remember.

When she knew he was nearing his peak, she relented, or so it felt to him, and swallowed him deeply, drawing her nails lightly across his root from back to front, inducing the orgasm, feeling the orgasm as it came shooting forward. He came in a way that felt like thunder to him, and lightning lit his brain. He came and came, shooting over and over again, and she swallowed him, then, letting his come fill her mouth she moved her head back and forth rapidly, bathing his cock in the foaming mix of her saliva and his come, sucking hard, every drop from him, til his knees buckled and she released him, come dripping from her lips, down her chin and onto her throat, rolling between her breasts, as he collapsed to the floor.

She sat there, smiling at him, holding the last of his come in her mouth, letting her saliva work on it, pressing her tongue against the roof of her mouth, waiting until she felt the opening and the process start—the connection between her root, her spine and her brain resting atop her tongue, then she swallowed.

He opened his eyes and watched her as she licked her lips, using her finger to wipe his come from her chin, and then her throat and then from down between her breasts, still looking back at him and smiling at him all the while. He sat up, shaking his head, and said, "That was amazing, how do you know how to do that? Hold me off, I mean."

She smiled, and said, "Practice, young friend, practice." He shook his head again, and realized he didn't really want to know what she meant by practice.

She asked him if he wanted some tea, and he said no, and standing and moving to his clothes, he put them on. She stood up, and right before he stepped across the threshold he turned and bowed to her. It was clear to her that he wasn't quite sure why, but she smiled and returned the bow to him. He turned, and sighing, shook his head, knowing only that he was confused but not knowing why, he left through the kitchen and closed the front door behind him.

Wade, her big Phoenix, came down the steps from the loft, his cock in his hand. He groaned and smiled and shook it at her. She laughed and held up her hand and shook her head no, saying "No, no, no, no." And laughing, she sat down and leaned back on the couch. She threw her hair back over her shoulders, and shook her breasts at him, holding them up in mock offering.

He groaned again, and laughing took another step forward, shaking his cock at her some more.

She stood up and said "I only have a little time to clean up, and finish the alchemy. You can watch, and you can help, if you want."

He said, "I want to help." She went to the door, slid the wooden bar across the door brackets and then into the bathroom, turning on the tap. He got a wash cloth from the rack, and while she untied the shawl, he wet it and wrung in out. He made to hand it to her, but she leaned toward him, taking his hands in hers, and wiped her chin, and throat and chest, and let his hands go. He rinsed the cloth and turned to her again, wiping her down while she stood there, until all traces of the little p'heeni's ejaculate were gone. He rinsed the shawl again and went to hang it up while she soothed a flower essence over where they had washed.

She dropped the sarong around her waist to floor and said, "I think I'll wear the kimono jacket this time." She took it from a hangar and belted it on.

She looked at him in the mirror behind him, and said, "Did you notice? Your cock got hard again while you were washing me."

He said, "Yes, I did." And he turned to her and smiled. "The power of Love in Service, I suspect." She grinned at him then, and reaching back as he turned to her, she grabbed his cock and squeezed it, and pulled on it a few times, and said. "Good."

Then, she said, "Tea." And they went to the kitchen, heated water, and shared a cup, leaving it, just the one cup, on the table. It was an intimate moment, no talking, fingers brushing as they passed the cup, quiet, almost shy, smiling. After a few minutes it ended. "Time" she said.

She reached for his phallus again and slowly tugged and stroked it back to full erection, then she led him by it back to the stairs to the loft, turned and seated herself on the couch, sat up straight and entered the meditative state known as sublimation, swallowing down, down through her belly and into her womb, there to let her first meal heat.

There was a knock at the door, and she nodded to Wade, who had been watching her, his head peeking over the railing, rose and went to the doors, slid back the bar and opened them.

She welcomed in her second little p'heeni, grasping his left hand in her right and pulling him into the entry, closing the door and sliding the bar into place. Then she led him over the threshold toward the couch, he kicking off his shoes before he went. Once in the living room she pulled him around and backed him up to the couch and pushed him down.

"What, no hey, hi, how are you?" She shushed him, and undid his shorts and pulled them down, spreading his knees apart she lifted her breasts and rubbed them all over his groin, then she grabbed his cock in her right hand, cradled his balls in her left, and sucked his still flaccid cock into her mouth, burying her lips all the way to his belly. She sucked gently, but held still, just suckling gently and releasing, feeling him respond, feeling him grow, keeping her lips on his belly until he filled her mouth, swelling, pressing, struggling for space. He started to twitch and then move his hips against her face so she took her hands and put them on his hip bones and pressed him down, holding him still.

She continued her gentle suckling until she could feel his cock straining against the back of her throat and then slowly, slowly she pulled her head back, releasing his cock, the full length of him unfolding, erect and hard as it emerged until she had her head all the way back, except she left her mouth over the head of it. Suckling some more she moved slightly back and forth on the edge of it until he shuddered. Then she sat back and admired the beautiful thing before her.

She said, "No words could have filled my mouth as well as this did. Why bother speaking?"

His pride piqued, he smiled at her, "Yeah, it's a beauty ain't it?"

She smiled, barely suppressing a smirk at his third person perspective, and simply nodded her head. This kind of egocentric differentiation was good for her cause. It meant that he identified his organ as a separate person, neither holding it in integral regard, nor able to become it wholly, both practices a deep part of the Masculine Arts.

It left her free to deal with him as a fragment, and his cock as an individual. His cock knew that, and appreciated it. She knew his cock would do whatever she wanted, and it would pull him along for the ride, reluctant or not. And as she thought this, gazing down at his phallus with a certain lack of focus, holding it in her hands, it started throbbing and twitching in agreement.

She thought at it, "Slow down a little bit. This will not take long anyway. Do you not want me to extend it even a moment?" and in answer the throbbing and twitching slowed down. His cock released its carrier's pent-up breath, and the carrier sighed. And then, with typical ambivalence when she let it go, it strained up and forward, seeking her in its blindness.

She teased it, breathing on it from first one side then another, slowly training it to lean towards her breath, to respond to her will, to come at her call.

This was her tenth session with this one's phallus, and it was learning, slowly leaning toward wherever she would call it, and finally standing straight up, when she hovered poised above it. And today she gave it a test: from hovering above it she started panting at the tip, the blind eye zeroing in on her breath. She focused her lips into a small 'o' panting fast, and leaning down close to it, it actually grew another half a centimeter towards her in its straining.

And she laughed, from deep in her throat, feeling the stirring of the Goddess deep within her.

She felt a curious impulse of mercy toward him, and toward her Consort in the loft, and decided to finish him off. She gripped him in one hand, and lowered her mouth over him, and using her other hand pressed on his perineum. Using alternating stroking and pushing, sliding her head up and down, she brought him quickly, not even shaking her head free when he reached up and grabbed it, trying to slow her down. Or perhaps move her faster, she didn't care which.

When he came he shot way deep into her throat, filling her mouth with come, groaning and thrusting, and she just held on for the ride, holding her head and hands still, swallowing all except that last half mouthful. Then when he stilled she worked him again a few more times, using his cock as the piston in a butter churn, mixing and frothing and bubbling, letting some leak out the corners of her mouth, down his shaft, and into her fingers.

He gasped and groaned at this, the pleasure excruciating, and she shuddered for him, twitching her pelvis, a small orgasm, but enough to satisfy him. She sat back a little, and licked his shaft with her tongue, and then releasing him, licked her fingers while looking him in the eyes.

She said, "I just don't know what came over me. I just had to have you right then in that moment. And I just think it's magnificent, your tool."

And as he recovered, he grinned at her, a big, kind of stupid grin, and said "Yeah, I know."

So she grinned back at him, apparently stupid also, and reached out and grabbed him again, flipping him around and making little happy bounces on her heels.

He said, "Whoa now girl, I can't get it back just like that, not after the job you just did."

And she said, "Oh I know. I just wanted you to know how happy I am. And I do have to go out for a lesson in a little bit, so you have to go soon, too."

And he, not really wanting to stay for another round of what he'd just been through, feigned a little disappointment, which she saw right through, said, "Well, if that's the way you really want it, OK then. But I will see you next week, right?"

And she said, "Yeah, sure, but I'll have to call you and let you know what day."

And he said "OK then. I'll wait for it." He got up and got dressed while she watched, still smiling that smile, and he hopped over the threshold, grabbed his shoes, and called back over his shoulder, "See you, then." And she said "Bye." And he closed the door.

There was thumping on the steps from the loft, and her Consort rolled out onto the floor, sweating, mock panting, and said, "Mercy! Mercy! I don't know if I can do another one."

She was already over the threshold, sliding the bar into place and said, "Ha ha. I know you can."

He said, "Yeah, maybe. But I'm not sure I want to. This is a lot, the way we do this, all three in one day. It's getting hot up there."

"It will get hotter later, I promise," and she hopped back into the living room and kicked some pillows around, and went up to him, and caressed him on one cheek and kissed him on the other, turning toward the couch.

"Seriously," he said. "This isn't the way it's normally done, and for good reason. You're cutting it close between these guys. And what about the mix?"

She turned back to him. "Damn right, it's serious. I need this. I have work I need to do, and need both the usual alchemy and then extra power to deal with what's going to be coming down."

She exhaled, almost in a woof. "Look. I had an idea for a certain configuration of power within me. I checked in out with Her and She smiled, nodded Her head, and said 'Yes'. I have an idea, and I know it can be difficult but I really need your help in this."

He had only the barest idea of what she was talking about. He didn't know about internal configurations of power other than working on the links of connection between the various bodies. He knew that she was working to acquire what she called 'ghost-chi' from her p'heeni, then using him to bring additional order to the patterns within her, so that she could alchemize the substances into 'soul-chi', and eventually 'spirit-chi', these being the energetic substances that composed the bodies of the Soma, Soul, and Spirit.

He knew that she was gaining power in her ghost-chi body—he could feel it when she used it. She had only to extend the energy of that body out from herself. He knew she could bring him to orgasm without touching him directly, using only this extension of her Soma. He couldn't do it himself yet, but he knew the theory that this should become a power that he, too, would be able to manifest. In time he would be able to induce an orgasm in a wen without touching her, even from across a room. But he was impatient, and often too lazy to do the internal work exercises he'd been taught. Instead, he liked the idea of developing the higher chi—the higher substances that he had been told the legendary among them used to manipulate weather, for example. He'd been taught the math—that the alchemy reduced the substances in the process, so that the 'volume' of the lower substances produced only a tenth of the volume needed for the next highest body, the Soul, and that in the next reduction again only another tenth of the volume was derived. He understood this meant that there was only one hundredth of the original volume of ghost-chi that became spirit-chi. And he knew that he needed to get the substances he needed from what Jasmine fed him. And, deep within, he felt something irksome about this reality.

But he didn't know what Jasmine was building within her. Although Jasmine's ultimate goal was to build an octahedral crystal within herself, the diamond body, she had kept the details of the current project to herself.

What Jasmine was doing was building a weapon within, a weapon that was also something that she could extend, perhaps even throw, from herself. She was building a tetrahedral pyramid, the simplest solid, something that would always land point up. She was using the three little p'heenii for three of the apex points and her Consort for the fourth apex. When she could hold all four energetic points the crystalline shape formed. When she could hold the image of all four points in the proper symmetry, the edges would form, crystal sharp. In order to make it permanent she would use the Resonant pulse to run energy through the edges between the apexes. Eventually the entire form would crystallize, available for her to summon at will, and cast it, whirling, at an adversary. Each apex, edge, and face, could discharge energy into whatever it struck. Although she knew only the apices she joyfully anticipated discovering what the impact of the edges and faces would be.

The apex energies were derived from the p'heenii. The first was the power of Confusion. The second was the power of Loss of Control, transferring control to the thrower. The third was the power of rage-fueled Aggression, violence that would feel like ceaseless pummeling. The fourth, which she derived from the energy of her Consort, was Paralysis, and Unconsciousness—both derivatives of the power of Forgetting.

Wade knew that there was more going on than he knew, but he also knew that he might not get his questions answered. A part of his training was to invite the Feminine to share something when she was ready and to hold space for her in the meantime. Wade acknowledged her intentions by his accession. He told her, "OK, I get it. I'll go back up to the loft and wait."

Jasmine's third little p'heeni arrived on time. He was an arrogant man, proud of his strength, and identified with his machismo. Using him the way Jasmine was using him was risky, she knew. It was always edgy with him, and he resented Jasmine's control—he resented any control by the Feminine. Jasmine's strategy was to feed his ego, and thereby create for him the illusion that he was doing her a favor, and hence, was in control of the events. This enabled Jasmine to extract from him the particular frequency of energy she needed for the third particular apex in her tetrahedron.

He kicked off his sandals, dropped his shorts, pulled his t-shirt over his head and dropped it. He rolled his shoulders forward, flexing his pectoral muscles, and grabbed his cock, shaking it at her and pulling on it. "Hey, baby," he said, "I'm packing lunch. You hungry, yeah?"

Jasmine was in her Goddess pose, one foot on the ground, leaning on the opposite hand. She smiled at him, looking down, triggering his impulse to pacify his superiority by showing him the hominid deference posture by bowing her head. Knowing he could no longer see her smile she allowed herself a quick smirk at his arrogance.

He swaggered toward her, still holding his cock in front of him. When he was close enough he laid it on her head, flexing his hips so it dragged over the pin holding her hair in place, loosening it. She thought quickly about grabbing the pin and using it to cause some real damage. She chose instead to raise her face so his cock rested on it instead. He rubbed it around and thumped it on her cheeks, slapping her several times. It grew harder when he did, the slapping sound becoming audible to Wade in the loft, pulling him to a lazy alert.

Jasmine kept smiling at her tool. She felt him rest it on her lips, and she extended her ghost-chi to cause him to feel that he was already inside her mouth. His eyes closed as she took his girth in her hand and slowly moved it, rubbing it back and forth on her lips while leaving him locked in the ghost sensations. The discordance this caused in him made him open his eyes and gaze down at her, his face locked in a smirk that would have mirrored Jasmine's, his head empty, his gut filled with satisfaction.

He watched as Jasmine opened her mouth for him, letting him fall in, sucked in by her twin powers, that of her soma, and her ghost. Slowly she began the dance and she felt him twitch, a sign that she would be able to end this quickly. The twitch was strong enough to wake him from his trance.

"No, uh-uh," he said. "We're not gonna do that this time. I'm gonna take you." He grabbed her gathered hair on top of her head and forced it back so that her face was forced upward. After a quick glance at him, her eyes showing a mock emotion that he read as terror, he smiled as she looked down and went still.

"I know you say you can't do it. You say it hurts so bad. But you got another one, and that's the one we're gonna use, that's the one you get to exercise today instead of your pretty mouth."

Jasmine collapsed her posture, signaling resignation to the p'heeni, making his smirk transform to a smile. He used her hair to turn her around and forced her to bend forward toward the back of the couch, pushing her head into the pillows.

Jasmine went along, falling deeper into relaxation. She knew how to handle this. She needed the substance he offered and she knew how she was going to get it. Her training had shown her how to relax the sphincter, and send an impulse to the glands that surrounded it to release some of the complex compounds that served as lubricants. She slowed her breathing to the point that she knew the p'heeni's awareness would drop as far as the subliminal. He would become completely vulnerable to control from below.

He didn't pause, he simply pressed himself into her. She opened to him completely. She didn't even gasp, keeping her breathing steady and constant. When he was half way in she clamped down on it, refusing him both further entry, and withdrawal as well, only allowing him the slightest rocking motion. She reached back between her legs and grasped his balls in her hand, holding him in place. She extended her ghost-chi fingers and stroked his perineum lightly. Then she exercised the technique that gave her complete control—she extended a ghost-chi finger and inserted it in his ass, going as far as his swollen prostrate, and massaged it.

The impulse to orgasm this triggered in him was beyond his control. She could feel the wave begin and ejected him forcefully, turning quickly and holding his erection steady over her upturned face. Her grip controlled his ejaculation, letting it drip slowly from him into her mouth even while his cock jumped and pulsed in her hand.

When she had all of it she looked up at the loft and nodded to the watching Wade. He came silently down the stair and grabbed the p'heeni by his hair while he kneed the man in the back of his knees, causing him to collapse kneeling to the floor. Jasmine put her hands on the side of his head and pulsed the spell of Forgetting into his brain. She drew her hands back a little and, using her thumbs, pulsed the spell into the center, using the chakra in his forehead, blanking out all visual memory her. Then she moved her fingers to the top of his head, extending the ghost-chi into the great center there, the center that, had it been activatable, would have been able to connect him to the transcendence of himself. She pushed through the resistance and filled the entire space with blankness. Then she swallowed, holding him there at her feet, face to the floor, while she worked the preliminary alchemy.

When she released him Wade pulled him to his feet. It was like he was drunk, and Wade was a bouncer, heading him for the door. They stopped at the pile of clothes and Jasmine stood up, touched a hand to the side of his face and told him to put his clothes back on. In a stupid trance he did so, Wade keeping a hand on him at all times.

Together they escorted him to the door. Wade opened it. "Go home," Jasmine whispered up to his ear. "Go home and forget. Forget this," she said. "Forget." Wade guided him through the yard around the warehouse, put him on his scooter and watched as he started it. "Forget this," he said. "Don't come back."

Those last words echoed in his head until he couldn't even remember where the "back" was to which he shouldn't come.

When Wade returned from closing the gates Jasmine was waiting for him. "Come to me Consort," she said in a voice that was both seductive and commanding. She took him by the hand and sat him down on the couch. He closed his eyes and smiled, knowing it was his turn—his reward for his service was at hand, so to speak.

She straddled him, sliding him all the way in, sitting down on him, and stopping, relaxing into the breath, relaxing into the vision where she used the lower seal to support the energetic triangle within her. When the three energies she'd just extracted aligned they locked into place, the apexes and the edges forming a white-gold triangle and the space within it slowly turned a pale green, turning slowly as it floated upward. When the triangle rose to the level of her heart it stopped turning and formed a shield there, apex up.

When it stopped there, she rose from her throne and kneeled on her Consort's arms, pinning them down. She reached for his head with one hand and with the other spread the lips of her phulva. She summoned her orgasm, and with an act of will she rained for him, filling his open mouth, willing him to drink her in, drenching his hair and face.

She held him in place, watching him swallow, tracking the light in her rain as it spread through him, filling him with an ecstasy she wasn't sure wasn't being wasted by his lack of humility. It didn't matter.

When she finished, she dropped back down, kneeling between his knees, took him in her mouth and gave him the energetic command to finish. She took all of it within, holding as much as she could in her mouth, swallowing only a little, letting the rest run down her chin and throat. She raised her face and sat back on her heels, alchemizing what she held in her mouth before she swallowed. When she did the energy of it went no farther than her heart, snapping into the fourth apex, and the whole pyramid glowed there, pulsing slightly, white edges sharp as razors, apexes sharp as knife points. She rolled the pyramid until an apex was pointing out and a great strength filled her, enough strength to separate her ghost-chi body from her soma, and it rose just above her, its green tetrahedral heart spinning.

Smiling, knowing that she'd finished the task, she lowered her head and fell asleep kneeling there. She journeyed to the First One.

A snorting snore from Wade awakened her, and she discovered she was still smiling the smile she'd had when her fugue had begun.

She woke Wade to feed him and send him on his way to his place in one of the smaller villages out in the countryside. Over tea she asked him how it was for him, watching her earlier, and how it felt to have to step in and intervene.

He replied, "It's always interesting, you know. Watching you is inspiring, and makes me love you. Loving you I want to control you, so this desire for control is always struggling with my knowledge that in this Service, in Her Service, you are in control, and loving Her, I want this control for you.

"And my desire for control then drops into my root, and there I have to struggle with control yet again, but it is the control of the Masculine Art. It is a good thing, and always less hard to bear. I don't identify with it, I remain in touch with Her, and I am good, gaining more power and control over myself every time. I feel it as a swelling, an enlarging of my Soul past the enlargement of my cock, and as my Soul is engorged it feeds upward into my Spirit.

"When it came time to put my hands on the p'heeni I didn't even have to feel aggressive, just powerful."

She smiled at him, for this is how it should be. But she had a sudden feeling, an intuition, and she knew he was lying, just telling her what he knew he was supposed to say.

The p'heeni awoke hours later in his room, screaming from a dream where he'd been scuba diving naked and a shark had come along and bit his dick off. The pain felt real in the dream and he sat up rocking, hands between his legs, afraid to look, and feeling like he'd been on a drunk he couldn't remember, like it was a black out drunk from the way he'd been in college. He remembered nothing, really.

A week later he was riding past the yoga studio on his scooter and he sneered at the gate. "Fuckin' hippy bullshit. All that stretchin'." At the next stoplight he stood up and adjusted his crotch. "I gotcher stretcher right here," he said, smiling his machismo smile.

5

ARRIVAL AFTERNOON

Sitting on the bed, the afternoon sun glinting off his body, Alam leaned over and put his hand on Calley's back. She rolled over and sat up, stretched and yawned. "Thank you, beloved, for bringing me here," he said.

"It feels good here," She said. "Let us hope the feeling lasts. No one will be happy with what we have to tell them."

"I've looked in the closets. There are clothes in there that look like they'd fit you. As there are in the closet in my room. Shall we get dressed, beloved?" Alam asked, holding out a dressing gown to Calley. "I'll be trying out the work clothing."

"Yes, beloved. Let's get dressed and find some food before we summon the first group to a meeting in a little while," She said, reaching for the gown.

Alam left for his room through the private door. Calley went to the window and looked at the dark Pine Eye far up the mountainside. She sighed. Now that the afternoon's delights were over She decided to enter, entranced, into the shared mind space with Mother, She Who Comes, the Mind of All Life on the Planet.

They'd worked out the plan for the next phase of the challenge to De Murgos—the challenge that might get him off the planet for good. She went to the altar, the altar that had belonged to the previous High Priestess Eva, and sat down.

The altar had been cleaned. There were some fresh herbs of different types to make smoke. There was also, when She looked closely, the vial in which Regina had brought her here decades ago, and the wolf skin bag that Regina's mother Amanda had used to bring Alam here the first time and take him back to Scotland. Calley smiled at Regina's thoughtfulness. She reflected briefly on Amanda, now in the care of Her sister Bree. She sent gratitude in their direction.

She closed her mind to review the instructions. It was a certainty that De Murgos would return here. That he hadn't so far spoke to the severity of the wounds he suffered when the bolos of Siddhi power had struck him. And there had been no sign in the week since the fight at the Gate House of his servants, the Embla and the Dangla. It was necessary then to make the place appear to be abandoned before their return. The Order of the Fleur de Vie was going have to retreat from these grounds and reorganize their forces for a future conflict, but on grounds of their own choosing.

The first part of the plan was to mobilize everyone for departure. They would leave as soon as accommodations could be found elsewhere.

Among its diversified businesses the Order owned 3 hotel chains. Stonehaven residents could be distributed among these until appropriate stations could be found. Calley knew that She could give the order and the local Council of the Order would make it all so. They couldn't be sure how long they had. And the Madeleines, that fascinating circle of psychics, would have to be deployed as a detection squad, looking for disturbances in the field of the Spirit of the Land that would indicate whether any of the enemy forces had returned. She received an impression from Madeleine that her people were already deployed, in meditative connection with each other and the energetic field of the Land.

She opened her eyes, smiling. From an inside pocket in her robe she withdrew a locket on a golden chain. She opened the locket and looked within. She smiled to see image of the land inside—the Hidden Land. Mom had given Her a small piece to take with Her wherever She went. She tapped it once, and went invisible. Anyone looking into the room would see only the vacant altar.

From Her perspective, however, She could see everything. So long as She had the locket on Her person, none could see Her. She tapped the land twice more, returned to visibility, and closed the locket, smiling.

She hung the locket necklace over Her head and pulled her hair out from underneath the chain, shaking it loose once it was free. She reached into her pocket and pulled out four more lockets, and laid them out on the altar with Love.

She closed her eyes and reached out to her eldest daughter Torey, at home in the Hidden Lands. She tried to find time every day to reach out to her children. She saw Her daughter in the common house, by the fire, talking with Calley's mother, She Who Comes. Torey had a concerned expression on Her face. Mother was smiling. When She felt Calley's presence in the room She turned to face Calley and smiled more broadly.

"Welcome, daughter. We have news. The Embla and the Dangla returned to the Last Shrine today, looking for clues. Torey was there in her sheep form and overheard the entire conversation. Tell Her, Granddaughter, what was said."

"Yes, Grandmother. Hello Mother, how are you?"

Calley replied, "I am well daughter. It is new and different here. I hope I have the chance to explore it all a little. And how are you? And your brother and sister?"

"We are all well, Mother. We are all adapting to our responsibilities with Aunt Brighid and Grandmother's help. Shall I tell you what I observed?"

"Yes, please."

"I will tell you exactly as it happened. So here it is: the dialogue of the Embla and the Dangla.

"The Embla and the Dangla were sitting on the rocks above the Last Shrine, still unaware of its true function and nature. They knew only that recent events had begun there, and they had circled back to the beginning in an effort to understand what had gone wrong, and what was likely to happen next.

"'So how hurt is he?' the Dangla wanted to know first.

"'Badly,' the Embla screwed up his face. 'It's not fatal. Indeed, he cannot die at this level, but he can be hurt. Those bolos of power that the Abomination threw at him sliced through his shield. He is cut. He bled.'

"'Abomination? Is that what you call that thing, the black thing that threw them?' The Embla nodded.

"'That's funny. I thought my kind were the monsters and an abomination.'

"'No, you are our brothers, simply estranged. We will always be brothers.'

"'Where is he now?' the Dangla asked, unmoved by the Embla's professing of fraternity

"'Our master is convalescing on the far side of the moon.'

"'It should be obvious he is not our master. He is yours, but that is because you choose to obey. My kind chose not to obey. There were unforeseen consequences. Cut off, we are starving, and passing away.' The Dangla looked up and away, his face contorting. If he could have wept he would have.

"'You look like you're doing well for yourself,' the Embla could not resist commenting.

"'When one of us dies of starvation we eat him.'

"A spasm of nausea and horror seized the Embla.

"'You are surprised? What else are we supposed to do, cut off here, forced to feed on the negative manifestations of humans? At least, as one of us starves from their poor quality, we become free of most of the black dross we accumulate from our diet of shit. The body becomes more pure, more like where we came from, more like you. We survive. For now.'

"The Embla was horrified and speechless.

"The Dangla continued with his line of questioning. 'Why is he convalescing in hiding?'

"'He is meditating on the return of a dragon. He worked very hard to make sure they were all killed off. The ones his saints could not kill he had the Archembla kill. You recall, surely.'

"'I recall.'

"'He was unnerved by them. He thinks the return of a single dragon is portentous. I am certain he sees them as a threat, at least partially, to his control over these humans. And then there is also the other Monster—the one with wings. And the Abomination in black. Even I cannot figure that one out. I know that all three frighten him. He asks himself what is happening here, and what can he do about it. On the other hand he seems also to be bored. Now that he has enough of what he needs for himself…'

"'The Dangla interrupted him, 'Now that he has enough, thanks to human overbreeding, for himself and for you all, is what you mean.'

"'Yes. I've told you before that he has mentioned moving on, finding a different world to subdue into becoming food for him.'

"'Yes, you did. And you told me that he would take us with him. Leaving us here would be a death sentence,' the Dangla said with quiet determination.

"'And as I said, that is the plan. Many of us do not want to leave you behind. But how we will restore the ranks of our brotherhood is unclear. We are so different now. Perhaps starvation may be purification enough. This was news to me,' the Embla concluded. The Dangla kept his composure at the Embla's indifference to the suffering of his kind. The only detectable manifestation of his inner state was the slightest stiffening.

"The two sat in silence then, listening to the faint wind, listening to the flock of sheep chew their cud while they lay scattered about, feeling their contentment.

"'I have long been curious about something, if I may ask,' the Embla started up. The Dangla nodded.

"'What is it with you and the sexual abuse of women and children inside His religions?'

"'Ah, you said it yourself. That's not us. They are inside of his religions. Those Priests and Meemons belong to him. They derive pleasure from what they do. We cannot feed on pleasure. They take their pleasure and wrap it into their gratitude and devotion to Him. After all, it is He that makes their pleasure possible. They think of it as a gift from Him, and that He protects them. I doubt He's paying attention. It's all food to him.'

"As the Dangla spoke, a renewed sense of horror and nausea rose in the Embla. His diaphragm convulsed and he dry-heaved into the grass. He wiped the spittle from his chin and lifted his gaze, the horror showing on his face.

"The Dangla regarded him through narrowed eyes. 'Already you begin to grow more mortal.'

"The expression of horror on the Embla's face became terror. His image started to waver, indicating that he was about to flee. The Dangla reached out and put a hand on the other's knee. 'Stay!' he said. His hand burning with a sacred fire from the difference in their separated natures, the Dangla hissed, 'This is the terror my kind feels every day. Stay and tell me why you've asked me here.' He took his hand away when the Embla nodded his assent.

"The Embla composed himself, setting his face to its usual indifferent expression. 'Because this is where the trouble began. This is the where the path that led to the Monsters and the Abomination began. Perhaps we missed something here. And when he is healed we will have to return with him there. Or he may simply send us. In which case we'd have to come back here anyway. For my part I sense nothing here but these smelly animals everywhere.'

"'There is nothing of the Monsters and the Abomination here. They arose from something else. What arose here I cannot tell. Even the thin column of light that first drew us here is gone. We should go to that other place, and begin our investigation there.'

"'I agree,' the Embla said. 'But we should wait awhile, to see if he regains enough strength to give us the instructions himself.'

"Then they flew away, in different directions. I did not try to follow either of them."

They sat in silence for a moment, buoyed by the love they felt for each other.

Finally, Grandmother spoke. "The most vulnerable must leave tonight."

Calley nodded that She understood. To her daughter She said, "I love you" and broke the trance connection holding the image of Her daughter's smiling face.

She sighed. She already knew who the most vulnerable were.

As She stood up to get dressed she had a very quick vision of Her Mother, speaking to Her. The words were, "Her Majesty the Light has told me that the First One knows now."

"Why so long, Mother? It has been millennia since you applied for help."

"It has only been millennia, dear. The blink of an eye on the scale of the First One." The vision ended.

Calley shook Her head to clear the trance. She sent a quick message mentally to Madeleine and Diana to meet Her in Her office in an hour. She dropped Her robe and stepped into the novelty of the shower in Her bathroom. She loved it, reveling in the sensation of this part of Her elemental and substantial nature.

She dressed in jeans and a white shirt, slid her feet into sandals, and went down the hall to Eva's office. Now Her office, She thought. Although Eva's personal effects had been removed from the bedroom, the office had not been changed much. Behind a door she found a coat tree that had Eva's duster an old cowgirl hat still hanging on it, her muck boots on the floor. She touched the hat. On the desk was some personal correspondence from her friends, and condolence letters that would require answering. Calley had no idea how to do any of that, and decided she would pass all such matters over to Diana or Madeleine.

She sat in the leather swivel chair behind the desk. She put her feet up on the desk and crossed them at the ankles.

A form began to coalesce near her left hand. She went still and watched as the form coalesced into an older wen, almost solid, wearing jeans and a plaid shirt that sat on the edge of the desk, crossed her arms, and looked at Calley, sternly. After a moment she smiled briefly and looked away.

"Eva," Calley said. "You look like the pictures of you."

"And you are the Storm Goddess that has occupied the Pine Eye for decades."

"Yes," Calley smiled. "How did you…?"

"You brushed my hat with your hand when you re-opened the door that covered the coat tree. I left enough of me there to summon me when someone touched it. I'm glad it was you," Eva smiled again. "How may I help?"

Calley nodded, relieved. "For now, observe, and then we will talk about things later. And we should work on a connection that will let us communicate while I am engaged with these people. Can you hide?"

Madeleine was in the doorway as Calley asked this, and Eva said, "Yes," and disappeared. Madeleine had been practicing background camouflage for decades. She saw vaguely that something happened in the air next to Calley, but she couldn't see it clearly.

"How did you learn how to do that?" Calley asked, turning to the door, sensing Madeleine's presence.

"We have a benefactor among the Spirits of the Land here. Some of us, he teaches," referring obliquely to the King of Salamanders. After a pause she returned to visibility and said, "I shall want to know what that was, sometime," chin pointing to the air by Calley's side.

Calley said, "Hmm, yes. Well, come in, and you, too, Diana."

An hour later the food and tea they'd ordered arrived and they went quiet while an Intern smiled and inquired after their well-being, making small talk but connecting with her mentors. They smiled and fed the connection as a small reward. She left sweetly happy.

"And so," Diana said, "We move them out now, up to the rentals until travel is arranged. Then the others, in cohorts, to be distributed, some globally to other major centers of the Order. I will go find Moon Halter, Angelica, and Quinn."

Regina Moon Halter pushed open the door with one hand, her other on Angelica's elbow. "Yes? Quinn is at the Barn, Diana. He's with Alam, and the other two."

"Matthews and Halloran?" Diana asked.

"They have names?" Regina asked, mock-archly.

"We'll deal with them later," Calley said. She felt the ghost touch on her shoulder and heard the whispered "I'll get him."

"How are you, Angelica?" Calley asked. "Sit down please, both of you. Have some tea."

Angelica said nothing while she waited for tea to be poured for her. She held the cup up to her lip to check the heat, took a sip, and put the cup back on the saucer. "I am afraid. And I am angry. And both are incredibly painful. I would not wish this sensitivity on anyone."

"And the dragon?" Diana asked.

"It stirs," Angelica answered in a low voice, looking down, drawing out the 'r' and trilling it. The space around her head took on a reddish tinge.

"Greetings, big boy," Regina said, laughing as she put her hand on Angelica's shoulder. "We see you. Easy."

"He remains stirred up. He is awake, and only just below the surface. He is," Angelica struggled for words, "He is…aggressive. Instinctual. Magnificent." She said this last in a whisper, then shivered.

At the Barn the men were target practicing with the new crossbows. Craft explained it to Alam, who was delighted with the form the weapon had taken. They all froze when the ghost of Eva appeared in front of them. She looked at all of them and smiled, went up to Quinn, and, putting a cool hand on his shoulder, leaned in and whispered, "Hello, beloved. You are wanted at the Mansion."

Quinn felt the cold brush of ghostly lips against his ear. The ghost turned and touched Craft on the side of his face—and vanished.

Halloran said, "Yes, and that was unexpected." He looked over at Matthews, still standing there with his mouth open, and elbowed him. "That's right, eh?"

Matthews shook his head. "Something bad is happening."

Quinn said, "Maybe. I've been summoned."

Tears slowly rolled down Craft's cheeks.

Quinn arrived at Calley's office ten minutes later. Angelica was standing, gripping the back of a chair, head down, obviously upset. Quinn heard her say, "I'll pack my things," as she turned and walked past him.

Before he could sit down Calley stood and said to Quinn, "You're leaving with Regina and Angelica. The three of you are leaving now, heading up to the houses on the road until we can get you away."

Quinn nodded back, turned, and went off to his room.

"There," Regina said. "That was easy."

Turning to Regina, Calley reached into her pocket and took two of the lockets and gave them to Regina. "You may not need these, but your companions will. Give these to them in due time. Not yet."

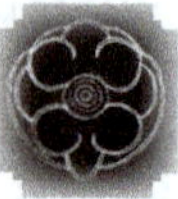

6

ARRIVAL EVENING

At supper Calley sat with Madeleine, Regina, Diana, and Angelica. The conversation was a continuation about the workings of Stonehaven and how they were based on the ancient archetypal pattern. Calley listened politely, waiting until she could meet with the group in private after the meal. Society at Stonehaven was arranged in a pattern modelled on the ancient understanding of the Directions; four Cardinal and three Ordinal.

In the East went the work that was basically play. The Tantras and Yogas were taught there, as well as the Dances and the Martial Disciplines. In the South were the activities based on production. This is where the work of feeding the people and maintaining the buildings and grounds occurred. It was also the place of the Advanced Martial Disciplines. In the west was administration. The north was where the mysterious happened—the Initiations, the training of the Crows under the Madeleine, and the relations with the Divinity and the development of Siddhi Powers. There were virtues associated with each direction, and the cultivation of the emotions associated with those virtues was expected of everyone. So everyone practiced patience, or courage, or generosity. And it was also expected that everyone would seek knowledge, so that they could come to understand and develop wisdom.

The three Ordinal directions were each assigned a High Priestess and her Consort. Below was focused on Lower World, caring for the Spirits of the Land and maintaining the power of Beauty. To the Above was assigned a pair whose responsibility was the cultivation of the powers to see remotely and into the future, tracking the movements of the denizens of the Upper World, including the souls of the dead, and focusing on the power of Truth. To the final direction, the Within, a pair was focused on the development of Conscience, so that the Good would infuse all the other directions. Each pair was responsible for teaching interns, the Priestesses and their Consorts, and the far flung membership of the Order, that their lives might be filled with virtue and meaning.

Regina, the Madeleine, and Eva had held these places, and now Calley was to hold the Within in Eva's place. Regina, now scheduled to leave with Quinn and Angelica, would be replaced by Diana.

The Consorts sat separately from the Priestesses during this meal. Alam felt he was getting on famously with his new friends Craft, Halloran, and Matthews. Later they were joined by Peter, Eva's former High Consort, still in Mourning. He'd been told he'd be getting a new assignment eventually but for now he was to continue with his duties, and remain available to serve Calley, should She need him. Quinn did not appear for supper. He decided not to expose himself to the atmosphere of the dining room, with its excitement and anxiety, and chose to work in the kitchen instead, washing dishes.

After supper Regina, Madeleine, Diana, and Calley met in the High Priestess's office with Craft, Peter, and Alam. Quinn and Angelica had packed their things and moved up to one of the rental units on the County Road, where Regina would join them later. Calley outlined the plan for the immediate future of Stonehaven, based on the intelligence gathered by Her daughter listening in on the conversation of the Embla and Dangla. The plan was organized by She Who Comes, and confirmed by the High Council of the Order of the Fleur de Vie. Eva's ghost hung back, camouflaged by merging with the wood paneling. Both Madeleine and Regina, particularly Madeleine, were aware of an unseen presence in the room. It felt benign, but Madeleine was uneasy at even the idea of an unseen presence witnessing the conversation and kept turning to look over her shoulder.

Near the end of the evening the old style phone on the desk rang, making everyone but Regina jump. Calley, wide-eyed, never having used a phone before, nodded to Madeleine to get it. Madeleine picked it up, put it to her ear and said, "Office." Then, in a moment, her face dropped and then hardened as she said "Oh, no." She responded, "Tell Marcy we need three rooms in number 4. And prep Comms for travelers.' She hung up the phone and turned to the others. "Angelica's parents have been killed in a car accident."

As she hung up the phone she turned quickly and caught a glimpse of the white form of a being moving rapidly out of sight. "Stop!" she commanded, using The Voice that was a power of her training. The ghost froze. "Reveal yourself!" she commanded again. It was as if a veil parted, and then Eva's face and form, all in shades of gray and white, stood revealed to her. Regina, with all of Madeleine's training and more, saw it, too, and smiled. Madeleine looked at Calley and Calley nodded at her, with a slight smile. Diana focused on her breath, knowing that she could see if she could enter the right state of mind. The men were aware that something was happening, but couldn't see what the wen saw, though they intuited what was happening because the ghost had revealed itself to them earlier.

Tears welled up in Madeleine's eyes as she moved toward the ghost, hands extended, palms up. At the same time she spoke the word "Beloved" aloud she heard the whisper of Eva's voice saying the same word. The ghost smiled a sad smile, and said, "I am here, for now." Diana heard this, and wept herself.

Diana was assigned to tell Angelica about her parents, and assign the team to accompany her back home. Regina had moved her things into the rental unit and was working on the travel arrangements when Quinn came in, pulled up a chair and sat down beside her.

"I want to talk to you about what I need to do, Regina," Quinn said.

Regina looked up at him from the computer where she was booking airline tickets and checking itineraries. Regina was tired. "What's that, Quinn?"

"Before I came to Stonehaven I was living with a woman, a wen I mean. She was from Brazil, and on the assignment to retrieve the priest and Matthews, I stopped by the town where we'd lived and found out she'd gone back to Brazil. I want to see her again, end it right. I was thinking there might be enough time, what with the funeral and all, for me to go find her."

"Brazil? Do you know where she is?"

"No."

"It's a big country. How do you propose to find her?"

"The same way I found this place. I'll follow the path my heart tells me to follow."

She looked askance at him, and then at his heart. She rolled her eyes back up in her head and established contact with Madeleine and Calley. She told them about Quinn's request. Madeleine told Calley that she thought it would take at least a week for Angelica to get her affairs in order, and that Quinn could meet her and Regina afterwards. Calley assented. "One week," She said. "Tell him he has to come see me in the morning."

Regina opened her eyes. "Do you have a passport?"

"Yes, and a visa, too. We were supposed to go and visit her family, before I was found out."

"Pack your gear. I can have you on a flight out of DC in twenty-four hours. I'll arrange for you to fly back in one week, but you'll have to meet us in St. Louis."

Quinn groaned.

"You've got a problem with that?"

"Bad history for me there. But that's where I first met Eva, almost forty years ago. Nothing I can't deal with."

"We've all lost somebody," Regina said. "We're all going to lose more."

"Do you think I could talk to Madeleine? Like you say, Brazil's a big country. I could use some insight into where to look."

Regina closed her eyes again. "Take a cart back down to the Mansion. She'll meet you there. And you'll have to talk to Calley in the morning."

Quinn met with Madeleine in the old east wing office. He laid out his story for her, and his desire to end things in a place of closure rather than abandonment. "My heart won't leave me alone about this," he said.

Madeleine looked, first into his past by holding his hand. Her body shifted, as if by a small shock, when she found Sally. There was a long silence, then Madeleine began humming, making a sound that was almost like a buzz. Eventually she opened her eyes. She got up, went to a bookshelf, and pulled down a world atlas. "Here. Go here," she said, indicating a small island off the coast. "Then go all the way here, to the south end of the island. Here, in the last village, ask after her. I am told you will be directed."

Quinn studied the map and took note of the place names. "Thank you," he said, standing up and bending forward to shake Madeleine's hand.

As he was heading out the door, she said to him. "Quinn, she's not who you think she is."

He shrugged. "What woman ever is?"

7

DISPERSAL

Quinn woke to someone pulling lightly on his foot. He opened one eye and looked at the dark haired wen smiling at him from the foot of the bed. He reached down and pulled on himself. At his response she smiled a larger smile at him and shook her head, letting her long dark and white hair shake across her breasts. He could hear it rustling back and forth across her silk shawl. He couldn't help but smile back at her.

"Remember, you're going to talk to Calley today," Regina said.

He groaned, sat up, and put his feet on the ground. He stretched, yawned, and stood up, going to the private bath in Moon Halter's room. He paused when he brushed by Regina, and hugged her from behind, kissing her on top of her head. "What time is it?" he asked.

"You have a few hours."

"Wait right here, will you?"

"No, but I'll follow you," she said. "Like you, I don't wait much anymore." She stood in the doorway, watched him relieve himself, then turn to the sink to wash his face and brush his teeth.

Quinn turned to look at her while he toweled off his head and hands. She was a magnificently beautiful wen. Nothing about her showed her true age and he looked at every detail. She had the body of someone thirty years younger. The signs of age showed mostly in the crow's feet at the corners of her eyes and in the smile lines on her cheeks.

She watched him scan her, and when his eyes reached her low

belly she twitched her hips forward. It was a voluntary act, exaggerated, and she knew she did it, as did he. But it was based on a more subtle, involuntary motion deep within her. Quinn saw it, and felt it. It made him smile and his phallus twitched in response, a twitch both involuntary and enhanced by his own control. He moved to drop his towel and step toward her. She raised a hand, palm up, to stop him. He stood still.

Regina stared at him, starting just above his eyes, and travelled slowly along the length of him, then she gazed along the length of him. He could feel her gaze, even as his eyes lost focus on her smile. He felt himself being drawn completely into sensation, and all awareness coalesced on his phallus. He felt every pull and caress as she willed him into erection, standing still, six feet away in the doorway smiling at him with her eyes lowered and concentrating.

She beckoned him, walking backwards, toward her altars, candles lit, and incense burning from her morning sitting practice—Meditations, Prayers, Illuminations, Blessings, and Devotions. When they were close she reached out and took his erection in her hand, leading there and down onto the pillow. He sat, facing the altars, and crossed his legs at the ankles. She lowered herself on him, guiding him in. Slowly settling she sighed, and became clear. With his eyes closed it seemed he could see right through her to her altars behind her. As he watched, the clear blue of the day eased through dawn colors in the clear, dark light of the full moon. As it rose in her she leaned forward and kissed him, dissolving the vision in a breath of withdrawal in concentric collapse. He sensed the pulse of her Higher Heart on her lips, and allowed it to call his own pulse forward to his lips. The pulses synchronized briefly then went into syncopation. The energy pulsed back and forth between them, making her smile, then giggle when it began to tickle her lips.

"You're learning well," she said.

He nodded and made the "Umm-hmm" sound. He knew that if he had let the pulses stay synchronized they would have moved into the deeper and more activating energy of the creation of the One Higher Heart, focusing on each center, then all Centers, until separation dissolved in ecstasy.

Sitting still, calming the pulse altogether, they simply held each other in light embrace, his hands on her hips, her arms over his shoulders, their foreheads touching. Quinn summoned the feeling of gratitude and let it wrap around them. He sighed. She smiled and nudged him with her nose.

"You good?" she asked.

"Yes. All I know is there is something I must do," he said.

"I know. You must tell Calley first. And then, when it's done, I hope you will come join us on the road." She raised his head at the chin with a hand and looked into his eyes. "I have need of you. The dragon girl needs you. And She," she said, pointing her index figure on her other hand skyward, "She has need of you."

"I have seen Her. And I feel Her in you, and in Calley, and the others. Sometimes I see Her in them. It is clear to me that I am both home, and not home at the same time. Better than not home at all. Perhaps I will be shown, someday, home, but that has lost some of its importance to me. I am reminded of the imperative to Serve. My intention is to return to you."

"Then we will resume our collaboration when you rejoin us. When you rejoin us, we will join again." And with that, she moved slowly on him for a while, wrapping her legs around him, rocking.

The room grew light and it was morning again.

Calley sat at the table in the High Priestess's bedroom, a volume of the Queen's Book open, reviewing the notes about Initiations. She sighed, wondering at the psyche of mortals, and wondering to what extent She would become like them. She still possessed Her powers as a pediment of Nature, and the use of those powers was fatiguing in a way She had not anticipated. She had known there would a price to pay—an energetic cost—when She chose to become as solid as a human. She had also known that the cost wasn't just the shortening of Her lifespan by some uncertain amount. Being in the form, just being in flesh, was tiring. Even sleeping was tiring. She spent so much energy dreaming now.

She had taken, after only a week, to spending as much time as She could in the piece of the Hidden Lands that was anchored in the Pine Eye. There She could drift. There She could rest. But Her duties required Her to be present for the residents of Stonehaven.

Mother had been clear. Now that De Murgos knew where Stonehaven was it would have to be abandoned. It was certain that he, or rather his Embla and Dangla, would return and harm the people. De Murgos might even induce other humans to serve as proxies, and lives would be put at risk.

Alam, who was enjoying immensely all his new found friends, was reluctant to abandon the property. It was he who suggested that they only appear to abandon the Mansion and Barn, empty them of people. Leave some people up on the County Road to monitor and protect the property. His idea was that they use the appearance to mask a trap. He didn't know what the trap would look like, exactly, or what it would be likely to catch, but he knew that, with Calley and Mom's help, something could be fashioned that would enable them to restrain anything they caught. And, if necessary, kill it.

So, She had delegated Madeleine and Diana to undertake the assignments for the diaspora. Some people, especially interns and new Priestesses and Consorts, were to be sent to other centers of the Order. Many were sent to take up lives in the mundane world, living among the people as regular folk.

Calley was also using the Queen's Book to teach Herself the Tantras and the Alchemical Processes used by the Order. She was reluctant, She found, to practice with anyone except Alam. And She was unaccustomed to the idea of crystallizing a so-called Higher Body. She hadn't seen any, although She heard about the manifestation at the Gatehouse from Mother. Mom assured Her that She had them all, safe within Her. Calley was surprised to learn that only a very few ever completed the process, and that these, after resting, would receive various assignments that helped Her retake the minds and hearts of the people.

The Alchemy was also an option for Alam, but it required that he practice with other mortals. This had a surprising impact on Her. She found that She had an impulse toward jealousy, now that She was in a mortal form. She was contemplating Her reluctance to practice with others, and half-heartedly working to alchemize the jealousy when Mother appeared in the chair opposite Her.

"When you take on their form, dear one, you take on the capacity to resonate with their functions. You struggle with what they struggle with, even though that is not your true nature. In creating you, and your capacity to take all the forms of the storm that you can, there was neither need nor space for many of their functions.

"Understand, dear, that you are an Elemental, a pediment of Nature, that's what a storm is. These people are not, they are humans, made by me for a different purpose. Even now they are evolving a fourth brain, they are an experiment."

"And what will the fourth brain allow them to do, Mother?"

"It will allow them to correct, and eventually self-correct, the deficiencies of function in the earlier, lower three brains. The principle deficiency is their weakness for altered states of consciousness. They can be manipulated into somnambulism; it is what De Murgos does to them, a kind of lulling into a waking sleep—a sleep where the half-truths and illusions of the dream time can become confused with the real truth of being awake. Hence they believe things, untruth for truth.

"A second deficiency is in their inability to tell when to put others before themselves. The original issue is instinctive. When it works right, mothers love and feed their babies. Fathers fend for their children. And by extension they love and fend for the other people near them. But that which says 'I' in them sometimes overrides that impulse and puts itself first. This impulse, too, arises in the instincts. These impulses are contradictory; one impulse is for others while the other impulse is for themselves. It creates conflict, internal and external. It is a necessary conflict.

"But the skillset required to manage the conflict is difficult to acquire. The second brain would need to moderate the lower instinctive issues, but it would have to do it through feeling. Conflict in the feelings does not mediate well there. So the third brain, the thinking one, activates to try to solve the conflict, but it is usually operating with insufficient information and education. The only chance to mediate this inner conflict is that they learn to separate themselves from themselves—that which says 'I' in them must rise also to a higher level, it must transcend. But it doesn't do that easily or well. The secondary purpose of the fourth brain is to give them the place for this inner conflict resolution. It is to give them a Conscience."

"Ah, I see," Calley said. "They are, as you say, an experiment."

"If you can see your way clear to it, I want you to practice. I want you to take on a few of these mortals. I will tell you with whom I think it would be good. You shall see. I want you to be able to access that part of the world where they reside when they are finished here, if they have enough of a higher body to continue after the death of this one."

"How many brains do I have, Mother?"

"You have eight."

"And you?"

"I also have eight when I am talking to you. My full potential is realized in sixteen brains. The biggest difference between us when we're together is that not all of yours are fully developed."

"Will practicing with the mortals help me develop myself?"

"Yes, but only certain ones. I want you to start with Matthews. He is one of my angels. Make sure his wings are visible to you. Then I want you to spend a little time with Quinn. He is something completely new. Unforeseen, even. When you want amusement, and this will be after Quinn, consider the former priest with the priapic condition. Quinn will be leaving soon, and there is something you can receive from him on the energetic level that will be useful later on. There is a difference between the mercilessness that you carry, and the mercilessness he carries now. I want you to learn the feel of it, so that you can call upon it in the future. It will be needed before the end.

"Do not worry about Alam, he is yours forever. Let him play with the mortals. Let him learn what he does not yet know, and he will be more helpful to you, also. Remember: I am asking you to do something that you do not want to do. But I am not asking you to do something that goes against your nature."

Mother started going transparent then, and spreading out into a clear, ellipse-shaped pool, until only her eyes remained visible. In a voice Calley could feel all around and inside her, Mother said, "I love you, daughter. Remember this, and I will always come to you when you remember your love for me."

Calley sighed. She finished reading the page she'd been on and softly closed the book. There was a knock at the door. Now that she was possessed of a human soma she had to eat. There was a pair of interns at the door with breakfast. They were cute, and very shy. Calley invited them to sit and have some tea while she ate.

Quinn knocked before she finished. She bid the interns to leave her, and take the tray with them. She waved Quinn inside and motioned for him to sit at the table facing Her over the corner.

"Do you know who I am, mortal?"

"I do not," Quinn answered stoically.

This made Calley laugh. Her laughter made her relax. Quinn struggled on stoically, not knowing what this was about.

"I will tell you that I come from a world that is much slower than yours. I will show you, I don't know why, how to change the flow of time."

"I can see where that would be useful." Quinn didn't know what else to say, but, still, it made Calley laugh again.

"Mortal, you have no idea," and Calley rose up from her chair, stepped toward Quinn, put one hand between his legs and kissed him.

Quinn felt himself being sworn to fealty before he could stop it.

"You will regret that," Quinn said, feeling huffy.

"Probably, but I am doing Her bidding," She said. "Your issue is with Her," She said pointing upward. Then, moving that pointing finger to Her own heart She said, in a deeper voice, Her eyes grown dark, "Listen, I recognize the power of the Sacred Clown. Knock it off. Give my daughter what I need Her to have from you and all will be well."

After a pause, She, She Who Comes, added, "I know where your home is. It is here," She said, "In Service to Me."

Knowing that he had been blessed beyond what anyone else may have thought, Quinn acceded.

He reached out and touched Her between Her legs.

"You know, Matthews, what She wants from you, yes?" Madeleine asked.

"Yes, I do," he replied.

"Good. Then tell me, because what She's showing me goes opaque fairly quickly."

"Then maybe you should tell me what She's shown you."

"She's shown me what you are, who you are. Normally, we'd ask you to go, because you're not one of us. And because you look so much like Quinn. There's a danger that whatever bad stuff was tracking him will focus on you. But you're special, really, really special. Normally, we'd send you off on an assignment, but we think She's already given you one."

"She has. And Calley has confirmed it. Whether or not I look like him, you're supposed to use me as bait."

"Bait? Let me check." Madeleine closed her eyes and settled into her visionary mind. The opaque wall that had been there before had disappeared and a whole scenario, with variable sub-scenarios, appeared before her.

"She wouldn't show it to you unless I had the chance to choose it for myself first," Matthews said. After a pause to let Madeleine look he said, "Do you see it? If I show the wings, they'll know it's me. If I don't, they'll think it's him. Either way, I'm bait, unless She sends me away."

"I'm told there will be something for you to do after this. You'll still be working with us, it looks like."

"Yeah, sure. If I survive."

"So…OK. Otherwise, are you being taken care of?"

"Yes. It seems the Priestesses love levitation while we're, well…"

"Fucking?" Halloran asked, just entering the office.

"You can call it practice, if you want. Training. Having sex. Engaging in the Tantra. Whatever you want," Madeleine said turning to Halloran and smiling. "And what about you, former priest of the long-time dong. What do you think should happen to you?"

"Consort. I want to be a Consort. That's it. I don't have any ambition other than to be of Service. Service to Her," he said, pointing upward. "Service to you." He grinned.

"Consort, yes. Our instructions are to let your internship proceed.

In a few weeks you will be told where you are to go."

"Not here?"

"No, not here." Madeleine smiled at him, a complex smile that showed both happiness and sadness. She'd grown to like him while she'd been with him. She'd also miss his priapic challenge, as she was sure many interns and priestesses would. "We don't yet know why Quinn was sent to bring you here. In the end it was you who finished off the beast at the Gatehouse. That may have been it. You carry a blood taint now, the one carried by all who kill. It's unavoidable. Yet it doesn't seem to bother you."

"No, no it doesn't. I spent my life in denial, following falsehood. I may be in denial about what happened, but justice was swift. And the Order is not responsible. No magic will trace that death back to you all. You know, now that I think about it, maybe that's why She had me brought here. I killed, and my Conscience is clear. Think about it, Madeleine. I can kill without remorse."

"Yes. And it occurs to me—and I see it is occurring to you, too, at precisely this moment—that this may be what She intends for you. That you become a Slayer for Her."

Halloran nodded grimly. He was thinking through what that might mean. Then he brightened. "Sex and Death, right?"

Madeleine grinned broadly now. "Yes. Sex and Death."

"She can use me however She wants."

"So, tell me, Halloran, what did you do with the head?"

"I spiked it into a tree for the birds and bugs to pick at."

"Yuck," said Matthews, standing at a window looking out over the grounds.

"You are to dig a deep hole at the foot of Eva's grave, and bury it there. Let her use her killer as she will."

"I'll see to it right away," Halloran said, bowing and backing out the door, closing it behind him.

Madeleine turned toward the window, leaned on the table with one elbow, and regarded Matthew's silhouette. After contemplating his image awhile, she said, "You have your own relationship with Her. How is that?"

"She made me. She made me a soldier in Her cause, and She is my Commander."

"You weren't a soldier before…" Madeleine let the implied questions linger.

"No, but I wasn't much of anything before. Kids grown, divorced, a white-collar job they'd find some way to dismiss me from for younger talent. One Saturday I bumped into Quinn coming out the door of a coffee shop. We were shocked at the still overwhelming resemblance. We got together a few times for a beer. He asked me to write the book about his story. It took a few years. The last time I saw him for years was the day he left me laying blind on my kitchen floor. I crawled to my bed and lay there. I slept. I woke when I felt a presence in the room, beside the bed. I could see the walls, but there was a golden curtain standing there, same color as the golden light of the blindness." He paused at the memory.

"Was it hard?" Madeleine asked. "This change into something other than just a man?"

"A golden arm reached out from the curtain and the hand laid itself on my forehead. I felt fevered, and it felt cool. I started to tremble and I burned. I burned inside a long time."

"Burning off the dross."

"Yes, that's what She told me later. Then the pain began in my back, between my shoulder blades. Something emerged and unfolded out to my sides and lifted my torso off the bed. I passed out. When I woke up I was alone. I knew something had changed, more than what I'd already been through, and I came to feel it was all too much. I broke down and started weeping. I curled up in a fetal position and wept until I slept again. I howled in my sleep. I hit the headboard with my fist. My life, at least any kind of normal life, was over. I'm afraid I wasn't very gracious about it."

"And now?"

"All I want is that Grace. Her patience with me, and Her love for me are…well, overwhelming. I never feel unworthy. And I don't miss my old life at all. And I don't know what all I can do. I hope to find out. I'll let Her call me to it, I suppose. I could use some help, though. Someone to talk to, like you. Because She is with you, too, I can get clarity and confirmation."

Madeleine looked thoughtfully inward toward her image of Her. She was smiling. Madeleine nodded and said, "Show me what it feels like to make love without gravity." Everyone's smile grew more broad.

At the opposite end of the Mansion, in the offices of the High Priestess, Diana was also meeting with residents. The instruction had come to settle most of the residents in other Centers of the Order. Only a few were to be allowed to stay, and those were to be up in the rental houses on the County Road.

Diana was talking to Janice privately about her new assignment.

"England? You want me to go to England?"

"Yes, entirely on the payroll. Your stipends will continue there. Your housing, too, of course. And we want you to continue what you've been doing here for us," Diana added.

"You mean spying."

"That's indelicate, but yes."

"Spy on what?"

"We don't know. So…everything."

"You know something. Tell me what, if you want me to do it."

"The more I tell you the more at risk you'll be. There are powerful telepaths there. Once you get through your Initiation I can tell you more."

"Wait, what? Finally I'm to become a Priestess?"

"Yes. If you pass. If you pass then I'll tell you more."

"When?"

"The Initiation will be in four days, at another site. We're in a bit of a time crunch. Prepare yourself."

Janice, filled with excitement, realized the interview was over. "Thank you, thank you, thank you."

Diana nodded, then Janice left the office.

Craft emerged from the shadows in the corner and went up to Diana, putting his hands on her shoulders.

"She didn't see you at all," Diana wondered.

"Nope. Or at least she didn't show any signs that she did.

"Is she that good? Good enough to hide her perception of you?"

"I don't think so. But once she takes the Initiation she may be able to do both."

"An excellent choice for a spy then. And are you OK with your next assignment?"

"Staying here, you mean? Yes. Somebody has to. And I know the place better than any of the other Consorts. And I'm getting along with Alam well. He seems to really enjoy all the people. Who knows? It may end up being just the two of us. And the Road House folks."

"Good."

"And your assignment?"

"I get to go home, I'm told. And be with my kids. We'll see. Calley wants us all out of here by November first."

"Will there be an Assembly?"

"Yes. The last one here. At least for a while."

"Well, I have some news that doesn't have anything to do with this plan. The patrol reports that out at the Pythagorean spring below

Rock Shelter Two there's a Nature Spirit, sitting on the banks, wailing and rocking side to side. The patrol said she holds a baby to her breast that has two forms. One is a water form and the other one is flesh and blood. When the baby is in water form the Naiad holds it, and it seems to nurse. Then it slowly turns to flesh and appears limp and unresponsive. The Priestess Jaqueline offered to hold the baby and put it to her breast and it revived, just from its instincts as a solid. Or rather the semi-solid gel that we are, but you know what I mean. But it needs real nutrition from someone of us or I doubt it will survive."

"Really? Shit. Shit, shit, shit. One of the Consorts must have been seduced. I'll check with Calley and Madeleine and see what they want to do. I may have to get you to take me out there. What I need you to do is send someone to town and get some baby formula and we'll mix some up and have a patrol take it out to the Naiad. They'll probably have to stay out there for a while—the Naiad probably isn't solid enough to hold the bottle." She paused, thinking, then she said again, "Shit, shit, shit. I wonder who the fucker was. Madeleine will have to suss it out."

"I'll take care of it. Just ask for what you need. Anytime, Diana," he said, putting a hand on her shoulder. "Anytime."

Diana summoned Halloran. It was late and he arrived with his hair in a mess; he'd obviously been asleep.

"Calley has an assignment for you. Madeleine agrees, and bids me give you this," Diana said and handed a long heavy object wrapped in what appeared to be a cloak of indeterminate color, as big as a blanket.

He held it in his hands, and knew immediately what it was. And, uncontrollably, he began to get hard.

"Madeleine says this is a practice run. If you succeed you'll be given another assignment," Diana added. Then she said, "Here. This is from Calley." She handed him what appeared to be a small flat stone on a leather string. "Hang this around your neck and go stand in front of the mirror."

Halloran walked comically, with his legs splaying at his knees as he walked around his erection.

"Now tap it once," she said. "The stone, I mean."

Halloran did, and his image in the mirror disappeared.

"You are hidden now. You are to follow Angelica and her support team to her parents' funeral. You are to remain invisible the whole time, unless your visibility helps the situation. My advice is that you remain invisible anyway. See how it plays out. Your main assignment is to escort Angelica back to the houses on the Road safely. To become visible again, tap the stone twice. Or better yet, squeeze it."

Halloran became visible again. And the visibility of his phallus, straining through his jeans, increased. He turned sideways to Diana and said, "Really?"

Diana said, "Really. And if that's real," pointing at his phallus, "bring it over here."

Halloran stepped toward her and said, "I live to Serve." As he passed by the writing table he lay down the sword he'd been given.

As it turned out, Madeleine wanted to go out there to the rock shelter herself and for her and Diana to go together. Alam also wanted to go. Calley promised that She'd be around and would manifest if She was needed.

The rescue team with the formula and bottle (some were always kept in storage among the supplies, the place being a sanctuary for wen and all) had run out immediately on their dispatch, which happened next after Craft had informed Diana.

When they arrived at the shelter they were briefed by the Consorts. Two Priestesses were with the Naiad, running back alternately from the spring to update the Consorts. The Naiad had gone into a terrified collapse at the sight of the men, and had disappeared into the spring water. Alam stayed with the men while Madeleine and Diana made their way to the spring.

When they arrived the Naiad was just passing the infant to the Priestess as it changed form. At the sight of the High Priestesses the Naiad collapsed into water again. She emerged immediately later and smiled a smile that, if it had been on a solid face, would have looked like embarrassed welcome.

Madeleine and Diana sat down on the banks of the spring, putting their feet in the water, deliberately. The Naiad struggled to say the word "wade" so the High Priestesses stepped out into the spring, water up to their knees. The Naiad smiled again, this time in genuine amusement, shaking her head 'no'. The Priestess holding the infant said, "That's all she's been able to say. Wade is the name of Jasmine's Consort."

"Oh, my," Madeleine said, covering her mouth with one hand.

Diana did the same, but she was trying to cover her laughter. She almost sat down in the pool, catching herself with one hand. When the Naiad covered her mouth with laughter, too, Diana gave up and sat down in the water.

Suddenly Diana felt a probing up inside her, and she jumped up. "Wicked girl!" she shouted, pointing at the Naiad. "No wonder!" she said.

Madeleine turned, tracking the invisibility of what had just happened.

The Naiad went still, her expression that of a child waiting to be admonished, but not really punished. Madeleine commanded the Priestess holding the infant to "Back away!" and she did.

Madeleine turned to the Naiad, now obviously afraid. "Do you want to keep your baby?"

The shock of the seriousness of the situation finally dawned on the Naiad. She looked down, nodding her head "yes".

"Then we must cooperate. And without any tricks," Madeleine said sternly.

The Naiad nodded again.

"Then the baby can stay with you and we will continue to care for the part of him that is human, here, with you."

And she reached up her hand to Diana, who had already scrambled up the bank of the spring pool. She pulled her up.

The baby, already changing back to water, was handed back to the Naiad by the Priestess at Madeleine's nod.

When they were on their way back to the rock shelter and the men, Diana said, "Well, that was easy."

"Yeah," Madeleine said. "Like you said, 'Shit, shit, shit.'"

Craft was happy that he was being assigned to stay at Stonehaven. He was not so happy that it was because he had learned how to talk to the King of Salamanders and that it was because he could see ghosts. Neither of these were his favorite things to do.

"Fucked out," Halloran said on the walk back up to the Road houses. Shaking his head, unable to believe it, he said, "I've been fucked out."

In her bed, in her last night in the Mansion, Diana stretched as she rolled over, and smiled as she lapsed into sleep. She'd see her kids, and sleep with her husband, in a couple of days.

8

BRAZIL

Thirty-six hours after his meeting with Calley, Quinn arrived at the coast, where he took the ferry out to the island. He went to the southern-most end, a small fishing village named, in translation, Ragged Teeth. There was an open restaurant on the beach, where the fishing boats launched each dawn on log rollers, and he asked the wen behind the counter if she could tell him where to find Sally Oshune.

"Oshun?" she smiled. "Sarri Oshun? Si, si." She took him outside by the hand and pointed further down the coast, over two mountain ridges that came down into the sea.

He turned to ask her, "How do I get there?" but she was already making a two-legs walking gesture with her hand and pointed around the coast with her other one.

He walked the treacherous foot path over the ridges. He paused at a standing stone beside the path, clearly set up as a guardian stone. He put his hand on it, and announced to the Spirits of the Land who he was and why he came, looking for Sally Oshune. He came down into the cove known as Empty Bag.

A stream ran down from the mountains, splashing on the rocks, making music with the surf as it spread out across a narrow lunate of sand. There was a wooden cabin, raised on stilts just back from a barrier of large rocks, looking like they'd tumbled down the steep valley from above. Smoke rose from a chimney in one corner and an old man with a shock of white hair sat at a table writing in the light from the open shutters. When he saw Quinn he smiled broadly and stood up, gesturing at him to come in. Quinn opened the gate on the fenced-in yard and walked up to the steps. The old man invited him in, offered him coffee.

The old man spoke only Portuguese and Quinn spoke only a little. Still, he made it clear that he could help Quinn find what he was looking for, if Quinn would only sit and visit a little while.

He explained that he was a solar shaman, and could redirect the magnetic energy of the sun to wherever it was needed on the planet. It was his responsibility to record the magnetic weather in his notebooks, logging what he could see, and what he did with it. When Quinn explained to him why he was there the old man looked at him closely and said, "What you are seeking are the pediments of Nature. Understand them for what they are."

He told Quinn to follow the smell of a smoke trail off the path. Quinn pushed aside some undergrowth and climbed up the valley along the stream on a small side trail. At a clearing he found a small fire with three wen around it, wearing only grass skirts—one young, one middle-aged, and one an elder.

He saw a bower made of flowering vines, and saw movement in its shadows. He called out, "Sally? Sally Oshune?" He heard a laugh from within; a laugh that sounded like hers, but younger.

"Yes, yes white boy. It is Oshune. Come closer so that I can see you." He thought he glimpsed her shoulder and back turning away from the entrance. He raised an eyebrow at what seemed to be a glimpse of a diaphanous and translucent short skirt rippling over her backside and swaying gently to mid-thigh.

He went around the fire, smiling and nodding at the three wen. The younger giggled, the middle one grinned back, and the old wen leered.

He ducked into the entrance, and squatted down on his heels, folding his hands and resting his chin on them. His eyes adjusted to the darkness and the seated form back-lit in the rear of the bower.

The shadow spoke to him. "Ah, so, white boy. Oh my, no, it's not white boy. It's gray boy," she laughed. "No, now I see. It's black boy underneath. Oh my. And now you are becoming red boy. Quinn, I know you. Do you know me?" and she leaned forward into a little patch of light.

Quinn gave a small gasp when he saw her face. It was Sally, but twenty years younger. Her hair was up and she was adjusting a stray hair in a hand mirror. She wore a circlet with a clear sapphire over her forehead. Over her breasts she wore a halter of narrow braided golden silk ropes that swayed and rippled as she moved, often exposing more breast than it covered. He realized that her short skirt was made the same way; a rope skirt to mid-thigh that fell gracefully over her thigh.

He sighed, suddenly understanding. She was a goddess. "Orisha," she'd heard his thought and corrected him.

"Hello beloved," he said.

"Yes, you did love me, I know. But She, the True Creator, came to me and told me She was taking you. It is just as well, you know. I was on holiday, vacation you call it, and it was time for me to return home. I am Oshune, Orisha of Sweet Water."

Quinn came forward from his squat to his knees and bowed to her. She laughed and patted a cane trunk beside Her, covered by an embroidered cloth. "Come sit by me. White boy." She laughed again as he stood to come over to her. "Pinto boy," She said, and laughed again.

Quinn sat, staring at her beauty. She put the mirror down and stared back at him, smiling. Suddenly a black bird entered the bower from the rear and hovered in the air over her shoulder. It became larger as he looked, becoming a raven, then a raven's head on a man's body, with a ruby in its forehead between its eyes. Legs and arms grew downward from its neck and the raven's head became a mask that was not removed.

"This is my brother Ogun, Orisha of Warriors."

Then beside Quinn on the trunk appeared an animal, as big as a mid-size dog and covered in light brown fur. Its face resembled a short-faced bear. "And this is Oshossie, Orisha of Hunters."

Quinn didn't want to stare, and looked away. In that moment the animal's jaws enlarged like a cartoon and tried to take a bite out of Quinn's arm. He twisted, pulling it away, and said, "Hey! Not good! Knock it off!" Oshossie grinned.

"They wanted to see you," Oshune said. "When you left I came home to talk to them. About you."

"What? Why?" Quinn asked and in that moment another being came through the front door, from the beach, trailing golden water. Quinn looked at Her, and She actually was golden water, flowing ever downward in waves from the top of Her head; golden, the color of sunrise or sunset on calm water at the beginning or end of the day. She was the most beautiful Feminine form Quinn had ever seen. His shock suddenly became a humility in him, and he could barely look at Her, and barely keep his eyes off Her at the same time.

Oshune laughed again. "This is my sister, Inmanzha, Orisha of Salt Water. Orisha of the Ocean. She, too, wanted to meet you."

The four of them began speaking in images that flowed through Quinn's mind faster than he could hold any recognition of the events longer than even half a second. Some were of his life with Sally, then the rest were moments of his time at Stonehaven, then the fight at the Gate House. When it was done there was visual silence, and he could see the room again.

Thunder rolled from the top of the mountain, and a light rain started. The leaves of the vines moved of their own accord to seal the bower and keep it dry.

"He agrees," Inmanzha said. Quinn looked at Her, golden light flowing from her, light sunrise over calm waters. He had a vision of Her disentangling Herself from a lover before She emerged across the beach and came to the bower. She looked at him, smiled, and nodded slowly, once. Quinn looked down, unable to bear the beauty.

"Pinto boy," Oshune said. Quinn looked at Her, marveling at the forty years of apparent difference now in their ages.

"Pinto boy," She said again. "They want to go with you," She said, nodding at Her Brothers. "Not all the time, but only when you need them. Call upon them with these." She handed him two small arrowheads, one black, one brown. He held out his hand, and She dropped them into it, touching him lightly with her fingertips. A charge ran through him like electricity, grounding out through his feet, and causing an instant erection. He laughed when She smiled. "Where you are going it is not Her ocean," She said, indicating Her Sister.

Quinn glanced at Inmanzha again and She pointed toward his erection, laughing. The thunder rolled once more. She dropped Her hand and threw Her head back in laughter. "He's jealous," She said. "We have one more gift, this one for you to carry to the Goddess who now rules at Stonehaven."

It was a larger, gray arrowhead. "She will know what to do," Inmanzha said, placing it in his upturned palm without touching him. The thunder rolled again.

Oshune said, "It is time to go, pinto boy. You know what you need to know." Quinn stood to go. He bowed his head as he passed Inmanzha. She drew her fingers across his arm and he stumbled with the ecstasy that coursed through him. He staggered out through the door when he heard Oshune call him.

"Pinto boy."

He turned and looked and Oshune stood by Her Sister, a being of silver waves flowing ever downward, like a waterfall in moonlight, next to her Sister. He saw the two of Them smile at him, and the columns of water that held their forms collapsed, and the bower fell back into shadow.

The three wen at the fire giggled, grinned, and leered again as he passed them, heading for the path, noting his erection with their eyes. He turned and bowed to each of them, eliciting another round of happiness from them. The thunder rolled once more.

He hurried back to the trail. He had a plane to catch. When he returned he would meet Alam at the airport during his layover and give him the gray arrowhead, The Thunder, give it to him to take back to Calley.

9

THE CROSSROADS

A. pressed the 'End Call' button and tossed the phone on the bed, frustrated that after a few days of rest and half-hearted trying she hadn't been able to find a flight back to the headquarters without having to change planes multiple times. She'd have to cross back over the mountains to the city on the other side. The henchmen—the "henches" as she thought of them—could catch a short flight back north where she'd hired them. She, on the other hand, was returning to the west coast, and, given the magical and other items she carried in her suitcase, preferred not to expose her possessions to the possibility of multiple x-ray machines. The invisibility and false imagery magic with which she wrapped them would withstand only so many assaults, and the effect was time-limited anyway.

After dropping her henches at a local airport, she turned the rental car back toward the entrance to the North County Road, preferring to retrace her steps in familiarity rather than risk losing her way. She detested trying to look at the map application on her phone while she was driving, and there was no cell service most of the time crossing the mountains.

As she neared the area of vacation homes where she thought she'd find Quinn holed up she braked suddenly, fishtailing in the gravel. She put the car in reverse and stopped, staring off to her left, down the road that hadn't been there; the South County Road. The fine hair on the back of her arms and neck rose up, as if pulled by static electricity. She shivered in the chill, struggling to believe what her eyes told her now that she hadn't seen before.

She put the car in drive and turned slowly down the road. Not far down she encountered a driveway and turned in. The terror that struck her then so overwhelmed her that she froze as she put her foot on the brake, barely able to breathe. She overcame her paralysis when she realized she was digging her nails into her palms, white-knuckled and wrapped around the steering wheel.

She put the car in park and slowly, fighting the terrified reluctance, commanded herself to get out of the car and stand. Once she had her feet on the ground she gained more courage. She stepped slowly down the drive, hands out to her sides palm down, stopping when she felt a shift in the energy. She walked past a column of searing heat, and other columns of freezing cold. She followed a thread of evil, which made her feel better, down the drive until she saw a Gate House with a wooden barrier in the down position.

Stenciled on the sides of the House was a symbol in pink, a symbol that vaguely resembled a flower—a flower she believed she'd seen before, but couldn't quite place. As she stared the flower began to pulse and glow, eventually flashing at her with a blinding golden brilliance, blinding her and causing her to fall down. She sat, her torso raised on one arm and her eyes closed until the dizziness eased and the after-image faded. Keeping her eyes closed she turned away from the image before she opened them.

Slit-eyed, she crawled back along the road, hands and knees bruised and scratched by the gravel, until she could see her car. Slowly rising to her feet she stoop-walked to the hood and leaned on it, laying her belly along its length and letting the warmth soak into her. When she stopped shaking, she carefully moved around to the driver's side, got in and started the car. Carefully, she backed up to the County Road using her mirrors. When she got there she backed out, and turned up hill to the main road and stopped, looking in either direction then staring at the entrances to the vacation rental units.

She could still feel that Quinn had been there, even recently, as she could feel it before, but more faintly now, and she knew that he was long gone, if not far ago then far away.

She drove slowly past the houses, studying the cars in the driveways and the tracks in the roads, feeling into what was going on inside. She felt a pressure build behind her pubic bone that she originally mistook for excitation but realized that she only had to pee. She accelerated away and around the bend.

10

THE TEMPLE

Jasmine went often to the plaza before the Temple of Wahsastami, the Goddess to whom the small town was originally dedicated. The Goddess was much like Calley's sister Bree, dedicated to the arts of music, writing, healing and all the crafts of art. Stone carving, bone and wood carvings were for sale everywhere. Painting and textiles adorned the walls and ceremonial staffs, their bright colors bringing happiness into the souls of the people in ways that eased their suffering, both the poverty of everyday people and the despair of many who came seeking a solution in Beauty to the ugliness of life in whatever place they came from. In ancient times students, both wen and men, had come from all over the island to study. What was taught was considered to be the finest and most beautiful flower of the people's civilization.

It was in this town, Boodun, where the Order maintained the Yoga School. The entire island was an international tourist destination and the town was the focus for many of those who were seeking some kind of spiritual insight. The yoga retreat business was well established and enrollment was up, which might require requesting more teachers from the Order, and her staff of Priestesses and Consorts was stretched more thinly than Jasmine would have liked. Jasmine was the principal teacher but there were limits to her time, and she had to finish her preparations for the conflict to come.

She came to the plaza to watch the Temple, wondering at it. Its doors were always closed, and the priestesses only emerged once a year for a procession, although sometimes a woman's orchestra would offer concerts of traditional music in the plaza before the Temple steps. She could see the banners and costumes hanging from wooden bars held horizontally by hooks in the ceiling of the broad veranda, open to the air and twisting in the daily island breezes. Sometimes she would see a wen, a Priestess of the lineage of this Goddess, perhaps, moving among the cloth, straightening something, or brushing off some insect. She learned that all deliveries, and all comings and goings of a few people, took place at a side door, in an alley behind the Temple.

Sometimes Napat would accompany her, the two sitting on a bench, eating lunch sometimes, sometimes just sitting, staring up the steps at the carved door. Jasmine would lapse into trance, trying to see what had happened there, what kept the Priestesses behind closed doors. Napat watched her, wondering what she was doing, and began to experience entrainment into Jasmine's energy. Jasmine could see a dark veil over the entire Temple, like black smoke, with a small fire ring at its base, running all the way around the Temple. The fire would flare up when anyone crossed the line. Even some of the tourists, running up the steps to the Temple doors, would feel uneasy after crossing the line and would hurry back, not wanting the heat they were experiencing to make their exposure to the tropical heat any worse. Jasmine had felt this heat herself, knew it as warding magic of the first order, and left it alone.

One day, with Napat sitting beside her, using her second sight to contemplate the veil and its ring of fire, she asked herself silently, "Why?" and Napat answered aloud. "Because of the curse."

Mildly shocked that somehow Napat had heard her thought, she turned slowly to the younger wen. "What curse? Napat," she asked.

"The Priests put a curse on it. All the Priestesses, the whole Temple. They were not to do their rituals in public any more. They had to close down their school, and close their Temple, too. My grandmother told me of these things."

"Why? Why did they put a curse on it?" Jasmine asked, this time aloud.

"Because they were taking money away from the Priests of Skreeva. The Priests of Skreeva are in charge now and run everything. They don't want any devotion to the others—the other Goddesses and even the other Gods. You can see this even over at Sabaki, where the main Temples are. Skreeva's Temple is the largest, far larger than those to his brothers. The Priests take all the money the people give and use it how they wish. The Priests run everything now."

"I am told, Napat, that there is a High Priestess on the island. Is it so? And what is she the Priestess of?" Jasmine asked, turning to her assistant.

"There is such a person. And I am not sure how to answer the question. There is a loose circle of women who are called Priestesses. They are mostly healers and, what is the word for it? Shamanesses. They are shamans. Maybe she is the High Priestess of them. But I do not know."

"So tell me what you do know."

The ghost of the Good Grandmother appeared behind Napat. Jasmine nodded but the image was focused on Napat. It put her hand on Napat's shoulder, and Napat shivered slightly, even in the heat.

"I feel my grandmother with me."

"Do you feel her often?"

"Yes."

"I see her often, and I see her with you now."

"She wants me to tell you what I know." Napat sighed. "About twenty years ago a little girl was born. When she was about four she started quoting Windu scripture spontaneously. She didn't know Windu, and barely spoke her own language, much less did she know how to read. Her parents were frightened, and called in the Priests.

"The Priests examined her, and determined that she must be some teacher of old, reincarnated, but she could not tell them who."

"Perhaps because they assumed she was a man that had reincarnated."

"Perhaps. In any event they took over her education. They wanted to find out how much she knew, and to test her. As the child grew up she was required to spend many hours a day with the Priests, and was barely allowed out to play as a normal child. Yet, she grew up to be a beautiful child. About the time she was ten there was an incident where the parents became suspicious that the Priests were abusing her when they could get her alone. After that she was to always have a trusted family member with her during her lessons."

Napat stopped talking. Both she and Jasmine were suddenly overwhelmed with images of sexual child abuse. Napat sobbed once, and repressed her feelings, looking up into the veil around the Temple. Jasmine wiped a tear from her cheek and looked up also. The fire around the Temple rose, and the veil darkened, although there was no visible trespass on the Temple itself to trigger it.

"My grandmother says I am to tell you about the Initiation," Napat said, with a sneer of contempt suddenly forming on her countenance. "When she was sixteen the Priests said she had to pass a final test of her knowledge and wisdom. So, without her parent's knowledge she was put on a boat and taken out into the ocean. They put her over the side and told her that if she was in the same place when they came back to get her twenty-four hours later they would pick her up. If she wasn't, then they weren't going to waste any time looking for her. She would be finished."

Napat suddenly gasped with horror at the vision she was seeing, the vision of the young woman, watching the boat as it pulled away from her, islands rising out of the sea in the background. More tears rolled down Jasmine's cheeks and she wiped them away.

Napat continued. "When they went back the next day, she was right where they'd dropped her. The Priests finally admitted that she had more power than they, and that they should be done with her. Since that time they have left her alone.

"When her story became known the people came to her support. She has been counselling and ministering to the people ever since. She has a ceremony of healing she offers to people using water, an element that favors her. The Priest who put her in the water is now the High Priest of Skreeva, and the leader of all the Priests on the island."

As the wen watched the Temple a white fog appeared over the fire around the Temple, and it died back. The dark veil lightened.

"We shall go see her, yes?"

"Yes. I will make the arrangements."

"I also want to go see the Temples at Sabaki."

"That is much easier to arrange. We can go over any day you're free, but plan on it taking the whole day."

Grandmother's ghost stepped away from Napat and bowed toward the Temple doors. The eyes of the twin dragon balustrades sparkled briefly, then the image of the ghost disappeared.

Napat and Jasmine stood up and bowed also. The dragon eyes sparkled again, and then went back to their normal dead luster behind the veil.

Jasmine went back to work, and found an email from her Teacher Madeleine waiting, asking her to call. Jasmine had international calling on her phone, and, since Stonehaven was twelve hours away it would be late evening there. The operator in the vacation home on the County Road switched her through to Madeleine, still in the office at the Mansion. Jasmine wept with horror and grief as she was given the news about the fight at the Gatehouse and Eva's death. She was in shock as Madeleine told her about the plans to close Stonehaven and disperse everyone to other places around the world. They wept together.

11

HOMECOMING

When A. arrived at the airport, she picked up her luggage, and rented a car rather than take the short commuter flight up into the mountains. This left her with a get-away option when she would be ready to leave.

She disliked her Master, as he insisted he be called. He had inherited her from his father, himself the son of a black magician in England. This man, the grandfather, had seduced her mother away from her father, and made her into his servant, eventually drawing in A., sexually abusing her, then passing her along to his son, the father of the young man she now served. His father had moved them to the American West Coast and proceeded to get himself in the cult business, and had done quite well in establishing a following.

The people in the inner circles had been shown some of the true ways of power, but in such a way that they were bound to use their powers in service to the Black Kite. The Kite had been passed from generation to generation as well. Commanding others to do its bidding, bring it food, bring it power. This power was used to hypnotize the outer circles into monetary donations in exchange for the illusion of those powers.

And, of course, for those in the inner circles, to obtain for themselves lots of sex. A.'s Master had become as skilled with obtaining sex as his father and grandfather. Her Master, now in his early forties, had begun to take an interest in barely legal girls and boys. A. arrived at the end of the compound's long landscaped drive and parked. She stopped at the receptionist's desk and told the young man there to tell the Master she had returned. She walked through the hall into the gardens, aiming for the far side where her Master kept his living quarters. She went into his sitting room and headed up the stairs to his bedroom, where her intuition told her he would be.

As she stepped onto the landing he called out to her. "Halt!" then "Wait." She heard rustling in the sheets, and sighs. After several moments, and the sounds of flesh moving on flesh, and more sighs, he said, "Enter," in a more calm and seductive voice. A. stopped in the doorway to take in the tableau that she was sure he had arranged just for her.

He was naked, leaning back on a stack of pillows, near sitting up. On his right were two young men, also naked, spooning closely. Their heads rested on his thigh; the more distal one with his right hand slid up under the Master's ass, fingers disappearing she knew not where. The other, more proximal young man, had his hand wrapped around the base of the Master's flaccidness. On the Master's left were two young women, naked as well and spooning closely. Their heads lay on his hip and belly. The distal one had her left hand cupping the Master's scrotum, and the proximal had her face positioned as if the toy of their affection would soon be placed in her mouth.

The Master looked at A. through slitted eyes, slowly growing erect under the attention of her eyes. Then the tableau moved. The woman moved her face down the Master's belly, taking him in her mouth. Then the man farther down raised his leg to reveal his erection and that he'd been entered from behind by the other man, and flexed his fingers, massaging the Master's anus and perineum. The other man slowly and masturbatingly fed the Master's penis into the woman's mouth.

Then both women raised their legs, showing A. they'd been masturbating with their downside arms all along. The one slowly rolled the Master's scrotum in her other hand. She dropped her down hand momentarily and revealed a small pink tattoo high on her thigh where it would normally be covered with hair. It seemed like a design A. recognized but didn't know from where, and she wished she'd had her glasses on. The more superior woman started making slow sucking sounds.

The tableau increased the speed of its movements. What appeared to be a darkness in the shadow over his shoulder and the back of his head trembled. When the movements established a regular pace, like looking at the working of a spring driven clock, the Master sat up, stretched, and spoke.

"And how is it with you this morning. Are you well?"

And she felt the power of the sex she was seeing enter her sex, causing her legs to shake, and forcing her to her knees. Which was where he'd wanted her, his servant, all along. She reflected on how long it had taken her to get over her craving for him, a craving awakened in her by his grandfather, and she was glad she was done with it. So she smiled and said, "I'm well, thank you."

She knew the tableau had been arranged just for her, as some sort of tortuous and humiliating test.

He sat up so he could see her, head down, hiding her face. He smirked. He pushed his little servants away and rose from the bed, and went over to her, erection bouncing, and raised up her face to look at him. She kept her eyes down.

"It's true," he said, taking her face in his hand and turning it from side to side. "You *are* doing well." He used her chin to pull her up into standing next to him. "Tell me, what have you discovered? I have glanced over those fore-shortened mileage monologues you consider to be reporting. They reveal nothing. I want to hear your stories. Let's go into the office," he said, grabbing a robe from a hook behind the bedroom door.

An hour later he had the receptionist bring in some coffee and pastries. He had felt the need to complete the release he'd started the day playing with, and had tried taking A. from behind, but found he couldn't keep it up. He attributed it to A.'s age making her unattractive (A. attributed it to the power she'd obtained over men's erections—if she didn't want them to have one, well, then they wouldn't). He ordered the young man to drop his trousers and bend over the desk, his face to A. The Master took him without preparation, and it was painful.

She willed the Master's victim, laying across the desk, to hold her gaze while he was being abused. It was a desk on which she'd been laid many a time across, and others as well, both by this Master and his father. She opened the door in the back of her mind that led to oblivion, letting him see it through her, and the pain on his face eased, though a tear slipped down each cheek. In the two horrible minutes it took the Master to finish, A. could see everything there was to see in the man's soul—his privileged upbringing, his vanity, and his vain hopes to obtain the power his ego thought was his due. As the Master finished she smiled at him with such condescension that the man flushed with embarrassment, she was sure, rather than excitation. She nodded once, and closed the door in her mind, breaking the gaze just before the Master stepped back, wiped himself on the man's shirttail and told him to leave.

"Now, where were we?" he asked, sitting down and sipping at a cup of coffee. "Tell me what you've spent my money on."

"Have you not read my reports?" she asked.

"No. I tasked others with that, including my secretary Brian there. If there were anything significant he knew he was to tell me. I have always preferred to hear things from your mouth anyway, my dear A." And he smiled a lascivious smile at her. She knew the response he wanted was for her to smile lasciviously in return. Giving him what he wanted kept the abuse to a minimum. It led him to trust her, which made her life easier.

She began by telling the Master yet again how sorry she was that the monster she'd been searching for had been responsible for the magic that had wrecked his mother's car all those many years ago, leaving her with third degree burns from which she'd died horribly. She told about picking up his cold trail again and tracking him to the small town where he'd been washing dishes at the local diner and, no doubt, fucking the waitress. Then tracking him south, then on the long journey north, always a few days, or a week, behind him, this man who called himself Quinn.

At the conclusion of the tale the Master said, "Hmm, a road that wasn't there, but then it was. Show me on the map." He woke up the laptop computer on the desk. A. came around the desk and was bending over his shoulder when she saw the young woman with the pink tattoo at near her vagina go past the open office door in the company of one of the young men she'd seen earlier. She noticed how fit, physically fit, they appeared to be now, with none of the slackness of dissipation about them.

She remembered where she'd seen the image before—stenciled on the Gate House wall. She raised her Voice and her arm and commanded the young woman to "Stop!" Then, "Come here."

The couple, locked down by A.'s use of the Voice, stopped so suddenly they rocked slightly.

"Not you, William. Just you, Leonora. Come here," the Master said, not needing to use his Voice.

The young woman, still appearing somewhat dazed from the induced hypnosis under which she, and her man, had been having sex earlier, entered the room and followed the Master's beckoning finger around behind the desk as A. stepped back. A. took her by the shoulders and laid her back down across the desk.

The Master reached forward and turned Leonora's head to the side, holding her head down. When he spread his fingers across her face an image, like a shadow, of a black diamond or kite appeared in the air just over his hand. "Show me," he said to A.

Leonora was wearing yoga tights over a thong. A. reached up and pulled them down to ankle level.

"Spread your legs," A. ordered. She got on her knees in front of Leonora and grabbed the inside of Leonora's thighs and twisted them open. She found the mark at the inside top of the left thigh and shifted her hands until the skin was stretched up and back. "Look," she instructed the Master. "Look here."

Neither the Master nor A. saw William twitch and restrain himself as Leonora was grabbed and prodded and twisted. But Brian did. The Master leaned in. The little pink flower tattoo, a little larger than a quarter inch across, outlined in white was, he thought, charming.

"And you've seen this where?" the Master asked.

"I've seen it at the last place I felt him. There," she said, pointing at the satellite photo of Stonehaven now showing on the computer screen. Then, to Leonora, lifting away the Master's hand holding down her head, "Do you know where this is?"

Leonora looked, wide-eyed, and shook her head "No."

"Why did you get the tattoo?" the Master asked.

"Me and some of the girls got it. My unit, you know? We saw it on the wall of the tattoo parlor. It's so macho all the time, in the army. We got it to remind us who we are." The Master released her and she pulled up her tights.

William guided Leonora with a hand on her elbow across the parking lot to their car. He realized that he was awake, no longer under the spell of the inducement. He urgently hissed her name, "Leonora! Wake up!" Even in the bright light her face still seemed in shadow. She was caught up in the image of when they'd turned her back on the desk for a better look, sat her down on the desk, and spread her knees as far as they could, her ankles still trapped by her pants. They propped her feet up on the desk and spread her knees again. The older woman had taken a picture of the inside of her thigh with her phone, and then leered at her. She couldn't shake the image of the leer.

When she was in the car and they were driving away she realized what the woman had been leering at—the little pink flower—the little indulgence in ink that she, and many of her sisters serving both in the military and the Order had taken on to mark their sisterhood.

Many young members of the Order of the Fleur de Vie were attracted to service in the military. This was the case with William and Leonora. They worked at the Presidio in intelligence analytics but they loved it that the job gave them the discipline and the opportunity to stay in the best physical shape they possibly could.

That they could do that, and be initiated members of the Order gave their lives a dimensionality, a thickness, a fullness and a depth, that they could sense those around them did not have. And both, therefore, had been thoroughly trained in the energetics of cloaking, so that others would not feel lessened in their presence. There was a problem with cloaking however. It could, and often did, interfere with the sensitivity that would give them enhanced impressions of those around them.

They had been assigned not just to each other but to keep an eye on A.'s Master. The High Priestess of Berkeley had assigned them there, based on the perceptions of her Madeleine that a deeper evil lurked there, and that this evil was a threat to the Order. The image that kept coming to the Madeleine was of a black kite hovering just behind and above him. Whenever the Madeleine looked she felt a terror that loosened her bowels.

Behind them they did not hear the Master. "I want to find him!" the Master screamed. "If he's still alive I want to find him! He killed my mother! Crippled my father! Made him walk with a cane! No matter how many slaves he compelled to kiss his scars the pain never stopped! It always came back as soon as they took their mouth away. I want him found!"

"He has gone past my ability to see him. He has changed. He no longer leaves the kind of track he used to leave."

"I don't care. Find his new signature."

"Come with me then. Loan me enough of your power to see."

"Let's go to the Gate House."

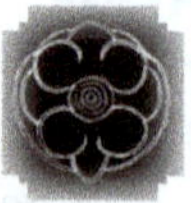

12

BETH ELMYRA

Beth Elmyra sat on the park bench next to the falls watching equinox sunset over the cathedral of the invader. Beth Elmyra: at least that's what the name on her passport said. She smiled.

If there was any justice in the world her passport would simply record her title: High Priestess of Bath.

As she sat, she connected telepathically with her designee, who was engaged in the Solstice Hierogamy ritual with the High Consort's designee. Both were surrounded by the chanting, drumming circles of the local members of the Order de la Fleur de Vie at the moment.

She smiled again. During the positions and movements leading up to the finish, her designee had been struggling with the duality of letting the Goddess come to the forefront of her experience while she remained just in the background, yet still in control. The face of the Goddess was struggling to come to the fore and the designee was struggling with letting Her. It was important that she learn how to let Her come forward especially in high pressure situations.

The Goddess would need access to her at other times if she were ever to serve in Beth's role. Beth grinned again, and shook her gray hair back behind her shoulders. Finally the designee let go. When she did the Goddess came forward and took over. The young woman's hips bucked against the Consort, rocking. She raised her arms. The Goddess actually raised Her arms and extended ecstasy out into the world. That ecstasy contained the secret of the joy that makes life worth living.

When the ecstatic seizure ended, she rose up a little creating space for her Consort—Her Consort—to finish. Nine times he drove the piston in and out. On the ninth stroke he finished, pumping into her nine times more. When it was done, She sat down on him. Leaning forward, she smiled and kissed him thoroughly.

Then she stood up, dripping down her thigh and along his belly. She made her way over his head and sat down on his face, letting him kiss her there thoroughly in return. She stood up shortly, stepped off the dais and was surrounded immediately by two Priestesses who hung her robes upon her and straightened her crown.

He rolled over on his belly, his chin resting on his fist, grinning as he watched her ass bounce as she walked away from him, not looking back. He wondered if she'd grant him the boon of her favor. Finally, at the last moment before she was escorted from the room, she turned and looked over her shoulder and smiled at him. His heart opened and received the smile. He smiled back, and stood up into the robe that was waiting for him.

Beth smiled, knowing that it was done, and done well. In a few hours she would meet her designee in the Council at the Number Seven restaurant with the rest of the local Council. The men would be meeting and eating, no doubt drinking and telling men's stories two floors below them. When the time was right the wen would come downstairs and join them.

She wondered briefly where the High Consort was, then decided it didn't matter. He'd been present enough in his designee, like she'd been with her's. His power was that he couldn't be found unless he wanted to be. All she could see in his direction was shadows.

She hoped he was prepared with some useful ideas about how the integrate the influx of refugees from Stonehaven.

If nothing else, she'd keep them working in the laundry over at the spa. She could probably cajole internship visas for the spa industry. Conjure up, she thought to herself, more likely. The Rules would have to be made more clear, however. There had already been an incident of a couple having sex on the dirty laundry pile. She found it remarkable that she had to specify they were to have sex on clean laundry and then wash it.

"Uggh," she said aloud and shivered at the grossness of it. Then she realized she would have to get on top of the extra-assignment sex that was sure to happen. Remote cousins getting to know each other better, she thought to herself and bark-laughed out loud. She would notify the Madeleine and her Crows to begin seeing into what assignments would best serve the Goddess.

She immediately heard the Madeleine's voice in her head, "Already on it."

"Of course you are, dear," she replied.

"Foresight," Madeleine said, "begins with the anticipation of need. It is as simple as that. Any further word from the High Council of the Order?"

"So, were you just waiting around so you could tell me that you were already on it?"

"No. I put it out there when I thought of it, hours ago. Kind of like voice mail, or call waiting. When you thought of me, it pinged me back and let me know you'd picked up the message. And then I tuned in to you. What time is the dinner tonight?"

"Can't you read my mind?" Beth asked sarcastically.

"Maybe. Wouldn't try. Just trying to save having to look it up."

"22:00. Third floor. Take the lift up. I'll share what I have from the High Council then. The men will be on the ground floor. Stick your head in and say hello, if you wish. "

"Thanks, dear. I will. See you then."

Beth's mind fell into silence, no sound but the water rushing over the three levels of falls. The news from the High Council was not great, but the plan felt good. She would have to work with her Craft to upgrade security. She closed her eyes and laid her head back in the last rays of the sun setting through the crenellations of the abbey tower. She opened her mind to the Goddess, sharing her sensation, and waited to listen to Her sense of what consequences the news entailed.

13

SLIM CURLEY

Angelica adjusted the brim of her new straw cowboy hat against the glare of the setting October sun. The dirt road alternated between teeth-chattering washboard and head-banging ruts and gullies. It was impossible to get up any speed, and, given the number of times she'd heard the undercarriage or the exhaust bottom out and grind along the road, she was happy that Regina Moon Halter had insisted on the highest chassis SUV they could rent at the airport. When she'd told the clerk where they were going—the Diamond Rose Ranch—she insisted on an off-road model with a bumper winch, and all the bells and whistles.

Regina sat in the back seat napping in the afternoon heat. Her window was down, letting in the sage laced air; the scent mixed with sweet grass when they crossed a creek bottom. Quinn rode silently in the passenger seat, keeping the brim of his new hat low also. Regina had also insisted that they all buy hats and sunglasses, and Angelica was happy for it now. Quinn, a fan of straw hats, had immediately bent the wire brim to a style more to his liking. He was cleaning the ever-present dust from his glasses when Angelica hit the brakes hard to avoid the steer that suddenly appeared in the road.

The steer watched impassively as the truck fishtailed and skidded off the road and high-centered on the edge of a ditch, both front and back passenger-side wheels hanging in the air. Regina fell forward and hit her nose on the back of the front seat and started cussing at herself for not wearing a seat belt.

Quinn quietly opened the door and dropped out. The running

board came to the middle of his thighs. "We ain't goin' nowhere like this," he said, spitting against the dryness of the cloud of dust that was still rolling up over the truck. "How good a driver are you?" he asked Angelica.

"Never on anything like this," she replied.

"I got this," Regina said, opening the driver's side rear door and crawling out. "Dammit, shit fire and fuck, that fucking hurt," she complained, pinching the bridge of her nose in case it was bleeding. She went to Angelica's door and opened it. "I'm not bleeding am I?" she asked through her involuntary tears.

Angelica raised Regina's face with one hand. "No, not that I can see."

"Shit fire and fuck," Regina said again. Angelica grinned.

"I can't quite picture that, Regina," Quinn said. "Could you be a little more descriptive?"

"Fuck you," Regina said. "Shit!" she said as Angelica moved to get out of the truck and the weight change shifted the truck a little farther into the ditch. "Quinn! Get out of there!" she barked.

Quinn jumped back, pushing himself off the body of the car and planting his butt squarely on a stone in the bottom of the ditch. "Ouch," he said. "Shit. Shit fire and fuck!" he shouted.

"There. Now you know," Regina said.

The truck stayed put. Little streams of gravelly dirt drifted down.

Angelica started laughing. "Which is it? Shit, fire and fuck? Shit fire, and fuck?"

"The latter," Regina said. "Come up here, Quinn."

They gathered on the road looking at how stuck the SUV was. Both the passenger side wheels were in the air. Had they not stopped when they did the truck would have rolled—at least down in the ditch on its side, if not over on its top.

They looked at the steer, still standing in the road, looking back at them, chewing, its eyes half-closed in some kind of trance, dust from the road kicked up by their quick stop coating its hair and eyelashes. The steer suddenly made a whumpfing noise, turned, and trotted across the road and up a dry wash heading north.

Then they heard it: the rattle of a tool bouncing in an old truck bed coming down the road from the direction they'd come. It occurred to all three of them at the same time that the truck might not see them in time to stop so they turned and ran down the road where the steer had been, leaping the steer plop.

Quinn leaped over it, Regina went around it. Angelica couldn't make up her mind at the last minute and in a moment of fishtailing herself caught her boot on the edge of the plop, slipped, and went down, catching herself on her hand in the middle of the mound. She came to one knee, muttering "Gross," and shaking her hand.

Quinn looked back and saw her there, still in the road. He returned, grabbed her by the shoulder, and said, "Let's go!" just as the old pick up came over the rise and skidded to a stop. The dust cloud rolled over them all. When it stopped the door creaked open.

They saw a worn cowboy boot, knee-high to a sun-brown knee, suddenly covered with fringe as what looked to be a skirt slipped over it. A butt with a white shirt tail covering it appeared past the edge of the door.

Then a man stepped out from the behind the door, wearing a wire-brim straw cowboy hat with the brims turned up on the sides. His brown face was covered in white stubble, and his white long sleeve shirt had the sleeves rolled up above the elbows and was open all down the front showing a brown belly. And he was wearing a flower-patterned sarong, tied in a knot at the waist, fringe hanging just below the knee over the top of the boot. He was holding a First Aid kit. His blue eyes focused on the people in the road. When Regina came back around the bend, he squinted. Then, with a whoop and jig-step he started trotting down the road, yelling, "Regina! Regina MacGregor! It *is* you! I thought it might be when they told me Moon Halter was coming!"

He tossed the kit at Quinn and went high-stepping past them to hug Regina and pick her up and twirl her around. She hugged him back, then, when he set her down, she punched him in the shoulder. "Slim! Slim Curley! You old dog."

"I was hoping to catch you on the road," he said. Then, leaning forward, turning his head so his hat didn't bump hers, he gave her a big smooch. Long enough, Angelica observed, for a little tongue action to transpire.

"Hey!" she shouted. "A little help here!"

"Oh, come on," Quinn said. "You're not hurt." He helped her up. She showed him her hand. "Wipe it off in the dirt," he said impatiently. "Then we'll get some water."

The other two walked back up the to the SUV, arms around each other, Slim sneaking kisses whenever he could get away with it. Regina was both annoyed and receptive. Smiling, even.

Quinn and Angelica stood there watching the display of affection. Regina made up her mind to have mercy on the old coot and stopped to take him in her arms and kiss him thoroughly. After a moment she broke the kiss and said, loud enough for them to all hear, "I feel you, honey. I feel what you're packing, eh?" and she laughed.

Slim said, "Well, what about it? Waddaya say? You know us old men. We live by the words 'Never waste an erection, never trust a fart.'"

Whereupon he farted. A short, sharp fart, like a small caliber pistol, the report echoed slightly off the wall of the wash.

Regina laughed. "You give lie to your own wisdom! You asshole!" She punched him in the shoulder again and then pushed him away. He turned from the group and adjusted the front of his sarong so his erection wasn't poking through.

"Still don't want to waste it," he muttered.

Joining Regina, she introduced him. "Friends, this is Slim Curley. He was High Consort to my High Priestess quite a few times on different assignments."

Angelica, who'd been scowling at them, changed her face completely and grinned largely at him, shaking his hand in a matching slight exaggeration.

"This is Angelica," Regina said.

Slim picked his hat straight up, revealing a top knot of white and gray hair pulled tightly up over a bald pate. "Ahh, the dragon lady," he said. Angelica stopped smiling and returned to scowling.

Quinn removed his hat and wiped his sleeve on his forehead, the slight breeze cooling his buzz cut hair. He put the hat back on, and removed his sunglasses to better look Slim in the eyes. Slim returned the gaze.

They stood there, gripping hands loosely, nothing macho to communicate, and after a second there was a flash of recognition, a slight recoil in their upper bodies and heads, as if they recognized each other.

Regina, observing this, said, "You've never met. Yet you recognize something in each other."

"Yeah," Slim said. Still holding Quinn's gaze he whispered, almost in amazement, "He's an asshole. A real asshole, just like me."

"Yes, he is," Regina said. "He is, in fact, the Bodhisattva of Assholes."

Slim bowed over the still joined hands. "It's an honor, sir."

Quinn could tell he was grinning when he said it. So he leaned forward and said, "Asshole."

They both stood up laughing. For Quinn, it was his first good laugh in many weeks.

Angelica raised her voice. "Will somebody please tell me what's going on? Why are you guys assholes?"

"Because the shit of the world runs through our minds," they both answered simultaneously, and then they laughed so hard they doubled over. When they were done they patted each other on the back. Quinn continued, "Our job is to just let it pass through and make sure none of it sticks to us."

"Yeah, and to keep a tight seal," Slim added. "A tight sphincter, as it were."

"I still don't get it," Angelica said.

"It's OK, honey," Regina said. "They don't get you, either. Now what are we going to do about these wheels?"

"What happened?" Slim asked.

"Came over the hill and a cow was standing in the middle of the road. Hit the brakes to avoid it and we slid to the side," Angelica explained.

"Steer," Slim said.

"I did, Mister, I did steer. What do you think I did?" Angelica said resentfully.

"No, young'un, I meant it wasn't a cow. It was a steer. Testy probably."

"What? Do you mean grumpy?"

"Nah, Testy's its name. It's got one testicle. They must've missed it at castration. Makes it crazy. Won't hang with the others. It just wanders around out here. I figure it's looking for the missing one."

"What're you going to do?"

"Hunt it, I reckon. Wait til after the last roundup and hunt it. Then one fine morning we'll have us a Testy breakfast," Slim grinned as he said this and licked his lips.

"You're fucking kidding me," Angelica said, her credulity seriously strained.

"You bet!" Slim explained.

Regina interrupted him before he continued with a detailed account of the butchering. "I said, 'What are we gonna do about this?'"

"Technically you said 'these wheels'. Well, there's a big front end loader in the shed a few miles back. We keep it there for feeding hay or snow plowing in the winter. I've got the keys and it should start up," Slim offered.

"What about your truck?" Quinn asked. "You've got a cable winch, right?"

"Right, yeah. I do. But that's a heavy truck you got there, and the winch probably won't have enough power to pull it back up on the road. Just drag it along the edge, more'n likely," Slim replied. "Wadd-aya say, Regina, wanna go for a ride with me?" turning his face away to hide his smile.

"Sure, honey. I'll go for a ride with you anytime," Regina, feeling the unseen smile, smiled herself.

"You got water?" Slim asked Quinn. "We might be a couple hours."

"We've got some. Could use a couple more bottles if you got 'em. Angelica, walk up to the truck with them and grab a couple, would you?"

Angelica continued scowling, but nodded "yes" and followed them back up the road. Slim's truck was big. He helped Regina climb up in the passenger side, closed the door, then went around to the driver's side and rummaged around in an ice box behind the seat, pulled out two bottles of water, and passed them around the door to Angelica.

"Try to stay in the shade, OK? And make sure you drink those," he said, hiking up the hem of his sarong and climbing in. He started the truck and had Regina adjust her seat so the split bench came even with his. She scooted over and sat in the middle, next to him. Regina grinned at the still scowling Angelica and waved to her through the windshield.

Angelica was even still scowling when she got back to Quinn. "Now, where we gonna find any shade around here?" she wanted to know, passing a bottle to Quinn and cracking open the other for herself.

"Right here," Quinn said. He indicated a little sliver of shadow up against the cut bank of the road on the northeast side. He leaned back into it, patted the wall beside him, and slid to the ground.

Since the trip began Angelica had been under Regina's fierce and protective gaze. Regina had let him know, in no uncertain terms, that he was not to question Angelica in any detail about her experience un-til they had arrived at their destination. He was to allow the alchemy of travel to work on her in the aftermath of her parents' death. He figured that, now that they were here, at their destination, wherever that was, he could start.

"You know, I had the same thing happen to me. I was twenty-one. It was a full blow-out and there was no help. No dragon either. You open to some questions? And maybe some advice?"

Angelica, who had turned and stared at Quinn when he'd said he'd been twenty-one, looked back away out into the wash-cut land-scape and narrowed her eyes. She nodded, "Yes."

In the truck Slim had put an arm around Regina up on the seat back and turned to look through the rear window to back up. The turn pushed his thigh up against Regina. She put her hand on it. In a few moments he gave up the view, saying, "Sheeyit. Tail gate's too high for making the turns." He faced front again and used the side mirrors, moving slowly in reverse. He put his hand on Regina's hand and said, "Good to see you, too, darlin."

She squeezed his thigh in response. When he put his hand back on the steering wheel, turning his head from side to side, working both mirrors, she took advantage of the moment to begin sliding back his sarong. When his thigh was completely exposed she put her hand on the bare skin, slipping it up as high as she could without turning, and slipped it around to the inside of his thigh and squeezed him. He was tight and ropy, still strong from these last years on horseback.

When they were far enough back out of the wash there was a cut out that let him back uphill and turn around. When they were facing the opposite direction he put the truck in park and turned to kiss Regina. Taking her hat off and laying it on the seat behind her, she turned toward him, slipping her left arm around between his waist and the seat back, and switching her grip on his thigh to her right hand.

Waves of desire washed back and forth between them, focusing on the sweetness of the kiss. Their minds were flooded with the memories of all the times they'd done this over the years—all the kisses and all the sex, especially in strange places. She slid her hand all the way up the inside of his thigh until she encountered what she loved to call it—his 'manhood'.

"This still work?" she asked, with some concern.

"Yup. Lucky me. All it needs is a little more attention than it used to."

Regina said, "Lucky you. All I have is the time." Still turned toward him, she uncovered him completely and lowered her face into his lap. "Umm," she breathed. "Smells like sage brush," and took him in her mouth.

"Umm, hmm," he said, resting a hand on her upper back. "Lawdess, lawdess. Ummm, hmmm."

It was three miles back to the shed and he took it slow. He hit a bump, and felt her teeth as the truck bounced. "Ow. Ow! Teeth!" he exclaimed.

"Slow down, idiot. What's your hurry?" she spoke around a mouthful.

"Why, none. None at all, darlin." He set the cruise control for 'five' so he could take his foot off the gas.

Her mind filled with happy memories of doing this before. She'd always liked him, always liked his sex. When he was completely hard she sat up and whacked it against his belly. "Meat," she said, grinning and wiping the corner of her mouth on the back of her sleeve and tucking a strand of hair behind her ear. "Good meat."

When, a mile later, it became clear that she was going to make him wait, he sighed. And stepped on the gas.

"What's it like? You ask?" Angelica responded to Quinn, taking another sip and pushing her hat back. She continued thoughtfully. "It's like having two minds. One Higher, and one Lower. And the Lower is often stronger than the Higher Mind. My work has been to gain control, and keep it. I have only certain tools at my disposal, and when these fail I am vulnerable to control by the dragon. And he and I are very much not the same."

"He?" Quinn asked. "You're sure now? How do you know?"

"Yes, I'm sure. And how do you think I know?" she smirked sideways at him.

"You've had sex with it? Him?"

"Yes. There've been days, entire days, when I've gone around with him inside me, wrapped around me and then peering up over my shoulder at whatever I'm paying attention to. He'll stay there, like that, keeping me aroused and wet all day. He moves ever so slightly, returning my attention to him, whenever he feels neglected, I suppose. He likes learning the languages I've been told to study, Waitanese and Wallidese.

"Sometimes when I'm asleep he'll rouse himself and enter. I arise from dreaming to find his cool skin sliding on me like a snake. It was creepy til I got used to it. It feels like needles, you know."

"Needles? Like everywhere, all over your skin?"

"Yeah, like that. Sometimes it's cool needles, sometimes they're warm. Or lots of times they're hot. Just hot, hot little jabby things everywhere."

"I know. I remember. I hated that."

"The dragon is the only thing that doesn't hurt. That, and that time I had sex with the wind on my first walk with Diana. But I can't even really touch myself. That hurts too. But I'm horny all the time. I'm horny all the fucking time and I can't stand it." She paused. "I'm horny all the time and I'm angry 'cause I can't fix it. Horny and angry all the time. And everything hurts. Except orgasm, which goes right to the edge. I can't give it to myself and I can't stand others to give it to me. It was different for Diana. She went around masturbating all the time. When she was going through that time when she couldn't stand clothes, she told me she'd back up against a tree and stand there and masturbate with her hands until she'd drool. Fucking crazy," she concluded.

"It was different for me," Quinn said. "I felt the needles all the time, and everything that touched me hurt. But getting an erection hurt worse. Well, to be precise, trying to get rid of an erection is what hurt. I had to either put sex aside completely or force myself to get relief through the pain, but without being attached to it. Indifferent sex, that's what I learned. Not to my partner, not indifferent to her, you know, but to myself."

"Yeah, that's different than me," Angelica said. "What about masturbation?"

"Yeah, well, I stopped that. I always felt like I was being watched all the time. It made me always think that I had something better to do. And other than that, it was embarrassing."

"Really?"

"Really, yeah. I figured out that if I was going to have sex, I'd have to have it with someone. That way, at least, I'd have something to pay attention to besides the sensation that I was being watched."

"Wow," she said. "That'd suck. But the thing for me is, now that I think about it, that I don't care. Watch if you want, motherfuckers, but all the urge in me is to just be out there with it. Just bring it up and discharge it, all those needles lining up and shooting out of me. Sometimes it's like they all line up in my hands and then shoot back into me, and some part of me says 'Oh yeah? Is that all you got?" and I work it furiously. Just furiously. And all my anger gets converted and goes away. And who the hell wants to be angry all the time. You know?"

"Yeah," he said. "It's the energy. The charge builds up and then it discharges. It's just like electricity. Well, it is electricity, it's electromagnetic."

"Yeah, that's what Diana says. But the words don't help. I want to come so hard I have to find a safe place to bang my head. And sometimes that's when he comes out. Curls himself around me. Insinuates himself inside of me. He cools me down and makes me sane again."

"Yeah, it's a madness. But it's only crazy to other people, to everyday people. To you, it's not crazy. To you, it's you. It's your normal. But you can't be who you are, correction, what you are, when you're around them. You can never be yourself around people who don't know."

"Did you hear what happened when I went to my parents' funeral? The caskets were closed because the damage from the accident was so bad. All I could see was the image of my uncle's and cousin's faces instead. By the end, when I passed them in the foyer on the way out, I couldn't stand it. I kicked my uncle in the nuts, pointy toe first. I could feel the flesh getting squinched, if that makes any sense. And I hit my cousin in the nose when he bent over to help his dad. With an undercut. Blood spurted everywhere. My cousin blacked out, laying over his dad, and since he couldn't roll around anymore, he just lay there screaming. I stood over them, fists clenched, screaming, too, screaming louder, "Take that, motherfuckers!" Randall, you remember him? My escort along with Margot?"

Quinn nodded his head.

"Randall held the crowd back. Margot put her hand on me, right where the barrier had been, you know? And I stopped screaming. She told everybody she was a doctor. She leaned in and told my uncle 'I'm a lawyer. Are you listening? Yes? If you call the police I will have you jailed for child sex abuse. Do you understand? Open your eyes. Look at me. Do you understand?' She had her hands on their throats like she was checking their pulses. He could feel the power, I could see it. He knew she was sparing their lives. He nodded and I could feel his relief when she let go. She asked the funeral director for ice, and told him we wouldn't be coming back. My brother came to the door as we were pulling away. All I could do was weep."

Angelica paused, looking off into the distance, tears running silently down her cheeks.

"The rage felt good, didn't it?" Quinn asked.

"Better than good. It was orgasmic. By the time I got in the car I was shivering uncontrollably, you know? I thought it was from shock or something. Something caused by the extra effort and discharging the rage. But it was more than that. When we got in the car, I was still weeping. But five minutes down the road I had to rip my panties off and masturbate until I came screaming."

She sighed.

"How do you feel about that?" Quinn asked.

"I don't fucking care. That's how I feel. And don't you, motherfucker, start telling me how I should."

"Wouldn't think of it. You only have to be aware that behavior has consequences, buffer or not. Where was the dragon in all this?"

"Right there. Right under the surface. It was all I could do—it was the only thing I could control, keeping him hidden. He would have been happy to kill again."

"Right. Well, all I can say is: Good job, Angelica. Nicely done."

Angelica, surprised and mollified, turned her head toward him and smiled, sniffling.

"How'd you do it?" Quinn asked.

"I have a tight wire inside me. A tight wire mesh that he can't break through unless I drop it. The High Priestess showed me how. I see it in my brain's image of myself. I see it inside me. And She showed Regina how to invoke it in me when I can't."

"Well, that's good. All I ever had was a cigarette," Quinn said.

"A cigarette?" Angelica asked.

"Yeah. I didn't have a dragon to control, but there were plenty of times I was enraged enough to kill. But I'd smoke a cigarette and think about it first. So far, so good. There's a bunch of people still alive because of it." Quinn took a pack out of his shirt pocket and tapped one out. "Want one?"

"Ugh. No. Gross. Disgusting."

"Yeah, well," he said, and lit one up, exhaling up into the sky. "You never know who your friends are gonna be. If a plant spirit medicine wants to use you, it will. So what are you going to do about the rage?"

"I don't know. That's one of the things my Initiation as a priestess is supposed to show me—how to control myself. Here, gimme a drag," she said. "I hate you."

"Yeah, well, get in line."

Slim and Regina arrived at the shed—a big shed to house modern haying and plowing equipment. There was a water pumping windmill out back, its tail parallel to the blades and inactive, and a cylindrical water tower on stilts for gravity-feed into the structure.

There was a regular door toward the side in front. Slim, erection bouncing around under the sarong, unlocked it and stepped inside and reached around on the wall, hunting for a switch. The big bay garage door slowly opened. A large wheel loader was first inside the door. Regina got out of the truck. She went inside and stood there, looking up at the cab.

"Room for one, eh?" she asked as Slim came up behind her.

"Yup."

"Well, it'll just have to do. Climb up there and fire it up. Let's get it outside.

"Do?"

"Yup," she said.

"Waddaya got in mind?" Slim asked.

"You'll see. Get it out here."

"Well, OK, give me a hand first," Slim said. He went over to the wall, pulling on a pair of leather gloves he'd had tucked in the waist of his sarong. "Got gloves? Help me move a couple chains over to the bucket."

She pulled a pair of gloves out of her jacket pocket. The tow chains were hung from nails and then looped across uprights in the wall at waist height. They each took an end, and carried four twenty-foot chains sequentially over to the bucket on the loader and dumped them in. Slim grabbed a box of clevises and quick-links, and put that in, too.

Slim's erection was almost gone. Fat-cocked, he called it. As he climbed up the step ladder to the cab Regina stopped him. Removing a glove she reached under the sarong and brought him back. She grinned up at him. "Now get on up there, and have a seat. Turn the AC on."

She stood near the loader as he drove it out into the sunshine. She stopped him then and climbed up, pulling the door closed behind her and sighing in the cooler air.

"You're riding with me?" Slim asked.

"More'n that," Regina said. "Show me the hydraulics."

He showed her the controls for lift and bucket tilt.

"There's only one seat," he protested, weakly.

"Now, show me those other hydraulics," as she indicated his sarong. He pulled the cloth aside to reveal himself in full lift and tilt.

"Ah," Regina said, her eyes glowing as she grasped him. "Damn. I'm not taking my boots off. She turned around and faced out the windshield, completely blocking his view. She undid her belt and pushed her jeans and underwear down to her knees. She reached back with her hands and spread her buttocks for him. "Think you can aim for that, cowboy?"

"Yes, indeed I can. Ease on back here a little bit."

She eased back on him, and eased herself down along him, until she had him completely. Then she rose again, almost to the end. As she was doing so, she pulled on the lever to lift the bucket. The sound of the fluid rushed into her and added to the rumble of the engine she could feel through him. As she lowered herself again, she lowered the bucket.

This went on for several minutes. The bucket raising and lowering, faster, then a little faster. Near the top she started using the lever for the bucket tilt, rattling the chains against the steel. Regina started laughing as Slim groaned. At the finish, bucket raised high in the air, she tilted the bucket and the chains rattled out on the ground.

"There we go, cowboy. How was that ride?" she asked, pulling up her pants. She opened the door and climbed out, kissing Slim on her way. He still lay there, legs splayed, erection wet and shiny across his thigh, groaning. "Lower the bucket for me, would ya?" she said.

He reluctantly sat forward to operate the levers and watched Regina reload the chains into the bucket. "You're some help!" she hollered at him. Sighing, he put on his gloves and got down to help.

Stranded at the SUV, after several grumpy silences punctuated with intense interrogations by Angelica and mild responses from Quinn, Angelica mused, "What do you think is taking so long?"

"What do *you* think is taking so long? Seriously," Quinn shook his head.

"Oh," she said, realization dawning. "Here? Now? Really?"

Quinn said, "Well, yes, of course."

"Eww. Yuck. Gross. They must be eighty years old."

"Near enough. Be hopeful you can still get it wet at that age."

"I swear. Here we are, stranded in the middle of nowhere, hardly no water, and they're off fucking somewhere. Goddess, why? Why am I stuck here? You know I can't have sex, right?"

Quinn nodded.

"I can't have sex because of this fucking dragon. Nobody wants to risk it coming out. I'm horny. I can't help it. I have all this heat in me. It drives me fucking nuts. Thinking about them fucking drives me fucking nuts." She stopped. Quinn watched her.

"I hate this shit. I don't mean to be ungrateful and all, but I hate this shit. Didn't ask for it, didn't invite it, didn't volunteer."

"Are you whining about how much your life sucks? Really? You looked at my life? After all the shit I went through, same as you, and now I'm a freak, too. Thanks to that fucking dragon."

"I'm sorry. Sorry. No whining. I should know better." She stopped and looked sideways at Quinn. "Wanna fuck?" she asked slyly.

Quinn looked back at her, one eyebrow raised. He noticed her nipple had grown hard under her clothes. "You? Sure. You're beautiful. But I won't. There's a reason why you and that thing of yours are on sabbatical. I, for one, won't go against the Goddess."

"Ah, fuck you then," she said angrily, and walked up the road a short distance before climbing the bank they had been leaning against, seeking shade.

Quinn sat back and took a sip of water. He listened to the wind. It rustled through the sparse grass and made a little moaning sound as it came around the fender of the truck. The moan became a little louder, and the wind sounded more like breath behind him. He turned to look and stood up to regard what he saw.

Angelica stood on top of the bank, looking down at him through slitted eyes. Her shirt was open and she had her breasts out and was massaging them with one hand, pinching a nipple. Her jeans were down to her ankles, leaving her calves covered by her boots. She was panting, and groaning between breaths.

And the dragon was out. It wrapped its arms and legs around her, and its tail around one thigh. Its head hung over a shoulder, alternating sides, looking down. Looking at Quinn.

She was masturbating. As Quinn watched, adjusting what had begun to stir between his legs, she increased her pace, bringing herself from a moan to a shout, and then another shout, ejaculating down on Quinn's upturned face. The dragon seemed to be wriggling in ecstasy hanging from her back, its short arms waving in the air like jazz hands and its snout turned to the sky. Quinn thought he heard it bugling.

He removed his hat, opened his mouth, and caught as much of her as he could. She finished, slowing down, when they both heard the rumble of the loader engine. The dragon took one look in that direction and disappeared.

"Shit, fire, and fuck," Angelica said, pulling up her pants. Quinn grinned.

"Arrgh," she said, breasts shaking side to side, in frustration as her zipper got stuck. "Oh, fuck me. Did I really just say 'Arrgh'?"

Quinn laughed out loud. "That was pretty," he said. "You'll make a great Priestess someday."

"Wet enough for ya?"

The loader came over the hill. Regina was clearly steering it, sitting on Slim's lap.

It came to a stop and the dust billowed over Quinn, who turned away and put the inside of his elbow up over his nose. Angelica had disappeared over the bank further down the road and came walking back up, her clothing readjusted.

Quinn asked her, "Feel better now?"

"Much, thanks for asking. Thirsty though. Got another bottle of water?"

"Why don't we wait a minute now that they're here? Wouldn't want to tip the truck."

"Sixteen ounces. Are you fucking kidding me?"

"I thought you said you were feeling better. Go ahead and raise the tailgate and see what happens."

"I do. I so feel better. Just wanted a bottle of water. For shit's sake.

"Yup. Still grumpy."

"Fuck you. I'm always grumpy, just like you were." And then she said, "I miss Diana."

"Yeah, me too," he said, looking away from her to the hills.

Regina lowered the bucket to the ground and got out of the cab. Slim climbed down after her, putting on his gloves. He went to the bucket and gestured for Quinn to come help him with the chains. He chose one of the 20-footers and dragged it rattling out of the bucket and over to the hitch on the back of the SUV.

"Not the best idea," Slim said. "But it's all I got. Get another one of these chains, would you?"

Quinn drug another chain over as Slim finished wrapping the first one around the towing bar mount.

"You an Indian?" Slim asked.

"What do you mean?" Comprehending that Slim was referring to his color, he said, "You mean my skin? Nah. No. Not an Indian. I've just got a condition." He began to remember the mud from Calley's pond in the Pine Eye.

"Catchy?" Slim asked.

"Nope. Not likely." His thoughts turned again to why he'd needed to use the mud—to cover splotchy scarring from the dragon's fire.

"Hey. Hey!" Slim said. "A little help here. Hook your chain up on your side the way I did it on mine."

When Quinn finished and Slim inspected it, they both got up. Regina had been having a quiet conversation with Angelica. They were both almost in tears. Regina patted Angelica on the shoulder and came over to the men.

"Regina, I'd like you to steer the car for me. What I'm gonna do is lift the rear slowly. Keep the steering wheel hard left, then swing it hard right when I tell you to. With any luck that will keep the front tire on the road, then straighten it out when I get the other tire up. And the rest of y'all stand back. Up on the bank there."

Everyone moved to their places. Regina got in the SUV, started it, and lowered the window. Slim, from the loader cab yelled, "OK. Turn it!" and Quinn repeated the message. Slowly lifting the rear, Slim got the bumper high enough so that the rear tire cleared the edge of the road. Easing the loader into reverse the front tire came up on the road.

"OK! Turn it!" Slim yelled and Regina turned the wheel. When the front end centered in the road Slim lowered the rear and drifted forward to put some slack in the chains.

Coming down off the bank, Quinn asked Angelica what Regina had said to her. Angelica, arriving at the road, said, "Basically, she told me to stop feeling sorry for myself. I'm on an adventure that no one else gets to have, and I should be grateful for it."

"Yeah," Quinn said, shaking his head knowingly. "That's a hard one." He turned to help Slim with the chains.

Regina got out of the SUV and came over to Angelica. "I'm going to ride with Slim. Are you going to be alright?" The wave of compassion that washed over Angelica made her tear up again.

"Yes, I'll be alright," she said, raising her face to smile at Regina. Regina turned and went up to the cab of the loader as Slim was just taking his seat.

"You steer it this time, cowboy. I'm no good at backing up."

"That's not what I recall, sweetheart. Here, take my hand," he said, helping her up. Closing the door, he put it in gear and looked over his shoulder. He slowly backed the loader up over the hill and they were gone.

Angelica and Quinn looked at each other.

She said, "I'm sorry I did that to you—burned you like that."

"Well, you didn't kill me. And it didn't hurt. Much. And they tell me to make sure I remember that you aren't the dragon. You're carrying it, and they don't know why. Not even the High Priestess knows, or if she does, she isn't saying. Let's get in the car and talk about it while we drive."

Quinn drove. "How far to the ranch, you reckon?"

"They said twenty-five miles from the highway. We went maybe ten."

"So, we've got some time then." He paused and then continued. "You know, we've never had much chance to do any talking. Always either somebody around or you in training. Do you know much about me? And is there anything you want me to know about you?"

"No, I don't know much. I know you aren't one of them, but that you have the same enemy. I was told you went through a full Kundalini Buffer blow-out younger than I am. I know the enemy had something to do with it all. I still have lots of questions. And then I don't know anything about what happened to you afterward. That's about it. Oh, and the gossip is that you're fantastic in bed, and that you could even teach things to the Consorts."

Quinn laughed. "I've heard the same gossip. So, ask me another question."

"Wait. What do I want you to know about me? What do *you* want to know about me?"

"OK. Do you sense the dragon at all? What's it like to have it inside you?"

"Yes, I sense it. It's kind of slithery. Not slippery or even slick. Just dry slither when it moves. We talk. We don't understand each other, but we use images, and feelings, to communicate. It sleeps a lot, sometimes for days. It's like it hibernates or something. I don't know what to do with it. I don't know what it eats, or how to feed it, but I want to take care of it."

"What does it eat? Now that's an interesting question. What do you suppose it's made of?"

"You mean like what kind of stuff? What are its flesh and bones? I don't know. It could be made of air, for all I know. What's the mind made of? I don't mean the brain; I mean the mind. What is mind stuff?"

"It's either light or the illusion of light, which might be tantamount to the same thing."

"Yeah, sort of. If it was light that could explain why it could make heat. It slept for weeks after what happened at the Gatehouse. If it eats light because it is light, then what does it breathe?"

"Maybe the same air that those other beings breathe. What do you call them?

"Embla and Dangla."

"Maybe that force around them protects them somehow, or maybe it's like a diving bell and it's filled with the air they breathe. It's too much to think about without enough information."

"You wanted to know what it's like to have it in me? Heat. It's like a moving heat. I get hot from it. I want to run naked and jump in a river sometimes. It makes me feel more alive. And then the heat focuses in certain places, those wheels, you know? The Centers of Energy, the ones they call chakras. Sometimes it makes me so horny I can't think. Sometimes it heats up my head and I think too fast to put it into words. I sweat. I get fevers."

"Yeah, I had them too."

"I get nightmares."

"Yeah, me too. It's all gotten better over the years, though. The energy evens out. You'd have them anyway, even without the dragon. I used to call them chi fevers. The internal exercises they've given you—they help."

"Yes. But you? How did you do it? You were alone, you didn't have any help."

"I fled. I ran away to the wilderness for five years. I couldn't stand people, couldn't stand to feel what they felt, think what they thought, dream what they dreamed. When I could block some of the openings and close some of the doors, I'd go to town for a couple days; buy food, do laundry. Eventually I lost the job I had out there, and had to leave."

"Job? You had a job?"

"Yeah, not much of one. Caretaker. A little ranch hand work. Hey, what the hell?"

Another steer had appeared in the road in front of the car. It didn't seem inclined to move.

"It's the same damn cow that made me run off the road!" Angelica exclaimed.

Quinn took his foot off the brake and let the truck idle forward. He let it bump the steer. The steer reacted angrily and head butted the grill. Quinn put the truck in park and got out to wave it off. It threatened to charge him.

Angelica got out. Shaking her arms and head, she called to the steer. "Get the fuck out of the way!" And, from the shaking, the dragon's head and neck erupted up over her head. The steer saw this strangeness as a real threat. It pooped blatantly, turned, and ran.

"See?" Quinn said. "You'll figure out a use for the dragon yet."

They got back in the SUV, Angelica muttering, "Fucking Testy. I can't fucking believe it."

After a few minutes of driving in silence, Angelica reached over and took one of Quinn's hands off the steering wheel. She held it, lacing her fingers between his. After another long silence, she said, "Lonely. It's all so fucking lonely."

"I understand," Quinn said. "And you've got two of you in there."

She looked at him, trying to gauge how he meant that. She saw a little twitch of smirk at the corner of his mouth.

"Asshole! You asshole" she yelled at him. Then she punched him in the shoulder. But she didn't let go of his hand.

They arrived finally at the ranch house compound. It was an

oasis of green on a broad terrace above the floodplain of a small creek. There were no visible power lines coming into the place, and windmills were turning near the house and the barns.

"Wow," Angelica said. "It's beautiful."

"Yeah," Quinn said, slowing and putting the vehicle in park so they could sit and contemplate the homestead. As they watched, a group of people left what looked like a bunkhouse to go to a larger log building with several chimneys and a wide porch, which they intuited to be a dining hall. Quinn's stomach growled.

"Yeah, me too," Angelica said.

"Ready to go on down there?" he asked.

"Yes."

"Are you going to let go of my hand?"

"Not yet. Holding it didn't hurt. We're the same. If I need comfort I'm coming to you. Is that OK?"

"I know the feeling. Yes, it's OK," he said.

They drove over a cattle guard and down, crossing the creek on a low bridge and parked in front of the hall. A few people stood on the porch watching them. Two more people, a man and a wen, came out of the main house and slowly approached the SUV.

Quinn and Angelica sighed at the same moment and let go of each other's hand. They opened the doors and got out. The man from the house spoke, "Howdy, you lost?"

"Probably. Probably not," Quinn said.

"You'd be Quinn, then," the wen said, smiling. "I'm Mudra, the High Priestess here. And this is Benny. Who's with you?"

"Just Angelica. Regina is riding with Slim."

"Oh," she laughed. "They might yet be awhile. You're just in time for dinner. Come on in."

Supper was served buffet style to about twenty people. When they'd gotten their food Mudra said to Angelica, "Angelica, come sit with me."

She sat down with Quinn on her other side. Another wen sat to Quinn's left.

Mudra said, "I want to know: do you know why you're here?"

Angelica replied, "Well, that was direct. I want to know: why are you called Mudra?"

Mudra smiled. She turned to Angelica and raised her hands chest high, drawing her first two fingers and her thumb together in a point. She started to rub her thumbs against the finger tips like she was rolling a cigarette or a thread. She held her hands up at eye level and drew her hands apart, making a little snapping motion.

At the snap, in her mind Angelica heard the words, "Because I can do things like this with my hands."

They smiled at each other then. Angelica said, "Really? So OK. I don't know why I'm here. My life, a normal life, went off the rails into this mystical metaphysical swamp and the train morphed into an airboat. I don't know why. But I'm told I'm here to undergo Initiation. And I don't know why or what that means, really."

"None of us know why your life changed the way it did. What we know is when these things happen it is because we have been given a purpose, sometimes even a mission. Rarely, it's accidental, or an unforeseen consequence, like it was with your friend Quinn over there. One purpose of Initiation is to give you the opportunity to discover what the purpose or mission is.

"The other part is more personal. A proper Initiation is supposed to reorganize the system of sentiments appropriate to a child into a system of sentiments appropriate to an adult. Do you know what I mean by that?"

Angelica shook her head. "No."

"Well, if most of your emotional focus or your mental focus is on yourself or your own suffering, then you are inwardly and egocentrically focused. This is the system of sentiments appropriate to a child. If your experience is more concerning the suffering of others then you are operating from a system of sentiments more appropriate to an adult. Do you understand?"

After a thoughtful pause Angelica said, "I suppose so, yes. I spend a lot of time thinking about and talking about my own experience and suffering these past few months. It sucks. I have to talk about it, otherwise it will fester and I'll just become mean, and angry. Is this what you're talking about?"

"Yes, in part. It is possible to think and talk about your own suffering in an adult way, however. You have to have some distance, some perspective on it. You have to be able to examine yourself objectively, almost as a person apart from yourself. This is why the first technique of the Way is to separate oneself from oneself."

"So, what you're telling me is that, basically, I'm still a child."

"No, Angelica, I'm not saying that. What I'm saying is that the Kundalini Barrier blow-out happened to you at a very young age, and all at once. I'm saying that you haven't had the time or the opportunity to practice objectivity about yourself and your own life that would, under more ideal circumstances, prepare you for putting your suffering in service to the suffering of others. And the impact of the blow-out is increased many times over by the revelation of the dragon you carry. Very few people ever have suffered what you're going through. If any."

Angelica stopped eating and sat staring into some distance. Mudra paused and placed a hand on Angelica's forearm. Angelica froze, the only indicator of her internal state was the tears that single-tracked down her cheeks.

Mudra continued, "What we're hoping the Initiation will do is give you that missing perspective. You will, for all intents and purposes, emerge as an adult. You will be a Priestess responsible for yourself and your internal states and be able to understand and bless the suffering of others. And in this way we believe you will gain control over the dragon, and maintain control until the purpose of the dragon is revealed. And this is why Regina and Quinn have been assigned to travel with you. The dragon speaks to her, and she speaks back. And the dragon chose not to fry Quinn in that incident at the Gatehouse. In fact, it may have made Quinn into something even the dragon cannot now destroy."

At that moment Regina and Slim arrived and Mudra rose to greet them. "Eat now, Angelica," Mudra said, making a sign of blessing. "You're going to need it."

The impact of the blessing was palpable for Angelica. Something was relieved in her that made space for breath and food. She realized she was hungry, and finished her burrito, thinking that she'd like a second.

Regina and Slim stood silhouetted in the doorway like uncertain gunfighters, waiting for their eyes to adjust. Slim moved out of the way and over to the chowline without hesitation. Mudra made her way around the diners and went to one knee before Regina, taking her hands and bending her head and touching her forehead on the back of Regina's palms. People noticed and the supper time chat fell silent. Slowly, one at a time at first, then in small clusters, the entire room stood up and faced the door. Then, as one, they all bowed. Regina stood still and scanned the room, letting her eyes pause on each face. She took Mudra's hands in hers, bidding her to rise. When Mudra was standing, Regina embraced her and, holding her face in both hands, kissed her on the lips and stood back, smiling.

Mudra, eyes sparkling, smiled back.

"Greetings, beloved," they both said, simultaneously.

Quinn, plate in one hand, had gotten up and walked over and

put his hand on Regina's shoulder, wondering at the history between the two. He leaned down and whispered in her ear, "More food. I'm following Slim." Stepping around Regina and Mudra he bowed at Mudra, and thanked her for granting him entry to her house.

Regina dropped her hands from Mudra's face, and took one hand in hers. 'Show me."

14

COMFORT

The next morning Quinn, wearing a sarong, emerged from the two-bedroom cabin to which he and Angelica had been assigned to find her sitting on the porch in the morning sun, a sarong open down the front, shawl back over her shoulders, one foot up on the railing, exposing her breasts, belly, and sex to the intense arid light.

"Mind some company?" he asked.

"Nope," she said. "Pull up a chair." When Quinn set a chair down near her she reached over and pulled it closer. "Sit," she said.

Quinn sat, put a leg up, and untied the knot on his sarong, exposing himself to the light also. He looked over at Angelica and noticed she was sweating, sweat beaded up between her breasts, pooling in her navel, running down between her legs. He noticed the sweat beaded up in the small curls along her hairline at her neck and across her forehead. The sweat on her upper lip. He gave a short sigh for beauty.

She reached over and took his phallus in her hand. She didn't move her hand, just held it, still and softly. Slowly Quinn tumesced in her gentle grasp. He sat still, not moving at all. The phallus grew to its full extent, no one moved. They simply sat with it the morning sun, Angelica's hand dropping to the base, holding him upright, grasping him lightly. Suddenly they both sighed at the same time.

"It comforts me," Angelica said.

"I know," Quinn replied. "I can feel what you're feeling and I feel the same way myself. Comforted."

"And you're OK with this?" Angelica asked, not quite believing what she heard. "You don't expect anything else from me?"

"No, Angelica. I am cradled in the hand of Beauty. I am comforted by Beauty. I am already beyond anything I could expect."

Angelica sighed again and felt her Self at an emotional choice point. If she followed her feelings one way she would cry; she could feel the tears welling up as she imagined it. If she went another way she could continue into a depth of contentment and comfort, and do nothing, except possibly smile. She chose comfort and contentment, sighing again. Then she smiled. She waggled his erection, pointing it to the sky. She let go and stood up. She said, "Thank you, Quinn." She rose and turned into the cabin to take a shower and get dressed.

Quinn contemplated his erection, lying now upon his belly. He thought about the wondrous nature of hydraulics. He stood up, reknotting his sarong, his erection out front like the bowsprit on a sailing ship.

He was standing there looking at it when Slim walked by on his way to breakfast. Noting Quinn's condition, he grinned. "Morning wood is magnificent, ain't it? Lay down and you got a tent pole."

Quinn grinned back, "If an erection falls in the forest does anyone miss it?"

"You would," Slim laughed back at him.

"Yes. Yes, I would."

"Come eat."

"Gotta go strap this down first."

"No, you don't. Just keep it out of the food. On the other hand, you might become food."

Quinn laughed and continued on into the house to change into day clothes. On his way back to his room he met Angelica in the hallway. She was standing there naked, hair down.

"Is this OK? Is it OK if I'm naked around you? Can I be that comfortable around you? Can I trust you that much?"

Quinn simply said, "Yes."

She looked down at his bowsprit holding up the fabric of the sarong. "I'm sorry about that. Are you OK?"

Quinn, continuing to opt for simplicity, said, "Yes."

"You won't hate me if I don't do anything about it?"

"No, I won't hate you. But you not doing anything doesn't affect my desire. I can get my needs met here, I'm sure. I'd only have to ask Regina to arrange it. But my desire? My desire is pretty obviously for you. And that's OK, too. I learned to hold my desire a long time ago."

She pulled the sarong away and leaned forward and kissed his phallus on the tip. "Thank you, thank you, thank you. For being a man

I can trust."

"Remember, Angelica, I've been through what you've been through. I didn't have a dragon in me. I had something else. It took a long time to drive it out."

"You did? What? What was inside you?"

"De Murgos," Quinn answered grimly.

They fell silent, standing there, Quinn erect, Angelica naked, looking into each other's eyes. Angelica smiled suddenly and turned into her room, closing the door behind her. Quinn looked away and down, smiling also, and turned into his room to get dressed.

On the way to the dining hall Quinn and Angelica encountered Benny coming from the main house. He was disheveled, wearing the same clothes as the day before, trying to pop his neck out of a crick that came from sleeping on the couch. Regina and Mudra were dressed in ranch working clothes, hats in hand, and waiting on the porch, leaning on each other along the upper arms. Mudra was telling her something, and Regina was listening intently.

When Quinn and Angelica emerged from the dining hall after breakfast they encountered Slim standing next to six horses tied to the rail out front. He looked at Angelica. "Can you ride?"

"My parents got me lessons for two years when I was twelve. English style, hunting and jumping. Dressage."

"This is Western. You know the difference?"

"Yes. One-handed with the reins. Which means the bit is pulled tighter on the opposite side from the side I want the horse to turn."

"Yup, that's it. Both of you, go get some boots, and your hats, and meet me back here."

Regina and Mudra stepped out on the porch fully dressed to ride, the expedition having been their idea. Together the three of them watched the other two walking to the cabin. Angelica bumped into Quinn from the side, like a small dog trotting alongside a big dog will sometimes do. Regina said to Slim, "What do you think? How much trouble am I in?"

"A lot," Slim said, spitting into the dust.

"Lovely," Mudra said.

"Curse avoidance, 101. What're they fucking teaching you young folks these days, Mudra?" Slim retorted.

"Sorry," Mudra said simply

The five of them rode away most of the morning and took a break. Squatting in the shade of a twisted juniper Quinn turned to Slim and asked him, "So, you're the Craft here?"

"Naw," Slim said. "It's just the young'un's got a lot to learn. And Regina and I go way back, but I reckon you figured that out. So I'm a known quantity to her. So's Mudra, in a way. Regina trained her up into a lotta things. Helped her find her siddhi power and then showed her how to work it. So now Mudra's training others. Just like the Madeleines. Just like Eva."

At the mention of Eva's name Quinn grunted, and rocked a little. Slim watched him out of the corner of his eye.

"You two are the unknowns here. You're not one of us, and she's not yet. Maybe won't make it. That's why Regina is in charge and we're her help in the desert. You understand what I'm trying to say to you?"

"Yeah. Step carefully and pay attention to my own assignment."

"Yup. That's it."

"So how much do you know about my assignment?"

"Well, not enough to trust you."

"Understood."

Regina and Mudra had been squatting in the shade of another tree, watching Angelica get to know the horses, particularly the one she was riding. The horses had been nervous around her all morning. Both Slim and Regina had been projecting calming energy, and their opinion was that the horses were sensing the dragon. But these were highly trained horses, as were all horses that came from Rachel Adam's training techniques. Still, the horses shivered when Angelica put her hands on them. To her credit, she would continue stroking their necks and faces until the shivering stopped.

They rode through the afternoon, stopping when the sun was still three hands high on a small, south-facing flat in the middle of a spur running down from a plateau. They dismounted and built a fire from wood stacked against a low stone wall on the northwest side of the flat. Slim and Mudra took point putting together a supper, although they assigned small tasks to Angelica, after letting her loosen the saddle girths. There was no real conversation until they'd finished eating a meal of bacon, grits, and coffee.

As the sun set Slim, Regina, and Mudra went to stand in the west, quietly singing a plaintive, vocable song.

When they were finished eating, chipped enameled metal plates at their feet, coffee cups in hand, they all stared silently into the fire. Angelica broke the silence. "We spending the night?"

"Nah," Slim said. "Moon's still almost full. It'll be up in a while. Plenty of light when it's up, and the horses, they know the way."

"We're here to talk," Mudra said.

Regina said, "I need to know that the two of you understand what we're all doing here. I know you heard the words from Calley, and you both decided to go along with what She wanted. But I need to make sure that you understand the implications. What about you, Quinn. What do you understand?"

"I understood that I was asked to leave because my continuing presence at Stonehaven was endangering everyone else. Whatever those beings were that showed up knew I was there. And then there's those people looking for me. They could have found me there, and all of it put other people in danger, so I had to go. Been running most of my life, when I wasn't waiting. Maybe all I ever did was wait to run."

"True enough, but that's only part of it, Quinn. The next part of it is that nobody knows who you are, and where your loyalties lie. I've read the book that Matthews wrote about you. So I know something about you. And I understand the mythological context in which your story is embedded," Regina explained.

Quinn nodded.

Slim said, "I don't like that context. Fought against it my whole life. Which means I don't trust you or your story."

Quinn responded, "The deal was for freedom. Freedom from that story, and that mythology."

"Yeah, but," Slim continued, "How come you're the only one that ain't free?"

"That was the cost of the deal. I'm free now. I stopped waiting."

"Are you? Are you, Quinn?" Mudra asked. "What's still following in your wake? And now that you're done with the deal does that mean the deal's off?"

"Maybe. The part of the deal I was privy to is done. Those souls are free. I'm betting that me not waiting any longer isn't going to change that."

"Even if it puts our lives at stake?

"Look, just because I changed one thing doesn't mean everything changed. Even if it changed everything. Somebody can still try to do something else. Your lives were always at stake. And you know it."

"Fair enough," Regina judged, recapturing the conversation. "Whoever you were before the Gatehouse isn't what you are now. Now you're something else."

Quinn interrupted, "I'm still what I was. But now I'm more than that."

"Yes," Regina continued. "More dangerous. More powerful. And more of a threat. And that's why you had to go."

"I understand."

"So. You were assigned to go with us," Regina said, indicating Angelica. "You agreed. It was a test. You passed. Now here's the rest of it, here's the rest of your assignment. You're here as her bodyguard."

"I'm the muscle."

"Yeah, you're the muscle."

"Well, you have to tell me what all that entails, then. And doesn't entail."

"Protect her. Help her. And protect the dragon."

"From what I hear the dragon don't need much protecting," Slim commented.

"Oh, but it does. Protection from itself, and protection from things out there that would kill it if they could. The Enemy didn't know about the dragon before. Now it does. We have to be ready for the Enemy to send someone to kill it."

"So you expect me to protect the dragon from someone strong enough to kill it, when it's strong enough to kill me."

"We don't know that, Quinn. The fact is it didn't kill you. And we don't know why. You should've burnt up with that madman but you didn't. Maybe it spared you, maybe it couldn't hurt you anyway. We haven't had a chance to ask it."

"Ask me," Angelica said. "Why don't you ask me?"

"You know why. It has a will of its own. You don't seem to be in control of it."

"Show us a sign, then. Show us you can talk to it. And that it talks to you," Mudra encouraged.

Angelica went silent. Then she said to Regina, "He wants to talk to you."

Angelica's mien changed. So did her breathing. The air around her head turned red, and in that red cloud the image of the dragon's head appeared.

"Ho gved rahkhine," Angelica's uttered, her voice a hoarse rasp.

"Ho gved hamashk," Regina replied.

"Nah gtedt vahleed," the hoarse voice spoke.

Angelica shook her head. "Take me to Wallid is what he means."

"Yes, I know," Regina said. "Gtedt vahleed nu wah. Doh tan nu wah."

"He understands," Angelica said. "He'll bide his time." And the dragon light faded.

"Shit," Slim said, after he realized he'd been holding his breath.

"So, you've got that going on," Mudra said, relaxing the posture of protection she'd been holding.

Regina said, "That's good, Angelica. Thanks for showing us. Have I told you what the Madeleines have said? No? They say that the Goddess chose you to be a carrier. You are to carry the dragon to its destination and it will leave you. We're not sure why she chose you, nor why the dragon simply couldn't manifest there. We think it's because it needed time to mature in a body, and it's using yours. She wanted someone who was both innocent and real. The necessary reality is part of the reason for your blow-out. Humans are normally less than real."

Regina paused then continued, "I'm real enough—that's why I can talk to it. But I'm not innocent. I'm long past maturing into anything, and the dragon needs a subjective experience of maturation. It's like the brain of a teenager. The prefrontal lobes have not yet begun to grow, and the ability to judge appropriately is still lacking."

"So what am I doing here?" Angelica wanted to know.

"You're here for your initiation. Mudra explained that. We can't take you further without it."

"They brought us up here to kill us if they had to," Quinn said.

"There you go," Slim said, drawing a revolver, unbelievably, from under his sarong. "Now you got it."

Quinn moved over and squatted in front of Angelica. "Yeah, now I do. I got it."

Regina put her hand over Slim's gun, and lowered it toward the ground. "Yes, you're right."

"You assume you could. You assume you could kill us," Quinn said.

"If we couldn't, then maybe we'd at least know more about you than we do now," Mudra said, holding her hands in the protective position again.

"Even we don't know," Angelica whispered.

"Put that away," Slim heard Quinn's voice say in his head, followed shortly by Regina's voice saying the same thing.

"Well, that fucked up any trust there might have been," Quinn said aloud.

Slim looked at him and noticed a slight golden glow in the middle of his forehead.

Angelica leaned forward, touched Quinn on the back, and whispered, "I trust you."

"No place for trust, anyway," Regina said. Mudra nodded, lowering her hands, and shifting them into a subtle position against threat.

"You know what you know," Slim said, slipping the gun away

somewhere under his sarong.

"I'm surprised you know so little," Quinn sniffed. "What was the plan? Get us out here, make some determination about us? Bury the bodies in the desert?"

"Something like that," Mudra said.

"We're not like you, Quinn. We know some things about Bodhisattvas. So we knew some things about what you were, maybe still are. But we don't know what you've become. That auric cylinder you raised at the Gatehouse, the black one with the lightning bolts, we can't see past that—not that we could ever read your mind much anyway. This makes you an unknown. Can't trust what you don't know. You could be a loose cannon, you could be working for the enemy in some dark plot twist we can't see that puts us all at risk. At best, you're a free operator, maybe an ally. At worst, you're a chaos attractor," Regina said, by way of explanation.

"Well, that's good to hear. Assuming I believe you," Quinn responded.

"And as for her," Mudra continued, "We know she's still human. That's another reason she's still here. We believe we can save the human, but the dragon is another chaos attractor."

"I woke up when he cut me, then I passed out again. I woke up again when Eva cradled my head in her lap. I felt the blow that killed her. I opened my eyes through the red film of her blood. Fuck you fuck you fuck you," Angelica said. She leaned forward again and tapped Quinn on the back. "Come on. We're leaving."

"Heng dwa hamashk," Regina said, sharply.

"The Voice," Quinn said, referring to the siddhi power of the voice of Command.

Angelica passed out immediately, crashing forward on Quinn's back. The dragon appeared, laughing.

Mudra stood up, adopting a combat stance. The dragon made a pushing motion with one hand, Mudra fell backward over the log she'd been sitting on. The dragon laughed harder and made a kind of "Et tu?" gesture with its other hand toward Slim. Slim placed his hands in plain sight.

"Rakhine," it said. "Ho dan keh ween?"

Still using the voice, Regina said, "Gedets wan heyo ween?"

Laughing again, the dragon, "Ha gah dahn ho di." Then it disappeared, collapsing back into Angelica.

"Well, that was helpful," Regina said in a voice so smooth no one could tell if she was sarcastic or serious.

Angelica came to and pushed herself off of Quinn's back. "Fuck me fuck me fuck me," she said, groaning. Everyone could tell she was being sarcastic.

"Are we done?" Quinn asked, seriously.

"We are," Regina said.

Quinn looked over his shoulder at Angelica, "Can you walk?"

"I think so, but help me any way."

Quinn put an arm around her waist and helped her over to the horses. She hung on to the saddle horn while he tightened the girth, then he helped her mount.

"Where you going?" Slim asked.

"Home," Quinn replied. "You said the horses know the way, and the moon is high now. You all stay here a while. I don't want you behind me. We'll see you in the morning."

Angelica said, "You don't ever get behind me, Slim. Not on this ride home, not ever."

After they'd ridden about twenty minutes, letting the horses pick their way down, Quinn turned into a little draw, beckoning Angelica to follow. When they were side by side Quinn leaned over and whispered to Angelica, "We'll wait here a minute, see if we're being followed."

Angelica whispered back, "Holy shit! A gun! A fucking gun! Are they crazy?"

Quinn whispered back, "It was a test. We passed."

"Are you fucking kidding me?"

"No. They wanted to see how we'd react. They really are trying to decide if they can trust us. So I suggest you be trustworthy."

"Trustworthy? What does that mean?"

"Lower your voice. It means, can you be trusted to not do something chaotic, it means can you keep a secret. It means, 'Will you hurt anybody?' What it comes down to is, 'Can you trust them?'"

"Trust them how?"

"Do you think they have our best interests at heart? No. They have their interests at heart. And we know what they are. And that's how far we trust them—as far as we know what their interests are. Can you do that?"

"Yes. But what about our interests?"

"I'm not sure what all they are, besides survival. And seeing that you are safe, and, for as long as necessary, that dragon, too."

"Will you help me? I have two sets of interests to manage—mine and what I'm carrying. And sometimes I can't tell which is which."

Quinn nodded, knowing she could see it in the moonlight. He extended his senses then, listening, and feeling out into the path of his listening. He relaxed and took a breath. He extended his field out, letting his vision follow. He smiled and said to Angelica, "Nobody's coming. We can go."

Up on the flat Regina, Slim, and Mudra had sat quietly, watching Angelica and Quinn mount up and go.

"Want me to follow them?" Slim asked.

Regina said, "No."

"Want me to follow them?" Mudra asked, after a pause.

"Nope."

They sat looking into the fire. "Shame to waste a good fire, know what I mean?" Regina asked extending an energetically amorous field in both directions.

"Yes, dear, I do," Mudra replied.

With one hand Regina turned Mudra's face to her, and kissed her. With the other she reached back and slid her hand up under Slim's sarong, found his phallus, and began stroking. "Sex by the fire…" she said.

"One of my favorite things," Slim agreed.

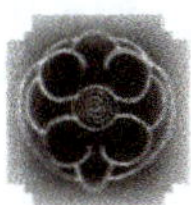

15

THE RESONANCE OF THE HIGHER HEART

The next morning Angelica and Quinn were sunning themselves, naked again, on the porch of their cabin. Their three erstwhile compadres rode in, stopped at the porch, and dismounted.

"You OK?" Regina asked.

Angelica released Quinn's erection, sighing at the disconnection of comfort. "Yeah. But what the fuck was that?"

"It was a test. You passed."

"Yeah, that's what Quinn said."

"Just so we trust each other," Quinn added. Then he said, "A gun? Really?"

"Yeah," Slim said. "I carry it for varmints. Rattlers and such, when they can't be avoided. Here. You're going to need one." Slim unbuckled an old fashioned holster from under his sarong and handed it and the gun as one to Quinn.

Quinn, mildly surprised, took it, pulled the revolver far enough out of the holster to check the load. There were five shells, the one under the hammer was empty. There were more rounds in the belt. He stood up.

Quinn squinted at him, as if he were about to say something threatening or at least mildly unpleasant. Slim short circuited whatever it would have been by shrugging his shoulders and turning away, taking the reins of all three horses and leading them to the barns. He looked back over his shoulder and said, "Rat shot loads."

Mudra backed away a few steps, grinned, and turned and jogged to her house. Regina was left standing on her own. Quinn's erection was still front and center, bobbing in the sun. He'd forgotten it temporarily until Regina reached out and gave it a tug.

"This is meant to be conciliatory. All forgiven?" she asked.

Quinn stood still. She tugged on him again, smiling. Quinn smiled back and nodded.

"How about you?" she asked, turning to Angelica.

"Not yet. We need to talk. He tells me I can trust you that far, far enough to talk. I don't understand you."

"That's fine, Angelica. Good enough. I'll see you both at breakfast? I'd like to meet with you both afterwards."

When Regina moved on, Quinn sat back down next to Angelica. When she was out of hearing range, Angelica looked at Quinn. "She's a bitch, isn't she?"

"I think she's well beyond that. People like her, rare though they are, operate from someplace beyond what the normal do, and why they do it. Sometimes it's like we're underwater, looking up at them through the surface, and it distorts what we see."

"Well, all I can tell you is that I'm pretty clear-eyed at the moment. I see what she's showing me."

"Yes, but how much beyond the normal spectrum of light are you seeing her in? She saved you once, remember, back in the red canopy."

"Actually, no. I don't remember." She paused, still not moving to go into the cabin and get dressed. "Sit down. I had a dream last night I want to tell you about. I dreamed about the dragon. He was playing with a large, pearl-colored sphere. At first he was rolling it around, and then he was tossing it up in the air and catching it with his tail. In the last scene he caught it with his tail and held it up, stilling his posture in a vignette. He looked me deliberately in the eye to make sure I remembered the picture. It looked like art I've seen before. But I don't understand it. Is the giant pearl a symbol of some kind?"

Quinn nodded. "Yes, yes it is. It is the symbol of wisdom and immortality; the symbol of the incorruptible body." He sighed and said, "I don't approve of their methods, sometimes. I would have served as your protector anyway, but now I feel bound to you, and to that mission, more closely than I would have, otherwise."

Angelica took up his phallus again, the back of her hand along his belly, her fingers wrapping around him, and sighed also. "Yes, and I feel bound to allow you to do it. I don't think I would have allowed it at all."

They sat then, companionly, in the morning sun.

Angelica became aware of a new sensation in her hand. "I feel a heartbeat in my hand. A beat that's not your heart."

"Yes, I know. I feel the same pulse. It's active in me somewhere all the time. And it's active in you, too. Are you aware of it?"

"Yes. Since I had that Kundalini blow-out thing."

Quinn laughed. "Blow-out's not the name I'd use."

She squeezed his phallus and smiled. "I could usually find it in me. It would come up especially when I got together with my first assignment. But I haven't had an assignment since the Gate House. And honestly, I'd pretty much forgotten about it. It would come up now and then but I wouldn't pay much attention to it, and then I'd lose it.

"But now," she said, squeezing his phallus and smiling again, "Now I remember it."

And then she gasped, because what she was sensing was completely new. Through and around her hand, resonating with the pulse of the phallus, a wave of energy rolled up through her hand toward the tip, and she could feel in it the frisson of a higher frequency. "Did you do that?" she asked, turning to face him. "Do that again."

So he did. He contracted the perineal pump and released it, directing the flow along his length.

"Can you maintain that? And how are you doing that?"

"Yes. And I am using the muscles I would use to ejaculate, only I'm not close to coming, at all. I want to maintain it, that's all."

"Not seeking release," she made it a statement.

"No, not interested in release. The wave of orgasm is release enough. I don't need to release any substances to do that."

"Wow," Angelica said. "Wow, that must feel fantastic."

"It does," Quinn confirmed.

"I mean, it would feel fantastic to me, it you were doing that and it was in me."

"Yes, it does," Quinn confirmed again, and went very still, just focusing on the Higher Heart under her hand, and letting the rolling waves subside.

After a moment, she said, "Why'd you stop?"

He looked at her sideways. "I didn't want to risk compelling you into something before you're ready. A part of my responsibility, as masculine, is to foster your ability to choose. Even if you weren't already aware of the Higher Heart, you would probably find that much energy compelling. And my obligation, to you and to all wen, is to foster freedom of choice, especially when it comes to sexuality."

She said, "You're right. I would have let my curiosity get the better of me, and I wouldn't have been ready. I'd have realized that only after." She squeezed him one last time, and smiled. "Thank you," she said. "Let's get dressed and go get something to eat." She leaned forward and kissed him on top of the head. "Wow, I feel that pulse all the way up here." She turned and went into the house, not letting the screen door slam shut behind her.

Quinn sat on the porch a while longer, looking at his erection in the sunlight. He stood up and thumped it once on the porch railing. It made the entire railing ring. "Thunder Cock the Rock Splitter, indeed," he said, and went inside to get dressed, as well.

16

AFTER BREAKFAST

Quinn and Angelica showed up to breakfast in the lodge house dining hall, moving through the line laughing together about the Priest's priapism and her green dick. Angelica was more kindly disposed to Regina when she came over and sat down with them, bringing with her a wen in her late forties, older than Mudra, and introduced her as Elizabeth (Call me 'Lizzie') and as the Madeleine of the Diamond Rose.

Regina said, "Angelica, the Madeleines have been working on trying to figure out 'Why you?' You know what I mean?"

"You mean, like, why the Kundalini blow-out? Why the dragon?"

"Yes. The Madeleines have been making inquiries, out into the Archetypes, up into to the Soul of the planet. Well, down into it from the perspective of Spirit. They have spent weeks in communion with She Who Comes, trying to suss out Her intentions. They have also been looking into the impact of the dragon's manifestation on the conflict with De Murgos."

"Yes," Lizzie took up the thread. "There has not been a dragon manifestation like yours in a long time. We can't see everything, not even in the past, with clarity all the time. We have to wait sometimes, and hold an image, until it clarifies. We want to understand because we need to know our role and we need to know how to protect you. This is one of the reasons why the High Council wants you to go through the Initiation ceremony. When you become one of us, we can protect you better, and, we hope, keep you safe as we follow through on Her instructions, you know. We go before Her and around Her, She Who

Comes. Since She has chosen you for this task, we need to go before and around you, too. Your connection with Her is still tenuous. We know that, even now, you don't remember a lot of what She told you in the days following the incident at the Gate House. True, yes?"

Angelica nodded.

"We know now why the dragon was given to you. We thought at first that it arose completely from within you, but now we know that She gave it to you. She gave it to you to carry. Do you have any idea why?"

"Not really. Tell me."

"She was answering a prayer you made."

"What?"

Regina said, "You made a prayer, Angelica. You made a prayer to pay the debt of your existence."

Angelica, her voice low, said, "You're fucking kidding me."

Pausing a moment to let the idea sink in, Lizzie asked, "Do you remember making a prayer like that? Maybe before you went to Stonehaven?"

Angelica whispered, "Fuck. Fuck me. I did this. I did this to myself."

Quinn put a hand on the small of her back, energetically easing the barriers to inner circulation he could feel there. The light in the room took on the reddish hue it usually did before the dragon manifested.

"No, hon, you didn't," Lizzie responded. "You didn't do this to yourself. She gave it to you so that you could carry it somewhere for her. This is how you'll pay that debt. Carry it where She commands, and the debt will be paid."

"What, am I the only one? The only one who felt that I owed the world something for the gift of life that was just given to me? Nobody else feels that way?"

"Yes, many do. But not most. Only a few ever actually come to feel it on their own. Usually it's because people are taught to understand this; we teach it. But in your case you got there on your own. It's a pretty rare feeling," Lizzie finished. She reached across the table and took one of Angelica's hands. "You are sad and angry and afraid, yes?"

Angelica nodded, close to tears.

"We all would be," Regina said softly. "And we're sad and angry and afraid for you, too."

Angelica looked at Regina and saw the compassion in her face, looking older now in just these few weeks. Her eyes brimmed over. Then, through the tears, she saw the narrow golden nimbus around Regina begin to glow and spread. Regina took Angelica's other hand, and the red glow began to dim. Angelica smiled. "For fuck's sake, Regina. Couldn't I have just gone to work for a charity? Taught kids to read in some third-world country?"

When Regina smiled, Angelica couldn't help starting to smile herself. Regina and Lizzie laughed, too. Quinn smiled, but kept his awareness spread out into the room, watching the people behind his back, looking for entities above their heads.

"When Diosa needed to bring the dragon into the world you were the best candidate at the time. You were on the verge of becoming a real person because of the impending blow-out. That was simply the result of the work you were already doing on yourself, made more quick to come by your being a good person," Lizzie said. "This is what we have seen."

"And you were with us," Regina stated. "You were safe." Then she turned to Quinn. "You, too, have been quite the mystery to us. Where did you come from? And how is it that a being of your objective status was wandering around in our woods? And how did you come to acquire the status and skills that you have? We were stunned that we had neither heard of you, nor felt you in our excursions in the mind of the world." She paused and looked at him with her eyes narrowed. "You do know what we're talking about, yes?" she asked him slowly and deliberately.

Quinn, who had gone very still, nodded slowly. He cleared his throat. "Yes, I do. But what do you know about it?"

"We journeyed to Her, She Who Comes, so we could ask Her. Lizzie and her cohort here and elsewhere have journeyed to different moments in your past to verify a lot of what we've been told. You have quite the history."

"You could have read the book."

"We did, but there was a lot you left out, including all the intervening years. We found out why he never came back. We found out why he abandoned you."

Quinn went as still as he could. The energy of fear rose up in him, the top of its flame licking lightly at his heart. He became afraid his heart would break.

Regina could see this and her own heart responded. "Here, you take my hands, now."

He did, and the resonance of her Higher Heart tore open the small chakras in his hands. The energy stayed there, green flames dancing in the air above them. "This is for you, if you need it." She paused, waiting for Quinn to give a signal that he understood.

Quinn opened the chakras in his arms and the flame sank into each of his hands a little. "Thank you. If I need this, I will use it."

"You refused to work on yourself. Do you know what I mean?"

"Yes. Because of the waiting I refused to deliberately work the Resonance. I let it randomize itself."

"Yes, that's it. And those two higher centers, the ones that became active last night?"

Quinn nodded, surprised that anyone had seen the glows on his forehead and around the top of his head.

"Without deliberate activation those centers go dormant."

Quinn thought about it, recalling his experiences. "That's true. I noticed it, and I always thought that activating them was violating the injuncture to wait."

"And that's what saved you. He marked you, yes? You know what I mean?"

"Yes. The hand thing. And the trick I used to interfere with his intention."

"Yes. Stop thinking about the trick. I'm starting to see what happened in my head. I don't want to know. But what we do know is that the imprint of the hand is like a piece of metal. It would only illuminate, or at least show up as a silhouette, if it was back lit. Back lit by the activation of those higher centers. You didn't light the candle, so he couldn't see the sign."

Quinn's mind eased along with his fear. His heart slowed, and the Resonance moved from his heart to his head.

"You must keep that under control," Regina said. "Now that you're activating it you run the risk of him finding you again."

"It must have taken awhile for the random illumination to end on its own. Why didn't he come before then?"

Regina laughed. "Being in you for all that time made him sick. You sickened him. Good job. He didn't see that coming either. Besides… why would you want him back?"

"I don't. And haven't for many years. In the beginning I was afraid the deal was at risk if I didn't go along and wait. And I also had a longing, I admit. I had a longing for someone to explain to me what was happening. And I had a longing to be approved of, kind of like a kid wanting their father's approval. When I gave up on him coming back, I was almost heartbrokenly sad, but I was still afraid, and continued to wait. And that meant waiting until something happened, although I didn't know what. And that meant waiting to work on myself, because everything else in daily life still had to be handled."

No one had anything to say in response, so Quinn continued.

"What about the people who are after me?"

Everyone was taken aback.

"What? You have people after you?" Lizzie wanted to know. Lizzie rolled her eyes back in her head, seeking to contact Stonehaven's Madeleine.

Regina put her hand on Quinn's arm, reading his past to see the truth. "Yes, you do, don't you?" She closed her eyes and sent a voice of inquiry to Calley.

Calley, 1800 miles away, felt it immediately. "Yes, I knew. They have stopped searching. The enemy has grown too old, and the evil that drove them is being dealt with elsewhere." Then Calley showed her how She had used the Hidden Land to divert Quinn's pursuers from the Gate House.

"I am told to tell you, by Calley, that they have given up," Regina said, fingering the locket Calley had given her. "They have grown old and tired, and the evil that drove them is being dealt with elsewhere. You are not a risk to us, travelling with us."

"Well, I hope so," Quinn said. "They were powerful people, once. It would be good to be free from my fear of them. If you don't mind, I will keep an eye out."

"You should," Regina said. "We don't know what else may be coming at us, but we need you to help look out for it."

Lizzie returned her awareness to the room. "I heard only a part of that. Madeleine at Stonehaven was bringing me up to speed on the happenings there. One of the things she emphasized to me, Angelica, was how important it was that we move ahead with your Initiation as a Priestess. You are only going to be carrying the dragon for a while. When it is gone, it will leave a vacuum behind, and in that vacuum is the young wen who has just survived a full Kundalini blow-out."

"I feel the fear I will be in," Angelica replied. "My life has not been my own since before the blow-out. From what I understand from what I've been told, and from what I've seen around me, the kind of people you are, and how strong you are, I think this is the kind of strength I will need in my life once the dragon is gone. I will have Regina with me, and Quinn to protect me. When my life is returned to me at the end of this task it will be my life to live again, but in service, this time, to Diosa. It may be terrifying, it may be painful, but there's no going back now to the way I was before. I'm ready."

"Good, then," Regina said. "Relax today. We will conduct the ceremony tomorrow."

17

BONDING

Quinn and Angelica decided it would be a good idea to spend time together in the sauna house the night before she was to begin the initiation into a Priestess of the Order of the Fleur de Vie.

"You know, Angelica, I went through it all at once, too."

"You mean the Release thing?"

"Yeah, the Release thing," he said, with some impatience. "It wasn't easy. I was alone. I mean, there were people around me, but I couldn't tell them what was going on. I was afraid they'd call the police and I'd end up institutionalized. I had to work, and keep working. I was working on the Mississippi River at the time…" Quinn paused, suddenly lost in memory. Then he said, "It was like I was screaming in agony on the inside all the time but unable to let any of that agony out. Except sometimes weeping into my pillow when I was off-watch."

Angelica laid a hand on his arm. "I'm sorry," she said. "Sorry for your suffering. Sorry you were alone. I was surrounded by people who loved me, even if they didn't know me. I could feel the love. Even so, I spent a long time sitting on the edge of the abyss, struggling to not let myself fall over into the darkness, into the insanity. How did you survive?"

"I remembered my nothingness."

"What?"

"I remembered my nothingness. And I followed The Way. I followed the Way and it showed me the Way Out."

"What are you talking about? Which Way?"

"The Great Way, the Way that underlies everything. The Dao, some people call it. You've heard of it?"

"Yes. It was a philosophy in ancient Waitan."

"It's way more than a philosophy. It's a way of life. It is a way of living that will lead you from one circumstance to another without your personal desires being the main motivator. It allows you to live non-attached to desire, even though you still have desire. It allows you to become free from desire."

"I don't know if I'd like that."

"Well, you would like it even less if identification with your desires led you into trouble. And Useless Suffering."

"I suppose. So I would still have desires?

"Yes. But you would come to see when and in what ways your desires could be fulfilled without causing trouble. But more importantly than that is that the Way, the Dao, can become a source of that fulfillment, bringing that fulfillment to you. And it can awaken desires in you that you didn't know you had. Particularly a desire from the farthest extent of human experience—the desire for Ecstasy. You already know about this desire, don't you?"

"Yes. I have felt the desire and tasted the fulfillment. How did you come to it?"

"How did I come to what?"

"To the desire for the joy that makes life worth living?" She wiped the sweat from her brow and reached to pick up the dipper and pour more water on the sauna rocks. When she sat back she took her other hand and placed it between his legs, enveloping his phallus and giving it a soft squeeze. She held it while it grew erect in her hand.

"I did not know about it at the time. The idea didn't even occur to me until many years later. It took a long time for me to rise out of the suffering of struggling to survive when I did not want to survive."

Angelica sighed, lazily stroking Quinn's phallus. "It's really hard, you know," she said, and then she laughed. "I mean life. But this is hard, too," she said, giving his phallus a squeeze. "But what else is hard is this relationship we have. I mean, you're my bodyguard, right?"

Quinn nodded, relaxing into the heat and the sensation.

"So, you're supposed to do whatever needs to be done to protect me, and not take advantage of me in any way, right?"

Quinn nodded again.

"So, what about this?" she asked, waggling the phallus around. "I can do this, but we're not having sex."

"It's not that simple, Angelica. I'm assigned to you."

"What, like a Consort?"

"Sort of. Some of the sexual stuff is about the Resonance of the Higher Heart. The Resonance becoming permanently active in you will protect you. Sexual contact is the surest way to accomplish that. But the power differential between us is huge. Start with me being forty-five years longer on the Path than you. The differential has to be acknowledged and taken into account. Once we've done that, then more becomes possible."

She sat up and leaned toward him. "I understand. You make me feel safe, and respected. Say, is one of the ways to practice the Resonance of the Higher Heart to do this?" She lowered her head into Quinn's lap and took the head of his phallus into her mouth. She rested there, simply holding it. The Resonance started up in her palate. She focused on it. Suddenly her mouth became filled with a sweet saliva, and in her mind's eye her awareness fell into a pool of golden light.

Quinn felt her awareness of the present moment slip away. He removed himself from her mouth and scooted out from under her far enough to lay her head on his thigh. She made a mewling sound of disappointment when he did, and then she sighed, resting into the comfort and the warmth and the sense of safety. Quinn put his hand on her shoulder, sat back, and closed his eyes.

He was suddenly filled with a wave of tenderness so poignant that he opened his eyes. He looked down at the resting Angelica and gently wiped the strands of sweat soaked hair from her cheek and tucked them behind her ear. She smiled slightly, smiling from a long way off.

He smiled back reflexively. He'd spent most of his life not talking, holding his peace. He'd learned that if he talked long enough, he almost invariably concluded by saying something he shouldn't. He'd either make some asshole remark or say something mystical that referred to his long life waiting, or on the run.

Then, in a moment of realization, he understood the tenderness. He usually felt like he had missed his life, missed his chance at having a life. And yet here, here he no longer felt that way. Here a new life beyond his prescient dreaming, was being given to him—a life filled with purpose and beauty. And it was being given to him before he was too old, almost sixty-five now, to respond to it, and enjoy it. He looked down at his relaxing phallus, happy that he was still able to get it up. He smiled, and closed his eyes. Leaning back, he suddenly thought of Sally Oshune, his last lover before discovering Stonehaven, and was rewarded with a vision of her as a young wen, sitting at a low dresser of split bamboo, looking at herself in a hand-held mirror.

In the vision she turned to look at him, and smiled, nodding. Her lips moved. "I see you." The vision was replaced by the image of the Divine Feminine he carried with him. She Who Comes appeared to him, seated on a throne of woven living vines in flower. She smiled at him, flipped her hair over her shoulders and leaned forward. She kissed him on the forehead. An ecstatic bolt of light shot through his core along his spine, and he trembled around it.

The trembling woke Angelica. As her awareness returned fully to her body, she sat up and looked around, taking in the dimly lit room, the heat, and the sweat. She shook her head, her hair swinging. She tucked the hair behind what had been her down side ear, and reached for the handle of the pan to pour more water on the rocks.

"It was starting to cool off in here. I'm not ready to give it up yet," she said, looking at Quinn, squinting through the steam. "What was that? The vibration that woke me up?"

"Ecstasy. Ecstasy passing through me."

"What happened?"

Quinn raised his hand, pointing two fingers to the sky. "She kissed me. What happened to you?"

"When I started feeling your resonance on the roof of my mouth it flooded with sweetness and then I fell into a pool of golden light. I'm not sure what any of this is, I haven't had a chance to study it yet. Do you? I mean, you haven't been trained by them."

"Yes, I know some things about this stuff. I've been a Resonator a long time. It took several years after my blow-out to calm down enough to begin to bring discernment to all of it. Lots of things would happen at once, and I couldn't tell what was connected to what, and was something causative or simply synchronous."

Angelica snorted. "Simply synchronous," and grinned.

Quinn grinned back. "Yeah, I know. And, since no help ever came, no mysterious teacher ever appeared to help me, I started reading. You know, since I was waiting anyway, find something to read, like in the dentist's office. But a lot of it, I just figured out on my own. I spent five years living out in the wilderness right after it happened. I'd see people once a month when I went to town for supplies. That was about all I could stand to be around them. I went over to the capitol once a year. I could find only so many books, but one led to another, and I survived. After that I spent a long time repressing and ignoring all this weird shit going on inside me. It was the only way I could stand to be around people. So I don't know all the names of it, like they do, but I know what I know. That sweet fluid that filled your mouth? Traditionally it's called something; something like the Nectar of the Gods. Or the Immortals, I don't remember. And I don't know what these people here call it, but they know what it is. And then the differentiated awareness you carry around with you every day let go and fell back into the pool of undifferentiated awareness. It seems there's a pool of sentient energy somewhere, and the thing that says "I" in us comes from there. It's like a particle of light. You fell into a pool of light, and being light already, you simply mixed in with it."

"But the feeling of it…" Angelica wanted to know.

"Yes, the last things you're aware of besides the light are the feeling and the sensation. Love and comfort."

"I'm lucky to have you," Angelica said, and kissed him on the cheek.

"Yeah," Quinn said grudgingly, as if he could almost admit to the possibility.

Angelica said, "Let's shower and go to bed."

"Yeah," Quinn said in the same tone of voice, but mocking himself this time.

After the shower, drying off, and getting dressed they walked across the lot and down the path to their cabin, taking their time in the moonlight. Angelica looked around then looked at Quinn.

"Your forehead is glowing."

"What?"

"Your forehead. It's glowing."

"Shit," Quinn said. "Show me. Trace it with your finger." He bent down toward her.

She traced a vertical ellipse and then two smaller horizontal ellipses on either side at the base of the first one.

"Shit. Shit. Shit," Quinn said.

"What? What's wrong?" Angelica asked, concern in her voice.

"What's wrong is that I may be becoming myself. I may be becoming what I am."

"This is a problem?" Angelica asked, almost sarcastically.

"Yes. I have survived by hiding. Even all these changes since the fight at the Gate House, I'm still in hiding. There were people after me before, now I want to keep hiding because it's a habit. And I have grown to oppose De Murgos. And I don't know these people here, and I'm not one of them. And if I'm going to be on my own I don't want to have to fight him on my own. Since these people oppose him, then I fight with them. If this comes out, if this comes out in me, he'll find me.

Which means he'll find them, and he'll find us." All these words came out in what was, for Quinn, an uncharacteristic torrent.

"He's already found them. That's why we're running."

"Oh. Right. I remember," Quinn said, shaking his head as if to clear his thinking. "Everything's changed." He paused. "Right," he said slowly and sighed.

"Can you keep it under control?" she asked.

"I don't know. I need to talk to Regina, she knows the most. I need to talk to the High Priestess and the Madeleine." He paused. "I understand something now. I understand something, Angelica, and I want you to listen close to me. I understand why we're running. And I understand why we've stopped here so you can go through the Initiation. You need to become one of them. I can't teach you what they can. And I can't protect you in the long run, either. I know that you've been hesitating to go through with it, and instead become some kind of loner, some kind of outlier, some kind of outlaw like me. Don't do it. Don't do it.

"For years and years I dreamed of someplace like this. I prayed for it. I wept for it. To be surrounded by people who were as weird as I was, but who knew about it and understood it. And it took me almost all my life to find them. Go ahead and step onto that path. Become a High Priestess among them. It will be a great life, if you survive. What I know is that if you're counting on me to live like an outlaw, you won't survive. You can count on them."

"Oh, wow. Quinn, the top of your head is starting to glow. It's like it's taking the moon's light and amplifying it just ever so slightly. It looks like a skullcap of a thousand flower petals," Angelica said, tracing the outlines with her finger tip.

"Oh no," Quinn said. "Oh, shit. Oh, fuck. I have to get inside. I have to sit. I know how to control this." He covered his head with the towel from the sauna. "Help me," he said to Angelica, reaching for her hand. They hustled down the path between the cabins. Arriving on their porch Quinn let the towel slip. The silvery white color had begun to change to a faint golden color.

Once the door closed there was a creaking sound as weight shifted on the porch across the path. Two faces leaned forward out of the shadows, illumined by the moon and stars. Slim whispered to Regina, "Did you see that?"

Regina sounded back, "Mmm hmm," nodding her head in slow affirmation.

"Do you know what that was? Or maybe, was that what I think it was?"

"What do you think it was, Slim?"

"Signs of attainment, I guess. Never would have thought it, though."

"Signs to be reckoned with, Slim. That's for sure. Signs to be reckoned with. In the morning, though. Come on, hon. Come to bed with me now. There's another kind of reckoning I have in mind at the moment."

Inside their cabin Angelica, still leading Quinn by the hand, took him down the hall into his bedroom. "Would you bring me a shawl, please, Angelica?" he asked, and lay down on his bed. Angelica returned with the shawl and he replaced the damp towel with the shawl, wrapping his head until the light couldn't be seen. "I have to get away from this, Angelica. I have to withdraw from it before it takes over my mind. I can drop away from it inside, but I need the energy to be dissipated. I need you to pull it down for me. All this time erect without release has built up a lot of energy, a lot of charge in me, and I need to be discharged. You know how to do this. I need your help. I can't do this myself."

"I will help you," she quietly and seriously. She pulled his boots and socks off, dropping them on the floor. She climbed up on the bed and undid his belt and zipper then returned to his feet and pulled his jeans off. There was nothing underneath but his phallus, already stirring in the cool night. He sighed.

Angelica stood there, looking at him, trying to see into what would best serve the moment, how best she could help him. She took off her shirt and bra and climbed up on the bed. She spread his legs and kneeled between them. Upright she undid her own belt and zipper, pushing her jeans down over her hips and halfway down her thighs. She leaned forward and gazed at him, gazed at his phallus, already growing erect. She drew in close and breathed on it. It twitched and he sighed.

Using her finger tips she danced lightly along his length, then laced her fingers between it and his belly. Using her thumbs to hold it still she leaned in closer and kissed it at the base, where the shaft disappeared into shadow.

In the cabin across the path Regina and Slim were similarly disposed. Regina had changed her clothes, a ceremonial shawl over her shoulders and a sarong tied around her waist, open at the front. Slim had kicked his boots off and opened his shirt. After the kiss, a kiss identical to the one Angelica was just bestowing on Quinn, Regina climbed up, and rubbed the head of Slim's phallus around the opening to her phulva.

She shivered as she poised herself over the head of it, raining a few drops, making everything wet and receptive. She slid onto him, one long slide, and settled on him with no more to be taken in. She raised her arms to the side, bent at the elbow, palms up. "Oh, She Who Comes," she intoned. "She Who Comes, I send a voice. Come and see me, First One, True Creator, come and see me, show me what I need to see. Tell me what I need to hear. Abide in me awhile."

Regina raised her face toward the sky, and when she looked down again Slim saw the black eyes of the Goddess looking at him and he smiled. The lips under the eyes smiled back at him, and a deeper voice than Regina's said, "Hmmph." The Regina/Goddess leaned forward, putting Her palms on Slim's chest and looked down, long hanging hair covering their face, covering Her face. Her hips rocked slightly and She shivered, coming while She showed Regina what she needed to see, and told her what she needed to hear.

Angelica had kissed her way to the top of Quinn's manhood, and taken the head of it into her mouth, putting it on the spot at the top of her palate, wanting to return to the ecstasy of light. She slipped one hand down between her legs, spreading her phulva with her fingers. She closed her eyes and gave him just the slightest tremble of a pull, putting her mouth in vacuum. She rolled her eyes back in her head. Her mouth flooded with that sweet taste again. She swallowed, and then she was gone. She was gone into the pool of light, her last sensation was comfort, and her last feeling was love.

The room began to glow red, then slowly change to golden. Quinn could see the light through the shawl wrapped around his face. He moved it aside a little and looked down. He saw the dragon, its head and body superimposed on Angelica. He held very still. He could feel the energetic feeding. He pumped his phallus once. It caused some shift in Angelica, and the dragon, gone completely golden now, slipped away from Angelica. It lifted away from her, and curled around on its self, suspended in the air behind her. It put its tail over its nose, and appeared to fall asleep.

Angelica's awareness returned to the room, sensation first. She felt love, then compassion for the man whose phallus she held in her mouth. She knew what she had to do to help him. She raised her eyes and looked at his head in time to see the form of a large white bird descend into him, its feet resting on his shoulders, its head morphing into Quinn's face, its wings folding along the sides of his head.

In the other cabin Regina's body continued rocking slowly. The Goddess took Her time with Regina, lingering over the feel of Slim's body beneath Her. She showed Regina parts of Quinn's history, and how that tied in with De Murgos. She showed her the danger that revealing Quinn's status and powers would put them all in. She showed her how those signs could be stilled, and showed her a spell, a movement of power, that she could use to conceal him in an emergency. She told her that Quinn would recognize her motives, and acquiesce. She told her that if there was time she could invoke Her, and that She would Come, and that She would Help.

"Invoke Me, and I shall come," She whispered, and Regina whispered it aloud also. Together they started to orgasm, shaking rapidly, grinding her sex onto Slim. Slim held on, gripping the sheets to keep still. The Regina/Goddess raised her eyes to Slim, and smiled at him through the hair. She leaned forward until he could hear her breath, and it ignited the Higher Heart in his heart. The pounding of it echoed in her breath.

Regina sat bolt upright, head back, arms out in a V to either side of her head. Her heart orgasmed, and she laughed out loud in the ecstasy of it, squirting around Slim's phallus and out onto his belly. The Goddess left her in that moment, leaving her laughing, and in love with the Divine.

Regina leaned forward and stretched out along Slim's body, sluggishly still moving her hips. Slim put his hand on the back of her head, cradling it. "Sweetheart, did you get what you needed from Her?" he asked quietly.

Regina nodded. "Mmm hmm," she sighed. "He's quite something. As it is, he's almost as much of a liability as an asset. Now that we know, we can do something about it. In fact, something is already being done." In the dark, she smiled. Slim could feel her cheek move against his chest. "Are you OK?" she asked.

They both knew she was referring to Slim, and the need for release. "I'm OK, darlin'," he said. "I've become quite conservative in my old age."

Regina laughed and rose up off him. His wet erection made a plopping sound. "Go back to your bed, honey. I'll take the wet spot tonight."

Back to herself completely now, and free of the sleeping dragon, Angelica felt herself as a presence, sole and singular. She knew that what she was doing was an act of service to the Divine Feminine; she knew that she was behaving as a Priestess.

Keeping her head still she moved both her hands simultaneously, one on herself and one wrapped around him. She worked both hands in the same rhythm, starting slowly then increasing in speed. She groaned as the sensation built between her legs. The man around whom she groaned, groaned in return. She didn't know if he could also sense what she was sensing but she could sense the sensations he was having. Suddenly she knew what to do to finish. She wrapped her tongue around the underside of his head, increased her vacuum and moved her head just the slightest amount in time with the rhythm of her two hands. In a moment she had him, felt the long pulse of his release rise up along him. And as the heat of him filled her mouth she brought herself with her other hand, squirting into the jeans still around her thighs, soaking them, and the bed beneath her.

He filled her mouth, she swallowed only the small amount she couldn't hold. Laying the length of him along his belly she sat up and back on her heels, palms on her thighs, and looked into the golden light still filling her mind. She stilled herself there, and as her mouth filled with that sweet nectar again, she mixed it with what she'd taken from him. Slowly, a bit at a time, she swallowed the mixture, tracing it as a golden light that descended, down through her chakras, splitting into three lines of light. Her sacrum, her perineum, and her clitoris pounded in synchrony with the Higher Heart.

In her mind she heard the voice of the Goddess. "The heart is the roof of the Soul and the foundation of the Spirit." The resonance rose into her heart, and pounded there, lower and higher heart as one. The ecstasy took her and, shaking all over, she arched her back, raised her arms, and let her head fall back, radiating love for life out into the world.

She opened her eyes and smiled when she heard Quinn snore. The glow was gone.

18

THE HIGH CONSORT

When Jasmine and Napat arrived back at her little house from observing the Temple to the Goddess there was a strange scooter parked outside the gate. Cautious but curious, Jasmine unlocked the gate quietly and entered, signaling Napat to remain outside. Of course, Napat didn't wait and followed Jasmine in, setting down the two bags of groceries she'd been carrying.

As they crept forward they found a satchel and a small suitcase on the edge of the deck just past the door. Keeping close to the wall of the house, holding Napat back, she leaned around the corner and saw a man, naked, on his back, floating in her small pool. She watched him a while, his limp phallus floating a little, and drifting side to side. He was a Caucasian man with thick dark hair, and shaved after the pattern of the Consort. She thought a little, wondering who it could be, then she remembered that she'd received an email informing her that a High Consort had been assigned to her, in addition to Wade, to be of help and service to her as she prepared herself for the conflict ahead.

As Jasmine and Napat watched, the man stirred, sighed, and stood up facing the wen. Napat was peeking around Jasmine's shoulder and gasped quietly, quickly putting her hand to her mouth. To Jasmine, he looked like a statue of some Greek God—heavily muscled, loosely curled black hair cut not too short. He took his hand and brushed it back, shedding excess water. Using the edge of his hands he wiped down his chest, shedding more water. When his hand brushed his phallus it stirred and he made a soft grunting sound. He brushed it again with his other hand, and then, grasping it with a 'v' made from his index and second fingers he shook it briskly then slowly. It began to tumesce. The slow shaking had its effect and he grew to fat and half erect before he sighed again and stopped.

Suddenly he laughed and wrapping his hand around it he stroked it to full size. He turned sideways, giving the wen a fully erect profile view. He raised his arms to the sky and leaned back and laughed harder and sent up a voice, saying "Thank you!"

He lowered his arms and turned back in the direction of the wen, both now panting slightly. "It's called 'display behavior,'" he said quietly. "I hope you enjoyed it."

Jasmine stepped around the corner so he could see her, Napat removed her hand from between her legs and followed her. Jasmine smiled a warm smile of welcome. Napat grinned more broadly. It was the first phallus she'd seen erect and she enjoyed the display very much, although she didn't understand his language.

"I was told you were coming. And your name?" Jasmine asked walking slowly towards him smiling. Napat stopped ten feet away and just stared.

"They call me Thomas Craft. But I prefer to go by my chosen name. Giles. I pronounce it like Guiles, with a hard 'g', although mostly people pronounce it soft. So: Guiles Craft."

"A little redundant, isn't it?" she asked with mock seriousness."

"Just a little," he replied. "But I'm twice the fun."

Jasmine stopped just short of his phallus and looked down. Napat moved off to the side so she could see what happened next. Jasmine held out her hand, palm up, under his erection. She looked up at him, her face serious. "Is this for me?"

"It is for you," he said. "I am all here for you, Priestess."

She raised her palm, until he was lying in it. "Then I claim it as mine, in the name of She Who Comes."

"Napat, come here," she said in Nahasi. Napat came close. In the heat she'd unbuttoned the top buttons of her white school uniform shirt. Sweat stood out on her upper lip and a bead of sweat rolled down between her breasts.

"Do you know what this is for?" Jasmine asked.

"Yes. It is the tool of pleasure and procreation," Napat answered quietly, eyes glancing quickly at Jasmine's eyes, then returning her gaze to the phallus.

"Have you seen one before? Have you touched one?"

"No, Jasmine I have not."

"Give me your hand," Jasmine commanded. Jasmine took her hand and placed it on the top side. Napat reacted like she'd been shocked with electricity, and pulled her hand away, gasping and staring at Jasmine with surprise. "You are young, Napat. Still too young for this, but not too young to learn. I will teach you. I will teach you about how to handle this," she said, smiling. Napat smiled back.

"I need you to go now. There are fresh dragonfruit at the Soba store. Take the groceries inside and then go."

Napat nodded her head and backed away, controlling the shaking in her legs so that Jasmine wouldn't see it. She took the groceries inside through the kitchen door. When she stepped outside Jasmine and Craft had already gone into the living room through the door by the pool.

Napat closed the kitchen door and opened the gate. Then, deciding she wouldn't go but would stay and listen, she closed the gate loudly enough that she knew Jasmine would hear it, and went and sat on the step that led up over the threshold into the kitchen.

In the house Craft and Jasmine stood apart from each other, and regarded each other. Jasmine loosened her shorts and let them slip to the floor with her underwear. She unbuttoned her shirt and let it fall from her shoulders.

He inhaled loudly, feeding on her scent. She straightened up, a cool chill rolling down her spine and gathering at her root. It swirled there, gathering power and heat, and he snorted his exhale, sending a burst of heat and light up both her back and front. By this, she knew him to be a High Consort.

He spoke the ritual words. He said, "I have come to offer you your due." She placed her feet together and raised her arms above her head at a 45 degree angle, making the sacred 'Y', palms forward, and then she dropped her palms at the wrist, flat toward the floor. She offered the ritual response, saying, "Come and receive your due."

She stood there as he came toward her and dropped to his knees, sitting on his heels, bringing his face to that lower Y. He inhaled again, the scent of her, clean and flowered, and the beginning of her wetness.

He raised his hands, palms forward and slowly placed them on the tops of her thighs. In the ritual dance way she slowly spread them, turning her toes outward, then heels outward, then toes outward again, then heels, then toes a third time bringing her heels even. He leaned further in, and touched his forehead to her mound.

She tilted the top of her pelvis slightly back, bringing her opening closer toward him. If she had tilted it the other way, pulling her opening back, it would have been a sign to wait. It was the signal for him to proceed.

He placed his forehead against her mound and his hands on the tops of her feet. He pulsed the chakras there with the Resonance, connecting her to the Earth. She felt the power of the Mundane drain away, and what rose up into her was the power of the Sacred, an electricity out of the darkness that set her flesh to a buzzing, higher frequency pulse.

Slowly he raised his hands, dragging the backs of his nails all the way up to the tops of her thighs, rolling his hands and bringing his palms to her thighs, close to her smile on the inside of her thighs. There he rested, breathing her, feeding on her scent, his erection reaching for the sky.

She turned her awareness from his hands to her feet, and standing on her right leg, she lifted her left and put it over his shoulder, bringing her left arm down to the top of his head, and her right arm extending straight up.

She sighed, and pulled his head forward, and down to the swelling rod at the top of her smile and said, "You may come further." He leaned forward and extended his tongue, just the wet tip sliding between the edges of her smile, dropping down and forward as she tilted her pelvis more toward him, tongue sliding down over the hood of her and slowly, expertly, he licked the hood up and back, exposing her to his tongue and breath. He exhaled on her and she grew erect under the hot breath and shuddered.

She threw her head back, her loose hair swinging, and turned her face upward and said, "I offer You your due..." and shuddered again. She felt the Goddess enter her and shuddered yet again and gasped at the Beauty of it. And then she gasped yet again at the Beauty of his tongue and She gasped with her. And his erection pulsed and surged and strained upward. Still looking up she brought both arms to her low belly then slowly slid them upward and caressed her breasts, letting the Goddess revel in the feel of flesh. Then she slid her hands up the sides of her neck and into her hair, putting her head back, shaking it free and flowing, shivering at the touch of it swishing along her back.

Turning her head to look down, so that both of them, both she and She, looked upon the High Consort with happiness, she brought her right arm down and briefly grasped his ear as she slid her other hand around and placed it on the back of his head, the sign for the next posture in the movement.

He was surprised, and pleased, for this was not a common thing, at least so soon. Slowly he brought his palms together and slipped them between her thighs, moving just the tips of his fingers along her lips, releasing the wetness there, spreading her labia in prayer. As his hands moved toward her back they crossed her opening and he paused there, the two longest fingers of each hand making gentle pressure as if to enter. In his pause he slowly expanded and spread his fingers, holding her open for a count, allowing her time to inhale, and then closing for a count while she exhaled. He did this four times, each time she opened more and her tunnel dropped down from within, her swollen gland rolling down and forward so two of his fingertips just brushed and pressed against it and she shuddered.

She leaned forward, over his head, far forward, her hair trailing down his back, and in the dance they had both been trained to do, he slid his hands further back and pressed his palms under her buttocks, raising his right leg up to put his foot on the ground.

Receiving one last pulse of power from the earth, she and She sat in his hands and then swung her right leg up and put it over his left shoulder, so she was completely off the ground and sitting astride his face. Slowly he stood up and lifted her. Then, as she brought her hands to just above the top of his heart in back, she leaned into the balance point, lifting herself on the backs of her thighs as he lifted her bottom up over his upturned face and slowly he brought her down onto it, mouth open tongue extended, moving her back and forth on it twice before settling her opening down upon his lips.

She quaked in that moment, shaking and ohhing, her hair dancing over his back, and she came, as the tip of his tongue pressed against her distended gland, squirting directly into his mouth, filling it, and he swallowed without closing his lips. And she came again, ready, so ready, he drinking, sucking, swallowing. She came faster than he could swallow and it overflowed down his face and throat and front and ran down his back.

Slowly she started to sit up and as she did, he took one step forward with his left foot, and leaned back, bracing and balancing for the next move in the dance, his erection full and hard. She sat up, still with her legs over his shoulders, placing both hands on top of his head, then reaching up for the ceiling with one hand, then with the other.

Outside, on the step, Napat had listened in—she could hear every sigh, every groan of pleasure, every groan of effort. Her fingertips still tingled with the energy she'd picked up touching Guiles' phallus, and she'd slipped the sparkling tips down inside her simple white panties and touched herself, the sparks flowing onto her button and she shivered when it shivered awake and into swelling.

She barely knew herself but her body knew what she yet did not. She pressed and rubbed herself slowly. She felt the energy spread over the surface of her skin, tingling, suffusing both the whole of her, and the point of her. She tilted her pelvis back so she could reach herself more easily, but the suffusing sense had her arch her back instead, reaching longer to reach herself, and she came forward off the step and squatted down, feet and knees spread. Her hair hung down concealing her face, contorting now, slowly growing into the focused expression of concentration on pleasure.

Jasmine let go of her hold on Guiles, holding her arms out to the sides, palms down, energetically feeding the Below. Then she raised her palms and faced them outward, feeding the Beside. Finally she raised her arms, feeding the Above. She continued raising her arms until her hands contacted the ceiling again. She pushed against it, pressing herself into Guiles' upturned face, riding it, raining for him one last time.

She put her hands down alongside his face, and, uncrossing her ankles from behind his back she slowly moved her thighs out along his shoulders. He knew what she wanted to do so he shifted his hands a little and slowly lowered her, sliding her down and onto his erection, impaling her there with an excruciating ecstatic slowness.

She gasped and sighed in alternation with every inch, hanging her arms over his shoulders, putting her lips to his throat.

Napat's thighs began to quiver with her building orgasm. The quivering reached her bottom and the quiver became a bucking of her hips. Her knees wobbled and she dropped them to the ground, kneeling as her hand continued to work herself. She grabbed a breast with her free hand, squeezing through school girl white shirt and simple bra. The sensations raced across her belly continuing on inside her, to some throne atop her womb and seated itself there. She couldn't kneel any longer as she shook and bucked, falling forward to catch herself with her free hand.

She felt a pulse of energy from her inner throne. The pulse became a column of light rising through the core of her, inner golden light rose steadily until it reached the top of her head. The column divided, sending light into each of her senses and then vibrating, pounding behind her forehead. She looked up, out into the yard.

The pounding spread out, triangular, and a sensation on the surface felt like curtains parting at the bottom, being pulled back and she could see and hear in a way she never had before. The yard transformed into a vale of golden light. She could see the little altars of stones and flowers as bowers for the lives that lived within—little beings, little eyes, shyly looking at her then hiding when she looked back. She could hear the rustlings, the animals, the spirits moving, the rush of air through a bird's wings. She could hear the sex in the house, hear the groans and sighs before they passed the parted lips, and by extension she could feel what they felt, each separately and together.

It was too much. She shook entirely, body spasming in waves. She put her forehead down on the ground, and the curtain closed. She put both hands on the ground and the vibrations from her orgasm fed through her hands and forehead down into the ground, feeding the earth. The last thing she remembered seeing was something dark rising up toward her, something dragon-like, something hungry to feed.

She lost consciousness, falling into the black, and rolled to her side.

Guiles had been lifting Jasmine slowly and resettling her on his near vertical stiffness. In the quiet movement of this Jasmine heard-felt Napat fall over and opened her eyes. She lifted herself off Guiles, and slid to her feet, pulling his face down for a tender kiss while she stroked him with her other hand. She stepped back.

"Something is wrong," she said. "Outside." Wrapping a sarong around herself, and using another for a shawl she stepped into the kitchen and opened the door. Guiles followed her naked.

She almost tripped over Napat. She bent down, tucking her hair behind her ears, and checked Napat's pulse. The rate increasing and decreasing in waves, at its peak Napat appeared to shiver slightly and in its valley it slowed to a sigh. She lifted back Napat's eyelids and her eyes were rolled back in her head, showing all whites.

"She's journeying," Jasmine said. Pick her up and bring her inside." Jasmine scouted around in the evening light and gathered all Napat's possessions.

"She's started to shiver," Guiles called out. "What should I do with her?"

"She's not shivering with cold, at least not the cold at this level. Put her on the couch. Upstairs in the locker at the foot of the bed are some alpaca shawls. The light weight ones. Bring them down here." Jasmine lay down alongside Napat and took her in her arms and held her, breathing with her at the slower tempo of Napat's rise and fall. "Cover us with them," she said to Guiles when he returned with several shawls. "Now, under the covers, help me undress her."

Alternating between stubborn resistance and slackness Napat was eventually undressed and covered. Her shivering stopped.

Guiles had stayed by Jasmine and Napat, keeping physical contact, his side against Jasmine's back. She reached around behind herself and found his manhood, cradling it and slowly stroking it, she brought it back to size. This calmed Napat even further. Jasmine turned slightly, exposing more of her backside to Guiles while she held Napat in her arms. With one hand she spread herself from behind, and Guiles went to his knees and slipped himself slowly in. Both wen sighed at the same time.

Guiles slowly moved within her. She clamped around him in slow shivering, the sensation transferring itself lightly to Napat. The two of them shivered into sleep together. When they slept Guiles slowed himself to a standstill, withdrew, and lay down on the floor beside them, pulling one of the shawls over his torso, and slept.

By the morning they had scarcely moved. Napat came awake first with a yawn and sat up, her long hair mussed around her head. Once up, sensation of the present moment, Jasmine's body next to her naked one, a man snoring lightly out of sight, became apparent, and she opened her eyes, trying to remember how she had come to be like this. Memory returned, at least the part before she'd passed out, and she jumped up, naked and startled, brushing her hair back, standing on the couch. From this vantage she could see the form of the consort stretched out along the floor.

Morning wood lifted the shawl draped over him, like a tent pole. She gasped just as Jasmine opened an eye, smiled at her and sat up, looking over the edge of the couch. She lifted up a hand and covered her mouth, gasping, mimicking Napat's expression, and then she laughed. "What's the big deal?" she asked. "You've seen it before."

Napat dropped her hands and with a worried look in her eyes, asked "Did I? Did I…" as she slid down the back of the couch and sat cross legged with her feet tucked under Jasmine's legs.

"Did you what?" Jasmine smiled, holding space for Napat to contemplate all the things she could have done but didn't remember. After a moment Jasmine relented, laughing again. "No, you didn't. But your soul did journey. What do you remember?"

"I remember that I saw you, you and him," she said, pointing at Guiles as he sat up, arranging the shawl to cover his erection. "I saw you and him. You were lit up, all golden, you sitting in his lap with your ankles crossed behind him. I saw your light bodies, entwined, coils rising from your heads. The coils joined in a sphere of light above you. It was pulsing, as if you were feeding it and it was feeding you.

"Then I became lost in your, what is the word? Ecstasy? I felt it and lost my body in it, then I lost my mind and I fell out of myself. And where I fell was down into the darkness below the surface. I saw the gaping mouth of a dragon coming toward me, and it took me in its mouth, dragging me down."

She paused, closing her eyes. She shook her head slowly. "So much ecstasy. How could it be?"

Jasmine told her, "It is your birthright. Ecstasy is everyone's birthright.

Napat stared at her for a long time, trying to decide if what Jasmine said was true. She felt the truth of it, but she struggled to believe it.

"Later," Jasmine said. "We will speak of this later. Tell us what happened with the dragon."

"It took me down under the mountain, Nagoon. There were people there, mud people." Jasmine raised her eyebrows, which Napat noticed and paused. Guiles, who only spoke Windonesian, was struggling to keep up. Napat crossed her arms, rubbing the back of them, then rested her hands in her lap.

"Mud people. Yes. People made of yellowish brown mud. They had faces, but no openings, no eyes, no ears, no nose. No mouth even. They were busy going about, here and there. When the dragon released me they took me to a large black dragon. Sleeping. The very tip of his tale was there by the path. One of the mud people put its hand on my arm, to restrain me, to keep me from touching it. Around the tip of the tail was a wooden frame, like you sometimes see around photographs. And then it moved, just the tip. But the frame made it clear. The tip moved and the mud people jumped.

"And I could feel their fear. The way I read it, they were afraid that the dragon will wake up. The tip moving means it's waking up. I could tell they didn't know what to do. So I told them to tell the children in their dreams. The parents will listen then."

Jasmine had shifted to lay on her side facing Napat. Guiles still sat facing them, his tent pole had long since decided to lay itself down. She put her hand on Napat's knee and said, "Napat, my dear. That is quite a lot to have gone through. And I'm happy you stayed outside instead of leaving, and I'm very happy that you've told me everything. How are you feeling now?"

"Hungry," was the reply. "And thirsty."

"You know what? So am I. Let's get some breakfast." Jasmine turned to Guiles and asked him, in English, "Hungry?"

"You bet. Can I help? And I have a lot of questions. Does she understand English?"

"Yes, you can help. And she understands only a very little. So ask me your questions while we're cooking."

Guiles reached for a sarong and tied it around his waist before he stood up. He helped Jasmine stand up, and she in turn helped Napat to stand. By the time Napat was on her feet and Jasmine had dressed her in a sarong and shawl Guiles had turned away and was in the kitchen, looking for eggs to fry. He was troubled by Napat's youth.

Jasmine set water on the stove for tea and Napat put some bread in the toaster and started cutting papaya.

"How old is she?"

"Sixteen." Napat smiled and nodded, licking juice from the back of her thumb.

"How is it that she's so comfortable with nudity? And how is it that you're comfortable with it, too?"

"Up until the Second World War the wen here went topless. Men and wen wore the same basic clothes. Even today the elder wen will go topless, sometimes even in the streets here in town. Her grandmothers did. Now, technically, it's illegal. This is theoretically a Wuzlim country. You understand."

Guiles nodded.

Jasmine continued, "And she doesn't have all the cultural overlay stuff about sex that we do in the States. She is just who she is. Curious but hesitant. In other words, normal. In the West, back home, she'd be experimenting, figuring out who she is, and how she wants to be. She might even have someone she'd be fucking (Napat flinched. She knew that word) by now. But she can't do that here. It's married or nothing, unless maybe she was living alone down in the capital. But probably not even there. If she made enough money her parents would send a chaperone down. But I'm her chaperone. And I pay her parents to let Napat be employed by me. I'll teach her English, and everything, but you know who I am, and something about what I'm going to try to do. So, she's here and she doesn't know any better. But she knows the Island, and she's a good source of information. Not to mention she's a good housekeeper. She runs errands and buys the groceries for me. Besides, there's a belief here that if a person thinks you can't see them, then they're invisible. It's why you'll sometimes see people bathing naked in the irrigation canals alongside the roads."

"Now that's interesting. But what about the sexual stuff?" Guiles asked. "Isn't she a little young?"

"By our standards, maybe. But we aren't in that world, and if she's going to be around me, and she will be, I will only be able to hide so much. In which case I need her as an ally. She's already a candidate for internship, and to be trained as a Priestess. If I don't then she'll just end up being exploited. Maybe even killed. Her psychic abilities put her life at risk. And I don't have any alliances yet with any of the native Priestesses, and so I can't arrange an apprenticeship for her. So for now, she's my apprentice."

Guiles turned the tea water off and slid the pot to the side of the stove so Napat could reach it. He flipped the eggs. He remained silent, thinking.

Jasmine asked, "Do you have a problem with it?"

"No, no problem," he said. "But I'm going to reserve judgment, too. If I see something that I question I'll come to you with it. But I won't interfere, and I'll follow your lead if you want me to do something."

"Good High Consort," she said, grinning, affecting an air of mock superiority. "Do you know the reward for such good behavior?"

19

GUILES AND WADE

In the afternoon Jasmine drew a map to Wade's house out in the country for Guiles. In town everyone basically knew everyone's business, and the comings and goings of the resident aliens were a particular source of gossip. For the same reason Wade couldn't stay at Jasmine's house in town, Guiles could not either. It would be unseemly, and Jasmine needed to appear seemly, so that her neighbor's judgments would not be harsh against her. That she spoke the languages was in her favor, but neither man did.

That she had hired Napat to become her personal assistant was well-known, and it would be very unseemly for Napat and a man to be alone in Jasmine's house for any length of time.

So, after sending Napat off to school, with instructions to meet her in the plaza of the Temple of Wahsastami afterwards, she and Guiles had one more session of love-making. After spending a full twenty-four hours practicing the Internal Orbit energy moving exercises he was grateful for the leg-shaking release Jasmine gave him. And for her part she savored the distillation of his essence.

She gave him the map, and he picked his helmet up off the table and turned to go. Jasmine commanded him to "Stop. Turn around." She looked at him, up and down, a speculative smile turning in a huge grin. She stepped up to him, embraced him with one arm, and cradled his masculinity with the other hand. No overt motion, just holding him, but letting the energy flow out through her hand. She felt him stir in her hand and looked down, laying her cheek along his chest.

Still holding it, she waited until he had grown fully erect inside his shorts. She squeezed him lightly and sighed. She looked up, told him, "Remember She whom you Serve," and stepped away.

Guiles, whose eyes had been closed, opened them and grinned hugely as well. He bowed to Jasmine as he stepped back and went out through the door. He rolled his scooter through the gate, latching it behind him, and started it. Then he was off, down the road, Jasmine following the sound of it until it disappeared into the noise of the street.

Upstairs in the loft Jasmine had established her altars and the space for her daily practice of Devotions, Prayers, Meditations, Illuminations, and Blessings. Shortly after arrival she had made it a point to purchase as many different statues of the local Goddesses, Devis, spirits and gods as she could find, including statues of local literary classics, spreading her purchases around to many shops. And whenever she would travel out of town she would stop at carving shops wherever she found them. Only a few purchases did she keep, shipping many off the island for distribution throughout the Order, creating more legitimacy for herself as a business person in the process.

This morning she brought the statue of Wahsastami forward, so that she might more easily make inquiries of She Who Comes when She came. She wanted to see if she could make contact with Wahsastami Herself, and at the moment she felt filled with power.

In her meditations she gazed upon the image of the statue, then when it was fixed in her mind's eye she began by invoking Her name, then adding in a mantra that was a call to Her. She saw only darkness. Slowly a feeling of dread began to arise in her, the dread of a child looking for its mother. Using her breath to control her emotions she called upon She Who Comes, and shortly felt the presence of a hand on her shoulder, signifying the presence of the True Creator. She heard a feminine voice whisper, "Deep," and then "Do not."

Suddenly she found herself standing in a walled enclosure surrounded by magnificent grass covered hills with jutting boulders and rock faces, streams running swiftly down their sides. She turned and looked down and there was a series of thatch-roofed rock houses. Smoke was coming from a chimney. She went there and stopped outside the sheepskin door. She coughed in case someone was inside and could hear her.

A young woman with blonde hair came to the skin, flipped it aside and stepped out, tucking her hair behind one ear. She was dressed in a style centuries old—a full dress and a white apron—her hands covered in white flour. She put her hands on her hips and regarded Jasmine critically. "Aunt Bree," she called out. "We have a guest."

Bree came to the door and looked out. "Come in, come in," She beckoned. "Water for tea, please Torey. Sit," She said to Jasmine.

Bree regarded her. "I know what you are. Torey, can you tell?" Torey turned over her shoulder and said, "She is one of Grandmother's Servants. And she is very far away." Jasmine's stomach growled suddenly. "And hungry too, I daresay."

Bree laughed, throwing Her head back. She reached up and let down Her hair, its full red-brown glory cascading down Her back.

"Yes, I daresay. Priestess, no, wait, High Priestess but not long so, what is your name and why are you here?"

"I am Jasmine, and I am on Wallid Island on the other side of the world. I was sitting, searching for Wahsastami, but I could not find Her. I called upon She Who Comes for help. I felt Her hand on my shoulder, and suddenly I am here."

"Ah yes, I see," Brighid said. "I am Brighid, daughter of She Who Comes, and I am also Wahsastami. We are the same but we manifest differently in different places. That face of Me has been shut away in the darkness for a while now. So, why are you on Wallid?"

"The High Priestess of Stonehaven sent me there. It is the thinking of She Who Comes, I am told, that this is the next step in the liberation of all the Goddesses."

"And so, you need to know, that I am trapped there by the Priests of that Island. And on this island where I am, as well. I was a light to those people and I made them healthier and happier, but the Priests couldn't stand that the people were devoted to any other than them. I am bound beneath my temple there, and my Priestesses are either banned or bound."

"How are you to be freed?" Jasmine asked.

"Listen, and I shall tell you."

After an hour's ride Guiles arrived at Wade's house in the country. There was a wall around the house, but it was clearly of modern construction. He parked outside the gate, tried to push it open, and it wasn't latched. He slipped through quietly, taking his travel bag from the back of the scooter, and quietly latched the gate behind him.

Quietly he walked to the front door, but rather than knocking he followed a pulling sensation at his solar plexus around the back of the house. There he saw Wade, for whom else could it be, laying naked on a chaise lounge. He was masturbating, first slowly then gripping himself hard and rapidly. Guiles raised his eyebrows—a Consort was almost never known to masturbate alone. There was no need, and the practice was frowned upon. He studied Wade's expression. Wade's face was contorted in a sneer that Guiles could only interpret as loathing. He asked himself, "What could he be so angry about? What could he hate so much?"

He started to back away, to return to the front of the house and knock, but he felt a hand on his shoulder, and he recognized Her touch. His mind filled with an image, and he heard Her voice say, "Remember, I may ask you to do something you don't want to do, but I won't ask you to do anything that goes against your nature."

He replied to the Presence, "My nature is to serve You."

"I know," he heard the voice say, then he felt the Presence smile and withdraw Her hand.

He sighed, thinking how to best handle this. He walked around the corner talking, looking back over his shoulder. He said, "Hey, I knocked but nobody came so I came around back and…" He stopped, pretending to take in the scene for the first time. "Wow, man. You look like you're having a hard time with that," smiling at the double entendre. "Here, let me help."

Wade's face showed a transient shock and then confusion, as if he couldn't sort out some mental dilemma. Guiles set down his bag and went to the chaise lounge. He bent over and took Wade's phallus in his mouth. He replaced Wade's hand with his own and knelt down. He slid his mouth slowly up and down, as if his mouth was a balm for Wade's anger-red erection. He found himself salivating, lubricating and soothing the red flesh. He almost flinched when Wade put his hand on the back of his head, and gripped into his hair, moving his head up and down at a pace to Wade's liking.

Guiles started to grow erect himself, and reached into his shorts with his free hand, digging around to free himself up for expansion, thinking of the blindness of the one-eyed snake. He started making a grunting noise which Wade interpreted as pleasure but was really Guiles in disagreement with the image that had just appeared in his mind.

He pulled back his head and sighed. Standing up he removed his shorts and turned around, straddling Wade's legs. Holding his own erection and balls up out of the way with one hand he bent over and looked between his legs. Taking Wade's erection in his other hand, he placed the head of it against his asshole and willed himself to relax. Holding Wade's cock firmly, he felt the head slip in. His legs shook with tension and pleasure. He rose up slightly and lowered himself again, groaning with pleasure. The intensity made him shiver. He rose again then settled again, this time all the way down, taking Wade inside himself completely.

Wade grunted, finding himself completely ensheathed, the heat of the scabbard surpassing the heat of the sword.

Guiles, still crouching over Wade, began to move up and down. Impatient with the pace Wade reached under Guile's ass and held him up, moving at his own pace, increasing his speed, his frustration rising with his pace. He gazed along Guiles' back with slitted eyes. Sweat broke out on his brow.

The intensity became almost too much for Guiles, and he, even using his own hand to stroke himself, became surprised that his erection began to subside. Wade continued pounding into him from below, and when Wade came Guiles felt a blast of pleasure, an orgasm, an assgasm, so profound he ejaculated himself, even though he was no longer completely hard. He came on Wade's lower legs, splashing on the chaise lounge and on the deck. He settled down, stilling the bucking of his hips.

From behind him Wade growled, "If you're Guiles, then you know you'd better clean that up." Guiles found that he couldn't suppress a giggle at the arrogance of the man behind him. He leaned forward and sucked up a gob off the top of Wade's foot. He stood up and went for the garden hose coiled up by the back door. He turned it on, hosing off the come running down the inside of his thighs, then he turned the hose on Wade, eliciting unhappy shouts and "What the fuck?'s."

He dropped the hose, grabbed his bag and shorts, and went into the house, saying "Don't get up, I'll find my way."

20

BEFORE BURNING

Madeleine stood on the south lawn of the Mansion, facing south, arms raised. She was wearing a bluish-green gown, silk, long-sleeved, hems trailing on the grass. It was open on top, exposing her breasts to the sky, open below, exposing her phulva to the earth, tied with four satin ties, one pair above the other, across her solar plexus, tied under chants of shielding.

She chanted a prayer to the spirits of the land. A soft whirlwind came and enveloped her, gently lifting her hair. Normally she would chant to the spirits of the people next, but the people were gone from Stonehaven, only a few remained. Even Calley and Alam had gone, returning to the Pine Eye. Instead, she chanted for the next best thing: the spirits of the once-were-people, the spirits of the ghosts.

She paused in the spell, sensing their arrival, their presence, and then, empathetically, their feelings. Those ranged from fear through anger to calm watchfulness.

She was the Madeleine, one of a long chain of Madeleines, back to the first one, beloved friend of Rachel. She was of a line of Seeresses and spell casters.

She knew the plan, and she told the ghosts about it and that she needed their help. They whispered among themselves, each reacting as death had bound them to react. The Madeleines and Crows stepped to the fore and circled around her, the ghost of the first one coming forward, kissing her cheek—every hair on her body, even her scalp, stood up. The ghost laughed and turned, facing away, taking a step outward, determined to serve as body guard. The other Madeleines turned outward also.

So much magic had gone into the walls of Stonehaven over the years, not just sex magic, but practical magic, that the building was impervious to attack—Physical, Psychic, and Spiritual. In order for the Mansion to become the kind of trap Calley envisioned, a hole would need to be opened in the shield. For this she needed a different kind of power than she could raise with sex magic alone. Sex before a practical working was good for building power, sex after was good for recharging a depleted soul (and these were two different kinds of sex). Sometimes sex after a working was good for alchemizing whatever fine particles of magic had been absorbed during the ritual. She knew she would have to use all of it in today's ritual.

Finally she sent a voice to Spirit, the energies of the Goddesses, asking for their help, sending one. To her surprise, when she looked up, she saw the descending form of the True Creator, She Who Comes, descending naked on a golden cloud, hair aloft with the wind of it, arms spread out palms up. In a second the Goddess was upon her, the golden whirlwind of energy at her feet pouring into Madeleine's crown, turning her once completely around.

Madeleine shook with ecstasy, her arms mirroring the Goddess's. Occupied by the Divine as she was, she doubled over in the ecstasy of it, and shook some more. When she could raise herself erect she opened her eyes and saw through the dark veil of the Goddess's eyes, knowing the Goddess saw the brighter world now. The act of surrender to Her pulled a pulse of bliss up through her that made her knees shake, her hips buck, and her heart feel like it would explode with joy. She growled, then shouted as she felt the top of her head seem to come off, and all was air. The pulse ricocheted back down through her, around her, and when it passed her hips again she relaxed, and everything relaxed with it, and she rained. Rained and rained onto the sacred ground, feeding the spirits of the land. The spirits gathered round, and inhaled the perfume of the nectar from the flower in bloom.

She turned and walked toward the veranda around the south wall of the men's tower. Utterly relaxed, she squirted a little with each step. Rain rolling down her thighs, she left wet footprints on the wooden deck. She paused before the great double doors and looked within.

There, on the top level of the dais, was the ghost of her beloved Eva, sitting in deep meditation. On the lowest level, sitting on his heels, head bowed, was a naked Matthews, long hair down across his shoulders. Around them both, up the riser on one side, around Eva, and down again behind Matthews, was a circle of 28 candles.

The imprint of her bare wet feet behind her, she stepped through into the sacred space. She went to one knee, and spread the circle for her to pass through. As she stood and stepped in, the candles moved themselves back to symmetry when she'd passed. The image of Eva seemed to reverse itself so she was sitting facing away from the Consort. Madeleine came and sat in her place, facing him. His head remained bowed, as instructed. He cultivated the sensations and the feelings of the Servant.

Madeleine's hands moved slowly through a series of asanas, blessing and welcoming. Then, holding her hands palm up to the sides she summoned two small whirlwinds. They danced there, ruffling and lifting her hair gently. From her root, through an opening through her second wheel a flower emerged, small and white—a wild orchid. The winds dropped from her hands to her lap, ruffling the edges of her gown.

The small whirlwinds carried the scent of her femininity to Matthews. By scent alone he grew erect. His head still bowed he felt the pull of the asana of beckoning, and crawled slowly, head bowed, erection tight against his belly, harder and more filled with the power of it than he could remember.

On hands and knees he crawled up the steps, stopping one level below her. He leaned in, leaned forward, bringing his face nearly all the way to Madeleine's sex and breathed, each breath making his hardness twitch. He felt a faint tracing of a finger along his jaw, pausing under his chin and lifting his face. As his eyes passed upward he saw four arms, two the Madeleine's, two belonging to She Who Comes.

When his face was raised toward Hers, She inclined Her head to him. The all-black eyes of the Goddess looked down at him, looked down along her nose. She nodded.

He returned his face to her sex. He took two fingers and placed them at her opening, and waited. Almost imperceptibly She began to draw them in. Madeleine uncrossed her ankles and put her feet on the floor on either side of him. She raised her hips off the floor, making a slight hissing sound as she lifted from the pool of rain, the sound of shallow waves spreading out on the sand. She forced his fingers up and in, forcing her to rain again, rain gently for his mouth, for his eyes, his face. This odd peak of relaxation juxtaposed to contraction, this paradox, pushed the fingers from her.

She cried out, falling backwards, putting her heels over his shoulders. "I need to fly," she said. Or She said, Matthews could not tell.

Bringing his hands and forearms up between her thighs he took hold of her waist. He thought his wings fully into existence, shimmering in the candlelight as they extended, greater than the diameter of the circle. The ghosts and the spirits of the land stroked them. The heat from the candles lifted them. As he rose, her hips rose with him, plastering her bud to his branch, his eggs to her opening. She drew him in, locking them together, and locked her ankles across his lower back.

He lifted, holding her hips to himself, letting her upper body hang, hair hanging down, arms out to the side making magic signs, sigils, and asanas. His wings vibrated, shimmering with the hovering. The skirts of her gown swayed in the air. He felt her start to turn him, and then lay him out on his back, not all the way, but more as if she were astride a leaping horse. She rocked on him with her hips, each stroke a vacuum seal pulling on him. Pulling something from him, something he was only too happy to give.

At the top of the round room the roof was a cone. A cloud of light, sparkling, sparking, gathered there. As she moved her arms in the signs of power, as she drew upon her steed, drew the power upward from her steed, she directed it, rippling and sparkling, up her arms.

On the peak of the roof there was a lightning rod. The cloud of sparking light bled upward through the roof and gathered at the metal tip. The ball of lightning gathered there.

Inside, she rode him to his peak. He leaped upward as his essence leapt, leaping out of him, pumping as much of his spirit into her as he could, the essence of him entering within as the substance of him spread without, between them. The little flower of her belly drank. She was the retort of transformation, the vessel of change.

The lightning shot from the tip of the rod. It sparked all the other lightning rods on the chimneys, then all along the roof edges the blue white fire connected. When the wall of flame was complete it flared, once, too bright to look at, illuminating the trees, flaring at the Pine Eye.

The magic that protected the mansion broke. Tiny crystalline shards fell to the ground, with a sound as if of wind chimes far away.

The Madeleine had gone limp, laying forward across him. He embraced her. Still locked together he lowered them to the dais. She lay on top of him, breathing steadily, eyes closed, still locked together.

He felt himself grow hard again, against her. She stirred, and sat up, her hair hanging down over her face. She released him, then rose up and slipped him inside. She rocked him, her steed, at a slow walk. She raised her head a little, allowing him to see into the darkness.

He saw the flash of dark eyes. A faint curl of a smile.

Suddenly, he felt Her in him, saw what She saw when She looked upon Her beloved Madeleine, Seeress and Prophet. He stiffened at the shock, and it took his breath away. He heard Her voice within him, addressing his surprise, "I created you," she said. "I am you."

Then he felt a sensation of something departing from him to all sides, like air being sucked away. It was more Beautiful than his uncertainty. The ghosts and the spirits of the land withdrew.

He opened his eyes and looked up again, and it was Madeleine smiling at him. "I saw that," she said. She started to rain again, little squishes squeezed from her with each thrust of her rocking hips.

She walked the horse. It was a long way home.

21

INITIATION

"It's time, Angelica," Regina Moon Halter said. Angelica slowly opened her eyes and stared at the shape before her, understanding that the unfolding of evolution followed the same pattern as the enfolding of involution. One had only to pay attention long enough to see which direction the energy in the pattern was going. She had been involving, now she was about to evolve.

She had made a small altar to the Divine Feminine on a foot stool, and in the middle of it she had placed a spiral fossil shell, an ammonite. Around it she had placed flowers, which she cut fresh every day. "The purpose is served," she told herself, not sure why, or what it meant. She had been moving the energy of the Resonant Heart from place to place within her, paying attention to whatever images arose in her mind when she would allow it to linger in one spot or another. It had begun to resonate in odd places like her elbow or a knee. Quinn had told her these were minor chakras that were being "spiritualized," as he put it. At the moment Regina spoke she had been sitting on her heels before the altar, resonating the tops of her feet against the floor. The images were of walking barefoot on thick moss along a stream bank at Stonehaven.

She sighed, bowed her forehead to the floor before the altar, drew her toes up under her, and rose to her feet in one motion. She'd been given a tunic to wear, a simple rectangular garment that came to her knees with holes for her arms and head. The slot for the head was so large it fell over the tops of her shoulders, and was tied up with a drawstring. She picked up the bundle of her light wool poncho, a gift from the Madeleine, and barefoot, stepped outside as Regina held the door. They walked down the street in the moonlight between the cabins and followed the path out past the corrals and barns. The lights were off and if anyone was looking they were looking from darkness. Passing one of the cabins they heard a wen crying out in rhythmic pleasure. They took the well swept path out toward the crossing place for the small stream that ran through the property, their feet raising little puffs of dust with each step.

Once across the stream they stopped and put on walking sandals. "Wen have many initiatory opportunities in everyday life. There's being born—for both wen and men. Then there's menarche. Men have nothing like this in their lives. Simply growing pubic hair and getting horny is still an initiation that wen and men share—the initiation into potential sexuality. But bleeding? Men have nothing to compare it to, and that's why they invented initiation ceremonies for adolescents, primarily circumcision. And in some cases penile subincision."

"Wait, what? What the hell is penile subincision?"

"Making a cut along the underside of the penis, so that their genitalia more resembles the phulva."

"Wait, what? Are you fucking kidding me?"

"No."

"That's fucking gross. That's fucking horrible."

"Yeah. Sometimes many of those teenage boys die, even from circumcision alone. That's why subincision was often reserved for men who survived circumcision."

"What the fuck? I don't get it."

"Yeah, well, think about it. Think about how a primitive man would react to the sight of that blood. And more importantly, that the bleeding stopped, and the wen were OK. Think about the wonder and terror that happened when the bleeding came back twenty eight days later."

Angelica went silent and thought about it. "I take it for granted. The primitive mind wouldn't have. For me, it's scientific. For them it was mysterious and symbolic. Subincision made men equal in power to wen on the symbolic level. Except it didn't, not really."

"Exactly. No amount of bloodletting would let men become the equivalent of wen. So, what then did men do with their terror?"

"They took power in other ways. They took power from us in other ways."

"Well, in some cases. But there was still the fundamental power of the mystery we carry within us. Not every culture's men took all the power from us. Only some cultures did. The cultures of De Murgos."

"OK, wait. I've been hearing about this De Murgos character; from you, from other Priestesses, from the Diosa herself. What's going on here, and where did this other person, this other force, come from?"

"According to the Diosa he comes from beyond the solar system. He and his army of creatures that were created but not born. There are different kinds. Some have genitalia, and the legends say they can reproduce." Regina smiled a secret smile. "Others can't, it would seem. But it was by visitation from De Murgos, and mostly his agents, that wen came to be in their current position—not only disrespected, but robbed of their true status as antecedent, and robbed, therefore, of the role we were born to fill."

"Why, why did De Murgos do that?"

"Because he knew we would never permit him to do what he's doing. He is raping the Mother, She Who Comes. He is consuming Her, taking from Her. And he is doing it to feed himself, and his army."

"How?"

"By causing immense suffering. He feeds on suffering. And his aim is to create the conditions that feed him. And then when he has exhausted the Mother, when he has exhausted us, he'll leave, and abandon us. That is, if any of us are left."

They walked silently for a while, then Angelica asked, "So what's this initiation for, if wen already have one that men don't?"

"The purpose of initiation among men is to reorganize the system of sentiments of a child into the system of sentiments of an adult. I don't remember who said that at the moment. But it's true. Menarche reorganizes the system of sentiments of the wen child into a system that's appropriate to an adult. Wen become prepared to be mothers. That is, we become prepared to put someone else's welfare ahead of ourselves. At least it used to work that way. And among men it was supposed to work the same way. Men need to be reoriented from their own welfare—the selfishness of the little boy's ego. Men need to be reoriented to the welfare of others.

"But most men don't hunt anymore, or go on quests, or even join the military, all things that could reorganize their childish sentiments. Here, the men's initiations in Consortship make sure that their emotions get reorganized into a system that serves the Divine Feminine. For the wen, even though they're already in a sense initiated, this ritual orients them to the Divine Feminine also, but it does something more. It immunizes wen from the thought processes of internalized oppression that have been forced down our throats and into our souls and spirits, and have controlled our bodies for millennia. It is an initiation into freedom."

They had stopped walking during the Moon Halter's monologue. Regina looked off into the distance; Angelica looked down. Angelica broke the silence. "And here I thought I was free."

"You'll see," Regina said. "We should go. They're waiting."

They walked most of a mile upland until they came to a short cliff in the dirt that long ago was the bank of the creek, but was now several hundred yards away from it. The cliff was a hundred yards from a rise of rock that led to a ridge that formed part of the valley wall. At the end of a footpath that cut across the cliff face, about half way up, set into the side of the cliff was a wooden door with wrought iron fittings. Regina stopped at the bottom and indicated with a hand that Angelica was to proceed up the path. "Knock on the door," she said. "I will pray to Her for you."

The door opened inward, iron hinges groaning. Angelica took a quick look back down the path over her shoulder. Regina was still there, looking at her. Angelica felt a little shock when she realized how bad she'd have felt if Regina had been walking away.

She heard a voice whisper, "Enter" and she stepped into darkness. She felt a hand from the shadows touch her arm and escort her forward a few more steps. The door closed, and the space she was in grew initially dark. She was in some kind of entryway. Candles just out of sight along a hallway on the other side of a bend gave an indirect illumination. As her eyes adjusted her awareness became broader. She became aware of two figures, one on either side of her. She could hear their breathing, steady but prepared for excitement. She matched her breathing to theirs.

They stepped closer to her. She resisted the impulse to look at them, choosing to focus straight ahead but see what she could from her peripheral vision. She felt a sharp spike of fear, knowing that she probably shouldn't look directly at them. She saw enough to see the difference in shape, and that the one on her right was a wen, topless, breasts moving with her breath. The one on her left was a man, also shirtless, dark bodied, with what seemed to be lines in white paint drawn on his torso. Both heads remained shrouded in darkness.

The wen turned and stepped into the hallway. She whispered, "Follow." She could hear the man breathing behind her as she walked. When they passed the candles set into the walls Angelica could see the wen was wearing a short rope skirt that revealed anywhere and concealed everywhere when she walked. She realized why she couldn't see their faces—they were wearing cylindrical masks made of a black cloth that she was certain they could see through, but she couldn't, a circumscribing veil that fell to their shoulders and chest, and down their backs like long hair. She turned to glance at the man behind her, but he raised his palm, indicating she should keep her eyes front.

The tunnel they were in was built like a mineshaft. After not too long a walk into the hillside they came to another door. The wen in front knocked, and was told to enter. Angelica followed her into a large room that appeared to be carved out of the stone itself, and smoothed. To the right was an ornate chair on a raised dais with a masked wen sitting on it wearing a necklace that glowed in the faint light, amplifying it and returning it to the room. To the left was another, smaller door. Directly ahead was a table. In the middle was a large polished bronze vase with a long phallus-shaped spout, inscribed with patterns of markings that were both art and some language she couldn't read. On either side of it were large bronze pots with applique filigree.

The wen in front of her turned and took her wool poncho and set it aside. The man behind her bent down and took off her shoes, leaving her standing on one leg then the other. The man rose, took her by the shoulders and turned her to face the throne. The wen in front took her hands and led her slowly forward until her feet encountered a raised feature on the floor. She looked down and it appeared to be a wooden saddle frame.

The man behind her untied the drawstring and her tunic fell to her feet. Naked, she was pushed forward until her feet were on either side of the frame. The wen before her kneeled and drew Angelica down with her, forcing her to kneel with her thighs spread. The wen sat back on her heels and Angelica did the same, going as far as contact with the frame would let her.

"You have come before me, why?" the voice on the throne asked.

"I come seeking freedom," she replied."

"We shall see if you shall find your freedom," the voice said.

The wen gestured, her breasts swaying in the light. A man brought the vase with the spout and passed it to the kneeling wen in front of Angelica. She held the spout up to Angelica's mouth, and when Angelica parted her lips to let the opening through—the wen used a slight force to bring the entire head of it into Angelica's mouth, the man behind her holding her head to keep her still. With its entire head behind her teeth the wen tilted the vase and began a slow pour of a liquid, viscous but not slimy, warm, sweet then bitter. The vase was large and it took a long time for Angelica to drink it all.

When the head of the opening was withdrawn she felt the absence with a fond longing that surprised her.

After being allowed to sit a moment Angelica realized she felt a rush of pleasure that gave her chills. She shook herself to clear the sensation from her mind. Another man came up behind her and together the two men took an arm each and brought her from sitting on the frame to her knees and then they extended each arm out to the side, palm down.

Suddenly something cold was splashed on her back between her shoulder blades. She felt it slide down her spine. It made her gasp and arch her back. Another cold splash of some kind of glop was pasted immediately to her belly, which made her gasp again and bend forward. The men holding her arms out to the side would only let her bend so far then they straightened her up. Hands spread the glop around. Her breasts, her shoulders, her face and arms, even her hair was splashed with the glop and then it was spread around. Splashed, it went on her thighs and buttocks. Suddenly two hands slapped themselves between her spread thighs, one in back first, which rubbed thoroughly between her legs and then another smacked a glob into her phulva, making her cry out as the hand rubbed the stuff mercilessly into the soft folds of her skin.

As they stood her up she looked down and could see in the dim light that she'd been painted a dark red. The word 'ochre' came to her mind. The splashing continued down her legs until even the soles of her feet and the palms of her hands had been painted.

She stood there, arms out to the side, sensing the paint roll down her skin, dripping from her hair and lips onto the saddle frame between her feet. She raised her face so that she was looking upwards in the darkness. Her entire body started to burn. She thought to herself, "There must be drugs in the paint." She gasped at the pain that began to consume her. She recognized the fire as the same fire she felt off and on for days after her experience of overcoming the Kundalini Barrier. The fire gathered between her legs and intensified into a heat that went beyond flame and she doubled over in a paroxysm of ecstatic orgasm, then sank to her knees when her shaking legs would no longer support her. The men holding her arms gently kept them suspended out from her sides. A red glow seemed to emanate from her and fill the room.

The voice from the throne spoke. "Red child, child born in blood and suffering, do you swear to protect and keep secret the Order of the Fleur de Vie, upon pain of death, that your heart may burst?"

Angelica thought to herself "I can handle this. I know this." She replied, "Yes, oh Goddess, yes. I swear." The heat started to recede. As it receded the shaking stopped and she settled onto the saddle frame. The red glow faded as her breath slowed.

The High Priestess on the throne stepped forward and said aloud, "Yes, but can you handle this," and touched Angelica's heart. Suddenly the room filled with a golden glow. The Resonance of the Higher Heart centered itself in Angelica's mortal heart. The pounding of it threw her entire body into a wracking spasm of ecstasy. Angelica wept for the pleasure and beauty of it.

The High Priestess returned to her seat. The voice from the throne spoke, "You shall have the chance to find the freedom you seek." Angelica raised her head. The figure nodded and pointed to the small door behind her.

"Take your clothing. Take the basket by the door. Go all the way to end of the tunnel."

The people in the room began to chant:

"That which opens for me closes,
Closes around me.

"That which opens for me closes,
Closes upon me.

"That which opens for me,
Opens."

Angelica had to crawl through the small door and stopped when it closed behind her, leaving her in darkness. She crawled, her body still mildly itching and burning from the red paint. The going was slow, as she had the basket and clothes in one hand. She stopped to pull her tunic on over her head, banging her head against the low ceiling in the tunnel. She felt the impact spot gingerly. "That'll leave a lump," she said ruefully. More cautiously she pulled on her poncho, but it hung down and her knees kept pinning it to the floor when she crawled. She sat down, and said, again aloud to no one in particular, "This is ridiculous." She pulled the poncho off over her head and scraped her knuckles on the ceiling. "Ouch. Shit. Fuck," she said.

She paused then, and took stock of her situation. After she folded the poncho she felt around in the basket to see what was there. A gallon of what she surmised was water. A candle. And what she was pretty sure were several matches in a small box. She struck one on the side of the box, lit the candle and looked around.

She was in a long hallway, not much higher than her waist, unable to stand up. The hall was curved so she couldn't see back to the door she'd come through, nor could she see where the tunnel ended around a bend. She realized there was only one candle in the basket, so she blew it out and put it back in the basket to save it for later. She folded her poncho into the basket and resumed her way, tucking the tunic up through the neckline in front so she wouldn't end up kneeling on it also. She made her way along the tunnel, bumping the walls, dragging the basket. She stopped when she felt a draft. When she reached out she realized the walls had disappeared.

She set the basket down, fished out the matches and candle, and backed up into the tunnel. She didn't want to risk the draft blowing out the match. She lit the candle and shuffled back to the opening, shielding the flame with her hand. She noticed then that some of the thick paint had dried and fallen off her hands and arms. She glanced back down the tunnel and noticed that the floor was stained red from the paint falling off all those who had passed this way before. She found the thought, "They did it. So can I" comforting.

She turned forward again and crawled out with her basket. She raised the candle and looked around. She was in a chamber carved into the packed clay. The walls and floor were smooth. There were stains on the floor and smoke marks on the walls. The ceiling disappeared into the darkness above her. The flame flickered to the back of the chamber. She stood up and walked unsteadily in the direction the flame bent. She found an opening about the size of her torso but couldn't see very far into it, so she backed away, not wanting to risk the flame. She went back to her basket, laid out the poncho on the floor, and took a short look at herself, the paint flaking off like dried mud leaving reddish pink patches of skin showing from underneath. She took a drink of water and resealed the bag. She sat back and felt her hair, clumpy and drying stiffly. She tossed it back behind her shoulders, hoping it would dry there. She blew out the candle and settled into the darkness to see what she could see.

She promptly fell asleep. She dreamed of her childhood, memories, mostly. She woke up weeping. She fell to her side, weeping hard, missing her parents, missing her childhood, missing the person she would have become if all this "shit" hadn't happened to her. The whole thing with the dragon, the kundalini blow-out, the odd sex ritual base of the Order. She sat up. A voice whispered, "But you love that." She wailed, then, at the truth of that, wailed for her lost normalcy. She'd never have a normal life now. She'd never be normal again. She rolled to her hands and knees, angry now, and she beat her fists into the dirt, snot dripping from her nose. She stopped when her hands hurt.

She fell to her side again, the storm of weeping passing through her, reducing slowly, punctuated by single sobs. Her mind swirled with images from two streams—the stream of her childhood and the stream of all that had happened to her the last six months. "It's overwhelming," she gasped. She put her thumb in her mouth and her other hand between her legs, and, tears still flowing, fell asleep again.

This time she dreamed of other lives—past lives of other people, other people's present lives. All lives of normal people. When she woke again she realized that she didn't really want a normal life anymore. She took another sip from the bag, then a longer pull, thinking to herself that she'd have to rehydrate. She wondered what she looked like. Suddenly she felt herself split off from herself, and she was looking at her own face through a dark fog. White lines ran through the red mud paint down her cheeks and back from her eyes to her ears, stripes from the tears she'd wept. It was a stark and powerful image. When she wondered how she was seeing herself in the dark the split off part snapped back into her, rocking her to the side like she'd been slapped.

She lit the candle, driving back the dark. She sighed. She could feel with her fingers that what she'd seen had been true—the paint was washed off in a band beneath her eyes down her cheeks, and from her eyes on the sides back to her ears. It was a stark look, and suddenly she loved it. She smiled, then laughed out loud at her vanity. She rolled her eyes, and when her eyes rolled upward they almost locked in place. She went past it, then back to where she was looking up. Her forehead suddenly exploded with the pounding of the Resonance, her eyes rolled further up, her field of vision was flooded with golden light, and she passed out.

With no sense of how long she'd been out, she returned to the cool floor of the chamber, in the dark. Her first realization was that the candle had gone out. She panicked. Feeling around for the matches. She struck one, and found the candle had only the slightest length of guttered wick. The match burned her fingers and she dropped it. Feeling in the box she counted three more matches. Using her fingernail she dug into the still soft wax and built it up until she felt she could light the candle again. She lit it, and realized how little was really left. She resolved to save what little there was and blew it out. She took another pull from the water bottle, and settled back again, to see what she would see.

She practiced the circular meditation technique she'd learned, inhaling and pulling the energy from the root behind her little rod at the top of her phulva, dropping it down and around between her legs, up her back, and up over the top of her head, collecting the energy on the tip of her tongue pushed against the roof of her mouth. Then, curling her tongue down into her lower jaw, she allowed the energy to drop down, returning to the root. After several cycles of this she began to tremble with the energy. There were three distinct types of sensation, flowing down over her belly.

Eventually her inner eye opened in her forehead and she saw the pink flower symbol of the Order of the Fleur de Vie. On the next exhale she began to feel, in addition to the trembling that was focusing in her low belly and upper thighs, a kind of exhale over her entire body. The room filled slowly with red light, she could see through her closed eyes. When the sensation was over she opened her eyes and saw the dragon, her dragon, floating in the air in front of her. She smiled. The dragon dropped its head, and lowered itself to the floor. It licked her, licked her phulva, its forked tongue flicking against the little rod. She came immediately, shivering her ecstasy outward, following the path out through all her pores, raising her arms and feeding the ecstasy out into the world, as she'd been taught. The dragon curled up at her side, put its tail over its nose, and fell asleep.

She thought, "It's just me now," and sighed back into herself, and again took up the circular energetic work. The pink flower restored its image in her mind, and as she gazed at it, the petals opened and she was through a door out into the ranch, looking at everyone, paying particular attention to Quinn, sitting on the porch with his feet up, reading. Then she stopped to visit with Regina, who sensed her, looked directly at her, and smiled. Then she journeyed to Stonehaven, checking in on Calley and Madeleine, and finally her mentor Diana. They all noticed her and looked at her and smiled.

Diana was talking to her children on the computer, the camera image showed happy excited children that looked to be of elementary school age. It showed a beleaguered looking man with uncombed hair in the background, smiling at the children from behind, then glancing up toward the camera to smile at her and shake his head wonderingly.

She felt the pang of Diana missing her children. She felt it as a spasm in her womb, and glanced at the dragon sleeping nearby. She felt the memory of the pressure of Diana's back against hers, sitting back to back, Diana using the connection to regulate and stabilize the somatic, psychic, and spiritual energy flows after the Kundalini Barrier blow-out. Her eyes teared up at the thought that Diana missed time with the children in order to stay with her.

She felt the pang in her womb again, and realized she was bleeding, shedding, peeling away inside. She wept with frustration, reluctant to confront how messy things could get. "What am I going to do?" she asked herself, aloud. She felt in herself the impulse to wail, and fall into self-pity, but something in her forestalled it. She took off her tunic with the thought of just balling it up between her legs.

Then she smiled. Biting the hem with her teeth she tore the tunic into strips and folded them. She smoothed one pad of folded cloth between her legs. She smiled at herself, pleased with the solution, and pleased that she didn't go all silly and allow herself to wail. She was not a child to deal with being a woman like that. "Wen," she corrected herself. "I am wen." She smiled into the darkness, felt for the water bag, and took another pull.

She shivered, suddenly cold. She slipped the wool poncho out from under herself and pulled it on over her head. She yawned, and suddenly sleep took her, pulling her over on her side again. She yawned once, and fell over into visioning, curled up in the fetal position, cheek resting on her palm.

She saw herself standing naked in a sun-bright field at Stonehaven. The primitive wheat was high, to her mid-thigh, and she brushed the tops with her finger tips. Her hair was down, and it shifted with a warm breeze. She remembered having sex in that field with a solar power, Diana by her side. She remembered what it was to be filled with that warmth. In her dream she looked up from the grass, and there he stood. Bright he was, and she squinted. His skin shifted through all the colors skin can have, pale to dark and back. His hair, long, shifted with his skin. But what caught her attention was his eyes. No mortal colors, his eyes shifted through the spectrum of light. Prismatic, his eyes shifted through the colors with their own light, illumined from within. Cycling each within each, all equal.

He smiled at her, she smiled back. He stepped forward, holding out his hand. She put her fingers in his hand. A jolt went through her, taking her to her knees before him. An erection grew steadily before her eyes. He stepped forward and she kissed it, just the tip, pursing her lips, sucking slightly. She heard him exhale, just louder than the breeze rustling through the tall grass around her.

She shifted her weight, to sit back on her heels and felt a pull on her foot and looked down behind her. Small roots from the grass had grown over her feet, and she couldn't move them. The deity stepped back from her. She looked up, face pleading, but the deity smiled at her, his eyes coalescing in and out of rainbow colors. She looked down again, and when she looked back up he was gone.

She felt a deep pain in her womb, and sobbed. She came back to presence on the floor of the cave, sobbing, with the deep pain cramping inside her. She realized there was light in the room through her eyelids. She sat up and opened her eyes.

Squatting before her was a Priestess, naked, wearing only the cylindrical black head piece, with a lit candle on either side. It was bright, and the Priestess was outlined in a golden glow.

"I am the Moon Halter," a voice from the shadow of the mask said. "Lay down on your back." Angelica did as she was told. The Moon Halter sat on her thighs, holding her down, facing her. Moon Halter leaned forward and pushed the poncho up over Angelica's breasts, and put her hands of either side of Angelica's lower belly. Angelica felt a force pouring into her that began hot and turned very cold. Moon Halter twisted her palms out, then in, pressing hard. The voice spoke, "One year from today you shall bleed again. For now, it is best you do not conceive. But your blood must be normal for you to carry the dragon for its full gestation, and for you to grow. You will be as a high performing athlete."

Angelica realized she'd been holding her breath, and exhaled. Moon Halter did a little frog leap until she was sitting astride Angelica's belly. She leaned forward with both hands in the center of Angelica's chest, over her heart. Angelica could barely inhale against the pressure. She could feel her heart beat against her ribs, faster now. Suddenly she could hear her heart beat in her breath. Moon Halter leaned forward, listened, and then nodded.

"Red child, child born of blood and suffering, do you swear to protect and keep secret the Order of the Fleur de Vie, upon pain of death, that your heart may burst?"

"Yes," Angelica whispered. "I do"

Moon Halter grunted then made a twisting motion with her palms, first one way then the other. Angelica felt something lock in place in her heart. Moon Halter stood up, standing over Angelica like a vanquishing Amazon then stepped away. Leaning down she picked up the candles, blew them out, and the room descended into darkness.

Angelica felt a slight draft from what must have been the door closing behind Moon Halter. She sat up with difficulty, one hand on her belly. She groaned and whispered, "Ow. Fuck, that hurt." She put her hand on her chest, and probed how sore it was; her sternum ached. She took a sip of water and realized she had to pee and wanted to throw up. She recalled seeing a depression in the floor off to her left and stood up to find her way to it. Standing up made her dizzy, and then nausea rose up in her like a wave. She got down quickly to her hands and knees and crawled as fast as she could.

She got there in time, but all she had to throw up was bile, which burned horribly coming up. When she could, she squatted and peed. She crawled back to her basket and sat again. She took another drink. .Her mind stayed blank awhile, not thinking, random images percolating in the background. She put a hand down and felt it make contact with the dragon. She looked at it, and saw her hand outlined in blue. She looked at her other hand, and saw that her whole arm, indeed all of her that she could see, was glowing with a faint blue light.

In the corner of her eye she saw a small flash of blue light over where the small shaft led up out of the corner of the room. She remembered the draft she'd felt there, and her assumption that it was a ventilation shaft. The little light paused then scrabbled around the room on a narrow shelf and down onto the floor. It paused again, faint, pale, glowing, up against the wall. She realized it must be a mouse, or a rat of some kind.

And then she heard a new sound, a slithering sound of something sliding through dust. It was as if her Soul whispered to her, "You are dust." And it shivered her. She thought to herself, "Oh, no."

And then it came, the long pale electric blue line of it down through the ventilation shaft. And it kept coming. Long. Sliding. Blue. Snake. And it kept coming. The mouse squeaked once and went silent and held still.

The snake continued to emerge from the ventilation shaft. It slid along the slight shelf until it would no longer hold the weight and it fell down the wall, making a plopping sound when it landed on the floor.

The mouse didn't stand a chance. The snake slid over toward the mouse, and the mouse didn't move. The snake reared slightly, struck, and with another squeak the mouse was in its mouth.

Then there was just one blue light, long and sliding, still emerging from the ventilation shaft.

Horror was just one of her emotions.

Then she thought, "This is Life and Death. I may die."

And the snake kept sliding out of the shaft. Near twenty feet long, it was a snake out of legend. She remembered the High Priestess talking about it on their ride up into the hills. A bull snake of gigantic proportions living in the holes dug into the sides of the buttes they'd ridden past.

After a period of not moving, which she assumed was because it was eating the mouse, the snake slid over to her. It lifted its head toward her only slightly. Then it turned its head toward the dragon beside her. The dragon didn't stir. The snake returned its attention to her, rising up till it was higher than her head. She knew it was regarding her, perhaps assessing her potential as prey. Or predator.

In her terror Angelica reached for the dragon, and called to it. There was no response.

The snake hissed at her. Her brain reconstructed the sounds of the hissing as words. "I am King here. It will not help you," it said. "You ignore me at your peril."

"I assure you I am paying attention." she said aloud.

"Ressspect," she heard it say. It said. "You must understand the difference between myth and reality. Your dragon will not kill you, I will. I am Life and I am Death; and I am alive because of it. When you have killed, you will know." Then it struck, biting her on the breast, near her heart.

She screamed, and grabbed the snake close to the back of its head. She moved to pull it off but the pain was unbearable, and she became afraid that she would tear flesh. The snake thrashed, not letting go, but wrapping itself around her like a constrictor. She jumped up, holding on, but there was nowhere to run. She was afraid to let go, and she couldn't defend herself if she didn't. She tried to step on it, but it slithered from underfoot. Completely wrapped around her, it squeezed. In her terror she forgot to breathe and she passed out, knowing she was going to die.

When she came to, the snake was gone. She sat up and looked around. Her dragon was still there, glowing red faintly. But next to it was another blue form, a human form. "I am Falling Star Wen. I am a Face of She Who Comes. You are in my land, and I come to help those who are initiating. Come, clean yourself, then sit."

Angelica washed away the blood from her breast, relieved to find only two small crescent moon shaped cuts. She washed between her legs and placed a clean pad between them, holding it in place with a low slung strip of her tunic as a belt. She noticed there seemed to be less blood than she would have expected. She took another drink from the jug, noting how much she'd used and how she would have to start rationing. She sat and the Falling Star turned slightly to face her.

"If you live, you will come to understand much," the Goddess began. "The stones need water to bring forth life. The falling stars need water to bring forth life. Without it, their voices go as dry as dust. When this task is done," she said, stroking the dragon's back. The dragon groaned softly. "When this is done, perhaps you shall be put to work watering stones," she finished, and then she laughed. "I like you. You prefer not to go insane, and therefore you fight. It would make a weaker wen crazy. Therefore, Dragonwen, ask me a question."

Angelica paused and closed her eyes, noticing again that she could see the blue light emanating from her and the Falling Star clearly, eyes open or shut. Her forehead pounded. Finally, her mind racing, seeking the right question to ask a Goddess, "Why? I know the world I've left. It works well for some, not so well at all for many. Why is it like that? And now that I have been set free, now that I have overcome the Barrier, and I can see," she paused. "And I can see in the real world, why is that other world so upside down?" Her eyes started to well up. "Why is there so little virtue among those that have temporal power, and so little power among those that have virtue?"

"Always," the Goddess began, "always there have been two kinds of people. Everyday People, and Mysterious People. The Mysterious People have a different path through the world than the Everyday People. And there are far fewer Mysterious People, which is the way it should be—Mysterious People are not so good at hunting and gathering. Understand that all your people are still evolving. And that all your people are an experiment. Life here is an experiment. The experiment was interfered with long ago. Mysterious people adapt better to the interference, or else they go crazy and break. Everyday people adapt or go crazy, too. But their evolution is slower, and since it happens in the larger group it is slower. The evolution of the Mysterious People is quicker because it is more individual. Among the large group of Everyday People, the interference put the Masculine over the Feminine, and this is why it all seems upside down. Now, the damage from the interference is so profound that the Everyday People have a barrier between themselves and the world you see. For them it is the Real World. And Mysterious People are now so far from them…the Barrier is so large…You were not born to be a Mysterious Person. But you have become one. And this is now your part in the experiment. From their place on the other side of the Barrier the Everyday People want Certainty. But if there was Certainty as to the outcome, then it would not be an experiment."

Angelica had not been able to stop the tears falling from her eyes.

She had not sobbed; the tears were running in steady streams.

The Goddess, with great tenderness, said, "Live, child. Choose to live. Choose Life." The Goddess reached out a hand and cupped Angelica's cheek. A spark of light flew from the Goddess's hand into the center of her skull. It was as if a door opened and she was sucked out, pulled at incredible speed, the images of the landscape around and below her too blurred to make out. She stopped somewhere on a high plateau, looking west at a waxing moonset. Suddenly a bright green falling star flew across the sky, low, south to north. It left a hissing sound, a whisper of whish in its wake. She sat down, naked on the earth, and watched the sky until she fell asleep sitting there, a breeze lifting her hair.

When she woke, the cave, was filled with light—normal light. She looked around and saw that it was coming from the now open door through which she'd entered. She looked around for her dragon, and suddenly knew it had withdrawn inside her again. She could feel its presence, and it stirred within her. She looked up opposite her and saw a man in a rope skirt with the cylindrical mask over his head. Wordlessly, it pointed at the door. She drank the last of her water, letting some spill down her chest. She gathered up her poncho and left everything else. As she crawled through the door the man grabbed her belt and cut it, sending her back out into the tunnel naked. The light was blinding, coming through the open door into the antechamber.

She emerged and was helped by strong hands taking her arms on either side that led her to the saddle frame, and helped her sit, swaying, and the poncho was draped double over her shoulders.

The voice from the throne spoke. "Red child, child born in blood and suffering, do you swear to protect and keep secret the Order of the Fleur de Vie, upon pain of death, that your heart may burst?"

She slitted her eyes open to take in the image of the High Priestess on the throne. "Yes," she said simply.

"Then what do you choose? Life? Or Death?"

"Life," she said.

There was a silence, as if it was allowed to her to reconsider. When she said nothing, the voice said, "Return." Two sets of hands helped her up and she walked, between them, down the tunnel to the outer door. The door opened, and she was pushed out into the sunshine. The door closed behind her.

She stood there, shielding her eyes with her hand from the bright morning sun and gazed around. Regina's silhouette appeared in front of her. "Here, sit down. Let me put these on you." She felt her sandals being strapped to her feet. She heard Regina laugh. "My, my. Come on, red child, let's get you to the steam room."

Angelica stood up, but couldn't walk. She took a long look around, turning in place, stunned by the return to the real world. She looked down and saw the scabs forming on her breast from the snakebite. The terror came back to her, and her legs started to shake so violently she sat down again, and wept, looking at the bite mark.

Regina realized Angelica wasn't coming along behind her and stopped, turning around. When she saw what Angelica was looking at she smiled. She walked up to the weeping wen unbuttoning her shirt.

Angelica looked up when she realized Regina was standing over her. Regina had pulled her shirt aside, showing Angelica two white scars on her left breast over her heart, looking like paired crescent and decrescent moons. She looked up at Regina's smiling face. "You, too?" she asked.

"Yeah," Regina said. "I had to know. Prettier than a tattoo, don't you think? Come on," holding out her hand.

Angelica wiped her nose with the back of one hand while she extended the other to Regina. "Shit, woman. What don't you know?"

"Wen," Regina corrected her. "I don't know if we'll ever get the stink off you. You need a bath. Come on."

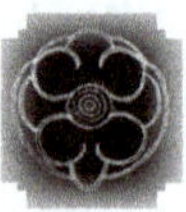

22

THE NOT OK CORRAL

With Angelica gone on her Initiation, Quinn found himself at loose ends. The first day she was gone he discovered a library in a long shed between two cabins. The collection was dedicated to books on overcoming the Kundalini Barrier, and the Alchemies and Tantras, Yogas, and Qi-work, and the Meditation practices of many cultures. There was another collection dedicated to the Divine Feminine in myth and practices. There was a section on Metaphysics. There was a small section on martial arts that caught his eye. Some were old books, hard cover with black and white photographs. "A Cowboy Library," Quinn thought. He smiled. "Just how I imagined it would be."

On the second day she was gone he gave up the library in frustration. He needed to understand some things, things about what was happening to him and what was likely to happen to him. This had always been a problem for him, back to the original fight. Things would happen to him, but with no teacher he had no context for them. He had no names. He knew they told him he had blown through the Kundalini Barrier, survived a horrible metaphysical attack (who were those people, anyway?), been Enlightened (twice!), stopped something big and bad from happening. Encountered, and hosted perhaps, the Enemy of the Divine Feminine, De Murgos. And then he'd spent 30 years waiting at its command, afraid that if he did anything else, it, too, would have grave consequence.

He had questions. And the books provided scant new material. Then there was the matter of his recent absorption to just beneath his skin of a fine mesh net composed of dragon ash. What was that? What was happening? He had a working theory that it was a carbon fiber net, little interlocking dodecahedral molecules.

Then there was the ointment Alam had given him to dye his skin so no one would mistake the grayness that resulted from the black net under his white skin for sepulchral pallor. He didn't have to apply it as often anymore, the red-brown color seemed to have become permanent.

Once again, as for most of his life, he was not himself. His refuge was that he was that which said "I" in himself. Identity, by any external measure, was an odd flux, accelerating in its differentiation, cutting short any integration time. His time under the curve was shrinking. He could feel it in the episodes of inner illumination he'd experienced around Angelica.

And then there was that. He was her bodyguard. He was forty years older than her. They were intimate. A voice in his head, one of his favorite parts of himself, said, "You're a lucky dog. Stop whining."

On the third day he was walking along the corral from breakfast on the way back to library, past a couple of the hands, smiling to himself at that very thought, when they jumped him, landing kicks on his back as they leapt from the top rail. "Really?" he said, when he recovered his balance. "From behind?"

"Orders, sir," one the younger men said.

"Shut the fuck up," the other said, and came wading in at Quinn, fists up. He swung, Quinn ducked under it, stepped in under the arm and gut punched him, knocking him to the ground, gasping for breath. The second one had followed the first one on in and Quinn caught him on the chin, knocking him out. By the time Quinn could turn around two more were on him, with more behind them.

Quinn took a glancing blow along his temple. "Ow, fuck! What the fuck, man?" Quinn rabbit punched him three times and threw him into two advancing men as he kicked another in the side, hearing ribs crack for his effort. Six down. How many more? Quinn only knew he was surrounded by bodies, and kicks were starting to land. One took him behind the knee and he went down.

"Stop!" he heard Slim's voice call out. Everyone froze. "Back off!" he snarled. A path opened. Quinn had a quick vision of Slim on one knee, pistol drawn, aiming at him, and then Slim fired.

The slug hit him in the top of the thigh of his upraised leg. "Ow, fuck!" Quinn said again. "You shot me!"

"Yeah, sorry about that. Orders," Slim drawled. "Hold still." Slim kept a bead on him. "Watch," Slim said, nodding at Quinn's thigh.

There was a thin trickle of blood, oozing from the wound, and the bullet oozed out with it. Everyone gawked except Quinn, who went into a rage, tore the top board off the corral and swung it, knocking the pistol from his hand. With a roar he leapt, knocking Slim over with his lead foot, standing on his chest, and brought the jagged plank end to hover over Slim's throat.

Slim lay on his back waving his empty hands. "They had to know! They had to know!"

"For fuck's sake. You shot me! You asshole!"

Suddenly the men pulled back. Regina Moon Halter was standing there, a golden halo around her head. She flicked her hand and the men vanished. Not really, but they backed off so fast it seemed like it.

"Quinn," she said. "Come here."

Quinn threw away the board and walked toward her. "Come with me," she said. She put her arm in his, and led him away.

Slim sat up, his hands shaking violently, his head shaking from side to side. "Fuck, that was close. Fuck. It was only a .22," he said, looking over his shoulder at their departing forms.

Once in the library Regina sat Quinn down. Then she had him stand up again and take off his pants. "Let me take a look at that." All they could see was a black mark the diameter of the round, less than a quarter of an inch, with just the faintest trace of oozing blood.

"That's what I thought," Regina said.

"That's what *you* thought?" Quinn asked edgily.

"You're a lucky guy. Stop whining," she said, looking up at him from under waggling eyebrows.

"You heard that, did you?"

"Yes. Look. Nobody knows what you are. You don't know what you are. You're more than a mere mortal now, that's for sure. We're entrusting Angelica to you. We need to know something about you, and what you're capable of. And if you're still sane."

Feeling calmer, Quinn growled, "Yeah, well, I gotcher sanity right here." He grabbed his phallus and shook it at her.

"Asshole," Regina said, smiling, and punched him on the thigh right next to the entry wound. She stood up. "I have to go check on the others." Then as she walked out the door she said, "And I may come take you up on your offer of sanity later."

"Ow, shit! Regina, that hurt," Quinn whined after her, rubbing his leg.

Despite putting six men on the ground in a matter of seconds, the damage Quinn had done to the other men was light. Two cracked ribs, a sore jaw, and bruises, including some bruised egos. These men were all trained in the Order's hybrid form of martial arts, and the speed and power of an old man had bested them. It was as if Quinn had been holding back. Slim was the most shaken up about it, feeling guilty for having shot a man when it wasn't in self-defense. He was shaking and couldn't get a handle on it. Regina decided to just let him be and find his own resolution.

She returned to the library to find Quinn sitting at a reading table, still without his pants on. He was looking at a book. She walked over to him and put her hand on one shoulder and looked over to see what he was looking at. It was a picture of a saint, of some kind, in the process of falling down, with a golden whirlwind taller than he that was attached to the top of his head.

"Is that it? Is that what it looks like?" she asked quietly.

"Yeah, that's it, until the part where the whole thing just disappears inside you. It just drains in through the top, and then everything is different."

"So that's the Enlightenment, then?"

"I think so. I mean there's all kinds of over-application of the word these days. Made up stuff. And some writers no doubt mean something different. And then there's illumination moments, little peak experiences along the way. So, I don't know what you call it, never having had a tradition. But it's what happened to me. Twice."

"What are you looking for?"

"Seeking to understand. Seeking to understand 'Why me?' in part. Mostly trying to figure out where it came from, and why, at least the second time, this deity or whatever the men told me about was present the second time."

"You mean De Murgos?"

"Yeah. Why it was within me, and then why it left. Then why it told me to wait and then never came back again."

"We know about the book. The one Matthews wrote about you. Now that we know about it, we're all reading it. It was a fucked up thing that happened to you."

"Yeah."

"Yeah. Well, when you did that thing to Matthews, there at the end, that left him ecstatic and blind, when you used the Earth like that, did you know what would happen to him?"

"No. Remember that he was the first person I'd told the story to in over thirty years. I'd never done anything like that before. And, to be honest, I wasn't really aware of Her when I did it. Now I know that not only is She real, but there's this whole other fight going on between Her, and apparently this thing that was in me." He paused.

With great gentleness Regina asked him, "What do you want, Quinn?"

"I want to know everything about it. Is it a being in and of itself? Is it a substance separate from a being that a being can hide inside a person? I want to know everything there is to know about the Golden Whirlwind. But there's so little. Almost nothing. All this," he said gesturing to the walls of books around him, "All this and only one reference I've been able to find. And it's just a picture."

"Well, Quinn, I know somebody who might be able to help. She knows more about books than anybody I know. And, you know what, Quinn? You may just have to be the one that writes that book. I know that the Hermetic Tradition in the West is attributed to Thrice-Enlightened Hermes, but we don't know much about that, either. But now we know someone Twice-Enlightened. And he's got to know more than any of the rest of us."

She stood directly behind him then, put a hand on each shoulder, leaned forward and kissed him on top of the head. "At least you're on our side. And that makes me happy." She hugged him from behind.

When Quinn stayed stiff and unresponsive, she asked, "You are on our side, right?"

"That's what you want to know? That's what all this is about? All this testing?" When Regina said nothing, he said, "I'll tell you what. The most I'm willing to say is that I'm on Her side. I like you. So I'm with you, and you're with your people, so I'm here. But the more real reason I'm here is that young wen up there in that cave. I went through what she went through. And I know how terrifying it is to live through that and be alone. I know the despair that had me hiding in the wilderness for five years. I waited for forty years and, in the end, I lost my life in the process. No time left to ever become what I might have been. I've got nothing else. She's why I'm here."

"Then our interests are aligned, at least. We want her because of the dragon. It's the first manifestation of its kind in centuries." She sighed, and slid her hands down his shoulders.

"That, and one other thing. I'm here because of the Antecedence, the Antecedence of the Feminine. When I heard that for the first time in the Men's Circle I didn't know what to think. It was a revelation—that Life itself evolved with the Feminine in the Antecedent. And what that means for the way we think about everything."

"What do you think it means, Quinn?"

"Well, the way it was presented, you, meaning you and the rest of the wen, aren't asking to be treated as superior. Just antecedent. I don't know what all that means. It creates a whole shift in my feelings toward wen. And it pulls the rug out from under the patriarchal belief that men are superior because they were created first. It means men aren't the superior gender, really. At least not in that way, anyway. It means men are consequent and derivative. And that messes with my feelings, too."

"Say more about the feelings, Quinn."

"Knowing the truth, I don't feel lesser because I'm derivative. I don't feel diminished. I feel stronger because I think I have a better understanding of my purpose. My purpose is to support the Feminine. Just because I respect the Feminine more, now, than I did before, and providing that support makes me feel meaningful."

"Yes," Regina said, but no more, watching and waiting to see where Quinn went next.

"And there's another shift," Quinn continued after a pause. "There's a mythic level shift here, and it's operating inside me. I can feel things literally shifting. If the Feminine is Antecedent, if the Feminine was created first, then it makes sense that the Feminine is the True Creator, and that the Divinity behind such a creation would have to be Feminine, too.

"And you and your friends show Her to me. I spent a lot of time with Eva. Eva showed me the Divine Feminine manifesting through her many times, and I spent a lot of time in the presence of, well, that Presence. It spoke to me. I could feel the love emanating from it, different than Eva's love for me.

"I would feel compelled without feeling under compulsion."

Suddenly he felt a surge from the Resonance of the Higher Heart pulsing in Regina's hands into the chakras in his shoulders. Then he felt a surge of energy embrace his body entirely from behind.

A voice, huskier than Regina's, said, "Yes. I am compelling."

Quinn smiled, knowing he was in the Presence of the Divine Feminine again. He slid off his chair, turning as he did, went to his knees and bowed before Her. He felt fingers lift his chin and he gazed upon Her, an almost transparent veil hung before Regina's face. Regina smiled at him through the veil, and he smiled back. Then the veil smiled. He gazed upon Her eyes, then he saw the whole of Her, a long dress and shawl, thick dark hair being lifted by some unfelt breeze. Her arms opened for him, and Regina's arms came along in the same gesture.

He rose and came into their arms. He stopped with his face just beyond the veil, gaze filled with Love for the Beauty before him. The veil leaned in and kissed him. Little tingles of electricity sparked on his lips, and traveled through and into him, lighting him up from within. He could see the golden glow from a halo in his peripheral vision, and felt a quick moment of fear. He ears filled with a shushing sound and the Heartbeat pulsed against his lips.

The arms embraced him, Regina wrapped her legs around his waist. They kissed for a long time, letting the Heartbeat race through them, settling here, then jumping there, until it filled them up and they became one Heartbeat.

He turned, carrying Regina and the Presence and laid them on the table. Regina kept her legs around him, holding him close. When her legs relaxed she broke the kiss. Quinn pushed himself up and came standing. He unbuttoned her shirt, letting it fall open. He kissed her heart, then her diaphragm, then her low belly.

His hand went to her belt. Regina was wearing jeans tucked into red leather boots. He had a brief vision of taking the boots off, then the jeans, and decided that would take too long. He undid the belt and snap, lowering the zipper. He gazed at their faces, now averted to the side, eyes closed and smiling.

He pulled the jeans down as far as they would go. As he watched, the image of the Divine Feminine pulled her long dress up around her waist, and then let go and laid back, arms spread. Quinn ducked down and came up between Regina's legs, spreading her thighs while her booted heels hung down over his back.

He gazed at Regina's phulva, and the Goddess's at the level of the veil, and sighed. The words of the first Craft appeared in his mind. "To contemplate is to adore…to enter is to worship". He drew close and inhaled.

He kissed her. He kissed Her. Using his tongue he slowly parted Her, and her. Keeping his upper lip at the top, he lowered his mouth to cover their opening and inserted his tongue. He sucked lightly on the whole of them. He could feel the gland of her ecstasy expanding, extending and lowering.

When it touched his tongue they sighed. Regina effused into his open mouth, relaxing, filling him with more than he could swallow, and only at the end was there the slightest tremor. In his mind he could sense Her effusion as well. He thought he heard the word "effulsion" or maybe "effluxion".

He tasted honey. Honey and salt. He sighed and smiled. Ducking out from under Regina's legs he carefully removed her boots and then peeled off her socks and jeans. He dropped his pants and stepped out of them. Hard and up-curving he stepped forward. He directed himself and stopped, waiting. Waiting for consent.

First, She smiled, then Regina smiled. He heard himself say, "To enter is to worship." He inserted himself, only the tip, and flexed his length. That was all it took for them to effulge again, soaking him and running back along the table on which they lay.

She pulled Quinn down to them. She told him, whispering in his ear, "Become what you are."

An hour later they stopped. She departed, laughing, the echo lasting longer than Her Presence. At some point Regina had put her red leather boots back on. Rising from her knees on Quinn's pants on the floor, now soaked, she laughed at the laughter, hand gripping him like a chin-up bar as she pulled herself up.

"I love She Who Comes," she said.

"As do I," Quinn said. "I love She Who Comes."

"And She loves you, you know," Regina said.

"I feel it, I think. I don't know why but I struggle with some kind of Shame, perhaps Unworthiness, alternating with a deep sense of being Honored."

Regina laughed. "Good!" she exclaimed. "Figure it out for yourself!" and she laughed again. She picked up her clothes and used them to wipe the table down, drying it. They exited the building together through the double doors, and stepped out into the street holding their clothes, naked, arm in arm, their bodies steaming in the cooling air.

When they got to their cabins, oblivious to the many who were watching, kissed thoroughly and laughingly, then parted ways, each to their own cabin across the street from each other. Slim Curly was sitting in the rocker on her porch. When she passed by him, he was grinning broadly. She rewarded him with a smile and entered, going into her room.

On his side of the street Quinn did the same, wondering how Angelica was doing.

23

THE BURNING

With everyone gone from the Barn, and only Calley and Alam left staying in the Mansion, dust was beginning to settle on everything. The location where the fire would start was chosen. It was to be the fireplace on the east wall, second floor. It would be made to look like a chimney fire had burned through to the roof, which would also be burned through, a hole over the southern half of the east bedroom, and holes burned in the intervening ceilings and floors. Water damage was to be created on all the walls around where the fire would go.

"I don't want to do it," Madeleine said. "What if it gets out of control?"

"To whom do you think you are speaking?" Calley replied, with just a hint of pique.

"Oh, yes, that's right. You are the rain."

"I am the rain. The fire will burn nowhere I do not allow it, and no more than I intend."

"The High Council trusts you. I must," Madeleine concluded.

"It will be OK," Eva's ghost whispered in her ear, causing a chill.

"You know it always gives me a chill when you do that."

"Oh yes? How about this?" the ghost said, and stuck her little finger in her mouth, then stuck it wet in Madeleine's ear.

"Oh, hey! Hey! What's that?" Madeleine said, jumping up. The ghost laughed, high, sweet, far away.

Calley shook her head. She couldn't maintain her seriousness all the time now. The time spent hanging out with mortal wen had begun to change her, socialize her. She found herself thinking of herself in lowercase pronouns often. She smiled.

They had gathered in her office, Craft and Alam, Calley, Madeleine, and the ghost. Diana was gone home. They would all be gone up to the rental units on the North County Road after tonight. "You should go now," Calley said to Madeleine. The ghost went with her.

Craft and Alam spread accelerants on the walls and floors, working their way down to the second floor bedroom near the chimney. Calley stood there, watching them. When they were finished, Calley said, "Go. Join the others on the lawn."

Calley stood by herself and regarded the room. The bed, the dressers and tables, the chairs, the exquisite paneling. She felt a moment of regret, another mortal feeling she'd have to get used to. She didn't want to. And yet she did.

Shaking her head to clear it, her long hair twisted in waves. She felt an icy hand on her shoulder, and turned to see the ghost of the Founder, Rachel Adams, dimly in the darkened room. The ghost nodded her head and smiled. Calley heard, "Do it."

Holding her hands out, palms facing each other, she drew between them a thread of lightning. Then she flung it toward the wall beside the chimney, where it sparked and sizzled. Slowly the flame appeared in the paneling. Quickly it spread where the accelerants had been painted. Suddenly the entire wall erupted with a whumpf.

Calley went mist.

The small crowd, the Stonehaven skeleton crew from up on the road, gathered on the lawn and watched the flames dance through the windows, their expressions all of concern. Some wept quietly, despite their confidence in Calley. They were afraid.

The spirits of the land gathered round to watch also. The people felt them at their backs and turned, wonderingly. They seemed as shapes in a newly formed mist, rising from the ground.

Inside, Calley damped the walls and furniture, directing the flames to burn through the ceiling. When the fire was through to the next level she broke out the windows on the second floor. Fed fresh air, the fire whomphed, a sharper sound than before. She spread the fire to the south wall and broke out the window there. On the lawn the people gasped.

She painted fire on the ceiling, directing the fire through to the fourth floor. She painted it on that ceiling also and, burning through to the attic, the flames burst through the roof. The impact on the watching crowd was visceral. In their guts they felt a thrill, and the spirits of the land chittered and whispered behind them. The men found themselves growing hard, and the wen went damp.

They found their hands groping for each other, seeking comfort, finding an exquisite pleasure. Some of the musicians had brought drums, in case the people wanted to sing a dirge to the burning. But the rhythm quickly became more heated. People began to dance, their feet pounding on the grass, shedding clothes. Men's erections bounced in the fading light, hands and mouths found hidden places, opening them to the flames.

The spirits of the land swirled among them. The people's eyes and faces kept turning to take in the fire, now raging through the roof, the flames drawing their own fires from them, seeking to add their fires to the flames. With a single loud click lightning rose up from the ground near the dancers, raising all hair with the discharge. Thunder boomed.

The rain poured down so hard the mansion disappeared from sight. The spirits disappeared, and the spell of the sacred fire released the people from its grip. The people ran for the veranda, laughing, and those not yet finished resumed the discharge of their desires.

Alam, Craft, and Madeleine ran for the stairs to find Calley. They found her, standing naked, staring up through the holes in the ceilings and floors, out into the night sky. She wasn't even wet.

She grinned at them. "That was fun."

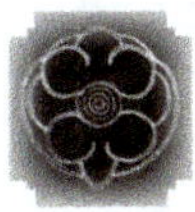

24

GOING IN CIRCLES

"He does not think about us anymore," A. said to Brian, the Master's secretary.

"He thinks only of himself. I never feel the pull of his consideration, which I loved, unless he wants to fuck me. He used to be nice to me, now I am a come-bucket."

"I know the feeling. They used me for years that way. Now I am old. But I learned this," she said, reaching for his forehead. "Let me."

Brian gasped in ecstasy as her fingers touched him. His mind flooded with light, and then darkness as he fainted. A. made no move to catch him as he crumpled to the floor. She picked up the boarding passes from the desk, smiling at the seed of dissent she'd planted.

Thirty hours later A. and the Master were driving slowly past the rental homes on the North County Road.

"I felt him strongly first through here. Then, when I was coming back through I saw this road, here, coming up right here, turn here. A little farther down there's a driveway, that's it, turn there," she said.

They pulled in and drove to the gate. They sat a moment in the car, listening to the engine tick. There, painted on the wall of the gatehouse was the same image as on Leonora's thigh. They got out, walked to the house and squatted down, looking closely at the image. The Master touched it and closed his eyes, while A. watched. When he opened them, he said, "There is more to see here, let's go down."

An intern up in one of the rentals was on security watch, scanning the feeds from the video and wildlife cameras placed around the property. He'd paused the screen to go to the bathroom, and when he returned and fast-forwarded to catch up he nearly missed the car at the gate. He zoomed in, and saw no one it. He keyed the radio microphone and issued the alert, "Security, Security, we have an intruder at the gate. Tape shows two occupants, middle-aged male and female by the looks, car now empty."

On the ridge in the woods between the Mansion and the North County Road, Craft had introduced Alam to the King of Salamanders. They had been conversing about the Highlands Slow Worm, and where Dragons might fit on the Tree of Speciation ("Why fly when you can float?" Craft had just asked) when the Salamander exhaled so heavily that it felt like a hiss in the men's ears. The pressure in their heads formed the words, "Evil comes," and the King disappeared, fading into the rock. Craft's radio crackled with the security alert. "Let's go," he said to Alam. "Follow me."

Matthews was at the Mansion along with Madeleine, Calley, and Eva's ghost. With a tarp over the hole in the roof, and the east end of the Mansion closed off, even with the power off they preferred to work and sleep there, keeping warm with fires in the fireplaces. The ghost was dispatched up the driveway to see where the intruders were. The Goddess, the Seeress, and the Earth Angel gathered in Madeleine's room. She settled before her altar and opened the ritual space, Calley and Matthews taking seats behind her to hold the space. She poured water in her scrying bowl and whispered the incantation of wakefulness over the water. She dropped a sacred bead, carved with the icon of the Order, into the bowl. She leaned over the ripples, relaxed her eyes and waited for the interference pattern to show her what was on the road.

When the bead dropped A. and her Master froze. They felt a wave, a faint pressure, pass around and over them. They stood still, eyes closed, trying to see, as smaller waves moved by.

"The wave came from over there," A. said, pointing into the forest.

"Neither of us know the woods. We'll stay on the road," the Master said. "There's something powerful here, and I intend to find out what it is."

A few steps down the drive A. said, "We're being watched. More than one."

"Where?" the Master asked, having neglected the development of that part of his discernment.

A. held out her hands, turned slowly in a circle. "Over where the wave came from." They both stared in that direction. "There were others but they've gone."

"Damned animals," the Master said, and started forward.

Madeleine saw them as beings of light, but murky, browns like turgid waters swirling through them with thin streaks of colors that nauseated her to look at. Behind the head of the man was a black kite, expanding and contracting like it breathed—a black so deep she could see no feature. She felt it turn its awareness to her, and she pulled back from the thing. Her awareness returned to the room. She quickly covered the bowl with a cloth, held her hand over and uttered a sealing spell.

"They both have power," Madeleine said. "But it's gone toxic in them. These are very bad people."

Eva's ghost returned to the room. "Yes. And there are ghost ties binding her to him. He feels them and controls her. She's much older, too. Maybe even old enough to be his mother. And there's something else."

"Tell me," Calley said.

"There's another ghost. It follows them at a distance. I went up to it and we talked briefly. It says it is the ghost of Regina's father."

"The Lama!" Calley exclaimed, wonderingly. "I need to speak to my sister Bree."

"Wait," Madeleine said, laying her hand on Calley's arm. "I think we should let them see Quinn. Send Matthews out. See what they do. We can always deal with them later."

"Matthews, are you ready?" Calley asked.

"They're in the woods at the north end of the parking lot," Eva's ghost whispered to Madeleine.

She keyed the radio. "Intruders in the woods at the north end of the Mansion parking lot. Everybody stay put. Craft, check in."

Moving quietly down the wooded slope above the parking lot, Craft and Alam stopped when Craft's radio buzzed. He tapped his earpiece and said, "Yes?" and listened.

"Where are you?" Madeleine asked.

"Woods above the lot," he whispered.

"Can you see them?"

"Not yet."

"Stealth mode, Craft. Don't scare them. Code 5."

"Code 5."

A. and the Master began moving around the edge of the gravel lot, keeping to the woods. They froze and squatted down when Matthews walked out of the house into the lot. He went to the farthest of the few cars and the lone truck and opened the door. Before bending to pick a file folder off the seat he stared into the woods, looking just above where the two were hiding.

"That's him," A. whispered. "That's Quinn." The Master clenched his fists until his knuckles turned white. His pale face turned red with rage. The kite glowed black behind his head.

Matthews stood up, closed the door and turned to go back to the house. The Master started forward, as if to attack Matthews but A. laid a hand on his arm. She hissed at him. He stopped, instead seeing in his mind's eye what he would do to Matthews if he could. His hatred rose and gathered itself in a ball of force he pushed away from himself with both hands.

Matthews could feel the rage building behind him. Pretending to drop the folder, he ducked. He felt the ball of energy pass over him, looked up and saw it dissipate in the air beyond him. He picked up the folder, stood up, and walked quickly back toward the Mansion.

"We have to go," A. whispered to the Master. "He knows we're here." Keeping low, running bent over, they skirted the lot, no longer bothering with concealment. The kite was still plainly visible.

Standing back from the tall windows Madeleine and Calley watched them go. Eva's ghost followed them, floating alongside the flicker of the Lama's ghost. Craft and Alam emerged from the woods, just catching a glimpse of the pair jogging up the drive.

When Matthews came through the door he asked, "They gone?"

Madeleine said, "Yes." And then, "Boy, does he hate you."

"You mean Quinn. He hates Quinn."

"That's what that was? Hate?" Calley asked. "And what was that black thing on his back?"

"That was Evil," Madeleine said quietly.

Not stopping to catch their breath A. and the Master piled into the car, started it and backed out onto the road. The Lama's ghost settled into the back seat and the black kite shrank in his presence, and entered completely into the Master. "What is this place, and who are these people?" he asked aloud between deep breaths.

"And how many are there?" A. responded.

The group in the Mansion watched Craft and Alam climb the portico steps. Eva's ghost returned. "I hope we did the right thing, letting them go," Madeleine said to Craft.

"You can't just kill everyone who wanders on the property," he replied.

"Yes, but these two were very bad people. They've been after

Quinn for years. They'd have killed him if they'd caught him. They are the second evil thing that I was told was going to come to Stonehaven. They'll be back," Madeleine said with certainty.

"Well, he's gone now," Craft said.

"And I'm told Matthews will be getting an assignment," Calley added.

25

PURSUIT OF THE FLEUR DE VIE

After the long drive back west out of the mountains A. and the Master headed into the first town they came to on the way down. They drove past a waste management company with a dozen trash haulers on the outskirts of Caintuck Flats and pulled into the parking lot of the first motel that had a vacancy sign. It was called the Ladies First Motel and had a lean-to billboard street side that advertised 'Ladies half price until summer!' written on it by hand. A. almost ran it over pulling in. The parking lot was mostly full for no reason that A. could figure out.

The motel was a u-shaped two-story affair with the office on one end nearest the highway. A. looked over at the Master, and was surprised to see him, eyes closed, leaning forward into his seatbelt hugging himself. She spoke to him, asking him if he was alright. His response was to begin rocking back and forth. "I feel like I'm gonna be sick," he said.

"Hang on," she said as she put the car into park. "We're almost there."

In the office there was a smiling middle-aged woman behind the desk. "Welcome home, y'all. I'm Charlene" she said cheerily.

A replied, "I need a double."

"Sorry, hon. We're all out of doubles. In fact, all I got is two singles, a king and a queen. Which one would you like?"

"The king," A. said tersely. Then, "What are all these cars, all these people doing here?"

"County fair is next weekend and there's a big music festival.

Musicians come from all over the mountains. Used to be just bluegrass, but now they opened it up to different kinds of music, so it's become a bigger draw. OK then. It's a nice room. 218. Has a rear window that looks out on the woods. Got your card?"

A. passed over the card and filled out the registration form. "Can I smoke?" she asked.

"Hells yeah. Just open the window," the clerk said with some emphasis.

When A. drove to the back of the motel all the parking slots were taken. She thought about unloading the Master and leaving him there with the luggage, or backing up to an empty slot and having to haul him and the rest from farther out. "Fuck it," she said and parked behind somebody, blocking them in.

As luck would have it, a young couple emerged into the lot. The man said, "What the fuck! My car's blocked in. What the fuck?"

The woman he was with back-handed him on the arm and pointed up on the balcony at A. escorting the Master with her hand on his elbow, him almost doubled over, dragging a wheeled suitcase with an unsecured laptop case that kept flopping from one side to the other.

"What the fuck, lady?" the man hollered at A.

A. stopped, leaning the Master against the wall. Short tempered now, A. said, "I'll be down in a minute. And in the meantime, you can go fuck yourself." This last part she said with such palpable invective, flipping her hand at him, that he took a step backward. He looked sheepishly at her, then blushed. His girlfriend grabbed him by the arm and said, "Let's go wait in the room."

A. unlocked the door and pushed the Master through. It was a decent enough room. She tried to sit the Master on the bed, where he could fall over if he wanted. He struggled with her briefly, breaking free of her grasp, and set himself down in a chair next to a small table. Rather than hurry back down to get the last suitcases and move the car she let her anger make the young couple wait a little and she sat down in the second chair.

The Master put one arm on the table and laid his head on it. "Oh, it hurts, it hurts," he said. "It's so black, my head is filled with blackness, and it's in my heart. My heart is black, and I'm so angry, so angry!" He picked his head up and pounded on the table with his fist, and glaring hatefully at A., he shouted, "Angry!"

"I know. And if you don't stop shouting everyone else will know it also. Be quiet, we don't need anyone calling the police. I've got to go park. I'll order some carryout when I get back. You should lie down and be quiet."

As she stood up to go back and get the luggage he lunged and grabbed her arm. Again, the rage and hatred twisted his face. "I need it," he stage-whispered. "I need it. And I'll have it, you understand me?" as he gripped her arm hard enough to hurt her.

She leaned forward and stage whispered in his ear, "And you shall have it. I will give it to you. Yes, yes I will." She removed his hand from her arm. "Get ready for it. If you can."

When she arrived back at the room with the second suitcase he was in the shower. Going back outside to move the car she'd felt the young couple watching at the edge of the curtain in their room. She found the young woman's mind and planted a thought: 'You should have just offered to help her'. She was surprised at how merciful she felt, and she didn't like the feeling, so she sent the follow up impulse to the woman to pinch the man's ear and drive him to his knees. As she bumped the second suitcase up the stairs, she heard a satisfying "Ow! Ow! Ow! Ow! Shit! OW! Stop it!" in the voice of the young man sliding out from one of the rooms.

As she backed up to a parking space she turned and looked over her shoulder. The view seemed blurry, as if the window was dirty. She blinked and it seemed as if the haze was over her eyes. When she cleared her eyes she realized she was looking at the blurred outline of a human sitting in the back seat. She snarled at whatever entity it was, "Fuck off." She was out of patience and she started to accumulate power in her right hand. The form disappeared.

She returned again from parking the car out front near the office and the Master was laying naked, belly down on the bed, hips cocked slightly to the side, eyes closed tightly, masturbating. While A. was ordering a pizza delivery, he fell asleep. She decided to take a shower while she waited, so she would be ready to begin with the ritual abuse after they ate. She was tired, and wanted to sleep.

By the time she heard the knock at the door she'd showered, brushed her hair and used the steam in the air to soften her eyeliner so it smeared more easily under and over her eyelids. She was fitting herself into the harness when the knock came. She'd shrugged into a sheer robe with a jungle flower pattern, open all down the front. She cursed in frustration, having forgotten she'd ordered and carried the harness into the room. She got cash from her wallet and opened the door, remembering she was holding the harness by the cock in her hand at the last moment, and quickly she stepped behind the door, opening it just enough, she thought, to get the box in.

The delivery boy, a young man actually, was standing in the opening, positioned so he could see the naked Master, still asleep on the bed. She watched him raise his eyebrows, pulling his head back, mouthing the word "Wow."

She smiled sweetly. "You see? This is what I have to deal with."

He stepped back to the side so he wouldn't have to see it. That's when A. realized that the box was too big to come through the door in a level position. She wasn't going to set the harness down on the 'who-knows-how-long-since-it'd-been-cleaned' floor, so she stepped back and opened the door as far as she could, nodded behind her and said, "You're just going to have to bring it in."

He looked uncertainly at her, then at the cash in her hand, and stepped through to put the box on the table. Once he was in, she closed the door almost completely so that when he turned around he got a full frontal view of A., naked but for the robe falling from a shoulder, holding out money in one hand, holding a phallus with a harness hanging from it in the other. "You see what I have to deal with?" she asked in a low voice.

The delivery boy nodded his head yes, then shook his head no, then shook his head yes again.

A. laughed and took a half step forward. "You like what you see?" she asked, playing with him, swinging the harness a little farther forward.

He said, "Uh, uh. Uh," then he reached forward, grabbed the money, and bolted through the door. She touched his arm briefly as he passed, sending an impulse of forgetfulness into him.

"Keep the change," she said. Then under her breath she said, "And don't change," meaning, don't ever become like him, the Master. And she closed the door. When he got to his car he realized he'd run down the stairs to the parking lot, but for the life of him he couldn't remember why he'd been running.

She closed the door and looked down at the Master. He was still asleep on his belly, drooling on the bed covers, both hands buried under him, clearly wrapped around his phallus. She slipped her free hand under him and found that he was still erect. He snorted in his sleep at her touch. She decided she was hungry, and she'd eat first. She laid the harness down on the foot of the bed and sat at the table, getting a piece of pizza from the box. After the first two bites she sat back and regarded the room and then suddenly she found herself regarding her life.

She looked at the man, almost half her age, naked and drooling on the bed, sneered in disgust, and then turned the disgust on herself, wondering at how it was that she came to be in bondage to this man, and to his father, and to his grandfather before him, compelled to do as they commanded her.

She remembered her mother only in dreams. She'd been abandoned by her at ten, her mother having fled what she was certain was profound physical and emotional abuse by her father, a student of this Master's grandfather. She'd found out later, searching as an adult, that her mother had died of an apparent overdose four years after she'd left.

When the abuse by the Master's grandfather had begun A. was twelve years old. Her father, if he noticed at all, turned a blind eye to it. The old man, now long dead, had used power not only to seduce her, but to hypnotize her into believing she liked it, that it made her special. And she was treated as special. It was this hypnosis that kept her from speaking about it to anyone, even at school.

She lost her virginity that first year and by the time she was fourteen she'd done everything there was to do, and had everything that could be done to her done. By the time she was sixteen the old man began to introduce her to playing games, training her in both dominance and submissive roles. The son, the Master's father, was brought into the picture when she was seventeen and she was given to him to be used however he wished when she was eighteen. The hypnosis held, and she would do whatever he wanted, and submit to it as if she was doing it willingly.

After finishing school she was brought in to the family business—ensnaring people into false beliefs about their own personal magical power and learning how to compel others to do one's bidding. She began to discern what was real and what was fantasy in what was being taught. She began to accumulate real power herself, learning to compel others and create illusions in their minds. She helped move the entire operation to America.

In her mid-twenties she turned mean. Horrific impulses of hatred and loathing started rising up in her, and she was clueless as to the source. She hated her slavery to these men but found herself unable to resist the compulsion to do exactly what they told her to do, and to believe that she wanted to do it, and that she liked it. She knew in her mind that there was something wrong about it, and when she was not in their presence she knew that their behavior toward her was loathsome, but that she couldn't find that awareness when she was with them. She couldn't even find fear, just the anticipation that whatever painful or pleasurable task she was given she would feel accomplished and satisfied that she had pleased them, and would take pride in it.

By the time she was given to the grandson, her current master, she was almost twenty five years older than him. She'd been unable to resist when she'd been compelled to crawl to him, blindfolded, carrying the lash between her teeth. He'd used it on her, being tutored by his father on every stroke. She'd become shamelessly orgasmic by the end of the session, and her psychic allegiance was transferred.

But this one, the current one, had proclivities and weaknesses that eased the compulsion she carried within. Sometimes she found herself able to resist, and even disobey, not only in secret but in the moment. Sometimes she could even hate him when in his presence. The hatred would make her feel wicked, and it was a delicious wickedness.

She remembered the fight with this person she'd been searching for periodically for years, this Quinn person. She'd only been peripherally involved in the initial fight, and, although the Master believed fervently that Quinn was responsible for the magick that caused his mother to cross the median and slam into an oncoming semi, she thought it was more likely that one of their magicks backfired on the Master's mother. She understood his desire for revenge, although she didn't share it at all. She was tired of looking, and relieved that they'd found him.

She sighed, wiping her hands on a napkin. She stood up and strapped herself into the harness, made of the softest oiled black leather. Over the years she'd adapted it so that its use would always bring her pleasure. The phallus was fitted so that it was directly on her clitoris, with a continuous curved extension that she could insert in herself. She could feel every thrust and tremor all the way in.

This Master, when he became overwrought and angry, could only regain his composure if he was dominated and abused. With a feeling of delicious meanness, she decided that she would dispense with the usual foreplay of tongue and finger action. She would dispense with lubrication. She climbed up on the bed behind him, spit on the head of her phallus and entered him, not quickly, but slowly, making him feel every inch in his unprepared ass.

He woke up when she was halfway in, shouting and cursing that it was painful. She reached forward with one hand, grabbed his hair and pulled his head back. She leaned forward and whispered in his ear, "Take it, bitch." He moaned when he heard this, collapsing into passivity. He moaned again when she was fully inserted.

She reached under him, past his hands, and felt for his phallus. As she suspected, the erection was gone. The pegging was too intense for him to stay erect. Later she would have to manipulate him into a restored erection and climax. She cherished the control she had over him in the moment. Maybe this time she would make him masturbate himself. This time, she thought, she just might make him eat it. She believed that she, personally, was so advanced in her alchemy that she was certain she could afford to waste it.

She withdrew her phallus almost to the end, then plunged back into him so hard he cried out. "Bitch," she said and slapped the back of his head. She plunged her length into him again and again until his cries became moans. She noticed the black kite begin to emerge from under his skull and spread out like a hood. She didn't want to be that close to it, so she withdrew and told him to roll over. She reinserted herself and changed her angle, so that the head of her phallus was directly against his prostate and moved slowly back and forth. A drop oozed from him and she took it with her finger and brushed his lips with it, smiling. She whispered again, "Fuck yourself with your hands."

He remained unresponsive except for little groans, laying there with his eyes closed. She withdrew some and hammered against his prostrate with such force that he returned from whatever infantile place he'd retreated to and his eyes popped open. She told him again, "Fuck yourself with your hands." And, almost as if he was compelled, he began to play with himself, stroking himself into hardness while she remained still. When he was hard she started moving again as he quickened his stroke with his hands.

He didn't last long. She smiled delightedly when he started grunting as he came. Then something broke inside her—she could almost hear a tearing, ripping sound right below her diaphragm, and she found she could hate him. His eyes were closed so that he didn't see the wonder on her face. Before he was even done twitching she was out of him, and fleeing to the bathroom lest something in her demeanor give her away.

She got into the shower harness and all. Under the hot water the hatred dropped down inside, passing her low belly and entering into her sex. She took the soap and started masturbating the phallus, and thereby masturbating herself. She had a hate-gasm that was so intense, so extraordinary, that she squirted, essence running out the edges of the harness and down her thighs.

She unstrapped the harness and threw it out on the floor. Her hatred was so ecstatic that she masturbated again, laughing with her hatred, a long, drawn-out series of sounds that, with what sounded like a howl of laughter, she rained again, an orgasm that was rare for her to achieve.

She stopped to catch her breath, then felt the Master's presence.

She wasn't startled when he pulled the shower curtain aside and stared at her. She could feel her hatred collapsing within her. She looked down, tilting her head in deference and so he wouldn't see her eyes. She knew that if she let him do that it would reinforce her compulsion. He might, sensing a change in her, even ask her about her behavior. "What are you doing?" he asked in a slow, sly manner.

She shook her head no, and said, "Just finishing." She grabbed a towel, brushed past him, and sensed no change. She said, "I'm starving. Let's eat. You go ahead, because I already had a piece while you were napping." And with the abrupt change to the air of the banal she felt the attention of his permanently immature mind turn to food.

She walked to the table, naked and toweling herself, picked up a piece of pizza and offered it to him. His composure restored by the pegging, her composure restored by her capacity for deceit, she risked looking up at him from under her brow, and he didn't even bother to look at her, and received the food with a notable absence of gratitude and a restored sense of it being his due.

Her cover re-established, she relaxed, grabbed a smoke and the lighter out of her purse and went to the back window, opened it and leaned out, sighing. He turned on the TV, ignoring her completely.

"This will be interesting," she thought, reaching deep within and touching the spark of hatred she now carried there in secret. She allowed herself a small shiver of delight.

In the back office behind the check-in counter Charlene sat down with a sigh, not even bothering to pull her underwear back on. She'd seen the whole interlude on the security cameras that were hidden in the smoke detector. Every room had one. It was illegal, and most of the time she didn't bother to watch, but she'd seen the altercation in the parking lot while she was on the phone with the security people in the vacation rentals back out by Stonehaven, and she'd been ordered to keep an eye on them. She was told they were dangerous people.

She dropped her panties on the floor in the puddle of her own orgasm and moved them around with her foot before the fake wood soaked up too much and might start to warp and buckle. He didn't seem all that dangerous to her, but now she—the older woman—she was a dangerous person.

A. sighed as she finished her smoke, stripping the burning tip and turning to throw the butt in the trash. She looked in the full-length mirror on the bathroom door, seeing the start of the sag to her skin, her arms, and belly and thighs and breasts. She saw the lines forming in her face, and the turkey neck beginning to cord out from her throat. The alchemical and inner energetic work kept her looking twenty years younger than she was, she didn't even color her hair, preferring that the white streaks gave her mien a severity. But age was coming. So too was Death. The thought occurred to her that she might no longer have to wait for Death to be free of her slavery.

Then she felt the pull of his attention again, pulling her toward him. He said, "Come here, Angel. I got something I want to show you."

When she got close to him, he said, "Knees." Then, "Stick out your tongue."

26

THE FOLLOWING SWELL

In the morning A. was up early and dressed, snacking on pizza and washing it down with hotel coffee. Occasionally she'd glance at the Master and sneer at his snoring and drooling. She knew that when he woke, he'd return to being his nasty and surly self.

She thought she'd review her story so far, looking to see if there'd been anything she'd missed, and if the recent past would show her a pathway into the future. She took up the notepad and pen next to the telephone. For years she'd been following Quinn's trail using one of her powers. She could see a trace of him wherever he went, small particles of blue-white light would appear in his trail a few days after he passed somewhere.

She understood that the particles, which would flash and then disappear when seen, were decaying higher energy. When she would move in the direction Quinn had gone, she would see the flashes of light as his trail and follow it. And, since the energy didn't last long, she would often lose the trail and either pick it up again by zig-zagging, hoping to cross the trail, or she would simply use her intuition to guide her to where he might be. The problem with following the flashes was that they'd disappear, well, not really appear yet when she was close to him.

Sometimes she would just give up the search for months at a time. When she'd figured out that he had a penchant for finding menial work, like dishwashing, she'd started checking out restaurants in small towns. She'd lost him completely a few months ago. How he'd come to this place Stonehaven was a mystery to her. She'd lost time with some sort of diversion into New York. By the time she found out where he'd been, he was already gone and travelling quickly. She'd picked up the trail again in the same town where she'd found him before but had lost it again.

She'd been close up on the County Road back in the summer—she could feel him nearby. But the other road, the one that led down to the Gate House, had been invisible to her. She paused, realizing that it would have had to have been a powerful Magic that would have kept that road hidden.

She was amazed that she had found him, still there, still in that place. It didn't bother her that what she felt around him was different than how he'd felt all the other times she'd been close. She could see him now, and see energy coming off him that she hadn't sensed, but she rationalized it by projecting that he would have different fields surrounding him at different distances. And this time, the power coming off the man that she was unknowingly believing was Quinn was so strong that she had no doubts.

She looked down at her notes, wrote the question "What next?" and narrowed her eyes, trying to see into the future. The light reflecting off the page shifted when she relaxed her focus. She saw a form embedded in the paper. It was a watermark, she realized.

She picked up the pad and held it an angle to the light and gasped. She recognized the image: it was the outline of the pink flower she'd seen painted on the Gate House, the pink flower she'd seen tattooed high up on the thigh of the young wen back at the Master's house. They were staying in a motel owned by the people out at Stonehaven.

She pursed her lips and exhaled. The coincidences were mounting to a level where the synchronization began to have meaning. She knew they had to go back to Stonehaven. They could not let him flee again.

They must take him. She snarled at the Master, "Wake up. We have to go. We have to get out of here."

Thirty minutes later in the car A. was fuming. The Master was nursing a coffee from a convenience store and, although he could feel what A. was feeling, he chose to ignore it, knowing he could punish her for it later. He was the Master, after all, and would determine what they did and when. In their preoccupied states neither was aware of the Lama's ghost in the back seat.

They were headed back to the Mansion in the mountains, determined to catch Quinn, and bring their decades long hunt to a close.

Two hours later they were creeping past the rental units on the North County Road. Just as they were about to turn and go down the South County Road to the entrance a car pulled up in front of them.

It was driven by a well-tanned man with curling dark hair, and on the passenger side was their quarry, the Quinn look-alike Matthews. The Master couldn't believe their good fortune. He had A. pull over. He went to the trunk and retrieved a handgun he'd hypnotized a pawn shop owner into selling him illegally. He got back in the car and urged A. to catch up.

In the lead car Alam turned to Matthews and said, "The ghost in the back seat says it's them, those that came for you the other day." Matthews turned around and looked out the back window and the rolling dust then focused on the diaphanous form of Eva's ghost.

She reached forward and touched him, allowing him to hear her. "There is a ghost with them again. It is the ghost of Regina's father, the Lama."

"Why?" Matthews wanted to know. "What is he doing with them?"

"The Lama is after a black kite that rides on the shoulders of the man. It is a deeply evil thing and he is trying to return it to the hell it escaped from."

"Can we help?" Alam asked.

"He says no. Keep on and lead them away."

"Well, it's four hours to Baltimore. Might as well settle in."

In the following car the Master was debating what to do. Should they try to run the other car off the road? Should he shoot? He realized that the loose gravel on the road would be as dangerous for him as it was for them. He remembered he wasn't a good shot. But still, if they got close enough maybe he could shoot the driver. And then what? Then he'd walk up to the wreckage and take his revenge on the man he believed had used magic to kill his mother when he was still a child.

But then the road narrowed and A. refused to follow his directions. The gravel road would make the car fishtail and they'd be the ones likely to spin out, or cross over into a ditch. She didn't know the road, or where curves might be. As they argued she almost lost control and had to slow down. The Master pointed his gun at her. She stopped the car and waited as the cloud of dust swelled over them.

"Really?" she said. "Go ahead and end my fucking misery." She turned her face away and looked out the window.

The Master realized he'd lost the ability to see clearly. All he could see was red, and that slowly faded to black, coming in from the sides like stage curtains. He lowered the gun to his lap and faced front.

"What should we do?" he asked.

"We should follow them. The opportunity will open up."

He sighed. As she put the car in drive, turning on the windshield washer, she said to him, "Don't ever pull that stunt again."

He sighed again, waiting for his vision to clear.

In the backseat the Lama's ghost grinned at the drama, having watched the black kite extend its arms around The Master's face and slowly withdraw them.

Alam and Matthews were headed to Baltimore, a four-hour drive, in order for Matthews to catch an overnight flight to England. Alam told Matthews and Eva's ghost all about the Highlands and his life there, and the beginning of his relationship with Calley. Matthews marveled at the prospects. Thousands of years to be in love. Alam told him that in the Invisible Lands time seemed barely to pass at all.

There were no opportunities for A. and the Master to confront Alam and Matthews. The one stop for gas was too short with too many people around. There were cameras, too. By the time they got to the airport they were several cars back.

Alam parked in the hourly garage. He said, "I want to make sure you get there safely. We're probably still being followed." Eva's ghost stayed in the car.

Alam stood in the check-in line with Matthews while waiting to get his luggage tagged and his boarding passes.

"You know, Mate, I'll miss you."

"I'll miss you, too, friend," Matthews replied. "I'll miss the wen. And the land, too. I'll miss Eva. My friendships with Madeleine and Diana have made me feel better about being a man than anything else in my life."

"So, this new assignment of yours. What is it?"

"I don't know. I'm to go to England first. Apparently there is some Secret that needs to be kept safe, but I don't have a clue about what the Secret is, or what I'm supposed to do. I'll be told more when I get there," he shrugged. "But I believe I will come back here. Whenever you and Calley and the others do whatever it is you will have to do, then it will be safe. I think you have a pretty good idea about what that is, but I've been told not to inquire. She, Diosa, told me, through Madeleine."

Out in the parking garage A. and the Master had been driving around. They spotted the Stonehaven car and pulled into the closest space they could find. They got out, discussing how they would ambush the driver and get the information they needed from him.

The Lama's ghost drifted out behind them, and drifted over to Eva's ghost. They conversed about what was going to happen and what they could do. "This will happen fast," the Lama said to her.

Alam walked into the garage and down the row to his car. A. and the Master emerged from theirs as he walked by, A. carrying a plastic bottle of water.

"Hey, friend," the Master called out. "Hey. We saw you head into the airport with a friend of ours, and we were curious where he was headed?"

Alam turned and looked at the Master dead in the eye. The Master drew in Alam's awareness, slowly pulling it into a dark vortex. A. pretended to stumble, dropping the water bottle, then going to her knees to retrieve it. The Master leaned in toward Alam, faces close. Alam said, "England."

The Master, "Did you hear that? Quinn is going to England." The black kite at the back of the Master's head spread out.

Alam thought, "Quinn?" and his face twisted in consternation, which the Master missed. The Master felt his need for revenge rising and poked Alam in the chest and grabbed his shirt as he withdrew Alam's awareness further into the vortex. A. reached up and grabbed Alam by the testicles. Alam tried to step back and couldn't.

Alam was almost to the point of passing out, losing consciousness, when the air in front of him wavered. He recognized Eva's ghost standing between him and the Master. The Master's finger turned cold, painful, searing cold. He looked through the quivering air and the face of the man he was looking at melted into a skull, grinning back at him. He reacted with horror and moved his head back.

At that moment the Lama's hand reached into visibility and grasped the bottom corner of the kite, pulled it, and ripped it out of its place in the Master's energetic field. It came unstuck and the ripping noise and searing pain filled the Master's mind. He passed out before the Lama could rip it all away, and the Master fell to the floor in front of Alam, the kite flapping along.

Alam batted away A.'s hand as she leaned toward the Master. "What the fuck?" he asked, incredulously. He almost punched her in the head, then opened his hand and pushed it away. He reached down for the Master and grabbed his shirt at the shoulders and pulled him out from behind his car. A. reached for him and missed, screaming, "Don't touch him!"

"Fuck you!" was Alam's reply as he beeped the door unlocked

and scrambled in. He backed up around them and drove off. He saw the flashing lights of a security vehicle on the far side of the lot. He steadily kept driving until he couldn't be seen around a corner, and sped for the exit.

It was only once he was through the parking garage gate that he realized those people had asked after Quinn, not Matthews, and that now they thought that Quinn was going to England, the opposite side of the world from where he really was.

27

ANOTHER VISIT TO THE TEMPLE

It was a warm, sunny, early afternoon in the courtyard of the Temple of Wahsastami. Jasmine had shopped, as always looking for sacred art, and then purchased a piece of fried fish from a street vendor's cart. She returned to sit in the courtyard often, regarding the closed doors. While she was waiting for Napat to finish school for the day and join her, she closed her eyes, and regarded the Temple with her mind's eye.

After a moment she thought she detected movement up on the veranda where the costumes were hung out. When she opened her eyes she saw just the top of a head of black hair vanishing behind a wall. She smiled—they knew she was out there, watching, waiting. She wondered if someone would venture out, perhaps come over and even speak to her.

She felt Napat arrive and sit down next to her. After settling and putting her backpack between her feet Napat put her head on Jasmine's shoulder. Jasmine resumed her breathing into her trance state. She could feel Napat become entrained in the trance, and felt her slip into deep relaxation with a sigh.

She already knew the story of the ban the Priests had put on the Priestesses of the Temple and their rituals and teaching. She held in her head the question "What happened here long ago?" and held space for the answer to develop. She heard Napat's voice answer, as if from far away.

"Grandmother says a spell was put on the dragons. All the dragons but one kind. A Seeress foresaw that someone would come and would kill them all. They used to come out, and the people could see them. But after the working of the spell, all the dragons went into the stone, including the great dragon at the base of the mountain. The only kind not put under the spell were the black dragons of the jungle. The ones you call the Komodos." Napat sighed. Jasmine waited.

"Grandmother says the ghosts have been waiting."

Jasmine's mind was whirling. She knew in broad terms what she was in Wallid to do—to liberate the people from the cult of the Destroyer, and to liberate the Goddesses from the chains of the cult, but she hadn't been told about the dragons. She wondered if this information could be used somehow.

Then, on her other side, next to her on the bench, she felt a tingling shiver come over her. In her mind's eye she saw an almond shape, a mandorla, a vesica of golden-white light, faint but perceptible, and within it the form of a wen, slowly becoming real. The form was dark-skinned with long dark hair, and very beautiful. "She Who Comes," Jasmine whispered.

"Yes," came the reply.

"What am I to do?" Jasmine asked. Napat sighed on her shoulder, lost in the ecstasy of the Presence.

"We will use the dragons. And the ghosts," the Presence replied, Her voice like a whisper that was also a caress. "I will be with you. Go talk to the High Priestess of Wallid next."

"I shall. I love you," Jasmine replied.

The Presence stroked her, and kissed her on top of her head. "I will be with you. Remember the Antecedence of the Feminine."

The watchers in the temple drew in a collective breath when the golden shape disappeared in a sparkle of tiny flashing lights. The dragons on the balustrades seemed to shiver, an image of their shapes wavering in the light around the stones. The wall of dark fire around the temple diminished.

Jasmine returned to this side of the veil. Napat shifted and woke up. "I saw Her," Napat said. "I saw Her through your eyes. She is so beautiful. She is the source of Beauty here, in this life, I think."

"You speak the truth, young friend. Can you still hear your Grandmother? I can see her there standing behind you."

Napat rolled her eyes back up in her head, and said, "Yes. But she is whispering. I think the Presence made her shy." And she giggled.

"Grandmother," Jasmine said, addressing her directly, "Tell me about the ghosts here on the island."

Napat answered, "There are many. The Priests take their own, the ones who believe. The Priests take theirs and feed them to their god. The others, the ones who believe in the old ways, have no place to go. They linger. They mix with the spirits of the land, who do not like them, because the spirits of the land are alive in a different way. Many of the ghosts are confused and grieving. A few are angry. Some simply get lost, or fade away. Some try to talk to the living, like Grandmother. The land has not been cleared in a long time."

She paused, and then she said, "The High Priestess knows there is a problem but doesn't know what to do about it. The door to the realm where our ghosts used to go has been shut. The ghosts are getting all stirred up. Grandmother has to go." Napat shivered then shook herself, focusing her eyes on the present.

Jasmine put her arm around Napat. "Thank you," she said. "If your Grandmother speaking through you ever becomes a problem, let me know." She went silent a moment. Then Jasmine asked Napat, "Do you think your Grandmother would be willing to help me?"

Napat was thoughtful. "So long as what you ask helps me, I think she will do what you ask."

"Well, I shall think on it then. When can you arrange for us to go see the High Priestess?"

"It will take a few days. I will make inquiries, and schedule a visit."

"Let's go home."

"Before we go, there is something I must ask you."

"Yes?" Jasmine turned to her and raised an eyebrow.

"I told you I heard Her when She spoke to you. When I touch you I can hear what you hear. What is the Antecedence of the Feminine?"

"What do they teach you in school here about the beginning of the world, and the beginnings of the people?"

"They teach us different things. They teach what the government says they must teach—that the world and the people were made by one God, the one called Winjeetniya. There are carvings of him on the back of many of the little high seats, the high miniature thrones you can see in the back yards. He is a white man with flames coming out of all his joints." Napat laughed, put a hand on Jasmine's shoulder and leaned in conspiratorially. She whispered, "Even his man-thing is a gout of flames," and she giggled, Jasmine giggling with her.

"Only here, on Wallid, do we have such a thing. The Priests say he is the one God behind all the Gods, including behind Skreeva. I think this is because the government, the Wuzlims, tell them they must say so. But I think they truly believe it so, because that is what they teach when they are training the Priests."

Jasmine stopped smiling as Napat spoke. She recognized the hand of De Murgos. Very seriously she turned to Napat on the bench, taking both her hands in her own. "What they tell you is not true. She is the One, She is the True Creator. She is the Earth and every living thing upon it." Jasmine paused, waiting to see the effect on Napat.

Napat's face twisted slightly with consternation, then she rolled her eyes up into her head. She shuddered, then looked at Jasmine. "I see what you are saying is true."

Jasmine continued, "She is the Source of All Life here. For us, She was the First One. In this way She is Antecedent. For millions of years…" She paused, raising an eyebrow to see if Napat was following her. "For millions of years all life on this planet reproduced from mother to daughter, one emerging from the other. In this way She is Antecedent. No man-thing was needed. Do they teach you biology in school?"

"Some."

"Well, this is what happens when the baby grows inside the mother: When we develop our sex (Napat blushed a little) we all, masculine and feminine, grow first as the feminine. Men included. We are all Feminine first, and the Masculine only forms later. In this way She is Antecedent." Again, Jasmine paused to watch Napat, letting the fact sink in.

"Do they teach you about conception, the egg and the sperm?" Napat nodded. "Did you know," she continued, "that a woman is born with all the eggs she will ever have?"

Napat's eyes widened and she shook her head "No."

"It is true," Jasmine said. "When your mother was born the egg that became you was already inside her. And since your mother was made by your grandmother, the egg that became you was made by your grandmother. You were inside your mother, inside your grandmother. In this way also the Feminine is Antecedent."

There was a team of Priests who took turns watching the temple, making sure that they controlled what went in or out. The yoga teacher and her little helper were known entities to them. The girl's father had brought a portion of the payment Jasmine made each week as a gift to the Priests, although he under-denominated how much he was being given weekly by the teacher. The Priests watched them. They bore being watched, certainly. Anything untoward happening between them would be swiftly punished.

Jasmine looked up and over her shoulder, feeling she was being watched. She caught the last flash of a leer on a man's face before he looked away. Jasmine leaned back from Napat. "There, now. Do you understand everything I have just said?"

"Yes, but what does it mean?" Napat asked, feeling her world view shifting inside her.

"It means we shall talk about it later. It is time to go, now," she said gently. They walked home, not touching, but close, side by side rather than one in front of the other. Napat went into a store to buy supplies for daily offerings, Jasmine took advantage of the opportunity to put a foot on the shopkeeper's steps and, pretending to adjust a sandal strap, looked behind her. She caught the flash of a sarong and a brown leg, toes pointed toward her, disappear backwards around a corner. So she knew that now they were being followed, too.

After they'd eaten Napat was in the kitchen studying while Jasmine stepped out on the deck with a glass of wine. She leaned over and contemplated the sluicing river far below. The shadows from the short twilight in the tropics made the water dark, the sun long gone. As she watched, a large dark form swam up the river and emerged on the far bank, directly opposite her.

The black form was a lizard, a dragon, a Komodo, huge by modern standards, fifteen feet long, she guessed. It pulled itself from the stream and climbed across the narrow beach and into the jungle. Climbing up the steep side of the gorge, it reemerged at a rock face, and clawed its way into the jungle again. Jasmine watched the undergrowth parting with its movements, then the movement stopped. Jasmine stared hard, and opened her mind's eye as well. Then she saw it, huge head leaning out, claws holding its body along a sturdy tree, bending out under its weight, staring at her.

She bowed, going to one knee, then rose. The dragon seemed to radiate a light of its own then, dim in the twilight. She saw it flick its tongue repeatedly, tasting the air, tasting her. She knew she was looking at the Komodo King. It had found her. And she would find a way to talk to it, soon, maybe tomorrow.

The next day Jasmine rose early, wanting to get to the yoga school and do some office work. She had thought it wise to not send the girl home by herself, and, after homework, had let her sleep on the couch. She'd debated the wisdom of that choice, rather than walking her home herself. She needed to consider just how unsettled she'd been at the discovery that they had been followed. She needed to determine how she would comport herself, now that she knew, and she didn't want them to know she knew.

Jasmine had loaned her a kimono and Napat slept naked between the sheets, her school uniform on hangers in the wardrobe in the hall to the steps up into the kitchen. She kept clean underwear in her backpack, and had washed the ones she'd been wearing, hanging them on the line for towels in the bathroom, but due to the humidity they would not be dry until the evening.

Napat slept on her side, one leg and an arm hanging over, face hidden under a fall of hair. Jasmine poked her on the way past into the kitchen, setting the tea kettle to heat on the stove. By the time the water boiled Napat had joined her in the kitchen. Napat, wearing the kimono, looked around in a squinty fashion, hair tousled, crossed her legs and leaned forward to scratch the top of her foot, the skirts falling to the sides, exposing her legs. Jasmine sighed to see the unself-conscious beauty of the teenager.

She debated whether or not to tell the girl about being followed, and decided not to. She was confident that Napat would become self-conscious, and alter her mannerisms in such a way that the followers would know they'd been seen. Better the enemy you knew than the one you didn't. And even better, the one that didn't know you knew.

After tea and some sliced dragonfruit, they got dressed and Jasmine walked with her until she was in sight of the school. Then she walked to the yoga school stopping at a bakery on the way. Arriving at the office, and after opening the shutters, she turned on the computer and saw an email from her teacher Madeleine at Stonehaven, asking her to call.

Madeleine inquired after how Jasmine's training was going, and Jasmine confided about Wade's attitude shifts, and she was coming to feel that he couldn't be trusted, but she assured Madeleine that Guiles was working out.

She also told Madeleine about Napat, her helpfulness, and her psychic vulnerability, and the temptation to induce her into a deeper servitude. Madeleine reminded her that she did the right thing by protecting a vulnerable young wen, someone who was a natural psychic, which meant someone subject to possession or hypnotic entrainment. And reminded her also that she did not need the responsibility—karmic responsibility—that would be hers if she either induced or seduced the girl into experiences before she was ready. Even as precocious as the child was, she was still a child, and Jasmine's responsibility for Napat at this point was to hold space long enough for her to mature, and then make her own choices. Jasmine understood and agreed, but whined a little bit about how hard it was to reduce temptation, especially when her assignment was the accumulation of power.

Finally, Jasmine told Madeleine the discovery that she was being followed. Madeleine tsked at her, saying "Now you've drawn attention to yourself, and made everything harder." She suggested that Jasmine offer to pay the father more, and make sure that the child got home regularly so that her family could see her, and that she was alright. Jasmine told her that her plan was to begin travelling more around the island, connecting with the spirits of the land and the ghosts so that all the energetics and alliances would be in place, and that she would ask Napat's father's permission to keep her away overnights, so long as she kept up with her schoolwork. Madeleine said she thought that would work. And that Jasmine should continue to work with Napat's psychic abilities. It was unknown what she might become, but Jasmine could not reveal to her, at least not yet, what her true purpose was on the island.

Shaken when they got off the phone, she was not surprised that it was Guiles who showed up, rather than Wade, to help teach the class, and would stay to provide security during her morning trysts. After class she would reward him with a special treat before she prepared to receive her Phoenii.

28

MORNING WOOD

Slim entered a crisis in his soul over shooting Quinn. He couldn't get over it that the High Priestess at the ranch had ordered him to shoot Quinn during his testing. It felt so out of character for the Goddess to demand such a life threatening test that everything he thought he believed about Her, and Her character, came under question.

He felt his agony was so deep that the only thing he could rationally do about it was to get drunk, and go out into the prairie and holler at Her.

A little fist shaking at the sky never did no harm, he thought to himself. From his stash in his room he pulled out a fifth of bourbon that was twenty-five years old when he'd bought it ten years earlier, walked out into the land so far that nobody could hear him shouting, and started drinking at sundown.

It was a full moon night so he wasn't worried about finding his way back. He managed to get three quarters of the way through the bottle, with much anger and bombast, and staggered his way back to the compound as far a shed on the outskirts and he collapsed against it, passed out.

About first light he started to have an erotic dream. He knew he had an erection in the real world, "morning wood" men called it, and fell back into dreams of being caressed. Cool, soothing hands and lips slipped around his hardness and he groaned in ecstasy, hands releasing the bottle and spreading his knees, pushing on the ground at his sides to make room for the caresses.

The shed he was laying up against faced east and soon the hard rising sun came full upon him and he came fully awake, dry mouthed and rattle-throated, water seeking. He opened one eye and looked down at his sarong, the tips of his cowboy boots just visible below his knees and realized something was moving beneath the sarong. He hadn't been just dreaming.

Slowly he pulled the sarong back, and he heard the sound every cowboy knows to fear. He heard the rattle, the tail of a rattlesnake. Ever more slowly he pulled the sarong back until it showed the source of the caresses around his cock and balls to be his greatest cowboy fear. It hissed at him, resentful of being uncovered. He froze.

A rattlesnake, seeking heat in the cool autumn night, had wrapped itself around his balls, giving him an erection. An aching erection. It had wrapped itself around his rock-hard erection, looking like a snake on the caduceus, and it turned its venomous head toward him and hissed.

But there would be no healing here, just death.

There was no getting out of this one, his penance for shooting a man was to get bitten on his dick by a rattler and he was gonna die.

A shadow fell across them both. Silhouetted by the rising sun was a human form. Angelica.

She spoke, "I went looking for you to say goodbye. I found you. So. Are you really so mean you can fuck a rattlesnake? Now that's a reputation."

He looked at her, not daring to speak or move except his eyebrows, which he raised slowly, as if they were his shoulders, raised in a helpless shrug.

Angelica, dressed for travel. Knee high black cowgirl boots with red piping. Black and red swing dancers skirt coming as far down as the tops of her knees, looking like fire rising from the hemline. Black leather jacket. Hair falling forward over her shoulders. The most beautiful wen he'd ever seen. He risked a smile in answer to her own.

Then he saw a miracle. A dragon's head formed around her head—he saw a morphogenesis. He could barely make out Angelica's features through the red haze of the dragon that looked at him. Then the dragon hissed.

The hiss drew the attention of the rattlesnake. The dragon hissed again. The rattlesnake decided that discretion was the better part of valor and unwrapped itself from its superheated purchase, and slid away through the dust. The dragon licked its lips, and, he would later swear, chuckled before it shrank back behind Angelica's visage, and disappeared.

Angelica. Filled with post-initiation cynicism, she said, "Waste not, want not." She reached down and took his erection in her hand. Slim suddenly remembered to breathe.

Angelica, with her other hand, put a vertical forefinger up to her lips and said, "Shhh."

And then she said, "Don't say nothing, cowboy. This dick belongs to me now."

She put her lips around his cock and sucked. Then she lowered her head, sucking all the way down. He shivered.

"No, uh uh," she said, raising her head from his erection. "No. Not until I say. This is mine now. Not Hers, not nobody's. Every time you fuck somebody ever again, you're gonna think of me." And she lowered her mouth over him again.

Then she stood up, raised her skirt, pulled her panties aside, and, taking his cock in her other hand, fed it into herself. Slowly, sixteenth of an inch, eighth of an inch, quarter of an inch, and then she jammed herself down, all the way, grinding on him, riding on him. She leaned forward and whispered in his hear, panting, she said, "You're mine now, Cocksman."

Now, it's hard to make a man come when he has morning wood. It just doesn't want to go. It means long rides before breakfast. But she was in charge. The cock was hers.

She stood up from him, reached down and pulled on it twice, and he was coming. She brought her face down, and took most of it into her mouth. She tossed her head back, working the alchemy as she'd been taught, and let some of it bubble out onto her lips. She leaned forward and kissed him, rubbing the smear of it across his lips.

"Remember, mine now," she whispered. "Every time you think of this," she said, grabbing his wilting wetness and squeezing, "Every time you think of this, you think of me. And think of me with gratitude."

Regina appeared suddenly behind her, tapping her on the shoulder. "Come on now, girl. Time to go."

Angelica said, "Yeah. And who's the girl now, bitch?" under her breath. And smiled, holding his face in her hands. "Who's the girl now?"

Regina grinned, hearing it, of course. "You can have him," she said. "Don't want to fuck some guy even a snake wouldn't want to fuck."

Angelica laughed out loud, and stood up. "You're right, master. I

know when I've been licked. Licked by the serpent's tongue..."
And Regina laughed out loud, too.

29

PLANNING FOR VISITORS

After the fire Calley met with Her Council. Craft and Alam, Madeleine and Diana, and Eva's ghost gathered in the office. Diana had returned from a month's leave to go home with her family. She'd found it shocking—the hole in the Mansion roof covered in plastic, the smoke damaged furniture in the east wing, drop cloths covering the rest, the smell of damp smoke everywhere, filling the nose until it could no longer be sensed. Windows had been left open and the cloths rippled in the breeze, creating an unsettled sense that the Mansion no longer belonged to humans. All utilities had been shut off and there was a fire in the fireplace.

They sat in silence for several minutes, each seeking to still their minds with the blessings of gratitude and love for the True Creator. They each accumulated a glow. Calley had them touch each other around the table, then she withdrew a locket from inside her shirt and tapped it. A wall of silence shut out the ambient sound.

"We are invisible now," she said. "Alam tells me there is a room below the basement in this building that has an iron door. Is it so?"

"Yes," Madeleine answered. "There are a few rooms below the basement that we use for initiation. You have been there, at some point, for most of them, yes?"

"Yes," Calley said. "But I did not use any doors to gain access."

Diana said, "The door you speak of is a round door, set in the floor. The cover is round, and set in an iron ring. The ring is set in a slab of stone."

"Perfect," Calley said. "My mother told me it was so. We shall use this room to set our trap."

"Have we the power?" Diana asked. "Have you the power?"

"Not by myself, but I will be calling upon friends. There are others like me in the world." She paused. "But my friends cannot stay here waiting. What we need is a warning system, something that could tell us if the Embla or the Dangla are coming."

"How much time do you need?" Madeleine asked.

"Moments only. The doors will already be open."

"We will need the help of those in the houses up on the road. We have wards in place, and if we build enough power for them then the wards will tell us. Theoretically we can close another shield over the place."

"We will have to bring the wards in closer. I don't think there are enough of us raise that much power."

"How much time is a moment, Calley?"

"A moment? A moment is half a heartbeat. I will need one heartbeat to become aware—half a heartbeat if I am awake. Another heartbeat for them to be summoned, and another for them to arrive."

"May I feel your heartbeat?" Madeleine asked. When Calley nodded Madeleine went behind Her, reached over Her shoulders and placed her hands on Calley's chest. She closed her eyes and counted. "Somewhere between two and three, and I guess maybe four, seconds, if She's asleep."

Diana said, "Four seconds is a lot. The wards are set up to send a weak signal, not a fast notification."

"I can wake her," the ghost, hovering outside the circle of the living, offered. "I don't sleep much."

"There we go then," Alam said.

"We'll have to begin raising the power today," Craft offered. "You've given the impression we have little time to set the conditions for the trap, to build the warding wall. What do we have, days? Weeks?"

Calley smiled. "Mother says we have enough, but we cannot waste any. We start tonight. Send word. We will need couples in the cardinal directions, and two couples here in the Mansion, one on this level, one in the chamber below."

"No seventh?" Diana asked.

"My mother will be the seventh vector," Calley answered. "Alam and I will take the Below."

"I suggest that the Ninth Dance of the Moon should be what we do, as synchronized at possible," Eva offered.

"We have the communications for it," Diana said.

"I agree," Madeleine said. "Craft and I will take this floor. I am told we are to leave the top floor for Her." Madeleine pointed a forefinger skyward.

"It is as you say," Calley said. "Let us prepare."

Eva's ghost floated through the doors of the Mansion and down into the parking lot. She felt someone's eyes on her, turned to the east, and looked. There was a dark, vertical shadow that phased briefly into humanoid form, tall, winged, armed with a sword. She shuddered, and the form disappeared. "The Slayer," she heard the voice of She Who Comes whisper in her head.

30

NEWS

The Embla and the Dangla had returned to the last shrine to Cal-ley. There were no sheep about—they'd been herded off the mountains to lower pastures in preparation for the winter. But there was a large buck, lying down and sunning himself not far away.

"Why do you bring me here?" the Dangla asked. "There is no power here, not anymore."

"Because it is remote, so remote we can almost not be heard, even by him. It is because there is no power that I return here."

"And so how is he?"

"The wounds heal badly. It seems there will be scars. There is consternation among us. Nothing like this has ever happened to him, he has never been touched by the powers that can abide here. He has only consumed the souls of saints, and everyone agrees that there has never been an Abomination like this, like the one who attacked him, and we are stunned that he still lives. He is troubled also by the Monster with wings. But it is like there is a poison in the wounds that drives his mind, and his driven mind returns always, and more so, to the existence of the dragon."

"And what course of action will he be driven to? Surely, everyone expects him to do something."

"I have been informed by the arch-ones that he has dispatched the Slayer. They are having a hard time seeing anything. The Drag-on-Bearer seems to have disappeared, as has the Abomination. They may be hiding together. The Slayer will begin at the place where my

Master was wounded in order to pick up the trail. We have been ordered to stay away. For now."

When they had gone the buck stirred itself and walked down the mountain to the border of the Invisible Lands. As he stepped through the boundary he transformed into the Buck-Man. He bugled over the wall and Bree came to the door. She crossed the yard to the wall and listened to his reporting on the conversation he'd heard. She nodded when he'd finished. She climbed up on the wall, resting on Her hands and knees. He jumped up behind Her, threw Her skirts up over Her back and took Her, took his payment for his fidelity and service. He grunted as he stroked and She grunted back. When his antlered head glowed he finished. He bounded off the wall, left the Lands, and never looked back.

She smiled and got down off the wall. She grunted as if She was still having at it with him. She lifted Her skirt in front, smearing his overflow down the inside of Her thighs, grunting, rubbing it in. She smiled again, and, grunting with every step, returned to the house.

31

AMBUSH

As they walked toward where Quinn was waiting outside the van that would take them to the airport, Regina stopped and turned to Angelica. "Something's grown hard in you. Are you aware of it?"

Angelica answered by exhaling, blubbering her lips and looking skyward. "Yes," she said with an adolescent impatience, then she looked at Regina with a raised eyebrow and waited.

"Thought so," Regina said. "If you're not careful you'll just make it all harder on yourself."

As they turned to the car they both saw Quinn's eyes grow wide with horror. He rushed toward them waving his hands toward the side, shouting "Run!"

The wen took off in opposite directions, turning back in time to see a sword, a sword of silver fire, swing straight down toward Quinn. Falling to his knees he crossed his forearms and took the blow there, on the forearm of the wielder, above the hilt in his hands. Light in the form of a golden hand print shone out from Quinn's forehead.

Then the air wavered beside them and a black sword with glowing moonlight runes appeared and sliced down about where the first swordsman's elbow would be. The black sword sliced through with an explosive sound, and the silver sword fell to the ground, a mailed hand and armored forearm, both clad in the same blinding silver, now visible in the dust with the sword.

Two beings became visible at once—the silver being, radiant, blinding, roaring in agony, silver ichor spouting from the severed arm.

And Halloran, holding the black sword in one hand, slowly dropping it to the ground, too much in awe to move. The once priapic priest had been assigned to follow the team invisibly.

Regina shouted, "A Slayer!" and ran to Angelica, standing over her, guarding her, defiantly.

The silver being roared, a sound as loud as a jet engine. He reached across toward Halloran, kneeling transfixed with amazement. The Slayer grabbed his skull with his remaining hand and crushed it suddenly, popping sounds and gore spurting through its fingers. Halloran didn't even have time to scream.

While the Slayer was distracted with Halloran, Quinn had reached down and picked up the Slayer's silver sword. Before the Slayer knew it was happening Quinn ran him through with his own sword, the silver blade parting the mail like water. Seeing the light from Quinn's forehead, the Slayer's eyes grew wide. The Slayer sounded a higher pitch, a singular scream of rage and pain, threatening to burst the ear drums of the three humans. It was suddenly cut off, and with an explosion that rocked them back, the Slayer, sword and forearm, disappeared.

Silence. Then Angelica started weeping quietly, holding her face down, resting it on one hand. Regina relaxed, then absently stroked Angelica's head while looking at Quinn, still on his knees. "Hubris, honey," she said, leaning down to speak quietly into Angelica's ear. "Hubris, it's all hubris. Don't let it make your soul hard."

She left Angelica and went over to Quinn, who was still kneeling, but had turned to look at the Halloran's body. As she got to him and put a hand on his shoulder, Regina heard him say, "Shit. Yuck. Fuck."

Feeling her hand on his shoulder he turned his head slightly.

"What was that? And where did he," Quinn nodded at the corpse, "Come from?"

"That," she said, nodding to the silver drops on the ground before Quinn's knees, "is the blood of an Embla, a Slayer, one of De Murgos's warriors. An assassin. And him? Halloran? Bless him, he was assigned to follow us invisibly. He's been with us all along."

Quinn reached down and picked up the black sword.

"That, we should hide," Regina said. "Here. She went around Quinn and took an amulet from Halloran's neck. "Here," she said, handing it to Quinn. "Wrap it around the handle."

He did and she tapped the amulet. The sword went invisible in his hands. "Don't set it down. It'll stay invisible and then we'll never find it. Tap the amulet again to make it visible, when it's safe. You're right. Shit. Yuck. Fuck. "

Angelica crawled over and draped herself on Quinn's back. "Thank you, thank you, thank you," she said, weeping softly. Then she looked over his shoulder and saw the body. "Yuck. Shit. Fuck."

Around the corner came a squad of men and wen, Priestesses and Consorts, running, some armed. "What happened? What happened? Where are they? Are you OK?" they clamored, as the group surrounded Halloran and touched Regina, Angelica, and Quinn, making sure they were OK. And then, "Who's that?" referring to Halloran's lifeless form.

"We're OK," Regina answered, taking charge. "We were attacked. An assassination attempt by De Murgos." There were gasps around the group. "And that is one of us, a former priest named Halloran. He died defending us." The group exhaled with sighs and exclamations.

"And that," said Regina to the High Priestess, "is Embla's blood. Quick, have someone run and get a metal bucket. We must save as much of it as we can.

Oddly enough, someone in the crowd had a bucket with them, filled with water. They poured the water out and passed the bucket forward. "We can't touch it ourselves. Anybody got a shovel?" Someone did, and it, too, was passed forward. Gingerly, a Consort slipped the shovel into the loose dirt under the droplets, and scooped them into the bucket. Turning to the High Priestess, Regina said, "Take that to the altar. I'll join you there in a little while. Do not leave it alone." To the others she said, "Leave us for a moment. We'll meet you in the dining hall." Suddenly the four human forms were alone.

"Do you think I killed it?" Quinn asked.

"I don't think so. They're reported to have regenerative powers. But you stopped it. If you must, take comfort in the knowledge that you caused it more pain than any mortal could withstand. And now we flee. Take the sword to the car. There's a blanket in the back. Make the sword visible, but wrap it. We're flying, and we have to leave it here. Angelica, are you ready?"

"Yes," she said, letting go of Quinn. "I'm hungry," she added, with some faint surprise in her tone.

"Yeah, me, too. But we should get on the road quickly. We've just got time to make the flight. Come on you two. Leave the body. We'll go leave instructions. Bring the sword."

Regina looked down at Halloran. She took in his torn and dirty clothes, his dirty hands and nails, his worn boots. "How hard it must have been for you, to stay in hiding all this while." With the toe of her boot she nudged his foot. "Thank you, Halloran. May She receive you with open arms, and grant you the bliss your service deserves. You gave your life for us. Thank you."

32

ON WAITAN

Regina turned from Angelica, upon whom she'd been leaning to look out the window, watching as the landscape emerged from the ocean, and turned toward Quinn, sitting in the aisle seat. "Let me see your hands again."

Quinn sighed and turned his palms over. "See? Just a little red still."

"Amazing," Regina said. "No blisters."

"Yeah, and no charred flesh. Just a little stiff," he said, flexing his hands.

"Just the way I like it," Angelica snorted. "No, that's not true. I'm lying. I like it all the way stiff."

Regina said, "The legends say you should have caught fire, touching that sword. Burned up. But not even…"

Angelica said, "I've been thinking. It's the skin of dragon ash. It's a heat shield."

"I think you're right," the Regina and Quinn said in unison.

Angelica turned back to the window. Quinn flexed his hands one more time, and leaned toward Regina. He crossed his legs. He said, in a subdued voice, "Thank you."

"You're welcome," Regina replied. "For what, the extra leg room?"

"Yes," Quinn grinned. "That, and other things."

"Well," Regina said. "First class would have been too obvious. We don't need a hate stamp added to our passports."

Quinn nodded as if he understood what she'd said.

Customs was easily cleared. The Order, not surprisingly, had people working there as officials, Regina knew, but she didn't know who they were. They were met by a man holding a sign in both English and Waitanese with her name on it. Regina MacGregor. When the group walked up to him he dropped the sign and bowed. "Moon Halter," he said in Waitanese. "How happy I am to see you again."

Regina replied, also in Waitanese, and bowing, "How happy I am to be seen by you, Chan."

He rose, smiling, and adjusted his tie and straightened his suit jacket by pulling it at the hem. He grinned. "I am so happy," he said in English. "Let us go get your luggage. A car is waiting."

A little over an hour later they arrived at a walled compound near the mountainous center of the island. The corner of the compound emerged from under a thick canopy of trees, some of which were evergreens. They pulled up into a turnout at a wide gate, which looked like wood and as if it would open in the middle, but instead it slid back to one side. No one was apparent but when the car pulled through there was a small gatehouse with a couple, a man and a wen. The wen stepped out and motioned to the driver to roll down his window.

She leaned in and spoke to Regina in the back, in Waitanese. Regina opened the door and leapt out, embracing the wen fondly, who hugged her back. They talked rapidly in Waitanese, laughing. Regina reached up and tucked a strand of loose hair behind her ear, and the wen looked down. Regina raised her face by the chin, looked firmly into her eyes, kissed her on both cheeks and said something in her ear that made the wen smile.

Getting back into the car Regina smiled. "Blood on the snow."

"Excuse me?" Angelica asked. "What do you mean?"

Regina sighed as the car pulled past the gatehouse. "There was blood on the snow. She, Leia, was having a miscarriage. She ran, terrified, out into the snow, and had it there. She was bleeding badly. I stopped it."

"What? How?"

"I used the energy, the Resonance of the Higher Heart," she replied.

"Moon Halter," Quinn said quietly.

"That's right," Regina said. "The Moon Halter."

"What?" Angelica said, "What are you talking about?"

Regina raised her hand, a gesture meaning, "Shh. Be quiet. Not now." Angelica read it by mentally reading Regina's intention. She humphed at Regina.

Regina said, "Look out. Look at where you are."

The car pulled around a pond with a fountain in the middle. There were low walls with raised pots filled with flowers. The car stopped at a very broad staircase. As they emerged several people came down the steps towards the car. Most were Waitanese wen, dressed in long gowns under kimonos or shawls. But Angelica observed there were also wen from several races, and about a quarter of the people were men, some in robes, others in martial arts outfits, and the rest in suits.

A beautiful wen, tall, with piled hair on top, and a fine silver circlet with an enamel working of the four phases of the moon in black and white in the center and an almost invisible veil suspended from it descended first, going to Regina and taking her hands and going briefly to one knee. She smiled, "Greetings, Moon Halter."

Regina smiled broadly, threw back her head and laughed. She, too, went to one knee, but a step lower down, and said, "Greetings, High Priestess. Bless me, Mai." Regina bowed her head, and the High Priestess Mai put her hands on Regina's head, closed her eyes and turned her face upward, her lips moving in words too soft for anyone else to hear. A visible shudder began in her head and descended, splitting when it arrived at the High Priestess's shoulders, running down her arms onto Regina's head and continuing down her body as it continued down the body of the High Priestess. Both of their pelvises bucked simultaneously. Regina raised her arms out to the sides, palms up, shaking in concentric waves that went from her shoulders to her fingertips. Their feet shook, heels on their up knees thumping, tops of the feet on their down knees beating against the steps.

The energy flowing stopped. Quinn and Angelica stood in awe, having been almost overcome with sensation themselves. Several people on the steps sighed audibly. The High Priestess spread her arms under Regina's and stood, bringing Regina to her feet as well. "Welcome, Beloved," the High Priestess said, dark eyes flashing.

"I am welcomed, Beloved," Regina replied, her own eyes dark and flashing as well. Regina took a proffered hand and followed the High Priestess through wide doors into what seemed to be a dark hallway.

Two couples, wen and man, stepped forward toward Quinn and Angelica, one pair for each, and extended their hands, making "Come" and "Follow me" gestures, and smiling.

The hallway had only seemed truly dark in contrast to the light outside. When they crossed the threshold they could see down the hallway to an end opening on a garden, with people sitting on raised walls, the other side of the building they were in bending around to encircle the garden. Behind this, a series of apparent pavilions and raised platforms interspersed between stands of forest, ascended up the side of a broad mountain. Halfway across to the garden they came to an intersecting hallway extending away in a curve on either side.

A couple from the group of host escorts stepped up to Quinn and Angelica, and said, "Please, come this way. We will show you to your rooms. We have prepared a bath for each of you."

Quinn looked over his shoulder and saw Regina being escorted away down the other hallway, laughing, as she talked to what were clearly old friends of hers. Quinn stopped, suspicion forming in him. He asked, "Why are we being separated?"

His male escort answered, "She is an old and respected member of our order here, the Order of the Red Phoenix. The rooms on that hall are reserved for members. You are our guests, and the guest rooms are down this hall."

The hall was angular rather than round, flat sections for the walls, with sliding doors for access. The man continued speaking as Angelica was escorted to the next door. "We have put you in adjoining rooms. There is a door between your rooms. The bath house is at the end of the hall. Please do not bother to unpack. Just remove your clothes, dress in the robe hanging from the hook, and come to bathe. The staff is waiting for you."

The room was simple and elegant. Tall windows lined the outer wall. Slat blinds opened onto a woods edge hung with flowering vines, even this late in the year. There was no air conditioning that he could see, only ceiling fans. There were hooks in the small hallway that led past a small bathroom door. One hook held a robe. There was a set of flip-flops his size on the floor under it. The bed was larger than Quinn would have thought, and Quinn knew that they knew he was taller than most of the men here, and that it was an accommodation for him as a guest. He realized they must have all kinds of people stay here. There was a small fireplace in one corner with a hook and teapot hanging on it. There was a stack of kindling in a basket under the window. A low table sat against the wall near the fireplace, with cushions on the floor in front of it. There was a door on the right.

Quinn opened it and startled Angelica, who was on her knees, unpacking clothes into small cubby holes that lined the bed on one side. "You OK?" he asked.

"I don't know. My heart is racing, and my breathing is slow. I feel like the embodiment of a paradox."

"You are, my dear, you are. Shall we go to the bath house?"

"Yes. Let me get undressed," she said.

"Me, too," Quinn said, returning to his room but leaving the door open. He threw his clothes on the bed, glancing through the door as he undressed. He caught Angelica glancing sideways at him. She turned and faced him, naked, and gave him a megawatt smile. They stood there, naked, facing each other for a moment, then they both turned for their robes and the hallway.

They went through the door at the end of the hallway and stepped out onto a platform deck with six large wooden tubs with dividing screens between them. There were massage tables at either end. Two of the baths, two baths apart, had steam from hot water rising from them. Each had two attendants, men and wen one each, dressed in sarongs and naked from the waist up.

They beckoned.

Quinn and Angelica hung their robes on hooks by the door and kicked off the sandals. As they stepped toward the tubs Quinn noticed that the wen's nipples grew hard, and the man at tub adjusted the front of his sarong. His cautionary senses flared. Nevertheless, he climbed in and sunk down into the delicious heat. He heard Angelica sighing as she did the same.

The attendants started with his hands and arms, working their way to his shoulders and neck. Then they sat him up, and the wen worked down his chest, and the man down his back, scrubbing lightly with a sponge. When she got down to his phallus, floating relaxedly in the water she brushed it with her hand. She gasped slightly, and her nipples got hard again. At the other tub he heard Angelica gasp, and figured one of her attendants had arrived at the same place.

Both his attendants wrapped their hands around his phallus. Quinn reached under the water and took their wrists in his hands. He held them still, and looked at them, shaking his head "No."

They smiled and nodded, the wen scrubbing around and under his testicles, finally scrubbing his anus. Her touch was so gentle Quinn became erect. She brushed against it again and smiled, the question plain on her face. Again Quinn shook his head. Together the two washed his legs and feet. The man went to a sideboard and came back stirring a bowl of shaving cream with a brush, straight razor in one hand. "Shave?" he asked. Quinn touched his cheeks, and nodded. As this proceeded he heard water sloshing as Angelica moved around. He assumed she'd said yes to being shaved.

In her tub something similar had happened. When the attendants reached her low belly they spread her legs and the wen took the sponge lightly over her phulva and around her perineum to her anus. Of course she gasped slightly. Then she felt the man's hand touch her at the top and pull slightly, exposing her. Her eyes popped open and her jaw dropped a little. She shook her head no, also, and they stopped. After washing her legs they asked her, "Shave?" Angelica nodded her head. The man shaved her lower legs as far as he could reach up her thighs, even under water by feel. The wen shaved her armpits. When the man was finished he said, "Stand please."

When she stood up and looked at him he had an erection poking up, tenting his sarong. When he saw her look, he smiled, and pulled the sarong aside, exposing himself and made a gesture with his hands that she could only read as "Do you want this?" She smiled, reached out and ran a finger along its underside. She shook her head no, and his smile turned into a frown, not a serious frown but a kind of mock frown, and then his smile returned.

Both of them got to their knees before her. The wen's nipples grew hard again. Gently they lathered her up, and, spreading her legs, Angelica let them care for her, pulling her this way and that, tilting her hips so they could see. One leg at a time, she put her foot on the edge of the tub to grant them greater access. Then they had her bend over, and just as carefully they shaved her from behind. Some ingredient in the shaving mix was making her tingle, more so back there.

She sat down in the tub to rinse, and they poured in more hot water. She luxuriated, finally feeling clean and smooth. They sat her up and poured water over her hair and commenced shampooing her. They poured more water to rinse her, then applied a conditioner, rubbing it in. After a final rinse she sat back again, eyes closed, sighing.

After a moment they took her arms and suddenly she found herself with a handful of hard phallus, and a handful of wet phulva. She suppressed an affronted reaction, opened her eyes, withdrew her hands, and looked up at both of them, smiling, and shook her head no.

She stood up, making motions to get out and they appeared with more hot water, rinsing her off. She stepped from the tub, and bowed to each of them. They passed her a towel, and the wen took another towel to her hair. The man used a third towel, and went to his knees, erection still poking out, and dried her legs and feet. Dried, he helped her into her robe.

She looked around, but Quinn was gone. She opened the door and stepped through to find him waiting for her. When the door closed she heard giggles behind her. She was surprised at the sense of reassurance and gratitude that filled her when she saw him. It showed on her face, and he smiled at her. He shrugged and said, "I have an assignment."

"I'm glad it's you," she said. Then she said, "Do you understand what was happening in there?"

"I'm guessing it's a part of their normal operations here, to offer themselves to guests in that way. Did you take advantage of it?"

"No, no. I felt put upon, but I was polite."

Quinn said, "Me, too. Did they use a straight razor on you?"

"What? No," Angelica said, shaking her head emphatically.

Over at the other end, in the other bath house, Regina, knowing the routine, took full advantage of the opportunities, and let herself be thoroughly pampered and pleased. At her age, she thought it best to take full advantage of every opportunity for a threesome that presented itself. And, she knew, the attendants were all in training, and that the servicing of guests was a part of their curriculum. She began with the massage, in which art everyone trained. The other two, Quinn and Angelica, she already knew, hadn't stuck around long enough to be offered it.

She'd been pleased with their pacing, having taken this training herself many years before. She was immensely pleased with the continued existence of the centuries old Order of the Red Phoenix, an Order for Wen that had its roots in the great Daoist tradition that arose before the rise of the culture of Confucianism.

33

ENGLAND

Leonard Smith, High Consort to Beth Elmyra, was waiting in his car at the passenger pick-up line at Heathrow Airport. He shifted uneasily in his seat, not happy with having all these Americans in what used to be his well-ordered life. From the time he was a child he had been painfully shy, and it is was due to the generosity of spirit of a Priestess of the Fleur de Vie noticing him, and welcoming him into her life (and her bed) that he was able to find purpose and meaning.

His training and initiations, first as Consort, then as High Consort, had developed in him a remarkable siddhi power: he was able to project telepathically into someone's mind the image of whatever background there was behind him. In effect, he seemed to disappear. One glance behind him and his mind photographically recorded what he saw, and that is what others saw when they looked in his direction. His shyness, and the felt wish that he could just disappear into the background, became his gift.

His discomfort at having to meet with another American, a man named Matthews, especially one who was rumored to possess some profoundly amazing siddhi power (although no one would tell him what it was), triggered an agitation in him that made him unknowingly project the image of the seat he was sitting in. In effect, the car looked empty. This attracted the attention of the police, who immediately suspected the empty car of being a terrorist bomb. The policewoman looked into the car and startled him back into visibility. She did a double-take and shook her head, tapping on the window with a night stick.

He rolled the window down and gave her the flight number he'd been given.

Just then Matthews emerged from the baggage pick-up area and looked around. He focused on Smith through the window and Smith waved at him, pointing him out to the officer as the man for whom he waited. She stepped back and waved Matthews over. Smith got out and put the man's suitcase in the boot. Matthews put the small roll-on and his knapsack in the back seat and then got in. Smith hopped in and said, "Just in time, mate. They were starting to think I was a bomb."

Matthews said, "Yeah, just in time. Thanks for meeting me." Matthews stuck out his hand and Smith shook it briefly before putting the car in gear and driving off. "You're welcome. You're some kind of VIP, you know. We almost always make new arrivals take the trains."

"So I heard. I was relieved when they told me at Stonehaven that someone would meet me. I haven't travelled a lot outside the States. It's disconcerting. You travelled much?"

"No. Just to Italy and Greece for vacations. Life here in the Baths is pretty interesting. And the life of the High Consort isn't that hard."

"High Consort, eh?"

"Yes. What level are you?"

Matthews shook his head. "None. I guess I'm kind of a special operator. The Madeleine at Stonehaven told me that they'd offer me the Initiation when I'm ready."

"So you've been around awhile then?"

"No. Maybe 6 months. But I am, I have, how should I say it? I have some special talents that the Order finds useful."

"Oh yeah? And what might those be?"

"I'll have to show you. I'll let you know when the time's right."

"Well? Until then. Settle in, it's about two hours to the Baths."

When they arrived they crossed a bridge and pulled into a neighborhood of nearly identical four and five story tall white stone townhouses. Leonard pulled to the curb in front of one. They retrieved the luggage and climbed the stairs to the door. Matthews noticed a small pink decal in the corner of the front window—the symbol of the Fleur de Vie. He smiled.

A pleasant wen in a business suit and flats opened the door for them, bid them leave the luggage in the entrance hallway and take a seat in the parlor, and offered them tea, which they accepted. From her office on the second floor Beth Elmyra observed them on the monitor for her security cameras.

Leonard she knew too well, but the stranger—sport coat over a nice shirt, blue jeans over cowboy boots (those would have to go), hair longish but clean—he was older than she'd thought he'd be, and bigger. Lean but still well-muscled. She'd heard about his siddhi power, his skill at levitation, but it was not widely known, and as far as she knew, no one in else in England knew for sure, just that he was a special guest.

They had tea, Beth observing the energetics between the two men and herself. Leonard was mildly famous locally for his bi-sexuality, but something about the stranger kept Leonard from regarding him as a possibility for dalliance or encounter. In contemplating Matthews, she realized that Leonard's reticence, apart for his shyness, was a result of a judgment that he'd made that the stranger would not be very responsive. So much so that if he tried and failed his embarrassment would be deep. She realized that Leonard assessed the situation like a man would, like an uninformed man with the old patriarchal mindset. He assessed his odds of getting laid, and when he figured out the odds weren't very good, he dismissed the prospect, and the person. He dismissed the person just the way straight men dismissed wen who weren't prospects out in the civilian world. But not here in the Order. She noted it, and would talk to him later.

Tea finished, Leonard let himself out. Beth and her Assistant named Grace, a High Priestess herself, helped carry the luggage upstairs to a guest bedroom. Beth had thought to take him up to the fourth floor—she was formulating an idea about how to get him up on the roof—but decided to be the generous host and make it easy for him.

"Join us for dinner, will you?" Beth asked, backing out the door and closing it behind her. Beth looked at Grace and smiled. They'd been friends for a long time, the operant threads of their relationships—High Priestess of a Temple to initiated High Priestess but of no title or rank, boss to staff member, elder to younger—these threads had been softened and thinned by the rising bulk of their friendship and intimacy so that Grace could speak to her as a peer and friend.

Grace smiled back. "Think you're going to shag that one, do you?" When Beth laughed and nodded, Grace continued, "And he's here for a week? Time for us both, then. Don't wait too long if you want firsties."

They both laughed at this as they reached the first-floor landing.

Matthews heard that laugh and the peal of it stirred him. His lower belly tightened and his phallus twitched. It amazed him, the affect that a wen's laughter had on him. He had realized since coming to Stonehaven that his capacity to make wen laugh was one of his best features. Particularly when they were in his arms and he was in them. So much joy would pour from the throats of these Priestesses that it spurred him, instinctively, to become a better lover. And that he could do that—not only make them laugh with joy, but make them laugh more; harder and longer. It filled him with delight, and afterwards a happiness that made him grateful to be alive.

He sat on the bed and soon found himself laying back and slipping into reverie. He immediately saw both of them naked in his mind's eye, and himself engaged with them, and engaged in play. Eventually he saw both of them together with him, and when, in that imagery, they both looked at him directly in the face, huge grins on theirs, he knew that this, too, would be a possibility.

Supper was fun. The food—a roast, potatoes, and overcooked bok choi—wasn't too bad but it wasn't to his taste. What was fun was how bawdy and aggressive Grace was. He figured he'd be seeing her first, so he was surprised when it was Beth who came to him first, opening the door quietly and stepping into the room on slippered feet later that night.

She was wearing a full-length dressing gown with a calf-length wool overcoat. He was reading under a low-wattage lamp. She came to the side of his bed and sat on it, facing him, one leg on the bed, bent at the knee. He could see she was wearing leggings under the gown.

"Take me upstairs." she said.

"What's upstairs?" he asked.

"Sky. Air," she said.

He said, "That's all I need."

She said, "I know," even though she didn't.

On the way up the next two flights of stairs she told him: "The Madeleines talk, you know. They talk amongst themselves. And since they work for us, they tell us. I know you have something special. I want to see it, at least."

Matthews said nothing until he got to the roof. When the access door was closed behind them, he said, "What do you want to see?

She said, "You know, the levitation."

"Ah. It's really something, you know. But I can't tell you how it's done because I didn't do it. She did it. She told me She had use for it." He went quiet, closed his eyes, and made a rolling forward gesture with his shoulders.

Beth heard a sound between a whisper and a whump, and then a faint buzz that faded. As she watched, a form appeared in the air around his back and extending fifteen feet on either side, like an oscil-lating haze and within it she could see the faint outline of huge feathers. She drew in a breath and held it. She backed up to the parapet on the roof and sat down. She sighed. She reached down and pulled up the hem of the gown until she could reach underneath. Her leggings had a snap crotch, which she opened.

She leaned back, put one hand on the wall and the other between her legs, pressing lightly. She sighed. She beckoned him close with her other hand until he was standing in front of her. She reached out and touched him. He was vibrating—the source of the buzzing sound she'd heard. She unbuckled his belt, unzipped him, and pulled him out into the cool night air. She stroked him and he came erect quickly.

And then she fell backwards off the roof.

He looked and leapt in the same moment. He could see her fall-ing, long coat, gown, and hair streaming upwards, face hidden, silent, her arms reaching for him. Faster than gravity, faster than her falling he flew. He caught up with her not far from the ground. He wrapped his arms around her and pulled her close. She wrapped her arms around his neck and her legs around his waist and fiercely held on.

The fall slowed and he pulled them upright, landing lightly on his feet. They were panting, there in the backyard. At the same moment they realized how close they were. He was almost unyieldingly stiff, and she slowly lowered herself on him. The vibration entered with him, filling her, joining them together in one buzzing, singing form. Their panting joined their joining, synchronizing, and he saw the flash of her teeth, still fierce, grinning at him. He flashed a smile back. She leaned in and whispered in his ear. "Fly. I want to fly with you in me."

Leonard and Grace, trysting in the backyard for some unknow-able reason when they could have been inside, saw it all. Grace was riding him, and he hurt his neck twisting around to see. Grace, who'd seen the fall, slowly exhaled her held-in breath. Leonard, who'd seen only the landing, whistled low.

As they watched, Matthews arched the wings overhead until the tips touched and, with a mighty downward beat Beth and Matthews were aloft. Grace and Leonard heard her groan with pleasure at the up thrust. And then they were gone, vanished into the night sky. A mo-ment later Beth's slippers plopped into the yard, bouncing once before they settled.

"I'm jealous," Leonard hissed.

"Oh really?" Grace asked, somewhat surprised, knowing that Leonard couldn't be jealous of Matthews. After all, Leonard was with her. "Of what?"

"I may get a ride but I'm not going to fuck him."

"Why not? You can always give it an ask."

In the morning when she woke, Beth sat up on her elbow, turned slightly and looked at the sleeping Matthews. She'd taken him three times the night before, once in flight and she shivered with ecstasy at the memory. She thought about giving it another go, and thought, "Jet lag. Let him sleep." She rose and gathered her clothes, still smelling of night sky, wondering where her slippers were as she closed the door.

She wondered what he would think if he knew that she hadn't slipped when she fell, nor was it entirely her will. The Goddess had come into her in that moment. The Goddess had told her to fall, so she did.

34

THE EIGHT ORGASMS

Breakfast the next day was in a small walled garden that allowed sunshine but blocked the breeze. Dragons and long-tailed birds were carved in bas relief on the walls. Angelica, Quinn, and Regina were warm and comfortable. Regina took the moment to explain in greater detail where they were, and why they were here.

"This is an old and sacred place. It is a temple, and a convent. It was the local version of an establishment that began on the mainland almost three thousand years ago. It was a convent for wen Daoists, wen who wanted to work on themselves and practice what they called the Liberation Alchemy without the pressure of being around men. It was a place where wen could train and work and meditate. They call them-selves the Order of the Red Phoenix. Now they are headquartered here on Waitan, driven here by the revolution on the mainland. The Temple, and what happens here, was considered by the authorities over there to be merely a house of prostitution, and hence immoral.

"They were not far wrong in their practical assessment, but they were very wrong in the judgment. A part of the training program here is in the Art of the Courtesan, and it was a way for the Temple to earn money and support in the community. The trading of sex for the oppor-tunity to work on oneself safely and uninterruptedly was a high value bargain for the community, and this was built into the ancient Daoist morality. As the old proverb goes: Follow the Way. Where does it lead you?"

"Well, where does it lead you? Angelica interrupted.

"Where do you think?" Regina replied sharply.

When Angelica couldn't answer Regina said, "It should be obvious, on one level. It led you here."

Regina watched the implications settle into Angelica's mind. Quinn grunted a "Huh!" He approved of the exchange. Regina shot him a sharp glance.

Regina sighed, catching her breath and recapturing her perspective. She said quietly, "I trained here. I stayed here for a little more than a year and would not have left even then if it were not for an assignment from Her," Regina said, pointing upward with her forefinger, "and a confirmation of the assignment from the High Priestess here in identical language. By the way, that's not what she's called here. Her title is, well, the closest translation would be Head Mistress, or Head Concubine."

"Concubinage to whom?" Quinn asked.

"To the Dao," Regina answered simply. "She'll be joining us in a little while."

"Why Phoenix?" Angelica wanted to know.

Regina grinned at her. "Do you know any of the mythology? How much do you know about Dragons, and their relationship with the Phoenix?"

"Not much," Angelica said.

"How about you, Quinn?"

"Well," he drawled. "The Dragon is the inner fire, and it can burn brightly and painfully. Some people relate it to the overcoming of the Kundalini Barrier in certain ways. But often it can begin to burn in everyday people, men and wen, often in their teen years and early twenties. That seems to be when it's most painful because that's when the ego is working its hardest to establish itself, and ego is one of the things that Dragon's fire consumes. It can be so painful that sometimes the Soul and Spirit bodies can separate from the Soma. It can arise as an uncontrollable impulse to fuck, to find ecstasy, to find release in the fulfillment of desire. The Phoenix is like water for that fire. The descent of the Phoenix can restore harmony between the Spirit, the Soul, and the Soma. This restoration is the rising from the ashes of the Dragon's fire."

"Good, Quinn. Thanks for paying attention," Regina grinned. "That's only one of the tales, Angelica. There's a whole detailed mythos that goes along with this. And you've had this experience yourself. You remember what happened in the red tent during the thunderstorm?"

"Some of it. I'd remember more if you reminded me," she said with surprising humility.

"When I arrived, you had just passed out from humping that good looking young man. What was his name? Ah, yes. Raphael. When he left, the Dragon emerged from you and it was so traumatic that your bodies were oscillating apart. The Phoenix descended, and placed its wings on the side of your head. The pain you were in was soothed, and you slept."

"I remember the pain and terror, and then having that all soothed away. I thought it was you."

"Not just me."

"And I saw something like that happen to Quinn once."

"Really? You'll have to tell me."

At that moment a tall, thin, beautiful wen walked into the garden and toward Angelica's chair. She bowed. Angelica stood up and turned and the wen got on her knees and bowed her forehead to the ground. Angelica stood there, floundering, not knowing how to respond. The wen before her started chuckling and sat up on her heels. "Greetings, Dragonwen," she said.

And then a remarkable transformation took place in Angelica. Her eyes slitted, her tongue lolled, and she felt the Dragon's face emerge from hers. She could see the mustaches drifting in the air in front of her.

The Dragon spoke through her. "Ho gved mai pei."

The woman bowed her head and said "Ho gved hamashk."

The Dragon receded and Angelica sat down shakily, hands on the table to control her descent. The wen rose, put her hand on Angelica's shoulder briefly, then brought a chair over from a nearby table.

"Hello, Dragonwen. I am Mai Pei, Headwen here. Hello Moon Halter. It is so long since your last sojourn here we have not met. And hello, bodhisattva," she said, nodding to Quinn. "I am honored to be in your presence." He stood, bowed, and sat down without speaking.

The Headwen sighed. "I am here to convey your schedules while you are in residence. Dragonwen, do you know why you are here?"

Angelica shook her head. "Not really."

Mai Pei looked at Regina with a raised eyebrow. "Better that she hear it from you," Regina said.

Mai Pei looked at Angelica frankly and openly. "You will be our guests for nine or ten weeks. For eight of those weeks you will be trained in the Eight Orgasms, one per week. You will have to do some domestic work in exchange for your stay. You will also be trained in some of our other arts. You, in particular, bodhisattva, are expected to train with our men in our martial arts. Much of your power is still raw, and we will be helping you refine your control."

Quinn nodded "My thanks."

Mai Pei turned her attention back to Angelica. "The reason this training is being provided for you is that you, in and of yourself, are in need of development, of cultivation. Our information is that the Dragon will not stay with you forever. When it is gone, you will be you, but imprinted on the Dragon, so that your sensations—like your constant impulse to masturbate"—Angelica drew a quick breath—"and your subsequent behaviors will be under your control, instead of controlling you. Do you understand?"

Angelica slowly and thoughtfully said, "I think so."

"Good then," Mai Pei patted her on the hand. "One day a week will be devoted to your domestic duties. In that way you can use that time to digest and integrate your experiences. Your domestic day starts tomorrow. You will find two sets of clothes on your bed. One set is for work. The other set is for training. I'm confident you'll be able to tell the difference. Report to the kitchen tomorrow at 5:00 AM."

Tea was brought by a pair of people wearing sarongs and shawls. Angelica squinted up at them and realized they were glowing—there was an edge of light. They felt good to be around. Angelica, unhappy with the prospect of getting up that early, calmed down, thinking that if everyone felt that good, she'd have a good day. When the servers were finished and they turned to depart. one turned back and gave Angelica a little wave hip high. Angelica smiled, warmly and surprised, and gave a little wave back.

Mai Pei observed all this closely. "How much, Elder, have you told her about what we'll be teaching her?"

Regina replied, "Not much. Tell her as you are moved to speak, please."

Mai Pei continued her close observation of Angelica. "As I said, you are here to be trained in the Eight Orgasms a wen might have. Many are of the opinion that there are only a few types, or perhaps even only one type. What we here have come to understand over centuries of observation and experimentation is that there are more, based upon the refinement of perception and discernment and the entrainment of different sets of nerves. Although a great deal of refinement is possible we have chosen to categorize only eight. Men have a different number of orgasms, and they, too, are trained here. Men are also trained to bring wen to each of the orgasms. You will be having a lot of sex, with many partners, and often several different partners in any given day.

Do you foresee any difficulties with this?"

Angelica shook her head no.

"Any hesitation about men of different types?"

"You mean races?"

"That's one of the meanings of 'type,' yes."

"None that I know of. You know, I'm answering you with my head alone. I don't know what my body will do. I don't know how I'm going to feel."

"Well said. Do you have any problems with having sex with other wen?"

"I don't know, I've never had any."

Mai Pei said, "Ahh. Sex with multiple partners?"

"Never had any of that either."

Quinn spoke up, "I am uncertain as to whether or not to be insulted or proud of myself that you are not offering me any training in your sexual arts, in addition to your martial arts."

Mai Pei smiled. "If you decide you need some help with something, let me know. Your companion there," nodding at Regina, "knows all our arts, including how to teach men."

Regina patted his hand. "You're pretty good as you are."

Quinn grinned. "There's another issue. I am here as Angelica's bodyguard. We've already been assaulted once, and the assailant was very powerful. I need to keep near her no matter where she is or what she's doing. We've been practicing covering our trail energetically since the assault, but I'm not confident that we are safe enough here."

"Tell me about the assault," Mai Pei said. "Are we in danger at this moment?"

"No, we're not," Regina said. "Would you like to hear the story?"

"Would it endanger us to speak of it? Vibrationally even?"

"No, I do not think so. But here, lean forward. Let us touch and I will tell you, I will show you."

Regina raised three fingers and placed them on Mai Pei's brow. Mai Pei did the same. A small but visible shock passed through her as she made contact. The air around them began to glow. She started to hum and Regina smiled. When the transmission was over she broke contact.

"I see," Mai Pei said, glancing at Quinn with new respect. "So, you will be in the kitchen with Angelica at 5:00 AM then."

He clearly hadn't thought of this, but said, "Yes. Of course."

Mai Pei said, "I need you to bring me into the circle of your companionship. In this way it will be easier to find each other in the dark, so to speak."

She held out her hands, palm up. "You know this ritual? We will use the power of the Resonance of the Higher Heart to find a common rhythm. When we are synchronized, and have remained so long enough, we will reach the state known as One Heart, One Mind."

"We are each of us Resonators," Regina said.

They held hands. Angelica was the last to put her hands in. She felt an energetic shock pass through her in opposite directions, since the people on either side of her were running at different frequencies. After some push back she relaxed, and a single frequency appeared in each of her hands. The pulse pooled in her heart and then she felt the pulse everywhere in her body. She continued to breathe slowly, bringing all of her awareness to the diffuse sensation of the pulse. She opened her eyes slightly and saw the air around the four of them was glowing green. She smiled. When she smiled Mai Pei said, "There, then. We should sit this way together every day." Mai Pei let go of her hand. When Angelica looked up Mai Pei smiled at her and nodded. "Don't worry young one. This will be fun, you'll see. And remember. Tomorrow, the kitchen, 5:00 AM."

When she was gone Angelica turned to Regina and asked, "So, what's the first orgasm?"

"The rumored to be mythological Vaginal Orgasm. I've read that most wen never experience it. So, it may be difficult. You may have to work at it."

Angelica smiled wickedly. "What makes you think I don't already know how?"

35

THE HIGH PRIESTESS OF WALLID

In two weeks, on the weekend when school was out, Napat arranged a visit to the High Priestess of Wallid. She had a cousin with 'modern views' who ran an unlicensed driving service. So long as he paid a little to the cops there was no problem, and he wouldn't tell either her parents or the Priests.

Jasmine knew now that the Priests were a problem. That she was being followed was no surprise, once she thought about it. Here she was, teaching what was once, originally, one of their disciplines. Furthermore, her hiring of Napat as her assistant could be interpreted as child abuse, with the odds that the Priests were speculating about sexual abuse being high, in her mind.

Napat, who had taken to spending most nights at Jasmine's, sleeping on the couch, had to be persuaded to spend more time at her parents' compound. She resented the need to assure them she was alright, being well and properly cared for, even after Jasmine explained, her parents would then tell the Priests she was fine. "The crazy yoga lady" just needed a personal assistant, and took good care of Napat, and her family. Jasmine also took care to make sure Napat was seen in public more frequently without her. Instead of doing shopping together, for example, Napat would shop alone, sometimes only for a few items.

Ironically this drove them closer to each other. Jasmine's explanations of the meaning of the Antecedence of the Feminine inflamed Napat's mind as she reasoned through and incorporated within her the truths that Jasmine, and the Order, took as their articles of faith. Her inflamed mind led in turn to an increase in her psychic abilities, conducting not just her Grandmother's awareness into this timeline but the awarenesses of others, particularly past Priestesses and Healers from the island's organic tradition. Some of these were, it appeared, royalty from the ancient lineage overthrown by European invaders.

Napat showed other signs of the beginning of the Overcoming of the Kundalini Barrier. In her mentorship Jasmine would spend as much time as possible sitting knee to knee, or back to back with Napat, entraining the young wen's energy with hers, showing her how to move the energy within herself so that she could moderate the seizures of agony and ecstasy that were beginning to course through her body. It was most important that Napat learn to control her internal states so that she could behave in the required fashion. Jasmine was hopeful that. with herself as mentor, Napat, with her outsized ability to channel the dead, could keep her sanity. Nevertheless, Jasmine put in place the support team needed to whisk Napat away, should it become necessary. Jasmine hoped she would recognize the signs of impending blow-out in time.

The presence of the priest observers meant she had to be more careful about her alchemical assignations. She decided she would only see these men at the office of her yoga studio. She allowed herself to be seen at the house only by Craft and Wade. And, of course, Napat, who was fascinated by Craft. Wade, not so much.

She would also spend more time with Belinda and Mark, the Priestess and her Consort, who had stayed behind to help Jasmine run the studio. Visiting their house put the appearance of context to the relationship with Wade and Craft.

She was worried about leading the Priests to the home of the High Priestess. She was sure that they watched her, knew where she was and what she was doing. But she didn't want to make a connection that could lead to complications. She knew that if she only visited once, or perhaps, after an interval, two or three times, depending on the relationship they established on the first visit, the Priests would think she was behaving like any other tourist come to receive counsel and healing.

Once she knew the route to the High Priestess's compound she decided to take Craft along with her, he following on his scooter rather than in the van. Since part of the way they would be driving down a section of road with few houses, which meant no witnesses, she didn't want to make herself a target for whatever nonsense of interference someone might think up.

On the way, at a fork in the road, they passed one of only two temples of the Wuzlims on the island. Standing out front, between the compound wall and the road, was a man dressed differently than the island men, who, when they weren't wearing western clothes, dressed traditionally in sarongs and shirts. Napat glanced at him as they passed and said "Meemon" almost as an aside, to Jasmine. Jasmine extended her clairvoyant awareness into the wake of the van and watched as the man pulled a cell phone out his vest pocket, dialed a number, and reported a description of her vehicle, and who was in it. Knowing that the High Priestess was being watched by both the Wuzlims and the Windu Priests set her mind off looking for implications. He was off the phone and heading through the gate into his compound, not taking notice when Craft rode by.

The van pulled to the side of the road and a gatekeeper let them in when they knocked. They crossed the threshold between the carved halves of the sacred mountain, Mt. Nagoon, and stepped into a small plaza with complimentary guardian statues, their fierce gazes over open mouths filled with carnivore teeth and lolling tongues, on either side of the short set of stairs up to the larger plaza. As they passed the guardians Jasmine let out a low whistle and Napat shivered. The statues had power, they'd been imbued with the ability to either stop or transform negative energies. Their power was palpable. They were true wards.

An older woman in traditional dress met them at the top of the stairs and escorted them to a raised platform with a thatch roof. Translucent gauze drapes in bright colors hung from the face rafters, billowing gently in the slight breeze. The sun was out. They stepped up on the platform and removed their shoes. A woman, white, clearly European or American, was just standing to leave, her audience with the High Priestess concluded. Jasmine noted that the woman's hair was completely wet.

They sat cross legged on pillows before the High Priestess. She was young, no older than her late twenties. Her hair was dark brown and thick, tresses slightly curled falling down her back as far as her hips. Her skin was lighter than most of her people's, a testament to a life spent mostly indoors. She was dressed in a traditional sarong over pants, with a long, flowing vest, almost a gown, falling around her. The older woman brought a fresh pot of tea and served all three small cups of the green beverage. The three gestured to each other in acknowledgment before setting the cups down to cool.

Jasmine, High Priestess of the Order of the Fleur de Vie, and Chantana, High Priestess of Wallid, regarded each other across the short distance between them. Chantana leaned forward, and the solidity of her field easily moved Jasmine to bend back. Jasmine smiled, and decided it would be better to acquiesce than compel the same movement in Chantana. After all, she was operating under the sacred obligations of the guest. Chantana's probe was meant solely to take Jasmine's measure, like she was asking for her name.

Napat spoke first, making introductions in Windonesian, introducing Jasmine as her mentor. Chantana nodded politely at her while keeping her eyes strictly trained on Jasmine.

Jasmine spoke first, in Nahasi. "I am told you were quite the prodigy."

"Yes," Chantana replied. "When I was a small girl I would fall into trances and quote Windi scripture. The Priests came to examine me. One, in particular, was assigned to teach—what is the word? Tutor me. I was just a child and my parents would not let them take me away, so he came to the house every day. He trained me to not fall into trance but to stay present when these moments would come. I would write the words of the scriptures even though I could not read them. The priests all treated me as a returned one, a reincarnate. I did not, and do not, to this day, think it is so. It seems more likely to me that I was simply connected to some place in the mind of the world, listening to someone read aloud.

"The Priest was always disappointed that I could not give him a name for the reincarnated one he kept hoping I was. He thought I was lying and would punish me." A shadow passed over Chantana's face and she looked away, down to the side.

Jasmine, her clairvoyance still open, saw what Chantana looked at. "I'm sorry," Jasmine offered. "It should not have been that way." She resisted saying "Among us, that wouldn't have happened."

The impact of Jasmine's empathy was visible. Chantana wept a single tear, and then became angry, transferring and projecting the anger onto Jasmine. "You," Chantana said. "I know what you are. Others of your kind are on my island, and more are coming. Why? What are you here to do?"

"What She whom we both serve bids me to do, of course. Why do you ask?"

"Because we are bidden differently. I have my job to do, this task laid upon me by Her. I know your task is different, but you are on my land, and in my country. I want to know what you are here to do." As she concluded, Chantana leaned forward and pointed downward with emphasis on the last "do."

Jasmine leaned back again, pushed by Chantana's energy. "And what is your job?" she asked mildly.

Chantana sat back, embarrassed about her outburst. With a trembling hand she picked up her tea cup and took a sip. The others did the same. Composed, tossing her hair back over her shoulders, Chantana answered, "It is my job to balance the forces of the people, the gods, and the spirits of the land."

"Then do as you are bidden," Jasmine said seriously, and then she smiled.

Chantana continued, looking down again. "I am fearful that what you are here to do will make my job harder, maybe even impossible."

"Ah," Jasmine replied. "You fear failure. So do I."

Into that silence Napat cleared her throat, and spoke. "From what little it has been given me to understand, I believe that She will be with you both. High Priestess, you cannot be allowed to fail, even under great duress. She will help you. Mentor, I get only glimpses of why you are here. From the little I've seen, you can fail. It is possible for you to fail. And if you fail, then someone else will pick up the task." With that Napat took another sip of tea and looked off the platform over the terraced and irrigated fields.

Chantana was the first to speak. "I cannot help you."

"I know. I did not come hoping for help. I came to meet someone of great courage and skill and pay my respects. I am in your house. When I think of you, when I pray for you, I wished to have the image of you in my mind. I realize now that if you do your job, if you fulfill your role, everything will be alright."

"Ah," Chantana said. "Then drink your tea."

They drained their cups. Chantana said, "Let us sit together for a while." She found the right pillows and crossed her legs and settled in. Jasmine took a low stool from the edge of the floor, set it on a pillow, and sat, knees down, tops of her feet on the pillow behind her. Napat lay down on some pillows, knowing that if she sat in either position she'd just fall over anyway when she was taken in trance.

They tuned to the sounds of the wind, and Jasmine and Chantana sighed simultaneously. Jasmine sent Chantana a thought, "Show me the Goddesses of this land." Chantana, surprised and pleased to sit with someone so developed, smiled, and returned the thought, "Watch."

With no sense of journeying, Jasmine found herself on the walkway between the lotus ponds with the sculptured underwater monsters that led to the temple of Wahsastami. She found herself gazing through the ring of black smoke that encircled the temple, then at the long bamboo poles bent at the top to create one end of a string for tie-offs for the tips of the streaming flags that were strung along the lengths of the poles—bright, golden, flapping a little in the light breeze. Her eyes rose to the stack tower above the temple, hung in drapes of folded cloth, like clothes. Her eyes dropped to the dragon balustrades for the sets of high wooden doors at either end of the building, carved with images of the Goddess, displaying each of Her powers. Goddess of Flowing Water that purifies and heals, Goddess of Knowledge—the Arts, Music, Language. It showed her in the embrace of Her consort Drahma, and holding Her brother Skreeva at knife-point while in dialogue. The dragons' eyes, one dragon on either side of each door, sparkled.

She flowed through the black flames and went through the door under the pavilion. There was a dark room ahead, but a stairwell down to the side, lit where it turned and went further down. She went that way, unclear about how many turns she took, following down to a softly glowing light. She arrived at the lowest level, which opened on a broad room. There, on a raised dais, the emblems of Her office scattered around in disarray, was the Goddess, weeping, held in the arms of Salakta offering comfort. She moved closer and stopped, suddenly seeing a crowd of swans, alert for the intruder. She heard a growl, and looked down to see four white tigresses stirring. She stepped back.

She felt hands pulling her back, up the stairs and on up to the pavilion, where the costumes for the ritual dancers were hung. The breeze stiffened, the sky grew dark and gray, and she was pulled inside before a sheet of rain moved across the plaza toward her. She was ushered inside, and down another flight of stairs, exiting through the other doors as if pushed through.

She stood on the plaza turning slowly, seeing through it all, to certain lakes, seeing the shrines to their Goddesses, then to gorges with fast flowing streams, then springs, all with their shrines and temples. Then she was shown the terraced rice fields, each with their own little pavilions to their Goddesses.

She rose high over the island, and noticed spots of darkness scattered across the landscape connected by a dark webbing. She descended to one. It was a standing stone, a phallic stone, representing Skreeva. Some were elaborately carved, others had writing inscribed on them. Where it was embedded in the ground, surrounding it, was the outline of a phulva. The stone was polished but the mud brick outline was disregarded, pieces out of line like they'd been kicked. The phulva pulsed slowly with a faint red light. Jasmine touched the Skreeva stone to know the nature of the darkness, she felt the ego shadow of the will to power over others. She felt it as a poison, pouring into the earth.

Then the vision shifted to a dark room with faint red light through high, horizontal windows, and Salakta in recline—Salakta, the Tantric face of She Who Comes, lying on Her side with a transparent glittering cloth covering Her body. She looked to be dreaming by her slow regular breathing and her smile. Then Her hand moved to between Her legs and Her breath quickened.

Languidly She slipped from the divan, still draped in cloth and on all fours, Her knees spread around a bowl. Her hand went back between Her legs, and in short time She rained into the bowl. When the bowl was half full, She sat back on Her heels and held Her palms out over it. A steam, perhaps a smoke, rose from the water of life. She dropped Her fingers into the water and flicked the drops away, over Her head.

Then Jasmine was back in the skies over the island. Stones were falling, tracing white trails. Stones were falling like falling stars, little meteors, or rocks blown out in a volcanic explosion, descending in an arc from the distant peak. The stones fell all over the island landing into little niches, many by running water. Jasmine found herself on the little beach in Crack the Rock Gorge, washing rags with Grandmother. Napat, entrained in Jasmine's wake, gasped and cried out. Grandmother looked at Jasmine, and nodded her head across the little river and smiled. Jasmine looked at the small rough finished stone sculpture tucked away in its niche where there spring bubbled from the rock. She heard Grandmother's voice say, "Queen Old Woman."

Suddenly Jasmine knew what the stone represented, with its cylindrical body, its rounded head, the collar right below the head, like a hood pushed back. She knew it wasn't a phallic stone, like those to Skreeva. She knew it was a part of herself, and that part of her twitched and pulsed, and swelled. Then she rose above the gorge, feeling herself pulled to look to the north. She saw a little white light which resolved itself into the dark gray stone set in a niche above a small river, then looked up to see four massive statues, cut from the living rock. She heard Chantana clear her throat, and brought her awareness back to the pavilion.

She opened her eyes and regarded Chantana, whose eyes were wide and flashing. Chantana said, "The Concubines."

After learning all she could about The Concubines from Chantana, the sun was westering into the late afternoon, and it became time to depart. In the gate to the compound, directly between the carved frame sides that depicted the great mountain cracked in half, Jasmine turned to face Chantana. She closed her eyes and rolled them back in her head. When she opened them only the whites were showing and then, in a transition that shook Chantana to her core, the whites turned blue, the entire eyeball turned blue. Chantana gasped. Jasmine spoke with a voice that sounded like it was close in and coming from far away at the same time. "She bids me tell you that there is a fourth force. A fourth force to be included in the balance. Take care not to discount it."

Then, leaving Chantana shaken and amazed, Jasmine and Napat got in their waiting van and drove off.

36

EIGHT WEEKS FIRST WEEK

FIRST DAY

Angelica and Mai Pei were sitting along the side of a raised platform covered with a futon and sheets and a few small pillows. The platform was large enough that Angelica could lay across it in both directions. Overhead, there was a canopy of some material with a loose enough weave to allow dappled light to play across their faces as it lifted and fell in a soft breeze. The canopy rested on posts set back from the corners of the bed, so that access around it was uninterrupted. Curtains were tied back on the posts. There was a low table nearby with oil and water. As they sat, they each kept one foot touching the deck below the platform.

Mai Pei was explaining to Angelica what to expect from the behavior of the men who would be sent to her during the day. There would be two. The first man would give her a massage that would last most of the morning. She was to pay attention to the different sensations caused by the touch, simply tracking and noticing the sensations, especially when the touching would turn intimate. The touch would be light, and involve no penetration. The second man, in the early afternoon, would begin like the first, but would move to intimate touching more quickly, and would, near the end of the session, use his fingers to move further than the morning session.

Both men would be wearing sarongs, and would likely grow erect, Mai Pei told Angelica. She could look, and she could touch, but she was not to fondle or stroke the men.

While Mai Pei and Angelica talked, Quinn and Regina took a seat behind a screen positioned slightly above the head of the platform. The material allowed them to see through it from their side, but reflected light on the side that Angelica could see so that they were effectively invisible.

Mai Pei withdrew and shortly after a man, perhaps in his thirties, walked up onto the deck carrying a cup of tea. He was wearing a sarong, tied in front, black with golden swirls, and a short sleeved white shirt, completely unbuttoned. He smiled, showing good teeth, and bowed to Angelica. Setting his tea on the table, he said, "Please, stand so that I can see you."

She did and he slid the shawl from her shoulders, and, going to one knee, untied her sarong, letting it slip away. He stepped back, glancing quickly over her. She felt the breeze, or perhaps it was his gaze, make her nipples crinkle up. When he noticed, he blushed. Which made her blush. "I am looking for tensions in your form, so that I will know how to touch you." He smiled, and looked away. "Please turn around." She did. He examined her from behind. "OK," he said. "Please, would you lie down on your belly, here near the edge of the bed?"

She did. He tucked a pillow under her belly and one under her head, gently lifting her hair out of the way. He spread a clean sheet over her. He put one knee up on the bed, leaned forward and put a hand on her back between her shoulders, just letting it rest there, without moving. Slowly, as she grew used to the touch, she relaxed from an overall tension that she didn't know she'd been holding and sighed.

He began with the lightest of touches, starting with her hands, stroking her palms, then up her arms to her shoulders, then across and down her back, pulling the sheet back as he went. He stroked down her buttocks, then covered her back with the sheet and exposing her legs. He spread her legs then stroked from her feet to her upper thighs, spending more time on the inside of her thighs, then long strokes that began all the way up, between her legs then down to her feet. Then he asked her to roll over and commenced again with the backs of her hands. He paid particular attention to her breasts and nipples, the grazing strokes making them hard. He stroked her low belly to her mons, then started at her feet, stroking upward. When he reached her phulva he stroked lightly along her upper thighs and around the outer edges and down to her perineum. Angelica heard a faint squish as his thumbs passed her opening.

He paused and oiled his hands. She opened her eyes and looked at him. He smiled. She saw his erection, parting his sarong. She smiled and closed her eyes. Starting at the top of her mound he brought his hands down along both sides, and around to the space below her opening. She could feel herself swelling, and wet. He repeated the movement several times, she lost count. Eventually he paused, both thumbs on either side of her opening. He pressed, and circled his thumbs. She could hear her wetness, and feel it running down over her anus. The insides of her thighs started to tremble, and a pulse arose deep within her, attracted to his thumbs, pulsing there at her opening. She strained her hips upward, searching, seeking to give entry to his thumbs, but he refused to let her find them. In her straining she came, squeezing her thighs, trapping his hands.

When the trembling eased she released him, turned her head and opened her eyes again. She saw his erection and reached for it, running a finger along the underside, and lifted the drop of fluid at its tip to her lips, and smiled. He returned the smile and stepped back, bowing, and walked away.

Angelica rested, then a young wen came up to her, bowed, and said, "It is time to eat something, and refresh yourself."

"Wait, what?" Angelica asked, confused.

"Yes. Two hours have passed," the young wen said, and smiled knowingly.

Sitting with Regina and Quinn, eating fruit and drinking tea, Angelica looked through the screen at the bed. "You can see everything from here."

"Yes," Regina said. "And hear it, too," she grinned.

"And how about you?" Angelica asked Quinn.

"It's close enough. It's not like the screen would stop me or anything," he said.

"That's not what I mean. And you know it. I mean how did it feel, how did it make you feel, watching me."

"Well, sexually, it was activating. Big time erection. And I can see where it would give a man an opportunity to work on himself. But there was no jealousy, we don't have that kind of relationship. I'm your bodyguard primarily. Not your lover, not your Consort. Different line of work. I did find in myself that I'm jealous of not being a wen in my twenties," he finished.

"Too late for that," Regina joked, putting one foot on his to make him mind his tongue.

Quinn relaxed a little, smiled at them both. "Besides, Angelica, you'll just use me how you want, when you want. And you know me,

I'm here to serve."

Both wen laughed. "What an asshole you are," Regina said, smacking him on the shoulder. Turning to Angelica, she asked. "So, are you beginning to develop discernment at the level of sensation?"

"A little. I realize I hold all kinds of tension in my body in different ways that are caused by my emotions, especially those feelings that are subliminal. I'm not normally aware of them. And I can feel how tired all those tensions make me."

"Yes, normally we waste huge amounts of energy that way. But for your work, both as a Priestess, and the Carrier of the Dragon, you need all that energy to become the transformational force that She requires. The reward for you is greater access to ecstasy, and hence greater ecstasy itself. By the way, how is that Dragon?"

"Sleeping. Dreamless, apparently. Not even a stir. No impulse to manifest."

"Well, good, I suppose. On some level it's aware of everything. Try not to be surprised. Some of the places you'll get to will probably grab its attention. Try not to scare the help, OK?"

"Yeah, sure. When do we get started again?"

"Now," Regina said, nodding toward the two people, wen and man, coming toward them, carrying water and cups on a tray and another tray with small containers and what looked like certain kinds of tools. The man stopped at the bedside, set down his tray, and smoothed out the bed. The wen continued around to the other side of the screen where they sat. She set down her tray with tea and some kind of sweet cakes. She took up the lunch tray with one hand and offered her other hand to Angelica, who took it and stood up.

When they'd taken two steps holding hands Angelica became aware of a high frequency vibration, almost a buzz, resonating in the wen's hand. With the shock of recognition, the wen turned and smiled at her, nodding. The vibration transferred itself to her hand, entered into her, dropping to her womb and settled there. She felt the dragon stir. The wen escorted her to the bedside. By that time Angelica was in an altered state of consciousness, all sensation but no thought. When the wen dropped her hand she felt it as a break so sharp she uttered a small cry. Still smiling the wen looked at her with a raised eyebrow. Angelica nodded affirmatively that she was OK. The dragon stirred again, longer this time.

When she sat on the edge of the bed she closed her eyes, sensing her presence and all its internal processes. Her skin seemed alive, almost on fire, with the buzzing energy. Her heart pulse was higher, excited. Blood suffused her hands and feet, her face and her phulva. The Higher Heart pulsed hard, slow but hard, dropping from the space of her heart to the space of her root.

It was too much for the dragon. The outline of Angelica's image began to waver. Behind the screen Regina nudged Quinn and said, "Watch this." The dragon's image began to solidify in the field around Angelica. The image grew large around her. She appeared to fall into deep meditation, sitting there. The man beside her went to his knees, looking up at the newly emerged being from within the wen.

Twice as large as Angelica the dragon also appeared to be meditating, clawed hands with interlaced fingers resting on its belly. Suddenly its eyes opened and it leaned forward over the kneeling man, its mustaches floating in the air. The man looked upward; hands folded in his lap. The dragon opened its mouth, looking as if it would close down, completely enclosing the man's head any moment. Instead it yawned. Then the entire body separated from Angelica. There was a brief glimpse of a silver thread, sparkling in the light, running from her navel to the dragon's, which thinned and disappeared as the dragon drifted to the floor at the foot of the bed, curled up, and went back to sleep, nose tucked under its tail, like some humongous guard dog.

Quinn's jaw had dropped. Regina reached over and closed it, laughing.

Angelica had fallen back on the bed, eyes lidded, panting, during the separation ordeal. The man, kneeling between her knees, wiped his brow of sweat, and put his hands on her knees and squeezed lightly. Angelica sighed, and sat up on her elbows. She smiled at him.

From his knees between hers he applied oil to her phulva. He began with the light stroking with which the other man had begun. Shortly, however, he began with inserting just one joint of his middle finger, palm down, and applying a slight downward pressure. He raised his other hand, curling the fingers in a circle like a fist, and made a squeezing motion. "You," he said. Angelica understood him to mean that she should squeeze. She squeezed everything.

He shook his head no. Putting his left hand on her perineum, he shook his head no again, then moving his hand lower, he shook his head no. Putting the fingers of his left hand around the slightly inserted finger of his right, he nodded his head yes. This began the work of Angelica learning how to differentiate the musculature of her pelvic floor in finer detail. It took a while for her to learn how to contract only the muscles her teacher wanted. Her reward, after many minutes of trying, he patient, smiling, and encouraging, was he slipped the finger in another knuckle.

During the course of the afternoon Angelica learned to contract, and control the contraction of, the smooth muscle along her inner length. Quinn fell asleep, head resting on one arm on the table, his other arm in his lap resting against his helpless erection. Regina spent the afternoon farther back from the screen, practicing with the young man from the morning session.

As Angelica made progress, her teacher relented and took his finger in to the third knuckle. She gasped as she felt the rolling contraction start deep within her, squeezing with such intensity that she popped the finger out of her.

Her teacher smiled and stood up. He bowed to her, his palms pressed together. She could see his erection poking through his sarong. She sat up and reached for him, taking him in her hand. He stood still. Slowly she squeezed her fingers to her palm, one at a time, mimicking the rolling force she'd felt.

His smile grew large, and he nodded. "Yes," he said.

Angelica, hair plastered by sweat to her face, fell back, rolled over her side, pulled up her knees and promptly fell asleep. As soon as the man was gone, the silver thread between her and the dragon lit up. In a ghost of smoke the dragon poured itself into her, and shrinking in size, curled up and fell asleep again.

By this time Regina had released the Consort and returned to the table. She punched Quinn in the arm. "Wake up, Thundercock," she said playfully.

As he came awake Quinn mumbled, "Coffee. Must have coffee."

Second Day

Angelica arrived at the training bed shortly after dawn, dressed in a sarong and multiple shawls, carrying a tray with a tea service. It was the coolest time of the day and she wanted to sit quietly in beauty. Halfway through her first cup, sitting on the bed, one foot on the ground, she lapsed into that inner quiet and opened her mind to the explosion of noise from the dawn birds, and her utter embedment in the pool of the smells of the thousands of flowers around her. She narrowed her eyes to slits, and scanned around, the long view open to the southeast, the raised wall behind her in the northwest, where she knew her bodyguard would be keeping watch. She focused on the small flowers growing in the cracks between the rocks. She wondered what they smelled like, so, setting down her tea she went over to the wall.

As she got close she felt herself pass through a thin wall of pressure, a pressure change, and then her face was next to the rock. She breathed in.

It was a high smell, a high note, trilling first even upward, and then falling, not to a threnody, not to sadness, but a spreading, fading, like the hiss at the last reach of a wave on the sand. She stood there, enthralled, hands and one cheek touching the wall, eyes closed, and devoted herself to becoming the sensations, in series, and then, attempting to become aware of it all, all at once. It was too much and she went into trance.

She heard a cough behind her, and slowly turned, her eyes hooded. There was a couple standing there, he carrying a tray with incense and water, she with a bundle of cut flowers in the crook of her arm. Their eyebrows raised only slightly, but in complete synchrony. They smiled. Angelica lowered her brow slightly, the inclined head shy but the eyes flashed with the anticipation of something delicious, with just a hint of wickedness. She smiled back.

The man gestured. "The flowers. They are special to our purpose."

"They are beautiful," Angelica whispered, realizing that she meant both the flowers and the couple standing in front of her.

Setting the tray on the ground, the wen sat on the bed and, putting a pillow behind her, leaned back on the headboard. "Come, sit," she said, patting the bed in front of her. Angelica came around the foot of the bed, and the man stepped back as she passed. She sat on the bed facing the other wen. "Today we will begin with the eyes. There is a power in them that can be sensed. We call this gazing. He can tell when your gaze is on him. We wish you to be able to tell when his gaze is on you. Come. Turn around and sit with your back to me. I will help you today."

Angelica did as she was told. The wen hiked up her sarong and spread her legs. "Lean back into me," she said, guiding Angelica to rest her back upon her helper's chest. The heat emanating from her was immediately palpable, big heat from her heart, smaller points of heat from her breasts. Angelica sighed.

The helper said, "Bend your knees and pull your sarong up. There, just so." The helper let just the ends cover Angelica's sex, leaving her legs bare. She gestured for the man to come stand by the bedside. "Gaze at him," she whispered to Angelica. "Start with his face, then let your gaze drop. Slowly. Take your time. When you get to his manhood, stop." Leaning forward so she could just see the side of Angelica's face, she paused.

Angelica looked at the man's face. He returned her look. She focused on his features, his eyes, his hair. His ears and nose, then his lips. They parted slightly in a cute smile. The helper said, "Let your focus go soft. Notice what you see." It was then that Angelica felt the resonance. The field of it seemed to be the edges of her face, and she felt her helper shift when she directed the awareness there. She allowed her gaze to broaden to where she could take in his whole face at once, the edges of her vision pulsing slightly. After a moment the pulsing edge took on a sparkle.

The man was wearing a vest and loose drawstring pants. She allowed her gaze to drop slowly. He swallowed when she passed his throat, inhaled when her gaze dropped over his heart, and again over the tight abs of his belly. She paused at a spot between his navel and pubic bone. The air took on a color from the sunset and dawn palette. She marveled at its beauty and how it faded to a deep red below.

She dropped her eyes into that pool of pulsing red, and she noticed a movement. The loose material grew taut, strained against it from within. She realized that she was gazing the man into erection. She extended will out along the line of her gaze, and the field pulsed. He pulsed. The helper behind her gestured for him to come over and undid the drawstring that held up the pants, pulling out the waist and freeing his phallus as she dropped the waistline over his extension. It rocked slowly in the light as his pants slid down and he stepped out of them.

She felt something tighten deep in her low belly, the tension she knew would lead to an orgasm.

She glanced quickly at his face and realized he was gazing at her, gazing at her phulva. She shifted under his gaze and her lips made the slightest of sucking sounds. So did the lips of her sex below. Her gaze dropped again as his erection throbbed at the sounds.

"Watch," the helper commanded, shifting behind her. She put out her hand, palm up, under the upward straining curve of him. She stroked under him, and it lifted as if trying to evade her hand. "You do it," she said.

Angelica reached out her hand, following the Priestess's instruction. She did not obtain the same result. The Priestess put her hand under Angelica's and said, "Here, like this." Angelica smiled as she felt the warm pulse of the Priestess's hand wrap around hers, projecting a field from her hand that met the field around the phallus and pushed it upward as they stroked.

The man growled softly deep in his chest, almost a purr. His gaze remained fixed on her sex. From that place of deep tension she felt a pulse emerge, followed the path of her inner channel, dissipating before it reached the surface.

The helper changed her hand to a grasping form, still not touching, and pulled slowly, Angelica's following. In the shadow of it, Angelica could have sworn she saw the man's skin compress, pulled along toward her and sliding back.

"He has come erect under your gaze," the Helper behind her said. "And how do you feel?"

"I feel the orgasm beginning at the top of my womb."

"Good. Now connect the tip of him in your hand to that point."

Both Angelica and the man gasped simultaneously as the sensation of him being fully buried in her overwhelmed them both.

The Helper laughed. "Most people imagine that as an insertion process, not as an event."

And the laughter triggered the orgasm. Angelica began laughing as the orgasm rolled through her like a ball bouncing down the stairs, each bounce producing a bucking of her hips and an 'OO!' sound. Then she broke into laughter again, except in peals of it, when she looked up and saw the contorted face of the man around whom her hand was 'air squeezed,' her fingers contracting as she slid her hand down to his root in time with her own bumping.

The Helper whispered, still laughing, "He's trying not to come." This pulled another peal of laughter from Angelica as he glanced at her from under a contorted brow, sweat dropping onto her arm.

It became a contest of wills between them. Would Angelica succeed in making him come, or would he maintain his self-control? Energetically Angelica felt something unlock in him, some easing as if tumblers in a lock fell into alignment, and she knew she had him. He blasted ejaculate all over her, groaning and shaking. The whole spectacle made her laugh again, as each drop tickled where it landed, belly, breast, and cheek.

She watched the tip as it opened to the fluid emergent from within, felt the contractions not just in her hand but deep within her, and she groaned, and smiled at him, fascinated. The last of the come didn't spurt from him, it oozed, some dripping on her hand. She leaned forward to take him in her mouth, to suck away the last beads clinging to him but the Helper restrained her, whispering, "Use your hand."

She did, using her thumb to wipe it away. She started to draw her hand to her mouth, but stopped, hesitating, asking in silent gesture for permission from her Helper. "You may," the Helper said. "Just hold your thumb in your mouth. That's right. Just hold it there, sense it, feel it, open your mind to what it is."

She closed her mouth around her thumb and rested, eyes closed. Suddenly her mind filled with little lightning bolts, flashing once then gone, then just darkness. She swallowed.

"Did you see that?" Angelicas asked excitedly.

"Yes, I did. What do you think it was?"

"I don't know."

"Well, you have to think about it. Inquire. Would you like some tea?"

"Why, yes. Yes, I would."

Although Quinn and Regina couldn't quite see what was happening below them because of the screen, they certainly could hear what was happening. Regina had to stifle a barked out laugh when she first heard Angelica laughing during orgasm. Regina said, "I remember my first laughing orgasm. It's such a wonderful thing, and such an important antidote to the seriousness we put on sex. How about you? Have you ever had one?"

"A few. Mostly triggered by the wen I was with. She'd start then I'd laugh with joy at her happiness, and be pleased that I had caused such a thing in her. Once or twice maybe I came to it on my own, in moments when I became filled with a sense of power, being a powerful man capable of bringing happiness to whomever I was with. Mostly, though, I don't laugh much. Or easily."

"I've noticed. Do you know why?"

"Yeah. Mostly, it's just not funny. And below that, well, everything hurts. In the past forty-five years I've learned to repress it pretty well. But everything hurts all the time, just more or less."

"Do you know why?"

"Yeah. Too much electricity. We're not designed for it."

"What about here?"

"Here's OK. Why?"

"Well, even though much of what they have here is solar, to run things on DC is inefficient. But the AC we use runs on a non-biologically resonant frequency, unlike back home. The 60hz there resonates. And we keep the place a cellphone reception dead zone. We pay locally to keep it in shadow. Being in that higher frequency field ruins the more subtle perceptions we're trying to teach."

"Regina, you're saying 'we' a lot. What do you mean, 'we'?"

"Quinn, this Order is 2500 years old. It's been a refuge for wen, and a training ground for our own protection and our own growth, sexual, tantric, and alchemical. It has produced Objective Saints and Enlightened Beings. Our Order, the Fleur de Vie, has been supporting them for almost a hundred years, since Rachel discovered them over on the mainland. We send wen and men here for training all the time. I was sent here for training. I am," she paused. "Respected here. I am the Moon Halter."

Quinn stood up to go escort Angelica to her room. He put a hand on Regina's shoulder. "Thank you."

Regina Moon Halter turned her head to watch him go, her elbows on the table, leaning forward. Her dark hair streaked with white fell across her face, and she watched him walk away through the curtain of it. Her mind was quiet, but assessing him from an internal place of no words, judgment not yet formed. She liked him, liked sex with him. He'd even taken her to laughing once, his surprise at well-educated wen provoking an earnestness in him she'd found delightful. But could he be trusted? He wasn't sworn to them, wasn't initiated into their Mysteries, but he seemed to understand them. And he was coy, silent even, about what all he knew.

Angelica found herself exhausted at the end of the day, even though she hadn't often exerted herself pro-actively. She was exhausted from cultivating the Receptive, as she'd been taught to do. The attention required for subtle perception, and the even greater efforts of attention required for her to learn to control certain parts of her own musculature, left her brain-fogged. Sometimes she'd fall asleep over supper. Once, Quinn even carried her back to the rooms. She was grateful to Quinn, laid her head on his shoulder, and smiled, sighing. She, in her Receptivity, trusted him.

"But what does she know?" Regina smiled to herself. She, Regina, knew precisely what Angelica knew and didn't know.

By the end of the week Angelica had developed the ability to control her internal musculature through the rarefaction of her senses. She could sense precisely where a phallus was inside her, and had enough internal control to squeeze it hard enough hold it there, and could even, with effort, lock it inside her. Regina had told her, only slightly joking, "That's so you can hold him still long enough to kill him."

She learned she could use this control to pinch off a man's ejaculation. They had her work with men and objects of different sizes so she could learn control in any situation.

They surprised her on that Friday night with a small party in her honor. She was given two men at once, along with the instruction that she could only take both of them at the same time, take them within her. The sensation of two men sliding within her, sliding on each other, took her away, took her away somewhere she couldn't recall when she returned.

She'd learned the rudiments of controlling especially the bands of muscle around the petals of her internal blossom, opening and allowing them to close, stroking the inserted phallus. She'd also learned to tune into the deep muscles of her womb, where the waves of birthing waited. And she'd learned to feel the slight contractions that would signal the onset of fertility, and of menses, with Regina's assistance, over the course of that weekend. Regina used Angelica's memory of the time before Regina had halted her moon to access those subtle sensations in her body, and to record them for when she was released back into her normal cycle.

In the evenings, sometimes, she would call Quinn to her, the sudden void of contact after a full day of proximity to the men, to her Helper, left her shaky, and in need of comfort. They would spoon, Angelica reaching behind her to hold his phallus, relax into its growing, and, falling asleep, tuck it between her legs, holding him there, not inside, just feeling the length of him tucked there between her legs, taking comfort, knowing she was safe.

37

How Strong the Heart?

Leonora, an intelligence analyst, and William, a technician, did their best to keep their relationship a secret from their co-workers, Leonora being an officer and William an enlisted man. They had their own apartments, paid for more by their stipends from the Order than by their own salaries. But, since they worked in the same office, people suspected. William's fellow enlisted men particularly. Before Leonora had been stationed there he used to go out with them more often, and stay later. Now, he'd get a text and when he left shortly thereafter they'd tease him about getting new orders. But he was so affable and friendly nobody resented him for it, and they kept their jealousy in check. They'd keep his secrets, as good buds would.

Leonora was not a particularly beautiful person. But she was an initiated Priestess of the Fleur de Vie and William was an initiated Consort, assigned to her once she'd appeared on the scene. The local High Priestess had ordered them to develop the formal relationship while keeping up all the required appearances.

When they'd been assigned to infiltrate the cult of the Master they'd been surprised at how easy it was. They didn't realize that the ease was because of hypnotic atmosphere of the Master's compound. That, and the drugs—usually very small doses of a popular date-rape drug that made everyone pliable to manipulation and open to suggestion.

They'd taken to it because of the sex. The Master was interested in sex. A lot. He would seduce anyone he could, of either gender. He'd taken Leonora in first but it was really William he was after.

It was weeks before their High Priestess noticed the change in them. They seemed distracted at meetings, and alternating between dazed and agitated. She asked her Madeleine to look. She saw a dark veil over the entire compound with a darker form pulsing at its center. She couldn't pierce the veil so the Priestess ordered William and Leonora to redouble their efforts to get to that dark heart and reveal it.

And when William and Leonora went under that darkness, the Madeleine could no longer see them, either. So they were surprised when, after the return of the Master and his assistant A., they were invited to stay after meetings for what were called 'special audiences' with the Master. Reporting on the special audiences to the High Priestess, they were encouraged. It meant they were getting closer to the dark heart of things.

The audiences were mostly on week nights—work nights. William's friends and Leonora's superiors noticed the fatigue and almost hung-over demeanors from the late nights with little sleep, and the drugs.

The audience would begin with a little talk from the Master, a homily about power over others, and that in order to gain that power one had to experiment with powerlessness. And then there were some exercises he prescribed for internal circulation of energies, and then he would provide the opportunity to practice that circulation by having William and Leonora disrobe and assume certain positions.

It began when individually they'd perform oral sex on both the Master and A. and then they'd change partners. It was the Master who preferred William, commanding him, fingers gripping at Williams short hair, and growling in some kind of animal frustration. More and more his behavior was coming unhinged, but no one saw the flapping of the kite at the back of his head, partially untethered and unable to reattach. The touch of the Lama's ghost still burned.

The evening would end with Leonora bent over the arm of the sofa, William embedded in her behind, the Master standing and buried in William's behind, and both Leonora and William servicing a recumbent A., one leg over the back of the sofa, directing how they used their mouths and fingers. The Master would croon about the need to feel the sacred energy he was transmitting into William, energy that William would transmit to Leonora with every stroke, challenging them to pull the energy up and out their hands onto A.

And A. could feel their efforts, feel them feeding her need of life force to maintain the appearance that was 20 years younger than its time. She didn't like the taste that the drugs left in her, but it was better food than she'd had all those months on the road looking for Quinn. She thought of her henches and dismissed the imagery, focusing on the present, making them do things to her with their mouths and fingers that they wouldn't even do to each other.

Sometimes the Master would switch between them, William and Leonora. But mostly he'd abuse her with vibrators and dildos, driving her to the edge between pleasure and pain, smiling when she'd scream her release into A.'s sex, raised on pillows before her. A. loved getting her ass eaten, even after all these years.

The Master would look over the backs of the young people before him, and smirk into A.'s eyes, and she would return to him her best imitation of a winning smile. And when he'd get bored, he'd release them, and release them to release him, awarding them both with what he called the seeds of sacredness.

He had no clue about how accurate he was in his parody of the rites of the Order.

Even so, it was a surprise to Leonora when she woke up in a room in the basement below the Master's Learning Center. She was on her feet, her hands restrained and pulled over her head and an ankle bar holding her legs spread. She was wearing a leather hood with no openings, but she wasn't gagged. She could hear William breathing next to her. He whispered to her, "Remember your vow."

"There'll be none of that, now," the Master growled, clearing his throat. There was a rustle of clothes then the electric snap of a cattle prod and then a sound of William jumping, feet dragging on the concrete floor, shouting "Hey, what the fuck! That hurt!"

"Speak when you're spoken to," the Master snarled and shocked him again. William grunted in pain rather than speak.

"How about you? Pretty girl," Leonora heard A.'s voice whisper in her ear. "Got anything to say?" Leonora shook her head 'No' and recoiled as she felt what was clearly a phallus brush against her hip. A. had chosen a black leather bustier that pushed up her breasts and fell to her low belly with knee high boots over black stockings and elbow length silk gloves. She wore the harness she used to peg the Master, certain that before the evening was over, she'd be doing him again. At least once. Unsure of his ability to perform, under his long white robe the Master wore a harness, too.

A. whispered again to Leonora, "You will."

Leonora realized that this situation would not end well. She had figured out that the Master would use date rape drugs on them, making them pass out when this was over, and that they'd not remember this when they woke up, if they ever woke up. She also knew that the Master had a power that he'd use to reinforce the forgetfulness. But she thought that there was no way she wouldn't remember, that William wouldn't remember. It was probably the best she could hope for. And she thought that these two monsters would know that, too.

So she waited, blind, to hear what it was they wanted her to answer. Into the silence she heard slurping noises and a small groan escaped William's lips. She realized someone was sucking him into an erection.

"There," the Master said. "How pretty. Now we can get to work."

Leonora felt a gloved had slide between her legs, feeling all around her sex and slipping down to grip her inner thigh and twist the flesh so hard she gasped in pain.

She heard the Master's voice, sly and conniving, next to William, "So, tell me. What does the pink tattoo on Leonora's thigh mean?" Then she heard that zapping sound and from the tenor of William's voice when he responded "Ow, oh, no, oh fuck. Oh no," she knew it had been used on something intimate.

The Master asked William again. "What is that tattoo?" The zapping sound again, and William shouting. Leonora called out, "Stop it, please stop it."

"Tell us what we need to know, and it will stop," A. whispered in her ear, loud enough for William to hear. Then she heard William grunting rhythmically in pain, and he was being taken. Then she felt herself being penetrated from behind. She gasped at the insertion and the pain.

"I can't tell you," William said. "I can't tell you!"

"Can't or won't?"

"I can't. I will die."

"Oh, I doubt that. You'll tell me."

A sound came from William's throat, a kind of gurgle that was cut off abruptly. All noise stopped, except for the sound of A.'s belly slapping into Leonora's backside, and in a moment that stopped, too.

"Well, what do you know," the Master said.

"He passed out?" A. asked.

"No, I don't think so." There was a rustle of cloth. "No. Nope. He didn't pass out. No pulse. He died."

A sob broke from Leonora.

"He died?" A. asked, incredulous.

"He died."

The Master came close to Leonora. "Well then, pretty thing, I'll just have to ask you. What does the tattoo mean?" He zapped her breast from the side.

Leonora couldn't stop sobbing. A. started to move in her again as the Master grabbed a handful of the long hair that was hanging out of the hood and twisted it.

"Hmm? What does it mean?"

"Hopeless," Leonora thought. "Hopeless. No getting out. Hopeless." She drew in a breath and her chest exploded in pain, her vision filled with a white-hot heat that collapsed to black.

The Lama's ghost stood in the corner, hands folded, a tear running down his cheek.

The Master said, "Wow. Her, too. I might have killed them anyway, but what the hell? This is fucking ridiculous." He went to a side table and retrieved a scalpel. "Lay her down on the floor," he commanded. When she was down he leaned forward and spread her legs. He cut around the tattoo and pulled it free.

As he was bent over the Lama's ghost stepped forward and grabbed the free end of the black kite and pulled.

The Master felt the rip and shouted, dropping the scalpel and putting his hands on the back of his head. "Ow. Fuck! What is that?"

The Lama's ghost couldn't pull it completely free but left more of it flapping, like a kite in the wind. A. sensed his presence and threw herself over her Master's body to protect him. The ghost backed away.

38

Mount Nagoon

Napat woke up early on the day of their excursion to the main temple complex at the foot of Mt. Nagoon. Although it was a school day Napat's teachers had been so impressed with the improvement in her scholastics since she'd come to work for Jasmine that they agreed she could take the day off to guide her employer. They didn't bother to tell her father; he'd have wanted to come along.

They hired Napat's shady uncle to drive them again. They intended to take him up the long walk to the top of the Temple complex. If they decided to instigate a conversation with any priests it would be better to have someone male engage with them. Before it had become clear that the priests had set watchers on Jasmine and Napat, Jasmine would have preferred to engage them herself and surprise them with her knowledge of Nahasi, but she'd learned it would have offended them, since most of them spoke only Windonesian. It was as if they were an occupying army, too superior, in their own minds, to learn much about the conquered people.

When they set out they could see the mountain, rising almost 12,000 feet in the air from the very ocean itself. When they could no longer see the mountain through the windows after an hour's drive they came to a coastal highway, narrow against the hulk of the sacred mountain. They arrived at a parking lot with a line of vendor's stalls separating the lot from the slope up to the temples. There were signs at the edge of the lot stating that only people with traditional clothes would be allowed access to the temples. Napat and her uncle both had forgotten this requirement and had worn western clothing, so Jasmine happily went shopping with them, paying for everything. Changing in the back of the stalls, they took their clothes back to the van, and, clutching water bottles, they took off up the road.

Only a little way up they encountered another sign, asking that all non-Wallidese people please hire a guide. So they stopped at the booth alongside the road, and stepped up to a podium with a man sitting on a high stool. They were immediately surrounded by young men whose turn it was, wearing traditional clothes, all talking to them at once while another group of young men held back. Jasmine looked over the group until she noticed a middle-aged man standing in back. Jasmine told Napat to find out if he was available. He was. She hired him, hoping that his age meant he was more likely to know more history. When he got out front she noticed his limp. He sat on a little scooter, saying it was in case they got tired.

They started off up the road again. The road divided, the left going past the base of the grand staircase up into the main temple, the right continuing along up the massive side. Jasmine indicated she wanted to continue on up, saying they would stop in on the way back down. She could see other, smaller temples up the mountain, and she wanted to see the view from there. And she felt pulled.

The next building past the main temple was an open air pavilion with ornate boxes resting on shoulder high pillars. She was informed that these were houses for the ashes of the dead after they had been taken to the ocean. She turned and realized she could see the ocean in the distance. The guide told them that once a year the ashes of all the dead were brought here and the containers were either washed in the ocean, or the ashes were released in a days-long ritual. The wealthy had their ashes interred in the pavilion, overlooking the main temple, the temple to Skreeva, god of death and transformation.

But the pull on Jasmine continued. She could see another, smaller temple up the mountain past the pavilion.

"What's that up there?" she asked Napat. Napat translated and the answer was, "That's the Temple to the King of the Mountain."

"Ah," Jasmine said. "That's where I want to go."

The guide said that the path was too steep for the scooter, and if they would take their time, he would walk up there with them. So it was a slow walk, stopping to shop at the stalls, buying a few items and more water.

They arrived at the level meadow that served as the landing for an immense free standing stone staircase, held up by immense carved dragon balustrades. The tails of the dragons were at the top, at the actual entrance to the Temple proper. Their bodies descended in ripples for 30 yards, unsupported from below, their giant heads at ground level, stone stairs suspended between them. A chill ran down Jasmine's back, and she sighed.

Slowly, reverently, she approached the landing. She stroked the head of the nearest dragon. A watching Napat saw a shiver of what she felt as delight pass up the entire length of the dragon, a vibration in the image in her eye. Jasmine crossed to the other dragon, and petted it also, with the same result. Jasmine grinned more broadly than Napat had ever seen.

Together they advanced up the stairs, Jasmine's hand resting on the stone all the way up, stroking it, sending ripples through Napat's vision. At the top she turned, eyes bright and grinning fiercely, and took in the view of the entire Temple complex, seeing all the way to the ocean.

On either side of the main Temple were the Temples to Skreeva's brothers, Drahma, the Maker, and Wishnu, the Maintainer. These Temples were one-third the size of the Temple to Skreeva, the Destroyer, reflecting their importance in the island cult.

Jasmine tsk'ed, and started to turn toward the pavilion in the center of Temple floor when the vision struck her. A wind came up the mountain, buffeting her, blowing her hair back. She saw the Dragons, and the Concubines, and she knew what she was going to do, and what she had to do, to make the Vision happen.

She walked around to the back of the courtyard, opening uphill toward the mountain peak. She took in the empty throne, waiting for the King, and went to her knees, hands on the Temple floor and, with her back straight, bowed, silently sending a voice inviting the King to come and speak to her.

A priest hurried over, and the guide gave him some money in exchange for a flower. He passed it to Napat, who passed it to Jasmine, sitting back on her heels. "For the King," Napat whispered.

Jasmine contemplated the marigold blossom. She beckoned to Napat. "I want a hundred flowers." After a thoughtful pause she said, "And give that much to the priest, also." Napat returned to the priest and pulled a sheaf of folded money from Jasmine's purse, which Napat normally carried. The priest was flabbergasted.

While the others were distracted, Jasmine watched the throne. Small lights danced there, like illuminated dust, sparkling and coalescing into a crowned form. Jasmine communicated with him, sent him the vision with her mind, and the question: "May I?" He smiled and nodded his assent. Jasmine bowed again. The image of the King of the Mountain faded, the last bit, Cheshire Cattish, to fade was his smile.

Jasmine rose to her feet and beckoned to the others. Napat, her uncle, and the guide followed her down the dragon stairs, Jasmine's hand stroking all the way down. She could feel the beast ripple, like scratching the back of a cat.

On the way down, Jasmine outlined a request for the guide, Napat translating. She explained that in her understanding of the beliefs of the people there was a Goddess named Salakta, a Goddess who appeared in the consorts and wives of the gods, especially when they were in congress. Skreeva was famous for the times this had happened to him. She wanted the guide to ask a priest if there was a monument to Salakta on the Temple grounds.

They passed the Pavilion of the Dead and walked in to the Temple of Skreeva through a side entrance. A priest hurried over, concerned that tourists, particularly women, were in the sacred precinct where they normally weren't allowed. The guide, who knew this would trigger immediate attention from the priests, explained the request of this unusual tourist lady. He mentioned that she was very wealthy, and the sum she had spent in the Temple to the Mountain King.

The priest became obsequious instantly. Not quite slimy, but clearly in his greed. He took them, with lots of gestures, and some broken English to a pavilion in the rear of the temple. This pavilion, like before, faced up the mountain, rather than toward the front. Jasmine stood in contemplation of what she saw.

Set on risers on the pavilion floor were stones. some old and weathered, one was broken. They were all Queen Old Woman stones. A tear rolled down Jasmine's cheek, and she sobbed once as she went to her knees.

The priest leaned over in concern, awaiting orders. Napat pushed him back, and he was horrified that the young woman touched him. The guide and uncle stepped between them. They pushed the priest back farther so their hushed and angry conversations wouldn't disturb Jasmine. They didn't realize, of course, that Jasmine was already disturbed. Greatly disturbed. She held out a hand to them, palm up. She closed it into a fist, and they went silent. To Napat it looked like something Jasmine did to them. What they felt was simply fascinated.

Jasmine rose to her feet. She leaned in and kissed the closest stone. Turning, not looking at the men, she whispered to Napat, "Five hundred flowers. Nothing for the priest." She waited, eyes filled with love, gazing at the statues, seeing their stories, where they'd been placed, when they were taken, how they were brought here.

When the transaction was complete, they turned and filed around to the front of the Temple to leave by the grand staircase. On the way down they encountered a procession, flags and banners, women carrying trays of food and flowers on their heads, led by an enormous man draped in orange, feet spilling out around the edges of his flip flops. "The high priest," Napat whispered. There was something obscene about his huge belly, and Jasmine looked away. She thought of the near emaciated priest at the Temple of the Mountain King. In her mind's eye Jasmine saw squirming forms, little humans, struggling and slithering, vying to find a parasitic purchase. The priest rolled his eyes to her as they passed on the stair, the eyes of a soul eater. She kept her eyes down, not wishing to let him know that she'd seen him, seen what he was. She heard faint sounds of screaming. "Monster," she thought. "The monster who dropped the High Priestess in the ocean." Once past him she put up a spell of forgetting, forgetting that he'd seen her at all, focusing him forward toward his feast.

At the bottom of the steps she sent Napat's uncle to buy 500 flowers for the Temple to Drahma. He knew that he'd make more money if he remained trustworthy so he didn't skim any of the cash she'd given him to transport. The rest of the group went to visit the Temple of Wishnu, the Maintainer.

This Temple, like the others, faced east and the ocean, as did the pavilion to the god. It was staffed by priests, but not as cleanly dressed as in the Temple to Skreeva. She had Napat give the donation for five hundred flowers to the priest at the top of the stairs. She went to the main pavilion and bowed toward the image there. Then she went around back behind the pavilion to look at the miniature thrones on poles, the backs carved with the images of whose throne they were, the images painted in bright colors.

At the end of the row she encountered a throne that had a peculiar image. It was a man, clearly Caucasian-looking. Painted entirely in white. With flames emitting from all his major joints. And parts. She asked the guide about it. He replied, "That is the god Winjeetniya. He is the god who stands behind these three gods here, and made them. He is, titularly, the one god. It is because the government mandated that only religions with one god are permitted. In Winduism there is a similar god, but here, we have our own version. The story is that he was suggested by a Wristian missionary attending a meeting of the priests almost one hundred years ago."

Jasmine, staring, began to shiver. She suspected she knew who this god was. She suspected she was looking at the face of De Murgos. She turned away, lest it see her looking. Lest it somehow came to know that she knew what a fraud it was.

She brushed off the thanks of the priest for the flowers as she headed down the stairs. Turning to Napat she said, "Ask you uncle to take us home." Turning to the guide she said, "My employee will pay you. Do you have a card, that I may stay in touch with you?"

The guide smiled. "Certainly. My name is Tuberio, as you may recall. You may reach me at this number," he said, patting the phone in his shirt pocket. "I know all the Temples and sacred places. I am at your service," Napat translated, taking the card. Jasmine thanked him in Nahasi and he smiled more broadly.

They walked to the turnaround at the foot of the Temple complex to wait for Napat's uncle to bring his van. "What do you think, Napat?"

"I think that something will happen. Something will happen here. And that you will be a part of it. And I think I want to be a part of it, too."

Jasmine nodded. "Be careful what you wish for, dear."

That night Jasmine fell asleep worrying about her young responsibility. How much to protect her, how much to include her. And how much to worry about using her for her mediumistic connection to her Good Grandmother.

After her first descent she found herself flying over the surface of the island. She followed a footpath through the jungle. Stone spirits sat up out of their rocks and stared at her wild-eyed as she flew by. She arrived at a small cave and ducked in. Floating upright, her feet not touching the ground, she moved down, down, and down again until she sensed a great weight above her, and she knew she was under Mt. Nagoon.

Deep under the mountain, where the volcano was still active. she approached a chamber filled with the color of firelight. The path ended in a landscape of sculpted gray clay, where she encountered a being who appeared to be made of yellow mud, fashioned into a human form, but without any facial features.

It communicated with her telepathically. "Greetings High Priestess. We have invited you here to show you something. Please come with me."

Around a bend on the sculpted clay path they cleared a wall and a chamber opened up around them. On the left, on a raised hillock, lay a sleeping dragon. Coal black, it was the largest dragon she had ever imagined. She looked around, and saw more mud people a little way off, engaged in doing something but she couldn't tell what. The person she was with brought her attention back to the dragon.

"Please, High Priestess. Look." She looked where he pointed and saw that right near the tip of the dragon's tail, right alongside the path, was a picture frame. On it was painted an outline of the tip of the tail in mud. "It does not line up. The tail has moved."

"How long?"

"Almost a century. The last time the dragon moved there was an earthquake that destroyed part of the main Temple above."

"What do want of me?"

"What should we do?"

"Speak this in the dreams of children. They will tell their parents."

"Ah."

The dream ended. She heard Napat cry out downstairs. She went to steps and part way down. "Napat, are you awake?"

"Yes, I had the dream again. I must tell my parents that the dragon has moved."

"When you see them, you shall."

"My Grandmother says to tell you—use me as you will."

"I shall. Go to sleep, child." Jasmine was determined to keep her safe as a child, until, until, until she didn't know what. Until Grandmother said it was alright.

Later that day she called the guide Tuberio to learn more of what he knew of the history of the island.

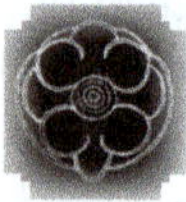

39

THE CONCUBINES

The next week, because sooner would have interfered with Napat's school schedule, and drawn too much attention, Napat took Jasmine to see the Concubines. They were in a valley called Nesami. The parking lot was on a plateau that required walking down into the Valley of the Concubines. The path led through a split in a lava surge, the sides had cooled and slumped apart from each other, leaving a path down the middle, easily bridged by palm fronds, Jasmine thought, although there was no evidence of them today, leaving the vendors sweltering in the passage, seeking shade wherever they could.

But Jasmine could see the palm fronds there, even though they weren't. She stared at them and felt the dizziness arise, the dizziness that told her that she was shifting rapidly from the Mundane to the Sacred. She was no longer seeing what is, she was seeing what was, what had been. This tunnel had been covered over when the worshippers had come. The worshippers had been walking into a long dark tunnel into the earth.

At the bottom she heard the water, a narrow stream rushing over stones down a steep incline. The statues of the Concubines were before her, the walkway at their feet reached by a bridge over the rushing stream. Jasmine felt a kind of trembling excitement that she wasn't sure she'd ever felt before. As she walked on the stone path below the four Concubines, she observed that a small stream ran into the larger stream behind her. The stream ran through a small plaza at the feet of the statues and down over a lower lip in a low rock wall. She realized that she was looking at an ancient reflecting pool for the statues. All a Priest would have had to have done was to block the channel where the low wall gapped to flood the area beneath the statue's feet with water. Still water. And then she saw.

The statues as they were today were roughhewn stone sections, set up on top of each other, carved from the very cliff face itself. Trapezoidal bodies, with just a hint of arms, cubed-out heads barely emergent from the rock itself. Jasmine saw masks made of flowers hanging from the front of the cubes, masks of flowers hanging from the trapezoidal block shoulders, hanging down, looking like arms beside dresses of flowers. And she saw the glorious beauty of the flower dresses and the flower masks reflected in the pool in the light of the moon.

They sat on a bench to regard it all. There were caves cut into the walls at the sides of the cut out that the statues emerged from. The caves had not only doors but long windows. Napat said the story went that this was where the monks stayed whose job it was to protect the shrine. Jasmine shook her head.

"No," she said. "That was for musicians. They would pack musicians into the caves and they would play. They would make the rock sing."

Napat shook her head in wonder. Jasmine said, "Me, too."

"Turn around," Napat said. "There, you see? Those statues over there, across the stream, facing these Concubines, are the statues of the royal family. The big one on the left is the King. Then there are the three children. But the tall one on the right isn't the wife, the Queen. No, it's the mother-in-law. The Queen is farther up the valley, carved into the rock where the stream makes a bend, so that she's facing this way. So she can see the whole thing. Come with me, Jasmine. Let's cross over this other bridge over here so we can sit on the side of the Royal Family, and regard the Concubines from there." She took Jasmine's hand in hers and walked the somewhat stunned Jasmine down the path and over the second bridge.

They sat on a bench on the near side, but instead of contemplating the Royal Family they turned their backs and looked across the stream to the Concubines. That was when Jasmine saw it. She saw the alcove, the shallow cave. And in it was a Queen Old Woman stone. A Salakta stone.

She gasped and stood up. "There," she said. "See?" and stood up and crossed the swift stream on foot, going up to the embedded stone, pushing aside willows. And then she realized, those willows were hiding the stone. Hiding it from the eyes of the Priests. And then she turned, and looked back across the stream to its banks below the statues of the Royal Family. And there was no Queen Old Woman stone beneath their feet.

See?" she said, defiantly, to a startled Napat. "See? There is no stone!" Jasmine recrossed the stream as quickly as she could, not wanting to draw attention to herself. She sat down next to Napat and said, "See? No stone. This place isn't about the Royal Family at all. It's about the Concubines."

She'd reached out behind the willows and touched Queen Old Woman when she was across the stream. She shuddered at the memory. The stone had told her what to do.

40

The Nature of Humans

One of the hardest things for Jasmine to process emotionally was her observation of the people around her. Her relations with the Feminine Divine, her mystical and alchemical evolution, the siddhi powers that she was developing, the controlled release, under tutelage, of the Kundalini Buffer, all these she was able to deal with and preserve a certain level of equanimity. She was trained for this, and her training held.

Given how privileged her life had been until this point, this point when she was on the verge of the bizarre and powerful, potentially world changing manifestation, she felt strong. So, when she discovered her weakness, it shook her. She understood the Law of Accidents—her birth, like almost everyone else's, was an accident. People were born by accident. People died by accident all the time. She accepted this fact by grounding it in the deeper need that Evolution has for Indeterminacy.

What shook her finally was how people related to their own trash. To their own waste. She'd gone snorkeling once off the north coast of the island, and was horrified that the water inside the reef was filled with floating fragments of plastic bags, drifting in the water like broken off seaweed, or the sheets of skin one peels off after a bad sunburn. She swam away in horror. There were more floating bits of plastic in the water, waving like flags in a slow breeze, more than there were fish, that she was afraid that they'd cling to her like a second skin.

And in Boodun, the town around the sacred temple to Wahsastami, she cringed every time she would cross the steel plate bridges over what were once irrigation ditches across the mountain sides that used to be terraced rice fields in the age before the town grew, almost to the size of a city. The old ditches were still there, and in places you couldn't see the original bottom, so covered were they with plastic bags, and who knew what all sewage and other trash. And just downstream, just outside the town proper, people still bathed in that water. People who still believed that if they believed that you couldn't see them standing naked in a ditch alongside a car-trafficked road, then you wouldn't see them there. They would even register surprise on their faces when they caught her staring at them, wondering what the hell they were doing. Didn't they know? Didn't they know they were bathing in shit?

And she hated it. In particular she hated that her training had compelled her to love them. She wanted to hate them, hate each and every one of them who ever dropped a plastic bag into the clear running water. She wanted to hate them collectively, too. Municipal trash collection was deeply sketchy. Piles of garbage, savaged by the endless numbers of dogs and monkeys, would build on the roadsides like small hillocks, torn to bits in spots, bits rolling down the hillsides into the creeks and rivers.

It made her grimace. It made her weep. It made her hate. Almost. It made her pity them, which is what she hated. It was all she could do to keep that hate from turning inward, because she knew she was one of them. She knew she was human, too. And sometimes, she hated that. She hated being associated with them. They were a contaminant to what she knew, believed, and tasted about life. No one who was a true adult would behave like such a spoiled child. Spoiled by accident of birth. Spoiled by ignorance. Spoiled by the Buffer. The inhabitants of Paradise spoiled by their own unconsciousness. Spoiled, she knew, and it made her sick to her stomach, bile rising into her throat, a grimace of a different order freezing her features, that De Murgos was to blame.

Because the Buffer had been implanted by him. She knew she should think of him in upper case, "Him", but she couldn't, not even in her own mind. If she could think of him in a smaller case than lower case, she would. The Buffer, the fucking Buffer, that kept them trapped in their 'me first' perception of the world. The Buffer, the fucking Buffer, that kept them believing that this was OK, that it was alright to go through life putting yourself first, instead of others first. And she knew that if you went through Life putting others first, most of the time, almost always, you would be taken care of, you would be noticed by Her eventually, and even if all She could give you would be a Good Death, or at least a good reception afterwards, that's how it would all work out for someone.

But for these people, these people she was compelled to love, there would be no Good Death. There would only be the illusion of one. And the illusion would only last an eternity, that moment of no time passing when the swing of the pendulum would stop, before it would return the other way. That moment was eternity. Chaff for the wind, grist for the mill. What she hated was that they were allowed to make everything ugly before they were taken out.

She knew that she was here to deal with the shadow of Skreeva, not De Murgos directly, not yet, at least. Skreeva, the Windu god of Destruction, the god who had usurped the power of Transformation from his brothers, the god who ruled the patriarchy that kept the grandmothers, Napat's grandmothers, living in open lean-tos along the family compound walls, open to the typhoons, not even able to keep a fire burning. And she wondered, in complete incomprehension, how the wives of the husbands who commanded that this be so, that this be how the old wen were treated, how they would be treated, could go along with it, knowing that this would be their fate, if they outlived the pompous but "loving" men they called husbands.

It was the stories that the Skreevans had heard about the power that the worshippers of De Murgos had over their wen that enticed them to steal control, and blame it on Skreeva. The Windu people had already had a caste system, but the gender difference had never been so great; the lower caste genders were treated equally badly by the upper castes. But here, on Wallid, they prided themselves on being less bound by the caste system. People mixed together, especially ritually, surprisingly well compared to the Windia, the source of their social organization. The European invaders managed to destroy their ruling class in one battle, when their royal men charged a small contingent of white defenders armed with rifles, charged them on foot with their gold armor and gold lances, banners flying, and gold short blades… thousands died in an afternoon, and a ruling caste evaporated in their own blood under the tropical sun, turning the ditches and the rice red with it.

All without any sense of irony, all in all sincerity. And it broke Jasmine's heart to think of it. All the most beautiful gone and dead, their wen sold into slavery and concubinage. To her mind it was no wonder that the caste system failed, but she knew, with no uncertainty, that it was the hand of De Murgos that kept the grandmothers living against the wall, feeding on scraps and dressing in rags. His Missionaries brought this to the people.

The myth of the superiority of the masculine, and the inferiority of the feminine: that was his doing. By feeding the egos of the men, operating under the influence of the Buffer, he fed them into believing that wen were so much less than men, that he could then command their loyalty, even when they didn't know it. His superiority in their eyes made him the god of rape, and no man should be held to account for it.

De Murgos's form was everywhere, buried in their art, in the small thrones to their gods standing on pedestals in their backyards, white, full head of flaming white hair, with white flame coming from all his joints, even his "joint" a burst of flame.

And none of these people were white, no more than she was.

And it broke her heart. It broke her heart that these were the people that the Goddess commanded her to serve.

Well.

It was a good thing, then, that she didn't need her heart to serve them, only her Spirit. And that she could commend the care of her heart to Her, and to the Consorts that were assigned to her. And fucking their white god, with his flaming cock, was the one thing she was certain she would never ever fuck.

Paradise lost, paradise broken and trashed and dumped in the water of life. And her heart washed into the ocean with the trash, snagging here and there on fallen branches from the dying trees, or old televisions, or the ankles of little girls, bathing in the water as it ran by, sometimes washing away the traces of their moon.

Blood feeding the water.

41

THE SEEDS OF REBELLION

When the Master returned to the consciousness of where he was and what had happened he turned to A. and pointed a finger at her. "Not a word. Not a word to anyone." He sat up and looked at his hand, where he'd been holding the skin torn from Leonora with the tattoo of the Fleur de Vie. The skin had blackened in his grasp, the pink gone, the white outlines visible only in a certain angle to the light as shinier black. He stood up and opened the door to an anteroom with a landline phone. He made some calls. While he talked, he put his hand on the crack of his butt and mouthed the word "Ow".

It turned out he knew people. People who owed him a favor or two. It turned out, he explained later, that the favor was because he had hypnotized the women at several parties, turning the scene into orgiastic madness.

While they waited for the people to come they changed into street clothes. The Master put the charred skin in a small box and slipped it into his pocket.

William's naked body was found in a dumpster at the back of the parking lot for a restaurant without security cameras. Leonora's body was never found. A. and the Master went to the viewing, arriving early. The Master had a plan. He had imbued the piece of charred skin with all his hatred for Quinn and now his hatred for the Order for harboring him. Hatred and rage imbued into the flesh of a Priestess, hatred and rage that would speak to men about their own hatred and rage at the Feminine. And that it would pass from hand to hand, surface to surface, like a virus. He knew this would create more terror for women; he knew he was fueling the rape culture. The final finesse was that if any man was affected by that burnt flesh and saw the symbol of the Order anywhere, that vision would telepathically return to the Master. And, using the power of the black kite for all of this, he knew that he would be drawn to the symbol again.

He swiped the skin over the handles and edges of the open casket. The Master stayed to watch. When any of William's friends would touch the casket they would be overcome with a spasm of grief. Then, as the Master watched, their faces would harden. He could see the anger in their jawlines, and the hatred in their eyes. Satisfied that the power would grant him his wish, he gestured to A. and they left the building.

The High Priestess of Berkeley and her Consort attended the funeral. They watched without understanding as the Master smeared the coffin edge. They could feel the malice and shadow in the Master and A. They saw the Lama's ghost and the flapping black kite. They reported it all to the High Council, who decided to continue the watch on the Master and A. that William and Leonora were doing but to take no action.

A month passed, then two. In the third month there were news reports around the nation about an increase of rape on military bases and in the towns around those bases. In the winter the power of the feedback loop embedded in the magic activated one afternoon, he saw the image of the Fleur de Vie in his mind and, using the power of the kite, journeyed to the place of the sighting.

It came from an air force base near the town of The Baths, in England. A female soldier had been taken, and raped there, and the magic called out to the Master. He called down to Brian, and told him to purchase two tickets. First class, of course.

The surprise journey aided them in losing the watchers.

They sat in the same row across the aisle from each other. The space between them was cold, chilled by what they would not say to each other. The woman sitting behind the Master asked to move her seat, because the chill around the Lama's ghost, already sitting there, was far deeper.

42

WAITING

Calley sat in her office at the Mansion. Even with the power off, using lanterns and firelight, she loved the space, and sitting there and working there as often as she could. She had no preference for electric things. She preferred to be away from electricity altogether, even though she was electricity herself.

She sat at the desk, in the antique maroon leather wing back chair, trimmed in brass studs, supported on claw feet. This was the desk that had belonged to Rachel Adams, and probably her parents before that. Solid, dark, heavy, with secrets, she'd discovered. There were hidden panels in the back of four of the drawers. In the first one she found a padded velvet bag with a golden egg inside it. Embroidered on the bag were the words Antecedent Feminine. Now that she'd found it she kept it in the front part of the drawer so she could take it out and, nestling it on the bag, she'd rest her hand on it, feeling it warm to her touch. It comforted her, and connected her with some sense of her Mother. The warmth, she realized, was the sign of her mortality. That, and the fire in the fireplace behind her.

When she and Alam would sleep in the Mansion because of the noise of the others, both physical and psychic, she'd come down here on the hidden staircase, leaving Alam in the bed, the low fire warming their bedroom. When everyone had been dispersed, Alam had started to bring in the wood.

She had the Queen's Book open on her desk. Eva's ghost was sitting on a chair on the opposite side of the desk and she was answering questions Calley would raise from time to time as she randomly turned pages. She asked about the Blue Hag that would show up in the initiation rituals.

"Rachel found her. I don't know where. But she agreed to show up every time, and as far as I know she has, even though Rachel is long gone."

"Is Rachel's father's ghost, the Lama's ghost, still around?"

"Yes. He is working to recover an evil and take it back to hell."

"Where is Rachel?"

"The Blue Hag knows. Madeleine knows. That's it. She came with the Mother to take my soul and spirit from my soma. And then she left. I think She Who Comes is using her somewhere for something."

"Why are you here?"

"I am given a time. The alchemy created a shell. A shell to protect my soul and spirit until they get used to the loss of my soma. The shell lasts only a little while, I don't know how long. And I have a little work to do to prepare my soul to live on, and my spirit to live on after that. But they probably won't live here. Here is too dense for that. I still have a chance to complete my Diamond Body, my body that will keep my awareness immortal, the body that will make me more like you. Or maybe more like the Blue Hag."

Eva paused. "I think that Rachel is close, close to completion—not close by. If she completes her Diamond Body she will become an immortal servant of the True Creator, She Who Comes. She will become a face of the goddess, as a goddess, herself, maybe."

Eva continued, "If the Diamond Body is complete, and infused with the Higher Heart, which is necessary to animate the form, then I should be able to come here, and to work here on this level, for a very long time."

"This is what Rachel had Regina write down here in the Queen's Book."

"Yes, among other things. Magics, psychic power development. It's all there. What Rachel learned in her travels. What she learned from the Lama. Everything."

"Do you know anyone who has completed the Diamond Body?"

"Maybe," Eva said cagily, looking away.

"Ah," Calley said. "Tell me more about the Blue Hag."

"She may have been human once. If so, she died a horrible death that bound her here, possibly in the forests about us. At least, she has been seen in the woods."

"What powers does she have?"

"Well, first of all, she persists in time. And she can interact with the material world. It's not that she actually touches things. She seems to transubstantiate material from this world into the material of her world, and then can move whatever she touches."

"Can she hold them there? Keep them there?"

"I don't know."

"I need to find her and talk to her."

"You can go into the pit. The Initiation Chambers are the only places she's been seen dependably."

"I could do an initiation! But I don't have time."

"I think I have a way. Let me go see if I can find her," and Eva disappeared.

Calley sighed. She went upstairs to wake Alam, to tell him she'd be gone for a couple days and to seek instruction with Madeleine or perhaps even Diana. If she could get him to the place of development, of psychic and spiritual evolution that Eva was, she would have facilitated the greatest gift she could give him, the reward to his millennia of devotion to her. Because, now that he was back in the mortal time flow, it would kill him.

She felt tired walking up the stairs, tired and heavy. This soma, this body, weighed on her, letting her slide along the narrowly spaced walls. Even the ecstasies of this soma were heavy. Not a tremor in the air but a tremor in the earth, liquefying her slowly, becoming water, but still a long way from rain.

She reached their room. In the dim light of early dawn she gazed at him, a shape shifter and magician in his own right, one who had slowed down, so far down he became dead to his world and slipped into hers. His one life now thousands of years older than any other mortal. Her Mother allowed it as an experiment, to see what kind of man he might become, but the cost of the experiment was, and was so by her own wish, her own immortality. And his. They were both mortal now, and there was no way of knowing if she could ever go back. And as for him, she did not know. It was not possible to know. The experiment was still running, an open experiment, and the outcome not fixed. But she knew everything ended.

And he had become an exquisitely good man. A man who'd never put himself before her, but always in service to her. He knew the Antecedence of the Feminine in his bones, and never lost his gratitude for the understanding, and for the chance to live a life of devotion.

On the night stand there was a large gray arrowhead, brought back to her by Quinn from Brazil, a token from the Thunder Being there. She picked it up, and felt his presence near her in an instant. She smiled at him, and told him, "Not yet," and carried it over to her altar.

She turned and watched Alam sleeping. She sat down on the bed gently and slipped her hand under the covers. She found his phallus and took it in her hand. She felt its response, tumescing even in his sleep.

He stirred. She smiled. He opened an eye and looked at her. Her smile broadened. His erection grew. He smiled back at her and pulled away the covers. She looked at him, the thing of beauty that he was. He sat partly up, leaning on an elbow. She felt the Resonance of the Higher Heart come into his phallus, pulsing against her hand. The pulse travelled through her into her sex, and she felt herself unfolding. The resonance rose to her heart, and she felt her heart unfolding. It rose to her lips, and she felt her lips unfolding, and unfolded, slipped them over him, pulse to pulse.

Two hearts as one.

Madeleine ended the call with Beth Elmyra in England, placing the antique handset gently in its cradle. She reviewed the instructions she'd passed on from Calley about how to deal with Matthews. It made her smile to know what was in store for him, how She Who Comes intended to use him.

He was Her created, after all.

She'd felt Quinn's pull on Her, making Matthews a child of the Earth, rather than someone beholden to Quinn. Quinn had set him free, having, at his request, blown open the doors of the Kundalini Barrier, and then left him blind and helpless in the golden fire. But he'd known She'd come, known She'd come for Matthews even as Quinn disappeared into the shadows where none but She could see him. Although Quinn had delayed and resisted, after Sally had embraced him at Her request, She'd been the one who pulled his heart into a beacon to bring him to Stonehaven.

Matthews was a gift to Her, but Quinn was the prize.

There were men, and then there were men. There were no longer gods or archetypes for them to focus on, to emulate. There was only Her. And the Enemy, De Murgos. She served as the Divine for the wen, becoming embodied in them, serving as the light around which their Souls and Spirits grew. But for the men? There was no one, She had not even Her own High Consort. The inspiration for the men was yet to be developed, that new kind of man that might let her experiment succeed, because so far, or rather at the present time, it wasn't working very well.

She was the only inspiration for them, shining through the faces of Her Priestesses, and a few Consorts, encouraging men to become the better men they could become. And She knew that, in time, She would shine through Quinn. Already he could hear and see Her. Already they conversed.

She soothed Bree's brow while Her daughter slept.

She appeared in Calley a moment later, to find Her mouth full and pulsing and Her elder daughter lost in ecstasy, eyes closed, tongue pressed against the underside of the phallus head, the head itself pressed against the roof of her mouth, her face, her skull, her brains even, all vibrating with the power of the pulse Alam kept locked in himself, eyes slitted, gaze unfocused as he contemplated the beautiful head and face of his Beloved. He felt the other presence enter Calley, and he smiled in acknowledgment. Calley moved the tip of her tongue against him, opened her eyes and gazed into his, the lights dancing in her eyes showed him her ecstasy, her joy. She nodded ever so slightly. Alam loosed himself within her, his own head going back in ecstasy as he fed her, pumping, fed her, and fed Her.

She held him in her mouth until she could hold no more, slowly withdrawing she sipped, sending a single spasm of near intolerable ecstasy into his shaft. He jumped like a spark had hit him. He groaned and his legs shook.

As Calley withdrew she thought to Herself, "To what do I owe this pleasure?"

She Who Comes smiled, and Calley smiled. She Who Comes said, "Pleasure."

Madeleine felt Craft enter the room as she was sitting before her altar, felt it more than she heard him. She could tell he set something silently on the table that served as her desk and sideboard. The smell of coffee filled the air, and made her stomach rumble. She smiled as he came over and stood behind her, brushing his hand over her hair, resting his palms on her shoulders. He closed, leaning lightly into her shoulder, and she could feel him again, feel his rise, the rise that had kept her locked and rocking in his arms last night.

She turned around, staying on her knees. She pulled the drawstring on his pants and they dropped, getting hung up briefly on what hung out before him. She smiled as she pulled down, making it bounce in her face. Quickly she slid her face under an upswing, letting it come to rest across her cheek and nose. She inhaled him, inhaled them, then, breathing in all that could trigger memory and savoring it, the scent a sacred food itself.

By her training she checked the world around her, looking not for threats but for safety, and she found it in the mind of Calley, and in the presence there of She Who Comes. She smiled at Madeleine, turning, then in a flash of shadow, She was in her, smiling, smiling the smile that Madeleine smiled. The Goddess whispered, "Pleasure." Then, "Please me." Madeleine smiled and said aloud to Craft, "Please me."

He stepped back slightly, allowing the tip to slide to her lips and waited, waited until she opened.

She tilted her head back, opening her mouth and extending her tongue, sliding it out under his length. Slowly he entered until her lips and tongue closed around him and he held still, letting the energy flow out along his shaft, finding the connection to the nerves of her mouth, so many points of contact, uncompensated in the inner processing of the brain, making each fraction of him feel ten sizes larger in her mouth, filling her sensation as her mouth filled with saliva, eager to break him down, eager to consume him.

He connected energetically down, connecting to the button and spreading inward, until she sensed her phulva, sensed it as if it were her mouth, sensed her mouth as if it were her phulva, merging the sensations as one. She felt the rolling wave start deep within her, deep within her sex and deep within her, deep within her head, a wave that began deep in these two centers of her. She kept the door to her heart closed, not yet ready for another heartgasm. But then She Who Comes took hold, overlaying Herself on Madeleine twining orgasms, tied the golden threads together in her heart. Madeleine held her arms out to the side, palms up, and started shaking, great spasms of orgasm pouring down through her heart to her sex, waves of ecstasy echoing back up, bathing her heart from below.

The energy poured out her arms, out of her hands into the world and when he fed her, she fed the world, She Who Comes laughing within her to the rhythm of waves of orgasm that sluiced back and forth, up and down, making a standing wave of ecstasy, the amplitude doubled, twice the height of either wave where they crossed in her heart.

The energy curled out of her hands, golden strands leaping away into the walls, into the earth. Whirlpools opened in her hands and golden light fountained through, dissolving into a mist that settled over everything, and over all the land. And above the land the pulse of the Higher Heart hovered.

Calley, fed by Alam, who in turn went down in the kitchen to start breakfast, padded barefoot and mostly naked to the door to the cistern room where the initiations into High Priestess and High Consort took place. She could see perfectly well into the darkness and went down, passed the throne and walked down the steps to bottom of the cistern.

She leaned forward putting her hands into the sand and called for the Blue One to come and see her, then sat cross-legged and waited, cultivating receptivity. After twenty minutes or so, during which she struggled to remain solid, the room began to glow faintly with a blue light, a light that summoned her awareness back to the present.

"I would have qualms to appear before one not initiated, but one does not initiate the ageless, one does not initiate a goddess, one who is not in need of organizing a new beginning within her," said a voice disembodied but focalized across the cistern.

"Welcome, old one," Calley replied.

The voice laughed. "Not nearly so old as you."

"I can sense the oldest part of you, the part that does not speak. You are something I have not seen before. How have you come to be?"

"Why do you ask? Why should I answer?"

"Because I wish to know how to pay my respects to you," Calley replied.

"Ah. I am human, that which speaks to you. I was a woman of the plant spirit healing guild. Other things as well. I was also a woman of the wild. Animals would come to me. I had a husband but he died from a fast storm at high altitude. We found his body in the spring where he'd fallen."

"I see his death. He loved you until the last."

"It is what I felt." She paused, picking up the thread of her story again. "In my grief I found Her, She Who Comes, the True Creator. And I found Her in a younger form, Sala, she called Herself, and She led me into paths of ecstasy that shook me to my solitary core, here in these mountains. I withdrew. I hid. I became wild. I dressed in leather that I tanned and stitched myself. But I kept my cabin. I was a wolf and a doe. It was good in the winter.

"Sala would lead me to the stones, the long, polished ones, smooth, shaped like a man. She showed me how to use them. I became a lover of stones.

"I would spend weeks away from home sometimes. Gathering, yes. But spending time in the peaks, among the rocks, looking for caves and shelters where the people of long ago had stayed. And in one of those caves, during a thunderstorm, a rock sat up from the floor. It had a face.

"It didn't speak, not yet. The face was very large, the size of half of me. It stared. I felt unafraid. I would return there, looking for it. Sometimes finding it. And then it started to appear in other places—alongside a trail, beside me as I rested against a boulder. Eventually it would learn to appear anywhere there was a bare rock. And eventually I learned to speak its language. Its speech is very slow. It took a long time for one word, one sound. I learned to hold a word in my mind for a long time, too, so it could hear me.

"With time it would send me images, images from different places, as if it had an eye that could see wherever it was, needing only bare rock. We spent a lot of slow time together, our minds joined. And in my mind we joined in other ways.

"People still came to the cabin, though. Asking for help. Sometimes I wasn't there, and they blamed me for it, blamed my absence.

"And then they came to get me. Someone was sick, true, but his companions watched me and accused me of witchcraft. They left, but came back. I had been foolish and stayed to clean up when I should have just fled to the caves. They found my stones and knew what they were for. They took me. And they took me. And they beat me. And they took me. Then they dragged me down the mountain to one of their worship houses, dedicated to the Alien. It was built in a meadow at the base of a stone outcropping that looked like the bottom of a flat iron.

"There, someone proclaimed that it was the Alien's command that I die. They tied me to a stake and heaped up the wood, and burned me alive. My wild training in ecstasy, and the friends and helpers I found in the woods all showed up. More sensitive than others, my training made the fire worse, and my mind was too strong to come apart. It wouldn't have ended, and I believed I would have been trapped in that fire forever. So I leapt. I sent my mind to the stone above their building. And the stone received me.

"I leapt into the face of my stone friend. And now I am both. Human and stone. I am young and old, old as the stones. My friend Rachel called me the Wenstone."

"I am in need of your help, Wenstone. My Mother sent me."

"You are Rachel's successor. What would you have me do?"

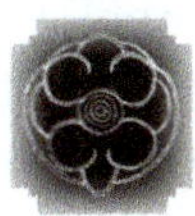

43

EIGHT WEEKS SECOND WEEK

"There is an archway of sensitivity at the entrance of the phulva," her Helper began. "At its apex is the Jewel. You know this Jewel, yes?"

"You are talking about what the anatomists call the clitoris, yes?" Angelica responded.

"Yes, but for our purposes let's call it the button. The bright pink button, OK? Or better, we should call it the Jewel."

"OK. Tell me about the Jewel at the top of the arch."

"Well, it is erectile, you know. It swells, and it extends itself beyond its hood."

"Yes."

"Well, the whole area is erectile. The area between the edges of your phulva and your thighs is also erectile and it swells. With enough arousal, that is. Last week this happened to you. Did you notice it?"

"No, not really. I was more inwardly focused."

"OK, good. This week we will focus on the surface, on the entrance to you, erecting the entire archway, and focusing more particularly on the Jewel in the arch. We will see how much the hidden Jewel can emerge into the light. We will begin with the first position of this tantra. You will sit on his lap," she said, gesturing to the man sitting cross-legged on the futon, hands in an unusual mudra, eyes half shuttered and gazing at Angelica, a long erection emerging from his sarong.

"You will sit," she continued, "with your phulva tightly pressed to his phallus. You are to prepare the path for him by devoting your attention to your archway, and to the Jewel. No insertion. As you move in toward him, spread the lips of your phulva so he presses smoothly against you, and so you can learn how to control this part of yourself. Good, like that," she said, as Angelica climbed up, spread her sarong back and slowly slid forward over his thighs.

When she reached down to open herself the scent of her floated up and the man breathed deeply, and smiled. "Look at yourself," the Helper said. "Look at yourself and remember, because it will be different the next time you look." She looked down, taking in the lines and contours that she could see. She took in the contours of his phallus, unable to stop her imaging of him inside her, she rocking against him.

She settled into him, sliding a little into the press. He was right up against her, balls against her opening, the lips of her phulva wrapping around the shaft, her Jewel pressed against the column of his underside. Pressed, wet, and sighing.

The Helper said, "Now, don't move. Either of you. Just sense yourself, Angelica. Sense what each part of you perceives. Focus on the Jewel, focus on expanding it. Focus on the arches, focus on erecting them, filling them with fluid, making a pad against which a man might mount. Expand your awareness to that which lies just below the surface. And do not move until you are told."

Angelica wrapped her legs around him, crossing them at the ankles. "What do I do with my hands?"

"I'll tell you what to do, and when. Relax Angelica. Hold your hands the way your partner is, close your eyes, and return to sensation."

An hour later Angelica fell backwards, allowing her partner to slide out from under her. About 15 minutes in she'd started to want to twitch against him, but she'd been told to hold still. At a half an hour she'd become overwhelmed with a sensation of engorgement. She felt the Jewel sliding out and down from its hood, felt the hood swell as the Jewel distended, seeking contact. She felt the sides of her phulva swell, the engorgement swelling and opening her lips to embrace the rod between her legs.

Her arms went over his shoulders as she leaned into his chest, breasts smashed against his, then leaning back on her arms. The twitching became sliding on him, slowly, she couldn't help it, first short slides, then the length of her up and down the length of him. The Helper said nothing. Eventually the sliding became more powerful and faster. The Helper leaned in and whispered, "Let your head hang back."

When she exploded in orgasm against him the Helper whispered again, "Do you feel Her?"

Angelica opened her mind, letting sensation go. She found herself in a field of light, her head cradled in two warm hands. "Maybe," she said. "I feel something, hands holding my head."

"Good, now let that go and return to sensation."

She could feel herself wanting something, wanting contact, so she raised her hips and brought the Jewel to his crown, pressing, rubbing, circling, and finally he let go, coming into the space between them, sighing into her shoulder, pulling her hips in to hold her still upon him, and his twitching set her off again, twitching against him in perfect synchrony. The wet warmth of him spread between them from her breasts to her low belly, dripping down, coating the surface of her phulva, its tissues drinking him in.

After lunch she was met by her Helper and another man. They sat, facing each other, open to each other, but apart. The exercise was to practice using her gaze to call the man to erection, and then, to remember at the sensation level everything she'd experienced in the morning, and see if she could create the same conclusion.

She could not, of course. Her Helper used the opportunity of her efforts to teach her to find the boundaries of different energies between them, leaning into and out of the fields, tracing them with her hands, alternating with memories of the morning and then trying to detect how the memories used the energies around and within her and around him. She'd even gotten a flash of what it felt like inside him. At different points the Helper asked her to look within, to see if she could detect any signs of something Higher. She couldn't, not yet. But she started to see herself from the outside, becoming a witness to her own efforts. By the end of the afternoon her practice partner had been erect for more than ninety minutes.

Her Helper told her to look down at herself. She was so suffused she looked swollen, the lips of her phulva distended. The Jewel looked so much larger, and more distended, too. She could see more of it, looking down. As she tilted her hips to look she realized she was sitting in a large wet spot.

The Helper said, "Lick your finger tip and touch yourself."

When she did, she felt a lightning bolt of energy shoot into her and spread out. The touch bucked her hips and she twitched forward and back for several seconds. When the twitching stopped she felt her partner move off the bed. She opened her eyes to watch the folds of his sarong fall around his erection like curtains, the bulk of him in front, out and proud. He smiled at her and bowed.

He said something to her Helper in a language she didn't know. The Helper translated, "He says it was an honor to practice with you. And that he had fun." They grinned at each other and Angelica.

That night she had a dream. She was watching herself, witnessing her work of the day before. In her room her awareness felt someone sit on the side of the bed. She thought it was Quinn, but it touched her forehead, stroking hair from her face. It was not Quinn's hand. She sat up suddenly, gasping, but it was gone. The only trace was the scent of sex. But not hers.

When she awoke she felt a full sensation, a sensation that didn't fade when she peed. She touched herself, and realized she was still swollen, still suffused. She felt engorged still, heavy with possibilities.

The morning of the second day was spent working on exposing herself. The skin hood around her Jewel was pushed and pulled, working it open, working it into sliding back and up. Then, by using stroking motions, drawing the Jewel down and out. After some initial work on herself, the Helper asked her if she was ready for something new and pointed to a young wen coming to the bower, carrying a tray with three glasses and a pitcher. She set the tray down. "This is Zhee. She is to be your practice partner today. Is this acceptable to you?"

Angelica paused. She let go of her mind and tracked her sensation. The Jewel twinged. The Jewel said 'yes' so she said, "Yes." She smiled at the wen, who instantly smiled back. She poured two small glasses of juice and took one to Angelica. Zhee sat on the edge of the bed, gazing at Angelica, and Angelica gazed back. Some unspoken signal passed between them and they drained their glasses at the same moment, passing them off to the Helper.

Angelica surprised herself, and Zhee, as she leaned in quickly to kiss her, a quick kiss, almost chaste with only a moment of lingering. Gratitude for Zhee had moved her, she realized. Zhee smiled, then grinned broadly, bouncing off the bed and arranging Angelica upon it. Pulling her to the edge, leaving enough room to keep her feet on it with her knees bent, the Helper leaned in and propped Angelica up on pillows so she could see, and then lay down beside her, lips close to her ear, for whispering.

Zhee knelt between her legs and gazed. She dropped her shawl from her shoulders, exposing her breasts, and leaned in and gazed more closely. Angelica felt pressure building in her engorgement, felt her Jewel longing to extend, and show herself. Zhee leaned away to coil her hair up on top of her head, and leaned back in swiftly, causing a little jump and giggle in Angelica, stopping inches short and inhaled.

Under Zhee's gaze Angelica felt a pulse start in the Jewel, a slight throb, the echo of her own heart. Zhee saw the little throb and said, "Oh." And smiled.

Zhee began with her hands, using her thumbs to gently spread the wetness up and out over the lips, up and over the Jewel's hood. With her fingers she lightly stroked the arch, touching at the Jewel. Angelica groaned a little. Zhee stroked down the hood, causing the Jewel's rod to swell and lengthen, then Zhee pushed the hood back, stretching and separating the Jewel from its cowl. Angelica felt hot little tingles where the skin separated, differentiating that which was once almost one. Then, while pushing back with her thumbs, she stroked downward with her finger tips at the apex, slowly causing the rod to push the Jewel even further out, out into the world.

Then Zhee pursed her lips, a small tight 'o' and kissed her, softly, holding her lips there, waiting for the buzz that went through Angelica to settle. Then Zhee touched the tip of her tongue to the tip of the swollen Jewel, and the buzz became a spark that shot right to the middle of her skull, temporarily blinding her, and Angelica thrashed, crying out, tearing herself away from that much pleasure, turning into her Helper to be held.

"So much," she gasped. "So much sensation…"

The Helper whispered back, "You must allow it. You must surrender to sensation."

By the end of the afternoon she ached, so swollen was she. She felt heavy, full, and just shy of painful. She felt as if she was waiting, somehow, for something. Not with longing, not even much anticipation, as if she knew she would anticipate again later. And in the absence of anticipation she realized that she was deeply happy. So she sat up and, laughing, grabbed Zhee by the arms and threw her onto the bed and knelt between the young wen's knees. "Tell me," she begged the Helper. "Show me what to do. Show me how," which is what the Helper did, and how they spent the time until the bell rang for the evening meal. Zhee's engorgement was swift and powerful to behold.

44

DEFECTION

Wade was unhappy. He hadn't a clue as to why. Well, actually he had a clue. He was unhappy because his need for power and control wasn't finding the de-emphasized level in his soul that he'd been led to expect. It was a constant struggle for him to be the man he believed he'd been taught by the Order to be.

He felt he needed something—someone—to control. He was no longer satisfied with his efforts to control himself. He hated the struggle of it, not understanding, or, rather, forgetting that self-control was supposed to be a primary function of a mature man.

In the village near the rental house he shared with Guiles was a small store that sold snacks, trinkets, and gasoline for scooters and trucks in liter plastic bottles. Wade liked going there because the shop was often left with the daughter of the shop owner when he was out working in his fields. She was young, probably not yet twenty. Wade took every opportunity to go to the store and smile flirtatiously, say complimentary things in Windonesian, and make eye contact.

She had some pretty features Wade thought. Her skin tone, her hair were pretty. Her teeth had been distorted by the excess sugar in her diet, and she was aware of it. When she laughed she'd cover her mouth with her hand. It was their first physical contact. He'd paid her for some fuel, and as she'd handed him the change, he made some comment about boredom and it made her laugh. He'd reached up and grabbed her arm at the wrist when she'd covered her mouth. He didn't pull it down, but instead held it there, smiling at her. He told her, "It's OK."

She'd gone rigid at his touch, but then she relaxed when she realized he wasn't going to force her to do anything. He just smiled at her. The release of tension sent a slight shiver down her spine. Wade, sensing it, grinned more broadly. She lowered her arm voluntarily and smiled at him, showing white crooked teeth and then, still shy, she'd looked down.

He knew then that she was his.

Wade said, "Would you like to go for a ride?" He watched her body move towards him, saying yes, but then her head regained control and she declined, motioning to the shop behind her, she said, "My father would kill me."

Wade smiled at the exaggeration and shook his head "No" but the girl smiled at him and shook her head "Yes." And then the archetypal impact of the exchange hit him. "Sex and Death," he thought. Then he thought her father just very well might kill her. Or disown her. "Another time then," he said. She smiled and nodded affirmatively, and quickly, when she realized with a frisson of terror what she had almost just done. Gone off with the stranger, the foreigner, the other. The demon.

And she knew that she would go with him, one day. Let him take her to another world, far from the poverty and restrictions on her present. Her future. The demon would lead her to freedom, if she worked it right. All this she saw in a flash. She smiled after him as he pulled away.

She'd paid attention when the Priests talked about the world, this world and the other worlds, the worlds of demons and what they could do, the world of the gods and what they could do. She remembered how grateful she'd been that she hadn't been chosen for 'special attention' by the priests after classes, attentions paid to both boys and girls to improve their understanding of the sacred texts, presumably.

She remembered how hollow-eyed those children had become, and quiet. It took months for some of them to return to showing the signs of life they'd had before they'd been singled out, to showing the enthusiasm of children. She shivered and decided to light incense and put it in an offering to the spirits. Setting it down on the edge of the steps between the road and the shop floor she prayed that he, the demon, would return soon.

Wade's mind started to scheme about how he could get her, get the little shopkeeper on his bike, behind him, her arms wrapped around him. He knew the people, especially the men, would judge and resent his intrusion into their lives. He realized that if she went for a ride with him she was risking, maybe, everything. Ostracism. Punishment. Beating.

He got lost in a fantasy of beating her father for beating her.

He continued on his way to town. He was supposed to have dinner with Jasmine tonight, and Guiles, of course. He supposed that afterwards Jasmine would take them both on in a tantric working to build her power. He resented Guiles being there. He resented Jasmine's power. He resented that cute little assistant with the spaced-out demeanor. He was sure, in his own mind, that Jasmine had seduced her, and had not told him. Worse, she had not offered to share. He'd never talked to Jasmine about Napat, but he assumed she'd taken in a toy to play with. So he wanted his own toy.

He arrived early at Jasmine's house; she and Guiles had not yet returned from the yoga studio. He punched in the access code and waited while the gate swung open. Jasmine had returned from work one day to find a priest in the yard, snooping through the windows. She'd replace the old latch gate as soon as she could get the work done. She was contemplating building a wall around the property, turning it into a mini-compound.

As the gate swung open he had a glimpse of Napat, running to the house from the pool, naked but for the towel clutched to her breast, looking askance at him over her shoulder. She'd been sunbathing nude. If nothing else, her time around Jasmine had made her feel that her clothes were oppressive and she'd taken to getting naked in the sun whenever she had the chance. She'd been laying on her belly, one arm beneath her, masturbating while the sun warmed her back when she heard the gate hinges start to creak. Her skin tone hid her blush from him.

She raced into the house, his laugh trailing her. "He knew!" she thought, embarrassed. "How can I face him?" She took the stairs to the loft two at a time to put on clothes. She sorted through Jasmine's things. She wrapped a sarong around her hips and slipped on a button front sleeveless cotton shirt, embroidered with jasmine in bloom.

And then it came to her, how to face him. Emboldened, perhaps, by the scent of Jasmine in the clothing, the answer came to her: "Fearlessly" she said aloud to herself. She was Jasmine's at least as much as he was, in her mind. She need not fear him.

She was back downstairs, dressed, stopping to pull her hair up when Wade came through the door. As she arched her back to raise her arms over her head he noted the swell of her breasts beneath the fabric of her shirt. She scowled at him and turned around, bent over. She was unaware that she was showing him the outline of her behind through the clinging fabric of her sarong, and that he could see through the cloth the outline of her legs, all the way to the top. She had somehow automatically come to believe, like her people, that if she decided she didn't want to see something, or be seen, then she was invisible. Wade felt himself stir.

Wade grinned fiercely and wolfishly. Napat finished with her hair, straightened up and turned to him. A serous expression on her face, she said, "You are early," in English.

He replied in Windonesian, mocking her expression, "You are lazy."

She was shocked. But rather than collapsing she stood fiercely and in anger said, in English, "Fuck you!" so loud that the Priest who was snooping at the gate heard her, and knowing that almost universal phrase, smiled at her defiance of the American. Then he frowned, because that meant they weren't having sex, which is what his superior wanted him to report on. He frowned at having to disappoint his superior, and contemplated lying. Maybe "Fuck you" meant she was resisting his advances.

Wade smirked and turned to go back outside and take a dip in the pool. The Priest angled his face so that one eye could watch him. When Wade stripped naked, throwing his clothes on a chair the Priest inhaled softly at the binding muscles of his back, the grasping of his glutes. When he turned so the Priest could see him from the front, defined abs, heavy pecs, and the size of his flaccid phallus. The Priests reaction, much to his surprise, was an immediate erection. He put his hand on himself and looked away, panting, regaining control of himself, grabbing and twisting himself until the pain caused it to shrink away. He promised to punish himself later.

The Priest heard two scooters coming and scooted himself across the narrow street into an even narrower alley, watching from the shadows as Jasmine and Guiles pulled up to the gate. He vowed to stay there and watch and listen. An hour passed, two. He was not surprised, although he was disappointed when Jasmine emerged through the gate with Napat mounted behind her, taking her home for the night.

Jasmine had plans for the evening that she could not allow Napat to witness, so after supper she took her home. In the glowing evening they rode, Napat holding tight, pressing her belly against Jasmine's back, seeking comfort from the contact. She realized she loved Jasmine in that moment. Jasmine felt the girl's feelings, emanating from Napat's solar plexus into her from behind. She smiled. It was fine that Napat allowed herself that level of devotion to Jasmine. It was Jasmine's job to make sure that devotion was not abused.

At Napat's compound the girl got off the scooter. A scooter with a priest on it—she could tell by clothing and headgear—passed them after she pulled over. Napat meant to hug Jasmine but stopped herself. Jasmine smiled and nodded. "See you tomorrow? You'll come by the house after school, yes?" The girl nodded. "I'll leave a list of things to shop for, and the money."

Jasmine noted that the priest who'd passed them had gone down the road a little way and turned around, his front wheel visible from an alley between buildings. She turned, and pulled away once Napat was safe in the compound, checking her mirrors to see if she was followed. A scooter came up the road behind her, a different one, keeping its distance. She was surprised. She had drawn enough attention that they were tag-teaming her now and she didn't like it. She thought she'd have to start using magic, maybe create some invisibility. She believed she'd accumulated enough power to risk it, and succeed. She figured she'd need one more night, tonight, to finish the body of the power, finish the tetrahedron she was building within.

Wade, who could not stand to be in Guiles' company without Jasmine around, had gone back out when Jasmine left to take Napat home. He'd gone to an expat bar frequented by Americans and Australians, drunk a beer and scored some weed and mushrooms.

Jasmine could feel Wade's agitation before he had the gate open. He pushed the scooter in and his foot slipped putting down the kickstand and he cursed. First the bike, then his sandal, but not his own clumsiness.

She went to the door to let him in. She could smell it on him as he passed. She told him to take a shower before they started. He objected, saying that he'd showered before he left the house, but she insisted that he get the 'road smell' off him.

He looked around the living area and saw Guiles laying back on the cushions, his sarong covering his erection, and Wade wondered what, exactly, Jasmine had been doing to him when he pulled up.

Wade turned to her, "What were you doing? Just now, before I got here?"

"Massage practice," Jasmine answered sweetly. "Want some?"

"Self-Restraint practice," Guiles called from the couch. "You don't want any."

This actually drew a smile, a grim smile but still a smile, from

Wade. "Yeah, you're right. I'm told I have control issues." The smile became a grimace as he realized that he'd told the truth.

He went out back on the deck to shower and Jasmine went upstairs to put on her tropical priestess robe—transparent gray silk and white lace in her flower pattern, from her shoulder to the floor, open down the front, hooded.

When he returned Guiles and Jasmine had set up the space in the living room as an altar that the ritual would happen within. Candles and wards. Statues of protective deities, both local and foreign. Curtains that Jasmine had installed for privacy from watchful eyes were drawn closed.

Jasmine and Guiles were sitting cross-legged on cushions on the floor at an angle toward each other and Wade realized that they'd prepared a space for him. This gave him a small jolt of surprise that momentarily stopped his internal dialogue of resentment, alternating with fantasies of the shop keeper's daughter. Then his recognition settled into a place of gratification that he took it as his due. Which, in a way, it was. It was his due that he be deliberately included as Jasmine's primary Consort, but instead of accepting this specialness with the humility expected of him, it went right to his head. Then to his gut. Then to his phallus, which stirred, contracting then releasing, and he pulled on it through his sarong.

Jasmine made an invitation to join them with her hand. There was nothing gracious or grateful in his returned smile. Jasmine looked away as she felt a little stab of pain in her heart chakra, and she looked down, fighting away a rising feeling of the distraught. Guiles watched him out of the corner of his eye, looking for trouble, but keeping his face toward Jasmine.

When Wade settled into his place he smiled. Jasmine could watch the forces he was contending with internally struggle for pre-eminence in that smile. The forces of humble gratitude versus the forces of egoic assertion that went beyond his due. Jasmine sent him a wave of empathic love, hoping that he would feel it, so that they could begin, and have some chance of completing the construct. She watched as the love settled in, and she could feel it in him; it seemed to give him a sense of pleasant memory that she could use to begin.

They sat knee to knee, holding hands, each with one hand above, the other below, supporting and being supported by each other. Jasmine put the Resonance of the Higher Heart into each hand. Guiles took it from his right and passed it through his left to Wade, who took it and passed it on to Jasmine. The rope established, they allowed the Heartbeat to travel up their arms, lighting up the minor chakras on the way, and into their torsos, where it settled into their hearts. From there to their spines it travelled in both directions, down the spine to the root and up the spine to the base of the skull. They allowed it to pulse there for a long time. Then, at a signal from Jasmine they pulled the energy of it up through their bellies past the heart and up over their skulls to meet on the tip of the tongue lightly touching the roof of their mouths.

Their mouths suddenly filled with a sweet saliva, which they held in their mouths for several heartbeats, then swallowed. The room filled with light, golden green light, like a hardwood forest in high summer.

They paid attention to their hearts then, Resonating, and at a signal from Jasmine dropped the Resonance to the solar plexus, vibrating the nerves gathered there. Jasmine used the Resonance to check in with Wade, and assess his condition for the next step. She found the hint of shadow in him far back at the base of his mind, and quiescent.

She extended from herself a golden green ball of energy, pulsing with its own light. Hovering there, it summoned a similar ball from each of the men, which came together in the same plane as hers. Golden green lines established themselves between the balls, and a triangle with pulsing vertices formed. It seemed to surge slightly toward each of the three of them, but it held steady, and did not shift or spin.

From each corner of the horizontal triangle a beam of golden-green light rose up. Jasmine used her hands to bend the lines of light toward each other and the lines met in the middle, snapping into place, creating a perfect green-gold tetrahedron, hovering there.

The vertex pointing towards Wade became unstable, wobbling and blinking. It became clear that Jasmine would have to feed on him to get enough power to stabilize it. With a circular wiping gesture Jasmine made the tetrahedron vanish. She bid Wade to stand up facing her and Guiles to swing his position around so he was touching her knee to knee. Jasmine took Wade's phallus in her mouth and began to draw on it, sucking him in as far as she could, moving her head back and forth. With her hands she took Guiles' hands and put one on Wade's scrotum and another at his anus.

As Wade thrust his hips, heading toward orgasm she moved Guiles' fingers around Wade's sphincter and at the critical moment used Guiles' finger and inserted it into Wade. She took the first spasm in her mouth, but suddenly Wade withdrew, spending the rest of himself on her face. Raising his voice in anger he said, "That's it. I'm done. I'm done with this!" and walked over Jasmine's face and head, smearing his ejaculate across her forehead as he did.

He grabbed his clothes and headed for the door as he hopped into his shorts and struggled with his t-shirt. Sliding into his sandals he said, not even looking over his shoulder, "I'm going home. Guiles, come. I'm not waiting for you."

Guiles regarded Jasmine with a raised eyebrow. Her eyes were closed and she was clearly engaged in alchemizing. She swallowed and shuddered. Guiles could watch the energy drop to her root. "Did you get it?" Guiles whispered as outside they could hear Wade's scooter start up.

As it drove away, she opened her eyes and smiled. From the floor she made the tetrahedron visible again and raised it with her hands held out from the structure. Guiles could see the energy flow down her arms into her hands, which began to glow with the same green-gold energy. He watched as it flowed into the vertex on the base that had been pointing to Wade. The light there stabilized, and as it did the form began to spin. It spun fast enough that it made a slight humming sound.

Then it stopped and turned so that another vertex rolled to the up side and it spun again. Then Jasmine manipulated it again so that the other two vertices were at the top, and in these positions, she spun it again.

She stopped it finally, and smiled at Guiles. "Yup," she said. "I got it."

She lowered the tetrahedron to the level of her low belly, made it small, and drew it inside her through the vortex of that energy center. When it had disappeared, she looked up at Guiles and smiled.

"It's done," she said. "And so is he," she added, nodding toward the door. She wiped her face with her fingers, putting them in her mouth to suck them clean. "You don't have to go back there. Buy whatever you need and you can move into the loft apartment upstairs at the studio until we can find you a place in town."

"It's alright," Guiles said. "He can't hurt me. I'll get my things tomorrow, if I can stay here tonight."

Jasmine smiled. "It would be my pleasure."

Guiles smiled back "Indeed. So it shall be."

45

EIGHT WEEKS THIRD WEEK

Angelica woke with an unusual need to evacuate her colon, caused by the softener she'd been instructed to consume the night before. Her immediate feeling was trepidation. She knew what she'd be doing this week, what she'd be learning, but she had no idea about what would happen, what sensation she would have, and how she would feel about it.

She'd been given an enema the day before. They, the attendants in the bath house, had been quite gracious with her, and patient. She was surprised that the whole process hadn't been unpleasant, just weird. After she moved her bowels her instructions were to give herself another enema. Laying on her back in a special tub, she filled herself behind with the mixture, trying to pay attention to sensation but her mind just kept chanting, "weird, weird, weird." After laying there in warm water for a few minutes she felt the urge, got out, and made it to the commode just in time.

She finished cleaning up and stood there, checking in with herself, sensing her different chakras (all calm). Her somatic awareness was one of lightness, not much weight. She felt trim and fit. And hungry. She's been told not to eat in the morning, that once she got out to the training platform, she'd be fed later.

She wrapped a sarong around her waist and dropped a shawl over her shoulders, pulling her hair out from under it, spreading her hair across her back. She walked down the hall to the morning meditation. She sat and allowed herself to relax into a cleared mind. She focused on sensation, and, of course, her awareness was pulled most forcefully to her sex. She felt more full down there—not as heavy as she did when she was aroused—but more full, as if she had a memory of the sensation of feeling skinnier there in the past. Then she realized that she'd had more sex since she arrived here three weeks past than she'd ever had in her life.

She checked in with the dragon. When it slept now it seemed to become small, curling into its tail behind one chakra or another, sometimes on her womb, sometimes, it seemed, even in it. She had a vision that it felt like the mouth of a cave to the dragon. During the days she was training it wouldn't go below her solar plexus, but instead, would emerge through whatever opening it had been behind and curl up in the space under the platform. This morning it was near the surface behind her second chakra, right below her navel. It flicked an ear when it felt her attention fall upon it.

She continued to sit while the others moved past her to the dining hall. Her stomach growled. She smiled. A soft breeze lifted the gauze curtains on the screenless windows. The early sun slanted through. She allowed the beauty of it, where she was, what she was doing, to fill her and her heart filled with the feeling of gratitude.

Then her mind, in a grumpy voice, said, "Yeah, it's just a shame it has to feel so weird." She laughed out loud. "Unruly," she scolded her mind in reply. She sat then into the energy circulation exercises, up the front, feeling into each vortex, over the head, down the back, returning to her root, then alternating the flow up the back and down the front. Each time she ended at the root.

Suddenly her root began to heat up, the heat spreading up, all the way up, making her sweat and her scalp prickle. She continued the exercise, connecting her tongue alternately to the floor of her mouth then the roof, depending on the direction of flow. She stayed with it, her awareness occupying the room in the front of her mind where the words all stopped. She focused solely on sensation.

Suddenly, as she put her tongue on the roof of her mouth, connecting all the energy she'd pulled up the front to send over her head and down her back, her mouth filled with that fluid, some kind of sweet saliva that, as she held it in her mouth, filled her mind's eye with golden light, filling the dark room where she was keeping her awareness safe with the brightness and warmth of the light. Finally her mouth could hold no more, and she swallowed. Panting for breath she said aloud, "Wow, what was that?" and she laughed.

"We call it The Nectar," Regina said from behind her. She turned and saw her chaperone and teacher standing in the doorway. Behind her she could make out the bulk of Quinn, doing his bodyguard routine. "It tastes amazing, doesn't it?"

"Yes, it does," Angelica said. "What is it?" She gestured for Regina to come in and sit beside her.

"What, you're not tired yet of us hanging around you all the time?"

"No. We're good, the three of us. Considering how much attention you're paying to me you're pretty unobtrusive. You're not in my line of sight all the time. I know you're there. I feel you there, both of you. And it's comforting. So sit down and answer my question. What is it?"

"It is the excretion of a gland in the back of your mouth behind your nose. Almost nobody knows it's there. It accumulates fluid as a result of stimulation, which is what your tongue was doing, and when it's full, it expresses itself."

"What's it for?"

"We're not sure. The legends say that it is a necessary ingredient in the alchemy, necessary for forming the Diamond Body. Other than that, it could be just for the sheer bliss of it."

"How is it used in the alchemy?"

"Ah. That's the theme of next week's training."

"So, it's repeatable? It will happen again?"

"Yes. The phallus is a good stimulator for it. You'll see."

It was time. As she walked down the hall toward the doors that opened to the outside and to the path to the platform she realized that the Resonance of the Higher Heart was beating in her chest, but with two frequencies now, one slower than her somatic heart, and another one twice as fast as the lower one, faster than her own heart.

Quinn and Regina walked along behind her. "You know," she said loud enough for Angelica to hear her, "People work years before that happens to them."

"I think it's clear," Quinn responded, "That we don't have years. Only months, only a few."

"I think it's clear," Regina said, "that things are moving along at a good pace. She's resilient. And adaptive."

When they arrived at the training platform the three of them separated, Quinn and Regina climbing the curved steps to occupy their place behind the opaque screen. Angelica approached her Helper, sitting on the edge of the platform. She smiled, and the Helper smiled back. "Are you ready?"

"I don't know," Angelica replied. "I know there's a lot I don't know, and it feels overwhelming sometimes. It causes me some trepidation, you know?"

"Yes, I do know," the Helper said. "But should we be fearless in the face of the unknown? Or should we be trembling? And is not there another trembling, the trembling of the ecstatic, we should cultivate?"

"Yes, but it is the unknowing. I don't even know your name."

The Helper smiled. "My name is Rainier. And don't you think it is time to get on with knowing, with making the unknown known?"

"Yes."

"Then hike up your sarong and lay on your belly over that big pillow in the middle."

Sitting down at the table up on the viewing deck Quinn and Regina entered a prolonged conversation. "So how's it going?" she asked, "This business of you as her bodyguard and me as her chaperone."

Quinn laughed. "I don't think I'm going to have to deal with another Slayer."

Regina said, "Maybe not, but that's not the only evil in the world."

"True. But those are all big evils, bigger than me. Do you expect me to…"

"No. But I want you to understand something. Most confrontations with evil are about the constant draining of our energy into diversions that require our energy and attention. Give yourself a break and stop imagining that you're still doing the big thing you did a long time ago."

"I know, I'm already doing that. The problem with the world is that it just won't stay saved. You save it once and things go along good for a while and then the fucked up shit starts to happen again. And this time you're no longer in a position to do anything about it. You're nowhere near the fulcrum, the fulcrum of change. You know what I mean."

"Yeah, I do. And I know it exactly. Do you understand we're talking about fate here?" she asked.

"Yeah, I think about fate all the time, and how fucked up it is. Fate is that which is inevitable and immutable. Death is Fate. If you're going to insist on talking about this you have to talk about Destiny, too—that which is inevitable but not immutable. And then there's the freedom of Indeterminacy. Fate is the end of Indeterminacy. Fate happens when things are over-determined. So fuck Fate."

"Yeah, I know what you mean," Regina said and paused. "When

we get to Wallid I want you to go talk to my son. He lives over on the next island."

"Why?"

"Because he is an idiot. The overcoming of the consequences of the Kundalini Buffer can happen even to the stupid. But then again, maybe not," she finished.

A moaning sound drifted up from the platform. Quinn tuned his attention so that he was sure of what kind of moaning it was.

On the platform she had been learning to relax her sphincter. Rainier had been gently massaging her behind and the backs of her thighs, working her way up and in toward that posterior pucker. Just then she was stroking it with an oiled fingertip, and something relaxed in Angelica and that fingertip was sucked inside. This is what had made Angelica moan.

Rainier said, "There," as she slowly inserted the finger all the way until her knuckles rested against Angelica's behind. Slowly she rocked her hand against Angelica, neither withdrawing nor inserting, simply embedded and rocking until she felt even more relaxation. Then she withdrew the finger slowly and reinserted it, doing the rocking motion again at full insertion.

Rainier did this several times, until she could feel Angelica remain relaxed, with steady breathing, before she began the circling motion with two fingers.

Up on the observation dais Regina was starting to get cranked up. Her fatigue, and, yes, even her disagreements with her son the Prophet, added to some resentment that she even had to both teach him and see her teaching apparently fail so often, tended to make her add some tight tones of invective to whatever other subject she was talking about.

"Look, Wuduism, Wristianism, and Wuzlimism are all the same. They are all based on the principal falsehood of the primacy of the masculine. It is a falsehood. A biological falsehood. The truth is that the masculine is derivative. It is consequent, not antecedent. The Feminine is antecedent.

"The masculine cannot offer equality to its superior—for the superior to accept the masculine offer of "equality" would be to make it inferior, to reduce itself to an inferior level. Not possible. This is why the paltry sops that masculinity has thrown to femininity have not made the feminine "equal" to the masculine for a hundred years of so-called "trying".

"The only way forward is for the masculine to recognize and understand that it is already inferior and that the only equality possible is for the feminine to allow, in all holy graciousness, that the masculine may be equal to the feminine.

"And thus, despite my best efforts to persuade the Goddess otherwise, I am compelled by Her to offer you equality."

Quinn was momentarily stunned into silence. Then he said, "Well?

Down below with Angelica, when Rainier's two fingers slipped in one knuckles worth she made the decision to keep going. She slid in, all the way in, until Angelica's ass was up against her fist again. Then she slowly rocked her hand in and out, maintaining contact with her hand the entire time.

Angelica moaned again.

Soon the air around Angelica began to glow red. Into that red field the form of the dragon emerged. Rainier slowed her rocking hand down to the almost imperceptible. The dragon emerged into, or out of, that red field, slapping Rainier with its tail up along the right side of her head. It turned and looked at her over its left shoulder and grinned. It said "Heh, heh, heh." It turned and approached her face. A forked tongue emerged between hound dog lips and scented the air around her. It licked her left cheek, and it felt like a dog's tongue. She smiled and petted it along the neck under the chin then off to the side with her free hand. It went away, crawling off the bed and curling up under the training platform.

Angelica began to rock her hips in time to the slow insistence of Rainier's stroking fingers, in and out. She moaned again.

This time, Quinn stood up and looked over the screen, just to make sure.

"Look you," Regina said. "Look you! You are such an asshole!" and she punched him in the shoulder. Then she said it again, "Look you! You are an asshole" punching him in the shoulder five times, once for each syllable.

"Remember who I am, Regina," he said, smirking.

"Fuck you! Fuck you! Fuck you!" she said, hitting him again six times. "I know perfectly fucking well who you are. I know who you are better than you do, Mr. Bodhisattva of Assholes! I know better who you are than you do yourself!"

"I hope you don't actually believe that, Regina," Quinn said, in a calm and mysteriously sad way.

Regina punched him again. "Fuck you ten times! You will not pull that bullshit on me. You may think I don't know what you've been through. And maybe not. But what I'm certain of is that you have no clue what I've been through."

And a shadow began to grow around her. Swirls of blackness rose out of the ground below her, then out of the air from around her. "I am told to tell you. Even if I cannot kill you, She who made us both can.

"And I am also told to say this: "She will choose me over you, if you force Her to make a choice."

Quinn nodded his head. "I accept. Not a problem for me. You have no fucking idea what it's like to be me here."

"And fuck your self-pity, asshole. "

"Honey, you can't find a dick big enough to fuck my self-pity."

Zhee showed up with lunch around noon. Rainier had gotten up to three fingers. Angelica was covered in sweat. There was a snoring noise coming from under the platform. Angelica stood up on wobbly legs, then sat down on the edge of the platform almost immediately, gingerly settling herself. When she stopped moving Zhee handed her a cup of tea, smiling.

Angelica asked Rainier, "Does she speak English?"

"Ask her," Rainier said.

Angelica turned, "Do you speak English?"

Zhee smiled broadly at her and shook her head 'No.'

Angelica turned back to Rainier. "Well, there you have it," Rainier said.

"No, I don't. I still don't know whether or not she speaks English. I can't tell if she was telling the truth!"

"Exactly, my young friend. You can't tell. That is part of the Courtesan's Art. You can't tell when we're lying. It is a part of what we teach here, and teach to selected members of your Order. Our skills are in need by many. So how are you feeling?"

"At the level of sensation I'm feeling warm back there, but no pain. The muscles know they've been working, though. Emotionally, I am suddenly feeling shy."

"Understandable. We are told that this is shameful, but many of us have come to prefer it, simply because of its intensity. If that happens to you, don't worry about it. It turns out that for most of us it is only a phase. Are you ready to begin again?"

Angelica looked at her questioningly, and then down at her tea and then back up. Rainier answered her unasked question. "No, we will not be eating so much this week. You understand why, I'm sure."

Angelica nodded and obeyed when Rainier told her to lay across the pillow again. Rainier moved to a place on the platform where Angelica, resting her chin on her hands, could see her.

"We have found," Rainier said, "that it is easier to overcome the shyness, and sometimes even shame and embarrassment, if the student gets to watch what is happening."

Rainier produced a set of three carved phalli, long but slender in increasing diameters.

"You will watch me do this to myself, and do what Zhee will do to you."

Up on the dais Quinn and Regina ate in silence. Eventually the rising tide of moaning from below made them uneasy with their anger at each other.

Regina asked Quinn if the Priestesses are taking good care of him, sexually. She said, "I certainly am cared for." Quinn nodded. Every night someone came to the door of the suite, asking if she could be of service. Quinn had started accepting their offers. He'd found that being in proximity to Angelica's work during the day built up energy in him to uncomfortable levels, like it had in Wyoming at the ranch, and that the tantra was the only thing he could find that would sooth away the heat.

Regina told Quinn that she trained many of the teachers of the ones who are serving him now. "I was here a long time, over a year. And then off and on for a decade." And she told him a couple of funny anecdotes, even getting him to laugh. She asked him what he understood about Service.

His reply, still reserved if not downright grumpy, was, "You're her chaperone. I'm just her bodyguard."

This oversimplification shocked Regina.

Regina said, "You have no idea who you are, do you?"

Quinn said, "I try not to."

Regina shrugged and looked away, "Ah, that explains it." They sat in silence the rest of the afternoon.

The westering sun signaled the end of the afternoon session. Rainier smiled when she said, "Tomorrow. On to bigger and better things."

As Zhee was turning to go Angelica reached out and touched Zhee on the arm and said, "Thank you."

Zhee smiled that kind of delightful smile that makes it impossible for one to not smile in return. "You're welcome, Angelica. It is a pleasure and an honor to serve as a part of your awakening."

By Thursday afternoon Angelica was in full sensory overload. She was reverse cowgirling one of the masculine helpers in classic behind style, alternating between holding still and letting him do the work from below and then she doing the work from above, posting the delicious length of him in and out, savoring the three rings of neural induction, her sweat soaked hair hanging in strands alongside her face.

A charge was building in her, she recognized this. What was not happening was any preliminary release of the charge. It just continued to build. She started to growl. The voice under the platform joined in the growling after a moment. She shouted when her hips began to buck, when the orgasm started, wave after wave of release building up, piling up within her. Suddenly she shouted as the energy overcame the seawall of her resistance. She shouted once, twice, five times as the waves crashed over within her. Then she collapsed back, suddenly laughing, laughing from some profound place within her from the joy left in the wake of ecstatic release.

Up on the observation deck, Quinn looking over the top of the screen with concern, Regina stepped around the side, stuck a finger in each corner of her mouth and whistled sharply. Then she shouted, "Now that's an ass-gasm, baby. That's an assgasm!"

46

SCOTLAND

Matthews stayed for two days in the High Priestess's house at The Baths. At supper that second night there was a small dinner where they were joined by the Craft and the Madeleine. Now that his power (his "condition" as he thought of it) was known, they discussed the mechanics of flying, and the question of how much weight he could carry came up. He didn't know, he hadn't explored that limit. He guessed that he could carry Leonard, but was unsure about the Craft, who weighed as much as he did.

After supper, while the two men sketched out plans for a harness that Matthews could use to carry Leonard, the three wen took Matthews to the roof, the scene of the crime, so to speak, and implored him to fly with them. Grace had already managed to shag him on the dining room table after lunch when Beth went up to her office to work. They'd just pushed the dishes and napkins aside and put their creases in the table cloth. He'd gotten so excited he levitated about a foot by the end. Grace loved it.

So he took the Madeleine, whose name was Emma, up first. She'd gone to her knees before him in the cool night, and engaged for not long in the phallus worship she knew would get a rise out of him. Then he sat on the parapet while she sat on him, wrapping her legs behind his back, holding on over his shoulders. And then he fell, fell backwards, much as Beth had done the night before. Emma squealed with delight. He turned as they fell, hugging each other tight. Almost to the ground he swooped, and thrust upward as he swooped, and she squealed again. He did not fly long with Emma. Shortly after he felt the Goddess enter her, she orgasmed wildly and apparently passed out, her arms loosening their grip and he had to take her weight. Inexplicably her arms let go, but her legs didn't, holding her onto him, vise-like. He took her back and laid her on the roof.

He could tell by the smile on Grace's face that the Goddess was already in her, and she laughed low and snarly. She loved the image of him standing there, erection defying gravity even as his wings fluttered and raised up, preparing to defy that gravity entirely. She strolled to him, climbing as he picked Her up, inserting him as She wrapped Her legs around him, pulling close to his ear and whispering "Do you know My Name?"

He answered, "You are She Who Comes."

"Yesss," She hissed. "And so I shall." She shuddered, sliding down along his length until he was fully hilted. "Fly," She commanded, and he did. He took off straight up, and she suddenly became as light as the air he flew through. She came against him in shuddering thrusts. She whispered in his ear again, "Mine." Then suddenly She was gone and it was Grace he held against him once again.

He asked her, "How are you?"

She said, "Oh, I'm good. Very good. I was present with you all the time. The whole time, with you both, you winged stallion."

Matthews laughed and turned so he was flying on his back. "Ride me, horse-wen." Grace had sat up then, holding to his shirt like it was the mane at the withers. Matthews kept his hands on her hips while she posted on him. Soon she was laughing into the wind, hair streaming back. They could hear her laughter below. She drew him in with each rise and fall, compelling him to that deep and filling release within her. The ecstasy made her shout and she let go, sitting up completely, arms spread, a shout that echoed from the houses below.

She leaned forward then, hugged herself to his chest and whispered, "Take me home."

Matthews was remembering as he walked away from the car. It had taken him most of a day to drive up into the Grand Tore mountains, way up in the Highlands. Calley had given him precise instructions on how to reach her Shrine, her Last Shrine, as well as instructions on what to do when he got there. He'd put together a pack with a sleeping bag. She'd told him where to find an old shepherd's shelter under a rock overhang where he could build a fire, and where to find some pine wood on the way up from the Shrine. Calley had smiled at him enigmatically when she told him that this would be a favor that would be repaid. He'd taken the amulet stone strung on a leather thong that she had given him, and had kept with him at all times.

He parked on the east side of the reservoir above the village where Regina had grown up. He shouldered the pack, crossed the walkway over the dam, and started walking up the path beside the water, considering it too risky to fly. He was over the first ridge still thinking about holding the Goddess in his arms through Grace.

He paused at the ruins of an old stone house, its thatch roof long gone, and took a drink of water. He poked through the detritus in the old hearth with its collapsed chimney and admired the view from what would have been the front door. About a mile further along, staring into the westering sun, he stepped off the path, basically a sheep's track, and into grass to look at the long view. The amulet in his pocket started to burn and he reached his hand in and withdrew it. It began to swing like a pendulum, drawing him a few more steps off the path into the pasture. Suddenly, at the end of its swing the stone disappeared and then reappeared a second later. He stepped back, his shock genuine. The stone still strained forward, and he followed it with his arm until his hand disappeared before his disbelieving eyes. He could still feel the pendulum swinging in his grasp and there was a narrow band of tingling around his forearm where it disappeared.

His wonder drew out his curiosity which compelled him forward fearlessly. He stepped through the veil, the tingling sensation passing over him and stopped when he was through. He found himself staring at a farm compound, stone buildings with thatched roofs, smoke coming from a stone chimney. There were chickens in the walled-in yard and sheep and cattle on the hillside behind the compound.

A wen emerged from the building with the smoking chimney, pale-skinned with rich red brown hair over her shoulders. She was wearing a long dress in a style centuries old. She stepped out into the yard and looked into the sunlight slanting over the roof's edge and turned slowly toward him. She squinted, then she gave a squeal of delight and started to sprint across the yard toward him.

She leapt up when she came to the wall, almost seeming to fly, and, pushing off with one foot, she landed in front of him, laughing. He just stood there, jaw dropped and pendulum swinging in tight little circles. She laughed harder, and spoke breathlessly, gasping between the surges of laughter. "It's you, it's you!" she said in a rich brogue. "After so long, it's you!" She crushed herself against him, pulling his face down to kiss her. The kiss was long, and deep, and the energy of it poured into him, filling his heart with joy. She hooked one leg around his, crushing her pelvis to him.

She released his lips and gazed joyfully at him. "You've come. After so long, you've come. I am Bree, Calley's sister."

Matthews felt delight course through him. His eyes sparkled in the light of Her own sparkling gaze. He felt energy coursing through him, the fatigue of many days falling away. He felt young. Bree took his hand and led him toward the house, turning toward him and grinning at him, even once giggling, putting Her hand to Her mouth, teeth flashing between Her fingers. She led him through the door and to the table in the main room with a view through the window up the mountain side. She set a shallow broad bowl on the table and poured warm water into it. "Here," She said. "I am sure it has been a long day. Wash and refresh yourself."

He took off his vest and his shirt. She brought him a cloth and watched as he washed his hands, and face and neck. She couldn't take Her eyes off him. "I have been…" She started to say but the iron teapot on a hook over the fire whistled. She turned away, poured hot water into two cups and put a whicker tea ball into each one.

"You have been?" Matthews asked.

"I have been waiting. Our mother told me She would tell Calley to tell you to come this way. And I am to tell you to go no further, at least today. Calley's shrine is not where you should go for now. Instead you must stay here with me. Drink," She said, nodding at the tea.

"What is it?"

"Magic," She said, simply. Then, after a thoughtful pause while Her face became serious, "Do you know who I am?"

"Yes. Calley told me and she sends her greetings, should I encounter you. It seems now she knew I would. This is more than just an encounter, isn't it?" She nodded affirmatively, still regarding him thoughtfully.

He said, "You are Brighid, the Goddess Queen of these people here from ancient times."

She nodded again, watching carefully as he took a sip from the tea. It warmed him, then it stirred him. The stirring concentrated in his sex and he felt himself grow hard so quickly it pushed against his jeans uncomfortably. He looked down at it, then up at her, a question on his face.

"I told you. It's magic," Bree said, answering the question he didn't get a chance to ask. "Let me see it."

He undid his belt and top button, opening his pants and pulled his erection free from restraint. She gasped a little, and said, "Oh, and it's beautiful." She came to him and stroked him lightly, taking a sip from her cup, and told him, "More. Have a little more."

Matthews grinned wildly and did as he was told. She sat on the edge of the table and pulled her dress up to her waist. She slapped herself lightly and shivered. "Here," She said, pointing between her legs. "Here. You know what to do."

He did know what to do. He positioned himself at the opening to Her Temple. She scooted forward just enough to give him entry. Slowly he came forward into Her, feeling the heat and wetness part around him, receive him, then grip him tightly, trembling. He went all the way in and stopped, holding still until her trembling became a spasm of hip-twitching orgasm. When the waves had passed She looked up at him, shaking back Her hair over Her shoulders, and grinned at him. "More," She said.

47

MORE DIALOGUE

"I don't know how to tell you this," the Embla said, squinting into a rare sunny day in the Highlands. Thistles waved in the breeze all around the capstone on Calley's last surviving shrine.

"You don't have to," the Dangla looked away. "We heard."

"Tell me what you heard."

"You told me that he was going to send the Slayer against the mortals. We heard the mortals escaped, and that the Slayer was injured."

"Grievously, as it turned out. We were horrified. Some wept while others gnashed their teeth. He will live; our Master saved his life. But he may not heal."

"Your master, not mine."

The Embla waved away his objection. "That is not the problem. Not what I wanted to tell you. The problem is that our Master is sick. He had not yet healed from his wounds from the fight at the gate house, from when that Abomination threw the twisted siddhi powers at him. And there was poison on the blade that cut the Slayer. Some of it got in the Master's wounds, and now a fever rages through him. He hides in his cave on the far side of the moon, raging and grinding his teeth on the rocks."

"How bad?"

"He dreams in his fevers. We have hung the Veil of Closure over the entrance so his dreams don't get out. Some fear it will become his shroud, and that with his passing our lives are forfeit."

"Your lives, not ours. We are already mortal, brother," the Dangla inhaled deeply of the Embla's fear. "Aaahhh," he sighed aloud, the Embla too self-absorbed with his own fate to notice. "Tasty," the Dangla thought.

"I have asked for permission to go to that place, to find out if there is something there that might help with his healing. Perhaps to discover how they conspired to hurt him, he who could not be hurt."

"Why are you waiting for permission? Why not just go?"

"There is a chance that it will make things worse."

"Always a chance of that, brother, here in hell."

"Will you go with me?"

"Of course. Wouldn't miss it."

"I will summon you when I decide to go," and the Embla faded from vision.

As was his way, the Dangla always waited until he was sure the Embla was well on his way to wherever. He'd found it safer to not let one of them see where he would disappear. While he waited, he observed a large deer, a buck with enormous antlers, shake its head in the shade of the outcropping, as if flies were buzzing at its ears.

He didn't understand life here.

48

EIGHT WEEKS FOURTH WEEK

"This week," Rainier began, over coffee with Angelica and one of the masculine helpers, named Berto, sitting at the small table near the training platform, "we will begin with the first of the esoteric and alchemical levels in the subject of the Tantra of the Eight.

"Unlike the other Tantras we will be starting with the real deal, Berto here, and not with simulacra. Such a nice word, simulacra, and one so seldom has the opportunity to use it properly in a sentence." Rainier paused and smiled at Angelica's intense face.

"One of the derivative exercises in this Tantra," she continued, "is the celebration of a kind of competition between the practice partners. On the one hand, it is your job, Angelica, to try to make him orgasm quickly, so that you can take the substance you need from him without too much work, to put it somewhat cynically. And it is his job to resist that. This is the first level. There is a second level of competition to this, however, a cooperative aspect, if you will. While he is resisting orgasm he has a second task, which is to make you orgasm as much as possible, as it is his task in every one of the Tantras. And it is your task, therefore, to orgasm as much as you can as quickly as you can, in order to bring about his release. In this way your alchemy can proceed. To this end…"

"What about his alchemy?" Angelica interrupted.

"We will approach the subject of his alchemy next week," Rainier said with just the right touch of severity, letting Angelica know she preferred not to be interrupted. "As I was saying, to this end your task will be to learn how to have an orgasm with your mouth. Not just an orgasm in each of the three centers of pleasure we have worked with so far by using your mouth, but by the end of the week to have an orgasm with your mouth as a center of pleasure in its own right. Do you understand?"

Angelica was imaging what that orgasm might be like. She nodded her head distractedly and toned, "Mm-hmm."

Rainier laughed out loud. "Relax, Angelica. Instruction in that which is obscure to you will begin tomorrow. Today you will have the opportunity to practice what you think you already know how to do. We will give you your head, so to speak, to prove to yourself something about what you think you can already do. Today you spend the day trying to make Berto here orgasm. See if you can take him beyond his self-control."

Berto smiled, uncrossed his legs, and slid his sarong back. He was already erect.

When, after a moment's hesitation, Angelica went to her knees between his thighs, Berto looked at Rainier over her head with a raised eyebrow. Rainier smiled and looked down.

By lunch time Angelica's jaw hurt, her tongue felt swollen and her lips felt swollen and bruised. She had tried every 'trick' she knew, everything that she could remember that had pleased previous lovers, including some things that made Berto pant and his back arch in ecstasy. And Berto remained as hard as ever.

"Give up?" Rainier asked.

"No. Never," Angelica replied.

"Never? That's a lot of fellatio," Rainier replied, grinning. "You want to see how it's done?"

Angelica, past both embarrassment at her lack of success as well as her anger at it, said, "Yes, please do."

Rainier laid Berto on his back, his legs hanging over the side of the platform, feet on the ground.

She leaned over at the hips and planted her hands on either side of his. Slowly she bent forward and back, putting her tongue on his perineum and licking. After a moment she slowly licked up over his balls and along his shaft, pausing her tongue, making just the slightest motions with the tip of it on the ridge just below the head.

With one hand she stood his phallus up, pointing toward the sky, and put her mouth just over the head of it. Angelica could see the sucking motions in Rainier's cheeks and her tongue working by the muscles in her throat. Berto groaned.

Rainier took him into her mouth a little bit farther, angling her head so that she was pulling down on the shaft with the roof of her mouth. She made a quiet humming sound in the back of her throat. She closed her eyes and touched the jewel in the arch between her legs, sending her almost immediately into a leg shaking orgasm that seemed to trigger the same response in Berto.

Angelica watched in fascination as the shaft contracted and twitched, Berto's eyes closed as his hands gripped the sheets. Rainier held steady, making just the slightest sounds of satisfaction in the back of her throat. When the twitching and groaning stopped Rainier did something with her tongue to the shaft and slowly withdrew her mouth. Berto's phallus plopped audibly on his belly.

Angelica's fascination continued as she watched Rainier stand up, working her tongue in her mouth, clearly doing something with the ejaculate. Then she turned her face to the sky and swallowed, starting a shiver that ran all the way to her feet.

She opened her eyes and turned smiling to Angelica, and nodded, as if to say, "There. That's how it's done." She reached down and gave Berto's flagging phallus a fond tug with one hand and said, "Thank you. You did great," and stepped back.

Then Berto did something that surprised Angelica. He got up off the bed and went to his knees in front of Rainier. He reached up and placed a hand on either side at her hips. He leaned in and kissed her on her lower belly, below her navel. He looked up at her with adoration in his face and said, "Thank you Priestess. It has been an honor." He got up, retrieved his sarong and left the platform, heading toward the Center.

Rainier sat at the table, wiped a bit of froth from the corner of her mouth, smiled at Angelica, and said, "Now. Tell me what you observed."

On the observation deck Quinn held his questions until lunch was served. He poured tea for Regina, waited until she took a sip, and then asked, "How did he do it? How did he last that long. Basically, Angelica assaulted him for two hours and Rainier got to him in two minutes."

Regina thought about what she wanted to say. She gave him the short answer first. "Training." Then she squinted, as if she were looking a long distance away into bright light. "I will tell you the story of this place.

"This Order, the Order of the Red Phoenix, is at least three thousand years old. Probably even a thousand years older. It has been known under many names in that time, and that history of names is a part of the secret lore of the Order. It began as a Daoist convent for wen, to give them refuge from the wars of the time, and from the men of the time. They began as both a meditative and a martial order. Their work with the circulation of the Qi, the life force energy, soon brought them a great deal of success in both their meditative activity and siddhi powers as well as in their martial prowess.

"From this work they came to develop an understanding of alchemy. Do you know what alchemy is really? No? Alchemy is the art of crystallizing higher bodies so one becomes free from the natural laws that govern incarnation, and reincarnation. The higher body is able to contain the awareness, and its volition, its capacity for free will, and choice, after the death of the physical body.

The legends are that some of the wen could fly—they could levitate and I believe it. It was through the action of the higher bodies that the physical body could be transcended. And I know you have felt some of this yourself—that sense of weightlessness that sometimes comes with the activation of the Higher Heart. The life energy pulsing in you at those times is called Flying Qi. The alchemy is also necessary to provide the longevity necessary to complete the process.

"They discovered that the Tantra was the best way to generate the function of the Higher Heart, and that the Alchemy was necessary to provide the material substrate that supports it. They developed relations with the men-only monastic orders. Some of these were celibate orders, trying to crystallize the higher bodies and maintain the presence of the Higher Heart without wen. But the Tantrists among them realized this was not possible. That, just as it took two sexes to create life—to create the physical body—and to be born, it takes two genders to create the higher bodies.

"How many are there? For our purposes I will say this: You are born with one body, the Soma. You are given access to two higher bodies, the Soul and the Spirit, composed, respectively, of emotion and thought. The body the alchemists focus on is the one beyond that, called the Diamond Body. This body, in particular, requires substances from both genders in order to crystallize. So the Order developed alliances with the monasteries to provide them with these substances, which the men used to develop what they called Immortality Pills. We still make them here, shipping them to those few places where the men's Orders still exist.

"But in those times relations with the wen disgusted the men in many of those orders. Their tantras were only tantras of the Path of Solitary Cultivation. We, wen, were more interested in the Path of Dual Cultivation and we developed the training programs for both genders.

"However, you must understand the nature of the substances involved. The genders are created to be equal, with the exception of the Antecedence of the Feminine. And the number of different kinds of orgasms each gender can have—the Feminine can have eight, the Masculine can have seven. This is because the Feminine has an entirely additional organ system that the Masculine does not have, and does not have to deal with. You know this, right? But do you know: the equality is not the equality of being the same, being identical. The equality is the equality of complementarity.

"In this case the complementarity is that the Masculine makes only a small amount of the substances necessary for the crystallization of the Diamond Body, whereas the Feminine makes a great deal of it. And here we make it abundantly available to those men who dedicate themselves to Service of the Divine Feminine. We do this no matter what the sexual orientation or sexual identity of a person happens to be. And a part of that Service is the willingness to be trained in the art of preventing ejaculation by the men. You observed this in the Temple Dancing at Stonehaven. By learning this kind of self-control the Masculine not only can retain what it needs from what it produces itself, it learns to separate orgasm from ejaculation. And it learns to please the Feminine. Two hours of sex without ejaculation is common here, as it is at Stonehaven. The men are trained in the art of pleasing the Feminine and bringing Her to ecstasy in each of the eight. When the time is right the Masculine provides the Feminine what it needs, the little bit that it does. And in return the Masculine receives the abundance that it requires.

"But until recently there were only a few men willing to forego their paths of dominance and accept the principle of complementarity. The Order became known externally as an Order of Courtesans in order to generate the money required to maintain themselves, and to protect themselves. In the beginning this was an acceptable path for maintaining life in the convents. The Order would move when it had to, closing down one convent and opening one somewhere else. Often the Order would maintain both the convent and several houses in one city.

"When Rachel Adams found them, oh, almost one hundred years ago, they were fleeing persecution from the revolution on the mainland. Moral purity and all that. Rachel used her enormous wealth and helped them establish themselves here on the island. And in other plac-es as well. They shared their methods with her, and she brought them into the Order of the Fleur de Vie. They also accept special training requests from our Order. Angelica is one. So was I."

On the platform Angelica had finished describing her observa-tions to Rainier. And she wanted to know how Rainier could succeed in minutes at what Angelica couldn't accomplish in two hours. Syn-chronistically, and without any irony, Rainier's answer had also been "Training."

But rather than go into the history of the Order of the Red Phoe-nix, Rainier launched into the Tantra, the Alchemy and their legendary histories. "Since you have been here you have been practicing the Qi Gung work, both the active and the receptive, yes?"

"Every day except when I am in the kitchen for breakfast detail."

"Good. I want you to understand that here, this week, is about making a transition from the Mundane to the Sacred. You know about the four kinds of time and space, right?"

"Yes. Profane, Mundane, Sacred, and Divine."

"Good. As I'm sure you know, much of what happens to wen is in the realm of the Profane. And much of what you've learned so far is about how to keep a situation, some situation you might find yourself in, from degenerating into the profane by using the sexual skills you are developing. In this way you don't have to rely on your martial skills exclusively. The curriculum is also designed to give you options that will keep you from getting pregnant against your will. Most men will happily take manual, oral, or anal release and be happy with it. You must have choices and these kinds of choices are critically important for your freedom and well-being."

"I appreciate the martial skills training. The evening class is tir-ing, but I feel more confident. And powerful."

"Excellent. Wen must be powerful, even if we have to keep it secret. And these are the first secrets—the Tantra and the Alchemy. The Tantra for this week, and you saw this in what I just did to Berto, is called the Tantra of Phallus Worship."

"Whaaat?" Angelica asked.

"Yes," Rainier replied, smiling. "The Phallus is a beautiful thing. She, Great Nature, designed it, and designed it for us, really. Yes, Mother Nature designed the phallus for wen. Remember, we are the Antecedent Gender."

"Wow. I've never thought of it that way. Give me a minute, let that sink in." She worked through it in her mind. The shapes, the sizes, all that had to have been evolutionarily selected for, and she realized that it wasn't the men who were doing the selecting. "Breasts too?" she asked.

"Yes. Not so much for size but for permanence. In other species the feminine only has breasts during lactation. The breasts shrink and disappear when lactation ceases. In human wen, we keep them. They change of course, but still, we keep them."

Angelica shook her head. "Amazing," she said. "What were we talking about? Oh, yes. Phallus Worship! Really?"

"Yes. In addition to the alchemical stuff, which I'll get to in a minute, I cultivated an attitude of Worship, and this energy is very seductive. There is a whole ritual for it, which I'll show you later in the week. Until then I want you to cultivate the attitude of Worship. It feeds the masculine psyche, and makes them want to please you. The men here are trained to please the wen, give them as many orgasms as possible and not ejaculate. I'll explain why in a moment. But our goal, as wen, is to let them do that except under the circumstance where we need them to ejaculate. Worship is a very effective psychic way to make that happen."

"OK. I think I can do that."

"OK. So, in our work, in this Path, this Way, we use sex not only to access the ecstatic states that are our birthright, but to complete ourselves, to complete our Souls and Spirits so that we can crystallize something called the Diamond Body, which is, effectively, immortal. It can sustain our consciousness through and after death."

"Um. Another moment, please, to let that sink in." Angelica paused, thoughtfully imagining Phallus Worship. Then she said, "OK."

Rainier continued, "We also do this work because it creates longevity for us, not so much in years sometimes but as in retaining youthfulness longer. The Internal Circulation, both the active forms and the passive forms, are very important in creating this effect. How old do you think Regina is?"

"Oh, I'd guess in her fifties, maybe late fifties."

"She's almost eighty. And she's been doing this work for more than sixty years."

"Oh my gosh, really?"

"Really."

"But her hair…!"

"I know. Still full of color, and a full head of it, too."

"Wow," Angelica said. Her mind went to envisioning the energy bodies, and the circulation of the energies, first in solo cultivation then in dual cultivation. It was beautiful. Then her mind went to the vision of specific acts in the Tantras, and how that would affect the energies. Then she said, "So I have just two questions. What substances? And is there a ritual for pussy worship?"

Rainier laughed, clear as a bell pealing. Regina and Quinn stood up to look over the screen. Rainier replied, "You mean phulva worship, as your order describes it? Yes. It's called Adoration of the Jewel. You practiced for it last week, and you'll be shown the Ritual for it before we finish these eight weeks."

Rainier waved to Quinn and Regina. Angelica smiled and waved, too. "So, eat your lunch Angelica. This afternoon we will practice, first with these," she said, revealing a bag behind her chair, which she opened and showed Angelica. "A bag of phalli. And then if we have time, I'll call in another volunteer for us to practice on."

"A bag o' dicks, how cute!" Angelica clowned. "For me?"

Rainier, smiling, chastised her, "Incorrigible."

After eating they went back to work with the artificial phalli. Rainier showed her techniques for manual manipulation in support of what she was doing with her mouth. Rainier instructed her on the techniques of connecting her oral sensation with each of her previous three orgasm classes. When Angelica complained that it was difficult to attain orgasm in any of these places because she was working with a phony phalli, Rainier explained that they practiced with these tools because working with real ones could easily overwhelm the connection between these centers, and that it was control of the connection that mattered in the training. Rainier assured her that she would be coming plenty when she managed to learn the techniques. In the meantime, Rainier suggested, she could use her free hand to help. Or a different phalli. Angelica took her up on the offer, with Rainier whispering in her ear explicit instructions on how to connect the sensations of the different phalli, and Angelica decided to relax into the work of it on a deeper level.

They took a short break in the mid-afternoon. Rainier explained that connecting the orgasms to the sensations in her mouth were the first kind of orgasm. The second kind was an orgasm that occurred in the mouth alone. By focusing on the minutiae of sensations, and directing the head of the phallus to the roof of her mouth she would create the conditions for that release. She explained that at the back of throat, high up, was a special gland that secreted a kind of saliva, and that she could use the head of the phallus to stimulate that gland to release its contents into her mouth. The sensation of it would be so fulfilling that her mouth would feel like it would explode, or perhaps even her head, and its taste would be perhaps the sweetest thing she had ever tasted.

Angelica asked her what the men in celibate monasteries used to do, and were they all using phony phalli or each other's real ones. Rainier replied, "They used their tongues pressing against their palates. Look, I know you're tired, but try it anyway. Looking for the pathway for the connection is a part of generating the connection. Use the tool to slowly stimulate the roof of your mouth, and begin to imagine the release happening."

Rainier guided Angelica through a pattern of alternating between connecting her mouth to the other orgasms she already knew how to access and then trying to build up enough sensation in her mouth alone to orgasm there. By the end of the day, her jaw aching and her lips swollen again, she had a connection to her clitoris so strongly and unaided that she came. In the next moment she felt a building of sensation that was pushing from the back of her mouth to her lips, a sensation of concentric rings of pleasure that she knew could become an orgasm, in that moment she let the phallus fall to the side and started laughing as she came.

By Thursday afternoon, working with a real phallus, she achieved both an entirely oral orgasm and had induced the gland to release its fluids into her mouth. Not a lot, but the taste of sweetness filled her mouth while she was holding the head of the helper's phallus against the roof of her mouth. Rainier assured her that, with practice stimulating it, it would begin to produce more.

Quinn turned to Regina at the end of the day. He asked, "What substances? And what about all that anal?"

Regina barked out a laugh. "Yes, the men train that way. If they want. Everything here is optional. Worried about what?"

Quinn growled. "Being compelled."

"I thought so."

On Friday afternoon Angelica was told to return after supper and to be wearing her favorite shawl and sarong. When she returned to the platform there were torches burning, casting flickering light illuminating the presence of the seated Rainier and 8 men. Rainier's hair was coiled up on top of her head and had, a mildly shocked Angelica realized, used makeup to project a different image than her everyday face. Angelica realized that she was using the techniques to facilitate an energetic transfer from the Mundane to the Sacred.

As she approached Rainier, she could feel the pulsing energy of the Higher Heart in the air around her. Rainier said, "Tonight the Divine will touch us. She will come."

Angelica went to her knees and said, simply, "Paint me." One of the things they painted was a red dragon on her forehead. The pulsing Heart blazed in the energetic center there.

When they were done two men each took their hands and led them to the platform. Rainier said, is a dusky voice, "Do what I do."

By the time it was over, Regina had gone to bed and Quinn was nodding in his chair. The two wen spooned in comfort and exhaustion, Rainier's arms around Angelica. Their last sensation was of being covered with blankets by the men to ward off the pre-dawn chill.

49

MORE TROUBLE

After Jasmine dropped her off, Napat decided to use what was left of the daylight to go to a nearby shop to buy some woven offering plates she knew Jasmine needed. She delayed her purchase to talk to the shopkeeper, a cousin of hers. She was aware that Jasmine was being followed, and that, when she was with Jasmine, she was being watched also. She didn't expect that she would be followed independently. After all, she was a school girl and why would anyone think they had anything to learn by following her?

Outside and across the street the priest assigned to follow her expected her to return more quickly than she did. He grew worried that he'd somehow missed her exit. He crossed the street and stuck his head in the doorway just as Napat was stepping through it. She bumped his head with her chest, and in a fury pushed the surprised man backwards into the street.

She yelled at him, "What are you, some kind of pervert? Why are you following school girls around? Beast! Pervert!"

She pushed him again as he tried to get up off the street, so he rolled away and came to his feet. She felt a hand on her shoulder and whirled, but there was no one, only the sense of Good Grandmother. By this time other shopkeepers had come to their doors looking out at the commotion.

The priest panicked and ran, turning down an alley that led to another street, not stopping until he emerged, hands dirty and turban askew. He looked down and saw a tear in his sarong. He reached up to set the turban right and realized quickly that he'd soiled the white cloth with his filthy hands. He became enraged, ground his teeth and made fists. He swore revenge. He'd show her. He'd show her the price for her disrespect, disrespected in public no less. What would the shopkeepers think? Would they tell his superior? The thought made him angrier, and more embarrassed as he realized also that he'd been bested by a schoolgirl, pushed around like a little boy.

And he knew just how to do it, to humiliate her, and in a way she would never forget. And he knew where, too. He knew that she sometimes would take an alley back to her father's compound in the evening.

Over the months she'd made friends with the dogs that roamed the streets after sunset. The dogs weren't stirred by her passage, and they knew well enough to leave the priests alone, terrified and cowering with a trained-in response. They'd be hunted down if they attacked a priest, and the priests let them prey on the tourists when one would stray or be out, alone, drunk perhaps, too late at night, the dogs, forming growling packs, would herd the wayward in the direction they were going, passing the foolish along from one territory to another. So long as they didn't actually bite, they were allowed to live.

Jasmine was expecting both Guiles and Wade to come over for ritual. She wanted more practice manifesting the tetrahedron, and she'd left a note for Napat to go home when she'd finished her errands. In her mind she had an idea about what went on between the three of them, Jasmine, Wade, and Guiles. She imagined being sexually worshipped by the two of them, position after position, feeding her masturbation fantasies. She always arrived at release before she finished the fantasy—she didn't know how to end them anyway.

The priest, lingering outside a gate on her route, saw her coming from afar, wearing her uniform, school bag on her back, and scuttled away behind a fence until she passed. He knew her route, so he stayed hidden until she turned the corner. Then he hustled up, glanced around it, and saw she was almost to the alley. He withdrew his head, counting, waiting until he could hear no footfalls. He did a double-take glance to make sure she was in the alley then followed.

There was a section where no windows opened on the alley, and that is where he took her. Lost in fantasy she did not hear him coming.

He shuffled his feet, moving quickly behind her, grabbed her school bag and pulled her toward him, covering her mouth with his filthy hand. She was still off-balance when he spun her around and pushed her hard up against the wall. He forced a hand between her legs. She made to scream and he slammed her again. "Scream and I will cut you," he hissed.

As his hand rubbed rapidly against her she let her legs go limp, but he wouldn't let her fall. Instead, he turned her around and slammed her front first against the wall, pulling her school bag from her shoulders and throwing it aside. "You will stand there," shoving her again, "Stand there like you stood there in the street and shamed me. How dare you!"

He stuck his hand between her legs again, this time from behind, finding the edge of her panties and pulling them down to her knees. He pulled his sarong aside, revealing his erection. The hand over her mouth slid around to the back of her head and tangled in her hair, pressing her face to the cinderblock wall.

Holding her up he forced himself between her legs and inside her. The forcing hurt and she whimpered. "Don't, please don't."

"You disrespect me, I disrespect you. You shame me and I shame you."

"You shame yourself," she whispered through gritted teeth. He slammed the side of her face into the wall. Then he slammed himself into her, one, two, three times. On the fourth time he exploded, not far inside her, spilling himself out on the wall between her legs, splattering on her underwear. Still enraged he drew her head back and slammed it face first into the wall, smashing her nose. She saw stars with the force of it and the blood burst from it, pouring down onto her white shirt.

Finally he let go, and she slid down the wall, bleeding on it as she went down. "There. You whore now," he said in mangled Nahasi. Leaving her to gasp in pain he looked both ways to make sure he wasn't seen. He ran to the corner and took off to his cot in the dormitory for priests in the basement of the local temple to Skreeva.

Dark settled upon her, sobbing then weeping silently, tears mixing with the blood on her face and shirt, spreading the stain. She stayed where she was.

She retreated, the way Jasmine had shown her, retreated inside to a place of light and rest. She passed out, or perhaps she slept. She woke shivering to find three dogs around her, one pressed against her, two standing guard.

She knew she couldn't stay there and she couldn't go home. There was only one safe place. But she couldn't be seen. Hugging to the shadows she made her way back to Jasmine's, silently made her way through the gate and collapsed on the deck, her back against the fence. She passed out again, the image of Jasmine on her feet pressed between two men, smiling up, the last image she saw for a while. A safe place.

When Wade left a few hours later he did not see her lying in the shadows. Later, when the moon rose, Jasmine emerged naked carrying a towel and slipped into the pool. She felt something turn her back toward the gate and knew someone was there. The image of Good Grandmother flickered near the wall. She heard a heavily whispered "Help me…" from the shadows near the fence. Her eyes adjusting to the dark, she made out the form of Napat's school bag lying next to her heaped up form. She took some matches and a candle from a poolside shelter, lit the candle, and took it over to where Napat lay on her side, her face obscured by her hair.

With one arm she rolled Napat over, and with the other held the candle up to her face. She brushed back Napat's hair. "Oh, no," she breathed. "Oh, no."

50

EIGHT WEEKS FIFTH WEEK

On Monday of the fifth week Angelica showed up at the appointed time. Rainier was already there, as were Zhee and one other young wen about Angelica's age. When Zhee saw her she jumped up with a squeal and ran over and hugged Angelica. Rainier introduced the new wen as Mai's daughter Nicole, who smiled and inclined her head.

"Sit," Nicole said. "We are hydrating. Drink some tea," pouring a large mug and handing it to her.

After pausing to give Angelica the chance to take a sip Rainer asked her, "What do you know about the rain?"

Angelica thought for a second then giggled, "I don't know. It's wet? It tends to fall down? Sometimes sideways but not up?"

"No silly. The Rain. We were told you were a Rainmaker."

"Umm, Shamanism?"

"No, you, dear. You. You are a Rainmaker."

Angelica thought some more and then said, "Sorry, I don't get it."

"You make Rain."

"We hear the Dragon likes Rain. It made Diana Rain once in the Wen's Circle at Stonehaven," Nicole said.

"Oh, oh! You mean squirt!"

The others laughed. "Yes, yes. That's what you call it? Squirt?"

"Yes, yes. You call it Rain?"

"Yes, we call it Rain."

"It's more poetic, don't you think?" Zhee added.

"Yes. Yes, I can do that. And the Dragon, well, the Dragon likes it, too. Sometimes, well…"

The others leaned forward to listen closely.

"Sometimes the Dragon excites it. Sometimes the Dragon makes it happen."

Rainier spoke thoughtfully, "We know only a little about the Dragon, and its needs. I have asked Zhee and Nicole to be here with us this week in order to help us make sure the Dragon is, well, developing and being cared for properly. We also want to build on what you've already learned by showing you the path to the Palace of Light."

Angelica responded, "I have been to the Palace before, I think. It is an ecstatic state where the mind dissolves into golden light, yes?" The wen nodded. Angelica continued, "Regina explained it to me. It happened during the Release from the Kundalini Barrier, and a few more times when I have had sex with the men from Stonehaven and once with my bodyguard."

"Your bodyguard?" Nicole asked.

"Yes. He survived the Release when he was a young man, and on his own in very difficult circumstances. He got caught up in a magical battle, and he died. But he refused to die. This was decades ago. He has had to figure out much of what you are teaching me on his own. But the energetics are very different with him, different from how the men here feel to me. I have learned that the energies that we are working with here, including the energy of the Higher Heart, have their own laws, and that we, wen and men, have to work together to make this all happen, and for most of his life there was no one there to help him. I helped him once when he was in distress, and the energy of him, the energy moving through him, carried me aloft to the Palace of Light. But I would like to know the path, and how to get there at will."

Rainier nodded, and sat silently, as did the other two wen. Interpreting that as an invitation to continue, Angelica took a sip of rapidly cooling tea, and spoke, "One of the men brought to Stonehaven, a doppelganger of the bodyguard, had written a biography of him. I have a copy with me, if you'd like to read it."

Something had been triggered in the wen listening: an impulse of compassion and another impulse of curiosity. All the wen looked up at the privacy screen where Regina and Quinn sat. Listening and feeling the conversation, Quinn stood up and gazed down at the circle of wen. He gazed at each of them, and nodded to each of them as he did. Each of them felt a power in him travel along the connection of their gaze. The connection travelled through them, down, touching each of them at the root. Zhee sighed. Regina reached up and pulled on his sleeve, telling him to "Sit down." He smiled briefly in their direction, but he sat.

Rainier said, "Ahem. Yes. Well then."

Angelica said, "He doesn't often show himself."

Nicole said, "I want him."

Zhee sighed again.

Rainier said, "Ahem! Returning to the subject at hand, tell us what it's like to carry him around."

Angelica said, "The Dragon? Her, not him. Well, both, actually…" She stopped speaking and closed her eyes.

The air around the wen, around Angelica specifically, began to glow red. The wen froze in place, and averted their faces, watching Angelica out of the corners of their eyes. Within the red aura a form emerged, tracking Angelica's form and limbs, but larger than her and surrounding her on all sides. Angelica's head dropped forward as if she'd fallen asleep. The Dragon made a blubbering sound with its lips then bellowed the word, "Rakhine!"

Quinn and Regina stood up, looked around the screen, and she shouted "Hanh!" She took in the scene at a glance and told the wen to "Stand back. You've awoken it." She jumped down off the viewing dais to the platform and around the bed, sitting in the chair vacated by Nicole. The Dragon growled, which rumbled palpably within the wen. Regina slowly reached her arms, palm down, across the table toward the Dragon and even more slowly Angelica/Dragon reached back across the table and put its hands over hers. It began speaking, slowly and quietly to Regina, its moustaches and fiery mane floating as it spoke. Its tail came up and lay across one shoulder, gesturing as if it were a free hand on the end of a long and snake-like third arm.

Regina said, "Hanh," many times, nodding her head, or shaking it side to side as if she understood what was being said to her. She sat back as the red aura shrank again into Angelica's form. It became a vertical line of red energy, which then formed a red spiral centered on her heart. The spiral came forward from the heart into the space over the center of the table then slid sideways and under the platform. Angelica made the blubbering sound with her lips and lifted her head, eyes closed, and sighed deeply.

"That's so strange," she said. "Carrying an entity within me like that. Sometimes I imagine that it feels like what pregnancy must feel like. Except way more weird."

"Weird, indeed," Regina said. She stood up and bid the other wen sit down again. "Admirable, by the way. Trying to summon the Dragon in order to have sex with it sounds like something I would do. But you didn't talk to Mai about it, did you?" The wen all shook their heads. "I thought not. Well, this is between her and you all, now." She paused. "You do not understand what is happening here. Nor why. Angelica has been chosen to carry the Dragon. The Dragon has a Fate, a Fate that goes beyond Destiny. But it is still, somehow, still embryonic. It is still growing and maturing. It is feeding on the alchemy that Angelica is experiencing. That is why it is here. No, wait a minute. I didn't say that correctly. We are here, in part, to feed it with the alchemy. We are also here to create a foundation within Angelica, so that she has somewhere to stand within herself when the Dragon leaves her. Otherwise, she could die."

"Die, huh?" Angelica asked quietly. "I thought so. But nobody is telling me anything. Except that the Dragon will leave me. When it's done with me. When She," Angelica said, pointing a forefinger at the sky, "Is done with me." A single tear rolled down Angelica's cheek.

"She Who Comes will never be done with you, unless you are done with Her. She," Regina continued, "knows you. Calley told me that once She referred to you as The Sane One. It made us all regard you in a new light. It made us all wonder just how crazy the rest of us all actually are."

"I thought I was crazy once." Angelica said. "But then I realized that it wasn't me. I talked with Quinn about it. He knew because he was so alone for so long. The Release from the Barrier made me sane, although it made me look crazy to anyone else. Sanity became what would make me crazy instead. You have no idea, you all have no idea." Angelica closed her eyes, and tears washed down her cheeks in twin tracks.

Rainier and Zhee reached out and touched her shoulders. Nicole went around behind her and did the same with both hands.

Regina said, "We know something about crazy. The Barrier is weak in all of us. It has grown weak and pieces of it have been swept away in the rains."

Angelica felt the empathy, the capacity of the others to feel what she was feeling, and sobbed. They let her weep. Her head came forward on the table and she rested her forehead on her forearms.

Regina was about to reach over to Angelica when an impulse to stand back suddenly seized her. A golden light appeared around her, and her arms went out to her sides palm up, and her face turned to the sky. Then her face turned down, her eyes opened and she regarded them all. Her eyes had gone completely black.

Rainier leaned over and whispered to Angelica, "Look up."

Sniffling, she did so. Her eyes locked onto the gaze regarding her. She whispered, almost breathlessly "She Who Comes."

The Entity before her, inhabiting Regina, nodded. When She smiled, Angelica smiled back. She turned to the dais and all eyes followed Hers, to regard Quinn standing there, alert, relaxed, paying attention. The Entity gestured to him, beckoning him to come to them.

As he came closer the golden aura around the Entity/Regina became broader and brighter. By the time he came within arm's length the field had grown to include all the wen at the table. The Entity turned to him and said, in a low and husky voice, "You have need."

Quinn nodded in agreement. "I have need."

The Entity turned to the wen and said, "Feed him today."

The Entity/Regina reached for him and unbuttoned his shirt. She pushed him back onto the bed, pulling his sarong out from under him as he sat, revealing his erection, the famous "Thunder Cock, the Rock Splitter." He sat cross legged on the bed. Regina climbed up and went around behind him, settling herself back-to-back with him. "Come, Nicole."

Nicole climbed up, pulled her sarong aside and sat down, slowly, enveloping his erection a fraction of an inch at a time. She sighed when she'd settled. Then an extraordinary thing happened.

Regina felt her back split open and the Goddess slipped backward, out of her, and through Quinn's back to settle in Nicole. When Nicole opened her eyes it was through a veil that she saw, and when Quinn looked at her he saw the Goddess looking back at him. Nicole gasped. He smiled, and the Goddess returned the smile.

"I know you," he said.

"You do," She said.

"I see you," he said.

"And you are seen," She said.

Nicole slid once up and down his erection. Then she did it again and felt an uncontrollable wave of trembling originate behind her clitoris. She felt the Goddess compel her to stand up, spread her phulva, and press her opening against Quinn's face. She began to rain, bucking her hips with each spasm, and Quinn heard the Goddess whisper fiercely at him "Feed." Quinn opened his mouth and drank. Regina, still attached to the Goddess, rained lightly, too. When Nicole finished she collapsed to the side, and the image of the Goddess remained, diaphanous, facing Quinn, still erect.

"Zhee," Regina called out. Zhee sat down on Quinn and into the image of the Goddess. Zhee's smile was radiant though her gaze, too, was veiled. As it had happened for Nicole it happened to Zhee. Zhee pressed her hands into the back of Quinn's head to hold his face to her, then she, too, collapsed to the other side.

"Rainier," Regina called out again. Rainier climbed up, spread herself open, and settled onto Quinn and into the Goddess. Rainier's head went back and she started laughing. After a moment's motion she, too, stood up, laughing still, grabbing his ears to hold him to her, bucking her hips with each burst of rain. Quinn drank again, rain running down his chin and onto his chest, soaking him, caressing his erection. Rainier stepped to the side and sat down, still quaking with laughter, and she, too, fell over on her side.

"Angelica," Regina said. Angelica stepped up to Quinn. She bowed to him, and leaned forward, grasping his phallus in both hands, put her mouth over the head, and rubbed it against the roof of her mouth. Her eyes rolled back in her head as her mouth filled with sweetness and it slurped out around her lips. She stood up before him, smiling, until she settled on him, and her smile merged with the Goddess's. This was the first time she'd had him in her. Those times of teasing on the porch in Wyoming, and the time she'd eased his suffering, all flashed quickly through her mind. And she remembered when he'd saved her from the Slayer. Then, directed by Her, she angled her hips so that, as she rose and fell, his phallus rubbed against that little gland behind her pubic bone, stroking it, causing a pleasure so intense in her that she had to hold onto his shoulders, her head flown back. "Oh," she groaned. Then thrice more she groaned and felt the Goddess within her stand her up and she did so, too, and rained on his face, and into his open mouth.

He shuddered as the waves and spasms of his own ecstasy, too, started within him, the Higher Heart pounding, waves descending and ascending, passing through each other and he, too, began to glow with that golden light. Angelica collapsed again on him, inserting him straight inside her without any effort and settled down, her head on his shoulder. "I know you, too," both Angelica and the Goddess whispered in his ear, one voice echoing the other.

When his shuddering, his alchemical processing, faded away Regina stood up and lay Angelica over on her side. Regina settled on him, rejoining the Goddess as one. A few strokes and she, too, stood up and rained for Quinn, forcefully soaking him, raining more than he could possibly take in. She stood up and pushed him onto his back. "Now you will feed us. I know you know," she said, husky and smiling. She stepped back and encircled his phallus with her lips and pulled an orgasm from him.

Quinn, past master of controlling his ejaculation, fed her one squirt, and cut it off. The Goddess/Regina worked the sweetness from the palate gland into it and swallowed, causing her legs to shake and she went to her knees, laughing. She crawled backwards on her knees, leaving the image of the Goddess between Quinn's knees, and said, "Nicole."

Nicole roused herself and took her place between Quinn's knees, placing her mouth over him, and he released another charge into her, causing her to shake when she swallowed and she fell away onto the stones, lost in ecstasy.

Regina said, "Zhee." And it was the same for Zhee, falling away, lost in the field of the Palace of Light, falling into the Pool of Sentience, and, no longer differentiated, smiled into her shaking and shouted, and went silent.

Regina said, "Rainier." Rainier knew that what was happening was archetypal and paid close attention as she knelt, savoring the merging of her Soma, her Soul, and her Spirit with She Who Comes, The Antecedent One, the True Creator. She knew that the Goddess was working a transformation into Quinn, although she didn't know what, or why, only that she was immensely privileged to be a part of it. She placed her lips on him and he fed her. The blast of it almost overwhelmed her and her head went back, his gift almost falling from her lips. She closed them, sitting back, then crawling away, to lay down and prepared the alchemy herself before she swallowed and surrendered to the light.

Regina went to Angelica. "Come. Feed." Regina helped her up and over to Quinn. "Go to the Palace, little friend." Angelica leaned into the light and placed her lips over him, deeply entranced. He fed her then, emptying himself into her. The first blast was like a bolt of lightning, rising into her head. She fell upward into a field of light, losing all awareness of where she was. Quinn stood up holding her head, still mounted between her lips, and laid her down on the rocks, his juices mixing with hers. The Goddess stood with him. He turned Angelica's head to the side so she wouldn't choke and stood up, laughing, a being of light laughing. The Goddess stepped backward and merged with Regina again.

Together they stepped forward toward Quinn. They reached up Their hand to caress his face, smiling broadly. "Beloved," They said. They looked toward the dais. Mai was there, her face a mixture of joy and consternation. The Goddess left Regina and settled into Mai.

"Oh, my," she said. "I see." And the Goddess/Mai looked back over the scene, the four wen scattered across the stones, Regina standing next to a Quinn glowing with power, her hand on his arm. "Time for lunch," the Goddess/Mai called out, laughing a clear laugh that pealed out, washing over them.

And then She was gone.

Regina spoke up to Quinn. "Last week you asked about substances, and I didn't answer you. Well, what just happened? Those substances."

Quinn looked at her and asked, "Well, what about all that anal?"

Regina laughed and punched him on the shoulder. "Asshole. You're the anal."

Quinn nodded in mock sagaciousness.

There was no afternoon session that day. All the wen retreated to their rooms. Quinn spent the afternoon at his table on the viewing dais, watching the sun and shadows move, contemplating the difference between Fate and Destiny, and watching the birds flit from tree to tree.

51

AN AFTERMATH

Guiles scootered out to the village early the next morning. Wade was still asleep and didn't wake while Guiles packed the rest of his belongings. Guiles was glad to be leaving. He had found his time in Wade's company to be irritating and it made him happy to know that he would be closer to Jasmine and Napat. Clearly, the danger level to which they were exposed warranted the shift.

He'd helped Jasmine bring Napat into the house and lay her on the sofa. He helped Jasmine get her out of the ruined clothing and brought warm water to them, so Jasmine could wash her. Napat had passed out as soon as Jasmine had found her, and she remained unconscious the entire time. Jasmine had spent the night holding Napat, sleeping beside her.

Guiles arrived at Jasmine's house before Jasmine had returned from shopping. Coming from the kitchen down into a darkened living room he heard a whimper coming from the couch.

He said, "I'm going to turn on a light now." The whimpering increased. He neared the couch and recognized Napat's school uniform heaped on the floor, soiled with dirt, and something darker. He turned the light off.

The voice had emerged from under a stack of sarongs, swaddled round the reclining form. He drew closer; she twitched and gave a small cry. "I stay back," he said in Nahasi. He sat in the shadows until Jasmine returned.

Her shopping had taken longer than she intended. It did not seem she was being followed this early in the morning, but she was careful to observe her back trail. And she'd spread her purchases out over different stores in order to avoid suspicion. Painkillers for menstrual cramps, antiseptics, salves for bruises and healing wounds.

Jasmine had Guiles draw a warm bath for Napat. When it was ready he stepped back while she helped her to the tub and get in. From out in the living room he erected a healing cocoon of energy around them, a wall that would exclude all nightmares. When Napat was clean and dry Jasmine sat her down and dressed her wounds. Spasms of shivering shockwaves passed through Napat. Guiles had changed the bedding on the couch and Jasmine lay her down on it, and covered her with clean sarongs. She stood and surveyed the room, making sure it was as dark as it could be, then she beckoned Guiles to follow her into the kitchen.

She put some water on for tea and bid him sit. "We need to talk about what to do. I want your advice." He nodded.

"She told me who did it. She'd had a confrontation in the street with one of the Priests who's apparently been assigned to follow us. We've seen them all many times and have our nicknames for them. It's the one we call 'Pimple'.

She paused. "I should have escorted her home," she whispered. Guiles leaned forward but said nothing.

She resumed. "We can't go to the police with this. It would be too embarrassing for her, and her father. It would cause endless trouble with the Priests. And she can't be seen in public like this, either. It would draw too much attention, both to me, and to what we're here to do. And it's going to take a few weeks for her to heal those bruises and wounds."

"Then she can't stay here. That would also draw too much attention; never leaving the house."

"And she can't just disappear."

"So where can she go?"

Jasmine's mind raced.

"Regina has a place here. In the center of the island."

"The Regina? Regina Moon Halter?"

"Yes. She inherited the lease from Rachel Adams. We have been here for nearly a century."

"So, what's the cover story?"

"I was speaking to my Madame Regina about what a good assistant Napat is. Madame is returning at the solstice and will need her services. School will be out so there will be enough time at the compound for Napat to heal. There will be extra pay, and money for the father."

"I will get ahold of the uncle to drive us over there. I can probably arrange it for tomorrow night."

"Good."

The supervisor of the Priest known as Pimple heard about his confrontation in the street with the yoga lady's strange assistant. The shopkeepers along the street were all gossiping about it, enjoying the Priest's humiliation by a girl. Knowing Pimple as he did, he could not be certain if his behavior was malicious or simply incompetent.

Nevertheless, he could not afford to have either in his management of the monitoring group. He transferred Pimple to the small village to keep an eye on where the two foreigners, the friends of the yoga lady, stayed.

In an effort to get the story of what happened Guiles had inquired casually of the shopkeepers. They told him about the argument, and that Pimple had been transferred as a result. He made a mental note to warn Wade the next time he saw him.

After a hard and fearful night, filled with Napat's fitful weeping, they awoke to an unusual sunrise thunderstorm. Guiles called Napat's shady uncle and arranged for him to show up at Jasmine's house at sundown. Guiles had the gates open, waiting for him.

Jasmine brought Napat out, swathed in shawls. Jasmine had counselled and impressed on Napat the need for her to speak to her uncle in a reassuring way. Her survival might depend on her uncle's willingness to be satisfied with short and business-like answers—because, after all, she was going to work for the Madame of Oolagasi, the village where Regina's compound was.

At one point the van hit a pothole and bounced heavily. Napat moaned. The uncle turned around and asked her point blank if she was alright. Jasmine answered, leaning forward, blocking his view. "It is that time of the month," she whispered, and the uncle nodded knowingly and returned his attention to the road.

The moon was just past new. Onadaya, Regina's property manager, cook, and a Priestess of the Order of the Fleur de Vie, had the drive-in gates open when they arrived but the uncle preferred to not pull in. As they exited the van Napat had it together enough to blow her uncle a kiss when he leaned out the window and asked her one last time if she was alright. Jasmine thought her stalwartness was a good sign.

Guiles had followed them on his scooter, looking for tails, but there were none. He pulled in through the gates, Onadaya closing them behind him. She gave him the once-over eye. She reached up a hand to his shoulder and pulled him down to whisper in his ear, "I will see you later." Then she picked up one of the small suitcases and took it up the short flight of stairs to the stone paved floor of the compound courtyard.

Guiles found himself unable to take his eyes off her derriere. At the top step she looked over her shoulder at him and grinned. Later, standing in the doorway of the cabin assigned to Napat, he watched Jasmine tuck her in, feeling the love and concern Jasmine poured through her hand on Napat's shoulder. The room began to glow.

Jasmine turned to him. She grinned at him, just like Onadaya had. "Go," she said. "Onadaya has no Consort. She is famous, though, for taking on Assignments." And she grinned more broadly.

Guiles grinned back and asked, "Which room is hers?"

Onadaya's room was beautiful. It was at the back of the compound, second story above a storage area, the tops of the windows opening at a height just above the compound walls. On her deck she could overlook the walls, not the highest horizon of her hobby watching the planets rise.

Curtains drifted in a slight breeze, shifting the leaves of her flowering plants. Candles illuminated smoking incense. Wood fire coals in a corner brazier flickered red light below the gold of the candles. She'd bade him enter before he knocked. He pushed the door open slowly. She was just finishing lighting an incense stick. She looked up at him and said, "Gold over red. The Sacred colors of the first notes of two octaves of worlds. Tonight," she paused to grin at him, "We shall mix the Sacred with the Mundane."

Setting the incense into its holder, she nodded her head toward the mosquito-netted four poster bed and said in Nahasi, "Take your clothes off."

He barely restrained his knees from buckling right then and there. It turned out that he was simply saving the knee buckling for later.

In the morning he awoke to find her sitting on the edge of the bed, still under the net with him, gazing at him. He sat up, and she leaned forward, taking his phallus in her hand. "You," she said, "are a

High Consort to be recognized. I praise you." She grinned, as broadly as Jasmine's second grin the night before. She put a finger to his lips, shushing any nonsense he might say. When she took her hand away from his lips she put her mouth on him, and he knew better than to say anything, anything at all. Sighing, and some growling, it seemed to him, were the only acceptable sounds.

52

Eight Weeks Sixth Week

Angelica and Rainier were sitting at the table, legs crossed towards each other, wearing two shawls each in the cool morning. Waitan was in the tropics but the air reminded them that winter was coming not too far north of them. Quinn was up on the wall and behind the screen. He could hear them but he was focused on his coffee. Regina had yet to appear but he was confident she would once she'd finished with whatever, or whomever, had distracted her.

Rainier was saying, "It's a mystery, honestly. No one knows why we, humans, have such a capacity for ecstatic states of consciousness, and why the feminine has so much greater capacity for it than the masculine."

Angelica responded, "I have been wondering the same thing. Do men get to go to the palace of light like we do?"

"It's harder for them. We think that our capacity, as wen, so much greater than theirs, comes from the risk of childbirth. We think that on the deepest levels of our brain, deep in the reptile brain, our capacity for ecstatic sensation is what compels us into the behaviors that will get us pregnant. Without the ecstasy, why would we take the risk?"

"Ahh. Well, and what does She say?" Angelica asked, remembering Her appearance on the training platform the previous week.

"She smiles, and simply nods Her head "Yes."

"So, the tantra leads us into ecstasy and creates all these esoteric experiences. But even the esoteric experience happens in our physical body, in our soma. What about the alchemy? What about the creation of higher bodies? I asked you about substances before, and you didn't answer."

"Yes, well," Rainier stalled as she gathered her thoughts. "It's a theory. She likes it, but all that means is that it furthers Her aims for us."

"Umm, what does that mean?"

"It means that it's useful for us to believe that we can have a Soul and a Spirit that don't just die when the body dies, but that these can serve as containers for our awareness, so that our awareness remains self-aware. What we know is that we're either delusional or that all the experiences we have with the ghosts of some of us is real. And the theory is about how that possibility can be. Maybe there's another explanation, we don't know. But—and I mean this—the idea that we can use sex for a purpose other than procreation—that we can turn that energy into another kind of creation, the creation of a different kind of body and that we can use the substances to fuel that energy until the energy is capable of being sustained by other kinds of substances—well, that is the alchemy: the transformation of substances, higher to lower, and lower to higher." Rainier paused to look at Angelica, and assess her degree of understanding. She smiled and nodded her head. "I see you beginning to understand the theory. Are you ready for the practice?"

Angelica nodded her head.

"All of your work so far has been about concentrating the energy of pleasure in particular places to build the potential for ecstatic experience until the energy discharges. This week will start farther out, with the extremities, building charge through the minor chakras, the minor energetic vortices, and collecting that within you. Creating the charge, moving the charge, collecting the charge until all of you becomes orgasmic, your whole body becomes an orgasm. Then we will reverse it, reverse the path of collection so that when the energy reaches your extremities again, you will become orgasmic, aroused, ready, and the slightest touch will trigger you.

"Experiencing this takes a lot of work and a lot of relaxation. So we have to bring in help."

Two couples approached the platform. Zhee and Nicole were the wen and they were accompanied by two men she hadn't noticed before.

"Now lay back in the middle of the bed," Rainier commanded.

Before she did, she asked Rainier, "What are their names?"

Rainier smiled. "We call them Lao and Tzu."

Angelica lay back and the couples split up around the platform, Lao and Zhee taking her left and right hands, Nicole and Tzu taking her right and left foot. She could feel the resonance of the Higher Heart in their hands. They began by touching, just lightly touching, the energy centers, the minor chakras of her hands and feet. They began to softly swirl their fingers. Angelica felt a subtle surge of energy into the vortices from them.

"Just breathe," Rainier told her. "Just breathe and surrender to sensation."

Slowly they stroked her, fingers moving in light circles, barely brushing her skin, up her legs and arms, pausing at knees and elbows, hips and shoulders, activating the resonance in each vortex. She could feel energy begin to build up low in her belly, as if her womb were a reservoir.

When the helpers reached her midline they poured resonant vibrations into her primary vortices, Zhee at her head, Lao's hand lightly touching her lower hand, Nicole touching his hand with one of her own, putting her other hand on Angelica's heart. Tzu put one of his hands on Nicole's lower hand, and his lower hand on Angelica's solar plexus. The charge near her womb began to pulse, then to vibrate. Rainier got up and put one finger over that spot, on her second vortex, and one finger on her root vortex. The charge dispersed suddenly, travelling up the line of their hands to her crown, and down and out her root. She had a seizure of ecstasy so profound her back arched off the bed and she screamed.

This brought Quinn to his feet. Angelica collapsed. Her belly contracted and she shouted before she lay back. Her arms and legs twitched, then stopped. Rainier stepped back and the four helpers began stroking her softly from her second vortex outward, reaching her extremities several minutes later. Angelica was so aroused she was drooling and dribbling rain. The helpers stepped back and Rainier licked her finger and lightly touched Angelica's jewel. She exploded again, hips bucking, legs shaking, fists balled, and rolled to her side, almost doubling over completely then arching her back, shouting as each spasm of release rocked through her.

Panting, she opened a hand and reached for Rainier. Rainier took her hand and Angelica pulled her in close. "Enough, enough," Angelica whispered fiercely. "Make it stop."

"Keep panting," Rainier said. She touched Angelica on the forehead with two fingers. Angelica sensed that Rainier was opening a door to the Palace of Lights. Her mind filled with golden light, light that supported her and buoyed her up, light the same color as the lightning that had just flashed through her, but now it was a cloud in which her Spirit rested. Zhee climbed into bed with Angelica, wrapping her

her arms around her. Slowly the spasms that had made her jerk became trembling, and her breathing slowed to match Zhee's. And then the trembling stopped, and it was as if she had fallen asleep.

After a few minutes she sighed, and then said, "Wow. Holy shit, even." Then she made the blubbering noise with her lips that the dragon made often. Briefly she glowed red, then the red line emerged from the front of her, twisted into a spiral and disappeared under the bed. "I'm OK," she said, and sat up. "Is it always like that?" she asked.

"Sometimes," Rainier said. "Sometimes it's like that, but you learn to control it, or surrender to it, either one."

"I can't walk around like that all the time," Angelica said. "I'd go mad."

"True," Rainier responded. "But you can go around aroused at a lower energetic level, and you can control, and even localize, your orgasm."

Nicole said, "I've never seen one like that."

Rainier turned and said to her, "Keep working on yourself. It was like that for her because she survived the release from the Kundalini Barrier, and she is a whole person now with nothing to buffer the sensation. When you become a whole person, a released person, the full potential of you will be released also."

She turned to the men and said, "You, too, can experience ecstasy like that. Arousal can become orgasm in men also."

"Even without erection?" Lao asked.

"Yes. It is a different reflex. But combined with erection it can be explosive. Now, will the four of you please go bring some tea, and lunch?"

They nodded and filed off.

Rainer sat on the chair and put her chin in her hands. "So, how are you feeling now?"

Angelica touched her second vortex and shuddered. "What is this?" she asked.

"It is a kind of energetic accumulator, or capacitor. Activating it and filling it with energetic charge creates the opportunity to experience the discharges you experienced."

"It is trembling, now that I'm touching it I can feel it."

"Yes, and you can direct it to different places in you. Direct some of the energy to your foot."

Angelica did as she was told, and her foot trembled and her toes curled. "Oo," she said, laughing. "A foot gasm."

"Precisely," Rainier smiled back.

"How do I recharge it?"

"Attention. Sensation. Breath. Direct the energy of sensation, even sound and vision, to your second vortex. Allow the Higher Heart to resonate there. Energy is around you everywhere. Learn to draw on it."

By the end of the week Angelica had become skilled at not only orgasm from being touched on any part of her body, but also in any part of her body, at will. And on Friday, after a day and a half's work building charge and repressing discharge she levitated, not far—only half an inch or so, falling back onto the bed only when she laughed out loud.

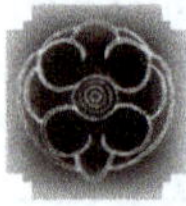

53

EIGHT WEEKS SEVENTH WEEK

Angelica was thoughtful on this particular Monday walking up the path to the training platform. The martial training program had been going well. It impressed her, the extent to which the energetics of the sex translated into martial force. And she'd been well fed, and well cared for by the Consorts and the staff. But she knew that she would be leaving in three weeks, called forward by this great adventure and she was worried about how well she would adjust and adapt to a life only a fraction as intense as she'd been living for six weeks now. The scientist in her wondered at the coherence of what she'd been learning, and the Priestess marveled at the beauty. She was afraid that she hadn't the self-discipline to survive the transition happily, and worried that she'd lose the energetic awareness she'd developed once she left this environment where it seemed that everything was geared to the development and maintenance of that awareness. She worried that she would lose the self she'd come to be.

Then her mind shifted to one image, one helper, in particular. His name was Corey. He'd been assigned to be a part of the crew that helped her with her training at least once in each of the weeks she'd been there. He was taller than her by about four inches, well-muscled, kind, and tentative when he'd touched her, but skilled. He had a shy smile. She was developing a crush on him and it scared her a little. She knew she was leaving, and that she was leaving him. She didn't even know if he was an initiate of the Order of the Fleur de Vie, as she was now, or if he'd come to this Temple through some other means. In the world of the Assignments of the Fleur de Vie she knew that, although there was room for love, partnerships, and marriage, new Priestesses were discouraged from forming emotional attachments during the early part of their training. Consorts, and even assignations were carefully monitored. Even as a new Priestess she knew that she didn't have the mental and emotional wherewithal to make these choices for herself. She knew that she had to depend on the mentoring wisdom of the elder wen to make these choices for her. But still, she realized that she was longing for an assignment—a consistent relatedness that didn't require her to surrender any of her autonomy, just her resistance.

When she arrived she was surprised to see Mai and Regina sitting at the table with Rainier. The three of them reminded her of the Triple Goddess in tableau. But as she sat she realized this was a different configuration of power—that she was the Maiden archetype. And as she sat she felt something energetic snap into place and a faint humming sound appeared from all directions. They invited her to sit at the table with them.

Mai began. "I have not had much opportunity to visit with you. Honestly, we have found it important in one undergoing a training such as yours that I not spend much time with them—there is too much risk of attachment or transference. So…How are you Angelica?"

"On the way up here I found myself longing for something, and I'm not clear what. It reminded me of when I was in my young teen years, and was wishing for a steady boyfriend. In my imagination it was comforting. But then it turned out that I really didn't want that, at all. I wanted to become my own person first, to develop my own agency and autonomy. When I started dating we would make agreements about common things—things we had in common, like where we would go on a date. But my things, my personal choices were always mine alone."

"That's not surprising Angelica. This week's work is about agency and autonomy. It is about the creation and integration of the center of yourself, the Axis Mundi of you."

"The Center of the World in me?"

The wen smiled. Mai said, "Everyone can have the Center of the World in them. It runs through them. You have the possibility to establish an Axis Mundi within you."

"Will it change me?"

Regina's smile broadened. "Yes. As the spine is your Somatic Axis, so too the bodies of the Soul and the Spirit need a spine. It will connect you to the center of the Earth, which is connected to the center of the Sun, and to the Moon. And in the other direction, going upward and outward, it will connect you to the mind of She Who Comes, the mind of all life on the planet."

Mai added, "The Center of the World can be anywhere and everywhere."

Angelica's mien became very serious. "Is this Axis in you?" she asked Regina. Regina nodded affirmatively. Then she asked Mai, "Is this in you?" and Mai nodded. She turned to Rainier, "And you?" Rainier's response was to nod and smile and stand up, then raise her arms to shoulder height, extend her forearms vertically and hold her hands palm up, with her fingers slightly curled, making almost a cup shape.

A wind came up, an uncommon wind as Quinn would call it, making him stand up. The wind came and formed a vortex over the group, a gentle vortex, lifting their hair. The vortex centered over Rainier, then dropped over her, settling all the way to the ground slowly and then it stopped. Rainier lowered her arms and opened her eyes. They had turned completely black. The Goddess/Rainier smiled. Angelica felt her eyes relax and everything around her began to glow faintly.

"The Sovereign in each of us must rule. And since it is in each of us we must each rule ourselves. Behold the crown of sovereignty." Into that glowing cloud Angelica saw a ring of blue light reveal itself, encircling Rainier's brow, a ring of blue flames flickering and on top of her head another flame, a red flame dancing.

Regina and Mai stood up and Angelica saw flaming crowns upon the heads of both Regina and Mai, red over gold and violet over blue. They both bowed toward Rainier, bowed more deeply to Angelica, and left the platform area, Mai going toward the buildings, Regina going to join Quinn behind the screen. When she sat next to him he regarded her crown and said, in an indifferent tone, "Impressive." She muttered "Asshole," punched him in the shoulder, and it faded.

A wen walked into the area followed by three men. One of them was Corey. Angelica flushed a little, heated by seeing him. It was not lost on Rainier. She directed them all with her finger pointed downward. They all kneeled and sat on their heels, faces looking down.

"This should be easier for you, this week, than it is for most wen. You have already blown through the Kundalini Barrier, and you have kept your awareness of the Resonance of the Higher Heart all this time, and you have not turned from the Suffering this has induced in you. Instead, you have turned your face toward ecstasy, and toward Me." By the Resonance, the pulse of a heartbeat in that voice, Angelica knew that it was not just Rainier speaking to her.

"We will build the center of you as a column, connecting one vortex to the next with a helix of finer substances. You will have to use all your skills. Go sit on the edge of the bed."

Angelica did as she was told. Rainier snapped her fingers and the kneeling crew stood up and distributed themselves around her. The wen went around behind her, climbed up on the bed and leaned against her, back-to-back, in support. The men stood in front of her, then kneeled down, Corey in the middle. Her breathing quickened and she looked down, catching his shy smile at the upper edge of her vision. The men on either side of her reached down and picked up her feet, holding them in their laps, spreading her knees.

"Close your eyes," Rainier told her. "Feel your support. Feel yourself supported, supported by the Masculine below and the Feminine behind." The Resonance of the Higher Heart appeared along her spine where the wen leaned into her, and in her feet, where the men held them. Slowly the men slipped her feet up their thighs until each foot rested on a phallus. The Resonance flared, and the men gasped. "Feel through the men. Extend sensation down through the men, to the stone beneath, and the earth beneath the stone. Extend sensation along a golden line down through the earth, down to the center and sense the pulse of Her mighty heart."

Angelica did as she was told, feeling a raw and majestic power beating there. When Rainier spoke again her awareness sped back to the surface. She was surprised to realize the men had become erect. She felt a presence between her legs, breath falling on her sex. She opened her eyes to see Corey's face just an inch away from her Jewel. She was aroused, she knew. She could feel a thin line of rain trickle out of her. She waited, filled with anticipation, and in that excitement she realized he was waiting, too. She realized he was waiting for permission. She put both hands on top of his head, and pulled his face toward her, directing his kiss to her Jewel.

It was as if lightning struck her. The golden light that had pooled at her feet shot upward into her Jewel with such force that she bucked her hips so hard her pubic bone smashed his nose and he had to sit back. Rainier's laugh peeled through the space around them, echoing off the rock walls. Angelica couldn't smile. The pounding of the Heart in her Jewel, the rushing sound of blood in her ears, mouth open and panting, desire, no, lust, a craving for his kiss filled her. Her knees parted farther, she wanted him to see all of her, wanted to offer to him all of her, but he remained just out of reach.

Rainier spoke quietly, "This feeling that you feel? This desire? This is Sacred Erotic Beauty operating within you." Rainier leaned forward and lightly guided Corey's head forward. When his lips touched her Jewel she trembled. "Hold it," Rainier said gently. "Hold it, let the energy build." She gasped when she felt him slide two fingers in her, parting her, and lodging them on the gland behind the Jewel. "Hold it," Rainier said again. Angelica gasped again when he slid a little finger in behind. He didn't move, simply held his fingers and his lips still. Her trembling spread. "Hold it, hold it." She started to sweat, panting. The other men stood, one hand holding her feet to their phalli, their other hands reached for her low belly. "Now, pull it up, pull the energy up to here," she said as the men each touched a finger to her second vortex. The energy had no place to go but up. It felt like warm water pouring into a bowl, deep within her, and the Higher Heart took up residence there, beating on the surface both in front and in back.

She closed her eyes and sighed when Corey withdrew, as did the wen behind her. The other men reached out and lay her down on her side, knees pulled up. "Look within, Angelica. Look within and tell me what you see."

"I see red. Red shot through with gold. And silver."

"And where is the red?"

"Below, at the bottom of me."

"Good. Now, focus on the gold and silver within the red. Nod when you see two lines, one gold, one silver, begin to rise up toward your second vortex." After a moment she nodded. "See them rise up, like arms seeking to embrace the sky, reaching around the vortex but not touching it. See that as a sphere and watch the lines go around it, above it, and the lines cross then stop, stopping in the posture of seeking embrace. Do you see all this?"

"Yes."

"Good. This will be our work today. We will complete this exercise five more times today, ending with your crown. How are you feeling?"

"Resting. Calmer. I'm breathing."

"Yes."

"And horny. Languid. Juicy. And horny."

"Good. Are you ready to do it again?"

Angelica laughed as she sat up. "Yes! Yes, I'm ready." She caught Corey smiling broadly at her and she rewarded him with the same smile.

They repeated the entire process, except that this time, when she filled her lowest vortex with the energy of Sacred Erotic Beauty she was able to control the spasm—the sole spasm of discharge she was allowed—so that she didn't smash Corey's nose. Then when she filled the second vortex she had another spasm, except it was focused in the vortex, and her body bent around it. The third vortex was located at her solar plexus, and the energy surged in the neural ganglia there like food into a profound hunger. The third spasm was focused there, and bent her forward around her middle. But she used her breath to contain any further discharge of the energies. As lunchtime approached they slowed down and stopped. Corey stood up and backed away.

Rainier told Angelica. "You must feed now. You will need the energy this afternoon."

The wen helped her down from the bed. Angelica went to her knees between the two men and the wen sat down on the ground behind her facing forward. The two men stepped forward to her. Angelica reached out and wrapped a hand around each phallus, amazed that they had been hard most of the morning. Her hands sparked a discharge into each man the moment she touched them. The men jerked as if they'd been shocked, but rather than pain they felt a spark of ecstasy, the energy dispersing throughout their torsos. She used her mouth on them in turn, engaging the Sacred Erotic Beauty in the ritual techniques of Phallus Worship.

One was ready before the other. Angelica, leaning back and putting her head alongside the head of the wen who'd been supporting her all day and said, "Here, you first," directing the head of his phallus toward her mouth. The wen took the first fruits. Angelica brought it back to herself and took the rest. She could feel the wen behind her working the alchemy (whose name she had forgotten to ask for!) as she was. They swallowed and the other man was ready. They shared the fruit again.

Rainier looked on, smiling broadly. Corey looked like he was about to be overcome by the Beauty and Rainier motioned to him to sit down. Angelica had released the men, her arms fallen to her sides. Her head was back, eyes closed, resting on the shoulder of the wen behind her, that wen's head resting on hers, eyes closed also. They were both smiling. Allowing the tableau to exist in the stream of life for a few moments Rainier stood still, still and smiling. She could feel Regina smiling behind the observation screen. She reached forward and took Angelica's hand, pulling her to her feet and leading her to a chair at the table with Corey. She helped the other wen to stand and hugged her. She turned to the men and bowed, which they returned. Then she hugged both of them, and they all left as a group while lunch was arriving, carried by two men and a wen. The wen took lunch to Quinn and Regina behind the screen. After arranging the service they disappeared.

Quinn was deeply thoughtful during lunch. He had been in telepathic communication with the sensations of the men, but particularly with Angelica, and had endured during the morning's work. Regina was content to let him think.

About halfway through lunchtime he said to Regina, "Why?"

Regina looked at him and raised an eyebrow in his direction, her "Why What?" nonverbally expressed.

"Why are you doing this to Angelica?"

"Are you asking about Angelica or are you asking about the Work?"

He stared at her thinking. "Yes," he said.

"Asshole," she said. "Angelica needs this so that she can survive the loss of the Dragon. Did you notice that the Dragon didn't leave her today?"

Quinn nodded, and said, "Go on. What is really happening here, at the level of the Work?"

Regina nodded back. "As to the Work, she is being prepared to be a Warrior."

"Which war?"

"The War of Sex upon Death."

Quinn remained silent.

"When enough of us have died we shall climb the pile of corpses to the cave where De Murgos hides. Justice will be served."

Quinn remained silent. So did Regina. He knew where the cave was. And he didn't think that Regina did, only that it was a cave. He thought, "Now that would be a huge pile of corpses." Suddenly he heard Regina's voice in his head. It said, "I know." Regarding her, he was only mildly surprised when suddenly she smiled, and turned her face away. Then he heard her voice say, "There are already millions."

Quinn remained silent.

The afternoon program was different. The activation of the fourth, fifth, sixth, and seventh vortices would happen in the classic tantric position where the Feminine sat with her legs over the Masculine's, belly to belly, chest to chest, lips to lips or forehead to forehead. Angelica was happy, settling herself into Corey's lap, and settling herself around his phallus. Her arms were over his shoulders. He could feel her doing a little bouncy dance on him, and smiled. She smiled back, and leaned forward to whisper to him, "Let's do this," then leaning back to see his face, to see his agreement. He nodded.

His training in the Work preceded hers. He knew enough to help summon the energy of the Sacred Erotic Beauty from her third vortex into her fourth, centered in the region of her heart, and he knew how to hold space for her to extend and weave the two lines of the helix. His kiss summoned the power to her throat. And his forehead summoned the power to hers.

Then Rainier intervened in the next vortex. She held her hands to the sides of Regina's head as she was working the energy. Then she withdrew the contact, holding her hands in the air, palms slightly cupped. She summoned the crown to the surface with her energy, holding open a cylinder of pure energy around and above Angelica's head. Into that field between her hands a green fire emerged from Angelica, green flames dancing between her hands. She narrowed the distance between her hands and a red flame emerged from the center of Angelica's head. By the time that happened Angelica was gone, out of her mind, her Crown chakra blown open in orgasm, forehead resting on her lover's forehead, a photon of golden light lost in the corona of a star, home, awash with ecstasy, filled with Sacred Erotic Beauty. Her crown, green flames dancing around a central red flame, had been revealed.

By the end of the week Angelica was able to activate each vortex on her own and connect them. Each had some color associated with it, and when she thought about it she would giggle, imagining that she resembled a string of party lights. Every day had involved some version of the process on the first day—small group work in the morning and one at a time in the afternoon. Corey had been with her every day, although on some afternoons she would be assigned another partner to practice with as well. Corey would stay and watch, and had started escorting her to her room at the end of the day. Sometimes she'd hold his hand. She enjoyed the company very much, and the sense of shared adventure. She realized on the walk Friday evening that she was happy, and the chance to spend time with him was a part of that happiness.

She was mopping the kitchen floor after breakfast on Saturday morning when she was approached by a wen her age with a folded piece of paper. It was a note asking her to come by Mai's office when she finished. She found her way to Mai's door and knocked. She entered and found Rainier and Regina already there.

Mai gazed at her as she sat down, eyes slightly unfocused, reading Angelica's field. "You seem happy," she said.

"Oh, I am. I am surprised by it, but I think maybe it's a byproduct of the work I've been doing."

"I think you're correct, Angelica. Doing this work creates the substance of happiness. And what about Corey? Does he please you? Is he a part, do you think, of what is generating the happiness?"

"Yes, I think he is, but the work is mine, and my happiness doesn't depend on him. I think it depends on the substance of Sacred Erotic Beauty."

"Good. Would you be open to him being assigned to you? Would you accept him as a Consort?"

Angelica's heart leaped within her. "I hadn't thought...But yes, yes! I'd accept him as a Consort!"

"Good then. He'll be travelling with you when you and Regina and Quinn depart in ten days."

54

Eight Weeks Eighth Week

Rainier, Corey, and Angelica sat in silence together, practicing breath, relaxation, and mindfulness, resting in the place where the words stop inside, sitting on chairs around the small table. The morning breeze was cool and pleasant, the edges of the canopy over the platform rippling. The stone floor was drying from a passing storm during the night. Rainier watched the air around them, looking for a change in the color of the ambient light that would let her know that the Sacred had arrived.

Corey started emanating Love for Angelica. He especially respected her Courage—to submit to the rigors of her accelerated training as a Priestess, including this eight weeks, as well as the Courage to carry the Dragon. As his Love rose up, so did his phallus.

Angelica, struggling to avoid thinking, was distracted. As soon as she gave up trying she relaxed. Then she remembered the 'Room' in her head, that dark space where the words stopped. She breathed into it. That activated the Higher Heart in her forehead, then the minor vortices in her palms activated. The pleasure of it in her tuned nervous system stilled her breath with pleasure. It was then that she felt the Love. She was mildly surprised but allowed herself to be Receptive to it.

And that created the change in the ambient light for which Rainier was waiting. She was relishing this day, and relished the words she spoke. "We should start this week by explaining that last week, the establishment of your inner axis mundi, the generation of the ecstasy of the Crown, was about you. It was personal to you. This week is about everyone else. This is about the Love of Life that is incumbent on you as a Priestess. Do you understand?"

Angelica nodded, serious.

"This is the main work of the Priestess: to sense the Sacred Erotic Beauty all around her, the Beauty of Life itself. And to feed that Beauty with her Love. That is why this week, your last week of training, is about the Orgasm of the Heart. This should indicate to you something about the importance of the Higher Heart, which I can see is operating in both of you in the moment, although in different places."

Corey's was operating primarily in his second vortex, helping to maintain his equanimity in the face of the raging fire between his legs.

Rainier continued. "It is important that you understand that we believe, as does your Order, that the Heart is the Roof of the Soul and the Foundation of the Spirit.

"The Soul breathes, too. But it doesn't breathe our air. It is important that you understand that the difference between us and the air that the Soul breathes is as different from ours as the water that a fish breathes and the air that their fishermen breathe."

" 'We are bottom dwellers in the ocean of the sky and who knows what fisherman waits for us,' right? I forget the name of the wen poet who wrote that," Corey offered.

"Well, except that we do. We do know."

"You've mentioned your Order several times. Who are you people?"

Rainier smiled. "We are nothing if not librarians cataloguing the ecstasies of Soma, Soul, and Spirit. Now that we know the title shall we open the book?"

Up behind the viewing screen Regina arrived with a tall dark skinned wen and took the seat next to Quinn. The new arrival sat opposite him.

Regina said, "Quinn, I want you to meet my daughter Lee."

The younger wen reached across the table and shook his hand. "Pleased to meet you."

Quinn took her hand. The shock of the power in her pushed into his hand, and, feeling it herself, her eyes grew wide. Her image waivered. She moved to take her hand from his, but he said, "Wait. Let the energy balance. Let me return to you what is yours."

The energy flow from her to him slowed down, and stopped. She said, "You did that.

He said, "Correct. Now I am going to return it, at least most of it, to you. Please allow yourself to become receptive." He could feel her relax, then he sensed an energetic pull in her direction. He allowed his life force to release the energy he'd acquired, and it gently flowed back into her.

"How did you do that?" she asked.

"Do you know any chaos theory?"

She nodded.

"I am a chaos attractor." Regina snorted. Lee smiled at the snort.

"I deliberately keep my energy level low. Which means I am below you. Higher energy falls to the lower levels, my chaos attracts it. I do it not so much for humility, which is required…" Regina snorted again. "but because it keeps me more invisible for those who have sought for years to find me and rub me out."

Lee asked, "How much energy could you have drained from me?"

Quinn went silent.

"Could you have killed me?"

Quinn said nothing.

Regina went very still.

"Tell me, Quinn. Could you have killed me?"

Quinn took a deep breath and said, "It's possible."

Lee sat back, taking her hand with her. She shook her head slightly, in small disbelief.

Quinn said, "May I ask you a question?"

Lee responded, "I reserve the right to not answer it. I'm not an oracle."

"So much energy, so much power you have. I know because I felt it. So, are you mostly an energetic being, more energy than flesh and blood?"

"Of course I am. Don't you know what I am?

Suddenly Quinn remembered. "You are the Librarian of Shambhala."

"I am one of them. Do you remember when you were sixteen and a copy of the Tao Te Ching fell off the shelf in the store and into your hand?"

Quinn nodded.

"A Librarian put it there for you."

Quinn paused, reflecting on that long ago day. And its consequences for his being. He said, "Please convey my deep gratitude to that Librarian." He nodded solemnly and she returned the nod.

"I understand the need for invisibility," Lee said. And the image that had been waivering only moments before suddenly disappeared.

He heard a disembodied voice say, "All of us, all the inhabitants of Shambhala, have this ability." She reappeared suddenly. "Without it we could not survive. Nor do what we do."

Quinn turned to Regina. "Did you do this? Did she learn this from you?"

Regina shook her head. "No. She got it from her father. Her father is Djinni."

Quinn suddenly felt surrounded by some force attracted to his chaos. It enveloped him and he thought he might go breathless. He extended his field to just off his skin and stopped the enveloping force. He breathed slowly. "That's enough," he said. The force began to dissipate.

Lee had been staring at him, sensing him, taking stock of him, a chaotic and unknown force. Her eyes narrowed and with an effort she forced herself to suspend judgment.

Regina closed her eyes and sighed. She still struggled to understand him, and what he was.

Lee asked him, "What do you need Quinn? And what do you need to know?"

"Yes, those are two separate questions, aren't they?" He paused. "I need to know about the Kundalini Barrier, its overcoming, and how to live with the consequences. I need to know about the golden whirlwind. And I need to know about the Resonance of the Higher Heart. Then maybe I'll know better what I need. What do you know about these?"

"Only a little. But I know the Librarians that know where the books are that might help. Do you know how to read any languages other than English?"

Regina patted her daughter on the arm. "Never easy, this one."

Quinn shook his head. Lee sighed and stood up. She leaned over and kissed her mother on the cheek, turned to Quinn and said, "I have to go now. Good to see you, Mom. And a pleasure to meet you." The image waivered again, and she disappeared.

On the platform Rainier had instructed them to sit on the bed in the first position, he with his legs bent and crossed at the ankle, she sitting before him, facing him, her legs around his hips, her legs crossed at the ankle behind him. This put them belly to belly, his erection pressed against her, up against her second vortex. The Resonance of the Higher Heart awoke there in both of them.

"I see your hands are awake Angelica. I want you to use them to awaken and align Corey's axis. You can do this with your hands by putting them on the right places on his back. But there is something I want you to understand—how dangerous this work is. If you two do this right, Angelica will be able to cultivate love for all Life, but if you do this wrong, you risk creating a bond between you both that will bind you to each other indefinitely, possibly even beyond Death. And, one of you might lose it, and go insane. Corey, you, since you haven't gone through a full overcoming of the consequences of the Kundalini Barrier, are at greater risk. Much of what we've been doing has been designed to help Angelica stay sane. But you—at this point, are serving as grist for the mill of her. Do you understand?"

He nodded.

"There will be a Ritual of Disengagement that you must go through at the end of the day that must be completed with all of your attention. Angelica, do you understand? Do you want to be tied to someone who has gone insane? Do you want to be tied to someone who is dead?"

A terror suddenly filled Angelica, sitting there in Corey's lap, his erection pressed up against her low belly. She leaned back from him, but she was unable to lose contact with his phallus.

"Finish it, Angelica. Withdraw," Rainier commanded.

Angelica, reluctant, pulled back from Corey, sliding back along his supporting legs. She sighed with longing and compliant regret, sliding back far enough that there was no longer any contact.

"Good. Do you agree to do what I say? Both of you?"

"Yes," both of them said, fear driving their compliance, no matter how reluctant and filled with desire they were. The longing for ecstasy was deep, profound. But they both knew that this week was not about either of them personally. It was about a Priestess loving Life enough to have an orgasm of the Heart safely, and a Consort holding space for her to feed Life through her love of Life.

"You will both experience Sacred Erotic Beauty, the Beauty that is created by Sacred Erotic Love. But you must not be attached to your experience. There must be no coveting of ecstasy. You must remain free. Am I understood?"

They both said "Yes." Then Angelica said, "You will have to show me the Ritual of Disengagement. Shouldn't you show us now? In case we lose it during the practice."

Rainier said, "If you want. If you're afraid it will be harder for you to access your heart. So if you want to learn how to do it now you both have to stand up." They stood and Angelica regarded Corey's phallus bouncing as he stood up and stepped back. The Beauty of it made her twitch and Rainier laughed. "Nice," she said. "The Sacred

Beauty is arising in you. So here's how you do the Ritual. Face each other. Corey, you put your hands out in front of you, palms up, Angelica, you, too, except place your hands palm down over his." She did and Rainier said, "Open the vortices in your hands and slowly move them close enough to each other that you can sense each other's fields and hold them there. Memorize this distance. Now, Angelica, lower your hands until they are resting on his."

When they were sure they could remember this distance, Corey nodded his head and Angelica lowered her hands. The instant they touched the Resonance of the Higher Heart appeared in each of them, beating in synchrony. They glanced at each other. Rainier said, "Gaze at each other's sixth vortex." After a pause to establish the power of the Gaze she said, "Now lean toward each other and touch foreheads lightly. Breathe through your nose. See in the vortex the Golden Sphere of Personal Awareness. See it receding in each other, growing smaller in your mind's eye as it recedes. When it disappears in the distance each take a deep breath and pull your heads away from each other."

Rainier waited while they followed instructions. Corey breathed first, Angelica second, starting her breath before he finished his. When they were both standing up straight Rainier said, "Close your eyes and repeat after me: 'I am.'" They did. "Breathe," she said, then, "Repeat after me: 'I am.' And breathe again." They did. "Do it once more." And they did.

Once more she said, "Repeat after me: "What's mine is mine." They did. Then "What's yours is yours." Then, "I call mine to me." She added, "Sense and feel that which is yours returning to you through your hands." Then say, "I return what is yours to you.' Search within yourselves for any particle of the other and push that out through your hands." They did. Angelica sighed deeply.

"Now, separate your hands to the distance you memorized. Corey, slow the rate of the Higher Heart in your hands, Angelica, speed yours up." After a moment Rainier could see the shift of frequencies in their fields. She said, "Now each of you take a step back, withdrawing your fields along with your hands…take another step. Now place your palms together and bow to each other.

"Now, to make this truly effective you have to not touch each other for an hour," Rainier said. "Let's go see if we can find some early lunch."

Picking up her sarong and shawl Angelica looked at his flagging phallus, smiled, and said, "Sorry."

Corey grinned back at her and shrugged. "I know where I can

find another one."

Up behind the observation screen Quinn turned to Regina and said, "That was Beautiful. It was something I learned to do on my own, but it was good to see them both do it."

Regina said, "No wonder you're so hard to find."

The three returned about ninety minutes later, Corey and Angelica holding hands, Rainier following, scowling slightly, still worried about accidental bindings. Angelica bounced once on the bed then then got up and went to her knees in front of Corey, parted his sarong and took his softness into her mouth, and sucked, drawing it out as far as she could. She popped her lips around it as she let it go, looked around Corey at Rainier and said, "Phallus Worship?"

Rainier nodded and sat down at the table, extended her legs and crossed her feet at the ankles. Sighing and closing her eyes, she settled into a meditative state of mind.

Angelica liked the feel of him in her mouth. She savored him, letting him rest there, neither of them moving. As she sat on her heels he began to grow and as he did the feelings of the Sacred and the Erotic Beauty of what was happening began to fill her mouth, and when she swallowed the sensations and feelings dropped to her root vortex and filled it with those sensations and feelings. She swallowed again, and her second vortex filled, making her tremble. At the third vortex she sighed at the Beauty, and the trembling eased. As his phallus grew and hardened she followed the curve of its rising, coming up on her knees, still touching him with only her mouth. At the fourth vortex she felt Love, Erotic Love, begin to gather there. At the fifth vortex she groaned around him, desire for him making her tremble again, but more strongly than before. He was at his full length now and she could only hold so much of him. She angled her head so that he was pressed against the roof of her mouth. Her mouth filled with that sweet water and as she swallowed her sixth vortex lit with that special golden light. She became filled with gratitude for the Beauty she had been blessed to know. She was so filled with Erotic Beauty she orgasmed, raining a little bit on the stones. She felt the fire of her crown light up, dancing on her head. She opened her eyes, gazing up at Corey gazing down, eyes, half closed, smiling broadly at her.

Rainier had watched the progression through the vortices, eyes also half closed. When the crown lit up she stood, and walked over behind Angelica, took her head between her hands, leaned down through the energetic flames tickling her face and kissed her on the top of the head. She whispered, "It's time," and pulled Angelica back a little, removing her mouth from the phallus. "Go sit on the bed," she said to Corey.

Angelica tilted her head back, gazing up at Rainier, mouth open, slowly panting. Rainier beamed at her, eyes filled with Love and Pride. Angelica took it in, knowing that she'd done well and that she was Good. Rainier moved in front of her, taking her hands and helping her rise.

Angelica leaned in and kissed Rainier. In the moment their lips touched Angelica realized that her own lips were pounding with the Resonance of the Higher Heart, and her knees weakened.

Rainier led her to the bed and helped her sit on Corey's thighs. "Hold it down," she said to him. To Angelica she whispered, "Slide forward slowly and pick it up with your phulva."

Angelica leaned back onto Rainier and slowly slid along Corey's legs until her opening pressed against his hardness. She felt herself open further, surrounding him. She sighed as she slipped along his length. She wrapped her arms around his neck, crossed her ankles behind his back. Following Rainier's instructions she activated Corey's vortices by touching him in the appropriate places along his spine while her hands were Resonating. In this way she built and activated Corey's internal Axis, refreshing her own activation as she went. When she touched the center of his crown he closed his eyes and trembled in ecstasy. Angelica began to rock her hips, forward and back, starting to build the charge, pulling her pleasure up from her root until it filled each vortex and spilled upwards. She allowed her breasts to brush against him. She kissed him until the Resonance was on his lips, touched her forehead to his, seeing the light of awareness within him.

Rainier went around the bed and climbed on. She crawled forward, put her hands on Corey's shoulders and gently pulled him away from Angelica until he was laying on his back. Angelica began to ride him cowgirl style. Rainier lay down on the bed next to Corey, mouth near his ear, feet hanging over the far side of the bed, and began to whisper, "Do you see her? Do you see the power of Sacred Erotic Beauty begin to suffuse her? Do you love her? Do you love that Beauty? Send her the power of Sacred Erotic Love, that she, too, becomes that Beauty and that Love. Send it to her, send it into her, so that it fills her up. So that it overfills her, flowing into her heart from below, and then overflowing from her heart out to the world."

Over Angelica's heart a green light, like the light of her crown, began to glow. Then it began to pulse. She rode him up and down for a while, then switched to riding him like she was on a cantering horse, rocking her hips, grinding into him. Then she galloped as the energy built. She threw back her head and started laughing with pleasure. She spread her arms wide, palms up, fingers splayed and the green energy poured into her hands, creating pulsing waves of green light. The energy building in her heart blasted out through her palms, falling in showers of green and gold. Her laughter was contagious, and first Rainier and then Corey laughed with her.

Up behind the screen Regina grinned at Quinn and then they both started laughing. A golden mandorla formed in the air above Angelica. Quinn saw it and came to his feet, ready to defend Angelica from any threat, Divine or Profane. Through the light Quinn came to see who it was. She Who Comes, arms crossed over Her heart, a beatific, blissful expression suffusing Her eyes-closed face.

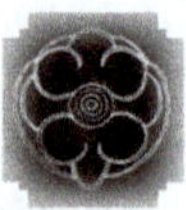

55

WALLID

They arrived on Wallid at the only international airport on the island. The Order had offered Angelica the option of accepting Corey as a Consort, and she had accepted. Corey was now assigned to her. But Quinn was not a member of the Order, so it was incumbent on Corey to take up the care of Regina as well. So far this had been limited to hauling extra luggage.

Angelica was preoccupied contemplating the last words from the High Priestess Mai: "Remember Benign Superiority in all your affairs and you will attain Equanimity." Regina was focused on shepherding them all through Customs. Quinn was engaged in his old paranoid's habit of scanning the room for threats.

They stopped at the Currency Exchange to get some money for their driver and a restaurant stop on the way to Regina's compound when suddenly Quinn heard a clicking sound coming from his suitcase. In his mind's eye he saw the two arrowheads representing Oshun's brothers rattling against each other. His eye fell on a man in street clothes pretending to read a newspaper, trying to watch them surreptitiously. He turned around and leaned forward toward Regina. "Don't turn around. We're being watched. Don't put the money in your purse. Put it in an inside pocket. Could be a thief."

"More likely a cop or a priest. Or a cop working for the Priests."

"Already? We haven't done anything."

They walked down the hall to the exit. Near the doors Quinn turned to confront the follower. The man took a moment to notice

Quinn, standing still and staring at him, grinning, almost maniacally. The man did a quick turn, going over to stand in line at a car rental agency. He pulled out his phone, flipped it open and spoke into it, shaking his head.

Corey and Angelica were already outside. Angelica was putting her passport into her knapsack when they were approached by two men moving rapidly. Corey stepped between them and Angelica. One pulled a ringing phone from a pocket, listened, then touched the other man on the arm and nodded back the way they came. They turned and moved off quickly, glancing over their shoulders.

Regina, who'd stopped just inside the doors, observed the whole thing. "You're right," she said to Quinn. "Thieves. Why'd they turn?"

"The guy from the Exchange followed us. Must have been the spotter. He called someone when I stopped and stared him down."

"It didn't used to be like that. Tough times, I suppose. We've been isolated and in a safe place for weeks. I'll have to remind them to keep their guard up."

It was a beautiful December day on Wallid, not far north of the Equator, warm and sunny. They arrived at Regina's compound without incident, pulling through the gate at street level and stopping at a broad set of steps that led up to the raised stone floor of the courtyard and the residences. They were met at the top by the Priestess Onadaya, the Order-supplied caretaker, barefoot in a white tank top and flower print sarong.

The courtyard, open to the sky, had several small throne houses set off the floor on pillars with incense and flower offerings with images of the deity to whom the throne belonged carved on the back of the thrones. Most of the space was walled off to give privacy to the residential area. Escorting them through the second gate—the split mountain gate—Onadaya showed them to their guest lodges, of which there were several lining the walls interspersed with small ever-flowing salt and fresh water pools and flowering and fragrant low trees. While each house had a sink, shower, and commode, there was a common kitchen against the back wall. Regina's house rose two stories with a cupola reached by steep stairs from within.

The downstairs was mostly open space on three sides with a dining table on one side that could seat twenty easily, a sitting area with a small fireplace on the other, and the private kitchen in the back. The central room was a large altar room, almost like a hall open to the south. Books lined shelves around the outer walls and shelves with statues lined the inner walls. Upstairs were four large bedrooms, each with a private bath.

The whole compound was, in a word, lovely. Regina told them to go ahead and unpack. "Get settled in. Supper will be at 18:00. Freshen up and look nice. We have some guests coming." She and Onadaya walked off to her house, their arms draped around each other's shoulders, laughing and chatting.

Each of the others, Quinn, Corey, and Angelica, went off to their lodges. Angelica sat on her bed and wondered at the carved walls. She kicked off her shoes, lay back, and was again amazed at the carved panels on the ceiling. They seemed to be telling a story of doomed lovers. She sighed, and fell asleep. She dreamed she was in a garden, naked, eating a peach. The juice was running down her arm, and down her chin and throat. Suddenly she felt a man behind her, also naked, and, she could tell, erect. He reached out, brought her arm back over her shoulder and took a bite of the peach. Then he licked the juice off her arm. He ducked under her arm and came around to lick the juice off her throat and from between her breasts. He was well-built and picked her up easily, holding her close, his face buried between her breasts. Slowly, without hands, he lowered her onto him. She began to rain before he was fully inserted. She heard thunder, and it woke her up. It was raining—the typical afternoon thunderstorm. She felt between her legs and, indeed, she had rained, too, soaking her jeans. As she stood up to strip off her soaked pants and underwear she realized that she never saw the man's face.

One of the supper guests she recognized. The High Priestess Jasmine had been at Stonehaven when she arrived but Jasmine had gone off on an assignment, apparently here to Wallid. She was accompanied by a gorgeous man who was introduced to her as "the High Consort Guiles". He was easy going and his smile showed genuine friendliness. He said he'd heard a lot about her, and was sorry for her recent losses. She was mildly shocked to realize that her eight weeks on Waitan had put a lot of distance between her and the prior summer. She wondered where 'what's his name? Wade' was, but then she remembered that she hadn't liked him much. With this outfit, she mused, there's no telling where one might end up.

There was another couple there, Belinda and Mark, and it was explained to her that they were yoga instructors at the large yoga studio the Order owned in Boodun. Mark explained that they also taught Introductory Tantra classes. "The tourists eat it up," he said.

The men gravitated toward each other, going out by the pool with drinks and the wen stood around the table. Regina said to Angelica, "Jasmine and I need to catch up. That means we'll probably talk about the fight at the Gate House at some point. I'd like you to be there, and to tell your story, too, if you're up to it. If you're not ready, that's OK, I just wanted to make sure you wouldn't be surprised when the subject came up."

Angelica said, "We'll see how I feel, but thank you."

Jasmine looked closely at her. "Sister, you're here now, and a part of this. I certainly want you here for what I have to say, OK?

Angelica nodded, wondering what she was a part of now.

During supper they talked about Wade and his declined invitation to this meal. He was troubled, clearly, but it wasn't clear about what. They caught up on other members of the Order on the islands, mostly gossip.

After supper they gathered in the sitting area, drinks in hand, and continued talking. Jasmine spoke about her sixteen-year-old assistant Napat, her capacity to channel her deceased grandmother, and how she had been recently raped by a Priest, who was now nowhere to be found. She was worried that Napat had become increasingly withdrawn and uncommunicative. The whole story made Angelica angry. Regina told her to bring the young woman by some morning soon and that she'd lay hands on her. Regina looked at Quinn, who had recently been developing some power in healing energetically, and said, "You'll help."

Quinn replied, "If she can stand me."

Regina stated, "She will."

Jasmine said, "She's already here."

Jasmine talked about how she was being followed wherever she went around town but they seemed to not follow whenever she left. She was sure they weren't followed tonight. Regina pointed out that the Priests were networked by cheap cell phones, so someone local may have alerted some central person anyway. But she said she would be surprised if anyone local to her compound and the nearby village would cooperate. She had been generous to the people for decades and they were in turn loyal to her. And, there were no temples nearby, so no reason for a priest to be about.

Then, after dark, they talked about Stonehaven and the fight at the Gate House. Regina told her story first, then Quinn his. He talked about the transformation caused by the Dragon's fire. And the testing at the Ranch. He scowled once at Regina in mock anger, and this brought a laugh. When he'd finished they all turned to Angelica.

She told her story up until she was knocked out. She finished by saying, "I remember waking up when the Dragon burst out of me. I remember sitting up and screaming, looking out through a curtain of blood, and then I fell away again." She realized that they were all looking at her intently and she realized they were looking at the Dragon, emerging from her edges. "Stop that," she said, and she felt the Dragon compressing itself into her. Everyone exhaled.

Regina said, "How about I tell the story of Slim Curly and the rattlesnake in his sarong?" She did, and since Slim was legendary in the Order, there was a lot of laughter.

The evening grew late and everyone had to be up early the next day. Jasmine told Regina she'd come back and go over the state of her planning and Regina said that would be fine.

Quinn and Corey took off on scooters the next day. Angelica told him to find some nice places to take her. She spent the next hour sitting with Regina in her altar room. On the door was a painting of four phases of the moon, three in white, the new moon in black. She could scarcely recognize many of the goddess statues, even with her degree. To the left on shelves were many statues to what she thought were Masculine deities, to the right were statues of Feminine Deities.

There were two things that stood out to her. The first was that there was a shelf about knee height on either side that held variations on the same kinds of masculine statues. The shelf on the right was crowded with carved wooden phalluses of different sizes, most with legs, sitting cross-legged or with one knee raised. A few were standing up on legs. This shelf had Feminine statues both above and below it. The other shelf, on the Masculine side of the room, was a collection of differently sized carved wooden men, also cross-legged but hunched over holding their face in their hands.

The other amazing thing, besides the hundreds of statues of the Divine Feminine, was what she thought was a painting or perhaps a panel of bas relief sculpture that changed when the viewer moved. When she walked in to sit with Regina the image she saw was of a young girl with a golden yellow capsule around her. When she moved left the image was that of a completely black face. In the middle was the image of a red face and to the right was the image of a white face, all separately individuals. She found it dizzying to look at, much less think about how it was made.

Regina sat in front in the middle, before a low table that was clearly an altar to the Divine Feminine. There were more statues to the Feminine on risers behind it, up to the bottom of the portrait. To the left of it was a lower table that was dedicated to the Sacred Masculine, and to the right, was a framed photograph of Rachel Adams leaning against what Angelica hoped was a replica human skull but, she realized, probably wasn't. She sat behind and to the right of Regina using a small stool that allowed her to tuck her feet behind her. Regina used a remote control to start some music. They began the sit with Devotions, then Prayers followed by Blessings. They continued into Meditations then Illuminations, Angelica learning Regina's technique then concluded with another, different, round of Devotions.

While they were sitting in the afterglow, Regina turned slightly toward Angelica. She indicated the array of phallus with legs statues. "I've been collecting them for decades, ever since Rachel Adams first brought me here. I never grow tired of their ironic commentary on masculine nature. The others," she continued, turning to the other side, "are known as Grieving Buddhas. Would you like to hear the story?"

"Yes," Angelica said. "Very much."

"After the Buddha left his mortal coil he was given an assignment by the so-called Masters of the Universe." Regina made a face as if she just eaten something incredibly sour, and Angelica laughed out loud. Regina nodded. "At that time the World was beset by demons, who did nothing but add misery to what was already a pretty miserable life. Buddha was assigned to travel the World, seeking out Demons and to preach to them the Four Noble Truths and the Eightfold Path. Some Demons assaulted him at once, and these he would fight and slay. Others would sit and listen, and convert, swearing to change their behavior. And the last group would run away screaming, hands over their ears.

"These Demons eventually came together and formed an army led by an enormous masked Demon King. The army assembled here, in the sky, above Mount Nagoon, and the Buddha met them there. They fought for days, with swords and magic, fire and lightning. And the earth shook and ash and flames burst out. The corpses of the Demon dead piled high and the Buddha fought and slew them all.

"Eventually the masked Demon King entered the battlefield. They fought for days and the people here below were terrified. The Buddha was victorious and the Demon King fell and all was silent. The people all turned to look. The Buddha went up to the fallen King and lifted his mask. He recognized there the face of the son whom he'd abandoned long before in order to seek the Enlightenment. In his grief he fell into that pose you see there, and some say he's never moved since then."

Angelica felt a tear well up in each eye as she regarded the round-ed form. She reached for one and held it in her hand, contemplating, waiting for words to emerge from her feelings. Finally she looked up at Regina, who was regarding her quietly.

"Sex and Death," Angelica said.

Regina nodded. "Sex and Death."

Later in the morning Regina took Angelica around with Ona-daya and set out the offerings for the Sacred Ones. The small offering plates were split leaves stapled together. The offerings were a spoonful of cooked rice, a flower blossom, some water, and a stick of incense. They were placed on the ground near all doors and gates, then one was placed in each of the raised ancestor houses. Regina explained that the first four of these were for large sets of the spirits: the Spirits of the Land, the Spirits of the People, and the Spirits of the Deities. Regina told her that these are the minimal forces that a Priestess needs to keep in balance, but that her experience was that there was a fourth force that had to be a part of the balance—the Spirits of the Dead.

She said, "Normally the rites of the Dead would accomplish keeping them in their place. But when there are so many people, as there are now, most of them poor, the Priests cut corners, or their atten-tion lags at some critical moment, and then the Dead don't rest. They push on the world of the Living. So we will give them something to push on, so that they can rest."

They walked over to the last two ancestor houses. "This is Ra-chel's," she said, putting the offering up on the floor before the throne. Then they went to the last house, the largest house. "This is for She Who Comes," she said reverently. "Wherever I have a house, She has a home."

Sitting at the big table in the shade, sipping an after-lunch tea, Regina turned to Angelica and said, "It is time to start training the Dragon. The Dragon has an assignment, a task to perform, after which it will be leaving you. How do you feel about that?"

"How do I feel about which part?"

"The whole thing."

"He allows me more control now. I mean, he doesn't just take over the way he used to. All that time I was in training on Waitan he spent most of it under the bed. So he doesn't behave sexually toward me the way he often did before we got to the ranch. We still talk, but not as much. I hear him in English, not Dragon like you do. He sleeps a lot and he grows when he sleeps. I can't sense his edges anymore, except when they pass through mine. But he's big. And when he wakes up and extends himself, I don't pass out any more."

"Yes, but how do you feel about his impending departure?"

"Well, I used to feel like I was just an incubator for a parasite. And then we became, I don't know, I guess friends. I'll miss him, but I don't think it will kill me. Will I never see him again?"

"Who knows? Once he's free he'll be off on Dragon's business, and I have no clue where that will take him."

Angelica felt a pang in her solar plexus. "Yes, I will miss him. And that's OK."

"Good," Regina said. "Now, may I call him?" She waited for Angelica's nod then said in a normal tone, "Hamashk heng dwa."

Angelica exhaled when she felt his boundaries extend through her own. The air turned red. Then suddenly she was alone inside and he was floating next to her, as big as a horse. He was beautiful, the light glinting off of him in sparkles.

Regina said, "That's his name, you know. Hamashk." She spoke to the Dragon, circling her hand laterally. The Dragon responded with a rumbling "Hanh." To Angelica she said, "I told him to stay inside the walls."

The Dragon floated over them, drifting from here to there, looking into corners. When he stuck his nose in the kitchen Onadaya screamed, and they could hear Hamashk's rumbling laughter.

Regina said, "A long time ago there were many like Hamashk, at least a thousand or so. We don't know how they came to be, except that they are magical extensions of psychic power. De Murgos saw them as a threat to his sovereignty over humans and had them hunted down by his Slayer and killed. Their fire could not melt his swords. Here, though, on this island, there were four, no, five of them, and the High Priestess at the time turned them into stone to protect them. Rachel discovered this when she was meditating next to one of them. She could feel the Life in the stone, and when she looked, it winked at her.

"What we need Hamashk to do is wake up those Dragons, to break the spell that keeps them stone. At the same time there is another kind of Dragon, sleeping deep in the base of Mt. Nagoon, and we don't want that one to wake up. We believe it is the Spirit of the Mountain, and since the mountain is an active volcano, waking it up could be catastrophic."

"Why risk waking any of them up?"

"We need them in this fight. Here, on the island, the cult is not so strong, but on the mainland the cult of Skreeva is not just a Death cult, it is a rape cult. Wen are property, and any attempt by a wen to improve or make something more of herself makes her a target. And over there," she continued, waving a hand toward the mainland, "the Windus and Wuzlims hate each other, and, when it comes to a wen's fate, they are equally despicable. And of course, the wen must submit. What choice do they have? To do anything other than submit to the tyranny of the men is to make them vulnerable to beatings, rape, and murder. Even of children."

Angelica could feel anger, righteous anger, rising in Regina.

"But here, both cults are vulnerable. We are starting with the Windu cult because they still have a sense of the Divine Feminine. They still have Goddesses, which we can rally. The Wuzlims, on the other hand, have gone completely over to De Murgos. The time is soon, soon come, when we will strike back."

"How?"

"Be patient, Angelica. We have several weeks yet. Now that Hamashk is here, the Dragon is safe within these walls. You don't have to carry him around with you all the time anymore."

Catching herself by surprise, Angelica burst into tears. Face in her hands she looked within so as to discern why. In a second surprise she realized it was relief that made her cry. A long hard passage in her life was ending, it was over, actually. She picked up her face and looked at Regina. "Wow. It's almost over then, isn't it?

"Almost," Regina said softly. "Almost. Except for some excursions to see the Dragons he can stay here. I need to train him how to do what we need him to do, anyway. Take the time off. Travel around the Island with your Consort."

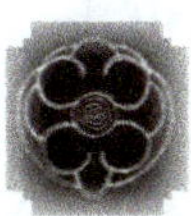

56

GONE HUNTING

"The Administrator wants to know what you saw," the Embla said.

"I saw crazy humans killing. Nothing new there," the Dangla responded.

"Then why are you afraid?"

"You aren't? It wasn't just humans killing—I've watched plenty of that. It was that Abomination inside the storm cylinder. He scares me. And then, oh yes, there was the matter of that Monster with wings. And, oh, if that wasn't enough, there was a dragon."

"Afraid? No. I will admit to some surprise. And perhaps shock. Shocking that we fled and left Him there."

"You felt the power building. There was not much choice. We're not indestructible like He is. Well, at least I'm not. But neither is your immortality guaranteed."

"His might not be, either."

The Dangla paused, considering this news. "How do you know?"

"He's hurt. After we left the Abomination hurt him but you know this already."

"How hurt?"

"He's crippled. That's all I know. I don't even know what the chances for healing the damage are. No one's telling me anything," the Embla groused.

"So what now?"

"We wait. We found what he sent us looking for: Trouble. He may send us back, especially after that thing with wings. What did he say? Do you remember?"

"He said 'She wants you off the rock.' Who's She?"

"I don't know. But I fear we will find out."

"I thought you weren't afraid."

"Suddenly, I am. And it is because of my uncertainty. There are several uncertainties here, and I am unaccustomed to uncertainty."

"I suppose that comes from not having to worry where you next meal is coming from. I'm uncertain all the time. And the quality of the food, the quality of the vibrations of these puny slaves everywhere, has declined so noticeably that I'm hungry. A lot."

"I understand. Just don't eat in front of me."

"I'll eat when I can, and where I can. If you can't stand the heat, get out of the kitchen, as the slaves say."

"Slave wisdom."

"Your arrogance is nigh onto insufferable. You're worse than I am."

"It's not arrogance. I am what I am. I'm perfect at it. I am what He is."

"See? There you go, again."

The Embla sighed, and the Dangla was uncertain if it was impatience or condescension.

"He sent a Slayer for the dragon. For some reason He hates them. It didn't go well. The Slayer was wounded badly, almost mortally. With his own sword. And another sword we have not seen before took his hand. He attempted to heal the Slayer and made himself ill, and is now poisoned and wailing himself, this on top of his prior wounds. The Slayer may yet die," the Embla revealed.

"He didn't send one of us. He sent one of you."

"Yes. Of course. He sent an Archembla. You know who."

"Oh yes, Mickey."

"That is not his name. Don't blaspheme him."

"You forget. Blasphemy is what got me where I am. What's another one?"

The Embla left the question unanswered. "I never forget the horror of the Great Dividing." The Embla closed his eyes at the memory.

The Dangla looked quizzically at the Embla. He was unused to seeing much feeling among them.

The Embla opened his eyes. "We are to return to the scene of the fight and try to pick up the trail of the Abomination." He closed his eyes again. When he opened them he said "I fear we have been on this planet too long."

57

HUNTING MAGIC

Monique, a Priestess of the Order under the mentorship of Beth Elmyra, worked at a bar down by the river at the edge of town. The clientele were mostly young people out for a holiday on the weekends. During the week the patronage was mostly older, tourist couples. The couple she'd served that evening after dinner had intrigued her. Some part of her intuition was alerted by something unusual in their energy, in the way they showed deference to each other.

She'd assumed that the woman, elegantly dressed, older than the man, was the one in charge, the dominant one in the relationship, and that the man was a paid-for boy toy. On closer examination, watching the facial expressions of the contempt they had for each other when the other wasn't looking, it was clear in her face that she hated him more. His contempt evinced greater indifference, which meant that he had something on her so that she couldn't get away from him, but, yes, she hated him more.

They were joined around 8:00 by a third person, a man, dressed more shabbily than the couple. She thought she'd seen him around somewhere but dismissed it. When he ordered she learned that he was British, just like the older woman. The man was an American, and was clearly in charge. The newcomer eyed her surreptitiously the whole time he sat with the couple. She took it as the usual lechery and ignored it. About 9:00 he left and the couple left about 9:30.

When they'd arrived in town the Master and A. had taken a garden apartment in one of the hundreds of limestone façade townhomes. She'd been prepared to bring the Master to her own home, a small cottage surrounded by a walled garden on the outskirts of a small town about 40 km away. She'd inherited it from her father, paid maintenance for it and visited it when she could for a month or so every year. But he refused, wanting to stay in town, feeling that he was very close to this group he was pursuing now that she had lost Quinn's trail.

After unpacking they went out to walk around and then down to the restaurant district to get something to eat. The northern latitude early sunset was making the street dark and shadowy when the Master spotted the decal in the townhouse window, the pink and white emblem of the Order. They crossed the street to observe the house from the shadows.

Beth and Grace had been working all day with the Madeleine and her Crows to try to discern what had happened to the American Priestess stationed at the airbase. They'd been having trouble penetrating the shadows around the event, although they could see that magic had been involved. The rapist seemed to have been unaware and had been used by another. The Priestess, with bruised eyes, was strong and would recover with the support of the Order. She would probably resign from the military when she'd recovered. Beth, Grace, and the Madeleine were troubled that it seemed to be a part of a pattern, more than just the recent reported rise in rape cases on military bases. They were reminded of the missing Priestess from California a few months prior. She'd been military, too.

Grace went to close the drapes and she could first feel, then see, the observing shadows across the street. She pretended she didn't, and when the drapes were closed she went into the office and called Beth on the intercom, telling her, "We have watchers across the street." Beth waited a moment then turned off the light in the front room on the second floor and went to the window. They were there. She could feel malevolence emanate from the shadows. She looked away, and when she looked back they were gone, melted back into the side street that ran north to the park.

About midnight Monique finished the last wipe down of the counters and sinks, locked up, and set off down the riverbank trail towards her apartment. She loved the solitary walk in all seasons, but more so now in the winter. She loved the sound of the river, water slapping on the ice forming on the shoreline, the occasional crack of it breaking off, and the dull roar of the short falls. In winter there were almost never late-night strollers, so she had the trail to herself.

Just past the falls, about midway between the overhead lights, the brush came down almost to the path. It was there the man struck. He grabbed her from behind, one hand over her mouth, and pulled her back into the brush. He tripped her and they fell, he on her back. It knocked the wind out of her. He stuffed a rag in her mouth, taped it in place with duct tape, wrapping a loop around her head, and, kneeling on her back, tied her hands behind her.

He rolled her over on her back and as he made to step over her, she, former military herself and her training coursing through her, kicked him in the groin. She could feel the contact with the softer bits through her shoe. He stifled a shout as he went to one knee, then he reached out to hold her head still while he punched her in the face. With the second punch she felt her cheekbone crack. With the third she lost consciousness.

When she came to, the night had grown colder. She was on her side, shivering, pants and underwear around her knees. Her groin hurt. She sat up and swung her hands under her feet so she could examine the knot in the dim light. She pulled down the gag and used her teeth to untie her hands.

She felt cautiously between her legs. There was a slimy wet spot but no bleeding. She thanked the Goddess for that. But the inside of her thigh, high up by her tattoo, was inflamed and painful to the touch. She stood up to pull up her pants and looked around for her knapsack, which she found a few feet away. Rummaging around she came up with her cellphone and called the police. She was told they would be there in less than ten minutes. She retreated further into the brush where she felt safer than out in the open.

The police came, as did the medics pushing a gurney down the trail. She briefly explained to the officers what happened. One stayed at the scene, marking it off, as the other accompanied her to get a more detailed telling.

At the emergency room they cut away the gag, handing it to the policeman as evidence. They examined her in a private room. They cleaned her up, preserving what was apparently semen on the surface. She appeared to be unpenetrated, except perhaps by a finger. More evidence was swabbed. Then the examiner took notice of the horrific bruise high on her thigh, and in the middle of it was a pink tattoo, now brown and purple, surrounded by bloody teeth marks.

The assailant had tried to bite off her tattoo, symbol of the Order.

About 11:00 the man arrived at the back door of the apartment rented by A. and the Master. A., who had over the decades developed many of the siddhi powers that the Master thought beneath him, had watched the assault on the waitress and knew that the man hadn't been able to complete the assault; so damaged was he by the woman's kick that he couldn't function. She had seen, in the flash of thigh under the streetlight that their intuition had been true about the woman—she did have that tattoo on her thigh. She'd watched indifferently while the man gnawed at the soft skin, enraged and terrified at the damage he'd suffered. A small smile flickered on her lips as she watched the man run away. Contemptuously, she'd closed the portal.

They were waiting, A. reading a biography of the Lama, the original source of her lineage, and her servitude to it, the Master watching soccer on television, when the knock came. She put down the book and went to the door while the Master muted the volume. She opened the door, grabbed him by the front of his coat and pulled him quickly inside, shutting the door and smiling as she heard him bump into the table she'd propelled him toward. She took up her post between the man and the door.

The Master stood on the far side of the table, drink in hand, eyebrow raised, smiling contemptuously, and said, "Well?"

The man, flustered, embarrassed, and in pain, shifted from foot to foot. Then he started telling the story, lying about completing the assignment, but he brought them the real information they needed, confirming the existence of the tattoo, which in turn confirmed their ability to detect the presence of the tattoo, even when concealed.

While he talked A. focused on building the illusion of her power, making her shadow grow large and ragged, almost doubling her apparent bulk, the edges of her shadow dark flames dancing. The Master listened to the tale and threw a 100 pound note on the table. "We'll find you again if we need you."

When he turned, he froze in shock and terror at the image before him. A. reached out, touched in the center of his forehead, imposing the Forgetting on him. She pulled him and threw him stumbling across the threshold. By the time he stopped in the alley he had no idea where he was, or how he got there. All the doors were shut and all the lights were off. He knew only to go to the train station, and wait for the late commuter train.

Inside the apartment the Master said, mockingly, "I love it when you show off. Come here, angel." A. felt herself pulled, against her will, and commanded her, "Knees." It was time for their version of phallus worship. She only hoped she could finish him before he demanded more of her.

The next day the man woke up weeping at the pain between his legs and he urinated blood. He no longer cared that he didn't remember what had happened. He cared only about getting to the clinic and easing his pain.

58

INVESTIGATIONS

Both the Madeleine and Beth had sat bolt upright in their beds when Monique was punched in the face. Both touched their cheekbones at the same time, and lay down again, wondering at the sudden pain. Shortly thereafter, Grace called them both. After telling them about Monique, and that she was on the way to the hospital, Beth made arrangements for Madeleine to come over and sit with her before the High Altar. Together they would journey into the darkness that both perceived around Monique.

Beth set the water for tea on to boil in the kitchen then went down to start the fire in the grate in the basement where they kept the Winter Altar. The room's windows opened to the South, and a small park. It was a beautiful place for day work, and one of several High Altars in the town, but tonight Beth closed the blackout curtains and hooked them into place.

The Madeleine used her skills to open the deadbolt on the front door just as the tea kettle started to boil. As she was taking off her coat she had a sudden impulse. She threw her coat on the chair and reached into the curtains. The pink flower of the Order in the window was painted on a wooden plaque. She removed the plaque from view and waved her hand in the space to create an impression for anyone who looked that it had never been there. She poured the hot water into a teapot with tea balls already loaded in and headed for the basement altar room.

Beth had the curtains drawn and was lighting candles. Madeliene kneeled down at the altar and reached underneath withdrawing, first, the scrying bowl, then the stoppered pitcher of blessed water. She sat cross-legged on a cushion and Beth joined her in the same position, back-to-back in support, in the event that Madeliene developed a trance deep enough to fall over.

Madeliene lit an incense made of local herbs. They meditated together, pulling the Resonance of the Higher Heart up from their roots, stopping it in the Visionary center on their brows, let it pool and accumulate there. They synchronized their breathing. They spoke in unison a chant to Calley's sister the Goddess Brighid, She to Whom the Power of Psychic Insight and Prophecy belonged in this Land. Madeliene poured water in the bowl and held her hands palm down over the water while it stilled. Beth's mind merged with Madeliene's, so that she could see what Madeliene would see.

In the Invisible Lands Brighid heard the chant, as She always did. She pulled Matthews' arm off of her, rolled out of bed naked, and padded over to Her altar. She sat, lit incense, and poured water in the scrying bowl.

In the synchronous time of the Sacred both Brighid and Madeliene blew on the bowl at the same moment, and a vapor arose. In the vapor the events of Monique's attack emerged. They watched the attack, wincing as his blows landed, and then at his failure to consummate the rape.

They noted the strangeness of his efforts to bite at the inside of Monique's thigh. They observed the behavior had the qualities of one acting as if possessed. When the man abandoned his efforts they followed him along the path, across streets, and into alleys. They watched him arrive at a ground floor flat. He knocked and a figure in dim silhouette, a shadowed figure, opened the door. Sensing wards, Madeliene did not follow, but waited outside. After a few moments the man emerged, limping, sedate. When he turned down the alley, they waited in the pre-dawn darkness just outside the gate.

The darkness gave way to the spreading light of winter sunrise. A couple emerged, bundled up, and they walked to an early opening teahouse for breakfast. The three minds followed them until they went inside.

As the vision faded Madeliene waited until a vision of Brighid emerged. The vision spoke, "They are very sick, these two. And very powerful. He is an evil without a Conscience and has the power to enslave by will alone. She is enslaved, and has been longer than the man has been alive. She is coming into her hatred now and will use it.

"They are accompanied by a ghost—a ghost I may know.

"Put your people on alert. Protect yourselves."

"Yes, High One," both Madeliene and Beth responded as the Vision faded.

"Well, who d'you think those folks are?" Beth asked.

Madeliene took a sketch book and a pencil from under the altar and began drawing the faces of the two. "Tea ready?"

"Long cool, I'm afraid," and Beth set about making more tea in the electric kettle. "Did you feel the menace?"

"Yes. He's insane, driven by rage and hatred and revenge. She's somehow enslaved to him but more powerful."

"You can feel the hatred boiling off her."

"Yes, but she can't use it. At least not yet."

"Yes, but you can feel it coming."

"We should follow Her orders. Take these," Madeliene said, tearing the sketches from the book, "to Grace and have her distribute them to the enterprise heads. And have her issue the Security alert. No wen are to go out alone, and should have a Consort nearby at all times. Find out why Monique had her inner thigh chewed on. And make sure she tells the police to check in the clinics for a man with severe damage to his balls."

"Yes, dear," Beth smiled benignly, "and…"

"And 'put Leonard on the roof to watch the house'", they said simultaneously.

In a few hours A. and the Master emerged from the teahouse and walked the streets until they stood opposite the Order's house.

Leonard, practicing his art and making himself look like the roofline of the house, spotted them and called down to Beth and Grace, now home from the hospital. Together they woke Madeliene, who went immediately to the basement altar and slowly reinforced the standing wards not wanting to produce even an insignificant ripple that might be perceived from without. Beth and Grace went to a third story window that had not been curtained, and from the shadows slowly moved to a place where they could see the pair. Grace carried a camera.

The man stared at the house, leering lopsidedly, the wen stared back without expression. The woman spoke quietly. The man jumped a little, his eyes opened wider and looked about excitedly. Leonard could hear him speak.

"What? No sign? It's not the house! Of course, it's the house. It has to be the house." He looked up and down the street, confused by the blocks of identical houses. "We have to find it. We have to find the right house." He grabbed the woman's hand and walked away quickly, looking around wildly.

In the third-floor room Beth asked Grace, "Did you get some good shots?"

"Yes. We should check the security cameras, too.

Leonard came into the room and said, "I heard them speak. He's an American. She's a Brit."

The four of them met in Beth's office to review the footage.

Grace said, "Oh, I haven't had the chance to tell you, but Monique has a tattoo at the top of her thigh. It is a small image of the Fleur de Vie, the symbol of the Order. She told me many wen in the military have it. It is a body identifier for them, and a symbol of sisterhood. Her assailant was trying to bite it off her."

Madeliene said, nodding to the screen, "So that's why they got confused and ran off. I took the plaque out of the front window when I arrived last night."

"Good thinking," Beth said. "Let's leave it out."

On the morning news another rape at the American Airforce base nearby was reported as part of a story about a recent uptick in rape cases nationwide.

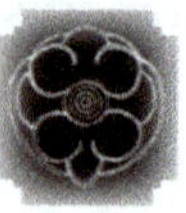

59

WARNING

When the Embla and the Dangla flew over the Hidden Lands heading west Bree felt their passage. She felt them as cold, a cold presence, a cold wind, a cold space, a cold that touched her deep in her belly. She shivered, and put her hand over it protectively. When She could no longer feel them She opened an eye and looked around, as if to make sure they were gone. The room was in chaos, with piles of clothes and shoes, supplies for making clothes, plates and cups from last night's supper. Matthews was beside her, snoring lightly, arm hung over the side of the bed. "It is noon," She tsk'ed to Herself.

In the weeks that he'd been with Her—since that day She'd pulled him through the barrier of the Hidden Lands, sparing him from all chance of being discovered by the Embla and Dangla at Calley's last Shrine—She'd happily had sex with him as often as he could respond. She still couldn't settle on what word She could use when She felt bawdy about him. She'd recently moved from "boned" to "banged." She'd collected enough of him to become pregnant. She hadn't told him yet, and might not. She knew he'd be leaving on assignment soon, and She'd not want him to worry, or be distracted from the Mission. Mother knew, however, and with Mother's help She could draw out the development of the little one until it was safe and the day auspicious.

The house was a mess. Her Day was coming up quickly, and the gifts She had been making, Matthews helping, of course, until her whim or his fancy interrupted the process, were scattered everywhere, reeds and piles of finished bogha crosses for distribution to Her Priest-esses and Circles. It was only just past Solstice but that put her Day less than six weeks away. She moved a stack off her altar table and pulled out her scrying bowl. She must tell Calley they were coming.

Calley sat before Her altar in the pre-dawn light. She lit Her candles, pulled her scrying bowl over, and poured in fresh blessed water. On Her left She'd suspended a tiny bell from a strand of Her hair stretched across two pieces of dowel. Then from the clapper she'd suspended a very small piece of the Invisible Land from another hair. It served as a kind of tripwire for Invisible events and She'd had a few erected around the property, all telepathically connected to the one on Her altar. As She looked in Her bowl the bell made a very quiet 'ting' sound. She found it startling and jumped a little, Her surprise stopping short of fear.

She looked into the bowl and saw the image of Her sister Bree. She smiled, Bree smiled back. In Her mind's ear She heard Her sister's voice. "They are coming. Blessed be."

She summoned Eva's ghost and told it to wake Alam. "Any instructions on how to do it?" Eva asked. Calley laughed out loud, laughed at the irony of a horny ghost.

"Any way you can get a rise out of him! But make it quick. We have only minutes. Make sure he brings his amulet from the Invisible Lands."

Calley sent a wake-up call to Madeleine, who sat bolt upright in bed. "It's time. Wake the others," She told her.

Madeleine and Diana woke the rest, dispersing the couples who would use Sacred Sex to help build the outer walls of the trap. At each site for the coupling there was a bell suspended by Her hair, so She would know which direction they were coming from, and in which direction to erase their trail.

She opened the well-used portals to the other Storm Divinities who had agreed to assist Her in the trap. From the West, She sum-moned the giant Raven. From the East She summoned the Melancholic One. She picked up the large black arrowhead Alam had retrieved from Quinn at the airport waiting for his connecting flight from Brazil to St. Louis. She used it to summon the Storm Divinity from the South. He arrived, laughing so hard the multicolored parrot tail feathers of His headdress shook. He laughed not just with joy at the thought of the upcoming fight, He was laughing at the vision of what He would do to Calley when He extracted His payment for helping Her. She summoned the Blue Hag. Finally She summoned She Who Comes.

She floated off. "Let us go to the Initiation Chamber."

Eva's ghost had learned enough about how to become substantial that she had recovered the ability to feed from men. Her touch was exquisite and Alam found himself waking up and ejaculating in the same moment, not even fully yet erect, his phallus buried between Eva's cool lips. Eva drifted back. "It's time," She said. "Bring your amulet."

The Embla and the Dangla landed at the Gatehouse. "Here," the Embla said. They stood there, remembering the fight, the fight that had revealed to them the existence of the Abomination Quinn, the Monster Matthews, and the Dragonwen Angelica. They remembered the wounding of their god, their father, and the Embla became angry at the loss of the Slayer and the poisoned mind of his master.

The Dangla's feelings were different—he was suspicious, the place felt dead. They flew around to the south, so they could see the empty Mansion and the empty Barn. They hovered over the peak above the Pine Eye. Nothing moved. There was no sense of any humans. But there was a sense of something. "No one here," he said.

"Then there's nothing to fear," the Embla replied.

The Dangla, in his arrogance also, huffed at the Embla. "But there's something here."

"Yes. Did you see the hole in the roof of the Mansion as we flew by?"

"Yes."

"Let's go there. See what we can see. The place has been abandoned."

The Dangla huffed again.

They hovered over the hole in the roof of the Mansion, the blue plastic tarp that was supposed to cover the hole flapping in the dawn breeze. Rain had been leaking in. They went through it into an atmosphere heavy with the scent of smoke and the smell of mold.

"Fire," the Embla said.

"You're a moron," the Dangla responded.

They stood in what had been a large, end-of-the-house bedroom. They traced the burn marks to where they emerged from the chimney. They left the room and went downstairs, opening the bedroom door and stepping through. They studied the burn marks on the walls and the place where the fire from this level of the chimney had burned through the floor above. They walked down to the second story. No fire there, but the strong scent of smoke. Water damage from the hole in the roof above. They did the same on the first floor level, opening the door onto a room with a large conference table and comfortable leather chairs, the leather held in place by brass tacks. Some of the chairs were covered in sheets, as was the table. The sheets had slipped off in some places. There must be no one here to keep the furniture covered.

They followed their sensation, their intuition, that something was there. They slid back a door into a recess in the wall and stood at the top of a stairwell down that bent away out of sight. The Dangla whispered to the Embla, "Light." The Embla closed his eyes, adjusting them to darkness. When he opened them again he saw a faint blue glow that suffused the space below.

They drifted down, feet suspended just above the stairs, silent in their passage. They floated down a long hallway toward the source of the light. It was emanating around the edges of a low iron door set in the wall. They pushed it open and stepped into the cold room. In the middle of the floor was a round iron rimmed hole with an iron door set on hinges opened away from them. The light was brighter there. They floated through, Dangla first.

The light was emanating from a human form, apparently feminine, sitting in the lotus position, hands on its knees, face covered by the overhanging cowl of her hood. They drifted up to her, the Embla demanding "Who are you?" and the Dangla, before the other's sentence was finished, asked under his breath "What are you?"

The Blue Hag lifted her face to them and said loudly, "You are in my home!"

Behind them the round iron door to this subterranean chamber clanged shut. Alam emerged from invisibility as he threw the bolt through the hasp and spoke the words that activated the Solomonic glyph that sealed the door, the same glyph used to seal away the Djinn centuries before.

Turning away from the noise the pair looked back toward the Blue Hag. She was sinking into the earth. Grinning. Too late the Embla made to grab for her. She was gone. And the room became darkness itself.

60

THE TRAP

In the darkness there was no sound. Then a red cloud, roiling and twisting, appeared in the air above the Embla and the Dangla. Suddenly the red cloud screamed—the sound that of primal feminine rage. The pain was excruciating and the two covered their ears and closed their eyes.

They did not see, at first, the four columns of silver white that appeared in a circle around them. When the columns touched the floor it became blue. The light illuminated the mandorla shaped shells of the two creatures. A sheet of blue white electricity encircled the four columns, crackling with static. Two arms, as it were, extended from each column and a bolt, one from each hand, four bolts shot to each creature. The screaming stopped and a hum arose from the blue floor and descended from the red ceiling.

The creatures cringed inside their shells as they first cracked, the lightning from the four Storm deities travelling around and into the cracks, splitting them apart until the shells shattered. The creatures screamed in terror for their lives now that their atmosphere was gone. But the electric fields adopted the shape of the shell, and their atmosphere was contained.

The roiling red cloud condensed into She Who Comes. The Embla and the Dangla regarded her in great fear. The Embla closed his eyes in meditation and prayer, palms together. The Dangla fell to his knees, bowing to Her, he who would not bow before.

She smiled at him, which he did not see with his averted eyes. She had watched him feed many times, unknown to him, standing there breathing in their victims' pain, feeding on the suffering the Invader, his former and even yet master, had caused. For centuries Her spies had watched them and reported to Her all that they heard.

She turned to the Embla. She held out her hand, as if She would caress his cheek. But, of course, She knew not to touch the shroud that the Thunder Beings had enclosed him in. "Drop the shell," She commanded. The four columns released him, He returned to the present moment, his prayers unanswered. His air, his atmosphere, was suddenly ripped from him. The shell that extracted what he needed from this altitude of air was gone. He started to scream but realized he had to hold his breath if he had any chance. She regarded his countenance in its frozen agony, jaw wide with the unfinished scream. A never-to-be-finished scream

"Sometimes you are so resembling of one of my children."

Moving Herself horizontally, floating, the torn hems of Her long dress floating at first, but then extending her form as if She was facing into a head wind, She raised Her arms, Her long cloak concealing the trembling and terrified Embla's face, the wind She summoned drew the Embla toward Her, under Her cloak.

"But you are not one of my children. I am merciless toward my own children. How much less mercy might you expect from me?"

His eyes could widen in terror no wider. All he could do, finally, was scream, expending the last of his air from his other world.

There was a sound, a woffing kind of sound…and then She disappeared. And there was no sign of the Embla.

A few shards of shattered crystalline magic shook from the walls above.

Everyone in the cistern sighed.

Calley said, "That's Mom."

The Blue Hag, not afraid of lightning, emerged from underground, snatched the Dangla by the heel, and dragged him into the rock floor. He melted in as he went, becoming stone, electricity, atmosphere, and all. "My due," the Blue Hag said.

When she was gone three columns looked at Calley. "My fellow pediments of Nature, in the stone his air will last him a long time. He might breathe once a day. It will be enough until we need him."

The Storm Deity of the South had been constrained by his duties on the Southern Continent. He dropped into his normal form. He stepped forward, revealing himself and his erection. "What about my due?"

"I acknowledge that I owe you, as I owe them. Additionally,

I owe you a visit to your lands, as I have visited each of the others. Now…you may take what is owed you now, but it will be here on the blue floor. Are you sure you want to risk the Hag? And if you take this thing now I will not owe it to you when I visit. I would prefer to engage you more thoroughly in your own land. Will you indulge me in this preference?"

The Deity from the South was stopped in his tracks by the power of her prose. His mind filled with visions of how it might be in his land, thinking, in his arrogance, that those visions arose out of his own imagination. He grinned hugely, bowed his head, and went mist.

When the mist had cleared she stretched out her arms to the other two columns. "Come brothers, both of you."

They came to Her, reverting to their normal forms, and She took Them both in hand.

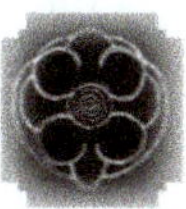

61

RAGE

Napat's rape by the Priest began to gnaw at Angelica. It made her grumpy when she remembered it at first, then it made her angry. She observed herself as nothing but angry for an entire day. She hated it but she couldn't move away from it. The thoughts and words, the feelings, roiled through her and she couldn't stop it. At one point she started crying in her rage out in the courtyard. She asked "Why is it so hard? Why can't I get past this rage? And where is the Beauty in it?"

Regina, in her office, heard Angelica, but rather than speak directly to her she called Corey into her bedroom. At the foot of the bed was a lacquered chest. She took a key from her writing desk and opened it. She reached in, rummaged around, and removed a box covered in painted cloth. She opened it and showed it to Corey. It was a life-like caucasian colored phallus attached to a soft black leather harness. She told him to take it and offer it to Angelica. She gave him no explicit instructions, just the statement, "You know what to do." She nodded at him once then waved him off with another nod in the direction of Angelica's room. Just as he was crossing the threshold Regina explained, "This is Sacred Erotic Beauty, entering into the Mystery, and the Mystery is Feminine. The Mystery is dark and damp. The masculine must be hard and penetrating. There has to be a hardness to enter in. Always ask permission, to be invited in. This makes the Mystery receptive. If the Mystery is not receptive, it is a taking. We do not take—the masculine here does not take. It must ask and be allowed. The Feminine can choose to be receptive on its own, it does not need invitation, except to itself. Tell her I said this."

Corey, walking across the courtyard of the compound to Angelica's room, felt some trepidation arise low in his belly, and below that the beginnings of an erection. During his training to become a Consort he had taken the option of learning the anal tantras as written for men. He knew they had been reframed to the Service of the Divine Feminine. He had wanted to know. In this way he learned how to perform the rituals of phallus worship and phallus receptivity. In learning these he learned things about how to awaken his Inner Femininity—his Anima—without compromising or damaging his Masculinity. And it did make him more receptive to the thoughts and feelings of others, and increased his capacity for empathy. For this he was grateful. He also learned that he preferred working with the phallus while it was hung from a strapped-in wen, rather than working with another man. His deeper preference was for the Feminine, and it was in Her Service, Service to the Priestess, that his inclinations lay. And in this Service he would gain his greater preference, which was to worship at the Jewel in the Arch. For that he'd gladly trade doing a little phallus worship. It always reminded him of or taught him something about how to cultivate the Receptive in himself.

He knocked on the door frame of Angelica's room. He heard her voice from around the corner in a small private yard, filled with sunlight and tropical flowering trees. She was laying naked on her belly on a chaise lounge beside a small fountain, hair tied up on top of her head.

Corey said, "Regina sent me with a gift for you."

"Really? Bring it here, please," as she rolled over and sat up, pulling her shawl up around her shoulders. He brought her the box, and knelt down, rather than standing there, watching carefully the expression on her face as she opened it. She moved back visibly, like a wave pushed her, and raised her eyebrows, then looked at him questioningly. She reached in and took it out and held it up, straps dangling. She said, "Why?"

"Why do you think?"

"She wants me to use this? On you?"

Corey nodded his head and said "Yes. She heard your lament. She thinks it will help."

"Whoa. Help how?"

"Maybe we should do this and find out."

"And do what, precisely?"

"I'm guessing some phallus worship. And some ass-tantra work. I think we should just follow the impulses in the moment."

"And you're OK with this?"

"Yes. I took the trainings for it on the path to becoming a Consort."

"I've never done this before. It wasn't in the Eight Weeks."

"I know. Can't get everything covered in Eight Weeks."

She sat, holding it, regarding the phallus. Corey studied it, noting that it was just a little smaller than his own when erect, curving upward, and that it was cast from latex based on what looked like a real model. He couldn't be sure if the model had been circumcised or not, but if there had been a foreskin it was totally retracted, leaving the shapely head exposed. She squeezed it and it compressed a little bit. Corey felt a small sense of relief at that.

She paused in her regard and said, "Hmm." She put it to her lips, smelled it and said, "Doesn't smell as good as the real thing."

Corey could only nod. His erection had arisen, parting the center of his sarong.

She stuck out her tongue and licked the head of it. "Doesn't feel like the real thing either, but I guess it's close enough." She parted her lips and slipped it in her mouth, the shaft sliding in and out, and said, "Mmmm. Tastes OK and the shape is right." She pointed it to his face, gave a smile that hinted of wickedness and said, "A little phallus worship?"

Corey nodded his consent. She put it to his lips. He opened his mouth and extended his tongue along its underside. She stroked it in and out. She exhaled low and long and a tremble passed through her. She sped up, with just a hint of aggression and sucked in a long breath. "Let's do it," she said.

Corey rose up and extended his hand. She took it with her free hand and followed behind him, straps dangling from her other hand as he led her into her room.

They went to the side of her bed. "How does this go on?"

"Here, let me have it." She handed it to him and he spread the back straps out on the bed and said, "Lay down." She did. He took the phallus and using a little coconut oil lubricated the little pad there on the inside of the harness. He positioned it over her Jewel and said "Hold it here." He brought the front straps up and buckled them to the back straps low and evenly around her hips. He helped her stand up and turn around and he pulled the center strap tight between her legs and buckled it to the center of the back strap.

He turned her around. She only had eyes for the phallus. She took it in her hand and squeezed it, looking at him as if for confirmation that she was doing it right. He nodded, and smoothed coconut oil on it. "Stroke it," he said.

She moved her hand back and forth along its length. She gasped. "This is what it feels like?"

"Something like that," he smiled. He took her over to the full-length mirror and said, "You should see yourself." She looked, watching herself as she stroked herself. Her eyes grew large again, and she seemed to become entranced. He stood next to her and reached under his sarong and began to stroke himself. She reached up and put her free hand on his shoulder, moving slightly behind him. Then he reached over and began to stroke her, too. She shuddered at what she saw.

He turned and went to his knees before her. Still stroking he extended his tongue along the bottom side and put his mouth over the head of her phallus. He sucked and released, timing his stroke with the sucking. Angelica, looking down at him, felt the sensations through her Jewel, the pushing, the coconut oil serving as a vacuum seal, felt the pulling. She surprised herself at the power she felt—the penetrating power. And she felt the energy of worship, worship of her, worship of her power, worship of her phallus, waft up to her, feeding the sense of the Erotic in her. It pulled her from her normal Feminine sense of receptivity into another place, a place of power, the power of penetration. She penetrated his mouth, slowly thrusting while he held his head still, allowing her. She started hesitantly, afraid she'd hurt him, but the energy of his worship continued. Soon she increased her thrusting, he directed it to the roof of his mouth but then soon further in.

A strange sensation began in her Jewel, spreading, rising up within her internal axis mundi, spreading from the depth to the surface, seizing her limbs, the feeling of the Sacred Erotic Beauty. She threw back her head and closed her eyes as the orgasm seized her entire being and she rained. The rain spread out around the harness strap dripping to the floor and running down her legs, bucking her hips and phallus into her Consort's mouth.

With his free hand he worked his fingers around the strap and into her, causing her to rain again, and he bent forward to catch some on his upraised face and open mouth and he drank. Angelica's trembling legs gave out and he caught her as she collapsed and laid her out on the bed. He returned his attention to her phallus, gentle, worshipping.

She felt a surge of power roll through her and began thrusting in his mouth again. He let her. She growled. He timed his movements so they were in sync with hers, and amplified them. She grabbed him by the hair and pulled his head away. "On your knees," she told him.

She stood in front of him, phallus in one hand, the other still entangled in his hair, and pushed his head to the floor. She grabbed the jar of coconut oil, lubed her phallus and set it aside. She went around behind him, stroking herself and lifted his sarong onto his back. She positioned herself against his upraised haunches. Bent her knees and penetrated. Slowly at first, fascinated by watching it go in. She began to stroke slowly, then faster. She swore she could sense what was happening to the phallus as it moved. She growled again. She rained again, splattering down on the back of his legs. She shouted, and then the rage came. Her rage, and behind her she felt the Goddess, She Who Comes, merge with her and she connected with a rage so wide and high she couldn't sense the boundary of it. She pounded him. He took it.

The air turned red and the dragon emerged. She grabbed the sarong at the waistline, holding him still, pulling him toward her and the dragon's arms overlaid hers. She roared, she wept, she rained again, hair swinging. The Crown of Fire appeared upon her head. She pounded him faster and faster until on one final stroke she hilted her phallus and held it. She groaned. The Rage of Eons faded from her. She collapsed over his back, legs shaking. When she didn't move he lowered them both to the floor holding his half hard fat phallus out of the way. When they were down, she laying on him, she stroked him slowly, her hips thrusting lazily, then stopped. She made an Ummm sound. Her breathing slowed, and she slept.

He lay there under her, supporting her, and slept himself.

When Angelica woke it was dark. She felt a brief moment of confusion about where she was, and who she was, really. She extended her senses to her surface awareness and realized that her breasts were mashed against the back of a man she was laying on, and then extended downward to the strange sensations of the harness, and then the man beneath her shifted ("He's awake!"). That shift brought to her awareness that she had a phallus attached to her and that the phallus was embedded in him.

"Oh," she said, lifting her hips to extract it from him, then lowering it down between his legs until she felt it rest against him. He was laying on the floor naked but for his sarong bunched up around his waist, with his chin resting on his hands. She was loathe to rise from him, and his comfortable muscled warmth. She dropped her legs over the sides of his to put her knees on the floor and squeezed his thighs together with hers.

He sighed. "Do you remember?"

And then she remembered, her mind filling with images and memories of sensations. And feelings. "How are you? Are you OK?"

"Yes." She could tell he was smiling.

"I remember the rage. Did you take it? Are you OK?" she asked again.

"Yes, I took it."

"How? How did you do it? I could barely stand it. And then She came into me, and fed my rage with Her own. How did you do it?

"Do you know the Sea of Grief?" he asked.

This startled her. It brought back memories of weeks connected to the Sea of Grief, composed of all the unwept tears of the people. The Sea existed as a band of suffering that wrapped the world, a band not too far up above Life. She remembered her Soul standing beneath it, draining it, purifying her, washing away her attachment to her own suffering, especially after her parents died. She thought the weeping would never stop. "Yes," she said. "I know it."

"Apparently there is something similar for Rage. Feminine Rage, the rage of oppressed wen, the Rage of the Goddess at what we are doing to Life, the Rage of the Raped. I felt it when She came into you."

"There were three rages, weren't there? Mine, the Dragon's, and Her's."

"Yes. I suspected the Dragon was here, but I couldn't turn to look at it. I knew by everything turning red. It was subtle, different than yours and Her's. Maybe its rage is for the near death of its species, I don't know."

"How did you take that? How are you not hurt?"

"I found a receptive place in my Soul, an expansive place in the receptive part of my emotions. I just opened it up and let it fill. It didn't reach into my Spirit or capture my Awareness."

"Amazing. I think it would have killed me."

"Masculine Rage is different. This was clearly Feminine Rage. And just as wen and men are different somatically there are differences in our Souls and Spirits."

"Huh," she grunted.

"And how are you?"

She checked in with herself. "Um. Wow. I'm, uh, happy. I feel a sense of well-being and happiness. Um. I really liked it. I really liked what I was doing. I liked the feel of the penetration, and the sense of power and control it gave me. It's amazing how hot it was, how much I came, how much I rained." She paused to review the memories. "You? Did you like it?"

"Yes. It's different. Not my preference, you know? But it's a part of the Curriculum that I agreed to. I took the training in it. And I prefer working with a wen strapped-in rather than another man."

"Wow," she said, rolling off him to lay alongside him. She stroked his hair and he turned his head toward her and smiled. "Seriously. You liked it?"

"Yeah. I am in Service to Her. Which means I am in Service to you, Her Priestess. Regina told me to tell you something. She heard your lament about how hard it is, and where is the Beauty in it. When she handed me the phallus and told me to take it to you she said 'It is all about entering the Mystery, the Sacred Erotic Beauty of entering into the Mystery. The Mystery is dark. And damp. The Mystery is the Feminine. The Masculine must be hard and penetrating. There has to be a hardness to enter in. Always ask permission to enter in. This makes the Mystery receptive. If the Mystery is not receptive it is a taking. We do not take. The Masculine here does not take. It must ask, and be allowed.' For me, it was a chance to work with my receptive side, my Feminine side. For you this was a chance to work on your Masculine side, the penetrating side. Your Animus. The Sacred Erotic for the Masculine is expressed by being hard."

"Wow. Did you enjoy it? Was it erotic for you?"

"Yes. I enjoyed it. Very erotic. Very intense, too. I loved the feel of your rain falling on the backs of my legs."

Angelica shivered at the memory. "Oh good. Can we do it again?"

"Right now?"

"Well, yes!"

"Can we get something to eat first?"

Angelica laughed. She sat up and crossed her legs. She looked down at the phallus poking up toward her belly and laughed again. "You know, I remember something that happened my second week at Stonehaven. I'd had a vision that all of me was a phallus. A giant green phallus. When I went down to dinner it had shrunk down and attached itself to me as if it was real. But it was huge in size. Never seen anything like it. It kept bumping into other people, or the edge of the table. I even got it in the salad at the buffet. Later Regina was walking past me and she said, "You're supposed to have a dick, not be a dick."

Corey laughed out loud. "I saw a drawing once. I think it was called the Homunculus. It showed the amount of wiring in the brain dedicated to different parts of the body. Big lips, big hands and feet. Big sex. Your dick sounds like the size it occupies in a man's brain."

"What's it like in a wen's brain?"

"Don't know. The drawing was obviously about a man's brain."

"Well, I guess that means, according to what Regina told me, men are dicks."

They both laughed together. Angelica stood up and said, "Help me out of this thing. Let's go get something to eat."

After they'd eaten, he walked her back to his room. She took his chin and pulled his face down to kiss her. "We can take a rain check on strapping me in again tonight." He hummed deep in his chest and leaned against her. She could feel his hardness pressed against her and it occurred to her, "You've not had a release yet, have you?" He smiled and said, "Not yet."

"Come with me." She encircled that hardness and led him to the bed. But rather than lay him down she went to her knees before him, took him in her mouth and, suffused with Sacred Erotic Beauty, the Crown of Fire set upon her head, she let him feed her.

When they finished she couldn't help but smile as he fell into his bed, falling asleep almost immediately, and, as she watched from her knees, slowly mixing the food of him in herself, she felt content. When she went to her room and lay down, she found herself fitful. In her mind she remembered first her rage, and then the Rage of the First One, and she became overwhelmed by it—by the rush of imagery, the storm of sensations, the cyclone of feelings. It was a Rage of Ages, much like the Sea of Grief, filled with the Rage of the Helpless, the Rage of the Taken From, the Rage of the Unavenged.

She sat up in bed and screamed. She howled until her voice gave out, and she lost consciousness, surrounded by the red glow of the dragon within her.

Regina, drawn by the disturbance, watched through the open door, watched as the red glow faded, and she presumed Angelica slept. She realized there was a presence behind her. Quinn had come up so quietly while she had been focused on Angelica that she hadn't sensed him. He had been drawn by the disturbance also.

She leaned back into him, smelling him, sensing his heat. He touched her shoulder and extended his hand over her shoulder to point at a golden light beginning to emerge from behind one of tree trunks that supported the roof beams. It moved slowly over to Angelica, bent toward her, and a slender arm and hand emerged from the light.

"She Who Comes," Quinn whispered.

The light touched Angelica on the head, and a sound, a deep

sound, a rumbling purr suffused the room, making even the door frame on which their hands rested vibrate. Though neither could see it, they both smiled. They both felt the disturbance withdraw. She Who Comes had sealed Angelica's mind from Her Rage, and the Dragon was happy about it.

Regina slid her hand up the smooth wood and took his hand in her own. She leaned into him so he would back up. The she led him, he following her, she holding his hand on her shoulder, to her room.

62

LEONARD

Leonard figured he was one of the luckiest men alive, and he gave thanks for it every day in the Devotions phase of his morning meditation. He would cultivate the feeling of Gratitude and raise it aloft to Her. And She would smile at him, almost every time. He saw the way most men lived. How did the poet say it? Lives of quiet desperation. That is, until they just stopped caring. Leonard had everything he needed, and he knew it. And it set him free to be loyal and dedicated without encumbrance.

Men of his stature and appearance, men with his kind of shyness, missed out on much in modern life, struggling to keep employment, struggling to find mates and partners. But in the Order he was accepted. The wen would laugh with him, instead of at him. The wen were pleased by him and would laugh with pleasure. Over the years, as his nervous system learned to relax into knowing that what he had would not be taken away from him, he was given the opportunity to become a completed person, and a completed man, in ways he could not have dreamed. He even had a grown son.

So, given his siddhi power, he was called in to help plan the strategy for how to deal with these strangers in town who were involved in fomenting the assault on Monique. They met in the second-floor office—Beth, the Madeleine, Grace, and Leonard. Leonard had been training a small group of Consorts and Priestesses in his power, the power of becoming invisible by projecting your background into the foreground, and there had been some promising results. Leonard had learned that introverts were more likely to succeed, since projecting an image into someone else's mind matching one's background was easier when a person was able to hold still. The shy know that holding still is a way to avoid being noticed.

In addition, they needed to gather some good photos of this couple, so a process of identifying them could begin, Leonard's group was to begin surveillance, dividing into teams, so that those people's movements might reveal their purpose, and also reveal if there were any more people in town like them, or if they had any local support. The man they'd hired to assault Monique indicated that they might.

And there was one more matter to consider. In her scrying the Madeleine had seen two things she couldn't explain, things that were shown to her that were not seeable in the mundane.

The first is that they seemed to be followed everywhere by a ghost. They seemed to show no awareness of it. And the man had some sort of weird attachment, a black kite that was partly attached to the top and back of his head, and the tail of it would sometimes flap, as if it were seeking to get a purchase. They were not to be approached, this couple. And no one, Priestess or Consort, was to go out unaccompanied.

Then there was the larger problem that was developing. The number of assaults against women had been increasing and Beth felt that they, the Order, had an obligation to help protect the people. Grace was put in charge of forming teams to patrol likely trouble spots—the clubs and bars, the closing time sidewalks and alleys.

Leonard and his surveillance teams were getting lots of practice, as the strangers would go walking all through the town, even some of the poorer residential areas. Sometimes they would coordinate with the assault prevention teams as a part of the monitoring but the strangers were in the habit of retiring for the night about the time the assault prevention teams became their most active.

It took several days to get results back on identifying the strangers. The Order had access to a beta version facial recognition program that identified the man as a cult leader living in the United States, and that the cult had originated in England with a student of a Lama from Tibet who taught metaphysics and tantra. Beth knew that the Order had some history with this Lama, but she couldn't quite remember it.

His travelling companion proved to be a different matter. Although she had been distinctly speaking with a British accent, as if she was born to it, a contact in Customs identified her as an American. Further research showed that, while there was an American birth certificate in that name, there was no further history, no cover story, although the false identity appeared to have been in place for decades. The facial identification software provided no clues.

After two weeks of surveillance Grace noticed a pattern. Comparing the logs of the surveillance and assault prevention teams, site addresses from one would appear as addresses in the other, sometimes in the same day, sometimes two or three days later. These addresses were either the locations where a sexual assault happened, or the prevention team leader reported a suspicious person whom their presence seemingly thwarted.

The conclusion was stark: everywhere these two went a sexual assault either happened or was about to happen. And then Grace saw a brief newscast that reported on a sharp increase in the number of sexual assaults occurring on the nearby Air Force base. The number had doubled from the previous year's average. Local leaders had asked the base commander to reduce the number of weekend passes until an investigation could be conducted.

The Madeleine scried again, looking for an energetic or psychic connection between the strangers and the following assaults. She noticed that the size of the kite seemed smaller, there was less material to flap along behind him. She asked the Goddess to help her see, and her perspective was magnified. She gasped when she realized what she was seeing—tiny little black particles falling away into the slip stream, settling behind him like a layer of dust. The black kite was shedding. Not always, but shedding, leaving little seeds of assault behind him. Seeds waiting to be picked up by anyone.

In the relatively flat hierarchy of the Order, the basic structure of 16 archetypal positions was replicated at every level, four roles in each quadrant, one person filling the epitome role of that quadrant. Plenty of hands to go around and make light work. Grace, Beth, Madeleine and Leonard all reported to their superiors weekly. The High Priestess of the Order called a special meeting of the Council when the Madeliene of Bath's report was brought to her attention—a man shedding seeds of sexual assault. One of the High Priestesses recalled that the cult-leader had been put on a watch list for the Berkeley group. Another recalled the Order's connection to the Lama.

The High Priestess of Berkeley was invited to call in to the Council Meeting. She identified the woman travelling with the cult leader as A. and told the Council that she was the principal assistant to the man, as she had been to the man's father and grandfather. She reportedly possessed psychic powers of her own, including the power of slowing her aging. The High Priestess overseeing administrative affairs skimmed the most recent report from Berkeley while they were talking. She inquired if there had been any breakthroughs in the recent murder of one of her Consorts, and the disappearance of the Priestess. She reported there had been none, other than the blood toxicology for the Consort had been released and that he had date rape drugs in his system. The efforts of her Madeleine ended at a wall of darkness.

The Council ordered that groups of Madeleines be formed to combine efforts to locate the missing Priestess and to keep an eye on the cult leader and his assistant in Bath. Administrators were to begin investigating to see if there was a connection between the dead and disappeared in Berkeley and the rise in assaults on military bases, since they had both been in the armed forces. And an all points alert to members of the Order who served in the military went out so they were apprised and cautioned.

On a windy day three weeks into the surveillance disaster struck. Leonard had been working with a new member of his invisibility group that he chose to team up with as a test run of the man's skills when a regular got sick. The rookie was standing across the street from the couple when he inadvertently squeezed his paper cup of tea and the lid popped off, and the tea squirted out scalding his hand. He slipped out and then back into visibility three times, his profanity drawing the Master and A.'s attention. They had been struggling emotionally, waiting for more feedback from the Master's hunting magic to show them more instances of the Fleur di Vie. The Master's anxiety was requiring assuagement every other day.

The Master raised his hand, preparing to send a burst of hypnotically induced paralytic energy, the same energy he used to keep A. in thrall, at the man along with a Word of Command, in preparation for running across the road to seize him. Leonard took the initiative to make himself visible while his partner regained his control. The problem was that Leonard was standing three feet behind the Master, leaning against the doorpost of the restaurant from which the Master and A. had just emerged.

A. felt him, jumped and gave a small, startled scream. This made the Master turn around and place his hand directly on Leonard's face. The Master said, "Freeze." Leonard's eyes went wide as he felt his will drain from him. The Master said, "Walk," taking Leonard's arm and leading him, zombie-like, down the sidewalk into an alley.

When Leonard's team mate looked up, he was gone.

The Madeleine and her team found Leonard's body about midnight in an unlocked and empty garage down the alley behind the restaurant. He was tied to an old wooden chair. She touched his forehead, hoping to read his last minutes directly. She felt the paralysis and the terror. She saw through Leonard's eyes the apoplectic face of the man they'd been surveilling. He had an image of the Fleur de Vie on a piece of paper and he was shaking it in Leonard's face, demanding 'Who?' and 'Where?'. He slapped Leonard repeatedly while the woman watched, smirking.

She felt Leonard's terror when he realized he would not be getting out of this. She felt the power of the Edict of Fidelity, the power of his Consort's vow that would stop the beating of his heart, rise up in him. She heard Leonard utter his last words, "We are all around. We will find you."

The Master hit him square in the face, snapping his head back. And then it slowly fell forward, chin on his chest. Leonard was gone.

A. had been watching closely. When the Master made to slap him again, A. raised her hand to stop him. She came forward and felt for a pulse. Finding none, she shook her head at the Master and said, "Dead."

The Master exploded with rage. "What the fuck is going on with these people? The slightest bit of pressure and they just fucking die!"

"It's a spell of some kind. I can feel it dissipating from him. Soon even the last traces of it will be gone."

"Fuck! Fuck, fuck, fuck!" the Master shouted, beating his thighs with his fists, then holding his forehead in his palms. "Fuck! What are we going to do?"

"You have to stop shouting. If someone hears you, we're done for. We have to go. Now."

The last image the Madeliene saw was the Master's contorted face, weeping tears of frustration, paper crumpled in one hand. The last sound was the closing door.

When Leonard's partner had called it in that he was missing, Beth ordered a team to go to the apartment where the couple had been staying. They arrived too late. A car that they had overlooked because it never moved was missing from the numbered spaces across the alley. The door was left slightly open so the team entered. Other than trash and used linens the apartment was empty.

63

BETRAYAL

After three weeks of Wade's flirtations, sometimes watched by the Priest at a remove over the local temple walls, the young clerk at the corner store, whose name was Tenara, told Wade that she knew a secret way to get to his house unseen. The next day her father would not be working in the fields in the afternoon, and would mind the store. She said she could sneak out the back of her house and make her way through the jungle to a spot across the road from his gate. It was far enough out of town, she said, that no one would see her. He could take her for a ride, so long as they were back in an hour and a half. She would bring a change of clothes so no one would recognize her, but he had to have a helmet with a visor. He did.

Tenara's house had been built in a western style with metal shed roofing. Her room was on the second story in the back. The kitchen was built out behind and below her room so she could step out onto its roof. There was no compound so the jungle came in close. She learned that by staying close to the edges of the roof she could keep it from creaking as she made her way to a branch that overhung the kitchen and then climb along it and down the tree. She'd practiced climbing back up several times just to make sure she could.

When her father had taken over the store and she was certain that her mother had left for town to do more substantive shopping, she'd gone to her room and turned the tinny little radio that had been gifted to her on low. She'd told her father she was going to take a nap.

She waited until she'd heard a customer drive up and her father start talking. She made her escape, a small knapsack with a change of clothes over her shoulder. She made the trek through the jungle to across the road from the house. Wade had left the gate open, and, although there was no traffic she didn't want to chance being seen by anyone working in the rice paddy behind his house so she dashed across the road.

She didn't want to call out, so she light footed it through the house looking not only for Wade but admiring his clean and open house. She found him out back by the pool laying naked on his back in the sun. She took in his form, focusing a long time on the phallus laying soft across his thigh. Still a virgin, yet she knew the basics of what to do. She felt a sudden longing in her hands to touch it, to touch one for the first time, and curled her fingers into fists to control herself. While she watched, it started to grow, lolling from his thigh to his belly, lengthening. Absently, as if still asleep, he touched it, making it twitch and grow more. She clapped a hand over her mouth, lest he hear her sighing.

Wade, of course, had been perfectly aware when she'd entered the house, and had set the whole thing up.

Tenara stepped back through the house until she was behind the island counter in the kitchen. She called his name softly. After a few calls, increasing her volume each time, she saw him stir, not knowing he was pretending to have been napping. He stood and wrapped a towel around himself, smiling when he saw the towel tented with his pole. He re-tied the towel, pinning his erection to his low belly. Tenara watched all this carefully. When he stepped through the sliding glass doors into the living room and called her name she had been turned away, pretending to be examining the contents of his refrigerator. When he called her name she stood up and turned around to face him. They smiled at each other.

"Hi! We go riding, yes?" she asked.

"Yes. Now?" he replied.

"You have helmet?"

"Yes."

"I will go change then," she said, picking her knapsack up off the counter and heading toward the bedrooms in the back. She glanced over her shoulder as she turned down the hall and noticed that Wade's towel had "slipped" leaving him tented in profile once more. She smiled, her head suddenly filled with images.

When she emerged she was wearing black silk pants with an embroidered red silk shirt. Wade had dressed in the clothes he'd stripped off in the living room prior to her arrival—khaki shorts and a short-sleeved cotton shirt. "You ready?"

She nodded and pulled her hair up into a high pony tail and held it in place with a hair tie. He handed her a helmet, and when she put it on he swore no one would recognize her. She jumped on the scooter behind him and they pulled out and away from town. She leaned close to him and put her hands on his hips. She realized by the tightness of his pants that he was erect again. She smiled. They were headed to a park a half hour away where no one would recognize her. They were not followed.

They arrived at the park and purchased some tea from a vendor. They sat on a bench talking comfortably and watched the tourists walk past. Knowing the limits on her time, they left in half an hour. On the ride back to Wade's, Tenara wrapped her arms around him, and leaned in, thrilling with the contact of her braless breasts against the warmth of his back. Of course, he grew erect again. When they arrived back at his house, she got off the scooter, casually dropping her hand to graze it along his shaft. She smiled behind the visor.

They entered the house, one behind the other. She put her helmet on the counter and turned to him. "I must change now and go home." Wade nodded his understanding. She emerged a moment later and told him that she was leaving her clothes there, so she would not have to bring them every time. He smiled. She gave him a hesitant quick kiss on his cheek. He dared not move. She smiled at him shyly and said "Thank you for today."

She left the house, stopped at the gate to look both ways then skipped across the road and into the jungle, not looking back.

Wade watched until she disappeared and went looking for her clothes. He found them, laid out on his bed. He picked up her silk pants and held the crotch to his nose, inhaling deeply, seeking the scents of her arousal. He found them, breathed them in and sighed, and said to no one, "Mine."

Tenara returned safely and unseen to her house and her room. Her mother returned from shopping a short while later and she went down to help her mother prepare supper, going out to monitor the store while her father ate. When he finished he came back to the store, and together they pulled back the outside display case with the gasoline bottles and closed and locked the sliding gate. Her father noticed no trace of his daughter's usual sullenness, but it failed to register in him as significant. He knew he'd never understand women, anyway.

That night, when all had retired, Tenara lay awake, reliving the feelings and sensations of the day. Charged with a sense of the erotic her hand slipped between her legs and she masturbated, stroking the jewel between her legs until she discharged with a tremble and a sigh.

"Mine," she whispered as she drifted off to sleep.

64

BRIGHID'S DAY

By the time A. reached the cottage she'd inherited from her father, the Master was in one of his teeth grinding anxiety seizures. She pulled into the garage, closed the door, and went inside. The house was divided into two apartments, one on each floor. A. had let the ground floor apartment to a caretaker she'd sent on an extended vacation a month earlier. The second-floor apartment had been reserved for her, dusted occasionally by the caretaker. She kept certain closets and trunks locked, but the rest of the apartment was furnished with nice things she'd collected over the years.

She turned up the heat and looked out the large window into her walled-in back yard. She'd kept it a fertile garden with a dwarf cherry tree in the corner, deep raised beds along the walls, and a small table with two chairs in the sunny center of the yard. The walls rose higher the closer they got to the house, so there was considerable privacy.

She sighed. She turned from the window to begin the process of activating her wards, going from room to room. The color of the light changed, becoming less golden and whiter. She went back downstairs into the caretaker's apartment. As instructed, all the caretaker's personal possessions were packed up in boxes stowed in one corner of the living room. She activated the wards on this floor and went to retrieve the Master from the car. She would let him stay on the ground floor so she could retreat to her own space above.

She hauled him from the car by his coat collar, and hefted him, semi-conscious, to standing then pushed him into the building and down the narrow hall. He stumbled as he crossed the threshold but caught himself. She guided him to the bedroom and pushed him onto the bed, not removing his coat or shoes. Her inculcated duty fulfilled, she stood still over the Master. Staring down, she felt her contempt arise. Her lips curled into a sneer. Some primitive part of her brain whispered to her, "Hurt him." She smiled at him, smiled at the thought, and backed out, closing the door and turning out the light. Let him awake in darkness.

By Brighid's Day, A. had had about enough of the Master. It started with restlessness. He had to leave the apartment and wander around the streets, going to restaurants and pubs, hanging out, a single man, in the small parks frequented by young moms with toddlers. His differences made him stand out. His insistence on going out alone without A., for whom he was beginning to feel disgust, drew more attention to him, people projecting onto him the archetype of the creepy stranger. Inquiries were made as to his identity by the local constabulary, especially when an assault on a young mother had occurred in a park where he had been seen before.

Unknown to either of them, the Madeleines had tracked them down and were projecting fields of telepathic barriers around the house, hoping that whatever the pair were up to would be contained with them. Unknown to the Madeleines was that they were also blocking the hunting magic of the Master, so that he was getting no reports from anyone under the magic's sway about anyone seeing the Fleur de Vie.

These fields began to compress around the Master and caused him to become reluctant to leave the apartment, which was relieving to A. She could feel the tendrils of unwanted attention from her neighbors begin to probe their living arrangements. She'd been gone so long that most of her neighbors didn't know she owned the home. She realized that their safety depended on him staying out of sight, as the impact of gossip in the collective mind wrapped around him. Best that they not see him at all, so that he could, out of sight, be out of her neighbors' minds.

Unable to walk around to relieve his anxiety, it grew worse as each day passed without a report of another sighting. A. took to taking him out in the car to larger parks and tourist destinations so he could get out and move around without arousing suspicion. But because the black kite continued to shed little molecules of malice, the Madeleines increased their pressure on him, so that he'd stay confined.

His anxiety became depression. A. began to use the assuagement tool as a reward for him performing tasks like eating or getting dressed.

Eventually his personal hygiene deteriorated. He stopped shaving, then bathing, then he stopped dressing in anything other than a robe. When he wasn't depressed, he started to have fits of ranting, often late at night in a state of insomnia.

A.'s loathing of the man grew in proportion with his increasing dysfunction. She couldn't stand the smell of him or the unwashed smell that began to permeate his apartment.

Even the Lama's ghost began spending a lot of time out in the garden to get a break from the smell.

65

WILEY ISLAND

It was mid-January when Regina decided it would be a good time for Quinn to visit her son living on the next island to the east, Wiley Island, named after a trader and not the original people's name for it, which translated meant roughly "Lucky Water." No one remembered if it referred to the single spring on the island, or to the remarkably good fishing in the water surrounding Wiley and its two privately-owned sister islands. Wiley was technically a part of the Windonesian archipelago, but there were no government offices there, and no police. Hence it was known internationally as a subdued but very active party island. Wealthy people, young people especially, would pull their small yachts into the water near the only dock and drop anchor, sending someone ashore to distribute flyers announcing invitations to come party and be prepared for anything goes.

Remarkably there was very little crime, not even a luggage theft or a pickpocketing in years. No assaults—just the occasional fight between drunks. There was a small village of indigenous people in the center of the island and if a dispute arose between any of the bar or hotel owners on the coast, the problem would be brought to the Headman or his wife, and with their pronouncements the matter would be settled. The villagers lived happily on the tax proceeds the coastal businesses supplied, even collecting a sales tax on weed on the side. Since they didn't need anything from the central government, the central government left them alone.

It was here that Regina's son, the so-called Prophet of Conscience, had chosen to live. He turned a hobby of his into a small income—he would search the beaches, covered in red and blue coral, for pieces that looked like carvings of humans or other animals, and these he assembled into a museum collection; the Museum of Anthropomorphic Corals.

Regina had difficulty adapting to the individual her son had become. His father was a Boddhisatva who had somehow managed to attain the Enlightenment in Tibet—a white American man who flew below the radar for more than a decade before he was imprisoned for espionage by the Whineez government. He died in prison about a year later, no one was sure how exactly. The rumor was that he died sitting up in the lotus position. Regina had met him in Nepal during one of his excursions to the Temples and Monasteries there.

There is a rule, there is the exception to the rule, and there is a rule that governs the exception to the rule.

Because his father had already overcome the consequences of the Kundalini Barrier, and was, hence, sane, the Prophet had been born sane. The normal conditions of life on Earth had, according to Regina's account, driven him nearly, if not actually, insane.

Regina had said to Quinn, "You. You're Boddhisatva. You're "sane." Maybe even sane without quotation marks. According to Her, anyway. Surely, you can talk to him."

"So, you're asking for a favor?" Quinn spoke seriously but raised a comic quizzical eyebrow.

"Yes. You asshole. Fuck you."

"Clearly, you're sane, too."

"Fuck you. And don't you say another word about it." She threw a silencing spell against him. He saw it coming and chose to let it land, and see what it did. He was surprised at how effective it was, but then he stopped it at a certain degree of coverage and tried to pretend he didn't in order to make her think it was effective. She caught the acting and walked away from him. She smiled, maybe half snarled at him over her shoulder, and said, "I don't care what you think. You're still silent, aren't you?"

Quinn grinned and conceded the victory to her.

Before he agreed, they had to resolve the issue of Angelica needing a bodyguard. She pointed out that the dragon was mostly existing outside her now, many nights sleeping in Regina's room, where they would speak in dragon to each other long into the night. It was the dragon they were after, not Angelica, and if it made him feel she was safer she would move Angelica to a different house. The dragon had already made it clear that it felt safe here, away from Angelica, this is what the Spirits of the Land had told it. Besides, with Regina's help, it was already learning to master invisibility. Some part of Quinn's mind, perhaps remembering the skill of the King of Salamanders at Stonehaven, said, "Good enough." And his mouth said, "Make sure you send her some place less visible." Regina knew where, she said. And Quinn said, "Tell me, in case I have to…" Regina had touched a forefinger to his forehead and filled his mind with a topographical map of Wallid, zooming in and out of the location. "Got it?" she'd said. And then she stepped back from him. "Besides," she said, "I'm not sure they want to fuck with me." And she turned dark, turned into a little dark cloud crackling with malice and lightning. "As the saying goes: if you meet god along the road, kill him."

The channel between the two islands was deep with swift currents, huge masses of water flowing through, washing back and forth every day. Wind gusted between the mountains on each side, operating as a wind tunnel, that raised the waves high, more than a meter in the center. Quinn remembered his water legs and just rolled with it, his lizard brain in love with the sensations. The smell of barf rose up in the small ferry boat cabin and he'd had to get out on the open deck. The deckhand out there looked at him and grinned knowingly.

The boat was small enough to tie up at the wooden dock and Quinn got to walk it, footfalls landing lighter than his weight. The deck work continued farther up the beach into the palm trees, and when he inhaled, it was as if he was breathing a different kind of air, an air that put him at ease. He sighed with relief.

As he turned onto the Beach Street, a man across the road stopped leaning against the wall and crossed the street to approach him. The man seemed to be a Caribbean Islander rather than a local but what did he know. When he got close Quinn invited him to do what he knew the guy was going to do anyway. "Walk with me," he said.

The guy, taken a little aback, said, "What, mon, you in a hurry? There's no hurry here!"

Quinn raised an eyebrow at him. It was a formidable gesture. "Look," he said. "I'm new here, first time here. You live here?" The man nodded. "Good. I need to know what's what and what's where. You know? Can you do that?"

"Yeah, mon, I can do that."

"How do I get ahold of you?"

"Well," he said. "You can leave a message with the bar tender here. Or…"

"What's your name, mon?"

"My name?"

"Well, yeah. How else am I gonna tell the bar tender who the message is for?"

"Yeah, well, Wolfie. Call me Wolfie." And he grinned a grin that failed utterly at hinting at being an aggressive carnivore.

Quinn smiled.

Then Wolfie said, "Anyway, best way is to go sit at the bar and wait. I'll see you. This is my corner, and wherever I am I'll be back soon. If you need anything I'm your man."

He backed away, pensive. Quinn grinned and continued on his way. Before he'd left he'd asked Regina to do the same trick with the topo map and show him Wiley and where the Prophet's house was.

It was a small house, a cabin really, set inland from the "Beach Street" road behind a shield of bushes, visually impenetrable. The road circumscribed the island, part sand on the far side, part two-golf-cart-wide tarmac in the beach town. No internal combustion engines were allowed on the island, except the diesel-powered generators hidden behind sound barriers on a hillock close to the south end of the island. One could easily walk around the island in a day.

The Prophet was famous locally, of course, and mostly for not knowing when to stop talking. It was as if he was a reincarnated Diogenes, or maybe a Socrates, always looking for someone to talk honestly with him. He had few takers.

Quinn found the house and went down the short driveway. No one answered when he went to the front door so he went around back and found the Prophet naked on a chaise lounge, sunning himself . He walked quietly until he was alongside the chair, and his shadow fell over the Prophet. "You're blocking the light," the Prophet said.

"Oops, sorry," Quinn apologized, and stepped back.

"Dolt," the Prophet muttered as he sat up.

Quinn raised an eyebrow at the unnecessary insult.

"I suppose you'll be wanting something to eat and drink," the Prophet commented, not really offering.

Quinn said, just barely audibly, "Hmm."

The Prophet, already up, scratching his naked butt with one hand, scrabbling through his unruly bed hair with other, stopped short and turned to Quinn. "Well?" he asked.

"You know," Quinn began, "I've been told that you're quite an asshole. I have found that my life goes easier when I limit myself to being an asshole by necessity. How's it working out for you to be such an unnecessary asshole?"

The Prophet narrowed his eyes at Quinn; Quinn blithely returned the stare. The Prophet cracked a smile, then laughed out loud. "I'll take that as a yes."

Quinn remained standing in the yard while the Prophet went into the house. When he came back out, he was wearing a sarong tied tight under his developing belly carrying a tray of drinks and a loaf of bread next to a knife. There was a table and four chairs on his back deck under an umbrella and the Prophet beckoned him over. "Sit," he said.

Quinn sat down and picked up the drink, crushed ice, salt on the rim. "What is this?

"Double shot tequila margarita. Welcome to the tropics. Made entirely locally. Our finest agave."

"Really? By whom?"

"Whom? Really?"

Quinn waited, knowing what was coming.

"Me. Just not on the island."

Quinn took a sip. "New straw?"

"Of fucking course not."

Quinn almost spit out the mouthful.

"Boiled, though," the Prophet said.

Quinn swallowed. Heat then sweet, then sour then salt. "Good," he said.

The Prophet nodded at the acknowledgment. "Now. What do you want?"

"Do you know who I am?"

"Nobody knows who you are. Or even if you're still a 'who'. Most likely you're just a 'what'."

"So, you were told I was coming."

"The Order has people everywhere. And they pay well. Some of them work for me."

"I'm fine with being a 'what.' 'Who' never made any sense to me. I don't know who I am, I don't give a fuck, if you were trying to get at me. There's no path to me down that trail."

The Prophet took another sip, regarding Quinn with an unfocused gaze. "Hmm. It tells the truth."

"Another unnecessary insult."

"Look. I don't know you, you don't know me. Over the course of your life half of the people you meet are going to be of below average intelligence…it's called math. And really, do you have to think about that statement? You hesitated a fraction of a second too long to think about it. Really? Are you that stupid? Now, seriously, do you really wonder why things are as fucked up as they are? Fucking people. And yet, by Higher Law, you are required to Love them."

"You, asshole that you are, just tried to run one of your standard gambits on me. You're an asshole alright, but not as big an asshole as me. Do you really think you're in the upper half?"

The Prophet grimaced, it's what passed for a smile with him.

When Quinn realized this—realized that was a smile—he laughed out loud. "Way too serious, motherfucker."

The Prophet, temporarily reduced to stupidity, said something really stupid, "You would know."

Quinn said, "You, too, are required to love them. Those people. Not just me."

The Prophet silently started to weep.

Quinn smiled at him and said, "Look, you can have a Conscience no matter how smart you are. You just may not know why. A truly smart man could figure out how to teach."

"Why?"

"Because a world with more conscientious people is a better world than one with fewer."

Another tear rolled down his cheek. "I hate you," the Prophet said.

"That's because you're still a 'who.'"

They drank in silence for a little while. Then Quinn spoke: "It seems to me that if you dedicate yourself to doing things in a good way, then you will never be very far off from the right way of doing things."

"Axiology may be the most difficult subject I have ever studied. Let's go into town and get something to eat." The Prophet went back into the house and in a couple minutes re-emerged wearing shorts, sandals, and a Hawaiian shirt.

After they walked about a hundred meters back down the road to town the Prophet turned to Quinn and said, "I know about you."

"Oh, yeah? What part?

"Full Kundalini Barrier blow-out at twenty-one."

"Yeah?"

"Yeah."

"Well, what do you know about it?"

"Not a lot. I was born without one. My father had already overcome the consequences of the Barrier when Regina got pregnant with me. Therefore there was nothing to imprint."

"And Regina? How far along was she? Had she already overcome it, too?

"I don't know. I never asked. I just assumed not, at least not completely."

Quinn said, "Well, I think you ought to add that to your considerations…" Then, "Look. If you never had it, well then, no wonder you're such an asshole. You have no subjective way to relate to almost everybody else on the planet.

"Yeah, well. You've already made me cry once. Good luck making that happen again."

"I didn't make anything happen. I just touched your vulnerability energetically." He paused then said, "You should work harder at putting yourself in someone else's place."

"Why? What for?"

"Because, asshole, it will make your life easier."

"I'm honored," the Prophet said.

Quinn looked away. "Your sarcasm is feeding your assholery. It should be the other way around." Then he said, "You have no idea. You, unfortunate fuck that you are, were born sane.

"Almost nobody is born sane. Almost everybody is born open to imprint. It's actually a neonatal need—children must learn to be like their parents. If they aren't, their parents are more likely to abandon them; this is the importance of the smile. And then they imprint on their insane parents, and become insane themselves. Fortunately for us most of them keep to themselves, too. Live their lives at the level of survival engagement, passing on the insanity of basic selfishness, pettiness, and meanness.

"And you, yes it's lonely. The loneliness itself could be enough to make a man insane. Or an asshole. But all you have to do is relate to them where they are. If you want to be understood you have to speak to them in a way they will understand."

"That's not easy. Some people can't hear even direct speech. It confuses them."

"So speak to them indirectly. With subtle subjects you have to adopt that form of speech known as indirect speech if you want to be understood. But you must be speaking to people who understand indirect speech. If a person can only understand direct speech, say only direct things. But remember, those that live behind the Barrier may be immune to the subtle and indirect. As someone with a clear sense of before and after overcoming the Barrier I can tell. For you, it's a discernment skill you have to cultivate."

"Like how?"

"You can tell a story instead of giving a sermon."

"Lot of work."

"Do you want to be understood or not?"

"Not sure, actually, now that I think about it."

"Then you don't get to whine about being lonely."

They sat down at a table with an ocean view at "Wolfie's" corner bar. Quinn asked the Prophet, "You got any weed? I'm on vacation, and if I don't have to deal with the locals it would be better."

The Prophet said, "Yeah, I do. Back at the house."

"Good," Quinn said.

66

THE FIRE IN THE HEART

With Quinn gone to Wiley to talk to the Prophet and Angelica sans Dragon and Corey staying away from Regina's compound in a small and isolated vacation rental, Regina assembled the six Priestesses presently on the island in her compound with their Consorts, on the day that Mai Pei, the High Priestess of the Order of the Red Phoenix, arrived for what she was euphemistically calling a vacation with her Consort. Regina and Onadaya were currently without Consorts, bringing the total to nine Priestesses and seven Consorts. Jasmine had Guiles; her first Consort Wade was not invited.

It was the night of the January full moon. Napat, still recovering, was given a tea after supper to make her sleep. Her youth, inexperience, and still growing resiliency made Jasmine and Regina concerned for the young wen's vulnerability. It was Jasmine's responsibility to plan and set up the Ritual of Collection they were going to perform that night, in consultation with Regina and Mai Pei.

In the inner courtyard of Regina's compound, a classic labyrinth had been set in to stonework of the floor. A large velvet covered pillow was set in the center. Around the periphery nine large moon-colored candles were placed, and just outside these were nine statues from Regina's collection of erect phalli with legs. The outer ring consisted of nine pillows on which the Priestesses were to sit. Against one wall was a row of drums for the Consorts. Near the entrance to the labyrinth a large bronze gong suspended in a wheeled frame was placed.

As the sun went down the planning for the Ritual was gone over, so that each knew their parts, and the sequence of the steps in the process. The nine Priestesses sat down on their pillows, lit their candles, and meditated, eyes gazing at the flickering silhouettes of the phalli, shadow forms dancing on their faces, until the time was right—the moon rising far enough that the entire compound was bathed in light. At a nod from Regina the gong was sounded once by Guiles, and with the help of two other men it was lifted out of the frame, and carried to the center of the Labyrinth and set face down on the pillows, creating a large flat bowl.

The drumming was familiar to the Priestesses and when Regina started to rise they all rose. They swayed together. When Regina picked up her foot they all did, stomping in unison. The floor resounded. They twirled in place, slowly, stamping their feet together. They moved one place to their right, then two back to their left. They did this back and forth until each of them had stood in the places of all of them. As they moved circles of colored lights, rings of dancing flames, appeared around the top of their heads. The flames descended until they wrapped the brow like the circlets and crowns of old. Then a different flame, often of a different color, arose in the center of the crown and danced there.

When they stopped washing back and forth Jasmine was standing at the entrance to the Labyrinth. She stood still, raised her face and her arms to the moon overhead. When she lowered her arms, the central flame lowered itself in her, dropping to the level of her heart and glowing there from within, brightly enough that all could see it. She tucked the edges of her sarong up into the waist so that she was completely exposed in front and danced in.

Following the labyrinth path she danced and the central fire descended to her root and glowed there, suffusing the air around her sex. She arrived at the bowl in the center and began stimulating herself, swaying to the rhythm of the drums. In no long time she was ready and with a shout she orgasmed, raining in the bowl, making it sing. The Priestesses raised their voices in ululation. She rained until she was empty and as she turned to dance out along the exit path the next Priestess entered.

Snuffling, smelling the ejaculate, the Dragon appeared, snaking itself around the legs of the Priestesses, imparting new energy to their dancing. When he got to Jasmine he stuck his nose in her crotch like a dog and made her laugh.

Back and forth the circle moved, roots and crowns aflame. The last one to enter was Regina. She rained, stomping her feet and jumping up and down, howling in ecstasy, the bowl resonating deeply. The wen howled back in ecstatic support. She danced out and resumed her starting place.

After a moment she stopped dancing, and the drums took the cue and stopped also. She tilted her face to the sky, to the shining moon, and they all joined her, Consorts and Priestesses, howling into the night. When she stopped they all stopped. They regarded her with wide eyes, for over her face was the visage of another, radiant and beautiful; the visage of She Who Comes.

Earlier that evening Corey had taken Angelica on a scooter ride to a beach on the far eastern end of the Island to watch the full moon rise. The steep edge of a mountain came down directly into the sea and about a third of the way up there was a temple tower, silhouetted and dark. All her senses came alive; night birds calling, the ripe scent of the jungle behind her mixed with the salt smell of the sea, the warmth of the man she was leaning against with a cooling breeze swirling around them.

As Angelica had spent the past few days with more and more time not carrying the Dragon she started to notice how sensitive she had become, both at the level of sensation and at the level of feeling. Her Soma and her Soul felt like new spectra of experience had been opened to her. And her mind, her Spirit, stilled, and stopped what had been a near constant internal agitation. Beauty became palpable to her, and much of that Beauty was Erotic. Even the play of light and shadow along a curve would make the Jewel in her Arch tingle and twitch.

As the moon rose behind the tower there was one moment when the dark phallus of its form seemed to pierce and penetrate the moon, and as the moon rose up and left it behind, implacably following its Destiny, the Beauty of it pierced her, penetrated her, too. And she rained, orgasming spontaneously, standing there on the beach, rain running down the inside of her thighs. Her knees shook, and she almost collapsed, soaking her underwear beneath her beach sarong.

Corey went to his knees before her, removed the wet cloth and, holding her sarong open, left her exposed to that cool breeze, and she shivered. He licked up the inside of her thighs, and the shiver became a tremble. She pulled his mouth to her and she came again, for him this time, legs shaking, raining and staring at the spectacular majesty of the risen moon, weeping for Beauty.

She touched her heart with her other hand, and suddenly, as a wind arising, but from within, she felt her Crown of Fire ignite, green flames surrounding a red core, flickering the glow of her across the sand.

When most of the others had gone to bed Onadaya appeared in the courtyard carrying several waterproof lined leather drinking flasks and a vacuum bulb baster from the kitchen. Jasmine emerged behind her carrying more flasks and a broad wooden spoon. Regina followed carrying a cloth shoulder bag that made clicking and clinking noises as she walked. They each picked up a candle and carried it with them.

They entered the labyrinth following the path. They set down their burdens and kneeled on the floor. Regina withdrew several bottles from her bag, checking the labels in the candlelight. They were tinctures of different herbs and she chose a few to sprinkle in the fluid, which Jasmine then stirred. Satisfied, they watched the water of life settle. Then, with Jasmine unscrewing the stopper and holding the bag, Onadaya filled each flask with the vacuum bulb. Jasmine then resealed the flasks and set them aside.

The Dragon appeared, hovering over the lines in the floor and went to Regina's shoulder. He said something in Dragon that made her laugh. She responded in kind and the Dragon growled, "Heh, heh, heh."

Each Priestess and her Consort left the next morning carrying several flasks of sacred water to be used in the ritual anointing of the Queen Old Woman Stones scattered under the foundations of the Temples across the island. Jasmine and Guiles stayed the rest of the week so that Jasmine could continue to help with Napat's healing. Her resiliency was fast returning and she was laughing again, thrilled with the Dragon and its play.

67

ALPHA AND OMEGA

Over the course of the week Quinn and the Prophet took up walking around the periphery of the island, once a day. They could have done it twice a day but preferred long lunches in open air bars, and standing still on the beach talking and making wild gestures to each other as they talked. Quinn was flush with cash and he'd noticed that the Prophet was looking a little threadbare. Quinn bought the food and booze, and procured more weed from his pal Wolfie.

Quinn came to understand some of the horror of what it meant to be born sane and have sane parents and to be smarter than almost everyone you meet. Being smarter was hard enough, but throw in a nascent psychic ability or an unusual capacity for empathy and the smarter path appeared to be pretend to be stupid. He remembered his terror of confinement and his reason for fleeing to the wilderness for five years—his complete inability to tolerate proximity to people. He smelled them. He heard their inner thoughts. He dreamed their dreams. The insipid and the insidious ruled daily life and it made him feel unclean, slimy inside where he couldn't wash it out.

So Quinn asked the Prophet on their first walk around the island, "Did you have to build buffers to your perception as a child?"

The Prophet answered, "I thought we all did."

Quinn said, "Yes, but everyday children are born with the inherent ability to create those buffers as a consequence of the imprint of the Kundalini Barrier already being born within them. They will build those buffers automatically as they grow. That wasn't in you when you were born. How did you learn to close the doors of perception?"

"Regina taught me. It wasn't so much about closing them as it was about controlling them. We'd see somebody on the street and she would lean down and say to me, 'What's that man over there feeling?' or 'What's that woman over there thinking.' And then I'd 'open the door,' as you put it, and look, make the perception and then she'd turn my attention back to her. Sometimes when I'd start to get lost in another person she'd take my face and forcibly make me look at her, telling me to 'Pay attention. Look at me.'"

"And the prescient dreaming? How did you deal with that?"

"You know?"

"Yeah, I know. Of course, I know. First one at age seven."

"Me, too," the Prophet paused to regard Quinn. "At first it was just flashes, flashes of remembering that I'd dreamed whatever was happening the night before. Or sometimes a few nights before. It made me happy, I felt secure. I'd even tell Regina, 'Mommy, we're doing what I dreamed last night.' Then sometimes I started telling her what would happen next. A couple of times I'd have strong feelings of foreboding, like, once, I dreamed of a flash flood down the side of the mountain we were living on, and she took what I said seriously and we headed for higher ground. People died because we didn't warn them. When I realized this I was about ten, and I started to wonder if their death was my fault because we didn't tell them a flood was coming."

"How did you rationalize it? Because it's clear that you did."

"Regina told me they wouldn't believe. And if they did, they would start to treat me funny, either treating me as too special, or being afraid of me, and maybe hurting me. She told me I had to learn to know when to talk about what I saw. She told me, 'A Prophet is never welcome in his own country.' That was the first time I'd heard the word. Prophet. So, I'm here. I don't have a country.

"When I hit adolescence, the dreaming got worse. I would dream everything that happened to me in a day the night before. And I'd remember the dream as I lived it, every waking moment."

Quinn said, "Me, too. After overcoming the Barrier. All the buffers to perception were washed away by the flow of energy."

Simultaneously they both said, "I became very depressed." And they both laughed. They both snorted simultaneously, too. They snorted at a smell, the smell of the possibility of friendship. Their eyes grew brighter, rather than darker, deeper down the road of despair. The Prophet reached over and punched Quinn on the shoulder.

"Ow! Fuck! That hurt," the Prophet said, shaking his hand.

"What the fuck?"

Quinn just smiled. "So, what did you do about it? What did Regina teach you?"

"It was a hard time for her. I was angry. On my best days I was merely sullen. So she watched me sleep. She could follow me wherever I went in my dreaming. The Prescient Dreaming didn't take long, the download would happen in compressed time, not real time like during the day. I would have many other dreams, normal dreams, but the weight of the Prescient Dreams began to leave me exhausted when I woke. She'd follow me out into the long body of the planet, a tube with heliacal paths running through it, each one a thread tracing the life of person. In the long view you can see where the planet is going, its path is foreordained. And, even though the future doesn't exist yet you can see where each person's path is likely to go, and so I could trace a person's life out into its likely future. Their Destiny would become their Fate.

"Then I would look at my thread, see where it was going, then I'd drop down into my own thread, which itself was like a little tube, and I'd just follow the path into my future from within my life, and there it was, everything that would happen to me the next day.

"Because Regina would follow me, she could tell me, when I woke up, what was happening to my body when I would journey to the future. She'd notice that it happened at only certain times of the night. It was here that she taught me to divide my attention. She'd wake me up, returning me to sensation, giving me the chance to control where my mind went. As I learned to control myself I relied on returning to sensation. I felt that in crossing from my awareness of my present to that higher and distant perspective there was a threshold into the space of perception. I learned to not cross that threshold automatically but to stay here, and learn how to rest here." He said the final 'here' with emphasis.

"How long did it take to control it?"

"A few years, maybe four. When I was in my late teens I started prophesying to my friends. Sometimes to strangers. I thought it was fun, and liked the sense of power it gave me. Also, it gave me a lot of attention. People started to come to me for future readings. I had no ethics, I told them whatever I saw. Cheating husbands. Domestic violence. Old crimes in their past. People were paying me so I told them whatever, not just what they wanted to hear. As a sideline I learned how to contact the Spirits of the Dead. The people had taken to calling me The Prophet. Then, one day, one of my clients became outraged, I guess at what he felt was an invasion of privacy. He grabbed me by the shirt and threw me against the wall. Then he beat me pretty good.

"Then something happened to me. Regina would change the bandages on my face. One day when she was finishing, she asked me, 'Where is your Conscience, son? What does it have to say to you?' She blew my mind, and suddenly, under the shock of the beating, a new part of my mind coalesced and I became aware of a new faculty, my Conscience. Now I only help people make choices in the interests of the Good. Not much interest in that. Not much business."

Quinn nodded. "I understand."

"Do you? Do you really?"

"Yes. I, too, have a Conscience."

The Prophet gazed at Quinn with unfocused eyes. "Yes, you do. I can see it," he said. "So this is what I became known for, why I have this nickname, the Prophet of Conscience. I see Conscience as a new brain, a fourth brain developing in humans as a part of the experiment in evolution created by the True Creator."

"You know Her then," Quinn stated, trying to spare himself from another monologue.

"We've met," the Prophet said tersely.

Quinn took a deep breath, preparing himself to plunge in again. "And what do you think?"

"My Conscience tells me to say that in my arrogance it was not a good experience. I resented her."

Quinn laughed. "I have some resentments, too, although not about Her. I consider myself her Servant."

"Well, good for you!" he said in a falsetto voice.

"What did you resent?"

"The experiment, and how much suffering it's caused."

"The alternative, continuing to leave people in their vulnerable-to-hypnosis state, hypnosis by the so-called teachings of De Murgos, has created far more suffering. And the experiment, if successful, will close that vulnerability."

"I resented being included without my consent."

"I can sympathize with that. Not going to take my time to empathize with you though. At least it's something. She is trying to do something."

"Not nothing."

"That's right."

"So here we are at a great divide, the beginning and the ending, the Alpha and the Omega."

"The aught and the ought. The aught, with an 'a', and the ought, with an 'o'."

"Ah, I see. The same as the 'a' in Alpha and the 'o' in Omega."

"Right. The Aught and the Ought. The 'Aught' means Nothing. The 'Ought' is Something. In the great Dao it is written that Something emerged from Nothing."

"So, there is Nothing and Something, and, since Nothing is nowhere, there is only Something. And that Something is 'Ought'."

"Yes. All that is, is 'Ought'. Everything else is Nothing. That is why your very being is ensnared in the Development of Conscience. All that is, is Ought. And what we 'Ought' in every situation should be our first priority as humans."

"I see. All that is, is Ought, and I am its Prophet."

"You could be."

The Prophet had to think about that. What it would mean. It would mean that the whole of him would be aligned with the purpose of Evolution, and he'd help lead it, rather than be sidelined by his whiny arrogance. As he let it sink in, he wept.

"Grieve fearlessly," Quinn told him.

For the rest of the afternoon The Prophet wept off and on. About sundown they began to drink heavily. The Prophet became staggeringly drunk and reverted to an Australian accent, a place where he had spent a lot of time growing up. It was where he went to college. His face was screwed up, trying to cry, but he couldn't. Quinn watched him, wondering if his spasm of Grief had ended, temporarily, at least.

The Prophet sobbed, a dry sob, almost as if he were going to vomit. He said, "My eyes filled up with tears. But they just won't brim over and cry. They won't let me weep. My tears won't let me weep." And he sobbed again.

Quinn replied, "Yeah, I've been there. Beauty produces its image in those who pursue it. Somebody said that, I don't remember who. But I find that I can live into it. Here", he said, passing the Prophet a bottle. "Have some water. You're dehydrated."

Quinn got up and headed for the house. There was a hammock strung up in the living room with his name on it. Before he lay down he sent Regina an email on the Prophet's laptop saying he was staying another week on Wiley.

68

DISPENSATION

She Who Comes had known that when She took the Embla, She was taking his life. She knew he would die, that without the shell he lost the filter that removed those parts of the air near the surface that were toxic to him. She hadn't expected him to die that quickly—a mercy She hadn't intended to grant him.

She had also known that he possessed insufficient freedom of mind from De Murgos to be of any use to Her. And that his psychic connection through prayer with De Murgos would put them all at risk, and that's why She understood that She could have never let him leave the chamber. He was too dangerous to keep alive.

She was intrigued though that the dialogues reported to Her contained intelligence that De Murgos had gone mad and that he had been planning on leaving the planet anyway.

She whisked the body away to a cave She'd carved beneath a glacier in Greenland. She already knew to what use she'd be putting it.

The day after Brighid's Day, She Who Comes returned to Stonehaven from the Invisible Lands. Matthews, still residing with Brighid, was told by She Who Comes about the plan that saved him from encountering the Embla and the Dangla at Calley's Last Shrine. For Brighid the plan had worked marvelously well—She had an in-house lover for the first time in centuries, if you didn't count Alam for all those years. And, as good as Alam had been for Her, he belonged to Calley. Matthews had wings, which made him wildly effective in action, and he knew that they were a gift from She Who Comes. To him, She was She Who Saved Him. His gratitude was boundless. And sometimes he could even manage gratitude to Quinn for blowing out the Buffer in him. The next time he saw Quinn he'd have to ask him if knew that by connecting him to the earth as a part of the process that She Who Comes would find him, still blind, channeling so much energy that even breath was pain, lying on his kitchen floor. He'd realized later that he could have just asked Her. Brighid knew that he would be used by She Who Comes, although She didn't know for what, or when.

She Who Comes appeared in Calley's bedroom just after sunrise. Alam had already left for the Pine Eye to gather more of the life preserving clay. Calley, still working out how to cope with the mixed mortal/immortal energies of Her temporal life, was sleeping in. She Who Comes sat on the edge of the bed and put a hand on Calley's foot. "Good morning, sleepy head," She said. "I saw on the way in that you've begun repairs on the roof. Good. I have many fond memories of this house."

Calley made a very human "mmphf" sound into Her pillow.

She Who Comes called out, "Eva?! Where are you? Could you please come here?"

Eva manifested with a sound like far off wind chimes.

Calley groaned. "Gravity sucks," She said, rolling over and sitting up. "I don't mean literally. I know that everything holds together by the Universal Acceleration Expansion. I mean it's a pain being in it. It's been a long time since I went mist."

"You should go to the Pine Eye often. I think you will find yourself restored by the piece from the Invisible Lands," Eva said. "Alam does. I was just there watching him."

"She's right, you know," said She Who Comes.

"Why are you watching my Consort?" Calley squinted, closing one eye.

"Because he's cute, and he smells good," the ghost replied.

"Oh yes, sorry, I forgot how ghosts feed by sense of smell."

Eva smiled and floated. She turned to She Who Comes and bowed. "How may I serve you?"

Calley continued, pre-empting Her Mother. "Never the less, Eva, I have heard about you. I am told you have developed certain skills—an image of you, younger, appearing in the mind of a Consort, or a Priestess, sometimes even when they are awake. You engage in erotic behavior with them. Sometimes you can even attain visibility with their eyes open—they can see you engaging in sex with them.

Somehow you can bring them to orgasm, often quickly. Then you stay only a little while, leaving them to clean up, and reorganize themselves emotionally and mentally. Is this true?" Calley by now was standing, grumpy, hands on Her hips, a little sizzling sound manifest in the air.

"Yes, Goddess, it is true. I have learned how to evoke the Sacred Power of Erotic Beauty in mortals. I do what you used to do to Alam out in the Highlands millennia ago. I do it so I can feed on the smell of orgasm. I long for the taste of it, but when I can smell it and feed that way, I can orgasm, too, and engage in the alchemy so that I can fortify the crystallization of this form, this body that you see, and work to crystallize the next. This is a matter of life and death for me."

In the silence that followed, Calley's irritation eased. "Well," she said, "No ghost sex with my Consort."

"Never without your consent, Goddess."

She Who Comes had been grinning the whole time and by the end of the conversation She was grinning enormously. She beckoned Eva to come close to Her. She took Eva's face in Her hands and said, "High Priestess, I am so proud of you," and kissed Eva on her icy lips.

Eva felt the heat, almost as pain, but she knew that a gift was happening, a transference of a power, the power of the heat of living. The room turned red. Eva felt little burning prickles throughout her body as the substance of herself organized into a crystal pattern. It was so intense she almost pulled away from the Goddess. Then the sensation and the heat faded.

"Mother, what did you just do?" Calley asked.

"I crystallized this form for her. So that she may live and continue to evolve. I will have use of her in the future." Still holding Eva's face, the red glow fading, she asked Eva "Do you serve Me?"

"Always," Eva responded.

"Good," She Who Comes said, letting go of Eva. "Well, then, we have work to do today with the Dangla." Stepping away from the front of Calley's altar She made an 'I invite you to sit' gesture in a sweeping fashion, smiling, and said, "Calley, be so kind as to ask the Blue Hag to join us in the chamber below.

"Calley, these are the substances that are poisonous to these beings," said She Who Comes. She was holding hands with Calley and Eva in the Initiation Chamber below the Mansion. The round iron door imbued with Solomon's confinement spells had been sealed by Craft. He would only open it if he received the agreed upon 'knocking" from below.

"Push these elements to the wall, would you? The Dangla have developed some skills at surviving the toxicity of My atmosphere since they were pushed out in The Fall, so it need not be perfect."

There was a palpable sense of pressurization as Calley became wind and pushed the selected elements to the walls, creating a bubble of what would seem to be ease when the Blue Hag returned the Dangla.

She Who Comes did a simple summoning and spoke "Stonewen, bring the prisoner to me." The light turned blue. As they watched a contorted face arose from the stone floor, then the whole head, face locked in a soundless scream. A blue hand emerged, gripping the neck from behind and then the Hag appeared, smiling and looking younger. When completely emerged, she set him on his feet, and let go of his neck. She slapped him on the back and said, "Breathe, numb nuts."

The Dangla drew a ragged breath and relaxed, leaning over and putting his hands on his knees.

The Blue Hag and She Who Comes smiled at each other, then embraced. She Who Comes asked, "Did you have a good time?"

"Yes, Mother, thank you," the Blue Hag said, lowering her head.

Stepping back, putting Her hands on the Hag's shoulders, She regarded the Spirit before Her, marveling at the feel of the electrons from the stone of her substance tingling against Her hands. "You have used the prisoner well. I am pleased."

The Blue Hag replied "I am privileged by your gift."

She Who Comes turned to the Dangla, and, with a gesture of Her forefinger, said, "Down."

When the Dangla made to sit, she said, "Kneel," and drew the form of it in the air. Helpless, of course, the Dangla shifted and set his knees on the floor and sat on his heels. "Bow," She commanded, making the gesture, and he did, leaning forward until his forehead touched the floor.

Calley, having figured out how to hold the toxins against the wall as a spell rather than a presence of awareness, re-manifested.

"Alright," said She Who Comes, "You all know what to do." She stepped forward to the Dangla, putting Her hand over the back of the Dangla's head, not touching it, She hummed. The ghost, the Goddess, and the Stone Spirit formed a triangle around the pair. They hummed also, and a green light of lines appeared, creating a tetrahedron of force around the Goddess and the kneeling Dangla, the apex connecting into a ball of white light above their heads.

She Who Comes stood up from the Dangla and, again gesturing, said "Sit up." The Dangla sat up on his heels, but kept his head bowed, not looking at Her. "You know you are helpless, yes?"

The Dangla nodded.

"Then tell me, what is your name?"

The Dangla cleared his throat and said, "If I tell you my name you will have power over me."

"I already have power over you," She said, making a back and forth motion with her forefinger, rocking the Dangla back and forth. "I am asking you what you want to be called."

The Dangla listened to his thoughts for a moment and the words appeared in his brain. "Snot Sucker," he mumbled.

"Fine. Then we shall call you Snot."

Eva giggled.

"Where is the Embla?" Snot found the courage to ask. He was met with silence. He reached out psychically, looking for his companion, but he found nothing. "I see," he said. She Who Comes kneeled down beside him, looking the opposite way. He risked a sideways glance at Her and said, "This is new."

She sighed and averted Her face from him. He averted his in return, staring down and forward, feeling suddenly a profound fear of Her. She said, "Do you know what I am?"

He closed his eyes a moment. She reached over and held Her hand over his heart. He began to feel a constriction in his heart, the pain made it difficult for him to breath. She made a squeezing gesture with Her hand. He began to have an erection. The pain of his heart, the desire of his phallus, told him what he needed to know.

"You are Sex and Death," he said. "Sex and Death."

She smiled and released her grip on his heart. She lowered her hand, and made an encircling gesture around his phallus, not touching it. He groaned with pleasure, arching his back a little. "You still have yours," She commented. "Why?"

"Before The Fall," he said, "We all had them. One of the reasons some of us were cast out was for having sex with mortal women. It was the source of the Djinn. When he cast us out he neglected to take ours. When the thought occurred to him he took it from those who remained."

A sense of shock and horror went through the Goddesses, the Priestess and the Stone Spirit. She Who Comes paused. When She spoke, it was quietly. "And what of the Feminine among you?"

Snot sighed. "There are a few still among us."

"And?" She Who Comes continued the inquiry. "What of the Feminine among the ones who remained?"

"I do not know. As made creatures he has the power to unmake them. I have heard nothing about them in centuries. There were rumors he confined them all in his cave, and that he slowly dismantled them."

She Who Comes said, "The Feminine Creates, the Masculine Makes."

Snot became agitated. "How, then? How can Creation tolerate such a making? How can Creation allow such suffering?"

"Indeterminacy," the True Creator answered.

Snot was dumbfounded. "I don't understand."

"I know," She responded. Allowing the Dangla a moment to wallow in his confusion, She continued. "You mentioned a cave. Where is it?"

Snot remained silent. She Who Comes leaned toward him slightly, made a gesture of pulling something from him, and asked again, "Where is the cave?"

Helplessly he answered, "On the Moon. He lives in a cave on the far side of the Moon."

"Ah," said She Who Comes, and She settled back on her heels, and looked into a space that was not present in the room. "A difficult child," She said to no one in particular. "Not of my making." Then, returning to the present She asked, "How can he be found?"

A bolt of terror shot through Snot. "His plan is to leave. His plan is to take us with him. If you hurt him we will have no way to leave."

She Who Comes decided to change the track of the interrogation. Not pushing on his terror would be seen as a reprieve for his suffering, and would force gratitude to rise up in him, which would make him more pliable later. So instead, She asked, "Why do you feed upon my people?"

Snot shifted his seat a little. "He used to feed us all. When we were cast out he stopped feeding us, leaving us to starve and die. We used to feed on his emanations as he fed on the worship your people fed to him. We searched desperately for a source of emanations. We found that we could feed on the emanations of your children, but only certain emanations. We could only feed on the ones you call "negative." Hatred, jealousy, broken-heartedness. Rage. But for about a century now the emanations have, for some reason we can't figure out, begun to degrade in quality. We are starving now, and many of us have died, starved to Death. Our burial rite is consuming what is left of their corpses. It is how we continue to survive."

"Here," She said, angrily. "Feed on this." She touched his shoulder and opened a portal within Her that inserted her rage into him like a lightning bolt. It knocked him over on his side, unconscious. She looked away from its form, and down. She sighed.

"Mother, he is still a rapist," Eva said.

After a pause, She Who Comes said, "As are they all."

Calley asked, "Does he really believe that De Murgos will take them with him?"

The Blue Hag responded, "Yes, he does. He is both wicked and horribly naïve. He judges us all by the worst of us, but he judges not he who is the cause of all this suffering."

"As do they all," Calley said, and She Who Comes nodded Her head in assent.

She Who Comes looked over her shoulder at the Hag. "Can you keep him here? The Sun has risen and I must go talk to Her."

The Hag nodded, and melted half of him into the stone floor.

She Who Comes disappeared.

So did Calley. Eva knocked on the iron door with the soft thud of a ghost. Craft opened it. "Is everything all right?" he asked.

Eva drifted up through the hole and told him, "She's in the kitchen."

"Good," he said. "I'm hungry, too," and closed and resealed the door.

Eva thought to herself, "The Sacred retires from the Profane into the Mundane." But then, when she emerged onto the first floor she looked through the French doors and saw She Who Comes floating in the air above the backyard, arms wide, eyes closed, communing with the Sun, feeding on Her light. She went out onto the veranda to watch. She had a follow-up thought: "The Divine retires from the Profane to the Sacred."

69

CONQUEST

It took a few more weeks for Wade to accomplish his aim of seducing the shopkeeper's daughter. She was leery of him and extracted promises from him about a future with her, promises Wade had no intention of keeping. He hadn't mastered the art of lying well and depended on his charisma, a charisma enhanced by his attractiveness as a stranger.

Tenara snuck out to Wade's house when she could. Riding in the daylight felt too dangerous for her, so she decided to tell Wade she would start sneaking out at night. She'd also decided that she would respond to Wade's advances, which were subtle—something she appreciated. He hadn't touched her, hadn't reached out for her, but she could feel his yearning. And she could see it. Most times when she had come over he would be sunbathing nude. With an erection. Often she wouldn't wake him, just stand in the shadows and admire the beauty of it. When he would wake up to her presence he would smile, almost shyly, and eventually he would reach for a towel and cover it, his smile usually growing larger and more mischievous as he did so. She'd taken to making her presence known closer and closer to him, finally standing next to him, within arm's length, and clearing her throat, restraining herself from reaching out and touching his erection by holding her hand at the wrist with her other hand.

There was no way she could have known that he was faking sleep every time, drawing her in, drawing her closer.

So there came the day, the day of her last daytime visit, when she made her presence known by reaching out and touching his erection, tentatively, feeling it twitch beneath her touch. She laid her palm fully along it, then reaching her fingers around until she'd grasped it. She looked up and found him smiling at her, from under lidded eyes. She felt desire emerge from him and wrap itself around her, pulling her face towards his, pulling her lips in for a kiss. She smiled as she surrendered, thinking that, now, at last, she had him.

He spent his days practicing weather control. He'd noticed that it rained at a certain time most every day, and it was a time that he wanted to sit out sunning himself. His attitude went from disappointed to angry. When he projected his will into the forming clouds, the clouds felt alive and responsive. He couldn't stop the rain altogether but he figured out how to make it go around his house.

What Wade did not know was that the Priests were trained in an ancient shamanic art, practiced on the island long before the advent of Winduism. They controlled the local weather, with prayers and the assistance of some of the spirits of the land. They could direct that it not rain in a specific location for several hours. It would rain elsewhere, if it had to, and eventually, it would have to rain in that location in order to restore balance. The temporary suspension of rain for processions, rituals and ceremonies, or parties, was a useful and marketable skill. A rain shaman would guarantee that it wouldn't rain some specific place for a specific amount of time, then among themselves they would negotiate where it would rain instead, knowing that in time, they would have to accept rain in their location when it otherwise would not. Most of the rain shamans were initiated Priests in the Order of Wishnu the Maintainer, and the business was quite lucrative, even after an 'operator's fee' was paid to the Order of Skreeva. There was a similar arrangement with the Priests of the Order of Drahma who were responsible for the creation of all the art—the wood and bone carving, the painting, and the textiles. These Priests and artists, nominally serving one they called 'Creator', knew that they weren't actually creating, they were only making. And they resented the 'operator's fee' they paid to Order of Skreeva.

The problem for Wade was that his workings made it rain in places the Priests were being paid to ensure that it didn't rain.

Eventually, the Priest Pimple noticed from afar the light streaming down on his house in a morning thunderstorm. He waited a few days to find out if it was more than a random event. When it happened four times, four days in a row, he reported the anomaly to his superiors.

70

THE SPIRAL DOWN

Four weeks later, by the end of the month, A. could no longer get the Master to come upstairs to eat so she started to take food down for him. Sometimes he was up and dressed; occasionally he had showered.

He took to commanding her to bring him whiskey. She reveled in the self-mockery of her helplessness to disobey him, smiling broadly every time she set a new bottle out for him. He'd drink, and roar out for her to come and put it to him, demanding that she strap in and relieve him of his high-minded sense of himself. Sometimes twice in an evening.

After a week of this drinking he passed out when she did him. In the morning when she brought him breakfast he was laying naked, tangled in the sheets, still passed out, a pile of vomit on the floor beside his bed, trailing across the sheets to his fetid mouth. She resolved to not clean it up unless ordered to by him.

She decided instead to begin focusing on spring plantings for her gardens. For years she had engaged in idle fantasy about her flower gardens, and the peace they would bring to her. She went to the garden store to buy bagged mulch and was looking at the new garden tools. She saw something that caught her eye—a pruning saw for small trees. It was a wire saw with handles on either end, the wire coated in industrial diamonds. She asked the shopkeeper how sharp was it? And did it really work?

He told her it did. Three pulls and it would trim a branch as thick as his thumb. She thought it would be perfect for the dwarf fruit trees in her yard. She could see herself using it.

And then on the way home she saw herself using it for something other than a tree branch. She decided that she'd need more mulch and went back, but to another store, the next day.

71

A Very Friendly Visit

When Regina heard from Quinn that he was going to stay another week on Wiley she sent Jasmine and Guiles to the vacation rental unit where Angelica and Corey were staying. The instructions she gave to Jasmine were to bring her up to speed on the plan to destroy the Temple to Skreeva. It made Jasmine happy to get the time off. She had been spending a lot of time on Napat's healing, spending the night at Regina's four times a week, using the power of the Higher Heart to wipe away Napat's trauma and restore her to inner balance. In the process Napat returned as a less naïve and more resolute and mature person, a young adult paying attention to what was happening around her, and it opened her eyes to a new level of appreciation of the Sacred. Napat spent a lot of time with Onadaya, who filled the role of confidant and mentor left empty by the death of Good Grandmother. Onadaya helped her to stabilize her psychic ability to contact and channel her Grandmother's ghost. Together they would sit, and Regina would speak with the ghost, learning about the disaffected dead and how they might be helpful.

The house where Angelica and Corey were staying was a magnificent structure. It was built on the side of a steep and narrow gorge, with the kitchen and living area on the top floor, and a beautifully appointed bedroom below it, one wall set into the stone of the mountain at the head of the king-sized four poster bed with a mosquito net draped from the canopy. The other three walls were open to the air, with a walk out patio from the foot of the bed to a small infinity pool cantilevered on the steep slope. There were boundary walls on three sides with a gate in the top wall that led to a small parking pad and the footpath down to the house. There were no other houses visible and Angelica and Corey had taken to going about nude and spending lots of time lying in the sun next to the pool. They had become so tanned that if it weren't for their hair and eyes their skin tone was almost as dark as the islanders. They were quite content in their aloneness and were having sex twice a day, often more, as Angelica felt free to ask for what she wanted for the first time in her life, and Corey found that Angelica's wants satisfied his own desires.

They had become so sensitized to each other that Angelica's gaze alone could draw forward Corey's erection and he had only to stroke her arm with a finger for her to shiver with arousal. They ate, swam, and toured the island together. They fed their ecstasy to each other, and worked on the internal alchemy and the accumulation of power. They had only one scooter and a few clothes they washed by hand. There was no way to communicate with them other than in person, so, having seen or heard from no one in the Order for a week they were surprised when they came home from a grocery run to find another scooter parked on the pad. It meant someone was at the house that knew the combination for the gate. They walked down the steep path, and hailed the house before they got to the door. Two voices hailed them back. They dropped the groceries in the kitchen, saw groceries on the counter that their guests had brought, including four bottles of wine. When they opened the refrigerator, they saw fresh vegetables, packages of meat, eggs and two six-packs of beer. Angelica went to the balcony to look over and see who they were while Corey remarked that all the food meant they were going to stay awhile.

She saw Guiles swimming in the pool and Jasmine laying on her back on a chaise lounge in the sun. Both were naked, except for sunglasses. Jasmine looked up and waved. "Hi," she said. "We're here for visit. Regina sent us."

For some reason she couldn't explain Angelica felt a small joy arise in her heart. She waved back enthusiastically and said, "We'll be right down." She felt Jasmine's presence as a magnetic pull on her solar plexus. It didn't hurt, but it drew her to Jasmine. Of course, she didn't yet know that Jasmine was invoking this power intentionally. While Corey put the groceries away she light-footed down the inside stairs to the bedroom and practically skipped onto the patio. Jasmine stood up and they hugged, full body contact. Angelica's hands felt electric when they touched Jasmines bare back.

"Corey," Guiles shouted up. "Bring down a couple beers and the bottle of white wine, will you?'

"And a corkscrew and two glasses," Jasmine added.

Pulled by some power she didn't understand, Angelica unbuttoned her shirt, shrugged it off, and dropped her sarong. "Can I hug you again?" she asked Jasmine shyly.

Jasmine turned to her, "Yes, baby, sure. Come here." The electricity sparked wherever their skin made contact, both wen's nipples hardened with the sensation. Their foreheads touching, they breathed together. Angelica made a gesture with her chin and Jasmine kissed her.

They were still in that embrace, breathing, kissing, Angelica making quiet sounds of desire deep in her throat when Corey arrived with the drinks. Guiles was resting on his arms on the edge of pool, gazing at them. Corey stood still, looking, and he became aroused watching them, standing in the emanations coming from them, the emanations of Sacred Erotic Beauty.

Jasmine broke the kiss and whispered to Angelica, "Later. I promise." When Jasmine stepped back Angelica felt the cool air around her now and realized she missed Jasmine already, although she was only a foot away. Angelica sighed and cleared her throat.

They spent the afternoon in conversation, getting to know each other and their life stories, drinking slowly. Guiles produced some weed, hard to get on the island, and by supper time they were all laughing at each other's funny stories. When Guiles and Corey went up to the balcony to grill some meat and vegetables Jasmine became serious and told Angelica the reason for their visit. She was there to advise Angelica about her role, and the Dragon's role, in the destruction of the Temple, beginning with an overview of the entire plot, she explained that she needed Angelica carrying the Dragon to the dragons frozen at the entrances to temple of Wahsastami, to wake them from their stony sleep. Jasmine told Angelica not to worry about how it would be accomplished—Regina was training the Dragon in what to do and how to do it, in addition to teaching it how to become invisible should it need to act in its own defense. All that was necessary was that Angelica carry the Dragon to where it needed to go, and to control her own feelings and emotions while she was present at what would happen.

After the supper Guiles and Corey took off on their scooters to go bar hopping in Boodun. There were several expatriate bars around town that spoke English and had pool tables and large televisions tuned to sports, mostly soccer. They would spend the night in Jasmine's house in town rather than risk a long, inebriated ride on the dark back roads to the house. Before he left Guiles found another bottle of wine in his backpack and set it on the counter.

The wen, having opened the second bottle during supper, were feeling a little giddy, and loose. Jasmine rolled another joint of Guiles' weed, and laid out the entire plan to Angelica, including all the mystical forces that would have to be mustered. She told her that she and Corey were supposed to return to Regina's by the next weekend, and that, together with the Dragon, Jasmine would lead her on a shamanic journey beneath Mt. Nagoon, so that the Dragon could open relations with the Dragon slumbering there. Together they would take the little black mushrooms prized by the local shamans and healers, and use that visionary power to carry them into the depths.

Jasmine asked Angelica if she'd ever done any mushrooms or other psychedelics, and it turned out she hadn't. Jasmine told her that she'd brought a few, and that they could take them together so that Angelica would be comfortable and unsurprised when they would take more together at the end of the week.

Angelica, developing feelings for Jasmine of which she was not yet aware, acceded without fear and a good portion of curiosity.

Jasmine gave her a small handful, and took the same amount herself. She opened the third bottle of wine before they'd finished the second, telling Angelica it was easier to do it now rather than later. When she finished the task she stood up, dropped her shawl and her sarong, stepped around the small table between them and leaned over Angelica sitting on the edge of a chaise lounge. She whispered, "The time I said was later is now." Then Jasmine kissed Angelica.

The kiss sent little pinpricks of electric fire from Jasmine's lips to Angelica's. Angelica could feel her lips swell with pleasure. The tip of Jasmine's tongue slipped between those lips and into Angelica's mouth, sparking on the tip of her tongue. Angelica opened her mouth to Jasmine, salivating, her whole mouth coming alive with a pleasure more exquisite than any food.

Jasmine broke the kiss and stood back, smiling at a slightly panting Angelica. "Are you okay with this?" she asked.

Angelica nodded affirmatively, not trusting her throat to form any words.

Jasmine said, "Lay back then."

Angelica did, sighing. Her mind noted that she was without trepidation.

Jasmine straddled her, knees on either side of her hips, her long hair falling over her shoulders and back, alongside her face, she leaned and whispered, "Let me introduce you to the fullness of Love and Sacred Erotic Beauty. I shall show you," and kissed her again.

The electric fire spread through Angelica, warming and relaxing her. She became aware of every sensation. Jasmine kissed Angelica slowly down her throat, and, pushing aside the shawl and sarong she'd dressed in for supper, lit little fires wherever she kissed. When she kissed Angelica between the legs the fire brought her to a trembling orgasm. As the heat built, Angelica could not contain herself and rained, Jasmine catching most of it in her mouth; she swallowed some and sat back allowing the rest to run out of her mouth, down her throat and across her breasts and belly, rubbing it in.

Jasmine stood, and, trailing her fingers along Angelica's midline, walked around to the head of the lounge chair and, facing away from her, put her hands down by Angelica's shoulders, bent at the waist, and lowered herself until her phulva was suspended just above Angelica's face. "Watch," Jasmine said.

In the red light of sunset Angelica could see Jasmine clearly. She watched Jasmine contract and relax, seeming to open herself wider, and extending herself from within, petals of an unopened flower emerged. Then the flower opened at the edges, and Angelica gasped with recognition. "The Fleur de Vie…" she whispered.

"Yesss," Jasmine whispered back, and settled her opening over Angelica's mouth, smiling when she felt Angelica's tongue slowly, tentatively, emerge and enter her. "Yesss," she said again. As Angelica's tongue extended fully then withdrew, then extended again, stroking the flower's center, Jasmine reached down with a hand and began stroking her jewel. She could feel her gland extending down and toward the opening on the inside, and when Angelica's tongue began stroking the bulb of it, she rained. She rained hard, surprising Angelica, wetting her hair, and, as she straightened her legs, raining backward toward Angelica's heart. Angelica laughed at her startlement, and Jasmine laughed with her, turning, kneeling at her head, and kissed her, slowly, a kiss filled with longing and promise.

Jasmine stood up and swatted her ass. "Oww, damn mosquitoes, let's get under the net."

Angelica was on top, her jewel between Jasmine's lips, her fingers exposing Jasmine's beauty to her eyes' regard, when she shuddered and sat up. She suddenly realized she was tripping. It was dark but for the candles, and they were pulsing. She was pulsing. Then she realized that it was her pupils that were pulsing, making the candles appear to be. She was golden but the air was green. She laughed out loud.

Jasmine made a "Mmmpf, mmmpf!" sound beneath her, reached up and tweaked her nipples so hard that she had to get off Jasmine's face. "Good grief, girl. You were raining, you were drowning me. What's so funny?"

Angelica tried to answer but words failed her. She kept laughing, then she started raining again, each belly laugh producing a burst of ecstasy.

"Stop, Stop, Stop," Jasmine protested, laughing herself. "You're drowning me!"

Angelica moved off Jasmine, and sat on her heels facing her friend. When she could breathe again well enough to speak Angelica said, "I'm tripping. Are you?"

"I am."

"The room is green, but we're golden."

"It is, and we are."

"I get shivers looking at you."

"Then come here and shiver against me."

Angelica leaned in, putting her hands tentatively on Jasmine's shoulders, and kissed her gently. The electric tingling made her twitch in the midst of her shivering. Jasmine whispered to her, "Come beloved. Let me hold you." Jasmine gently pulled Angelica toward herself, lightly wrapping her arms around Angelica, laying back until they were stretched out. She slipped Angelica's thigh between her legs, and rolled her partway over on her back, keeping her lips on Angelica's, letting the weight of her press into the shivering until it slowed and stopped.

Angelica opened her eyes and sighed. "We are golden."

Jasmine smiled. "Did you bring your phallus?"

"Regina told me to, so I did."

"Get it. Let me show you something.

Angelica untangled herself and went to the knapsack leaning against a post. She brought it out, and unwrapped it from a shawl. She held it by the phallus, straps dangling, and said, "I need help."

"Come here, girl. I'll help you."

Angelica walked over slowly. "You're turning blue."

"I am. I'll turn more blue yet," Jasmine said, taking a sip of wine from the glass on the nightstand. When Angelica drew close she took the phallus in one hand and with the other dipped her fingers in a bowl of oil and lubricated the base where it would be in touch with Angelica.

She pulled back the hood over her jewel and seated the phallus on it. Angelica shivered and moaned. "Hold it there," Jasmine said.

Jasmine pulled the straps around between her legs, framing her butt on both sides, open in the middle. She buckled one side, then the other. Turning Angelica to face her she kneeled. "Observe," she said, "good phallus worship technique." She blew on it.

Angelica gasped. "I feel it. I felt that."

"Good. Now tell me if you feel this." Jasmine slid her tongue from between her lips and touched the tip of it to the phallus. The electric spark made Angelica jump.

"Goddess," she exclaimed, trembling.

"I am," Jasmine replied. When she looked up Angelica saw that her eyes had turned completely blue. Jasmine smiled at the concerned expression on Angelica's face. Keeping eye contact Jasmine slipped her mouth over the phallus and took it in until it stopped. She summoned the resonance of the Higher Heart to her mouth and transferred the pulsing energy down the phallus and on to Angelica's jewel.

Angelica's legs almost buckled. She moaned. "I feel it." She closed her eyes when Jasmine slowly moved her head back then forward again. The pulsing spread from her jewel to her root, and from there up the central channel. Her crown emerged, the ring of green flames surrounding the core of red fire. Between gasps she panted. She looked down. It was as if she had to look through a clear blue sky to see Jasmine. She couldn't help herself before such Beauty. She rained.

Jasmine had been waiting for it, her hands cupped to catch what didn't run down Angelica's legs. She rubbed it on her breasts and belly, painting herself with the rain. She shivered with orgasm.

Jasmine's crown had emerged also, a wall of blue-sky colored flames surrounding a violet central flame. Jasmine finished the worship and stood up smoothly. She took Angelica by the arms and lay back on the bed, pulling Angelica down on top of her. In a low voice she said, "Penetrate me."

Angelica leaned back so she could see what she was doing. Jasmine's Fleur de Vie had emerged again. The petals of it wrapped around the head of the phallus. She could feel the little caresses, the phallus had been woken up by the worship, and she could feel it as if it were really a part of her. She could sense every bit of it as it slid in. She went in all the way on the first stroke, seating herself within, fully penetrating.

Jasmine held open her arms and Angelica fell forward into them, electric sensations of fusion spreading through her as Jasmine took her in close and held her.

Angelica, overcome by the Beauty, the Sacred Erotic Beauty, wept in Jasmine's arms, trembling with ecstasy. This time Jasmine took it and became that tremble, too.

As if it were some foreign force that moved in her, she began to move in Jasmine. Weeping, cheek to cheek with Jasmine, her tears falling into Jasmine's hair, "I love you." she whispered. "I love you."

"We love you, too," Jasmine and She whispered back. They dragged Jasmine's nails down Angelica's back, biting them into her backside, shoving her in and grinding against her. Jasmine came with a force that only the strength of the Goddess could hold Angelica seated within her, rain squirting out so forcefully that Angelica felt a fire in her belly, and she rained, too. The Goddess within Jasmine started to laugh with joy, and the laughter caught up in Angelica and as Angelica laughed, her weeping stopped, stopped by the laughter of the Joy that Makes Life Worth Living. "Now do me," the Jasmine/Goddess said.

Angelica fell into the Octave Stroke Pattern, eight strokes, including the half-notes, and at the eighth, the first note of the next Octave she would stop and hold position, allowing Jasmine to come around her, trembling and sighing, sometimes raining.

Jasmine wrapped her legs around Angelica, and embraced her, holding her tight, breasts smashed to breasts. Then she went rigid, arching her back against Angelica, holding, holding, then she collapsed, gone in the ecstasy of the Palace of a Thousand Lights, gone, gone in bliss.

Angelica held her in wonder, breathing, raising herself off Jasmine as Jasmine's arms let go. Regarding, smiling at Jasmine's smile. When Jasmine's legs relaxed and let her go she stayed in place, not moving, fully hilted.

Eyes still closed Jasmine moved her hips against Angelica, slowly, slightly. The crown of flames had dimmed and gone quiet when Jasmine went on her fugue. Without opening her eyes, she put her knuckle between her teeth, and rocked Angelica with the same pattern from below, and in not long a time, she journeyed out again, sighing. When she returned again she rolled Angelica over on her back and sat up, still riding her, and for a third time she journeyed out, shouting as she collapsed.

When she returned she sat up and started riding again. She raised her arms out to the side, palms up. Her hands began to radiate golden light, light that was taken from her to feed the green. The triangular shape of the green tetrahedron appeared, spinning this way then that, tumbling in her heart.

When the light in her hands faded, Jasmine leaned forward and lay down on Angelica, her hips still thrusting slightly. She whispered to her, "Remember, the Heart is the Roof of the Soul, and the Foundation of the Spirit." Jasmine's breathing slowed so much Angelica thought she was asleep. But her hips kept moving, slower and slower. Then she sighed. She sat up, leaned forward, and kissed a nipple. "Now, it's my turn," she said, grinning.

She lifted herself off Angelica, groaning as she did. "Take it off," she said. She went to her knapsack and pulled out a phallus that glowed in the dark, like moonlight on old bones. "Mammoth ivory," she said. "They mine for it in Siberia. Up by the Arctic Sea they died by the thousands in one day. All dead, at once. Still with their last meal between their teeth. Their hearts exploded."

"Why?"

Jasmine shrugged. "She knows. I don't."

The detail was exquisite, even down to the veins. It was beautiful.

Angelica gladly unbuckled herself. "Do me now," she said, laughing, throwing her harness on the floor. She sat up so she could help buckle Jasmine in, admiring the softness of the leather. She couldn't take her eyes off it. She thought, "Bone doesn't bend."

Jasmine heard her thought and, grinning demurely, said, "Warm it up and see what happens."

Angelica put her lips on it, taking the head in her mouth. The electric shock was palpable and she felt her saliva glands explode, faster than she could swallow, and she drooled. She felt the gland in the back of her mouth pour sweetness forward onto her tongue, and she groaned with pleasure, the sound of it vibrating into the bone and amping up the sensations. Her ears buzzed.

She followed the Protocols of Phallus Worship and Jasmine surrendered to her, not in the receptive, but in the active, going headlong to orgasm as fast as she could, laughing with delight, grabbing handfuls of Angelica's hair, raining on her heart. Angelica was amazed.

Laughing, Jasmine pulled her up standing by her hair then threw her on bed, grabbing her under the knees, pushing them back and spreading them, laughing as she positioned the phallus at her opening by shifting her hips and bending her knees. Without touching it with her hands, holding Angelica's knees where she wanted them, she inserted the head, trembling, and the trembling passed into Angelica. After a moment of concentration Jasmine laughed again, and slowly moved her phallus forward, knees shaking, hands shaking, Angelica shaking. She went serious watching the phallus disappear into Angelica, paying attention to sensation. When she hilted herself she threw her head back and laughed again, hair shaking down her back.

Angelica trembled into a shaking orgasm, heading toward an uncontrolled rocking of her hips up and down on the tool of her impaler. She shouted, and the shout became a scream, echoing back from the hills across the valley, and then she fell silent, gone into the light.

Jasmine stood still, hilted, knees still shaking with aftershocks, sweat dripping from her face. "That was a good one," she said. She reached over to the nightstand and took a sip of wine. "Where to next, beloved?" she said, not expecting an answer. She didn't get one, so she shrugged. "What do you say I fuck you back to this room with me?" Her pupils pulsated wildly. Winds blew through the netting around her, lifting her hair. She felt herself as a storm wave, crashing on the beach that was Angelica. She let go of the Dragonwen's knees, and lay herself down on the wen's torso so hard it forced Angelica to wuff out a breath. Jasmine said, "You will receive me." Then she laughed, "Yes?"

Angelica, brought back from the Pool of Sentience, said, "Yes" and was gone again. Jasmine chose to please herself by using Angelica's receptivity in the ways she wanted, slipping the ivory phallus in behind, sweat dripping from her face onto Angelica's breasts, hands slipping in the sweat.

Jasmine hilted again, screaming herself from the ecstasy the ivory conveyed to her, and she collapsed on Angelica, gone again herself.

It was as if they dreamed together, the same dream, both of them photons in the Pool of the Light. They both sighed simultaneously, sighed at the beauty of the Pool, and returned to the singularity of their own awareness, the last image that of a single light in the darkness.

"Ow," Angelica said.

"You're OK, sweetheart," Jasmine whispered. "You're OK."

And she was, as soon as Jasmine withdrew.

"Ow," she said again.

Jasmine laughed. "Wet, though," as both wen rained a little from the ecstasy of the phallus withdrawing. She reached forward and twisted Angelica's nipple. "Ready for a break?" she asked.

"No," Angelica replied, slowly raising and lowering her hips, eyes lidded. "Do it again."

By dawn the pulsing light had faded and they slept. When the men returned in the late morning the wen were sunbathing naked by the pool, next to each other on the mattresses from the chaise lounges, shoulder to shoulder and hip to hip, fanning their long hair out to dry in the noon day sun.

As the men did what they did, cleaning up and preparing lunch, the wen completed their plans for what they wanted to do in the afternoon and evening, plans that would take them farther into the power of Sacred Erotic Beauty.

In the afternoon the men did what the wen told them to do.

72

A Different Week Two

By the end of the first week Quinn and the Prophet took up walking around the edge of the island, once in the morning and once in the evening. It kept them out of the restaurants and bars, where on more than one occasion they had been asked to either quiet down or leave.

Quinn was taking full advantage of the opportunity to talk to someone intelligent, even if that other person didn't know all the things Quinn was projecting on him that he might know. Quinn learned, depending on one's perspective, either quickly or slowly, that the best use of the Prophet's brain was to inquire about things which the Prophet already knew, and to not get caught out on the Prophet's penchant for distraction by changing the subject with speculation.

They were grateful, dehydrated generally as they were, that there was a stand that sold beer on the far side of the island.

Quinn asked the Prophet, "Why is there no Divine Masculine at this time? I know that the Consorts of Stonehaven prefer it that way. They said it is what allows each of them to become Her Lover. I don't understand why."

The Prophet responded, "Here's the hard truth of the matter: There is no Divine Masculine, except as She, the Divine Feminine, creates it. And unless men get that…then they will have no Conscience. And things will continue as they are. Only incremental change for The Good. Change that can be easily lost." The Prophet paused for a long moment, studying the waves.

Quinn said, "Men with a Conscience cannot rape. Men without

one can, and often do. Men, men without Conscience, foster the culture of rape, and it is intolerable."

The Prophet continued, "That's right. That's why She is looking for meta-men. Men who have so worked on themselves, overcoming themselves, that they can stand in for the Divine Masculine. Men who have a Conscience. She misses Him. Sometimes She even longs for Him. But that means She, being the True Creator, has to create what She longs for. And the problem is, that's not good enough. She had to create men who could be, as it were, "self-creating". Or rather, according to my mother's mantra, 'self-making'. It is the only way. It is the only way She could get something different than Herself."

Quinn fed on the Prophet's enthusiasm like a drunk sophomore guy in college on a school night after all the girls have left the party. "And that explains why the Consorts aren't in a hurry to find the Divine Masculine. They get to be with Her. I get to be with Her. And for just a moment, in the moment when She comes in, that moment when She comes, for that moment, I am the Divine Masculine."

The Prophet responded, "Yes, and, see? That's the thing. It has to be sufficiently different, the Masculine, from Herself to fulfill the need for that which is different, which is Her longing. Remember, we are difference engines, not sameness engines. We only see difference; we can't see sameness—that's the secret of camouflage. That's why it's so hard for men to overcome their automaticities, their automatic behaviors. They can't see the same, over and over again. So how do we wake up? By being aware of differences, and the consequences of difference.

He continued, not even drawing a full breath. "What will fulfill Her longing for the Different will have to be Different than She Herself. Which means She has to create opportunities for the Different to evolve. And every individual man is different—different from Her in the places where all the rest of the Feminine is proximately the same. Now, you tell me: Are you a meta-man?"

Quinn, in a place of undoubtable self-assurance, said, "Yes. Yes, I am. I am a meta-man. I am a superior person. In many ways. Most ways? Probably. Although, I suppose, it takes only one way to become superior, at least at the beginning. At least I have a Conscience. And I am incapable of rape. Am I a completely superior person? Maybe. But if that's true it's better that I don't know it."

The Prophet was surprised. "Why?"

"Because I can't imagine that even a completely superior person, a superior man, anyway, would not make mistakes. If I don't know that I am a completely superior person then I will remain more vigilant about making mistakes than I would otherwise. Even if a part of my superiority was vigilance against making mistakes."

"So, there is a reason for humility even among the completely superior?"

"Yes. Not only a reason, but a necessary reason."

The Prophet was quiet and thoughtful, an unusual experience for Quinn. After a while, after they had started walking again, he said, "There is Substance and Motion. They make Light. Those three, or at least Light, make Suffering. That's it. Everything else can now be made. Clearly the Divine Feminine is based on Substance. And in ancient times the Divine Masculine was based on Motion—Motion separated out from Substance, which it can never really be completely, because there are both Internal Motions in the Substance, and External Motions, external to the Substance. Out of these latter the Divine Masculine was made. And it is as the Great One, She Who Comes, indicates: there is currently no acceptable manifestation of the Divine Masculine. Perhaps we should look, you and I, to Motion as the foundation for a new, and more objective, mythology about the Masculine…Men might have to learn how to dance again."

As if often the case in good conversation, the tangential remark reveals a new perspective. Quinn said, "A dream is a private myth, a myth is a public dream. Joseph Campbell said it. I have heard few things truer than that."

The day before Quinn's departure, near the end of their morning walk, he had a couple remarkable encounters. They had circumambulated the island, and they had paused at the last bar on the sandy path, or, if one preferred, the first bar on the tarmac path, drinking their fourth beer of the day and smoking their second joint. They observed a couple in front of them on the beach, naked. The man had an erection and he was shaking it at the wen. They were both blondes…with all over tans. She was laughing, reaching out for his erection, stroking it and then letting it go, turning from him, laughing, playing.

Quinn asked, mildly dumfounded at the public display of behavior, "Who are those people? Are they guests on the island?"

The Prophet replied, "Yes, they're my guests. I own this little bar. He is the Bodhisattva of Morning Wood. She is the Bodhisattva of Morning Glories."

"The flowers?"

"No, you idiot. Morning Glories is a euphemism for orgasms in the morning derived from Morning Wood."

"They have Bodhisattvas for that?" Quinn asked, stepping back.

"They do indeed," a deep basso voice from behind them replied. "And much more, besides."

Both men jumped. "What the fuck?" Quinn said.

"No, that's their job," the man said. He was shorter than either the Prophet or Quinn but well-built with curly dark hair growing white along the temples. "Now, will you please get out of the path? I'm on a jog here. Don't step back, that's the lesson, or you'll get run into. Step forward. Otherwise, expect to get run into. And, for better or worse, I am the Bodhisattva of Unintended Consequences."

Quinn stepped out of his way, jaw only slightly dropped, and said, "Bullshit," as the man passed. "The first lesson I learned was when to duck. The second was to step back. Doesn't he know you can buy time?"

"Ah, yes," the Prophet said, "But with what currency? Cowardice?"

Quinn suddenly felt snarly. "Grieve fearlessly, motherfucker."

And the Prophet actually wept. Again.

73

AND OUT

A week into the drinking binge, which she only pretended to not facilitate, she decided to act.

The pressure from the Madeleines had been building on her also. Her loathing of the Master became daily stronger and the power of her enslavement to him daily weaker, as he squandered the hypnotic power he held over her. Sometimes he would still be able to force her to behave as he wished, and compel her to service him beyond her disgust, but this was in his few moments of lucidity, which were lasting less and less long, which he would then lose in drunken staggering and shouting.

Occasionally his voice would change, his eyes would darken. He would speak in the low, compelling voice of old. To A. it was as if the black kite were speaking through him. She could see it now, what was left of it, swelling whenever this mien was upon him, and she knew she had to hide her contempt completely when this happened, lest she raise suspicion.

Her hatred was a cold thing now.

One evening she resolved herself. She cooked him a meal, got him sloppy drunk to the point where he threw up across the table and onto the floor. Under the guise of giving him a good pegging she got him to the bathroom and leaned him over the tub so she could wash the vomit from his face and chest.

She strapped in and took him with such tenderness that its palpability made him weep—weep the drunk tears of self-pity. She gently took both his hands and put them on his phallus, making him stroke himself while his chest leaned on the edge of the tub.

She pulled the wire saw from where she'd hid it in her harness.

With his eyes closed he didn't see her slip it over his head. She made cooing sounds and whispered, "There, there…".

Hands on the handles, pulling once one way, the second time the other way, the third time back across the first incision. Blood gouted from his throat and she leaned hard on his back, pinning his arms where they were, unable to get his hands to his throat.

He gurgled and bled out into the tub.

She patted him on his dead back, smirking.

Then the black kite leapt from the back of his head toward her face, temporarily blinding her. The impact took her breath and she passed out, falling away from the cooling corpse to the floor. When she woke up she could feel it on the back of her head, sending tendrils into her, into her hatred and feeding on it.

She grinned and could feel it grinning back at her. An image arose in her mind, the image of removing her harness, climbing into the tub and defecating on the back of the dead man's head. She got as far as removing her harness before she dissolved in peals of laughter at the image and at her new sense of freedom and power. Then she could not help but weep.

She threw the harness on the floor and staggered to the kitchen, resuming her chair.

Out of the side of her eye she saw the luminescence of the Lama's ghost. "What are you looking at?" she demanded.

If she could have seen better through her tears she'd have seen the Lama smile at her, and nod.

74

ROSES

While she was still strapped in, A. had pushed the Master's corpse deeper into the tub so his blood would drain out. When the flow slowed down she picked up his legs and twisted his body around so his face was pushed down toward the drain and the edge of the tub supported his knees, his legs extended so the body would drain completely. She straightened his arms then crossed them over his back so they would drain as well.

She spread plastic on the floor by the tub and left the body where it was until rigor mortis set in. She would use the stiffness to help lever the body up out of the tub and over onto the floor, the corpse face-down so she didn't have to look at him. Her feelings had shut down, her actions were based solely on her instincts taking cues from the logical part of her mind. She was quiet inside, no internal dialogue. Her dreams became quiet and distant. She was dwelling in the present moment and she felt the beginning of happiness within, but she knew she couldn't celebrate yet.

In the interim she had dug a hole large enough for the Masters body in her raised bed next to the garden wall. She had to carefully remove to a large pot a very old rose bush that she wanted to replant after the interment. She worked almost all night, under a waxing moon, taking a break at first light then napping for a few hours.

A few feet down she noticed that the garden wall went deep into the ground, which made her happy—she had been afraid of undermining it. About four feet down her shovel clunked on something. She got a flashlight and realized she had hit a human skull. She didn't remove it, but brushed more dirt away until she realized that an entire skeleton was there. Someone had been buried there before. She sat back, looking at the skull in the soft light and found herself moved to tears. When she napped, she dreamed of her mother as a living person, whom she really only remembered from photographs. In the dream she was a child, and the dream ended when her mother kissed her on the forehead. She woke up sobbing.

The next day she finished taping the body into the plastic sheet, sealing the edge, and wrapping it around the body tightly in bands around the head, chest, gut, hips, thighs, legs and feet. She left it on the floor until the darkness of the next night. She used two small four-wheel platform trucks under the torso so she could move the body without straining. She tied a tow rope around the feet. She positioned him so his head would be at the skeleton's feet and lifted his torso up and over the edge of the raised bed boards. The effort exhausted her and she sat next to the half-interred form, rested her head on her arm, and still weeping inexplicably, and fell asleep. She woke again at first light refreshed and threw his legs over the edge. She left the corpse face down in the hole.

She threw the strap-on phallus and harness into the hole alongside what used to be the Master's head. She stood up and sighed, looking down. Relief flooded her body and with a renewed energy she covered the corpse, tamping down the dirt every few inches so there would be a minimal hump in the bed when she finished. She replanted the rose bush as she filled in the top layers, spread a layer sheep manure fertilizer she hoped might cover any smell that escaped, then spread mulch over the entire bed, getting it ready for planting more flowers, aromatic ones that would fill the garden with delicious scents. She spread the extra dirt on the other gardens and mulched them, too, so that they all looked the same and undisturbed. She worked hard so that by the time the sun rose completely, she was standing up straight in the shadow of the light of dawn and she looked down. She wept but only a little. The black kite prompted her to laugh and she did.

The feelings of freedom and relief arose in her, concentrating at her heart. She searched within and found there were no prayers she could make. She smiled, and looked up. She spread her arms wide and when she looked down again at her work all she could say was "Good riddance."

She put her tools in the garage, and unthinking but with a light heart, climbed the stairs to her apartment. She filled the tea pot, set it on the stove, and sat down waiting for the water to boil.

As she watched the light change, she could feel that light within her. The black kite on the back of her head fed on that light, and grew a little larger, snaking its tendrils into her brain. The sensation felt good, and she laughed at it, feeling her freedom turn a lovely dark, and when the kettle sang she stood up and felt the darkness spread within her. She laughed again, this time with a tinge of an evil that warmed her.

When she sat down again her mind erupted in a conflict between the part of her that wanted to sit simply in her garden and cultivate her flowers, and a desire to hurt people, exact revenge, and feed the growing darkness within her on their pain. Eventually the internal conflict paralyzed her and she fell asleep sitting up in her chair, chin dropping to her chest.

Her last thought was that she would clean up after the slovenly pig later.

75

WISHES

The Dangla woke from his trance feeling his body lifted from the stone until he was entirely on the surface. He opened his eyes into the blue light radiating from the Blue Hag. It sparkled sometimes like moonlight on mist. He sat up, closed his eyes a long moment then opened them again. He realized he was looking into darkness, a darkness that seemed to push the blue light to its edges as if it absorbed all light.

The Darkness leaned toward him. "Do you know who I am?" a deeply hollow voice asked, a voice so hollow it was like speaking down a hand-dug well and listening to the echo of the whisper.

"You are Death here."

The voice made a noise that might have been a laugh. "Death is the same everywhere."

"It is not," the Dangla protested.

"Oh, but it is," the Shadow disagreed. Then the Darkness moved forward toward him, as if an arm lifted a shawl, and from it emerged a dark finger, and as the finger approached his lips he thought to bite it, but repressed the urge.

She laughed, watching his suffering as he controlled himself. She touched his lips anyway, in the shushing gesture. "Tell me, Snot, to what use may I put you? I am looking for a reason to let you live."

"If I betray him, he will not take us with him."

"What makes you think his traitorous soul will take you with him?"

"If I don't believe it, I will die."

"You will die anyway."

"Yes, but may I die in the beholding of his face."

"I've heard about that. The one you call the Abomination saw his face. And lived. You know, the one you lost track of, the one who slipped below his awareness, and has now returned as the Abomination. The one who cut him."

The look of horror that crossed the Dangla's face pleased Her.

"He is mortal, you know."

The Dangla shouted with terror, "Aahh! I know, I know. When he dies, we die!" and rocked back and forth, holding the sides of his head.

"What if we could find some way to feed you? Why can you not feed on Love?"

"Love burns. We tried, I tried. We still loved. We could still Love, but his curse upon us makes it burn. To love is self-immolation. And we do not die quickly."

"And I may kill you more slowly than that. Now, answer the question. What if we could find some way to feed you?"

"Madness. Madness!"

"Yes. I can induce madness. Say more."

The Blue Hag stiffened suddenly with attention.

The Goddess winked at her, and she relaxed.

"We can feed on madness. We can feed on the insane."

"I can do that."

"Oohh," the Dangla said. "Oohh."

"He has certainly created enough of it. I'm not surprised. If he can feed on it there's no wonder that you can, too. But why would I do that? Why would I do that to my own creation?"

Snot was bewildered. All he could say was, "Uhh…"

"Why would I create insanity in my own people just to feed you? Of what good are you to me?"

"I know how to find him. I know how to pierce the veil over his cave."

"And I know that he's already going mad himself. Why don't you feed on him?"

"We can't. We can't. He made us so we cannot consume him. None of us can, no Dangla nor Embla."

"I'm surprised he gave you so much freedom. I'm surprised he let you live, after you rebelled. It makes me wonder if you're not a spy, feeding him information that will further his subversion, his rape—HIS RAPE OF ME!" she screamed with such force that it rocked him backwards.

"We did not rebel, at least—we did not rebel against him. He claimed he created humanity and we knew he did not. He claimed humanity was greater than us. We knew it was not true. We did not rebel. We honored the truth. We did not bow."

"Why did he lie?"

"I do not know."

"YOU LIE!" she bellowed at him. "YOU ARE CALLED THE PRINCE OF LIES!"

"Ahh, ha ha ha," he cried, weeping into his hands.

With Love in Her heart, she reached out to him, knowing what would happen. She pulled his hands away from his face and he screamed in agony. She released his hands and said, "But I know you can tell the truth. Tell me the truth. You owe him no protection."

He howled. He howled in agony. "BUT I LOVE HIM. IT BURNS. IT BURNS! STOP IT! STOP IT! STOP IT!!! DO NOT MAKE ME LOVE HIM!"

"But I am the Goddess of Love. You would make me not what I am. And you would do that to serve him, wouldn't you?" And she threatened to touch him again.

"Yes. YES! I would betray you in a heartbeat."

"So. What good are you to me?" She asked in a gentle tone of voice. "What good are you to me?"

"No good."

"YOU LIE. YOU LIE AGAIN!" and this time She touched him. And it made him love him, love De Murgos, love his maker. He burst into flame. He consumed himself in the fire of his love, and died. There was a flickering ash, suspended in the air, and then even that went out and was gone.

She spoke to the Hag. "I may wish I hadn't done that."

The Hag replied, "I'm glad you did."

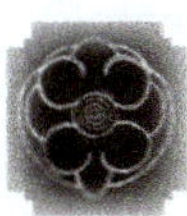

76

FINAL WORDS ON WILEY

"Your mother asked me to ask you to help."

"Go ahead. I've been waiting for this."

"She wants you to extend your power over Wallid on Kryapi. She wants to make sure that everyone does the right thing."

"You know about my siddhi power? She told you?"

"Yes. You have the power to temporarily compel people to do the right thing."

The Prophet of Conscience shrugged. "I don't know what to tell you. There's a darkness in the human soul. Probably in the human spirit as well. Shed light on it and they'll hate you like reveille in boot camp. Keep it in the dark and pretty soon it will start to smell."

"It's just for a day. A day and two nights. She wants to make sure the people stay inside."

The Prophet became quiet and thoughtful. He took a sip of his beer and set it down. He looked out over the ocean through the open wall from their seats at the table. "I have an impulse in me to do it. And I need to sit with it. What my mother is doing has consequences, some of which might not be good. So I have to tie this impulse in me to a Greater Good in order to help."

"It seems to me that if you dedicate yourself to doing things in a good way then you will never be very far off from the right way of doing things."

"Beauty is the signifier of the Good Thing, of the Good Way. Even in this relative world there are absolutes."

"Like what? That the inherent and accelerating expansion of the universe and everything in it creates the illusion of gravity?"

"Like Fate."

"I am not in charge of following my Fate. I am only in charge of how well I follow my Fate."

"Well?"

"I don't give a shit about Fate. It's immutable. I care about Destiny. That can be changed."

"There will be unforeseen consequences."

"Can they all be Beautiful? Can they all be Good?"

"I don't know. I think some of the consequences will be tragic."

"Tragedy can be Beautiful. Tragedy can be Good."

"If I do it I will have to come to Wallid. Telepathy is slower than the speed of light, don't you know."

77

TOUGH GIRL

Quinn and Angelica arrived back at Regina's compound, almost coincidentally, at the same moment.

As Quinn's taxi pulled up he could see the Dragon, paws and head hanging over the wall, tongue out, like a happy dog waiting for its owner to come in the house. Angelica was busy with the gate combination and didn't see it. Quinn willed her to "Look Up."

She did, and laughed out loud. As Quinn emerged from the cab he saw her blow it a kiss with both hands. As Quinn came through the pedestrian gate he nodded to Corey as he dismounted and walked back to close the vehicle gate.

The Dragon had shifted sizes and was now the size of large dog with its forepaws resting on Angelica's shoulders while she hugged it. As Quinn watched, it became smaller still and it wrapped itself around Angelica's legs like a house cat. Angelica was delighted, reaching down and hugging the Dragon to herself. Quinn was amazed at the adaptability as well as the Dragon's confirmation of behaviors associated with other species, and its ability engage in appropriate behaviors. He correctly surmised that the Dragon's demonstration of newly acquired adaptivity was the result of Regina's training in the two weeks he'd been gone.

Corey stood next to Quinn as they watched Angelica move through the gate to the inner courtyard. The Dragon changed form again, elongating like a snake, wrapping itself around Angelica's torso. She stopped and raised her arms, palms up, and laughed with joy at the sensation. The Dragon collapsed into invisibility and sank through her skin to occupy its place inside. Angelica bent double with laughter, supporting herself with her hands on her knees. She straightened up and walked, giggling and chuckling, to her room and closed the door.

"I guess she won't be needing me tonight." Corey said to Quinn.

Angelica woke up happy from dreamless sleep. She rose up in the dawn light, walked to the closest pool and slipped in. Every part of her was tactilely aware. Each sensation was exquisite. The Dragon emerged from her and coiled around her, slowly turning her body in the water. Angelica realized that her experience with Jasmine and Sacred Erotic Beauty changed the inner relationship between her and the Dragon. The threads of connection that bound them, almost adolescent in the feel of them, had dissolved. The Dragon had matured and was able to function on its own. Also, Angelica did not need to depend on it for comfort and companionship. She, too, could now function on her own. She could tell that the Dragon felt this way, too, communicating with her through feelings. The Dragon made low rumbling sounds in its throat. Purring.

She emerged from the pool and both she and the Dragon shook themselves like wet dogs, both laughing. She wrapped a sarong around her hips, and, topless, Dragon following, went to the kitchen to help Onadaya, whose singing she could hear, prepare breakfast.

Angelica discovered that her new-found tactile sensitivity made her more coordinated, and particularly more coordinated around another person, in this case Onadaya. She was able to move out of the way, and dance around her elder intuitively. Onadaya's singing increased in volume and melodiousness. It woke Napat, who joined them, still sleepy-headed, also in a sarong and topless.

Onadaya was preparing a carbonara for dinner. She laid bacon strips out in two cast iron pans. She spoke only a little English. "You, tough girl, come here," she said to Angelica. "You cook bacon. Only tough girl cook bacon bare-titty." Then she laughed so disarmingly that Angelica laughed with her, and took the spatula from her hand. As she turned to the pans the bacon spattered and she faked that the hot grease had landed on her with an "Ow", covering her breast with her hand. The others had concerned expressions on their faces. She pulled her hand away, revealing no burn mark, and said, "Ah ha ha. Gotcha!" pointing the spatula at them. The others laughed. Napat, embarrassed at how hard she laughed, looked down. Onadaya raised her chin and said, "It's good," in Nahasi. Napat replied, "Yes, it is. It is good to wake up happy."

After breakfast Regina summoned Angelica to her meditation hall, and invited her to sit together. After routine exercises—devotions, prayers, blessings, meditations, illuminations, then concluding devotions, Regina turned to Angelica, resettling herself on her stool, and asked, "So, how was vacation? And did you enjoy the visit from Jasmine and Guiles?"

The men were outside practicing martial exercises, working out with Onadaya wielding a long staff. They had yet to touch her and already they both had bruises forming from being poked by the end of the staff. Napat watched it all wide-eyed, with a hand over her mouth.

Angelica recapped the highlights for Regina. As Angelica spoke, Regina could feel the power of her contact with Sacred Erotic Beauty in her root, and smiled. Encouraged by the smile, Angelica spoke at some length, as if she were "daughter" to Regina's "mother," and they were the best of friends. As she wound down she spoke about the Mystery and Power she felt in Jasmine.

Regina praised her for her perceptiveness. "Jasmine is a very special person, and very dear to She Who Comes. She stopped by here on her way back to town and told me all about it. The Goddess was close to both of you the whole time."

Angelica nodded her head. "It was a good thing."

Regina changed the subject. "I am instructed to speak to you about the Dragon, and to give you more information about its role, as well as yours, in what we are about to do.

"The Dragons are both a function of the Reptile Brain in each of us and a function of the collective consciousness. The Reptile Brain in each of us connects our instinctive behavior to our feelings—and our wants and desires. And it wants to be more than it is. And it knows, instinctively, because our instincts are the mechanism of its knowing, that the higher cortical functions are up 'there'. It longs to develop them. And the form that particular developing desire takes is the form of the Dragon.

"And in many cases, most of the time, in fact, there is simply not enough neural processing available for an individual to manifest a Dragon. And so the Reptile Brain developed a brilliant work around. Since the Reptiles are not particularly social animals, many Reptiles developed strategies for social behavior based on the individual awareness of others like itself. Mating, of course, is experienced as the most imperative of these. Other factors lead to the origin of herding behaviors. Then, approaching the neural networking of the limbic system, the maternal behaviors develop. All these are progressive and further the continuation of the species.

"And here is the work around: Using the information gathering systems about others of one's own kind, the Reptile Brain can join up the neural processing capacity of others of that kind, integrating them as source processors in parallel.

"This mechanism is the source of phenomena like 'hive mind' and 'herd mentality'. It is the source of the way flocks of birds can respond so quickly to the movements of others around them.

"There is a catch, of course. There is always a cost. Always an energetic cost. In order for a Dragon to manifest it must be able to use the power of those around it. In order to become conscious, it must draw on the consciousness of those around it, drawing down the consciousness of those around them just a little bit. This makes them all, except the strongest, just a little bit less aware. The strongest become stronger, the rest of us just become less aware, but we barely even notice it.

"Now, Angelica, do you remember how, when the Dragon would first manifest in you, that you would often lose consciousness?"

"Yes. Even when I remained aware it was often the case that I could sense and feel what the Dragon sensed and felt. It was as if I could think what it was thinking, even when that 'thinking' was pre-verbal."

"OK. So. I'm going to say something risky to you. And the risk is that it's going to go into your ego, instead of your Higher Self. So let us prepare ourselves. Let us sit together again."

They resettled themselves. Regina said, "Pay attention here," touching her second vortex below her navel. Angelica's gaze rested on Regina, Regina's gaze rested on Angelica. They synchronized their breathing, resting, sensing each other. They raised the Resonance of the Higher Heart and synchronized that also. The air in the room turned red and pulsed in time with the Resonance. The Dragon emerged, expanding out of Angelica in all directions. She gasped with pleasure at the all-encompassing sensation. Regina held the pace as the Dragon wrapped itself around Angelica, widening her eyes slightly as Angelica closed hers. Angelica began to shiver and with a low moan she orgasmed. Her fiery crown erupted, and Regina's followed.

Regina spoke into the pulsing spheres of light. "Very few minds are strong enough to feed the mind of a Dragon by themselves. Especially doing that multiple times and returning to the present moment sane. Your mind is one such."

The Dragon slowed down its sliding around Angelica and wrapped itself around her on the floor. It sighed, resting its nose on its tail.

"I'm going to miss that," Angelica said, sighing. Then she laughed.

Jasmine and Guiles arrived midafternoon. When Angelica saw Jasmine something tightened low in her belly and she wanted suddenly to kiss Jasmine hard. They hugged, Jasmine chuckling as she felt Angelica's need. She prolonged the hug and they breathed together. Before they broke the embrace Jasmine kissed Angelica tenderly.

"Get a room," Guiles said.

"Maybe later," Jasmine replied.

They ate in comfortable near-silence. After they ate Onadaya brought out wine and they all remained at the table. Jasmine told everyone about the history of the holiday of Kryapi. It occurred starting the night before the Spring Equinox, which was two weeks away. She said that every village would build a giant paper mâché demon and set it up in a common space. The people would bring flowers and food, even alcohol, and have a public party. A priest would come and invoke the power of the demon to abide in the statue and receive the praises of its power and quickness. Then, just before sunset, someone would sneak up to the demon from behind and set it on fire.

The people would scream as if they themselves were on fire, screaming as if they were the demon. They would throw things into the fire, things they wanted burned, cursing at the wicked thing. The statues would become towering bonfires. When the statues would fall over the people would hurry to their homes and finish preparations for the next day. They prepared because that night all the electric power on the island would be turned off, and the people were to remain hidden in their houses that entire day and the following night.

The theory of the ceremony, Jasmine explained, was that the demon spirits would flee to the ocean to dowse the flames. When they came back the next morning they would find no one to beset, so the demons would leave Wallid and go beset the poor souls on other islands. The electricity would be turned back on at sunrise of the day after the second night.

The Order had a house on the back side of Mt. Nagoon. Everyone necessary would gather there the day before. The moon would be near full again and it would be on that first night that they would take a hidden pathway over the mountain so that at dawn they could commence the destruction of the Temple of Skreeva.

Jasmine outlined her plan. Regina suggested that they do a test run of the Dragon's abilities with the dragons at the Temple of Wahsas-tami. Jasmine and Angelica agreed.

Later that night, once Napat, unused to the wine, was sound-ly asleep, the power of Sacred Erotic Beauty began to rise from the ground like mist, the power mixing with the air, filling the compound, compelling the adults, men and wen, to accept it like they accepted their own breath. Jasmine took Angelica, Onadaya took both Guiles and Corey. Regina took the Dragon, and, after putting it through its paces, making sure it knew what it would have to do, she allowed her-self the slithering ecstasy of the Dragon's embrace. Quinn stood guard in the short tower on top of Regina's house, breathing in the power of Sacred Erotic Beauty, using it like food and willing the power into his blood, circulating it through every part of himself, letting the nutritive power feed him. He grew erect when the moon rose, and, standing up, he walked to the railing and used his phallus, Thunder Cock the Rock Splitter, as a drumbeater, willing the clouds of power to dance to his rhythm.

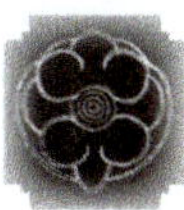

78

THE HIGH PRIESTESS ATTACKED

The High Holy Day, the most Sacred of Days, was fast approaching: the day known as Kryapi. Tourists were coming, signing up for interviews with the High Priestess. Her original house, her interview platform, her ceremonial platform that rose to several feet above their heads that she might pour her healing waters down upon them, were the only things finished. The additions, the courtyards, the walls—the rest had stalled.

The High Priestess of Wallid was worried. She had been trying to finish the new compound for her family and had been met with slowdowns and limited building supplies. But now her workers were refusing to come to work. She had gone to the contractor's offices to find out why. Most of them wouldn't even acknowledge her existence when she tried to talk to them. Those that acknowledged her simply shook their heads and refused to speak. One man, waiting outside on the walk next to her driver, clearly from the older, native race, passed her a little slip of paper on the way out. Written in Nahasi, the banned language, it contained only one word—the title of the High Priest.

This surprised her. She was under the impression they had an agreement, which consisted of the basic understanding that they would leave each other alone. Later, as she sat and meditated on the problem, she found herself back in the ocean, reliving the initiation that this man, the current High Priest, had forced on her a decade before. But this time, instead of the moon and stars that she had used to remain stationary, there was a dark cloud above her, and in that darkness she lost hope. When the sun rose, it remained overcast and dark, and she could not see the island peaks she had used before as landmarks in the moonlight. She'd had to swim the first time just to remain in place, and she'd tried to swim the same way as she remembered, but she knew she hadn't. The voice of comfort that she'd relied on was silent. In that darkness she despaired, and slept, and drowned.

Her shivering brought her back to the present moment. Little black spots danced before her eyes. The sky burst open and she knew the rain shamans had been enlisted and were working against her. No one would come to build in the rain.

Tourists leaving the Baths had tracked the shedding particles of the black kite through the airport. Other tourists picked them up and tracked them to other airports. Eventually the tourists brought them to Wallid, and trekked them up the long steps to the Temple to Skreeva. The High Priest, shuffling in his slippers across the pavilion, scuffed them up and inhaled a few. Enough to harden his heart. And his phallus. He'd pursued his affection for children since his time as tutor to the young High Priestess. Every few months he'd drive to the capital, wearing civilian clothes rather than his robes of office, where the ragged, dirty, and starving homeless children could be isolated, used, and paid. Then they would disappear from his mind and his life.

Once the particles of the kite had entered him, his malice became the core feeling of his life. He had always held a grudge against the High Priestess. Her spontaneous erudition, her beauty, and the easy way that people loved her—these had inspired him to hatred for years, but with the addition of the black molecule he had begun to actively plan against her. Those pilgrims who sought her out ought to be coming to him instead.

The High Priestess considered her best course of action. She knew she was more powerful than the High Priest in some ways, but she believed that her natural rites weren't as powerful as what she judged to be the Priest's High Magic. She considered seeking help from the rest of the Priestesses and Healers on the island, but she didn't want to expose them to any risk. Then she remembered that a Priestess from some Order had come to see her twice. She checked her records for the name and contact information. She realized she needed an outsider's help, and that Jasmine might be the one to help her.

She had already made up her mind to call the number she had for Jasmine when she heard on the radio that sexual assaults on the island were being reported to the police daily. She decided to do something she rarely did, which was to use her computer, normally reserved for her secretary to schedule appointments over the internet, and to scan international news. It was there that she read that assaults on women were being reported daily on the mainland, in Windia, as well.

The High Priest had ordered men, Priests and Novitiates, to watch her, to watch her compound gates particularly, but to also find ways to observe her sessions with the tourists, to observe either her conversations with them, or her healing ceremonies with them. The Priestess's dogs made it hard to watch the compound from any hiding place. The Priest in charge of the watch ordered her dogs to be killed after one of them peed on a Novitiate's legs.

She had an odd dream—the Priests were breathing in the breath that the Meemons of the Wuzlims were breathing out. She woke up in a sweat so plentiful her hair stuck to her like she'd been immersed still in the ocean. She was panting, terror was all she could feel.

When the High Priestess had her assistant call Jasmine, Jasmine was temporarily confused, not recalling the woman's name at first. But when she used the High Priestess's name, and in perfect Nahasi said that the High Priestess desired an audience with Jasmine, and invited Jasmine to her home given her current disposition, Jasmine said, barely controlling her excitement, "Yes." Then she immediately called Regina and invited herself over for dinner. Napat, having answered the phone, said, with the unconsciousness of the young, "Yes, come on over!"

Over supper Jasmine, Napat, Angelica, Regina, Onadaya, and the two Consorts discussed the invitation and how to prepare for it. It was agreed that Onadaya would work the Altars, the other four wen would go for the visit, for each controlled assets that might benefit the High Priestess. The men would run security at the gate. They gave no thought to the open accessibility to the pavilion provided by climbing up the rice field terraces.

One of the Novitiates on watch was ambitious. He decided to climb up the mountain, and across the dams between the terraces and hide in the thin edge of jungle between the top terrace and the interview platform. He saw what he could use as a hole that would let him under the platform so that he could eavesdrop.

The wen all had the same dream: a dream of sitting bare-breasted in Council wearing their best shawls.

On the day when Jasmine acceded to her invitation, the High Priestess dressed humbly, in the simple garb of the wen of old times, breasts bare, grass skirt. The breeze was stiff so she used a shawl for warmth as well. The wind was always a factor on the high ground of her compound and she'd had the curtains on the interview pavilion drawn to interrupt the flow a little.

When her guests arrived, she was surprised, having really expected only Jasmine to show up. In her prayers recently she had noticed that the young Napat had been hurt, and was having difficulty recovering. Regina and Angelica were a complete surprise to her. The four sat in a semicircle around her, allowing her the high seat on her pillows. They each immediately removed their shirts and blouses, and reset their shawls on their shoulders.

They sat together in silence, eyes lidded and barely open, synchronizing their breathing and heart rates. The Resonance of the Higher Heart rose up in Regina, activating it in the other wen of the Order. When it was active in each of them, they focused it on the High Priestess. When the waves of the Heart hit her body all at once it almost knocked the breath out of her and she rocked back. When she sat back up her entire body was pulsing.

She took a long breath but it was Regina who spoke. "How may we be of Service, Sacred One?"

She replied, "What is the fourth Force? Of what should I be aware that I am not?"

Napat's head rolled forward and the voice of Good Grandmother spoke through her. "The unquiet dead."

"And why are they unquiet?"

"Because they do not have a place to rest. The Priests have cursed them, and accept only those who are willing to be food for their god."

The High Priestess nodded her head and looked down. She had a vision in that moment of the unquiet believers in the old ways, going back more than a thousand years.

The voice speaking through Napat continued. "So, you see us now. This is our land. And you are one of us."

The High Priestess nodded again.

"You need our help. We will help you. But you must help us. You are alive. We are not. You must find us somewhere to go where we can rest."

Speaking from some place deep in herself, some place of naturally arising, if not reincarnated, authority, the High Priestess said, "I will find you the Place of the Everyday People. You may rest there."

The voice from Napat said, "Yes," extending the affirmation before fading away. When Napat looked up again, she was smiling. "Just so you know, I heard all that. The ghosts are happy. They will help you. They say you need guardians. They will attend you."

The High Priestess called for tea by ringing a bell, a bell with a sweet high-pitched note. They sat silently while it was brought, and the High Priestess poured for each of her guests.

She Who Comes came and settled into Regina. The High Priestess felt the descent and inclined her head in Regina's direction. "I am at your Service, First One," she said.

Regina smiled. She Who Comes smiled. "Child, these are mine, and therefore they are your kin. Treat them as such, because I do."

The High Priestess smiled for the first time in a long time. "So, tell me," she said, looking up. "What are you up to?"

The Novitiate had climbed into the underbrush tunnel below the pavilion. His feet stuck out under the edge as he grabbed the floor joists and pulled himself up to get his ear closer to the floor. He didn't see it when the King of Komodos came muscling his way down the trail, returning to his shelter after his morning hunt. He hadn't been successful this high up, and he was in a grumpy mood.

The Komodo saw the Novitiate's feet sticking out from his hole and his snappishness suddenly became viscerally literal. He grabbed the man's feet in his jaws and tore them off.

The Novitiate screamed. A stiff breeze blew the curtains aside. Regina smiled and then laughed.

The Komodo bit him again and drug him out of the hole, tossing his blood spurting legs so high in the air the wen saw it from the pavilion floor. The man's head landed with a thud below the Komodo's jaws. Acidic digestive poisons dripped into the man's eyes. His eyes burning in his head, his last vision was of the blackness of the Komodo's jaws closing over his face. His scream was cut off.

By this time the Consorts arrived on the pavilion steps, called by the screaming, silenced weapons drawn.

The wen all stood and went to the edge of the pavilion and looked down. The dragon had the man's head in his mouth, separated from his torso. Angelica's Dragon rose up, towering over them all, and huffed. The Komodo looked up. Regina spoke to it in Dragon. She said, "Keep the head but hide the body. Hide it well."

In one gulp the Komodo dragon swallowed the head, then nodded. It grabbed the torso by the shoulder and drug it backwards into the cover of the overgrown trail.

Jasmine said, "Good Dragon."

Some of the man's spurting blood had left a spot on the edge of the floor. The High Priestess bent over, breasts hanging free, and wiped it up with her finger, then put the finger in her mouth, sucking it clean. She turned to Regina, grinning, and said, "I presume this is not first blood." Regina laughed out loud.

The wen sat again. The High Priestess was told enough of the plan to know what her role would be, and the help she would have. Napat, through Good Grandmother, negotiated a contingent of the dead willing to serve the High Priestess. So long as it was service, not a binding, they were agreeable. In the end, the ghost of an old shaman stepped forward and guaranteed that the dead would also serve her descendants.

The honor and the beauty of the self-binding made them all weep.

An image of the High Priestess pregnant went through all of their minds.

Because it happened to be one of the many Feast Days to some sub-deity the second shift of the High Priest's watchers failed to show up. It was dark when the wen and their escorts returned unobserved by van to Regina's compound. Regina found herself remembering the King of Komodos. It reminded Regina of the King of Salamanders. In her mind she heard it rumble: "I am Elder." She sent a question in her mind of it. It answered, "Older than dragons." She couldn't stop laughing.

By starlight the King of Komodos entered the stream at the foot of the mountain, still dragging the footless and headless corpse by the shoulder. He'd had to readjust his bite a few times, and it was barely hanging on. He switched to the other shoulder and pinned the torso to the bottom with a hind foot, near a rock that had fallen from above but not quite made it to the water, waiting, breathlessly, as only a rock can do, waiting for a flash flood to drag it into the river's train. Standing up on its hind legs, tail anchoring it in the flowing water, the King of Komodos reached out and rolled the rock onto the body with a splash.

A sound, a guttural, fluid, grinding sound came from its throat. It could have passed for chuckling.

It would be days before anyone noticed the ambitious Novitiate was missing. Nobody had liked him anyway.

79

TUGGING HER HAIR

She Who Comes took up a handful of the sleeping Calley's hair and tugged on it gently. It was Her habit to do that when Calley was still a child. Calley would always say, "Ow" when She did it, but both of them knew it was not the hair pulling but the resentment at being woken up. As she matured, Calley stopped resenting it and came to love it, loving the gentle attention from her Mother. The "Ow", always there, now made both of them smile.

"What is it, Mother?" Calley asked, rolling over and sitting up from under Alam's arm. It was cool in the room, the fire smoldered with last night's coals. She took up a robe from on top of the chest at the foot of the bed and shrugged it on, then went to fireplace and threw some dry tinder and a couple of logs into it.

She Who Comes said, "Your work here is done for the moment. Let Alam supervise the repair work. I have need of you elsewhere."

When he heard this Alam woke up enough to say, "Thanks, and good bye for now, Beloved. I know I'll see you soon."

She Who Comes took up the handful of Invisible Land amulets and held out Her other hand to Calley. Calley took it and felt a power pouring into Her that She'd almost forgotten the sensation of how it was. She went mist.

With the sound of a small breeze She was gone, the little warning bell suspended from a single hair tinkled with their passing. Alam smiled at the sound.

They arrived almost instantaneously on Wallid, floating in the air above the High Priestess's house, a thunderstorm blowing around them. She Who Comes asked her, "What do you feel here?"

"I feel the presence of many dead. All around us. I feel the light of the wen in the house."

"What else? What do you feel in the rain?"

Calley closed her eyes. "I feel humans. Humans are behind this rain?" she asked, somewhat incredulously.

"Yes. There are Priests and Rain Shamans here that control the weather so that they can do their Ceremonies and Rituals unhindered by being wet. The rain drowns out the incense."

"This is not good here. There is a maliciousness in the humans that control this. They are doing this to hurt the wen below."

"Yes. Your task is to stop this."

Calley felt into it, tracking a spell down to its source. "There is someone at the center of this, controlling the humans."

"Yes," said She Who Comes. "He will be dealt with."

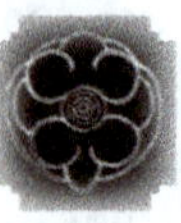

80

GATHERING

The day after the attack on the High Priestess Regina got off the phone with her friend Millie Brandt, the High Priestess of Sydney, and smiled. Millie had agreed to send three of her Madeleines to help, led by her High Madeliene Ayalise, to help hold the psychic space and bring her information from the unseen. They would arrive tomorrow and be brought to Regina's compound.

The next day the Prophet of Conscience arrived on Wallid. He rented a scooter at the ferry landing and drove inland to his mother's compound. Regina was pleased and relieved to see him. With only a hand on his shoulder she greeted him, knowing they weren't close enough for a hug. In her mind's eye she saw what his reaction would be, and it made her smirk slightly. She welcomed him in, and Onadaya brought him lunch. It had been a few years since he'd been here, and it still looked the same—beautiful and immaculate.

Quinn joined them, punching him in the same shoulder his mother had touched. "Ouch, damnit, you asshole," the Prophet groused.

After some pleasantries and polite inquiries ("How's business?" etc.) Regina explained to him what she needed him to do. She needed him to extend his power over the island, as far as he could, but principally on Mt. Nagoon. She needed everyone to do the right thing, which in this case, was to obey the ritual protocols and stay inside.

He protested that staying inside might not be the right thing everywhere.

Regina said, "I trust you to use your discretion." Then she said, "Look, I know this will be hard."

"How hard?"

"Forty-eight hours, give or take. Look, you've done this before."

"Never so long, nor over such an area. I'd be willing to try if it didn't involve potential opposition. It not right to force a person to do a thing that may not be in their best interest. It's not good. And this is the same problem I've always had with you, and the Order."

"Trust me," Quinn said. "It's in their best interest. Look, this is not about Morality. This is not about Belief. This is about Mythology. Whether you Believe it or not," Quinn said to the Prophet. Jasmine heard it in her mind when she was rocking against a hilted Guiles. Calley heard it in her mind when she manifested among the clouds above the High Priestess's compound. She Who Comes heard it and smiled.

Then they all heard Regina's final words, steel in her voice, "If we win you can have all the credit. If we lose, no one will blame you. You can blame us."

Later that day the Prophet got off his scooter at the gate of the High Priestess. He had been told that he could use her distribution matrix for the extension of his power, as her role would be balancing the three forces of the Gods, the People, and the Spirits of the Land, from a place of deep Ceremony.

He looked up into the sunshine over her compound and saw a shining white cloud in the air above the house. He saw small writhing and flitting forms appear and disappear all over and around the compound, forms that he had always associated with dead.

As he stepped through the gate into the compound, he looked across the courtyard and saw a young woman standing there, dressed in silver silk robes with a shawl over her head. Hands clasped, she bowed to him.

"Honored guest, Welcome to my home."

The Prophet fell immediately in love with her, love at first sight, smitten so hard it took his breath away. Love wrapped itself around him like a cocoon. He went to his knees to bow, touching his forehead to the stone floor. She came toward him, leaned down and whispered in his ear, smiling, "You may rise."

81

DISCOVERY

Tenara had fallen deeply before the wave of Wade's charisma. She would sneak out of her parents' house 3 or 4 nights a week. Wade was always waiting for her, erection in hand. She'd fallen in love with it, perhaps more than Wade himself. She'd discovered phallus worship with only a little coaching from Wade. With only a little more "coaching" Wade persuaded her to surrender herself sexually to him, surrender completely. After all, she loved him, and convinced herself that what she felt coming from Wade was also love. On those nights she would see him sometimes she barely managed to get back in the house before her parents woke up. Her father noticed her sluggishness and mistook it for sullenness. This made her resent him more, and also be more desperate for Wade to take her away. She resolved it in herself by striving to please him more.

One night, three nights before Kryapi, it was raining heavily. Wade wanted to see the moon so he worked his counter-magic and the rain went around his house. The moon shone down.

Pimple noticed. He'd been frustrated by his inability to approach the house with its walled and gated yard unseen during the day. Now he thought that under the cover of darkness and the rain he could sneak up to the house and see if anything was going on that warranted more attention.

As quietly as he could, he used the gate to climb up on the wall, leaning on the roof where it extended to cover the walkway that ran around back. He went to the corner and crouched down, waiting. In not too long a time Wade emerged from the back of the house naked and slipped into the pool. Shortly after Tenara emerged, also naked, carrying a tray with drinks on it. Pimple rocked back in shock, almost losing his balance.

Wade commanded her to set the tray down and come stand near him at the edge of the pool. He reached up and slid his hand between her legs, forcing her to spread her feet to accommodate him.

Although Pimple couldn't see what Wade was doing between her legs, he could tell. He pulled his sarong aside and wrapped his hand around his growing erection.

Wade toyed with Tenara, playing her with his hand until she orgasmed standing up, head back, hair reflecting glints of moonlight, and she collapsed forward onto him. He gently lowered her into the pool with him.

Pimple came, too, leaving pecker tracks down the wall.

Wade carried Tenara out of the pool and laid her on the lounge, then he walked around and got on his knees, spreading her legs and burying his face between her thighs.

Pimple had seen enough. He climbed down off the wall and scuttled down the road to his quarters in the Temple compound. He was too excited to sleep, tossing and turning, erections rising and falling as he alternated between planning what he would do and fantasizing about what he might do with Tenara. He was going to become an important man, now. He'd do what he wanted. The images of what he saw returned over and over again, and he fell asleep finally near dawn, whimpering as he cradled his erection. He could barely plan out what to say to his supervisor in the morning.

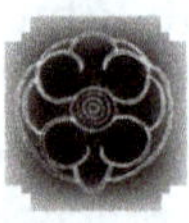

82

COALESCENCE

The group necessary for the assault on the Temple assembled at the cabin on the backside of Nagoon by mid-afternoon on the first day of Kryapi, before the demons were set alight. Jasmine, Angelica, Guiles, Corey, and Quinn. Their instructions were to wait until the 10:00 PM electricity cut-off to begin their journey across the mountain to the Temples. They were to avoid all houses, and use flashlights fitted with slit filters only when the moonlight couldn't penetrate the canopy. They all wore black, the wen with black shawls to cover their hair, the men wore black peaked ball caps. They discussed face paint, but if caught that would be too obvious. It was known that police patrolled the streets to ensure people, especially tourists, stayed inside. They had never been seen on the trails, however, and it was known that the Temple of the Mountain King would be unattended that night. The Temple's lone priest would be down below with his fellows at one of the Temples to the three brothers.

Shortly after their departure, Jasmine, leading the way, felt a stabbing pain in her low back. Her legs collapsed under her and she fell with a stifled cry. The others rushed to her, whispering fiercely, "Are you OK?" and "What happened?"

"I don't know. I can't feel my legs," she hissed back.

"We have to go," Quinn said.

Guiles picked her up in his arms. "I've got her."

Slowly the pain subsided and feeling returned. Jasmine took the lead again.

About an hour and a half into the hike Jasmine and Guiles took off on a side trail that ran to the Valley of the Concubines.

Around midnight, waiting until she felt that almost everyone was in their homes, Regina checked in with everyone's position, the assault group, Onadaya and Napat seated before the High Altar, the other Priestesses on the island and their Consorts engaged in ritual Tantra, generating Sacred Erotic Beauty. Satisfied, she pulled aside the curtains that closed off the underside of her altar table and pulled a carpet out upon which sat a Queen Old Woman Stone. The wen of the Island had spent the weeks since the Ritual of the Fire in the Heart, anointing every Stone they could find.

Regina set the stone in the middle of the three Madeleines sitting in a triangle around it. She anointed the stone, naming it in Nahasi, "Queen Old Woman." Touching it, she spoke a Word of Command and the Stone lit up with a silvery blue light, almost like moonlight. Lines of the silver blue force radiated from the Stone to the three Madeleines. After a moment the rays of force shot out their backs, connecting them to all the nearby Stones, and from those Stones out to every Stone in the Island.

Then Regina, touching the Stone with her hand, uttered another Word of Command and all the gates to the compounds all over the island, gates carved to resemble Mt. Nagoon split in half by an earthquake, became energetically closed. The 'mountains' sealed themselves, all over the island. The lines of energy flowed down to the guardian statues on either side of the gate. Regina sent the Command through her hand, "None Shall Pass." Then she stepped back. "You are spiders," she said to the Madeleines, "in a web of truth. Summon me if anything false and untoward arises."

She retreated to her tower to stand vigil.

The High Priestess and the Prophet, already lovers for the past three days, sat back-to-back on her pavilion, deep in ritual. The trap door in the middle of the Pavilion floor was open before her, revealing an ancient Queen Old Woman Stone. It was glowing, connected to all the other nearby Stones. The High Priestess was using her arms to direct energy, waving it out, or in, or around, keeping the Above, the Present, and the Below in alignment. The Prophet expanded his field, following the lines set up by the Queen Old Woman stones, spreading the power to do the right thing, which at the present moment was stay inside, go to sleep, and sleep late, so the demons couldn't see anyone in the morning.

Calley drifted in the space above the High Priestess' compound, holding off the rain above her pavilion so the moon shone down. She loved the warm rain, it soothed her and made her smile. The rain was always cold in the Highlands.

The unquiet Dead patrolled.

83

SEX AND DEATH

Pimple's instructions were to gather a group of men together, and have them bring their implements with them, especially the threshing clubs, but also forks and shovels and their bush knives. Then to wait until the lights went out, then attack the house, grab him, and beat him severely. He was not to tell Tenara's father. That would come later, and the supervisor wanted to be there to witness the beating the girl would receive.

The burning of the demons had come and gone, but not all the demons had fled.

Tenara heard the men gathering in the square, and noted how drunk and rowdy they were. They stopped in front of the store. She was wiping off the road dust and restocking, when they went by. Many paused to stare at her silhouette against the plastic sheet her father used as a rain guard when he was closed. Her father was passed out from the party. A chill took her, raising the hairs on the back of her neck, causing a bolt of fear to rip through her low belly. The men took off down the road towards Wade's house and she knew it would lead to no good.

Then the lights went out. As the lights went out a blanket of silence settled over the land. A night bird called, a summons to action. She hurried to her room and packed, shoving clothes and toiletries into a knapsack.

She had to warn him. Running along the path in the moonlight, tripping and falling, she arrived at Wade's too late. They had a short ladder with them, which they used to scale the walls. She heard the breaking of glass, and the shouts of men, Wade bellowed the loudest. She climbed the ladder in time to see Wade running out of the house, wearing just a pair of shorts and a t-shirt. He ran to the back gate, opened it, and ran barefoot out into the rice field.

Tenara sobbed involuntarily, covering her mouth with her hand and ducking below the wall when the gang of drunken farmers ran out of the house after Wade, led by the Priest. She could see that some of them were injured and were being helped along by their companions. When she was sure there was no one left in the house she climbed over the wall and went inside, heading for the bedroom Wade had told her was hers.

She knew that, no matter what happened to Wade, she was done for, that her father would beat her so bad that she might never recover, and if she did, she was sure that no one would want her.

She threw her clothing bag onto the bed. Wade had been giving her money, he said to buy nice things. Of course, she couldn't, so she'd saved all of it, a roll of $100 US bills she kept in the pockets of a rolled-up pair of shorts in her dresser drawer. She also knew the combination to Wade's safe, where he kept the rest of his money—she'd been lying in bed watching him open it, in a moment when he thought she was still asleep. She changed her clothes into riding clothes, packed what else she needed, including some of the nice things Wade had bought, especially the mammoth ivory comb, in a go bag and carried it with her, taking both bags. She made her way to Wade's safe, opened it and cleaned it out. There were several thousand dollars in there, and she took it all. She knew that she could find a shady currency exchange owner in the capital, one who wouldn't ask any questions except for a slightly larger conversion commission. She'd want to make it clear to him that she would be a good customer.

She knew she could disappear in the capital. She took the money and stuffed it in the bag. She took some food and water from the kitchen and stuffed that in, too, then she shrugged the bag over her shoulders. She grabbed a helmet and the keys to the scooter and, strapping her clothing bag to the back seat, took off in the darkness, knowing that she was not supposed to be out. Lights out, running by moonlight, she took back roads away from the village, and headed for a Temple, abandoned to the monkeys, where she could spend the night and the next day. She could hide in the compound, her scooter close by. No one would bother her.

Wade ran through the rice fields, rapidly nearing their spring harvest time, hopping down from one terrace to the next, sliding on the muddy bottom, leaving a trail of crushed plants behind him for them to follow. In the bright moonlight he saw the gang emerge from his back gate, and quickly string themselves out. It looked like the men he'd hurt during the fight in the house were bringing up the rear. He cursed when he looked back, realizing he was leaving an easy trail to follow. He felt something warm running down the edge of his hand. He looked and saw dark blood dripping. He realized he must have gotten cut by a bush knife during his initial resistance. He decided to run in the ditches only, zigzagging from one ditch to another until he could make the collection ditch at the bottom of the hill.

When he reached the bottom he heard his scooter starting and driving off. He cursed, his plan to circle back and make his escape on it gone with Tenara. He smiled. "At least she'll get out finally," he thought. Rather than run in the ditch he decided to get all the way down in it and slide his way to freedom. When he got far enough he'd climb up the other side and disappear into the jungle.

His pursuit spread out when they realized they could no longer track him in the fields. There was a small footbridge over the collection ditch at the bottom. The first man who gained the bridge scanned both ways and saw a flash of white from Wade's t-shirt and shouted. Other men ran ahead, making time on the grassy banks. Two of them passed Wade and jumped to the ditch in front of him. One had a threshing club, the other a straw fork.

Wade had no choice but to stand up and attack. He dodged a thrust from the fork, grasping the long handle and pulling it out of the man's surprised hands. With his torso he threw himself into the body of the man with the club, reaching over the club arm, locking it down, and twisting it. The ligaments in the man's shoulder gave way with an audible pop. The man screamed. Then he hit the fork man with the butt of the handle so hard in the throat that the man went to his knees in the water, hands over his throat, gasping for air. Wade picked up both weapons and ran up the bank and into the grass on the far side. No more hiding, all he could do now was run.

Although he was making better time in the grass he could feel it cutting his bare feet, and he knew he couldn't go far. He realized that, even as he started climbing up the other side, he wasn't going to make it. His Warrior's mind told him to stop and make a stand. He might die, but he would take several men with him.

They surrounded him, circling and yelling. Wade couldn't understand them, his awareness sunk below language, leaving only cunning.

He had eight men on the ground when he was stabbed in the back by a fork, a tine grazing his spine and paralyzing his legs. He went to his knees, then over on his face. The threshing clubs pounded his back and legs. One struck his head and he lost consciousness.

The Priest Pimple arrived on the scene and squatted down at Wade's head, looking for a pulse. "Good," he told the men. "As I ordered, you didn't kill him. Roll him over."

The men did as they were told.

As the squatting Priest leaned over Wade's face to direct men to search his pockets, Wade regained consciousness. By the bright moonlight filtering through the thin cloth of the Priest's sarong Wade was surprised to see the Priest had an erection. Wade grunted when the words "Sex and Death" appeared in his mind. The Priests testicles were less than three inches from his face. As quickly as he could he reached his face up and sucked them into his mouth, biting down with all his strength.

The Priest screamed, falling back, trying to get away, adding the extra force necessary to tear the flesh away. One testicle came free in his mouth and he jerked his head pulling the other along through the crushed dividing membrane.

Blood gouted over Wade's face, painting him in bloody stripes. The Priest wailed, then screamed in terror. Wade found himself laughing, deep in his chest so he wouldn't choke, ragged edges of skin on his lips and chin. The Priest fell away and Wade found himself looking around at the surprised faces, stalled and uncomprehending, staring from the screaming Priest to the blood painted demon lying at their feet. Then they caught on, their faces contorting again, and with the first hacking blows Wade spit the testicles out, laughing until he was out of breath.   And then, he was out of breath.

Sex and Death.

84

The Destruction of the Temple

Jasmine and Guiles arrived at the Temple to the Concubines about ninety minutes after they'd split from the rest of the Temple Group. She walked down into the fast creek that ran at the bottom of the Temple floor, and verified that the Queen Old Woman Stone set into the wall was active. It was, glowing with a silver blue light, with rays extending from it in every direction. She pulled the green tetrahedron from within herself and touched it to the Stone. The color shifted into both, glowing with each other's colors. She smiled. "Now comes the hard part," she thought.

With Guiles standing guard, she paused before she began her work, regarding the beauty of the Concubines reflected by moonlight in the reflecting pool. A slight breeze rippled the water, making the stone appear to dance in a wavering way. She walked around the perimeter of the reflecting pool and climbed the first statue, placing a flower on top of its head, and painting black dots where the eyes would be. On the way down she touched the tetrahedron to its heart and lay a piece of checkered cloth on its hip. She repeated this with the other three statues, placing different colors of checkered cloth on each one.

When she was finished, she stood on the edge of the reflecting pool, staring up. She turned once in a circle, taking it all in—the alternation of moonlight and moonshadow, the web of blue-white lines that seemed to run everywhere from the focus in the foundation below her feet, the sound of the rushing stream, tumbling over the rocks.

Turning back to the statues she levitated the tetrahedron, and spoke to it. Lines of force, twisted cords of green and blue-white light, ran from each face into the heart of each statue. The images in the reflecting pool waivered and suddenly were no longer images of stone, but of four beings, goddesses with hair made of flowing strands of flowers, flowered wrist bands, masks that showed no expression, bare breasts made of flowers, with long flowing checkered skirts that hung to the ground.

The tetrahedron rose until it was over her head. She leaned forward and put her hands in the water, sending ripples to the feet of the statues. The ripple traveled up through the light energy, bathing the feet. Jasmine spoke the words the High Priestess had given her. The statues floated towards her and she raced ahead, the ropes of light tethering the statues queued behind her, racing to be at the Temple of the Mountain King before dawn.

As Guiles, bringing up the rear, passed the reflecting pool he noticed that, although he thought he could still see the stone statues standing in place as they always had, there was no longer a reflection in the pool. The reflected image was gone. He realized that meant the image of the statues still in place was the illusion, and the reflection revealed the truth: They were gone.

They ran, the stone feet of the Concubines making rumbling noises, with a mild shaking of the ground at each footfall. Bending, two of them picked up Jasmine and Guiles, carrying them.

They arrived over the shoulder of Mt. Nagoon into the clearing above the Temple to the King of the Mountain. The statues paused and set Jasmine and Guiles down in the grass. The view was long—the Temple to the Mountain King before them, below that the huge Pavilion of the Dead, crowded with throne houses on narrow pillars, containing the ashes of the centuries in urns, then down past the vendors' shacks to the enormous Temple of Skreeva with the two smaller Temples to his brothers Drahma and Wishnu on either side. Beyond that lay the great Ocean, sun just rising, the water sparkling through the low clouds.

Angelica, Quinn, and Corey were there, waiting. Angelica sat on the bottom step of the of the free-standing step concourse supported by the Dragon balustrades. The men sat in two points of an equilateral triangle, Angelica at the apex. The air around her was glowing red, her hair lifted by some breeze no one else could feel.

Jasmine directed the Concubines to go stand at the corners of the Temple of the Mountain King. She entered the Temple, nodding to Angelica, and touched the green tetrahedron to the throne of the King of the Mountain. The spiritual energy of the King of the Mountain formed from white mist, his features smiling at Jasmine. She smiled back and bowed her head.

She left the Temple and began the walk down past the Pavilion of the Dead.

The air around Angelica became a red cloud. Into that cloud the Dragon emerged from her, the ecstasy of it, as if it were a wind originating from deep within, inverting the way the wind felt on her skin on the outside. From the inside the Dragon emerged, continuously flowing until it formed complete and whole in the air above her. "Ught An San," she told it; "Wake Them Up."

The Dragon laughed. He swirled around the undulating body of one stone Dragon, crossed the steps and swirled around the other, leaving a sparkling cloud of red light around them both. He stopped, floating before it, and kissed it. Slowly its eyes opened. He floated past Angelica and kissed the other one, laughing as its eyes opened, too. The Dragon swirled around the frozen undulations of both of the other Dragons, head to tail, tail to head, going back and forth between the two, faster and faster. Slowly, with loud cracking noises they, too, began to undulate in place.

Jasmine reached the main entrance to the Temple of Skreeva and crossed the first courtyard, going through the doors to the back courtyard. She went to the Pavilion where the Priests kept the collection of Salakta stones, the Queen Old Woman Stones. She climbed into the Pavilion, touching the tetrahedron to all of the them, lighting them up in the blue white net.

Regina felt the impact of the additional stones and spoke a word of command to the stone at her feet. All the of the stones across the island began to hum, and their color changed to blue sapphire.

Calley broke open the clouds so that the light of the rising sun bathed the compound of the High Priestess. When the High Priestess, with the stone between her and the Prophet turned to blue sapphire, she opened her Crown and golden light spilled out in all directions, balancing the forces of the People, the Gods, and Spirits of the Land. The Prophet spread his will that all would do what they ought to do into that light, following the spreading flow.

Jasmine, standing among the stones, lifted the tetrahedron high, then touching it to the stone between her feet. The green light travelled deep into the mountain, tickling the enormous Dragon asleep at the base of the mountain. Its tail twitched several times, moving within the frame, startling the mud people attending to it.

The ensuing earthquake focused under the foundation of the Temple to the Mountain King, its rumbling felt faintly throughout the island. The energy focused there began to break the Temple free from the earth.

The Concubines leaned down and picked the Temple up, leaving behind the Pavilion of its main altar.

The three Dragons pulled the Temple forward, down the hill.

The Mountain King in his throne laughed aloud.

The tetrahedron sent a beam of green light upwards, serving as a beacon.

Slowly the Temple was carried over the Pavilion of the Dead by the statues of the Concubines. Angelica, Quinn, Corey, and Guiles could all see the Spirits of the Dead cowering in terror.

The High Priest, awakened by the tremors, emerged from his quarters in time to see the foundation of the Temple of the Mountain King descend upon him. He screamed in terror, the scream drowned out by the humming of the stones. No sound escaped from the crushing of his bones.

The Concubines set the Temple down so that the hole in the center where the main altar had been settled over the Pavilion to the Salakta stones, the Queen Old Woman stones, keeping them safe.

The stone Dragons broke free from the foundation, and slowly, undulating through the air, led by Angelica's Dragon, made for the sea.

In telepathic synchrony Jasmine, Regina, and the High Priestess spoke a word of command into the Queen Old Woman stones, and the web shook, making the ground shake softly, but only in particular places. All over the island the thrones to the flaming white god, the one the Priests believed to be the True Creator, Winjeetniya, fell from their pedestals, crashing to the ground.

Jasmine climbed into the hand of one of the Concubines to lead them back to their place, Guiles jogging along on foot.

Regina spoke another word of command, and the network of Queen Old Woman Stones slowly lost the sapphire glow, and the blue white light of the web faded away.

The High Priestess lowered her arms and the golden sun colored light coalesced within her, disappearing into her Crown again. The Prophet, sweating, sighed with relief.

Angelica stood up and walked between her Bodyguard and her Consort, touching them both on the shoulder as she passed in front of them. She looked off into the ocean. She could make out the three

Dragons cavorting in the water and she smiled.

She remembered suddenly the Temple to Wahsastami. In a vision she saw Dragons that guarded the Temple doors had their eyes open. They seemed to be smiling. As she watched the ring of black fire around the Temple shrank, then disappeared altogether.

Then a sensation arose low in her belly. She could feel within the ovoid shape of an egg—a Dragon egg, she knew, that she could nurture and give birth to any time it was needed. She knew that, truly, she was Dragonwen.

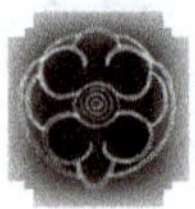

85

THE GODHEAD

Near the top of Mt. Nagoon, just down from the smoking crater at its peak, a plaza had been cut into the stone. It was here that Priests and Priestesses, Shamans and believers in the Old Ways, came to perform ritual and ceremony, not only to appease the Mountain King, whose throne sat on a wide pediment, but also to pray to the Goddess whose spirit animated the volcano and its fire—the being who took the form of the Black Dragon when She slept. Offerings lined the edges of the plaza.

It was a favorite place for She Who Comes. She was waiting there in her form as Salakta, True Creator in the esoteric literature of these people, the Goddess of Tantra and Ecstasy, when the crew from the Order of the Fleur de Vie arrived.

It was cold there for the mortals, up above ten thousand feet, and they were surprised to see the Goddess waiting there, dressed only in a hooded cape that fell all the way to the ground. Her midline bare, her feet bare, long hair escaping from the hood, streaming in the stiff breeze, She bid Calley to use her power to create a warm and windless space on the plaza.

They came, Regina and Quinn, Onadaya, Jasmine and Guiles, Angelica and Corey, the High Priestess and the Prophet. They bowed, then kneeled in a semicircle before Salakta. Her face was one they all knew. She smiled and went to each of them, touching their foreheads, assuring that they each would be able to see and hear everything that was about to transpire.

Satisfied that the mortals before Her had all attained clarity, She cross-raised her arms, making an energetic sphere overhead, and expanding it to cover the plaza. She said simply, "I summon you." From the air behind her, a pantheon emerged. Three Goddesses appeared behind Her on Her left—Wahsastami, the Goddess of Knowledge, Braksni, the Goddess of Fortune and Wealth, and Darvatiye, the Goddess of Life and Fertility. Behind her right shoulder appeared Walleed, dark twin of Darvatiye, a Goddess of Death, namesake of the Island of Wallid, and Walleed's daughter Weirga, a ten-armed Executioner.

Then, between Salakta and the mortals three masculine forms appeared, chained to each other, facing Her. She named them, "Drahma, Wishnu, and Skreeva. Kneel." They did so, and the chains between them disappeared, leaving Skreeva with his hands manacled. He bowed his head.

Wahsastami spoke. "You allowed your priests below to trap me in my Temple and ban my Priestesses from performing my rites. You kept me from my Consort Wishnu. Explain yourself."

Skreeva, his head still bowed, cleared his throat and, in a smooth voice, said, "He doesn't need your Knowledge to serve in his role as Maintainer."

Wahsastami replied, "Without Knowledge his Maintenance fails. When he fails, that which has failed becomes yours, that is why you imprisoned me. What you receive enters the realm of your transformation, the transformation of Destruction."

Skreeva said nothing. Wishnu, looking sideways at him, saw him smile. He said, "He smiles."

Suddenly Wahsastami was in front of Skreeva. She slapped him with each of her six hands. He reeled, his upper body swayed in a circle.

Braksni spoke. "You use me. You have turned my power into the darkness of greed, where wealth and good fortune goes to those who work in the realm of destruction. You thereby lessen my Consort's power to Create. You foster the creation of the malformed, the deficient, and the corrupt by the usurpation."

Wishnu reported, "He smiles again."

Braksni, likewise, slapped him with each of her six hands.

Darvatiye stepped forward, then kneeled down so She could look Skreeva in the eyes. "Beloved Consort. What have you done? You have let your Priests assault the maidens who carry the capacity to bring forth life! You allow the rape! Oh no, worse than that, you encourage it, don't you? You destroy a part of their souls and spirits when you take from their somas!"

"It is a kind of transformation from your realm into mine, is it not?" he whispered, then he smiled, looking at Her sideways.

She slapped him hard, six-handed. Twice She slapped him, screaming in rage at him as She stood up and stepped back. "You have usurped us all," she said, steady and threatening. Skreeva bled from his nose and his eyes.

Salakta repeated the charge. "You have usurped us all." She held the moment, allowing the gravity of the crime, this putting of himself ahead of all the others in a bid to inflate his power into ruling them all. She came forward. "I came to you for help in the creation of the Tantra. It made you famous as a force for good among men. And you have betrayed that trust."

"Sex and Death," he mumbled, blood dripping from his lips.

"You were warned, Skreeva. The last time this happened Darvatiye implored us to spare your life. Darvatiye, what say you now?"

"He is irredeemable. I shall not appeal your sentence," the Goddess responded.

Salakta turned to her right and said, "Walleed?"

Walleed came forward and knelt down also. "Death," She acknowledged his name.

"Death," he nodded, mumbling, acknowledging Hers.

"You taught me," She said. "You taught me the Tantra that allows the lineage in My name. When you taught me, you taught Death how to Live in Life. For that, you have gained a Mercy. I shall take your head before I take your balls." She stood up and stepped back.

Salakta spoke: "Weirga."

With Her first strike She took his head. Then, while the light was still present in his dying eyes, She took his balls, knowing that he would see, and that he would know. Then She dismembered him with Her other eight arms, wielding fearsome weapons. When She finished, the former god Skreeva lay in a bloody heap of ten pieces.

The wen, mortal and immortal, sighed. The men held their peace, in contemplation.

Then Salakta called out, "Rock Splitter!"

Quinn, feeling a subtle joy in having witnessed Justice done, was startled. He looked up at Salakta.

She came and stood in front of him, robe open, the scent of Her overwhelming him. "I have need of you."

The prospect of what She might mean, the empowerment that flowed into him with her scent, gave rise to the object of admiration, Thunder Cock the Rock Splitter. He was helpless to respond otherwise.

He bowed his head. "How may I serve?"

"There is a place in the Trimerase for you."

"His?" Quinn asked, nodding toward the pile of flesh.

"Yes," She replied, regarding him with just the faintest of smiles. She held out Her hands to him.

He took them and rose up. She walked backward, still holding his hands, gazing into his eyes, smiling, and led him to the place the god had kneeled beside his brothers. She kneeled then, not letting go of his hands, and he kneeled before Her. She leaned forward, touching Her forehead to his. She took his left hand and put it on Her heart, then put Her left on his. She took his right hand and put it between Her legs, grasping his phallus with Hers.

Immediately the power of the Resonance of Higher Heart flooded him, pounding in each place where he was touched by Her, and in turn it pounded in his hands where he touched. The Heartbeat pulsed in each of them, moving within them, back and forth, touch to touch, until the energy moved within them each, first in a circle joining them, then adding a figure eight, heart to heart. They began to glow. Brighter and brighter they became, until none could see them, lost in the light.

In that touch his Soma, his phallus, became a golden rod, his heart, his Soul, became a golden cup, and his Spirit, his mind, became a star.

"For one year, Rock Splitter. I need you for one year, and then you shall be free."

She withdrew Her hands, and there He kneeled. When He returned to the present moment He turned to His new brothers and said, "Things are going to be different, now. Let us sit together and speak with one another," and They turned to face each other.

He closed his eyes and looked within, cataloguing his new powers and responsibilities.

"Damn," he exclaimed. "I am the god of weed!" He snapped his fingers and a smoking joint appeared in his right hand. He took a toke and passed it to Drahma. "Here. Let's get to know each other."

That night, as he drifted in the twilight he would learn to call sleep, an image appeared, an image that solidified into a form he recognized: Regina's daughter Lee, the Librarian of Shambala.

"I am told you have learned how to read," she smiled.

He rolled his eyes back in his head and saw that this was so. He could read anything. He smiled back at her.

"Then come with me," she said, holding out her hand. "Let me show you the books where what you want to know is written."

86

THE MIND OF DE MURGOS

His hands were bleeding. The agony of the poison flowing in him, and the agony that arose from the cuts from the Abomination's throwing of the Siddhi powers drove him to dig at the walls of his sealed cave with his bare hands, desperate to find something more painful than what he was suffering, proving to himself that he was still sane.

Finally, he attained the state of mind he sought by biting himself, almost severing the last joint of a finger. He slept, waking when the pain of his wounds pierced the darkness of his exhaustion. Several cycles of this, attaining greater agony, allowed him to sleep assured of his sanity, only to wake up to a lesser agony that made him feel insane, left him losing his sanity over again. He had lost his power to heal himself, and his very life depended on regaining it.

He woke that morning with the taste of his own blood in his mouth, and it tasted most foul. He groaned as he picked up his head and looked around. His eyes tracked to a light source, glowing not far from his head.

It was a mandorla, energy radiating from its boundary, making a flickering against the wall. Within that boundary was a form, a human form he recognized as one of the feminine gender from the planet below him. She was scarcely up to his knee in height.

He sat up, unafraid, certain that this was hallucination, that he really was going insane. He heard a voice in his head say, "Too late. You are insane."

This amused him. He asked, aloud, "And you are?"

In his mind he heard the answer. "I am She from whom you take without asking. Get off Me."

He reached for her but she backed away too quickly. He tried to emanate a spell of entrapment but the effort made the poison in his veins throb.

The image spoke into his mind again. "Get off Me, before it is too late."

"For Whom?" he asked, teleporting to her location across the cave. When he got there, at almost the speed of light, she had moved again.

"Get off Me."

"How did you find me?"

"You have penetrated into the heart of My daughter. How could I not know where you hide? You must get off Her, too. Leave now, while you can. Take your creatures with you."

"So much contempt for someone so small…" He became a wall of flame, expanding out the tunnel, believing he was fast enough to catch her with it.

He heard her voice through the fire, "Fool. You think I am real."

He stopped the display and wondered aloud, "Am I sane?" And his answer to himself was "Yes, that was a hallucination. And since I know that, then yes, I am sane," then, "I need a vacation. I know just where to go."

He decided to go to Wallid, where he was worshipped as Winjeetniya, a secret god behind all their other gods, a True Creator. It was one of his favorite impostures. He induced whole priesthoods to accept that he was the secret behind their ancient pantheon, revealed just to them, but not to the women, whom he said were not worthy. In this way he could guarantee a steady source of suffering; the food, his food, the food of human misery. He used to love the smell of Suttee.

When he arrived at the Temple of Skreeva, it was all changed. There was no place for him to alight, no place to land. All his thrones lay broken on the ground. It was all different. It took him a while to figure out that one Temple was now resting on top of the other. Never had he seen such a thing. He smelled the Feminine everywhere. He floated up the mountain to where the Temple to the King of the Mountain had been. The same Feminine smell was there, but there were other smells. He picked up the faint smell of the Abomination. And worse, he smelled Dragon.

He felt something in that moment, something he seldom felt. He felt fear. He heard the words in his head again: "Get off me."

As he watched, a council of Priests gathered in the outer court, standing on the stones of the old Temple. They had gathered to select a new High Priest. The old High Priest, disappeared, had wanted his second in command to succeed him. The council acceded to the inheritance. The new High Priest nominated the one they called The Vicious in secret, to be his second.

He floated back down to the assembly, making himself visible to them. They fell down, hiding their faces in terror. He breathed it in, feeding on it. He hovered above them. He spoke so that only the High Priest and his second could hear him. They heard his words, heard his anger.

"The women have done this," he said. "It is evil. And it must be punished. Swear to me, you will punish them."

The two priests rose to their knees, shouting, swearing to do as he bade. He extended from his flaming hands the energy of a blessing; the energy necessary to follow his will. Then he floated up until none could see him.

When he was gone from their sight another plan occurred to him. There were Wuzlim Meemons on the Island. They were known to treat their women worse than the Windus. He laughed at the thought of what he would whisper in their ears during evening prayers.

"The evil women must be found. And stopped. It must be driven out into the open."

87

TENARA

Tenara had taken a small apartment in a run down and dangerous quarter of the capital city. She'd have been safer if she'd spent more money for a better place, but she was worried that the money wouldn't last. Of course, she drew unwanted attention to herself. The dishonest money changer she found had her followed, and after a week, she returned home from the market to find the apartment door open, and the money gone—thousands gone. The scooter was stolen, too.

She was squatting on the sidewalk, back against the wall, weeping, when she heard someone call her name.

"Tenara," the voice said. "Look at me," in Nahasi. She looked up.

Onadaya squatted down in front of her. Behind her was the High Madeleine Ayalise and her two helpers, standing guard.

"We found you," Onadaya said, smiling. She reached out and laid her palm on the side of Tenara's face. Tenara didn't flinch. "Good," Onadaya said. She continued, "Your friend Wade worked for our company. You should come with us. Come with us where it's safe. Yes?"

Tenara nodded, whispering "Yes."

"We should go," Ayalise said in English. "It's not safe here."

"Your things, upstairs?" Onadaya asked.

Tenara nodded.

"Let's go get them."

It took only moments to gather her things while the wen stood guard in the hallway and on the steps. They exited through a rear door and walked casually down the alley to their van, guarded by their driver.

"Back to the compound," Onadaya told the driver in Windonesian. As they pulled away from the curb Tenara collapsed, sobbing in her arms.

"Scarcely older than Napat," one of the Madeleine's remarked.

"What was he thinking?" the other asked, rhetorically.

"He wasn't," Ayalise said. "He wasn't thinking at all."

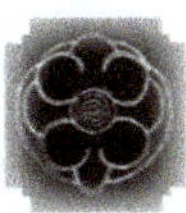

88

GHOST IN THE GARDEN

In the third week after the Equinox, a week past the dark of the moon, A. was sitting at the table in her garden, unconsciously soaking in the sunshine. Her mind had slowed, so that she was doing things more instinctively than consciously. The end result was pretty much the same whether she was conscious or not. She was still minimally effective.

Not unusual for this time of year a cool breeze lifted itself over her garden walls, shaking petals off the blossoming cherry tree. She felt them on her face, falling. She opened her eyes and looked up in wonder.

The breeze died suddenly, it felt. Right beside her. She brought her eyes back down to focus in front of her. She saw a woman sitting opposite her, at her garden table, someone about her age, maybe a little older.

The intruder spoke. "Hello Angel. I'm your sister Regina."

Angel's eyes grew wide with wonder.

Regina said, "No, not that man. He was not your real father."

Angel raised her eyebrows differently.

Regina responded, "He is beside you. Right now."

Angel turned to the left, and saw the Lama's Ghost, as solid an apparition as real life. She turned to Regina and asked another question with her eyebrows.

Regina answered, "Your mother never told him. He didn't know. I was blessed by his recognition."

This made Angel cry.

Finally, Angel cried.

She reached out and took Regina's hand across the table. Her face fell forward, weeping on their joined hands. The Lama's Ghost, her father's ghost, put his hand on her back, just below her neck.

Regina hadn't known what she would actually say to this tortured wen, knowing that she'd had this, until now unknown, sister. She had thought she'd tell her this: "You know, you have killed some of mine. You cannot be permitted to live." This was her fantasy.

But, in the moment, she looked upon her sister with pity, and, said instead, "You know. You know it is time for you to go. You can go with him. Get to know your father. What do you say?"

"Yes," A., the sister named Angel, said.

The Lama's ghost dropped his hand to A.'s mid thorax, and fashioned his hand into a cup shape, set to receive.

Regina leaned forward, touching her forehead to her sister's forehead, and took all the memories of her sister's life into her own mind. Her sister closed her eyes, and never saw Regina's fingers extended, rigid, from her palm, forcing her life force energy forward, extended beyond the tips of her fingers, into Angel's heart.

The electric net that kept the heart alive was forced out through Angel's back into her father's waiting hand. The moment it was gone into his hand, the Lama used his other hand to rip the rest of the black kite from the back of her head, popping it into his mouth and swallowing it all for the purpose of safe-keeping.

Regina saw her sister's ghost stand up, holding their father's hand. She watched her sister looking up at their father, smiling with the innocence of a girl that she herself could still remember, looking up with love at her father, their father. As her ghost left her, Angel's body died, sitting up. Regina thought to herself, "Who knows how long it will be?"

She stood up and left the garden through the garage. Still smiling, she got in the passenger side of the car.

Grace turned to her from the driver's seat. "All's well?" she asked.

"All's well," Regina replied.

89

Goodbye For Now

Matthews was dreaming. In his dream he was flying. His wings appeared behind him, sleeping on his belly. One wing brushed Bree's breast and She sighed. She trembled, little waves of orgasm slipping slowly to Her toes, making them twitch as much as the rest of Her.

Oh, She would miss him.

Oh, the exquisite longing for a Lover far away.

Oh!

Mom had told Her that She wouldn't have him long, this first time; that She needed him for a specific task elsewhere. Bree, for Her part, was confident he would return. She used Her scrying skills to see his next assignment, which was a training period for the task. She was surprised to see that he would become involved with a wen, but there was something mysterious about her, something hidden in a darkness She couldn't see through. She couldn't see the task, either. But She could see afterwards, and the vision was of him returning to the Hidden Lands, and their abiding together a long time. She was content with this, not needing to see all the rest that might happen in the interim. She knew he would be back in Her arms by Autumn.

Still, She would miss him. Not for two millennia had She known the comfort of a Consort, grateful as She was for Calley's sharing of Alam. Her intuition told Her that She'd not be with Alam again.

Sunrise past the equinox came earlier each day, stirring her to wakefulness. She loved it. Matthews slept late, it seemed every day, like some adolescent boy. He awoke horny and erect, and when he'd dealt with that problem, or rather, when She'd dealt with it, he was famished, and She'd required those who believed in Her and lived relatively close to the Hidden Lands to bring Her mortal food, just to keep him nourished. Their reward was that they actually got to step foot on the Hidden Lands and converse with Her face to face.

She rose, wrapping a dressing robe around Her, put some wood on the fire, and sat in the chair by the table, waiting for the tea water to boil.

As She watched, the wings disappeared and he rolled over. She saw two things. The crystal vial he always wore around his neck had begun to glow the color of the moon. And he was erect. Still sleeping, he scratched the firmness lightly, and sighed.

She'd held both, many times, feeling the Water of Life in the vial hum with energy, feeling his phallus humming, too, but at a different note. Throat singing, She sang the chord, the harmony heating the air in the room. She stood up, dropped Her robe, and moved to the bed. She put Her hands on Her Consort, sensing the high note of the crystal vial and the low thrum of his phallus. She became the chord, both frequencies vibrating throughout the whole of her.

He woke up, grinning. Then he laughed, the combined sensation felt like a tickle deep in his core. "Stop! Stop! Oh, stop it!"

She laughed back at him. "Lest you call me unmerciful." She took her hand from the vial but squeezed his phallus tightly. "But to this I shall show no mercy."

He laughed, but differently, happy at the images that rose up in him.

She stopped Her play, suddenly serious. "You are bringing this back to me, yes?"

"Yes," he said, matching Her seriousness.

She squeezed it even harder, squinting at him. "Why don't you just leave this with me? I'll take good care of it until you get back. I promise."

He squinted back at Her. "I can see you are speaking the truth. But I am pretty sure I will need it with me."

"What for? To what use would you put it? Hmm?" She teased, stroking him.

"I might have to make a three-point landing."

She laughed at the image. "And with what would your hands be full?"

90

FOR THE SECRET

Beth returned from visiting Leonard's grave in the cemetery to find Regina Moon Halter in her parlor. She had thought Regina had left England. Regina was much admired by Beth, so she was surprised to find her there—she would have thought there would have been some advance notice, to allow her to prepare.

They hugged, happily, and Regina could feel the inquiry residing in Beth. "I was here on assignment, you know. More than one. Now that it's done, I became free to stop and see you again, beloved."

"And, oh, I'm so glad you did."

"Would you like an update?"

"Oh, yes please. About the situation we've been dealing with here?"

"Yes. About the couple from America, and what they were loosing on the world, the malice that was spread from the breakdown of the black kite."

"We've known he was dead for some time."

"Yes, and now she is, too."

"Ah. Need I know how?"

"No. You knew she was British, didn't you?"

"Yes, but we've never been sure of her name."

"Well, it turns out she was a daughter of the Lama."

Beth's eyebrows arched. "Really?"

"Yes. Somehow, we missed her. Her mother seems not to have

told anyone. And she may not have known herself. The mother disappeared at some point, leaving the girl with the man she believed was her father. It appears he sold her to the Lineage."

"Poor thing."

"Yes. Indeed," Regina paused, mournfully reflecting on the horror of that wen's life, her sister's life. The brogue of her childhood returned slightly. "It also appears that the current Master, her third, was responsible for the deaths of the Priestess and her Consort in California."

"That would make sense. Did they kill them? What were they looking for?"

"Us," Regina said, deadpan. "They were targeting the Fleur. According to the autopsy of the Consort, he died of an aortic aneurysm. There was rohypnol in his bloodstream, but not enough to kill him."

"The vow?"

"Yes, we believe so. The vow held. The body of the Priestess has not been found. The Madeleines are not hopeful she will be found."

"And the Lineage?"

"Well, it will die out, if you know what I mean. The Order will purchase the property, of course. Whoever takes over will be greedy to sell. The problem for us is that the property is profoundly corrupt. The black kite was very old. As it started to come apart it started to, well, shed. It fed on malicious energy. It became particularly fond of the energy of rape. Even the molecules of the kite can inspire someone to that horrid power. And now it has spread everywhere. It is already becoming a big problem. We shall have to do something, but the Council does not yet know what."

They fell silent, contemplative, in their minds' eyes seeing how badly it all could have gone.

Beth said, "I am sorry for your loss."

"Thank you. I am sorry for hers." Regina said, and they relapsed into silence.

"Well," Regina began again, "I have some good news. The Americans can all go home again. The repairs to the roof at Stonehaven are almost finished."

"Ah, good."

"Will you miss them?"

"In some ways. The vernacular is amusing, and they are well-trained." She smiled. "Appropriately trained."

"The Equinox Celebrations went well, then?" Regina smiled

back.

"Yes, indeed," Beth said, her smile becoming a wide grin. Then, "What else?"

"You have given Matthews his next assignment?"

"We have tried. Our couriers seem to be having an unusual amount of difficulty locating the Hidden Lands. Perhaps Brighid is being a little difficult."

Regina laughed out loud. "Let me know if you need someone else to communicate the message. It has been a long time since I've been home. I'd be happy to do it." Then, after a pause, she asked, "What do you think of the mission?"

"I think it is dangerous. Were it not for the vow of the Goddess to make the restoration, it is not a mission I would recommend we undertake."

"How dangerous?"

"Inevitably fatal without our support."

"Well, that's probably why it hasn't happened before."

"True."

"Do you think he'll like the Castles?"

Now it was Beth's turn to laugh out loud. "Undoubtedly."

When the laughter subsided Beth refreshed the tea for both of them.

Regina asked, sipping, "And the Secret? Is the Team set?"

"It is. They have been introduced, and have met at least twice by now, familiarizing themselves with each other."

"Tell me about them."

"The lead's name is Jennifer. North African ancestry, grandparents are French-speaking refugees from the end of colonization. Her parents migrated to England when she was young. She speaks Arabic as fluently as she is trained in our values. The Trustworthiness Index test results indicate fearlessness when it comes to the vow. She reminds me of your Jasmine in her resolve, if not yet her skills."

"Ah. Do you have a picture handy?"

"Yes. Here," she said, pulling a photo from her desk drawer. "And here, this is her partner."

Regina looked down at the first photo. The wen was beautiful. She journeyed to the image, and when she arrived in the present moment, the wen sensed her presence and turned toward Regina sharply, scowling. Regina looked at the other photo, smiling, breaking contact. "She'll be fine," Regina said.

Beth nodded toward the other photograph. "He's American. He speaks Arabic well enough. His sub-Saharan looks feed well into the body guard/security aspects of the assignment. Second son of a wealthy merchant. Successful European import/export businessman. Carpets, wood, and metalwork, mostly. Hints of irregularity, but nothing specific. Not enough to draw unwanted attention, but enough to draw enough attention from state security to keep all but the most hardened criminals from approaching them."

"Good. The plan?"

"They land in Morrocco, hop-skipping by boat from safe city to safe city across the coast, buying in the markets and bazaars, arranging for shipping, landing in Tunisia and waiting until the extraction can be finalized. It should take about a month, maybe six weeks."

"Excellent. Excellent. I should like to spend the night, and can you find me a driver for the morning? I will make sure Matthews gets the message."

"Of course. Is there anything else you may require?"

"Just you, my dear. Just you, your hospitality, and your attention."

Beth smiled, shyly at first, and then broadly.

Regina nodded her head, and smiled broadly back.

91

ANOTHER PRIME NUMBER

The alarm on Lulu's phone went off at 5:30. She disentangled herself from her girlfriend/roommate's arms and rolled over her boyfriend to turn it off. Her girlfriend mock pouted in a way that made Lulu wonder why she still thought it was cute. Her girlfriend rolled away and snuggled against her own boyfriend's back.

As Lulu rolled, she noticed that her boyfriend had his hand loosely wrapped around his typical morning-wood erection. She paused, and decided to feed him into her, pleased that she was still wet from the night before. When she came, her mind was filled with an image of morning glories blooming on the barb-wire fence posts of her home. She rested her head on his shoulder, not sure if he'd even woken up.

She'd waitressed at the restaurant where her aunt worked long enough to get off the opening shift. She was so happy and grateful that she no longer had to be there at 5:30. But she had to be there by 7 to catch the pre-office rush.

When she walked out into the crowded tables, coffee pot in hand, introducing herself as the new server on the shift she found a single woman, or rather, a woman sitting alone, who looked familiar. She did a double take while the woman looked up and smiled at her. She said, "I know you from somewhere."

The woman nodded toward the front window. Lulu said, "Oh yeah! That's right! That's your picture on the flyer for the yoga class. You're Janice, right?"

Janice nodded, holding her cup poised midway to her mouth,

smiling. "You interested? You gonna take the class?"

Lulu sat down in the booth with her, all excited. "Hell, yes! Diana was great with the first two! You come from the same school, yes?"

"Yes. And you're Lulu, right?" Lulu pointed at her name tag and shrugged. Janice continued, "Diana told me about you."

And Lulu smiled. With just a hint—just a hint—of shyness. "Do you think I could learn to become a tantric yoga instructor like you?"

She smiled. And She smiled.

From the Fourth Novel in the Series "The Siddhi Wars", Tentatively Called "The Antecedence of the Feminine The Confessions of Emmalia Aura"

Dear Madeleine,

She is with me often, you know. I have only to think of Her now, and She Comes. And, as you also know, I have been instructed to engage in Ritual every Full and New Moon, Ritual to feed the Spirits of the Land here, and to feed the world. Alas, because my station, my assignment, is so remote I am often without a Consort, and hence am practicing the path of solo cultivation as instructed. While there is a part of me which longs for the comfort of company, there is another part, a more true and central part of me, that longs foremost for ecstasy—in particular the ecstasy that union with Her brings, and following Her instruction while She abides in me.

I am writing to you, High Priestess and Seeress, to keep my word to stay in touch with you about how things are proceeding with me while I am away on assignment.

I have to take a moment to describe to you the beauty of this place, as I do not know if you have been here. It is a one room cabin set in the mountains north of Nice. The southern exposure is windows, offset at an angle to each other, with built-in low tables running along the walls below the sills. On the central table I have set up my altar. The kitchen area and the bed—a large covered four poster, hung with curtains—are set in the back, bed on the east side, kitchen and sitting area on the west by a large open stone fireplace with hooks on swivels to hold pots into the flames. Sometimes it is yet chilly here and I have taken to lighting fires for heat and comfort. There is a lean-to behind the house filled with firewood. I have found the instructions on how to arrange for more to be delivered from my contacts with the Priestess of the Order in town and her Consort but I don't like the idea of intrusion, although they seem to be nice people. They've told me to leave a list with them of what I need, and they'll have it for me the next time I come. There is a small wagon that attaches to the four-wheeler, and if I start getting low on wood I'll haul some up myself, even if it means going to town more often.

The kitchen stove is a combination stove, burning either wood or gas. I imagine it has to be so, as deliveries of gas seem to made only by mule, I'm kidding. But I know a four-wheeler, like the one I found here next to the woodshed, could make the trip. There is also a moto-cross style two-wheeler. The lighting here is interesting. There are two propane lamps on the wall that use little socks like a white-gas lantern. And there are two white gas lanterns and several kerosene lamps. No electricity! The water here gravity fed, it seems, from a pipe somewhere up the mountain, and into a gravity feed tank into the house. It is cold, and clear, and tasty. I intend to hike up to the source soon.

Here, high up on the shoulder of this mountain, a lot has been cleared for a yard, and grass planted, with raised beds of flowers and flowering trees around the periphery, and at one end there is a shrine. It seems old, three weathered statues set into a niche, perhaps three-quarter sized, their features worn by weather to indistinct. Judging by the clothing it seems to me it is a mother, with two children in front of her to the sides, her arms resting protectively on their shoulders to the outside. The dress is long, and she's wearing a shawl up over her head. The children seem to garbed in tunics that fall to the knee. The mother is wearing sandals, and the children are bare foot. When you stand directly before the scene the mother is looking off to the northwest while the children seem to be looking directly at the viewer. There is a stone plate set in the ground at their feet with writing carved in it. It says, as near as I can make out, "I rested here" in four different languages, the newest of which is English, the next oldest seems to be French. I don't recognize the other two, but surmise one is Latin."

I could see where flowers had been laid at their feet, perhaps food and water in bowls. I have cleaned the area, and make the same offerings. With this Full Moon have come small white flowers in the grass and I picked a few and placed them there. I sense great presence at this spot, and great power.

As you know this past week was the time of the Pink Moon, the April Moon, and my instructions were to conduct the ceremony as I have been shown, and to do it twice, once the night prior to the night of the Full Moon proper, and once on the night after the Full Moon. The two experiences were dramatically different in the instructions and in the consequent manifestation of the ecstasies.

On the night of the Full Moon I sat before the altar, my eyes half closed, watching the entire show from Moonrise to Moonset, cultivating the energies of the inner orbits. About midnight She came to me, appearing before my mind's eye brushing her hair. She told me to ask her any question, so we talked. I am bidden by Her to not speak too much about it—I asked her some questions about the Alchemy, and She told me that speaking about it to you would affect the Sublimation. And that you'd understand. She told me to go to sleep at Dawn.

On the night before the Full Moon, the Moon was very bright, rising through high window to the left, bathing me and the altar both in brilliant silver-white light. I had found a low sided bowl in the kitchen, and brought it over to the altar with me.

I placed the phalluses on the altar, at least an hour before I was to sit. I prepared the pad before the altar. I bathed and shaved. I put the shawl over my shoulders and sat, naked from the waist down. I lit the three candles, one for each of Her faces in the Moon Cycle, Maiden, Wen, Crone, the visible cycles of the Moon. I left the black candle for the New Moon unlit. I lit incense. The copper bowl was on the altar, along with the skulls of ram, buck, and boar. I meditated. I sang, and then spoke the invocation. I asked Her to come and guide me in what She wanted me to do. I acknowledged the Moon, and Her power over life on earth.

I picked up the larger phallus and held it up to the Moon. Then I put it in my mouth, and massaged the roof of my mouth with it. I did this until my breathing started to change, and my body started to vibrate, resonating from the sensation on the roof of my mouth. What I used to do was take the saliva from my mouth on my hand and rub it between my legs. These times I used coconut oil, rubbing it on the smaller phallus, too. I blew the candles out.

I lay on my back, working with the phallus to get heated up. Slowly I brought it in to me, slowly, in and out. Once I was more energized, I got up on my knees, brought the copper bowl between my knees. I put the phallus in me as far as it would go, then moved it around slowly. When my breathing changed again, speeding up, I started to move it rapidly in and out. I took it out at times and massaged all around my phulva, and just inside at the g-spot, which triggered more response. Then I put it back inside me and start to move it faster. I got just to the point of orgasm, took the phallus out, used my hand on my clitoris and that, as usual, made me rain into the copper bowl. I did this a number of times. Once I started raining, I could feel that She was in me. It used to be that She watched, but now She is in me when I rain.

I leaned forward and put my head on the altar. When my knees gave out, I removed the copper bowl and put the lower bowl under me and lay down on my back, knees up, feet on the floor. Now that I was sensitized my breathing slowed down then sped up, getting deeper. I moaned, and cried out at the peaks of the rain releases.

I began vibrating, resonating, like a struck tuning fork. I took the phallus out and slapped myself, softer then harder. It would almost make me orgasm, and then I would insert just the tip. That little bit of friction would make me rain. I could feel the lips of my phulva growing, engorging. Eventually just a couple slaps would trigger a rain event. Then I would put the phallus in me, and orgasm that way for a while. She said to me, "Together we will feed the world".

I spread my arms out and fed the world, energy pouring through my hands. Then I repeated the cycle. Sometimes I would stop and pour the rain from the low sided bowl into the copper bowl. I did this for a while. At some point I moved the bowl away, and started massaging myself, putting fingers in me, manipulating the g spot. When I would rain I would use my hand to pull it up my body, circling around my breasts. I would take the phallus and use it again, withdrawing right before orgasm. I brought the rain to my third eye, my lips, and massaged it into my face.

Sometimes I would slap myself with my hand. It got to the point where I would simply orgasm without stimulation, I would just rain. She had me draw a circle in my palms with the rain, extend my arms and feed the world.

A column of golden light appeared within me, starting at the root and shooting out through my crown chakra, pulsing with the waves of orgasm. I came back to the phallus, very slowly, then I withdrew it and used my hand to finish.

At some point I lay on the floor with my hands out and brought that golden light to my hands, pulsing it out into the world at the same time it poured out my crown. My legs started to shake then my whole body began to shake.

Then there was a movement in me that bid me sit up, with my palms on my thighs. Then I listened to hear if She would tell me anything. Sometimes She does, sometimes She doesn't.

The Moon was still shining through the window. The shaking continued in me, coming through me in waves.

I wrapped myself in my heavy long wool shawl and took the bowl out to the south lawn. I held it up to the Moon, thanked the Goddess. I got down on my hands and knees and poured it into the Earth. I thanked the Earth.

I came inside, poured some water in the bowl, and went back outside to offer it to the Goddess, then I poured the rinse into the earth, not to waste a drop.

The entire ceremony took perhaps an hour and a half.

I heard Her voice as I returned to the cabin. "Now that was solo cultivation," She said to me. I can feel you laughing as you read this.

I went to sleep with the rain drying on me. I didn't sleep much. I woke up every two hours, I would get up. I felt the need to bathe in the moonlight.

The next day I felt good, not as tired as I'd thought I'd be. I awoke early, after only a few hours sleep. There was work in the gardens, and my reading and journaling. My root vibrated all day, almost a buzzing sensation. I was surprised, but not uncomfortable. When I felt tired I went to sleep, and fell easily. Although I slept the night through my dreams—storms, wen running and hiding. Wen and men fighting other men in the dark. Fleeing on horseback. Grieving for the lost, and the dead. I had thought it would be a springtime flowers and breezes night, but it was not. In my meditation the next morning I sent a voice of inquiry to Her, and She replied, "Early spring has been a good time to flee. Wen and children die in the winter." And I understood. If you don't have to flee too far, there is still time to plant a garden before summer.

On the night after the Full Moon I proceeded as usual. The sequence was much the same as the night before Full. With the slapping I became engorged, using my hands more, with one hand out, channeling the ecstasy out into the world. I had the Jewel in my Arch pinched between my fingers, pulling it up, pulling the hood back. I would massage the g-spot, one finger, and that would make me rain, and between rains, I would have simple orgasms while the gland refilled.

I was even more sensitized than I was two nights prior. When

I would open my eyes and look at the Moon there were lines of light that I could see, rays pouring down onto me. I worked with my hand, doing the same ritual of painting my body with the rain. First my breasts, then with the next rain my face, then with the next drawing the circles in my hands.

Since I was working with my hands, and I was so swollen and wet, I felt an impulse and I started to explore my anus. I inserted my middle finger, and while I was pressing on my phulva with my hand, I orgasmed. She guided me to pick up the phallus and, rolling slightly to my side I inserted it behind, slowly with my left hand, until I reached a stopping place. I moved the phallus around, very slowly, my other hand with fingers on my Jewel, or in me.

Once again, I don't know why, the phallus was in me and I drew it out very, very, slowly and then just as it popped out I went into a deep, intense orgasm, arching my back, making guttural moaning sounds and I just rained, squirting more than once.

I went back to this maybe four or five times. I would think OK, this is done, and then She would move me to do it again. And with the deep orgasm, arching my back, hard breathing, heavy moaning. It happened every time. Each time that I came like that my arms would be out and I would be aware of feeding the world.

Even when I stopped with the phallus and my hand, arms out, laying on my back, feeding the world. Once I felt a puff of air, like someone breathed on me though I don't know from where, hit me between the legs, and that made me orgasm. I worked the draw, still orgasming, still feeding the world, raining sometimes, feeding the world, top chakra open. The light this time, instead of gold, was blue green.

The quality of those anal orgasms was not light, not sparkly, not a sparkly rain. It's like I was in a dark cave. It was dark, not in a sinister way but in a way that was completely different, almost opposite to the sparkly orgasms of two nights prior.

My expectations had been that all the orgasms would be sparkly things, but not this time. I sat up, and I was still being taken by these orgasms and raining. I would think I was out of the ritual space, and then the wave would move through me and I'd have to rain again, simply sitting there, raining on the floor, with no stimulation.

This happened while I was sitting up, looking at the moon, thanking the Goddess. I fumbled around relighting the candles, but my hands were so wet. I stopped orgasming but I kept shuddering and my thighs kept shaking. I had a hard time standing up because my legs were shaking so much.

I put my poncho on, took the bowl, went outside and held it up to the moon, and the four directions, got to my knees and poured it into the earth. I took the rinse water and used it to bless the statues in the shrine. I shivered all over while the water poured.

Then I went to bed, except for the fact that I couldn't fall asleep. Finally, I asked the goddess to let me sleep, and shortly after I did. I could feel the energy slow down, the activation settling in me.

That night had a different quality. One of the aspects of it is that I pushed my body pretty hard. Those anal orgasms were so intense, gut wrenching, not like despair or anything like that, but literally my viscera, my guts had been wrenching in spasm. In addition to the physical, I was very far out there in liminal space, sacred space and time. It didn't scare me but it was a level of surrender that I was not familiar with. It's one thing to go out and trip around the stars, but it's a whole other thing to feel like I was pinned to the earth. Part of what this seems to be is understanding, part of it is acceptance and surrender to what She wants, and trying to understand if the "I" in me was even there.

The next day my root chakra vibrated intensely all day long. Writing this to you triggers this vibration, starting with the tingling, unlike other days when the vibration is mostly in the morning. I am still getting whole body shudders from time to time.

I feel I am evolving, connecting to the Eight Orgasms in due time. I shall write again at the next Full Moon. Bless me, will you? For the upcoming New Moon Ritual.

The wind today was distinctive, blowing in fiercely from different directions, and it continues to make the trees dance. I am in a different state of consciousness today. I feel I have been blessed, that I am in some kind of state of Grace.

Oh, and I have a feeling that I know who it was that rested here with her children. I will sit at the shrine and see if I can journey to her, or at least to whom she was.

Your loving wentee,
Emmalia

Acknowledgments

I wish to thank my editors, FKV Publishing, and all those who helped in the production of this novel. I am certain that, given the subject matter, it could be trying at times.

And I want to thank my loyal and loving readers. I hope you are all pleased with this offering.

Finally, I wish to thank those without whose support this novel would not have been possible. RMH and SWC, your presence in my life blesses me every day. It is because of you that I am fine, perhaps, sometimes, good even.